BECOMING *Adam*

THE TRUE STORY OF A PERFECT LOVE GONE RIGHT

BOOK 2

⁓

*…come to these books with a willingness
to read beyond the expected.*

MICHAEL DEMERS

 www.trafford.com
North America & international
toll-free: 1 888 232 4444 (USA & Canada)
fax: 812 355 4082

Introduction

"It matters not where my consciousness centers in this life or the next, or what anyone teaches differently, or however I may be challenged and criticized by others who see it differently and want to sway me to their way of seeing it, or who say my dream is impossible. As my soul roams the universe it will always be with the utmost thought and fixed determination that I am becoming or that I AM Adam!

Only in that manner can I create the reality I want for myself. Only with that strength can I attract the Woman to me who shares my dream exactly. That's what I want, that's what I am becoming regardless of any other soul who would tempt and beckon me into worlds of their own choosing. I am not theirs, they are not mine. The gods keep the timing, when the time is right for me, my well-beloved Eve will appear, and we will be ONE..." Michael Demers

Michael Demers retired comfortable, built a dream home in the Mojave Desert near Las Vegas, Nevada USA and settled in with Jen his beautiful wife. Baby boomers both they had worked hard, built a successful investment business and were about to enter their golden years. The marriage had been sweet except for a growing malaise in the last two years. No longer busy business partners they were spinning their wheels and not spinning them fast, Jen on mindless activities, Michael on the sofa reading.

Resentment was growing. Jen left his bed for another room and he didn't chase her, even when she beckoned from her bedroom door, bathrobe falling open, relaxed and ready, naked body steamy from a hot bath with candles. That was unusual for him, his sexual needs had always been strong and she had fulfilled, content with her man. They loved to spoon naked, mornings had always come with a smile as she did her makeup. Sometimes he stood behind her and brushed her hair, he was gentle, they were in love. But now with neglect she was growing distant, his mind was beginning to wander. Perhaps without knowing it they were preparing for what was to come, who knows how such things work...

Then for the third night in a row Michael alone in his bed had a recurring dream. He heard a voice telling him he'd become Adam and live forever if he could find Eve, the woman with a matching dream. It left a powerful waking impression, he felt that he could no longer ignore the voice, he had to do something.

Michael abandoned his retirement home, his enviable lifestyle and his wife. He bought a motor home and set out across America in search of adventure and Eve. Michael had always wanted to be a writer, his rational mind told him he was updating Steinbeck's *Travels with Charley* but he soon abandoned that too. There was something else driving him, pushing him hard, he was getting older, *he had to find Eve!* Along the way Michael kept a journal and made it public, it's a *delicious* read, I think you'll like it.

As we follow Michael we'll peek often into his private emails and we'll know in the end if he found Eve and became Adam, and what became of Jen left behind alone in her garden. Was Adam's Eve all along the woman growing roses, the acres of diamonds in Michael's back yard? Or is this story of a perfect love gone right the story of Michael and another woman he picked up along the way? We'll find out because this story is true, it really happened....

Let's dip into Michael's journal right here, a year after his adventure began. By now he has leased out the motor home and is living alone, a single man, divorced, renting a modest apartment by the sea in Victoria, British Columbia Canada. He's creating a series of books out of the million words he wrote into his journal as he traveled for a year. When an email begins with "M" it's a message Michael sent to someone. Here's how Michael wrote it himself.

M: (to Elaine) It was pleasant chatting with you over coffee today, I always appreciate your company and your time and counsel, you are dear to me. As we chatted I pretended you were my book editor, your every word needing to be preserved, in this case scribbled on a napkin. I will enjoy making the changes you suggested, they are valuable to me, a woman's point of view on my male writing, most of my readers will be women. I think my readers will eventually come to like book character Michael, I mean once you get to know him what's there *not* to like? But in the beginning yes, he did buy a motor home and leave home with the intent to travel for a year and write a book, an unfulfilled dream he had for decades. His wife could have traveled with him had she wanted to, but she chose instead to be offended, rush to a lawyer and secretly file for divorce. He didn't find out he was being divorced until after he'd hit the road. His wife's regretting her choice to divorce now but it's done though they keep in touch. Like the plot? Michael

I must tell you who are thinking of buying this book, this is not *"Fifty Shades of Grey"* but it's, well, you'll see, I never lost my sexual drive, I bare it all. Or at least most of it, I do embellish the sexual scenes for your entertainment. If you want to find out what *really* went down you'll have to talk to the woman involved, I respect her privacy, mostly. You'll find in my journal: adventure, travel, romance, love, sex, betrayal, rejection, heartbreak, spiritual insights, joy, the meaning of life maybe, the way to immortality maybe, unforgettable true stories told by a real life hospice nurse of children and adults living out their dying with an angel at their side…

Did I miss anything? Did I mention romance? The end will be sweet when we get to it, I'm not there yet myself but I think we're going to like it. It's got to be sweet or I'll have lived and lost and I've always been a winner. I'm sure you'll wish you were there at the end and knew Michael in real life, yes, he's real, he's me. Got tissue? Did I say there's romance in my books?

This story begins in Victoria with Jen my ex sending me an email message. Are you ready for this? Get yourself comfortable, my journal's thick, it's a long delicious read. There's romance and love to come, bathtubs and candles. And for men there's the adventure of a real life quest, a man going somewhere for a woman, and sex. Well, that's a guy thing, you ladies wouldn't understand how powerful a drive it is for us. Once we get the scent of a woman we'll follow her *anywhere* to drink from her fountain again. Try us, you'll see, just beckon, a whispered phone call in the night perhaps?

Let me tell you right now, I'll love you if you buy my books. I poured body and soul into living and writing them for you, treat them gently, enjoy me, love me, read me again, my sweet story could be *yours…*

Chapter 1

M: (to Jen): I closed Book 1 today, we are now living Book 2 live. Book 1 has only about half of the pages I want for a novel but I'll cut and paste flashbacks from the past year. I'll probably continue doing that, a live book until we've lived about half the pages I need and then cut and paste flashbacks from my year of traveling alone. It was a wonderful Thanksgiving Day today in Victoria City of Victory, City of Magic, *WOMB OF ME.*

M: (to Jen) I just sent the following message to Elaine:

Elaine, I thought I should tell you that today I asked Jen to marry me and she accepted. I think you saw that one coming all along, thanks for being my dear friend. You did so much for me that you may never even know, you were my angel for sure. I will understand if you choose to never see me again, I'm not available on the singles scene anymore. But it will probably be months before Jen and I can make living arrangements maybe here in Victoria. So if you'd like to continue as friends I'd like that. I hope your day off was relaxing, I think that was today. Take care dear one, you were and remain precious to me, an ancient soul, surely the angel your dad meant you to be, helping this other ancient one along the way in his time of need. Michael Demers

Jen: Thank you. This is a kind message.

Elaine: Congrats! I should have been called Cupide! I'm happy that you and Jen are getting married. Of course we can continue as friends. You two were meant to be together all along. Cheers, Elaine

M: Thanks Cupide, good aim. Sharpening arrows today?

Elaine: OK So how is it that you are asking Jen to marry you, when your last emails say Jen filed for divorce, and that you don't want to talk with her one minute, marrying the next. Are you strangely confused or bipolar or something? It's really odd... but good luck anyway. Perhaps the protein smoothies I recommended and you bought will help! Elaine

M: Honey it WAS the smoothies that did it, I began to THINK again. Yes, Jen and I have disagreements and a few bones of contention we can choose to gnaw upon while safe within our secret closet or dog house, or to throw at or to the other on occasion, or make soup, or feed

1

the dog, or happier thought, to ignore. But all that recent sometimes heated interaction with her over the last few days as she went through a time of crisis brought on I think by the death of one ex and the thought that another could follow served to keep her in mind much longer than usual. And with that, being capable of harnessing emotion I shut down feeling and turned for an hour to primordial (or is it) heartless reason. In that state I concluded that at our age we would be *foolish* to not get together again.

Jen and I were married for 18 years, almost all of that was good. We were busy business partners, we were acceptable to the other, we had our peak experiences and shared love and family, we traveled a lot. We made our million together, built a lovely retirement home and retired with goodly golden year prospects. If either of us started over again with someone else and the baggage that person would come with, we would be almost 90 years old before we'd arrive at the point where Jen and I can BEGIN TODAY our together life experience. Our baggage has the same name tags, it's colored familiar.

I found that I could not argue with raw reason, it was simply a matter of quietly putting up with each other's nonsense and tweaking the quality of living in a positive direction as best we can. Rationally that came across as the better thought. And since the happiness part is a matter for the individual, we'll do that by our individual selves anyway. I'm on top of mine, I am in excited anticipation and expectation of a better life than before. She and I are capable of co-creating such, I believe we will.

Jen *instantly* accepted my proposal of marriage. She was ready, she had forgiven me for running off to write a book and I she for the divorce, she loved me, she wanted me. We'll most likely marry early next year. It will be several months before she can adjust her affairs and we live full-time under the same roof. My guess is that our living arrangements will include a modest place in Victoria, it is my desire to be Canadian eh. Perhaps you and I and maybe she will be long-term friends, I'd like that. Sorry, Canadian eh but not confused, not bipolar, just smoothie RATIONAL. Granted, strange.

But then, you and I would not have become friends if we didn't share a bit of that like attracts like strangeness eh? Enjoy the day sweetie, let's not be strangers, I thoroughly enjoy your company, and your food. Michael

M: (to Jen) Here's how Elaine replied to my message informing her that I had asked you to marry me and you accepted.

"Congrats! I should have been called Cupide! I'm happy that you and Jen are getting married. Of course we can continue as friends. You two were meant to be together all along. Cheers, Elaine"

It is my hope that she and I can remain friends and get together occasionally and that you won't be jealous of her. I assure you that we never came anywhere near having sex with each other and now that you and I are engaged it's simply *not* going to happen. We both know that, our relationship will remain platonic as it always has been. Please allow that, she's important to me, she's important to my books. I love you, thank-you so much for accepting my proposal of marriage. It will put a whole new perspective on your visit next week. Prepare for some really tight hugs my darling, I *must* have you in my arms. Well ok, that too, *and in my bed*. Your Michael in Victoria

M: If in real life Elaine remains my friend and we get together at least occasionally it will create some lovely tension and suspense for the books. What with the death bed scenario and how you so passionately reacted to it, readers will be on the edge of their seats wondering as the story unfolds if Michael and Elaine ever DO IT!!!

Just be yourself, you are so excellently playing the role of "Suzanne", better in some ways than the first one from Texas even. She backed away and left a void for you to fill at exactly the right time, she had played her part well, scene one was done. Your cue was sounded and prima dona diva you came out from the wings, the audience standing and clapping and cheering at the sight of you. They know they are in for a treat tonight as the performance continues after the break. They await and I in eager excited anticipation of how you will delightfully forget the script and flub and ad lib your lines as you always do, and what will become of it, how will Michael adapt? You've always been Number One, you've always played at my side. We're the best, we're the stars, our pay is in planets to populate with children we make in our own image and likeness. Make children with me? It's painless, the curse is gone on those better planets, you'll *love* playing Eve with Adam. *Somebody's* got to populate new planets, might as well be us...

But now as I write this leaping effortlessly from fantasy to reality and back as I always do (fiction writers are good at that) the very thought of you and I married in real life is *exhilarating*. I sooo want you as my real life wife my darling sweetheart, *you* the one in my bed each night, my hand on your breast as we succumb together to the safety of dreams. Life's unfolding as it should, it's unbelievably good, incredibly *alive*. The ancient trees are still, I no longer hear their siren song to come lie under them and never again rise, just yours. I love you pardner. Your Writer Companion Partner Husband Michael

Elaine: So, what you are saying is that, even though you were married for 18. Years, you did get divorced and are now RE marrying! Otherwise that part didn't make sense. I thought that you were separated, and she was still filing. How could you then marry.......? The human emotion part of it makes fine sense though, and of course, we can be friends. I think that we were spiritually attracted, having many same interests there, and some intellectual commonalities... some gentleness too. All good. Must be off now. Talk later... working to wee hours after normal today... stamina challenge! Cheers, Elaine

M: Jen and I were not just separated, our divorce was final many months ago. Jen secretly filed for divorce maybe the very day I left to buy a motor home and begin my year's journey to write *The Great American Novel*. I didn't find out until weeks later and that from a business customer that I was being divorced. Her lawyer had written my customers to stop making payments on their real estate loans to cut off my income. Nasty, but all is forgiven, raw reason has prevailed, emotion follows. She was thoroughly provoked because I'd always let her control the flow of cash and knew I needed to have one of those revenue streams to take care of my needs, so I cut her off from it. She got riled and hastily dropped the atom bomb on my head, divorce. Can't blame her really, we never did communicate properly, maybe we'll have learned our lesson now, she says she loves me more for that year of apartness.

Re the stamina, I recommend protein smoothies, they will greatly help with the challenge. Got some? I have an extra if you need it, just ask, I'd be happy if you took it now that I know where to get more. Be well dear one, come soon and visit your not so starving writer, that stuff's good. *You* are good for me. Gentle Writer Me What's There Not to Like?

Jen: This is all that I ask when it comes to other woman. Knowing that Elaine understands we are getting married. I have no problem with you being her friend. True friends are platonic and wish their friends happiness with the love of there life. My maginficant writer, sweetie Jen

M: (to Elaine) My Bestest Friend, Jen goes home on December 10th to prepare for Christmas with her family so I'm wondering if you'd be interested and available to be my date to *"A Sentimental Christmas Carol"* with the Victoria Symphony on December 12, 13, or 14? My great reward will be to hear you sing along and see you in your short skirt again! Hey, just because we're platonic doesn't mean I have to stop *looking* does it? I hope you'll still read to me too sweetie when Jen's not here, it warms my heart so. I *like* the way we were, your pacing turned out perfect. *And I do love to touch my precious angel, sweet little kiss now and then?* Let me know about *"Messiah"* too at UVic, I've never seen it live, December 19th, it would be extra special to go with lovely you.

It is my great hope that if Jen comes to live in Victoria with me some day you two will become good friends, walk and talk and do things together. Being new to this city she'll *need* a good friend like you to get away from me when my fingers are working the keyboard as they so often are. Would you like it if it came to that? She likes more fun than I am usually willing to take the time for. And she's big on art and artists, *she's* the one to take to the galleries, she's good for the tickets or I am, Vancouver, Seattle wherever you two decide, I'm sure you'd enjoy each other's company. She'll look up to you in more ways than one (she's 5'2") and she would find your conversation stimulating. She could learn a lot from you my friend from ancient days gone by, you'd be her angel too. Just trying to plan your life for you as usual sweetie, but however it goes I hope you will remain in mine, I enjoy you so much. M Dreaming

Elaine: So much to think about... I'll get back to you. Mind is open to all, why not, just need to get schedule.... Best of the evening to you. Elaine, friendly one

M: (to Jen) If you find my overcoat, the one I took to China, please bring it. Leave room in your suitcase to take yours with you, or leave it here to wear when you're in Victoria. Please bring some clothes to leave in my closet. That would be comforting for me to see when you're not here, might make me think I'm a married man. I threw away all the women's clothes I already had sometime ago, need some new ones. Gotta nice skirt to leave behind maybe?

Jen: I just went out and looked. I was hoping to find it to bring. Will look later though the clothing in garage. I will see what I can do. Don't have to many clothing that fit my nicely. I have been wearing them a bit big. Guess I will have to go shopping.

M: How's my wifer woman today? Enjoying your family for the weekend? I'm keeping real busy with the rewrites. I've added a lot of pages and it looks so far that the first one is going to settle into a book of about 550 pages, quite long actually, might be a good thing, might not, we'll see. If the manuscript gets picked up by a good agent who finds a major traditional publisher for it we could make a lot of money. We'll have adequate with our present combined income but eventually could live very well from book royalties alone, that's my hope. I'd love to do a luxury world cruise in a large suite someday. I could write about it and write off the expense most likely. Anyway, enjoy your day, I'm about to go for a walk, need one. I love you. Your well ok guess it's true FIANCEE.

Jen: I just got back from Christmas shopping. Sounds like you are quite busy. Do you have fun as you write. Like smile or laugh at some of the situations. Love my Magnificent writer fiancee.

M: I LIVE to write Jen, I feel so honored to have the enormous amount of spiritual help it must take to arrange complex circumstances and events so well for me to receive the inspiration I need exactly when I need it. And yes, I smile, I laugh, I weep as the words take shape and have meaning to the conscious mind. I have always wanted to be a writer, just allowed myself to sink into making money the traditional way rather than trust I could do it with the pen. But that gave me experience that brings a wealth of associations to mind when something cues them on stage. (Theater of the mind.) Life is so good, it's *magnificent* really.

M: When you are here I will of course take you out to dinner for your birthday. But for Christmas would you be interested in a 4 day cruise from Los Angeles? If you're ok with an interior room it would be my treat, a gift for you. There's one leaving January 7th. That would give us time to visit my son for a few days, then San Diego then get to Los Angeles and cruise. Then Vegas Baby Maybe, or your place or wherever.

P.S. How close a secret are you keeping our engagement? I'd prefer if we announce it together maybe in January? Let me know.

Jen: Sure the cruise sounds great. Any place with you will be fun.

M: And the secret? Should we announce our engagement by email when you are here next week? Or would that tip off your family too soon and you'd prefer to keep it a secret as long as possible?

Jen: No decision until we are together and talk. I have the kids. My youngest daughter's on a date. I have no time to even thing with so many people in the house. Tried to trim a Christmas tree disaster. Everything came out of boxes before I could get them off the shelf. Trying to sort thru and clean up the mess. Went down stairs and almost could not see the carpet. Have not had my oldest daughter alone to talk. She alone knows we are meeting. Please put those concerns aside for the moment. I don't think I am going to have a minute to think or rest until I claps into your arms. Love you my sweet.

M: Works for me. My arms are waiting for you, cuddles and spoons coming up. Birthday surprise awaits and a cruise for after Christmas, all is well, you'll be here soon. See, told you all along - *I'm WORTH it!*

M: Our cruise is booked, 4 days leave Los Angeles January 7.

Jen: Wonderful!

Jen: I forgot to tell you another good friend of mine died a week after my ex. I am so glade I went and saw her when I heard she was not doing well. Seems like this last month several people I knew well died. Love ya

M: It has been hard on you. But it brought about the crisis in your life and my look in the mirror that has resulted in our engagement, so all is well for us...

M: (to Elaine) You volunteered to be my "pseudo editor" and the following is not something that I can run by Jen for her opinion. It would be most helpful to me if you would give what I wrote below careful consideration and write to me your woman knowing about the situation. I'd very much like to include your feedback in the book I am writing, it desperately needs the female point of view. Please keep in mind that although my books are based on real life situations, they are fiction. Your name of course will be changed before publication and your privacy protected. (Unless you want the fame.)

M: (to Elaine) You mentioned coming today but it's nasty out there, below freezing and snow. Much as I'd love to see you, I don't want you to take a risk for me. Please stay home if you can and get rest. I care lots about you sweetie. I'm having a lazy day today, up real early sipping white or nettle tea and writing, but back to bed. As I doze I think the books are being fed to me. It's a happy comfy warm feeling as it flows, but only short videos come into awareness. I don't seem to care if it's that way, I'm willing, I accept, I know life is unfolding as it should. I'm allowing it and went back to bed a second time, same thing.

Jen and I swap a couple of messages about finances. M: (to Jen) We'll do well sweetie, we'll travel together again I'm sure, no worries. Frosty snow on my car this a.m. two degrees below freezing, don't like that part of living in Canada but it comes with the territory, I'll stay in. I have a few activities planned for us and it's going to be rainy the first few days you come so bring a warm jacket, you'll need it as soon as you step off the plane. Enjoy another family day, only four more sleeps alone and we'll be together, can't wait for that. I love you lots my darling.

Jen: Thanks for the message. I to am looking forward to seeing you. Took the kids to a great free children's museum today. To tired to cook so we had pizza and salad. Thinking of going to bed. They are playing games. Love you sweetie, The magnification writer.

Jen: I know, you will keep me warm. Looked in the garage could not find your coat. Love you

M: Elaine's working tonight, haven't heard from her in a long time but got a message one minute before yours, often works that way. Loving the way my book is shaping up, I think it is going to get published if not too intellectual for the dumbed-down TV mob. Maybe they're different than the ones who read. Sweet dreams, sleep well.

Elaine: i'm at work now again, on the laptop.... the dialogue you sent is very intricate and complicated. too much for me to think about, but just like my last email, where i said i will get back to you when i can really think about it... until then, stay safe and warm... kind regards and kind wishes... from a. waif caretaker

M: Thanks honey, thinking of you, be well this night.

Jen: Send me another page. I enjoy reading them. to My magnificent writer.

M: I forgot what I sent you. Send the last couple of paragraphs and I'll return added to.

Jen: I think this was the last page we talked about.

M: You already have the introduction and it has not changed since I last sent it to you. That's as much as I want to show anyone except a literary agent or publisher when it gets to that point. There is time enough to read my book in whole when it is published, it would spoil the plot to give you more at this point. Just be assured that in my opinion it is publishable material. It has the potential to generate a goodly flow of royalty revenue over time because as you know I am a MAGNIFICENT writer. I'm quite happy with the way the Book 1 manuscript is shaping up now whereas I had many doubts before.

Most of my book is email conversation so you have already read a lot of it in the messages we have swapped. If you are still interested when we are living together full-time I may share with you what I wrote the day before as it goes along. By then you may be fully engaged in creating "Suzanne". You're already doing a good job of that with your messages just the way you are and people change, you can make a changed person out of "Suzanne 2". The first Suzanne didn't do it any better except the sex scenes and hospice stories, she was good at both. I'll copy a hospice scene below. I don't share my manuscripts with anyone else either, as you know I'm shy about someone reading over my shoulder as I write, and that's what I am doing right now with the rewrite. The first book will take less time than I thought it would, I already had it well along the way to copy and paste from various files. But it may take a year to find an agent who finds a publisher who makes and markets the book, we'll see how it goes, I expect the best.

Enjoy another day with your family, much as I know you love them my guess is that it will be a relief to see them go and get your house cleaned and tidied again after Thanksgiving. Only three more sleeps until we sleep together, I love you.

Tales of a Hospice Nurse - Extracted from Becoming Adam Book1

As Suzanne brought her powerful SUV to a stop in front of the farm house, one hand automatically switched off the audiobook she'd been absorbed in, and just as automatically her mind switched to present time and what she was about to do. She already knew that Mary was dying, that's why she was there. Mary, dear dear Mary, she didn't have long to wait now, she was already well into living out her dying.

Mary loved nature, most of all birds, she had traveled the whole world bird watching. She had taught English in Africa, worked in the Peace Corps, loved nature. Mary was a Texas woman and Texans love their guns. She kept a small pistol in the window seat by her rocking chair where she sat day after day watching her birds, enchanted with their movements, their interactions with one another, and their song. Mary's heart was always on her sleeve when birds were near. She had feeders for all types of birds and almost daily delighted in the sight of foxes, skunks, deer, and possums near the farm house. They knew they were safe with Mary.

But if an uncivilized creature like a cow bird or a grackle came to disturb her paradise, she'd pick up her handgun, quietly slide open the glass door, and take that sucker right out of her paradise, blow it into a different one altogether. Now it was Mary's turn to face paradise. Suzanne was here to help her do just that.

Suzanne stepped out of the SUV, walked around to the passenger side and grabbed her bag, thinking all the while about Mary, bracing herself for what was about to come, putting on her professional face, opening her heart full wide. Suzanne is a nurse, a Registered Nurse with a Bachelor of Science in Nursing. She works hospice, driving to homes already marked with death, and there tending to the needs of the dying. Suzanne used to work the other end, joyously welcoming into this world new life, life pushed laboriously, painfully from a mother's vagina. But now Suzanne worked sadness and sorrow, immersed daily in the full spectrum of emotion oozing silently from loved ones standing next to the death bed, waiting for it to happen, it always does, the mysterious transition to a world forbidden to those living.

Mary was an amazing woman. If she wasn't bird watching she was knitting caps for sick children who had lost their hair to chemotherapy. Suzanne had immediately felt a deep love for Mary the first time she visited, had felt that love even before she opened the door and walked into Mary's home. Suzanne was focused, in tune with death and those dying. She knew what to expect.

But it wasn't all sickness and sorrow, not at all. Several weeks after Mary's passing, a family member gave Suzanne a letter from Mary, thanking her for the laughter she'd brought to her in those final hours of her dying. No, Suzanne's full heights and depths of emotion were well exercised by now. She knew what emotion was needed at any given moment, and was capable of instantly filling that need. She had become a master of emotion.

Suzanne has many stories to tell. We'll tell them all in this series of books, I hope you enjoy it. The book's a labor of love for both Suzanne and her writer. And, yes, it's true, Michael and Suzanne met online on a singles site, and Michael's already in love with Suzanne.

Suzanne describes herself on that singles site as *"a very relational woman"* who loves her family, loves animals and gardening, is a great cook. She enjoys art, theater, music, and discussions about life and death. She is kind, loyal, compassionate, and wants to travel to enjoy life's beauty and diversity. She's a Texas girl, born and bred, and loves to dance. Michael lives by himself in a motor home, so even though he doesn't dance, Suzanne's desire to travel instantly elicited a positive response from him. As did too the character she describes, and other things such as her tallness and slimness, and the pretty face in the photos. (He'd learn later that she's well endowed, even in middle age turning men's heads and thoughts to more familiar things.)

Suzanne once wrote to Michael: *"And yes, I am a farm girl. I can cook, can, kill and dress a chicken, ride a horse, rope a steer, raise a garden, shoot a rifle, kill a rattle snake, drive a tractor, hoe a cotton field, and make love til the sun comes up."* She's also a nurse, a hospice nurse, and a good one, maybe even great.

As she approached the house, Suzanne noticed that the birds were strangely quiet, none at the feeders, nor, she recalled, had there been for the two days previous. The red fox was still under the porch. Suzanne writes to Michael about the hours that came after she entered Mary's house that final time.

"Two does came to the sliding glass doors and looked in at Mary. Her daughters at her bedside said, "Mom, when the deer leave, go with them." And within a few minutes the deer left. Mary took her last breath and the red fox under the porch left. The next day the birds returned to the feeders. Her husband said, "What mystery did I witness?"

Mary was an atheist, not into church but served. She loved the birds and the beasties, and they loved her back. Mary left in peace.

Suzanne: I like it... I knew the fox was there because Mary's husband saw it come lie under the porch. He had left water and food for the beautiful creature since he chose not to leave these last days of Mary. The story is there, maybe we need to look at the flow, seems choppy at times.

M: Ok, I'd love to look at the flow! Smile dear, that was for the audience – you know I love the *whole* of you. *Hmmm...*

M: (to Suzanne) There was a time when you were angry with me because you thought I was searching for a new "Suzanne". I wasn't, but I was communicating with another woman at the time and you were very much connected with me so you felt and personalized what I was feeling about her. She would not have been "Suzanne" but could have been a different book character, she was quite a character, the wealthy one with connections.

True to the feelings you expressed when I showed you my home city along the way to Zion National Park and you said I was "not available" because I was still in love with my ex Jen, she and I are now engaged to be (re) married. That will most likely happen in the new year but it will take a few more months to arrange full-time living together. I love Victoria so if we have two homes, one of them will be here.

I understand that you have felt for several months that your role playing "Suzanne" was complete and you left the building. Jen has become the new Suzanne. Below is a message I sent her this a.m. responding to her request last night to read more of the Book 1 manuscript. Book 1 is totally different now, I think it's publishable and I'm willing to rewrite if an editor requires that. I'd love to include more of your hospice stories in Book 2 if you'd allow it. Book 1 is about 550 pages, Book 2 will most likely be about the same, and Book 3 is largely in my files.

I hope Thanksgiving was fun with your family and that you are doing well. We're not so connected anymore but I thought with your last messages you were expressing concerns about money. I will never forget you, when my books are selling well there will be benefits for those who helped me write them, you were the best.

Are you still trying to sell your house? New men (or women) in your life? I never did know for sure if real life you was bisexual or if that was just the book character you were creating. I tended to take everything you wrote as true, the same as was everything I wrote to you but later embellished for the books. I think rather than ever saying you were actively bisexual you only told me in response to a question that you were *capable* of making love to a woman.

Victoria is a small city of culture. I'm attending symphony and will take Jen to the Nutcracker next week when she comes to visit for seven days. You would have liked it here had you come to visit. As I recall, you were hinting about us going to the Nutcracker together when I was living in San Antonio. My good friend Elaine in Victoria remains that, it's platonic but we enjoy each other's company. She's ten years younger than me and likes it that way. I guess she knows that I'll always see her as young because to me she always will be. She's an artist among other things and sometimes brings home-cooked food to feed this starving writer. After we eat she sits on the sofa and reads aloud to me as I massage her feet and calves. It warms my heart so, and I suppose her legs. The book she reads is metaphysical (hypnotic regressions to past lives) and we discuss as she reads.

I don't think Jen is jealous of Elaine but we'll see how it goes after we marry. I always loved the way you were willing to share me with other women, DeLeon in particular. DeLeon's still in Florida, hasn't changed much I don't think, still writes about the same things and the man who was once for her *"Magnificent Lord and King"*. We played well together she and I and you, it's in the books.

Enjoy the day, I miss our close connection but I understand that it was time for you to withdraw when you did. You're always welcome back as a friend and contributor to the *"Becoming Adam"* series of books. Readers will love your hospice stories, everyone I have shown them to ask for more. And of course everyone's dying to know what was in the bag when you came to Loa that magical night in San Antone, the night we made love as best I could at the time. (Getting better now - still watch and listen to your *"A Little Fun with Suzanne"* vid sometimes.) Will you ever tell the contents of the heavy bag that came to Loa Land, or will you always be a tease? You're so SUZANNE you know.

I copy a message sent to Jen.

"You already have the introduction and it has not changed since I last sent it to you. That's as much as I want to show anyone except a literary agent or publisher when it gets to that point..." (etc you've already read it.)

I get an instant reply from Suzanne. It's uplifting and hopeful that she will play with us again, hospice stories and maybe even come out of her toy box at night toys in hand? She's fun, you'll quickly get into her game I'm sure, she's bisexual and without shame or guilt bares it all. I like that in her, *mmm*.

Suzanne: The last months have been challenging to say the least. I've not been writing. Really I've been working a lot. I've had a few dates but nothing with chemistry or promise. I'm delighted you have rewritten your book, the changes as far as I've seen are good ones. I'm delighted you and Jen are remarrying. Maybe our stories are not what we envisioned, but it makes them no less beautiful. We are much more than the sum of our scars. I'll write more later.

M: Dear Suzanne, You write: *"We are much more than the sum of our scars."* From the little I know about you that would be you for sure. If we do come back to physicality for many lives of learning, and come with scripts and contracts as I expect we do, then in this incarnation you (an ancient soul) have cast yourself into the refining role of daily dealing with multiple challenges, perhaps living several normal lives in one. By overcoming the barrage, you have opened your heart to approaching a fullness of LOVE, the purpose for being. In my belief, the more we love unconditionally the more we become like God, which in the Ultimate Whole is the love that dwells in each and all of US. The more we love, the more we enlarge *ourselves*.

In my opening scenario, I think there were lines in your and my contract to help each other along the way, as we most likely did countless times in our long past lives history. Our souls are entangled irrevocably I think, that's how we chose to be, twin souls. Sorry you but you got *me*, get used to it sister. From the constant challenge of rubbing up against difficult you I learned to grow a thicker skin, a better protected heart. I needed that for what I was here to do with my poet heart. And you my sweet and bittersweet angel provided an abundance of challenge.

You have encouraged me today darling with your prompt and pleasant reply. My writer's heart leaps to the hope that perhaps Suzanne will reclaim her starring role as book character "Suzanne" and Jen keep hers as Jen Wife of Michael. She's better at that, she won't write of sex where *you* are superlative. Our readers demand it, they crave the image of you emerging from your toy box at night toys in hand to find a balance to deadly serious professional days. I love that part of you Suzanne, *I love it darling, I love it!!* It's as if I am there with you at night when you come out, sharing your earthy pleasure. How could it be any other way when we're so connected body and soul, my seed once planted within you?

Our readers would delight should you fill in the glaring gaps and mysteries in our story. For example where you were for the missing 45 minutes after you landed in Las Vegas and I couldn't find you. I thought until I phoned that you had missed the plane in San Antonio. You came to meet me in Vegas to find out if my love for Suzanne was also my love for Real Life You, and yours for me. Perhaps you spotted me from a distance sitting by the carousel, saw in me an older man and knew in that instant that my love for real you was not the same or yours for me. You knew that the next five days and nights would not be the wild carefree careless abandon I'd been painting it to be. My imagination for the missing time puts you in a bar fortifying yourself for the real life encounter with this man who you already knew did not love you as much as he loved Suzanne, or you him. Am I getting close to what really happened?

When I sensed you finally approaching from behind, I turned and in that turning also knew that Real You and Suzanne were very different beings. Our subsequent days in the City of Sin were cool but the nights in bed with naked you were desirable, I looked forward to them with excited anticipation. For me that one night in particular is never to be forgotten, the *fulfillment* of what I wanted, to place my seed inside your body. You pronounced that moment "good" and I was content with the days.

With my manuscript rewrite I am *savagely* slashing characters whose stories never turned out to be anything much. All who remain as characters in my books are: Michael, Suzanne (the irreplaceable), DeLeon, Carrie (I've never met her, she's writing a novel based on me), Jen, and newly emerging Elaine, another angel for me, she showed me how to change my books and brings me food and the comforting touch and attention of a lovely caring woman.

15

It is still my fond hope someday to hold that gala event or just bring us all together for a few days and nights in some exotic place. Whether we play the Suzanne Goddess scene or not, it would be fun. In the meantime I am hoping that you will someday allow me and Jen to take you to dinner and chat for a day or two or three, sip some wine, reminisce, and compare real life notes of how it was for us as our roles were played to a standing ovation in the Big Theater.

I want to meet Carrie too, she's a major player. Now that I'm married (soon will be) maybe the unreal tension will dissipate, it's no longer needed, *I don't think!* I'm hoping Jen and Elaine will become friends. I don't know how to fit DeLeon in yet, we were closely entwined there for a while. With your bisexual earth energies with us enhancing what we had how could it have been otherwise? Thanks for that (bittersweet) experience with a tantra goddess, a good writer, another ancient soul, dear DeLeon Fountain of Youth in Florida.

Here's a recent clip from my journal. By "journal" I mean the myriad disorganized files I keep in Word Starter. From those I cut and paste into my book manuscripts. Messages from *you* though go instantly into a manuscript never to be lost. They are most precious to me, pearls of great price. You see, you haven't lost your touch or timing darling, my response to your brief message today is working itself into a dissertation. Here now from my journal. It's a recent message to Elaine as yet unresponded to. I'd very much appreciate receiving your wise woman perspective on it too.

M: (to Elaine) You volunteered to be my "pseudo editor" and the following is not something that I can run by Jen for her opinion, she can't know about it just yet. It would be helpful if you would give what I wrote below careful consideration and write to me your woman knowing about the situation. I'd very much like to include your feedback in the book I am writing, it desperately needs the female point of view. Please keep in mind that although my books are based on real life situations, they are fiction. Your name of course will be changed before publication and your privacy protected. (Unless you want the fame.)

As I rewrite Book 1 early this a.m. long before daylight the thoughts flow into mind about how Jen reacted to the pretend deathbed confession I ran by her. That scene seemed to me to be a perfect ending for my books, the culmination of a beautiful life, the fulfillment of a perfect love gone right. In real life it seemed so poignant that I wept uncontrollably as I wrote and reread it, pacing mindlessly in my little one bedroom apartment in James Bay. Here's how it went down.

M: (to Jen - flashback) As I prepared to shower today a scene floated into mind, the last paragraph to end the *"Becoming Adam"* series. The scene is you lying in bed about to die, we're very old. I'm sitting there holding your hand about to tell you a secret, something I'd kept from you all those many years after Victoria. I never had the courage to tell you before but now with your eyes shut looking like you'll take your last breath any moment I confess, *"Elaine and I made love you know."* Your eyes flicker, the hint of a smile creases the corner of your lips, you open your eyes, look at me for the final time in mortality and hoarsely whisper barely audibly, *"I'm glad you did, she told me you had a long time ago."*

I was about to send a glowing message to Jen, anticipating that she would agree that the above is a perfect ending for my books. But we're so far apart she and I that I don't even want to communicate with her maybe ever again, she's just not good for me, she thinks me a failure. Here's what she wrote about the death bed scene that had me weeping for an hour. My phone is off again, I don't want to talk to her.

Jen: *What a betrayal. To the reader he would be a shit head, her an angel, and he does not deserve this Eve. Otherwise quite a twist in a love gone wrong. Adam failed his Eve.*

Now that I've abandoned the religious notion that sex is a matter of heaven and hell and instead believe that sex is beautiful, Jen's point of view seems almost incomprehensible. In the hypothetical deathbed scene, Michael has carried the burden of guilt not that he had sex with Elaine many years before, but that he hadn't until she was on the verge of death told his wife of many years about that love making. In the scene, Jen having matured in those years and learned to forgive, had long before accepted that Elaine was Michael's angel and in Jen's absence had taken Michael from his loneliness and given her body to him as a comfort.

But where Jen is when I ran the final scene by her she is not only unforgiving of her husband even as she slips away forever, she considers because of what he thought was a beautiful act of sharing many years before that Michael's entire life has been a failure. She thinks he has betrayed his Eve, twisted his perfect love gone right to wrong, and that you the reader think him a "shit head". How can it be that *anyone* would have come to that conclusion? Is Jen so steeped in religion, or is it that she is hopelessly mired in the western notion of monogamy and sexual "faithfulness", the demand of a western woman that her man keep his body exclusively for *her*?

Or is it perhaps that for Jen everything between male and female is about who has the power? She did everything she could to force Michael's pre-marital promise from him not to have sex with another woman than her. And he refused to yield to her control until they were married or living under the same roof. Did Jen in her own eyes fail to get the power, and never forgave Michael for his adamant part in her self-imposed failure?

What evil forces in sheep's clothing have played upon Jen to bring her to such a sad conclusion that her Adam is a failure in the end because he made love with another woman years before, that because of that beautiful sharing of bodies with Elaine, regardless of the way he has lived his life and the man he had become, Adam has betrayed his wife. He doesn't "deserve" his Eve so he doesn't get her, she walks away and never looks back in the end. And because of that betrayal, regardless of how she may have lived her life and never learned to forgive and thus to love unconditionally, Adam, Jen concludes, has made of Eve an angel.

If fail he did, was Adam's failure that he had given in to raw reason in a matter that should have been decided by the heart, he had married Jen knowing she was his "greatest temptation"? Was Adam's failure, the great tragedy of his life that he stopped his search too soon - *HE NEVER DID FIND EVE?*

Ok, I'm male, I understand if you are a western woman dear reader that you might agree with Jen's point of view. Where I am today it is a *tragedy* that you do. In Jen's conclusion I see a life filled with jealousy, a life in which she never learned gentle forgiving where forgiving is thought needed after judgment. I see *her* life in part as a failure.

I sincerely want to become Adam and find Eve, the woman whose dream is identical with mine. Or is it that I am using reason when the subject's entirely a matter of heart? And heart knows nor needs logic to be right? Did I just see a whole bunch of female heads nod up and down in unison? Michael's becoming Adam, turn over the corner of this page? I do love women so...

I also know that there is much about a woman that I do not understand because I'm male. Perhaps a wise and giving woman will take me aside privately some day and enlighten me about my reasoning and conclusions above. I'd like to learn where I went wrong if I did.

Good points for discussion? Debate anyone? Class assignment? Topic for survey and research – the 20th century western notion of monogamy and its impact on the quality of human life and death? Dissertation? Michael Demers's strangest notion? Who's Michael Demers?

Enjoy today sweet and bittersweet Texas one, you are most precious to me. Your Writer

M: (to Jen) Suzanne writes this morning:

> *"The last months have been challenging to say the least. I've not been writing. Really I've been working a lot. I've had a few dates but nothing with chemistry or promise. I'm delighted you have rewritten your book, from what I've seen the changes are good ones. I'm delighted you and Jen are remarrying. Maybe our stories are not what we envisioned, but it makes them no less beautiful. We are much more than the sum of our scars. I'll write more later."*

You will not have to play "Suzanne" just Jen, you're much better at that. I think Suzanne's back now, she may study her part a while but has been cued onstage with a new script because of your expressed discomfort writing about sex, there's no need for that anymore. Just be you the way you are and who you are becoming. Suzanne will take care of the sex, she's real good at that, sex is beautiful to her. She's always willing to share in writing (and sometimes videos to keep me going, it works.) And she's bisexual, she creates vivid dreams for both male and female readers. You couldn't do that. But who knows what the future will bring as you lighten up and *live* your life without fear, knowing eventually that you may be among a company of traveling ancient souls, stars of a great drama now playing in the Big Theater among the stars.

The audience is going wild with anticipation of a grand climax at the end, a really big show. They paid good money to get in, we're going to give them a big bang for their buck, we're known for that, it's what we do best. That's why they pay us in planets...

But in *real* life, get that cute butt and shaved lower cleavage *here* sexy babe, you're good in bed with *me*. I want you and your naked body and what you do for and with me desperately. Your Writer Fiancee Loving and Lusting for You - it's *all* good.

Jen: I love the writing. It does keep me hooked. You really are doing a magnificent job. Keep going sweetie. This is a million times better than the first time I read it or I am reading with different eyes. I crave to know as a reader who Michael is. Where he is coming from? Why he does what he does? Please share his complicated personality and emotional needs so I can understand the bad boy and the good boy. So I can relate one way or the other. He is the main character and I want to know the depth of his sole. Can you reach down inside of Michael and pull him out? You did with Suzanne. You are sharing her many sides to the reader. It is beautiful writing. I want the same from Michael.

You say you want me to be your Suzanne. I can not be this Suzanne. I assume you are referring to a different character in your book. What does the name Suzanne represents what to you? Please understand. No one has ever read the first draft of your book that I have or any of your emails. It is our private world. I delight in this world of Michael and Jen. Lets keep it that way and have fun. You are right. I commented below.

Since I don't know who or what you have explained about Michael before this or later in the book. I ask from this paragraph. What was Michaels emotional state at this time and what is he searching for on these dating sites where he meet this wonderful hospice nurse. When he states his journey was to write a book. Was Michael's secret purpose to meet and write about his sexual rendezvous. Then realized a broader deeper purpose. What was Michaels emotions and draw to this hospices nurse? Was he looking for a sex goddess at night and an angle by day.

Which makes for good writing. That would appeal to both men and women. Why does he search in this manner? What did she write that caused him to feel love (was it his need not meet) or does he fall in love with the idea of love. Was it the words she wrote or the words he wrote in (emails) that evoked tears of emotion. Did Michael realize it was like being on a stage? As actors preform and evoke emotions and laughter and finally it ends and they embrace tightly with tears fall from their eyes, the curtain goes down, the music stops and each walk in opposite directions.

My request would be, I WANT TO KNOW MICHAEL! He is so important to all that read this book. He is important to me. I want to go to bed and dream of him. You have done a marvelous job with Suzanne the hospice nurse. Go to it my Magnificent writer and make me fall in love with Michael. Don't apologize about your writing. If you think it is choppy than fix it. Add or take away. Use your poetic licensee. It really is a beautiful story.

Before I could respond to the above from Jen she does it again – WALKS AWAY! I think her questions about "Michael" are not to improve the book but to gather rocks to sling at me. She seems to have a desperate need to hurt or punish me. Perhaps my analogy about me jilting her in a past life was true. Perhaps rather than dear fiancée she is truly my greatest enemy. But then, they say to hold your enemies closest to your heart so you always know what they are doing. That simply does not work with her, she never lets me get close for any length of time. Is the engagement off? Is she coming next week? I don't know, and now maybe I don't care a whole lot either.

Chapter 2

———◦❈◦———

Jen: The past is the past and the presences makes a difference. If you have a need to have Suzanne write to you to create the organism you crave from her than you have no need for me. If you need a woman to be an angle on one side and one to dirty talk to you to satisfy your urges on the other, than you have a new type of life style I will not fit into comfortable. I thank you for being so honest. You are pushing me aside again to fulfill your need with these ladies. I don't want to wake up in the night and you masturbating to Suzanne's emails or new video's. This hurts me deeply. You fall at a drop of a hat into these women's beck and call. The writer ask to much of me. This is not real life for these women but it is for me. These women play in the fantasy box with you then leave for a filled life elsewhere. I don't. This is all I got. I am going to say what you want me to write. Maybe we should not talk about marriage until after the book's are finished, that is if either of us is available. There I wrote the script for you. Are you happy now. Just be the writer you want to be.

M: It seems that you will never be able to live with a writer. But at least you are true to yourself, YOU WALK AWAY EVERY TIME!!!! Does this mean the engagement is off, that you are going to find yourself a *fifth* man to eventually walk away from like you always do? Why did you prolong this divorce and the pain of it so long when you knew all along it wasn't possible for us to live together for *"many many reasons"* as you plainly told me? Why did you accept my proposal of marriage, or was that too just another lie to deceive me as you openly admit you do? Who have you become in the last year? Did I ever know the real you, or you me? Are you still coming on Wednesday or should I ask Elaine or someone else to come over to console me since you are not capable of anything as fine as that? Jilted in Victoria

Jen: Well enjoy her videos. It is obvious you prefer videos to masturbate to. I can not expect you to be anything more than what you choose to be. You really played me. You really want to get even. I do not believe for a moment you told these women you are engaged. Can't believe you set me aside again for your selfish desires. I do not know who you are. I do not like him. Delete all my emails and pick up with Suzanne. She plays it much better.

M: I have never lied to you. Elaine and Suzanne both know I asked you to marry me and you accepted. (I thought.) You read their response word for word. It is YOU who lies and lays in wait to deceive, even your poor sorry self-pitying self. I don't know what you have become. Perhaps it's just a desperate lust for the taste of another man that keeps you throwing me away when I had so much to give you and you knew it. I assume then that the engagement is off, you walked away again.

Jen: I am not going to marry a man that will slip to his computer to read emails from another woman to masturbate to. Would you want me to do that with another man.

M: Why would I ever do that if sexy you was at my side? The problem all along is that you would not allow us to live together, you should know that. Let the readers masturbate if it helps, I won't have any need to if you are in my bed where you properly belong each night. I still love you, silly silly you. I hope you'll change your mind about us, again. Since June it has never been me who moved away, it's always you, and then you blame me for it. If you were with me there would be no other woman at my side, just in my books where they properly belong. Can't handle your man being a writer can you? I should have known, fell for your deceit again, silly me.

Jen: Stop lying. You know my age and I do not have a sexy body. Those are words you use to bate me to play your game and go along with you having other women. Lies, Lies, Lies. You should know you never, never proved yourself to be worthy of a man I would live with and that's why we are not living together. I will not marry you if you need her for your sexual fantasy. Then expect me climb in bed with you to finish what she started. How would you like it if I talked on the phone to Al about our sexual fantasies with each other. Then climbed into bed and said, will you finish me off Al's big hot hard dick really got me going. Or I just said I need a big toy. Al really got me going. Sick isn't it. Get real. Its you that will be masturbating. I never changed my mind it was your doing with such an email that got what you wanted and that was to get me to call the marriage off. I can not play your games any more. Just delete me.

Jen: Jilted? No, No, No, you jilted me with that email. It's the words and your plans you want with this woman. Words saying I love you but lust for Suzanna's sexual emails. I can not go there. You have no right to do such a thing to any woman you might choose to marry. You said you would be faithful. This was not the email of a faithful man that plans on being faithful to his wife. What else will pop out of the closet.

M: You write *"What else will pop out of the closet."* Whatever Muse chooses to cue onstage will "pop out" of an infinite cast of characters and events when an epic novel is being written. There can be no other way to do it. It's sad that you cannot see that and just let it be, accepting your role of great woman behind a great writer. I often don't think it's in you though. You're not ready for me, maybe never will be, you're too selfishly absorbed in yourself and your sad pity-me blame someone else game. And in your obsessive fixation on SEX IS EVIL EXCEPT THE WAY *YOU* CHOOSE TO DO IT.

Yes, that's where you are, think about it, your entire complaint all along is that you don't have exclusive possession of my body and you demand it. I thought marriage and living together would solve that for you. What if I never tell you what's in my books and you never read them? Would that be an acceptable solution to your problem and get us together again where we belong?

M: Anyway, get your body here sweetheart, we need to cuddle and love again. I have not walked away, you know where I am. Coming? P.S. age or not, you'll always be younger than me, so you'll always be sexy to me, I want you and your bod.

Jen: What could possibly be going on in your head that would make you think I could live with such a man. Not one of the woman you dated would do the same. What a foul you are to even think so. Your daughter is right. You slat situations to your favor and actually believe you are fair. This is not fair. Or you are really stupid to a wife's needs. YOU NOW HAVE YOUR WISH. YOU, YOU, YOU, BY YOUR ACTIONS WANTED ME TO CALL THIS MARRIAGE OFF. How inconsiderate you are and a liar. I stupidly believed your email that you sent to my other address. That man I wanted to marry. The email that this man sent, I don't know. He breaks my heart with what he writes. I think I am just a part of your plot in your book and my heart does not matter because I was never real. I am a real person. You let the boom down. Saying in one sentence I love you best but I lust for her and her and who's next. I can not take it any more.

Since Suzanne is back and has taken my place, by your choose, I will cancel my plane tickets in the morning. Best to delete me from your book, can't play the game. My life is to real. Thanks again for all the put downs. I wish you the same from others that you dished out on this woman. I did think we had a great chance and you stooled it from us. For the lust of a lady.

M: Atom bomb time again, you're so good at it. Deliberately misinterpret an email or two and it's divorce or walk away for you. You are pitiful really, there's little if any love in you for me that's for sure. If you loved me you'd be here cuddling instead of what you are doing again today, same story. Your excuses as always are groundless. You invent a life that is not real but does contain tragedy and self-justification for being the shallow person you really are. I hope some day you'll find your place. By YOUR choice yet again it's not with me. I think you knew that all along, that's why you set these things up and deceive me. Enjoy yourself Jen, you deserve you. I wish you well my former and almost again wife. You *could* have had me all along, but you never came, you walked away instead. *Cute butt though,* I could have gotten into that. Just me alone, used to it...

M: As you should know, it's always the same story, you pretending you are offended by something I wrote that you irrationally misinterpreted the intention of and reacted to. And you using that to justify extreme nastiness and the dropping of atom bombs on the man you say you love. If you were ever able to think rationally you might question your preposterous interpretations of what I write. Would such a scheming deceitful (that's you) man have gone to great expense to plan a future with you that includes two expensive ($200) tickets to the Nutcracker Ballet on Saturday night for your birthday and a cruise in January for Christmas, *all nonrefundable?*

Silly man to believe you were telling the truth and sincere about marrying me this time huh? If you truly loved me, NOTHING would have interfered with that engagement, let alone a single email that you twisted to satisfy your desperate need for tragedy and heart break instead of love and joy, Eve Mother of Nations. Every single thing that you accuse me of is justified only when it points back to *you*. Your fight is with yourself, always. You have little love left in you, it seldom reaches the surface anymore. Who's REALLY irrational and filled with jealousy and wrath? You with your silly accusing heartbreak (yours not mine) stories about what I write in a single email that never actually says what you say it does? Or the man who does REAL things for you like proposing marriage and actually buying ballet and cruise tickets to share lovely times with you? Think about it if you are capable of thought anymore. It would be easy for even a child reading our emails to know who is right and who is wrong in what you are so callously doing to us. You do not believe in success, you are fixated on failure and blame. Blame yourself for that, it's an attitude, your choice.

Nothing more from Elaine now, I guess she too was deceived by your sickening plot to accept my marriage proposal when you can't believe we'll ever live together again and are determined to sabotage that if it ever becomes a possibility. So, in your twisted bad news way you may have taken her too away from me, not sure yet. I'm so gullible, I can never successfully fight you, don't want to, just wanted love for us. Anyway, please confirm right away that you will not be coming next week and will not be going on the cruise so I can find someone REAL to go with me and hold my hand, thanks.

I forward the ballet ticket receipt to Jen with the caption: *"See I'm real, you're not"*. There is no logic or valid reason for what she did today but being woman I suppose she can still get away with it, sure I'd have her back, silly me. She'll think that she doesn't need reason to justify what she does, she can turn it into a matter of the heart, which a male has to accept, we can't fight such a thing with any expectation of coming out winner. (Please don't be offended dear female reader, I love you like crazy, I can't live without the thought of you or someone like you in my life, just telling a story here from the male point of view.)

It's most likely premature to examine motivations but what else can I a male with mere reason at my command think other than she does not really want to marry me, or is not ready and wants to taste other men first? Will she turn to Al tonight when her company's gone I wonder, and unload her "heartbreak" to his strong and eager arms and kisses, making me into a villain? Is that what she's after, that "big dick" she so unusually wrote about in her angry mails today? Will she cuddle close to him when it could so easily have been *me* her fiancée had she really wanted me? *Why am I still allowing us to drag out this divorce?*

Jen: I ask one thing. Are you going to encourage Suzanne to send sex emails back and forth for the two of you. Being friends and sending occasional emails are ok. Sexual content is not.

M: Suzanne is a character in my books, has been there since the beginning. I allow her creator to move that character along as she wills. The only censorship I ever placed on her was redacting some of the paragraphs she wrote that I figured were too erotic for my audience. Her husband turned out to be gay so to keep sane she turned to writing erotic stories of fantasies with him that could never be, she sent some of those to me. Her life has not been fun Jen, even her retirement was stolen from her. To get a balance from the REAL tragedy in her life she becomes fictional "Suzanne". I like her that way much better than the deadly serious hospice nurse she is professionally, that fell apart for us instantly when we met in Las Vegas, there was nothing there for us in the real world. But we write well together and we get the sex into the books that will ultimately be what sells them, like it was for *Fifty Shades of Grey* that sold millions.

I will not censor the creator of Suzanne in spite of your demand because you can't handle jealousy regardless of how irrational it is. (The woman lives in Texas, thousands of miles away for goodness sake, we're not about to hop in bed together. Get real!) Either you accept me for the writer that I am or we never get together again. Right now I'm ready for either, you are so *not* looking good to me today. You are coming across as barely sane, did you know that? You're so hung up on no sex or sex your way or not at all it's sickening, *lighten up will you? Real* life is beckoning you, you could choose to *live* instead of wanting to possess raw power over the man you say you love when love and accepting and sweet gentle feminine persuasion would get you whatever positive it is you want much better.

Why are you trying to censor and control a writer of fiction and those who help him write his books instead of calling him magnificent when you know he is, and cheering him on? You need never read my books, I can cease to tell you about them. That should address all of your current concerns, they are irrational and preposterous in my opinion. But ok, I won't do the same to you as you try to do to me, be yourself just the way you are. I'm still willing to marry you and love you, it will just be that you are not involved in the writing of my books, that's all.

STOP FIGHTING ME PLEASE IT DRIVES ME AWAY!

Fighting is what my first wife chose to do. Had she loved me instead of ceaselessly attacking and trying to destroy me (like you are doing today) she could have had me for life, and in the Mormon dream, for all eternity. What is it YOU want Jen? If it's this man, you've already got him, he's your fiancee, *he* hasn't walked away.

Jen: I think you should apologize to me for assuming I would wish you well for the following. *Suzanne will take care of the sex, she's real good at that, sex is beautiful to her, She's always willing. to share in writing (and sometimes videos to keep me going, it works.) And she's bisexual, she creates vivid dreams for both male and female.* What in heaven made you think you could write such thoughtless words. Then when you find out how hurt I am I get a response of horrible put downs by you.

Jen: You did it again. You knew what it would do before you sent it. You send me down to the depths. The worst part is. You take no responsibility for your actions.

M: I rest my case. If you love me and want me the way I am come get me. Otherwise please tell me you are not coming so I can be with someone who *does* want me and will learn to love me just the way I am. I'm happy with me...

Jen: If you loved me you would want to please me and not do those things that you are well aware that would break my heart. If you loved me you would call me and reassure me that Suzanna will not be the woman that pleases you through her emails.

I go out to smell the roses in the darkness tonight, bundle up in the cold (Elaine's scarf) for a walk to Inner Harbor to see the beautiful Christmas lights on the legislative building, Christmas music from the open air skating rink on the lawn of the Empress Hotel, and a display of teddy bears at the Grand Pacific. Slipped in to the grocery store on the way back for almond milk to mix the protein shakes Elaine recommended, and three messages from Jen are waiting. A quick glance and none of them are pleasant, she cannot see that what she accuses me of is *her own* weakness. Surely what she really wants is to get rid of me permanently, possibly her intention all along but she had to find some way to blame *me* for her walking away, it's a pattern. Maybe it's for the best.

Still nothing from Elaine when she said she'd bring me food yesterday or today. Perhaps with that announcement about my engagement she has gone off to another more promising man? I wish her well, I am calm with me. The worst that could happen is that I live alone but I've been there before I can handle it. I just need to *permanently* close the door of possibility to my greatest temptation. She's still not available for me, may never really be, all along she's been lying and deceiving to lead me on, she admitted to that. Fool that I am for not believing her when said she lies and deceives. When I think of her I think of her as a very different person, one capable of even a perfect love. A very few emails in the past have led me on to think that, but the last few weeks she has not displayed that, just a desire to make me over in her own preferred image and likeness.

Jen: The man from California. that put on the dating site he wanted a wife. Called a couple days ago and I did not answer the call. He called a few minutes ago and told me the elderly lady next door sent two missionaries to his house. He said they wanted to recruit him into the church. I told him they want to invite him to listen to their message. He called to get my opinion since he knew I was a good Mormon. We had a great conversation about the Church. God does care about me. That phone call lifted my spirits so much. After we hung up I text him back and said thanks for calling I was really down tonight and you lifted my spirits I think I will call you my angle. He test back, is that all it takes. I text back, sometimes that's all it takes. So I am feeling better thanks to Henry. Maybe he and I can talk.

M: Lovely, you have another man on your list of people who cheer you up when this man apparently cannot, that's just the way I am.

Jen: What case are you talking about closing? If you love me and want me the way I am call me. Otherwise please tell me you don't want me and I will have a good cry as you set me aside for another waiting as you put it. Thanks for reassuring me you do not take responsibility for your actions. Yea for some people they would think that is happiness.

Jen: (writing about the ballet tickets) It would have been wonderful. I am sorry you are so determined to ruin it for us.

I thought it was completely done with her but here's a new message.

Jen: That Suzanne is the past. You are such a wonderful writer. You do not need trash to write a good book. Write the things that will make your children and friends proud of you. Please don't resort to such writing. Look at your daughter's book. She is good, you are a better writer in some things. You are magnificent writer. Stay email friends with Suzanne but please let go of the trash talk. It is a habit of your to threaten me. I want the man I love to respect me and my wishes and I will lighten up. I never associated a magnificent writer with books filled with sex scene's. Some is OK but not to the level you want with Suzanna. Everything else you write is magnificent. I can help with the few sexual scene's not Suzanna. We can act them out. Much better than emailing them. I am good at in the moment scene's. I will come but can't make promises. As much as you choose to hurt me, I will try. Start being a better man for me and I will reward you in everyway.

You assume to much, your first wife did not want you. Your wants and ways did not make her happy. She is now happy with her children and grandchildren. She has a secure retirement and a home paid for. If she does not have a man, well she just may not want one. You well know what I want. You are the character in the book and I want him to be a magnificent man.

Jen: I give up. Please write as you please and with who ever you please. God bless with great success.

M: (to Jen) After a day like today what better thing to do than go out in the night to smell the roses. I bundled up for the cold, long johns and tuque that I bought, jacket a gift from my daughter, and scarf a gift from Elaine. Yes, there are people who love and care about me just as I am without needing to make me over into their own preferred image and likeness. Your love is always conditional, it comes with strings attached. I just got back. But I see that while I was out for a walk fickle you has given up and walked away again, maybe forever this time. That's what you wanted all along wasn't it? However it is I simply cannot live with contention and nastiness, the stuff you create with your seemingly desperate need to hurt and blame me and keep us from ever getting together. I would have responded to love, acceptance and happiness, it doesn't come from you. My own comments were always factual rational responses to yours, not just making up tales to blame me for your walking away yet again, throwing away the people you say you love. You see life through a very different lens than I do. My focus is on tolerance and love and joy, yours seems to be on intolerance, fear, and guilt. It's not clear to me now, are you coming here next week and are you going to cruise with me? Please respond so if need be I can plan (yet again) a life without you in it, thanks.

M: On closer look perhaps it's me who misinterpreted what you wrote this time. Maybe when you said *"I give up"* it did not mean you had given up on us as I originally thought but that you had given up on your demand that Suzanne and I only exchange messages that meet your approval? Anyway, I really do want to try holding and loving you and see if that gets us anywhere closer to reconciliation and eventually living together. Please come honey, I love you.

M: Those sexual desires in me that you condemn so harshly are precisely what keeps me alive and moves me along the way to becoming Adam. It is the secret that was revealed to me years ago as the way to avoid boredom when eternity sets in. For me there is no other way if I am to remain male, which I am determined to do because I am becoming ADAM not Eve. You may never understand, so if all you do is be neutral on the matter and stop trying to impose your female perspective on a male, that would work well, we could live in harmony.

Please forgive as need be, I feel that it was you who did the provoking today not me, but I accept that you see it the other way around. It was never my intention to hurt you, it's not in me to deliberately do that, though of course you can interpret what I write however you will. I look forward to holding you in my arms, caressing your cheek, and whispering love to you. Please tell me you are coming to me.

M: Is your company all gone, can I call?

Jen: I'm all alone. you can call.

We talked, it didn't end well. I'm not meeting her needs but I think she's coming on Wednesday. Let's see what comes now with that abrupt outburst at the end and the disconnect. I'm still not seeing her as a happy thought but I know when we're physically together I'll be loving and gentle and tender, that's the way I am, the solution seems to be for us to live together. I think she's moving towards that for the first time since June. But I cannot promise her happiness, she has to find that within herself. Her choice is either me or her fears, that's how I see it. I still want us to live together but to avoid formal marriage if she'll go for that, at least for a few years. That way if need be we can just walk away instead of being forced to accept what some judge has decided is best for us to do with our assets. I don't want that ever again, it's a feeling of powerlessness, the kind of feeling that takes away the desire to live.

Jen: You want me to call you Magnificent to make you feel good about yourself, and I do. I want to see a magnificent man when I am around you. Will I see that man when I visit. You should of heard the kind things I said to my cousin about you. What about Jen. You may not think it but your beliefs and statements make me feel like I am a peace of shit. Who never see things your way. Who is going to tell me they like me? Who is going to listen and make me feel understood. Who is going to make me feel safe. Who is going to call me magnificent?

M: Perhaps with my arms around you I will feel that you are magnificent, today I'm not there, tomorrow maybe I will be. We've played this game before. All I can say right now is I love you and want to hold you again. Try not to live in your fears so much, you attract what you are thinking about the most. Expect the best for us and we'll co-create that and get it, works all the time. Like attracts like. The way you are today is not attracted to me that's why you think I'm something you couldn't live with. That's true you couldn't, I do not have a contentious spirit, I live in love and happiness. You could come there and find me. You can become chronically happy, love conquers all, you needn't fight anything, just find love inside yourself. Try it? You'll be glad that you did. Think only love and kindness, it becomes a habit after a while and you won't want to be anywhere else. Pretend your body is vibrating faster, you'll feel love. The fastest vibration is pure love, that's where God lives. Go to Him, you can, you'll be amazed at how good you look there... Feeling like a piece of shit is your own choice, don't ever blame someone else for it when all it takes is a little mental shift to feel good about yourself.

Jen: My earlier email before you called. True, Henry is another man waiting in the wings. He keeps in contact on rare occasion. I told him to keep meeting with the missionaries. To let me know how the lessons are going. That it would be worth it. My cousin called a bit before him. I told her that I loved you and you loved me. I told her all the wonderful sides of you that I love. She said, do what will make you happy.

M: My guess is that you felt happy as you were telling your cousin good things about me. See, it's easy to be happy, speak only love.

Jen: I am glade you stated God lives. That I believe is true. Your comments are good advice. Not sure if they come from understanding Jen. That's OK. You don't have to understand me as long as I do my job making me happy. I don't have to please anyone unless I want to. They are responsible for their own happiness. No worries. Be happy! If I want to stay up all night every night and watch movies I can. Of course I would go dancing or if you wanted you could tag along. That I would find joy and be really happy doing. We don't have a place hear to go. But was looking at taking some lessons to build my stamina. Do you know a place in Victoria I could go dancing at. Ballroom is my preference. I could do that twice a week. That would really make me happy.

I could develop some art talent and do charity work. That would please. I could plan a get to know your neighbor party. That would be lots of fun and keep me from getting board with you on the computer all day. Maybe we can invite Oresha and friends in. You could have a bit of wine with them. Sounds like fun and a happy time. I love my soft nighties. The material makes me feel warm and safe inside. Don't you think I should wear them every night if it makes me happy. Thanks for the advice. With all this activity and my body vibrations rising I would soon be on my way to happiness. From this day forward I make me happy. On for the ride. Each seeking their own happiness. What will you be doing for happiness. Oh I know writing. My magnificent writer. He is going to be rich. I do love you sweetie

Is this raw sarcasm? It sure seems that way. Oh well, whatever makes her happy.

Jen: I do not think you should demand me to make a choose between seeing you or missing my doctor appointment. That appointment is important for me to keep right after surgery. I tried to arrange it at the earliest time. So we would have as much time as possible together. I can not dictate your son's schedule. Neither can I risk my health by missing my two week appointment. I will be supper busy with catch up paying bills and receipts and deposits and so on. love you sweetie.

Happy married life coming up, loving devoted wife, Eve Mother of Nations? Hmmm….. I guess I'd better do some fine tuning on that happiness of mine, right now I'm not looking forward to being with my greatest temptation. Could I live alone for years more, not bother to get a live in? I'm doing it now and it's not such a bad place to be. At this pre-dawn moment I'm kind of favoring that. I trashed my singles site profiles so I'd have to make new ones, start all over again, no word from Elaine, yes a whole new me. I wonder what would be best? I guess I need to put my arms around Jen and see how that feels. It's sure not feeling good from a distance. Do I need her at all? Does she need me? It seems a constant battle between us, not exactly a good foundation to start a marriage is it. It does seem obvious that we aren't 'meant' for each other, whereas I was quite happy before I sent that proposal of marriage, it's quite a struggle now. What do you advise?

Jen: This is a suggestion. You may want to give Elaine a bit more time to adjust to the relationship being confirmed as platonic friends. Its ok for her to say we are friends but to have a man say it could hurt some women's ego. Just don't jump to conclusions the silence means the friendship is over. Good morning

M: (to Jen but not sent) You know what silence does to me. Silence has always come before being dumped by women I am growing fond of. Elaine has not contacted me for several days, I'm missing that friend connection. Maybe it *was* all about romance for her, just her going slow. Otherwise why would recent events have suddenly changed her from warm to cold to gone if she was just thinking friend, like you apparently were with Al though he was thinking bed because he's male? But yes, I think it would be best that I don't contact her either, just let her be. We've drifted far apart since I announced you and I are getting married. Are we? Can't say that I blame her for most likely favoring another man now, this one's not available.

These are just early morning musings. I haven't meditated for a few days and am not on top of things like I used to be, I'm not usually down and doubting like this. I'm still not seeing my future. I hate the contention between us, it doesn't feel at all like I have attracted a loving devoted wife Eve Mother of Nations, far from it actually. Where we are

I find only anger and guile and selfishness. It's confusing. But ok, blame me for telling you the way I am feeling this moment and putting you into yet another rant that may result in you not getting on that plane. You dropped a hint on the phone last night that you might get so busy you'd miss it.

That would be like you being almost two hours late picking me up in Las Vegas a few weeks ago. You never did get to the airport, I took a cab to the hotel, you said you'd been busy. You've never been like that before. Were you resenting my coming to visit? Are you resenting me being in your life? Is that why you say I'm not taking responsibility, because I'm leaving it up to you to make or break this relationship? And you are feeling an *obligation* to continue with it, rather than a happy desire to do so? Even yesterday you asked for a decision from me, said you'd have your "cry" and get on with life. Yes, I'm beginning to see what I'm doing, I think you want to be free of me. (*That's pretty clear to you dear reader isn't it?* Is that what she really wants, for me to break this off once and for all?)

I may not send this to you, probably shouldn't, ok, I won't, there, relief, don't need more accusations of nastiness because I told you where I am. You're wanting me to tell you how grand you are when I really don't know you, you're like a stranger now. I was unable to find anything to say when you asked last night what I found grand in you, you were not a happy thought at the time after a day of nasty messages. Let's get together physically and see how it goes, that would be telling. I'm sure that you would react badly to my telling you the way it is for me as I awake this morning after being on the phone with you until midnight. Neither of us were bubbling with joy because we were talking to our lover and fiancee. (Are we fiancee?) This is feeling like before I married my second wife, a big mistake with no joy in it. We married but it didn't last long. I should be following the happiest thought, you're not the happiest, right now there is no happiest, I'd better start searching for one. Where's that eager joyful anticipation that my lover's coming two days from now? I think only of the negative ways we were. You told me yesterday that you would come and visit but couldn't give any promises. Well I can't either. We both know where this is going don't we?

That settles it, I'll not be sending this message to you. I'll put on a false face and send a cheery one instead. I don't want to be blamed for destroying us with yet another sabotaging message, I thought that was *your* job, you've been doing it lately and seeing me as the one doing the sabotaging. The more I think and feel about where we are the more doubts I have about us co-creating a successful marriage. I need to learn from my second marriage mistake, a rebound for both of us, most unhappy, very short. Ok, as I write, the option of not marrying at all flows into mind as the best thing to do, we're not ready for each other, it's just a convenience thing. But who knows, maybe I can find more love for you with my arms around you when you are here. Will I? Right now I don't think so, but I know I can work on it and get there, for a while at least. Loving you as wife again is not coming easy, maybe we should just go for friends.

My sister asked me last week why I don't just live like she does, single? That has its attractions and it's not forever. I don't *have* to live long, finishing these books is the main thing now. The ancient trees are just yards away in case I get in a rush to pour my soul and life into them the way it was done anciently, it would be easy I just know it. The thought of heaven is always a most happy feeling, it's a great place to be, for a while, but we rush to get back for a fresh start in physicality, the grandest state of being.

Let's wait a couple more days and see what happens when we're physically together. I know we won't be deliriously happy though, at least not for the whole seven days. Sometimes with you I think the Als and the Henrys are calling much more strongly than I am. I am not *fighting* for you and you know it. I'm dumping responsibility and leaving too much of the final choices up to you: ok to marry, ok to not, have it your way kind of thing, and you playing that right back. I'm filled with doubt about this engagement. (Are we engaged?) I'm filled with doubt about the thought of marrying you again. (Are we getting married?)

Henry in California may become Mormon, the missionaries are visiting him. I'll bet that's hugely attractive and you felt real good talking with him on the phone, you thought God was rescuing you from *me*. Where's the joy for you in *me*? I awake this morning and read your messages, some of which I interpret as sarcastic and I wonder again if we are doing right by trying to force a remarriage? You keep saying that I avoid responsibility. Much of what you are judging is simply me not thinking I've done something I need to be "responsible" for, it's you who places your own meaning on what I write.

But ok, I don't *really* want to marry you, at least that's how I'm feeling this morning. But then again, you haven't been a happy thought all along, *why are we dragging out this divorce?* Maybe I should tell you that outright instead of sending a proposal of marriage. *Why did I send that proposal?* Just wanting to end this one way or the other? It was of course motivated by your saying you love me and would be the best thing ever for me, how could I be responsible for crashing that? Then the next moment you're off in an unhappy rant blaming me for something. I think at the moment I wrote that proposal it's not happiness I had in mind, it was the feeling of *inevitability* that I had succumbed to, it seemed foolish that we not, not happy that we do.

You'll find other men easily as soon as you get those 'I'm available' pheromones pumping out again. (Did they ever stop? Bet Henry felt them on the phone with you last night. Did you take down your single sites profile? Bet you didn't.) The worst thing that could happen is that I never find Eve, and never marry again. I guess I could handle that. And if/when my books sell and I get wealthy I'm sure I'll have women knocking my door down to get in anyway, my pick, my choice from among them, pick none, pick a dozen... Tall, classy, feminine, graceful, beautiful, intelligent, loves me unconditionally? (Where's that in you?)

Your advice to me is to *take the sex out of my books!* What would be left for the reader then? A text book of personal philosophizing maybe? That would hardly be a viral or a virile event. I'm the Writer, I must take full responsibility for what I do and I must do it my way. I was hoping for encouragement but from you I have to ASK for that, it's hardly encouraging.

I'm just letting you know what I'm feeling this a.m. It's certainly not a joyous anticipation of a happy married life, though we could make it so perhaps if we *worked* hard at it. Ready to work hard? Happy thought? Or would Henry in California who you've never met but says he wants your body from looking at a photo and may become Mormon be a happier way of thinking? Henry my dear will expect you to put out for him. If you don't, he'll dump you like Al I think has. Though Al being local of course he might still have enough hots for you that he'd come should you beckon and invite him to come to you in the privacy of your home. What man wouldn't?

Anyway you haven't changed a lot, you're still in "woman" mode *thinking* about things you don't disclose. It's still possible that you will take many months before we actually start living together, nothing has changed *really,* you were just jealous of Elaine, and then Suzanne. Is that correct? No, today I'm not seeing us getting married. Today I'm thinking we are not at all right for each other, just caught up in post-divorce trauma, dragging it out, jealous when others step in to take our place, not letting go....

Yep, down a bit today, won't send this, maybe reader will find it interesting, where's Michael with Jen this a.m.? Now you know.

Jen: Thank you for planning a wonderful Birthday for me when I visit.

M: You deserve it, so do I. *Ballet?* Am I gone nuts or something? Oh well, bringing me a pink tutu to wear?

M: Good morning. I've been writing in my journal for several hours already today, trying to get the clarity of thought that I think will only come with being in each other's presence. You say you aren't coming with promises and I understand, you broke the 'engagement' off is my understanding, correct me if I'm wrong. Instead of each of us knowing clearly what we should do about us we're in a state of confusion. I thought your other message this morning was quite sarcastic and provoking, but then I don't want to get in to misinterpreting what you write, we've been there done that a whole lot too much already. Let's see how it feels when we get our arms around each other, right now we're anything but deliriously happy that we're getting married. Are we? I don't think we're even engaged. Are we? You'd think we should be unquestionably happy if we were on a good path, no doubts at all. We'll take this one very slowly I think, that's what you've always had in mind anyway. I don't think anything much has changed for you regarding timing, you were just jealous of Elaine and then Suzanne. Right?

Silence tells me that I have lost Elaine but I've been to those kinds of places already, I'll survive without her. I won't blame you for the loss, it was me who sent the marriage proposal then told her.

Enjoy the day sweetie, that's the best I can come up with this morning, a bit down after that call until midnight that's all. I'll recover, always do, so will you. Still love you, just again not at all certain about marriage, being honest, let's get together and talk about it. If when we talk marriage it doesn't seem the happiest thought, we could still cruise in January, just be dear friends having fun like we had planned anyway until I sent that proposal of marriage. That was probably much too hasty don't you agree? Maybe the best loving relationship you and I could have for years would be friends and lovers, we'd never forget each other and become like the other spouses that way. That feels a happy thought to me. There will always be Elaine and Al and Henry and numerous others for both of us. (If I ever get motivated to get back on singles again, I destroyed my profiles, I doubt that you did yours, I always jump in too fast too deep, foolish in the things of this world.)

But we'll know more clearly what we want after we've felt each other's nearness again, that seems to work well for us, at least for a while. We don't have to be married for that but I'm still willing if those seven days bring us closer than I feel right now. We'll see how it goes, no promises, I'm looking forward to touching you again dear one. I want the best for us both I'm just not sure right now if that would be marriage with each other, let's talk. At least as friends and lovers when others crash upon us we'd have each other to run to, touch, make love, and comfort with for a while. Not so shabby a thought huh? And there's always the *possibility* of marriage should it ever come to that and it becomes the happiest thought for both of available us.

I do love you Jen, I do want to be with you often, I do want us to be dear friends and lovers, I don't know for sure if marriage is the best thing for us right now. That's where I am starting out today. Now get that cute butt of yours into my space will you, *that* I could get into....

Jen: (re the tutu) Pink or white.

M: Why pink of course. What a strange question, doesn't every man want pink?

Jen: Don't go nuts until you see the nuts cracking in the NUTCRACKER then decide if it is something. I am very excited about seeing it. For some craze reason when in China I was attracted to the Chinese Ballet. I was able to see the exact control of the song, sound and the movements. I could even tell when they were very good or average. Does not mean I understood it. What a crazy thing to find some level of joy from. I do love you.

M: You're the one who's nuts I think. But maybe there is a culture crazy lady hiding in there somewhere and none of your husbands indulged that. I can't promise that I'll like ballet but will give it a try. I hope you like it, and me for the birthday present. Birthday suit when we get home?

I do not like the notion of you not being naked in bed with me. Naked would be an enormous treat after all those many years of it being forbidden by the Mormons that husbands and wives sleep naked together. No wonder you have control issues with that example of blind obedience *for what?* Think about it. Naked is not evil, it's beautiful, sex is not evil, it's beautiful, God gave us that. Control for the sake of control is evil. Come with clothes on to my bed where I lay naked and I'll soon strip them off you, promise. I'll never again be somebody else's puppet dangling from their strings on pain of hell or a lesser heaven if I don't follow their every command. *I now think for myself.*

Jen: What do you think a woman wants when she climbs in bed with you. I would say do it.

M: Love that attitude. You get right down to the naked truth sometimes.

Jen: No the engagement is not off. I never said that. I am wearing my wedding ring. Sometimes I was jealous. Give Elaine time. She will most likely be back as she adjust. I don't want to call our engagement off. Maybe we need a bit more time. That's all. Do you want to call the engagement off.

M: What I want right now is you in my arms and naked in bed each night. We'll take it from there.

M: Our cabin on the cruise is M62. I surely hope you will be there for me, sometimes I wonder when the bombs are dropping thick and fast. There seems to be a (most welcome) lull in the battle so far today, hope it lasts... No more contention or power grabs? Touch of humility? Be my Eve Mother of Nations *always* loving? I think you are capable of that, just not sure yet if you are willing.

Do you remember that old chocolate bar jingle? *"Oh Henry...."* Do you like the hope of new flavors of chocolate a lot? Several choices of Adams chewing gum appeal to you? Keeping a list and counting it twice? Still searching for the best you can get? I'm not searching, not yet anyway, hot date coming up this Wednesday should be fun, like her a lot, hopeful, always expecting the best, thinking of *her* with *mmm* in mind.

Jen: (speaking of the cruise) This will be great fun.

M: Oh what a beautiful morning, oh what a beautiful day. She's playing nice in my sandbox today. Maybe I'll let her pull me around in my little red wagon, by the handle. I think she likes that, kinda grows on her I guess.

Chapter 3

As I strolled the park today and watched the ducks walk silly on newly frozen pond water I did some future thinking. At this point it's just fantasy. To become real would require the acceptance and availability of both Jen and Elaine. I could not run these ideas by Jen until she and Elaine have become friends, which would require Jen living with me for a few months before the plan is executed. If Elaine comes back to me as a friend I could run it by her almost anytime, telling her it is subject to Jen's approval. Here's the hypothetical plan.

On October 1st next year, Jen and I leave Victoria where we have lived for several months and go to Hawaii for six months. Elaine moves in to my apartment where she will live by herself for six months. Because she is house sitting and storing my furniture and stuff, she pays only half the rent plus utilities. Optionally I pay her return flights and she stays with me and Jen in Hawaii for three weeks in January just because she's our best friend. In April, Jen and I return to Victoria and share the apartment with Elaine. We get the bedroom, she gets a queen air mattress that inflates and deflates in moments for the living room floor, or buys herself a day bed. Should Jen and I get up too early for Elaine, she can finish her rest in our bed. During those six months I pay the utilities.

It's important to Elaine that she swim every day. She would have the use of the heated outside pool here during the warm months when it's open and could join the Victoria Athletic Club and use their indoor pool less than ten minutes from here on foot.

It is my hope that we would be the best of friends and this arrangement would go on for years or until Elaine moves on. My affection for her would likely be expressed with a quick kiss in the morning, a hug at night. She and Jen would work out their own arrangements.

What do you think? Silly, or viable plan? Would Jen be too jealous for that? Right now I think so, but if those two become best of friends, maybe it would work out for all of us.

I've been thinking a bit today about what really is it that keeps a man with a woman. I'm going to give you the male point of view ladies, you may be disappointed, it's quite different than the way women think I think. What I have to say may be just me and not common to all men, but here goes me. I have observed that when I am feeling sexual need I yearn for and think fondly of Jen. It's her specifically because I'm not a run-around, don't use prostitutes, and she is the one most likely to fulfill my need. When I am not feeling sexual need I may have occasional thoughts about Jen but it's not a pressing thing. Sure, I can feel love for her anytime, that's a given, I'm sure she feels love for me too, but there's more to it than that for the male.

When a man lives with a woman it's not likely that he is going to run away just because he's not feeling sexual need at the moment. They're there for each other in the myriad other things that come with western life besides sex. But Jen and I are not living together. So for me, at least at the physical level of awareness, it's those sexual thoughts that are *vital* to my connection with her. I can if I search inside find other connections, but they are not so powerful as to often cause me to think of her, I need to go looking for them.

Conclusion. I must tell Jen this because she's not getting us together anytime soon: IF A WOMAN WANTS TO KEEP A MAN, LIVE WITH HIM AND/OR GIVE HIM SEX WHEN HE WANTS IT! That's how I see it today ladies. Like it or not, sex is hugely important not just to the males of all ages past puberty, but also because of that to you unless it doesn't matter if you have a male around for long. Does it matter?

So how do women see it? How does a man keep a woman? I don't dare run that by Jen or Elaine or Suzanne today, I don't think I'd get a response from either, maybe later. I suppose a glib response from a male to the question "how does a man keep a woman" might be:

"How the heck would I know? Her chemicals foam and fume, her emotions are up and down and all around hour by hour, she's never the person I think she is, I'm going out with my buds for a while dear, see you later."

Did you hear the sound of the door softly shutting or slamming behind him? At her age she can't use PMS as an excuse, but for me it would suffice if she simply said, *"I Am a Woman!"* I'd understand.

That's just one man's point of view and it most likely does not apply to all women, women of course run companies, design buildings, build bridges, fly airplanes... I love you ladies, you're complex, you're mysterious, you're beautiful, you buy my books, I NEED you. Am I getting close to right about mystery you?

Ok, it's much later now and I haven't heard from Jen since early a.m. She should have been home today I would have thought, unless she's visiting her daughter, but all day? I wonder if Al's off work today and she's with him? Yes, it's not a sexual thing I'm feeling right now, I'm missing her, *I'm PINING for her!!!* Is *that* what you ladies call "love"? I copied this paragraph into a message I just sent to Jen. Hope she's ok. Sent the following too, missing her a lot, wouldn't want to lose her in spite of all the stuff we go through together.

M: (to Jen) Will you be overnighting in Vegas tomorrow or driving there in the a.m.? I plan to be at the Victoria Airport in good time to pick you up for your 3 p.m. arrival Wednesday December 3rd. I'm really looking forward to being with you again Jen, should be good. Even the weather is now looking better for your time here, at least the first few days.

Busy today? Plans to see Al before you come? Just curious, your business, wondering if he's still in touch now that he knows your company is gone, is he wanting to see you? Sure, I'm still a bit jealous, it will pass. You'll have two weeks alone before your Christmas company arrives, lots of time to get lonely after you go home, can't blame you if you want to be with a friend, I would. Whatever came of that other man in Utah who wanted to see you? Is Henry the guy that asked for sex the first time he called or was that someone else? You felt real good talking with him, but that could have been just doing missionary 'work' and feeling good about yourself?

I haven't heard from Elaine I think she's gone, but maybe you're right and she'll be back later? I'll have almost all of December and Christmas to go before I see you again so I sure hope she comes around as a friend and we can go to some Christmas things together. There's nobody else I want to see, I've pretty much written off Oresha and her friend, haven't heard from either for a long time and don't expect to. And I'm off singles now completely so won't meet anyone new.

Elaine coming back would be a beautiful Christmas gift for me in your absence. There's even less chance that she and I will get more involved than we have been now that she knows you and I are engaged, so you should be comforted by that. Just wish her back to me I don't want to be lonely, especially at Christmas. I'm not close to my second sister, I have no desire to go for Christmas in Nanaimo, unless she calls and invites me. And the one who lives in Victoria will be away for Christmas. I've missed you today, you must be real busy or away from your computer, haven't heard from you since early a.m.. I hope you're not angry about something I wrote and are doing ok with us. Love you lots.

M: (to Jen) Suzanne did it all the time, she manipulated my emotions by going silent and also by getting angry at something I wrote and not telling me she was angry or why until a long period of silence had passed. I know it's only a few hours of silence from you today and I'm sure it's not deliberate, you're not at your computer. But not hearing from you in my loneliness (no Elaine) and especially you often getting angry at something I wrote has me doing what I called with Suzanne *"walking on eggshells"*. Everything I wrote to her I screened carefully to be sure it wouldn't offend her somehow but I invariably messed up, there was no winning for me. For example I once told her she "needed someone younger" than me in her life. After the compulsory silence she roared back that I had no right to ever tell her what she needed! So the way it is now I welcome your messages but I sometimes cringe thinking they are going to be nasty to this already oversensitive poet's heart. (I know you don't believe that, but that's how I feel about myself.) You now have me programmed to walk on eggshells with you. I hope it doesn't last. The cure of course is to *never* write anything angry or jealous or accusing or critical of me. Just love, that's all I want from you, choose love, and let me know you do.

I hope to hear from you soon and how your day went. My loneliness is making me think you're off with some man, probably Al, but logic tells me it's not likely. But then again, I hardly know you anymore... Talk to me soon please, I'm needy right now. I don't dare phone because I know you hide me and I don't know where you are or who you are with. Anyway, I much prefer email as you know.

Well, that worked, always does, three messages from Jen came in exactly as I was writing the above.

Jen: (re the little red wagon and oh what a beautiful morning song) I did listen to the music plus a few others.

Jen: What naked truth's will you share in a couple night from now.

M: I'm not shy, I don't have any hang ups, I'll even go all the way if that's what you want and I am capable in that moment. You can do *whatever you want* with this male body, I think you know that. The only rule is no other males in the room, that's the naked truth.

Jen: I was thinking we should be able to share anything we are thinking with kindness and consideration. That is ideally. Can we look at some methods that would help defuse us from both parties. If one is offended. What rules should be in place to handle it. If the other is offended at the others response. What would be a good rule to follow so it does not turn into a battle. Just don't say come from love. That's a unrealistic place of that moment. I am talking about defuse methods. That would help us get back to love. I don't have the answer at the moment.

I don't feel jealousy any more or not at this moment. I was never jealousy that you communicated with Suzanne or her with you. It was a couple sentence that up set me. Has she contacted you again. She seemed to be busy. Does she write her sex talk when she is drunk. We know drinking causes people to let their guard down to say or do things they would not do otherwise. Would you let me see you lightly drunk so I could see how you would act and possibly I would encourage you to chased around the bed. I think it would be fun for the both of us.

M: Please understand as I've told you before, I WILL NEVER DELIBERATELY INTEND TO HURT YOU. You can easily choose to be offended or insulted at some things I write or do, anyone can do that, it's choice of attitude, sometimes an honest misunderstanding. But if you stop to think for a moment before you write back that this man you say you love never *intended* to hurt you, maybe you can get a grasp on your emotions before firing at me or dropping a bomb. There are times when I will write a message to you but never send it, just record it in my journal with that notation because I know in your mood at the time you would take it wrong. Oh yes of course, I do defend myself and speak the truth as I know it to try to get an understanding, and you roar back at that because I'm not calling you grand or addressing your needs with those words. But however, it's never with the intent to hurt you, I just don't go there, I am not capable of that. That's how I see myself, I'm sure you would differ.

Strangely you ruled out the one thing that in my opinion would always defuse any situation. You or I could write back with nothing except THE THREE CODE WORDS – *"I LOVE YOU"*. That's the best I can do to respond to your message right now. Tell me about your day? I was home alone except for a short walk in the park.

I have not heard from Suzanne, it might be months, I never know, what I really hope to get from her is more hospice stories. Since Las Vegas I don't know when Suzanne is drunk, I observed that she drank heavily but never showed it. She did not often talk of sex, I think only two nights when she asked me to help her to a climax with written words when she was home alone, and I did. You way over-rate the sex in my books, there's not a whole lot, but I'm hoping enough to keep readers coming back for the next book. I insert sex deliberately and don't see anything wrong with it anymore, it's the Mormons who take pride in calling themselves "peculiar". They're a lovely people but indeed are peculiar in some things, like not drinking coffee or tea or alcohol and hung up on no sex or even nakedness. That's very strange to most others.

I have not been drunk since I was a teenager in the military. But if you're buying and I don't have to drive or walk somewhere, sure I'll drink your alcohol, just not sure how much or how fast, I don't think I'll like to be hung over next day. Are you planning to sip some wine with me? Do you really think I need to be drunk to chase naked you around a bed?

Jen: And this we will see. Love you lots my love I am sorry I did not get to read those pages. I do intently enjoy reading what you send me.

M: Are you saying you want to read sex scenes from my books? *You asked me to take the sex out of my books!* Are you starting to loosen up from your rigid attitude about naked bodies doing sex?

Jen: I can get turned on as well as anyone that reads a sex scenes that are not vulgar.

M: Define vulgar.

Jen: I have a rule also no other women in the room. Yea and my naked truth looks better.

M: Sure, more than one woman in bed at the same time is a fantasy, most likely one shared by most males though they'd never speak of it like I do. Do you honestly think I'd bring another woman to our bed? That would only happen if *you* did - I'd be shocked!

Jen: Since that knowledge of men has come to me. I see it in movies and have asked other people and they say yes it is most men's fantasy. Most just don't say it is.

M: See, men live rich fantasy lives because church and society (and their woman) won't let them do what they secretly want to do.

Jen: I am busy getting ready to come for our visit. I shaved today. Went shopping to get a few things to wear on my slimmer body but not there yet so don't want to buy any larger. I am going to take back tomorrow the size 14 pants I purchased. My two new pairs are size 12. It would make me happy to be a size 10 when we meet in December. My daughter's mother in law is visiting so I went to their home for dinner. I was not going to eat tonight but did because of them. I was thinking today. I don't want you to walk on eggshells with me. Hope we can cure that soon. No time for other men. Please don't worry. I am not in contact with Al. Have not been in two or three weeks. I got my phone bill, the extra phone calls to you are costing me $300. You are worth that and more.

M: Thanks for shaving for me, you're getting me excited. I'm pleased to hear about the absence of men, I was hoping, just not knowing. If I phone you is the extra cost the same? If not send me a mail when to call and I will.

I fried myself three eggs today, first time in a month or more. Maybe I was thinking of taking pleasure in throwing out the shells. Just be nice *always*, that's the way to win me, you then align with love and joy which is where you'll find me when I meditate. A few days before the great war to end all wars while we were on the phone I think you caught a vision of me on the way to my spiritual home. Keep such things in mind and it will be easier for you to love me. I am not the nasty scheming deceiving lying man you sometimes color me as, never have been, never will be. Color me nice, I am. I love you.

Jen: (re my comments about what a woman needs to do to keep a man) Ah... what Purdy words. Thank you for writing this. It is a beautiful description of one mans opinion and that is very important especially to me. It would be interesting for women readers to know other men's view or perspective on this. Yours might be the most generous. I don't really know.

Jen: I will drive directly to Vegas early morning. I hope the weather is better. Trying to decide what type of clothing I need to bring. Will I need gloves. You could go home with me for another week. My surgery is the 17th. You could stay till the 19th or the 20th. I don't want you to be alone. If you come to see me till possibly the 21st could you leave and go see your son and stay with them. Till we meet. Or maybe use the motor home until after Christmas. I don't want you to be alone. I hope Elaine will call and you can do a Christmas event. Like I said I am very busy getting ready to be with you. please rest-a-sure my thoughts are love toward you and every moment I am thinking and planning when demanding work does not call me away from those thoughts.

M: Yes, you will need gloves unless you plan to keep your hands in your pockets. I have some really good ones my daughter bought me that you can use because my hands are invariably in my jacket pocket when I'm outside walking. I was astonished at how cold minus three feels to me now. As I was complaining to myself I spoke with a daughter in Alberta who said it was minus 30 where she is, I shouldn't complain. You do have that winter coat here but will still need a warm sweater under it. You can buy a scarf and a tuque or winter hat here if you need one. It won't be colder than minus 5 (five degrees below freezing) or so, hasn't been that low yet, so you know what that's like. I have umbrellas for the rain. But it does not warm up much in the day like it does where you are.

Jen: I was outside today and felt the warmth on my bare feet and touched the warmth of the house that was warmer than the air. It felt good. Wore short pants to the store but when the Sun went down. I went home and put long pants on. A light jacket works well in the evening. I will look for my gloves.

Gosh darn you know, I think she's serious about having me. Makes for a change of heart on my part. What in the world were we fighting about anyway?

Jen: Must go for a bit and take care of a few chores. Be back in a bit.

There, see, I tell it ALL like I said I would in the beginning of my book, the whole naked truth, even right down to that last two sentence note from Jen. Happy now?

Elaine: Sorry I haven't been in touch, but I had a bad weekend, in that I went skating on Sunday and fell on one knee, which took all the weight and it been swollen and painful. I've been putting ice on it and resting. I had to go out, get groceries and such, but have been laying low. I have to hobble off to work tomorrow.

How are you keeping? I can't begin to think of outings or editing right now... I just want to get my knee better so I can walk again! So, forgive me for being very quiet. I will be able to concentrate in a day or so. Until then, I'll be thinking of you, from time to time! Elaine the knee blasted limpy leg!

M: Oh honey, I'm so sorry. Wish I could come and kiss it better. Send your address and I'll have flowers delivered if you think that would help. Forgot what your favs are, remind me. I've missed you a whole lot, getting withdrawals about now. Please don't feel that you need to respond to those lengthy emails ever, I get carried away sometimes as you know. Ignore what you want to, just please keep in touch often, thanks.

You've warmed my heart with your contact tonight I was starting to think I'd lost you and it wasn't just Hawaii colored blue. I understand about the outings, let me know when you're ready to go out again, or preferably come here for some quiet time after Jen leaves December 10th, she arrives Wednesday this week. I hope you two can meet sometime, maybe not this visit. Speaking of you coming here for quiet time, today I received my purchase of all nine of the Vladimir Megre, Anastasia *"The Ringing Cedars of Russia"* book series translated from Russian to English. It might take a year but I'd be in heaven if you would read those aloud to me, I love you reading to me so. You are healing and rejuvenating for me especially as you allow me to touch you, I need to touch and be touched so much.

I'm pretty much determined to stay in Victoria at least until my lease is up July 1st and may extend it. Jen is burdened with her properties in Utah so I don't know when she and I will actually get to live together, I don't want to move back there. I'm not big on formal marriage either, don't know for sure what's going to happen there, we'll talk it through when she's here and I'll be seeing her in January. I'm hoping she will stay here a few months when the weather warms.

And then and then, Elaine will move in for half rent and house sit my place for six months while Jen and I are in Hawaii. Of course you can visit and stay with us in Hawaii, I want you to remain in my life at least until the next guy makes his claim on you and you accept, you're precious to me. When we're both available and nobody better is there for you I'll for sure be your date Elaine, count on it. Just tell me what you want to do and when, I'll get tickets if needed. The only condition is you wear your short skirt now and then, what a visual treat that is, who needs art? Thinking of you sweetie, be well.

M: (to Jen) You were right about Elaine. I got a short but nice note from her tonight and already I'm not feeling so lonely about after you leave. She was ice skating and hurt her knee, has been in pain and nursing it, not wanting to do anything else. I don't know her other boyfriend situation (if she even has any) but I think she may be my date now and again, maybe we'll get to some Christmas events. I hope she and you will meet and become friends someday if you come to live in Victoria for a while. You'd enjoy her conversation and she yours, walk and talk and visit art galleries and museums while I'm writing maybe. She's a really good artist, used to sell in galleries, she could teach you a whole lot about art. My ideal is still to live six warmer months here then rent something for six months maybe in Hawaii while someone house sits my place and furniture and stuff here. Could you see that fitting in with your plans for us? Of course you can get away and visit family anytime.

M: (to Jen) I'll want to stay with you and the warm weather as long as I can so I'll return to Victoria January 27th then? Going to bed now, will answer in morning. Sweet dreams honey, I love you, not lonely now. Bringing your new toy with you?

Jen: (responding to my "define vulgar" email) Inflicting pain, force, anything that takes dignity from a person or the sexes. I like playfulness and chasing each other. Scene's that involves both can hardly hold back the deep need for each other. Sex in unexpected locations that include risk. Scene's where he is at her apartment and after a morning jog he goes in to shower and she opens the door of the shower and he turns and all the good stuff begins and does not stop until all they ever wanted is complete. You could fill in the details.

Maybe a scene where they meet some romantic place that fits their personalities. I remember the big cowboy I dated years ago took me camping and he laid a blanket on the ground and then a double sleeping bag. We slept in our clothing but I made sure I was wearing something he would enjoy looking at, feeling and cuddling up to. But more than anything that outdoor sweet mountain air invited all his male sex hormones to rage. Of course he liked the woman standing in the moon light. It made him so hot that he just about went crazy. He got up walked around and came back got in bed and remained a good Mormon man. We were in our twenties. It could have been one of the best moments of his life.

Not for me. I'm not a cowgirl. I just kind of chuckled. Nothing in a whole year of dating brought that out in him or did it ever again. We did manage to go to sleep and woke up the next morning with cows all around us. He was a real cowboy and loved his horses and evidently cows to since then I wondered if it was the smell of cow paddies that got those hormones raging. This is a true experience I had. it could be made into quite a funny situation because I was unaware of his first choose of sleeping arrangements was under the stars. Maybe I will work on this more later.

We traveled on the next day and I remember trying to find a secluded place near a fast moving mountain stream to undress and clean my body but I felt his eyes were not just on outlook duty seeming I was concerned about a stranger coming upon us. Like I said he was a good Mormon boy that was not resisting taking a peek. When I have time I should spend some time thinking about what happened and write about it. It was funny when I think back. I did have a bit of fun with him.

M: (subject – the big cowboy – a night of stars and goddesses) Thanks for sharing that Jen, it's an idea that could be shaped into an interesting story. I'm more into intellectual analysis and philosophizing myself, that's why it's vital for me to add sex scenes and female points of view to my books or they'd never be read. Few people would want to read my dusty stuff except in eager anticipation of further scenes of pleasure along the way. Suzanne made this book *possible* to market and made it possible for me to be a writer, be grateful for her. When she climbed into Loa that night in San Antone and we embraced, her compelling woman sounds invited more, she was become my goddess.

I went consenting into that hug, a man controlled by religion not expecting who would emerge. In that never-ending hug I experienced a renewal, a cleansing, a *baptism*, a writer and new man was born in the caring arms of Suzanne. I felt washing over me a spirit of absolute peace, a *knowing* that what she and I were about to do was wholesome and good. *It was right with us, it was right with God!*

Since that intense experience I have never again felt the religious demand for fear guilt repentance confession and forgiveness. There was no sin in what we did, the sin all along was in the cruel command of religion that we must deny ourselves to get to heaven. Ever read the Old Testament? There's not a lot of sexual denial there, they *lived* their lives, patriarchs sleeping with prostitutes, daughter with father, a man spilling his seed upon the ground rather than have sex with a woman he did not want, but spill he did. Did Jesus come to punish and control? Or did he come to love and free and it's men who twisted that message, well-intentioned or not. I do not hate them for it, there must be an opposition in all things or we could not know good from evil, light from darkness, pleasure from pain. It's just that so often evil is called good and good labelled evil.

Jesus taught to judge by the fruits they bear. As I see it the fruits of religion include fear, intolerance, guilt, denial, frustration, anger, hatred, self-righteousness, bombs exploding in the market place, crusades, war, bloodshed, the list could go on. And of course there are good fruits too, a lot of them, it's the *abuse* of religion that causes many of the faults of it. The fruits of nakedness and sex by consent, often forbidden by religion, can be pleasure and fun, contented afterglow, tenderness, connectedness, LOVE. And of course sex like fire can be abused, there must be moderation and consideration in all things. We're here to learn unconditional love. We must have evil to know good and which is our greatest desire. The universe is benevolent, love conquers all. That's my personal philosophizing this early a.m. To me sex and nakedness is beautiful, I see no virtue in denial for the sake of denial when there's consent. I love women because I feel free to look upon their lovely bodies with delight instead of taking only furtive guilty glances like I once did.

You Jen could have been Suzanne for your big frustrated cowboy, you had it in you. But you were young then, you didn't know your role.

He could have made delicious love to you that night in the sleeping bag under the stars, the memory of what could have been could have been the memory of what was. You could have forever been in memory a lover, instead of just a lovely woman in the moonlight who never reached out hand or mouth to release his "raging male sex hormones." You did learn your role later though, I *know* you did, mmm, coming tonight?

Not only does sex sell but the thought of it flows life through an older man and gives him a reason for living. Your advice to remove the sex from my books so my children would be proud of me did not strike me as wisdom but did reveal how mired you are as was I in the mud of sexual self-denial. Being Mormon your big cowboy was forbidden to get naked in the night with the lovely woman on her back oozing pheromones into his sleeping bag on the ground. You *had* your "unexpected location", the man was there and the stars were calling. But that very scene in the mind of the strange and peculiar ones who control religion and its followers would twist it from romantic to *"the very appearance of evil"*. It's off to the stake with *you* witch, be gone!

The best writing creates *images*, pictures in the reader's mind, preferably unforgettable ones. "Big cowboy" of course invokes a sexual image as does you wearing something he'd enjoy cuddling up to, and you standing siren silhouette in the moonlight. You naked bathing in the mountain stream with your raging man taking a peek is image provoking. I'm sure he liked what he saw, but it turned out to be only added cause for frustration, he couldn't touch your tits. (Was that last sentence vulgar to you?)

If the night scene on the mountain that you paint led to fulfilling sex and contented afterglow in each other's arms the next day, that big cowboy body having pounded away on your willing craving body lying perhaps on the sleeping bag under a tree, our readers would be satisfied, they got bang for their buck. But for most of them it's 'vulgar' unless they're into masochism to think of the frustration that cowboy must have felt and you his woman doing nothing about it. He took you to his paradise cow paddies and all because he *wanted* to have sex with you, and you never made it happen, he couldn't force himself upon you.

To most people there is nothing virtuous about denial of that which comes natural when both parties are consenting, as should be assumed with the two of you alone in the mountains overnight. Only to a deeply mired religious person could your story be satisfying, and even then I'm sure in the recesses of their mind it would be bittersweet. Even as a strict Mormon, when I read a fiction story where a man and a woman were falling in love I always looked forward to the time when they finally DID IT! It was a warm fulfilling feeling, a flowing of love and well-being, instead of one of frustration such as is your lonely cowboy story. You and I were Mormons when we first dated so we did not dare go 'all the way'. *But we sure didn't settle for frustration!* There was plenty more that we could and did do so when we went our separate ways late at night it was sweet dreams and hopes for more that we took to our less lonely beds that night.

You could have served your cowboy better. He would have loved you for it, and as I will always love Suzanne, he would have remembered with fondness lovely you and the special star-studded night given you both on the mountain, the gift refused because you bought religion instead of yourselves and love.

That's what I get out of that promising story. It should properly have continued into the next day, the double sleeping bag drawing both your eager glances as you neared a secluded bluff of trees, his jeans shrinking with every step, no longer able to contain what was growing inside them. You're the woman Jen, tell me what *she* was feeling as she sneaked a peek at her big cowboy's jean-draped butt and the trees drew nearer.

Good foreplay, hugely unsatisfying sex, poor cowboy, lovely woman but a cruel one when she knew the man's raging struggle and didn't help him burst into a new world, a world of delight and contentment, a world filled with deeply satisfying memories for when he rocked himself to his final sleep. His goddess failed him on the mountain that night. But she learned her lesson I know, she's *my* goddess now and I am content. Maybe your cowboy didn't fail *himself* when he walked around, you innocent on your back in the sleeping bag not knowing that a man sometimes *must* pleasure himself when his woman won't do it. Perhaps the flowers were extra bright in that spilled spot the next Spring. But as you say in recompense, your cowboy remained "*a good Mormon man.*" Huh?

If a woman wants to keep a contented man at her side, *give him all the sex he needs...*

If a man wants to keep a loving woman at his side...

You're on sweetheart, your cue's been called. Write me about it will you.

See what a rampage you have evoked with that short story of yours? That's what I mean by playing "Suzanne". She's a counterpoint so I can point. She sends short messages and I the Writer respond with longer ones. That's my job, I've already written millions of words, I'm better prepared to write the dissertations. Point counterpoint works well for me. And you Jen do not have to get into sex, we already have the taste and scent of *first* Suzanne, we'd follow her anywhere now, I hope she comes. In the beginning during the troubles you would not allow me to print your words. But now you have become a major player in my books. You rank right up there with Suzanne, DeLeon and Carrie, and newly emerging Elaine should she continue to play with me. Just play "Jen" from now on, I'd like that, she's the one in real life whose bed I sleep in at night. Or *will* that is when she's gets her lovely butt over to my place and plays naked with me, I could get into that.

I copy the above two messages to Suzanne with the words: *I'm hoping for hospice stories from you sweetheart Suzanne, they are beloved by our readers, they fit my books well.* And I forward it to Elaine with the words: *Do you like this kind of writing Elaine? Make you want to read more? Should it sell? What do you think?*

M: (to Suzanne) Which of these paragraphs is most likely to cause a woman to want to read more?

1. That's what I get out of that promising story. It should properly have continued into the next day, the double sleeping bag drawing both your eager glances as you neared a secluded bluff of trees, *his jeans growing smaller with every step you took.* You're the woman Jen, tell me what *she* was feeling as she sneaked a peek at her big cowboy's jean-draped butt and the trees drew nearer.

2. That's what I get out of that promising story. It should properly have continued into the next day, the double sleeping bag drawing both your eager glances as you neared a secluded bluff of trees, *his jeans shrinking with every step, no longer able to contain what was growing inside them.* You're the woman Jen,

tell me what *she* was feeling as she sneaked a peek at her big cowboy's jean-draped butt and the trees drew nearer.

3.   That's what I get out of that promising story. It should properly have continued into the next day, the double sleeping bag drawing both your eager glances as you neared a secluded bluff of trees, *his jeans shrinking with every step, no longer able to contain the swelling seed bursting inside them.* You're the woman Jen, tell me what *she* was feeling as she sneaked a peek at her big cowboy's jean-draped butt and the trees drew nearer.

Play with me again sweetie, for the fun of it? Or just send hospice stories? I care for you.

Jen: To describe me in my late 20's I would say. I was very a perfect built woman with perfect portions on a 5'2" frame that weighted 115 lbs. When I walked I was aware my hips wiggled at just the right speed for eyes to follow. I guess I wanted that. I was once told by a female co-worker that the men loved looking at my perfect shaped butt when I walked by and often commented on it. When someone would find out I had 3 children they would say no way. One time a male co-worker told me I had the most perfect lips he ever saw on a woman. Twice I had men come up to me and just kiss me on the lips out of the blue and walk away. My long chestnut hair hung almost to my butt but I would lift it and tie it upon my head most days except I let it down when night fell. The few times when I wore my hair flow down my back. Jealous comments would come from a few women that would say as I walked by your hair is not real. I would turn smile and say yes it is.

For a time I worked with a beautiful 21 year old girl that had the most beautiful slightly turned up breast and went braless. With her perfect breast and nipples perturbing through her tight fitted shirts cause men to stop and often peak into our small department door moving their heads back and forth as they watched us move around the room to complete our projects. Silly me at the time did not realize. It was not just her they were looking at. I was very innocent to my effect on men even when I was told so I did not understand that power. I think for some men that was part of the attraction they had for me. I was a good girl and many wanted and few were allowed to touch. I have always been a one man woman. All my sexual energy was saved up to be unleashed with one man. Real life it did not happen but that is what I always wanted.

M: What a dream you must have been to that big cowboy. *And what a frustration!* I'll take you now babe, with delight. You're younger in years than I am, you'll always be young to me, and you'll always be a WOMAN to me.

Jen: I just reread what you wrote and I laughed. That's what readers want to do. He was not only a cowboy he was a big buck. I sure am glade I never got banged. Would rather it be you.

"If the night scene on the mountain that you paint led to fulfilling sex and contented afterglow in each other's arms the next day, that big cowboy body having pounded away on your willing craving body lying perhaps on the sleeping bag under a tree, our readers would be satisfied, they got bang for their buck." I like the first two sentences.

M: I'd rather it had been me too sweetheart but I'm too serious to be a cowboy and I'm not likely as well hung as that big buck of yours. Tomorrow night almost a half century later you get another crack at the big bang, hope it's a loud explosive one. Your M

Jen: Did you really find your Kira. Did you let go of your search for her back in the 1980's. I was just wondering how that turned out for you. Is Kira gone for now or do you expect another Kira?

M: There is no other Kira, the one who came fulfilled that dream. It's just that she was not Eve.

Jen: What was it about her that allowed that dream to be let go. She is gone because she loves another.

M: Yes, you wrote it. She has another Adam.

Jen: How often will that happen?

M: Probably every time I become fond of a woman who is not "given" me in the same sense as women were "given" to Joseph Smith Mormon founder. (I'm trying to speak a language you will understand.) I don't really know though. I think now with you seriously in the picture as Eve (I hope) that the stories will change, the same major characters will remain onstage and we will move towards that perfect love gone right and becoming immortal. But on the physical level of awareness I don't allow myself to know the whole script though I've obviously read it, maybe wrote it, it settles in in dreams but only in chunks. I simply offer as little resistance to what's happening as I can and let it flow moment by moment, you get used to living that way. It never ceases to amaze me how the stories unfold unexpectedly day by day. It's truly delicious, a fairy tale way to live life without fear, knowing that only good can appear.

When you get too focused on my fantasy please bring to mind that in the Mormon dream you will for sure have an Adam who has more than one wife, that's a given. It's not a punishment or a curse it's a blessing. It's not talked about anymore but in the original Mormon dream it's the true order of heaven that males are married to more than one woman for eternity. Brigham Young said a man could not be exalted without having more than one wife. In my particular version, all of us in my eternal family are equal spouses, all married to the other, that's how I see it. Now please don't go ballistic on me again and walk away, I'm trying to help you better understand "Michael", that's what you asked for. I LOVE YOU!!! Just one more sleep and we're together. Your M

M: (to Jen) I will send you something shocking. I do this because you mention in a secretive way your "he" who apparently is a spirit man who recently asked you to choose to die so *he* could be your "Adam". And because I want you to know too that there are mighty forces writing this epic novel that you are helping create. We're not alone in this, it has taken a lifetime of preparation for us to get to the point where it became possible. You play a starring role in this play that is unfolding. But as always, you can choose instead to walk away. That choice will always remain yours. You can fight your role at my side and be contentious, or you can relax into it, choose a perfect love gone right, and let it unfold trusting that it is unfolding as it should. You cannot do wrong either way, the story *will* be told and your ancient soul will be well.

The following is a true story, it happened in 1984.

As I took a break from the rewrite to use the washroom today into mind floated a scene I'd long forgotten. It played out here in Victoria Womb of Me, James Bay again. I was flowing with a spiritual initiation that would affect my entire life when I emerged whole and new from it. The test posed by my spirit teacher that day was: *"How important is the question WHAT DO I WANT?"* The answer was: *"Life Giving."*

I learned that lesson when on impulse I took a pair of sharp scissors out of a kitchen drawer, sat on the floor of the apartment I was renting on Quebec Street, faced the balcony, and positioned the scissors as a death dealing instrument inches away. I held them in two hands with the intent to quickly and mindlessly plunge them into my abdomen. I was living alone, I would have bled out quickly. Nobody would have come looking for me until the rent was due days later.

In the moment of movement an angel overshadowed me and gently whispered in the kind loving way true angels always do: *"WHAT DO YOU WANT?"* I thought a thought and replied, *"I WANT TO LIVE."* The lesson was learned and filed to come forth for this book. Maybe that's why I so often ask Jen, *"What do you want?"* What would have happened had I ignored the question? I would have died. My dear kind brother would have smiled, put his loving arms around me, and taken me to heaven where I would have rested and prepared to come back for another try. I had not failed, I never could, I had simply exercised the greatest power given man, I had CHOSEN for myself.

What do YOU want dear reader? When you are decided, don't hesitate, DO IT and don't look back! The universe steps aside to let pass a man or a woman who knows where they are going. Do *you*? Ask yourself the question *"What do I want?"* Choose the happiest thought that comes to mind and the universe will conspire for you. Mighty forces will come to your aid to make sure you get what you want and expect. You are CREATOR. *And so are we all...*

Jen: No it did not shock me. Thank you for sharing that. I am glade you choose to live. You would of hurt many and been missed by your family. Your life must have been very difficult at that time. Was real life just not working the way you felt it should. And it brought you to that point. What gave you such pain. How did it change your life from that point on. Do you see a benefit from it or is it just part of the earthy experience. My question is what was the difference of you killing yourself then my experience of just letting go and nature taking me. You had a angle waiting to take you to heaven and you told me I would go to hell because you felt he was not a good angle. I think he was.

M: There was no pain or confusion, the universe was unfolding as it should, I was being taught things that I needed to know to fill my mission in life. In this case it was the importance of the question *"What do I want?"* which leads to the making of a *choice*, our greatest power, our greatest tool. It is our greatest gift to give birth to a desire that creates a happy feeling, that manifests and enlarges the universe as we move towards unconditional love, the awareness of God. I was reborn as I always am when staying a length of time in my womb Victoria. I was reborn a new man, but one in disguise until a year ago, one prepared to awaken and write an epic novel that could potentially influence and change the thinking of many people, bringing them closer to an understanding of who and what they really are.

I doubt very much that I told you that you would go to hell, I do not believe in any such place. Your experience is your own, perhaps you will share it fully with your Adam if you choose to continue with him and forsake the hope for any other, a complete irrevocable commitment, no walking away possible. I think you were recently placed in circumstances where you had no choice but to make a choice. I'm not sure yet but I think you chose ME as your Adam. Did you? Or are you still pondering that one?

Jen: I am not going ballistic but if in this life, Adam has more than one woman. I walk out the door. I suppose that won't be a big deal with Adam. He is always looking and replacing in this world. All the Adams outside the church are doing that. I saw that in my ex's world of friends. Those Adams were really missing the boat and the big thing they all had in common they talked about just love and don't judge. For you and I we will dream of the budding Eve's of the next life. None are invited to our world now until we are in the next. Do you agree with what I see for us.

M: Your love remains conditional, there are strings attached. You do not commit, you reserve the right to walk away. We have not yet embarked upon the journey to a perfect love gone right. You continue to want power to control, that is your weakest link but it is your present choice. I am aware of the difference between real life and fantasy Jen, you should know that. And please, I've told you this before, do not compare me to your other husband and his friends and their beliefs. I'm not them, I'm me.

Elaine: (commenting on the big cowboy mail) Very interesting! I knew that's where you were coming from. It's tricky, knowing your children will read it. But just be yourself. There is a genius in bravery, or so said Goethe. Cheers, Elaine

M: Thank-you for your encouraging counsel to be myself dear one, I do need that kind of support. It's difficult and often lonely to be the writer of an epic novel, trying to hold in mind a gigantic picture that to see whole one must stand too far off to see clearly.

But your words *"It's tricky, knowing that your children will read it"* reaffirm that you and Jen will get along well, you are in agreement that my books should not be shown to my children. Sure, it's tricky I agree, especially because with one exception they are all immersed in Mormonism. For them it's easy to judge and condemn but difficult to give up curiosity and sexual feelings once indulged. When I had my other books published I knew one daughter was buying some of them surreptitiously. She may not have been ashamed of what her dad writes, she may have actually been fascinated by his story. *What, MY dad write that? Impossible. But I love the story!*

I'm curious to know how many of my children have read *"Fifty Shades of Grey"*, maybe some have. When the musical movie *"Jesus Christ Superstar"* was playing, Mormon leaders counseled their members not to see it. My guess is that's because in the movies Jesus had a wife, or at least a lover. Such a thing is just not acceptable to harsh religion, it's *got* to be evil. Being the rebel that I am, I saw the movie a few times, loved the music, most likely rubbed shoulders with other Mormons in the theater. That's human nature. Thanks for the feedback. Brave M

Jen: You told me you would be faithful. If you bring other women in that is not being faithful and you need to know my stand before we become one. I am committed totally to a faithful husband not one that abandons me for other women then expects me to be waiting at home for when he returns or expects me to welcome them into our home. Please tell me the truth do you have those plans down the road. If so let me off because you are not committed to me or our future. I will never be OK with you getting together with other women alone. In groups yes.

M: I have told you several times that as soon as we are married or living together with the intention of it being full-time or at least permanent, I will be sexually faithful to you. Any other demand from you just takes us right back to the war that was supposed to be the one to end all wars. You have not changed Jen even though you said you had given up your demands. I should not have expected you to change, you want control of me, there are strings attached to your love, it's never unconditional. Even in this present message you threaten again to walk away, hardly the stuff of commitment along the way to a perfect love. Tonight, just hours before you touch me and I you it is your fears instead of your love that you let take control of you. You are not disciplined, you indulge in weakness, your focus is not on love. But here goes a try at the code words I thought might work for us. I LOVE YOU!!!

Jen: Commitment is now to ensure the future. If you do not invest in me now then there will be no investment to take care of the future. I see you as now and I invest in you now to insure a future. Anyway how can you talk. I went shopping and you were imagining me with Al. You get just as jealous as I do. The only demands (or respect) has to come from you.

Ouch, the spirit of contention lives. Is she truly my Eve Mother of Nations? Is she the one with an identical dream to mine? Oops, shouldn't have wrote that, think I gave away the answer...

Elaine: Your email is very kind! I appreciate it. I will do my best to make time to meet Jen... and would definitely visit you two in Hawaii! But give me a chance to heal up in regards to my blown out knee. It is getting better day by day. I hobbled about today at work... fast paced, smothered with tons of info and head crammed by end of day, thankfully 4 o'clock. Same for tomorrow. Thanks for the thought of the flowers... no need, because the thought was beautiful! I will see you and read to you, sup too.... just have to get comfy with all the stuff I'm learning and get my Kneebone well! I will get back to editing when I am with you... easier that way.... then we can exchange chat! Oh and by the way, no guys have claim on me right now and anyway, in that case, I still want to remain friends. I do enjoy your company... our communication and thoughts that jive... and the fact that you are so easygoing.... easy to be around. So, stay tuned. We shall get together again. Go out and stay in, whatever. Take care yourself, it's going to warm up in a day! Faithfully your friend... Elaine

M: You sign your mail "faithfully" and truly you are, far beyond any other so far including Jen. From you I am always encouraged and feel support, from others I often feel criticism and doubt. I don't think you are a perfect angel Angel, but I wasn't expecting that. I don't want you on a pedestal, I want you on my sofa reading to me. Be well sweet one, let's get together soon after or the night of December 10 if you can fit some time in for me. Thanks for telling me about the no guys, I like that. Your M

Jen: Thanks for explaining the purpose of your angle. Mine was also for my good and what I needed. But you saw it as something horrible. That I don't understand about you. Similar situations and yours is wonderful and mine are made out to be bad. I am just pointing this out no need to explain its just a fact. I often see this pattern in our communication. Can't wait to see you tomorrow. Expect a big kiss in front of everyone.

M: I saw "he" as the greatest threat I could ever have. As a spirit man with no body he could fly circles around me, he has had your attention and maybe devotion for years, perhaps decades, has made love to you when I was there your husband in the same bed and you too asleep to give consent, he feels certain of you regardless of your daytime vision on the phone when you saw ME taking you through the veil. Does that not count for anything with you, *must* you walk away? Do you feel that is your destiny? Is that why you said it was "impossible" for us to be together? I must know these things Jen, I have every right to. Are you MY Eve or are you not?

And in that instant when we exchanged the mails you refer to, "he" (does he have a name?) was urging you to take your life and be his "Eve" (or one of them if he's Mormon.) What greater threat to me could you come up with when I was wanting you as *my* Eve Mother of Nations? Why would I not see that as "horrible"? But please please please make your own choices and make them soon. *What is it you really want Jen?* The same applies to me about the future. I could take you into my bosom, expect you to remain there forever, and any moment you could fly away, even kill yourself to be in paradise with spirit "he".

Public displays of affection are always welcome.

Tonight Tuesday December 2, 2014 at 9:45 p.m. in Victoria Canada City of Victory I submitted a query with attachments to a literary agent to represent me Michael Demers for the epic series of *Becoming Adam* books. This query will be a turning point for my books. I expect acceptance of my offer. If not, I will conclude that my writing is not as good as it needs to be for traditional publication. But of course it could simply be that I queried an agent who has no interest in that kind of book or is too busy for me. I expect a reply within two months. Wish us well. Here's the query letter.

"*Becoming Adam*" is an epic series of fictional books based closely on current real life people and events in USA and Canada, as embellished by the author Michael Demers. Book 1 is ready for submission. Book 2 will be about the same size. Book 2 is within three months of being ready for submission. Book 3 is almost certain and could be ready if needed in less than six months. Book 4 is possible, as is Book 5 within two years. Each of the above books are about the same size, each are part of the same epic series with the same or similar characters, all are current events within the last 18 months of today's date. Attached are extracts from "*Becoming Adam Book One - The True Story of a Perfect Love Gone Right*" by Michael Demers. And also extracts from Book 2.

I request literary agent representation. Thank-you for considering my epic series *Becoming Adam* by Michael Demers. Enjoy the day.

It's now Wednesday a.m. and I haven't heard anything from Jen since sending that message about "he" so I don't even know if she will step off that plane today. We're hardly happy with and trusting of each other, always up and down. lately mainly down. Yeah, she makes a good Suzanne! I'll do my part, I'll be at the airport this afternoon and hope she arrives. And hope too that she looks and feels good to me, I'm not even sure of that.

I'm sure curious about that spirit man that has such an influence on her, it seems almost a 'religious' thing but she never learned it from Mormons or from me. If she comes today I'll try to get her to talk about him. I'm glad at least that I have discovered his existence, there was no hint of it before a short while ago. Could she have known "he" since childhood? She says "he" is good so he's really under her skin. And what a threat to me, an entity that would take away my Eve and make her his, and who would take away her body. What greater threat than that? I never knew that woman. Do I want to? It seems completely unreal that we're (apparently) engaged to be married, it doesn't ring true. I must demand to be told about "he" before she leaves, if she comes. Crazy huh?

M: (to Jen but not sent) I haven't heard from you since sending that message about your spirit man so I don't even know if you are coming, but I'll be at the airport just in case. Please understand if I'm confused and don't give you the joyous welcome I had thought to. You seem a stranger to me, you're not at all happy with me and I'm not happy with you. That's very strange for two people who say they love each other and want to get married. I'll try but I'm not sure how I'll be when we meet, just being honest.

I hope the good feelings return but we're so volatile and up and down with each other, there's very little trust or confidence. It's the opposite of the happy excited way we should be if we're headed to a happy marriage. I think it may be a long time before we'd be smart to formally marry, don't you? But we'll discuss everything if you come today. I hope you do, your silence leaves me on a limb. At least if you don't arrive I'll know you have chosen your other 'Adam' and not me. And if you do arrive I'll need to talk before I can throw myself into sex with you. Sorry, I was feeling good for a day or two with you but late yesterday again the spirit of contention fell upon you and you were not looking like Eve Mother of Nations, far from the loving image I have and hope for her.

I have no idea what happened to the sweet wife I once knew, or the happy woman who was last here in Victoria with me, she disappeared the day she left and not just physically. You allude to having an experience on the hill, I wonder if that is what has changed you and made you so contentious? I am going to insist on knowing more about "he". If I'm to share a bed with an invisible man who can take away not only my Eve and make her his own but also her physical body, then I must know as much about him as you do. It's GOT to be that way Jen, you must tell me about him. You accuse me of wanting to have a second woman in our bed, well, you have a second man there, it's just that I can't see him, can you? This is so weird, certainly not Mormon, certainly not from me. How long have you known that entity, and why do you call him "good"?

Ok, I just decided not to send this to you, it goes in the journal as representative of my feelings towards you this a.m. the day you are supposed to arrive in Victoria for a seven day visit.

M: (to Jen) I haven't heard from you for a while so I'm not even sure if you are coming. But I'll be at the airport just in case.

Jen: heading to the airport now.

M: Fly safe sweetie, see you soon, I love you. Your Man

For those who are interested in how this book evolved in the real world, as I write this it is 9 a.m. December 3rd, 2014, I just started a load of laundry. Jen's flight arrives at 3 p.m. today. I'm living this book *live* right now, no leaps ahead or back, this is real time for me. I'm as excited as you may be to see how this epic story unfolds. Jen's my fiancée but an image of Elaine just flashed into mind, she's thinking of me, I send love back. I'm very fond of her, dear soul, I guess I love her. I'm still uncertain if I've found my Eve in her or Jen or neither.

I just got a call from Jen, she missed her flight in Las Vegas and will now be arriving in Victoria about midnight. She did mention that she might get too busy and miss her flight didn't she? I guess she needs her man at her side, I've been telling her that for six months. Anyway, it will be straight to bed for us tonight, about 1 a.m. before we get back to my place. She'll be tired but she'll do sex I'm sure. As always I'll be gentle with her, maybe we'll both be mellow by then. At least she's on the way and I've got a whole day ahead to work on polishing Book 1. Somehow I thought I had that done but it was only the first 40 pages of the 500 I had ready for the literary agent query. It will take a few weeks of polishing but I don't expect to hear back from the agent for that long anyway so all is well. Book 2 is shaping up real well. Back to work...

Jen: Will leave Seattle on flight 2334 arrives at 8:11 PM in Victoria. The agent must have been looking at the time on the next flight. Glade it is earlier. Let me know if you got this email.

M: I guess I needed contact with you because after we talked I lay down on the sofa and the next thing I knew it was almost 1 p.m. I saw that 8 p.m. flight and thought they might get you on it. I'll be there waiting sweetie, see you soon, I love you lots. Your M

M: (to Elaine) I'm thinking of showing Jen that photo of you with your two daughters. Do you mind? About how old is the pic? She missed her flight in Vegas and doesn't get in until 8 p.m. tonight. Hope that knee is improving sweetie, thinking of you.

As I showered this afternoon I thought of the following scene in Book 1.

M: (to Jen) As I lingered in the hot shower today with the bright heat lamp on, a glowing pearl appeared on the shower tiles before me. Perhaps it was symbolic of a Pearl of Great Price, maybe Eve, maybe just a water drop. It ran a bit as a teardrop, stopped and morphed back into a glowing pearl. I thought of it as a gift for me. And then in the telling of the story to you it became symbolic of the choice you make, we to be or not to be, that choice made only after the shedding of tears over a period of time. And most likely truly made only after you make YOU the highest priority of all, and live your life regardless of the way others think you should. I wish such a fearless attitude upon you.

Have those tears been shed, or are they yet to come? I *do* want Jen, I continue to think at our age after 18 years of marriage that it would be smart for us to reconcile and live together again. But we need a time of healing after having lost our trust and confidence in each other. She just called, she's in Seattle, I'll hold her four hours from now, we'll spoon naked tonight.

But sometime during those seven coming days we must talk about her spirit man. I need to know if he's a childhood friend, or when he arrived in her life if not. I need to know how much he has influenced her life and how much he currently does. I didn't know until a few days ago that he even existed, but I did remember her having sex with a spirit man in the night and finding it delicious. I just didn't know he had a face and name. A man that can with impunity rape my wife in the night when her husband is lying unknowing beside her, call her from her home to the desert at night, tell her she must urgently choose between him for Adam or me, that she must die to be with him, and she gives that careful consideration – *is my greatest threat!* I must know my enemy. If she shares fully with me then we have a chance for us. If not, I must logically conclude that as the years unfold my fondest hope, my perfect love gone right, my Eve could be suddenly called to another Adam by her own choice because she knows and loves him more. She would have died for *him* and I would not have known it, just her absence when I went looking for her in the worlds of spirit and discovered that in the end she had *walked away*, her full intent all along, she knew that it was impossible for *us* to be, she had covenanted to another man, she loved *him* best.

Where's my Eve? I never fail. This story must have a happy ending I promised that. Should I still be searching for Eve in this world or is she in the next and that's where I must go to find her? Or have I found her and all along she wore other clothing beneath the lamb skin? Will Eve betray me like Kira did? Is another man her Adam? But that would make my books a tragedy, it must not be that. There's got to be an Eve for me. Or are there *many* and they set the pace for themselves like Elaine does and we're not ready for each other yet? All I know is that in the end I WILL succeed, I will go on until I do, it's just not in me to do otherwise, that I *know*.

Elaine: Hi, yes you can show the photo, although I look slow and sad, because it was taken at my mom's funeral. The girls look good though, so go ahead. Cheers, Elaine

Elaine: Oh thanks for thinking about my knee. I can bend it 50% now, which is great improvement. Nobody knows about it, because I can disguise my limp... just looks like I'm a little tired. But the computer training all day with 10 million details all crammed quickly into ones head is a mind scream to a calm and gentle person like me! So I'm resting, but the weekend comes soon. ps the picture is 1 and one half years old... Elaine, limpy

Jen: Flight going to belayed to 8:40 says on the board here.

M: Ok, thanks, was just about to leave home. I can watch it on the internet. It's showing 8:40 arrival in Victoria. See you soon baby.

Later.

I did some polishing in Book 1 as Jen was in the shower and since I was writing about "he" a few paragraphs above I thought I'd paste in the following from Book 1.

Jen: It was interesting, I read a bit of an email you wrote a few days before my desire to drift off, where you wanted to give up and be absorbed by the welcoming trees and when I read that I called you on the phone with fear. That fear was, I could not let that happen unless I to were absorbed laying next to you. Then being a part of that absorption we would be as one. Here's my response to this comment you made in a email a week or two ago. *"That remains to be seen. And meanwhile I will live my life as best I can as if I am becoming Adam, I'm still not certain of that."*

My response, You will be a Adam. I, as a dear friend loves you much. I will go first if need be and prepare that Castle for you Adam, a place you may rest until you are ready to call your Eves and I will step aside as a loving friend and smile as you go forward. For *another Adam has waited since before I was born* to choose and take my place. Must be why my greatest trials have been the men in my life. You have been the greatest trial because I have loved you the most by far and time is short and I much choose, for he awaits. Good night my handsome writer. PS: How often do we really get in another what fits us best. I am the few that had that with you!

M: This is good sweetie, you are more like the woman I like to converse with again, no blames or put downs. That is good news indeed. But I'm curious to know what you intended to convey by writing: *"I will step aside as a loving friend and smile as you go forward. For another Adam has waited since before I was born to choose and take my place."* And, *"time is short and I must choose, for he awaits."* Does this mean that you will only ever be a friend to me and never be a "Sister Wife" or "Eve" because there is *another* man waiting for you somewhere and you must soon choose him or me? (Why *soon?*) Or is your choice already made for *him* and you're just now getting around to telling me about you and him?

If so, at what point in time, or is it after death, that you think you will be getting together with your other man? Would that be the one you saw in the temple who was most likely not me, or the invisible one who had sex with you in the night while I was lying beside you? I'm very curious about this, please clarify, it's important especially since you've been saying for months that you are my Eve and now I don't know if that is so anymore. Were you deceiving me all along? Or did something change last night? You constantly surprise me at what a stranger you have become, I don't know you at all except that I can certainly no longer count on the undying love and loyalty you've been writing about until today. Why would you lead me along about being my Eve when all along you knew there was another man "waiting" for you somewhere? Is that man in physicality and you are now searching for him? Is he Mormon, and if so will he have other wives as Mormon men do in the eternities?

Is our getting together in January now off because you have another man hiding somewhere? Are you clear thinking and rational Jen? You've had powerful emotional stresses lately, it can't be easy to attend the funeral of a man who fathered one of your children and whose penis was inside you a thousand times (if that means anything anymore, I suppose it could.) You've got me hugely curious. What changed overnight? Or am I simply misinterpreting what you wrote?

Jen: Just sharing what is my problem. As I go through this grieving process I manage to dance to Christmas music with my young granddaughters. As I smile and sing along with them my heart is breaking in two and often I stop when the pounding of my heart takes my breath away but up again I dance. I keep thinking how did we get here and how does one give their sweet kind long enduring and adoring husband away that he insists must be. But knowing you must let go as he searches for His Eve's. But knowing you must learn to be a better person and wish him and them happiness, while wishing it was you that was filling his heart with joy. Must let go! Must Must Must let go! But as you said wish the other well and happiness. But as we both know this will pass and my Adam will step forward to take me home. He's glade I did not sink into those beautiful welcoming trees with you. Jen signing off as Jen

Later as I persisted in knowing more about her spirit man she wrote:

Jen: I started to write about Adam three times and deleted it. I am told something's are not to be talked about. You should know that.

She's here with me in Victoria as I write this, at the kitchen table on her laptop, me nearby on mine at 4:30 a.m.. We made kinda love last night but it wasn't all that good, she won't do all the way, good Mormon girl you know. Maybe her wanting to be Mormon temple ready is a clue that her spirit man is Mormon too and they are both buying into the Mormon Dream? Could that be a big part of her wanting to be faithful Mormon? I suppose if she and he become "resurrected" beings their bodies could make children. But in the Mormon dream it would be spirits not physical bodies that they'd make. Adam and Eve had *mortal* bodies when they had their children on this planet. My dream calls for making *physical* bodies on other planets as did Adam and Eve on this one.

I got an hour's sleep maybe and when she got up I got up to work on Book 1. I'm amazed at how important her other "Adam" is to her and how clearly she lets me know. She just won't tell me about him. Hopefully there will come a time before she goes home six days from now for such a discussion. It's vitally important for me to know if she is *my* Eve or another man's. Her messages make it clear that she belongs to another man even though she wants me with her in this life.

We spoke a bit still dark outside about her spirit man. We are now calling him her spirit "guide". She can't remember, but as I jogged her memory we came to four times when she recalls "Guide" communicating with her. He gave her choices recently when he was in her home office. I understand the choice of life or death of her physical body, I don't yet understand why Guide would offer himself as her Adam, making her choice of Adam him or me. Ok, can't write more it's just not coming except a feeling that I could accept living with Jen as my wife and her walking away with Guide or another as her Adam in the end. In that scenario Jen would have helped me gather my Eves plural. Yes, it's plural.

Disappointed? Take another breath, there's another moment coming, for Michael Demers there always is…

This is a good place to get you up to speed with why I am living alone in Victoria and where I'm coming from. Come leap back in time with me, it'll be fun. Nervous about it? Here, hold my hand you won't get lost we'll get back to Michael and Jen before this book ends, promise. *Here we go….*

Chapter 4

Suzanne seems to have found a local man. In Book Ten she glowingly writes:

Suzanne: I know... I keep waiting for an answer about vacation time to go to Paris with you. So why did you cancel the cruise with DeLeon? What's happening? I had dinner with a new friend whose wife died recently with liver cancer. Grief is such a painful journey. I'm a good listener. People need listeners in their lives to feel a sense of worth after such loss. He told me I looked beautiful tonight.

M: DeLeon and I are getting together for about ten days but we're not cruising, may drive to Asheville, or go to Costa Rica, not sure yet. Your new friend speaks the truth about you, I'm sure you must be a great listener, especially to those in need. And of course you are a beautiful woman. I'm pleased you were told that, it must have lifted your heart, I'd like to have seen your return smile. I'm glad you are getting out. Any possibility of romance with him do you think? I'd be happy for you if you found someone local who was genuine and long-term good for you, not just lonely and needy. I think that is what you are wanting. But I'd sure miss Suzanne if it came to that. I only wish I had the means to rescue you pretty woman, show up with a limo to take you to my helicopter to take you to my yacht to take you to Eden. But even my vivid writer imagination can't see that manifesting this month. I do love you honey, but I love you enough to let you go if that's your choice and it's not just loneliness that could easily be cured with but the beckon of a finger in my direction. You do seem happy and upbeat the last few days, you look good in that, I'm thrilled. Your Michael

Carrie: I woke up in the middle of the night with a nagging realization, however... and, that is i really can't afford to work for free - not even for a little while i need to generate some income immediately. this whole thing is, of course, very new to me as i only found out ashley's ideas on monday... it's taken a while to actually digest her plan, which i love for the long run, which is for she and i to create a business together handling the social media presence of businesses... i can see the financial reward that is possible with that and actually already see far beyond just the 20 clients that she has envisioned so far...

i spoke with a friend of mine in the san francisco bay area who is part owner in a co-op bakery and he said they have to take turns keeping their page up to date, as it takes time everyday and no one wants to be responsible for it everyday... he's a very savvy internet guy and thought this was a much needed business, so that's very good verification for me... in the meantime, i am working for you... i am working to get these folks onto your page and to promote your book to them... i have a huge family of friends who are healers, teachers, leaders, body workers, etc... all metaphysically oriented and into everything you would like to promote through your books... i will promote to them personally as well as through the fb pages, yours and mine...

i know you gave ashley "a small budget" so i don't imagine she is in a position to pay me for my time right now... but i need you to consider doing so yourself, as i see where this is going, how much time it's going to take and how much value i am going to add... i don't expect to get what my time is actually worth, as i imagine that would be too much for you right now... that said, i also can't work for nothing, as i'm sure you can understand... so... please give this some thought...and let me know what's possible thanks, carrie

M: (to Ashley) Please find out how much Carrie is going to cost us and let me know, thanks. I don't want to pay her directly, her financial compensation should come from you. I'll need to approve each increase in your marketing budget, it's all coming out of my savings at this point. So please do your best to get e-commerce enabled on our site as soon as you can so we can start selling books directly.

Carrie: ashley...my email was to michael for him to pay me, not for you to do so... i cc'd you to keep you in the loop, as i am now doing with michael did he already respond to you and not to me? for even the time i've put in is less that 5. per hour and won't really work for me, which is why i asked him to consider paying me directly for my time and said i didn't expect to be paid by you right now from your "small budget" i expect to be paid from you for the work i do for our other clients, the ones we charge 100. per month for, but this is starting from the ground up and all my focus is on michael at this point, so i don't expect you to pay for that... it seems more appropriate for him to pay me directly for my time...

i'd like us all to be on the same page, so if he did respond to you, i'd like to know what he said and, michael, if you haven't discussed this yet with ashley, i'd appreciate hearing directly from you regarding this, with a cc to her thanks, both of you carrie

M: (to Carrie and Ashley) Financial compensation is going to have to be worked out with Ashley. Please understand Carrie that I am financing this entire project out of my personal savings at this point. I don't mind doing that, I have enormous faith that what we're doing will succeed beyond our wildest co-creative imaginings, but until the legend is 'out there' and we start selling a lot of books, cash on hand will remain very limited. Did you know that there are 8,000 new books published every single day? So it's vital to get out there and push push push to get our books noticed and flying off the shelves. Once we get the attention of media (most likely with the legend you guys are creating) they will take over and do much of our marketing for us free of charge. It's like a snowball near the top of a mountain, big push needed to get it over the top but then it picks up its own momentum and gets bigger and bigger as it travels. The people who become loyal readers of the books will grow exponentially. One tells two, two tell four, that leaps to eight, sixteen, etc. it will grow very fast once we've done the muscle work needed at the beginning.

We're on the way to Eden Seven! All I personally want to do is write and make sure we have plenty of fresh product to sell, I could do that for years. I deeply appreciate you two for taking care of marketing, I could not do that and write at the same time. It is my hope that someday you will know as well as I know, and will gratefully appreciate the vision and the power behind the project. At the moment we are focusing on financial success, but we're truly on the way to immortality. *That's* what is being taught in our books. And that will be the result from them as more and more people begin to believe immortality - living to a thousand years and more - is possible, and *expect* it! This is way beyond money for me, it's a vital mission for our time. I came here and prepared for this doing, left a beautiful home and comfortable life style behind to cast off into the unknown and do this. The right people to help make this project manifest are being attracted as we go along. I can't buy the land yet, but I expect to be in Costa Rica just a few days from now to look it over. *That's how serious this is!*

That's what Source is moving along through those of us who are willing to do the part we are asked to perform. Every single day I see miracle after miracle happening to move this along. We're not alone here, the power that creates worlds is on our side, conspiring for our success. We only need to *believe* and do what we individually feel inspired moment by moment to do. The reward was previously thought impossible, the fountain of youth has been discovered. The name "DeLeon" is from the man who says he found such a fountain in Florida centuries ago. The Goddess who today proudly bears that name and in real life calls me "Magnificent", "King", and "Lord" lives in Florida.

Be bold, and mighty forces will come to your aid. You who are truly New Thought will understand better now that you are not *just* selling books for money - you are a big part of moving this world and its people back to Eden, this time not only for the happy first couple...

Carrie: michael... i appreciate that You have a vision for Eden Seven... i don't really even understand what that is or how it is going to lead anyone to immortality... but this is Your vision and Your goal... i am willing to work my self silly for Your vision but as i said, i can't do it for free you want me to push, push, push without getting paid to do that... please take one moment to put yourself in my place i doubt you would do what you are asking me to do, if you were in my position... there seems to be some tunnel vision here that doesn't support your goal that you are unwilling to make any effort yourself (pushing this off on the "small budget" you gave ashley), for me to receive some value for the value i am providing, belies your philosophy... i find it a bit incredulous that you feel it's ok for you to use my time, energy and resources without offering any compensation for them how does that fit with LOA? you get something very valuable, but the one giving it gets virtually nothing... something very wrong with that picture... and, at least you have personal savings... if i had personal savings or an income, i could choose to offer my gifts for free... i would be delighted to "some day" appreciate the vision... actually i appreciate Your vision now... however, i do need to eat, pay rent and pay bills

i'm very happy to give you my all in this for however long it's needed and wanted as long as some of my needs are taken into account as well... the universe requires balance and equity for it to continue to provide LOA doesn't allow for one to prosper at the detriment of another... you know that.

M: Carrie, you rant about something that is not real. You build a straw man and then seek to defend it by creating something of me that I am not, for your personal gain. You would be happier and much more successful if you would trust and properly apply Law of Attraction to manifest all the money you need and desire. I have great hope for you, we were attracted for a purpose. Would more quiet meditation (raising your vibrations) help take you back to where you used to be? The truth is that I *expect* to have to pay you money for your work because I know you are desperate for money and that belief in scarcity is keeping you from manifesting the abundance that is already in your vortex. You seem to have abandoned peaceful non-confrontational conversation like we used to have when we were best virtual friends.

Ashley: I'm having an online meeting with Carrie at 5. I'm trying to help her think positively about the money. I truly believe we can make some money her and I with the social media work, but it will take a little time to get things going.

M: I wouldn't mind paying her a bit if you think what she is doing is worth it at this point in time and that's what we need to do to keep her. I do feel for her situation being on her own like that. We were once virtually close but something changed at her end and she started sending criticizing messages, so unlike her. I'd like to have the 'old' Carrie back as a virtual friend, it was fun then. If you decide to pay her, add her fee into your next budget request or invoice me separately and I'll pay it, thanks Ashley.

Ashley: Ok. I'll add it into the next invoice and take care of it for you.

M: (to DeLeon) I had an unusual lack of clarity last night so something was missing. I feel this morning that instead of driving to Asheville we should fly to Costa Rica, even if only for three or four days. I really want to get your woman feeling about locating Eden Seven in that country. I'll try to set up an appointment to see the land I sent you the link to. But we'd be out of country, would that work for you? Even more importantly, I want us to learn some Tantra together. The last I heard from her, Tantra Healer was able to see us on the 15th, I can try to schedule that for two hours. If you think we should also see the other one, please try to make an appointment with her on the 14th. We would then be free to fly to Costa Rica on the 16th, the flight is only three hours I think. Depending on when we get back, there may be time for another two hours with Tantra Healer if we both feel that would be beneficial. *Wow, tall one, just wow...* Your thoughts?

DeLeon: Okay, now that I've gotten used to/adjusted to your flying with the wind.... It Works For ME. And Darlin, I've got the passport! All sounds good. I'll connect with the other tantra instructor - to see if she has any openings on the 14th. I like the idea of seeing both - why not get the best from both. And then off to Costa Rica on the 16th. Okie dokie. Tall and do-able and it 'taint boring" Glad you came back to Costa Rica - feel that is a masterful part of your journey of creation - which then would keep inspiring you on other levels. I've reached out to a friend of mine - she has a home in Costa Rica.... it's not on much land. but I hear it is beautiful. Have asked her about this area - and feedback in general. Waiting her response. Going forward.. Happy and peacefully.

M: It's better to fly with the wind than against it. I love that you're tall and beautiful and slender and long haired and blonde and Goddess of Bling and DeLeon Fountain of Youth and Lioness and fun and flexible and spontaneous and open and and *"do-able"* did you say? *This is going to be such fun..* I'll see about getting our flights booked for four nights in Costa Rica from April 16th returning April 20th, and getting an appointment to see the land. I'll also check with Ashley re our itinerary, she runs a tour company in Costa Rica. We'll combine her ideas with those you come up with from your friend.

DeLeon: Sounds marvelous

Tantra Healer: Yes, absolutely. I can meet with you and your friend between April 12 and 21st. to teach you both Tantra together and to help you give her more pleasure and to help her awaken to her own ability to experience more pleasure. Have you read my website? This is my specialty. I can come to her home in Boca to see you and there won't be a travel fee. Please call me to further discuss your vision for the session and to make an appointment. Love and Light

M: Thanks for the prompt reply. I'll check with my friend and get back with you. She has a room-mate so would you be willing to meet with us for three hours in a hotel room close to you? We'll probably travel within three days of my arrival in Fort Lauderdale on April 12th. Would you be able to meet with us, say April 13th if my friend concurs?

Tantra Healer: You're welcome. Yes, I could come to you in a nearby hotel room for three hours. I'm not available on the 13th or 14th. On the 15th, however, I could see you between 10 am and 5 pm. I look forward to hearing back from you once you speak with your friend. Please show her my website.

M: I haven't heard back from my friend yet but we may be flying to another country and would have to leave on the 13th to have enough time there. I arrive in Fort Lauderdale on April 12th at 4:30 p.m. We could drive from there straight to a hotel near you if you could meet us on April 12 after 6 p.m.?? I want to have your session behind us *before* we travel if possible so I can have that knowledge and added confidence that I can please and pleasure my sweetheart better during our vacation. Can you meet with us on April 12 after 6 p.m. if she is ok with that?

DeLeon: Agreed - 3 hrs. is better - given our situations - if workable. Michael - what are ramifications of moving your arrival time up a day or so... provided, she could work us in her schedule. If not, and in the mean time. Would you want to connect with the other instructor - as she does a similar thing. Perhaps get one of them at the beginning - other at the end. Tell her she had been referenced to me by another doctor. May help wiggle in. Do you want me to connect with Her? If I'm not invading your space - share with me the emails you sent Tantra Healer - so I know how you presented it. Another day hungering for you.

M: (to Tantra Healer) Please schedule me and my lady friend DeLeon for two hours on April 15th. We may be staying at a hotel in Delray Beach. Would that work for you? Or could we come to your home? After your session we'll most likely fly to another country for three or four days and may want to see you for another two hours when we get back if we can get that scheduled. But we'd like to make that decision while we're away, so we'll have to take our chances on you being available. Please confirm April 15th and the best time for you, thanks.

M: (to DeLeon) The last time I checked their website though the Inn at Boynton Beach was only showing rooms with two double beds. As I recall we had a queen when we were there. Would you like to give them a call and try to reserve a room with queen or king bed for us April 12, 13, 14, 15? I think we were in room 320? Try to get that one??

M: (to Real Estate Agent in Costa Rica) I'm not ready to buy anything yet but it's possible that I and a lady friend may land in Costa Rica on April 16th and stay three or four nights. We want to see the cloud forest but would it be possible to see that property while we're there also?

M: Ashley, I'm going to be visiting my friend DeLeon in Fort Lauderdale, Florida a few days from now. It's not written in stone but it's possible that she and I may land in Costa Rica on April 16th and stay four nights. I'll try to arrange with the agent to see the land I sent you the link to that might work for Eden Seven. I want to get her and my feel for it (she was a real estate broker) you will be there when it comes time to buy. Do you have any ideas for us? We don't have a lot of time, I'm on a budget, and my friend is not up to anything extreme. (Heart problem - good doctors there just in case?) But I'd like to see the cloud forest and hear the howler monkeys again. How would we reliably get there and back to the airport? Where should we overnight? How much time do we realistically need for such a trip? Should I try to arrange more than four nights in Costa Rica? Can we do this without speaking Spanish?

DeLeon: The Inn in Boynton Beach - had one room only - two twins - and I said nope. So, we are in Boca Raton at Best Western University Inn Plus. I'm familiar with area. They also have "minimal fee" shuttle service to airport. They do have room service, breakfast. So, think that is better being in Boca, for Tantra Healer sake (and yours $). And yes on my credit card. All Done!

M: Thank-you my love. It is there then that we will do Tantra and I will best love you again for the days allotted us. But you may want to call back and put your own name on the reservation, remember the hassle when I presented a credit card with a different name than on the reservation? With you standing there it will not be a problem, I will be sure to take care of all expenses.

DeLeon: okay - will do.

Tantra Healer: That's awesome Michael. I was still trying to figure out how to make the 12th work. Yes, Tuesday the 15th is much better. Delray Beach is just as good as Boca Raton, especially if it's east, near the ocean or I-95. I don't do 2 hours for couples, we don't want to rush

Tantra, it's counterproductive. 2 1/2 hours is my minimum, 3 hours is better. My healing room is too small for seeing a couple so I would come to you. I am available on Tuesday, 4/15 until 5 pm. So we can start as early as 9 am or as late as 2 pm or anywhere in between. Let me know what works for you. Love and Light

M: Please book Michael and DeLeon for three hours on Tuesday April 15th starting at 1 p.m. in our hotel room. I'll email our room number sometime after we check in. I'm really looking forward to this. We haven't known each other long but DeLeon and I quickly established what I think is probably a "tantra-like" soul connection when we first met, some rough edges, but lots of love manifest. We're getting on in years and neither of us had known such a thing before, it was pleasantly astonishing. So DeLeon's already a goddess to me, she represents Divine Feminine. I want to be sure I know how to treat her as such continually, and her to know how to best draw out from me what she needs to get to where she wants to travel. I know I'll know when she arrives. And I know I'll be richly rewarded for having done my part in getting her there, I'd like nothing better, she's a joy to me. Can you send me an invoice?

Tantra Healer: Beautifully stated Michael. I'm so happy for you and DeLeon. I recently worked with a couple who were also experiencing the highest love and passion of their lifetimes thus far and they were both in their 70s. It's my honor and privilege to work with you. I can see you at 1 pm on the 15th. However, in order to send you a Paypal invoice I need to know how much time you want to book. 2 1/2 hours is $500 and 3 hours is $600. Please let me know how much time you want. My experience has shown that 3 hours is best if you want my support in awakening DeLeon's Divine Ecstatic Response as well as an energetic Kundalini Awakening for yourself and instruction on how to transmit more energy to your Beloved through your body. Love and Light

Ashley: This is exciting!!!! 4 days is tricky. I would recommend at least 5 nights. I have a very good private driver you could use and he speaks english and can potentially meet you at the airport. He could get you to the property and definately knows his way through the cloud forest. I would recommend having him to get you to a destination from a hotel in Alajuela the next day after arrival. Take you through the cloud forest to the Baldi Hotsprings for the day and one night to relax beside the volcano. Then take you to the property the following day, stay close by in a hotel there for 2 nights to see if you like the surrounding area, and to see the property and feel out the vibe, then have my driver pick you up from that hotel to return you to a hotel in Alajuela for one night to catch your flight back the following day. If you make a decision and have dates picked, I can start making the arrangements, getting prices, contacting the driver and the hotel in Alajuel. You would only have to worry about making the arrangements with the property owner or real estate agent and a drive to the property from your hotel. Taxi or the owner or seller of the property.

You can do it in 5 days I would say would be more realistic, but still not very long. Not including flight, you should be able to manage with under $1000 for two of you for 5 days with driver, hot springs, accommodations and food. But you will have to not splurge. Cheers!

M: (to Tantra Healer) We'll do three hours.

M: This sounds wonderful Ashley. I'll copy DeLeon in and ask for comments before I commit, we can do five nights. Do you book the hotels etc. and I pay you for everything except food, tips, and the Goddess of Bling's essential Costa Rica bling?

M: DeLeon, Please comment on Ashley's tentative schedule for us. Doing five nights in Costa Rica from the 16th would get us back to Fort Lauderdale on the same day that I fly to Yuma. I think I leave for Yuma at 5 p.m. so the flights might work. But it would be nice to have a few days together to rest and discuss after our experience in Costa Rica. Would you be ok if I delayed my return to Yuma say four or five days and I slept on your couch for economy so you don't have to dig out the trundle again?

Ashley: I book the hotels and driver, and you pay as you go! You will make a small $40 deposit towards my time and to ensure your seriousness, but other then that you don't have to give me any cash. I know them well, and they compensate me when they can with a small commission or a favour in the future and I've worked with them for many years. So its a safe and guaranteed system built to work for everyone.

M: I haven't heard back from DeLeon yet but we'll most likely do the five nights you outlined. Perhaps you could work your fee into the marketing invoice so I can easily write that off, our trip is certainly for the book business, thanks. Will USA cash work or do I need to convert to Costa Rica currency? How much USA cash do you suggest I have on hand? Will you bail us out if we break some unknown law and go straight to jail? Blue jeans and all casual, shorts etc. be ok? What kind of shoes? Will we need a jacket anywhere we're going?

DeLeon: It would be good to delay - and... you are not going to sleep on the couch!!! It's not that difficult to get the trundle out... I would go insane with you here.... and in a different room than with me!! END OF STORY!!

Ashley: Alright, I will get back to with all your answers!!!! How exciting!!!! You are quite the character... remind me of me! Haha

M: I was worried about that. You're just not NORMAL Ashley.

DeLeon: Just got back from driving Roomy down to Fort Lauderdale - and back, worn out, need to walk my dog and rest - so more later.. all sounds good - you know what your doing with all of that. And I trust your decisions....for us.

M: I love you baby....

Chapter 5

Suzanne: I am discovering Suzanne, she is not going anywhere. No romance. In fact he wrote me today and advised me to seek a much younger man due to my appearance and high energy level. I was only myself and said nothing about sex. So what's up? I think oft self as ordinary, nothing special, just me.

M: Every time you write to me in such a personal manner (I think you call it getting "naked") it doesn't matter where my mind may have been when I opened your message, you draw out from me a great love, a joy, a big smile of happiness. That of course does not mean that we are somehow 'meant' for each other or that I am possessive of you. I do think you should continue your search for the right man and take your safe pleasure when and where you will, with male or female. It simply means that I feel a whole lot of *love* for a certain nurse in Texas. That love began with our first hug when you came to Loa. It was not the raw earth sexual feelings I at the time had hoped it would be. It was a higher vibration, a kind of spiritual bonding, an *"all is well, all is very well"* feeling that has never left me. Just a mere thought of you renews that love every time.

But ok, I think you are asking for my opinion about what may be "wrong" with you because you're not attracting men who are likely candidates for a long-term relationship, or when you think they *might* be and you're willing to go along, they abandon you?

With regard to the man who recently called you "beautiful" it seems that he was older than you and most likely looking for marriage. And if so, yes, my darling you can be daunting for an older man. You are very attractive, don't show your age, and have delightful high energy. The man asks himself how he will ever keep up with the likes of you, in bed or not.

I will never in this lifetime forget the first time I touched your naked stomach as you sat on Loa's couch. Your skin felt so soft and smooth it could have been a baby's skin. I commented on how soft you are and you said *"thank-you"*. Do you remember that darling? You appear exceptionally young looking and should be able to attract men quite a bit younger than you if you so desired. That might not work long-term though, don't know, but could be good for short-term pleasure if safe and you guard your heart should it be wise to do so. I expect that all males find you sexually desirable, your breasts as I recall are perfect, your legs are long and lovely, your body is proportional, your face is comely. You know and can do all the woman things and most likely many of the things men do in Texas to. And I understand you're an outstanding gourmet cook. *You have a heck of a lot going for you Suzanne!*

Your *"nothing special, just me"* darling is not ordinary at all. You may not see yourself that way but you are an exceptionally attractive woman in many ways. It could be though that the raunchy ones only out for sex for a brief time and prepared to tell lies to get it, would find the radiant light of love and goodness that shines from you hospice nurse a bit daunting. (They don't know *Suzanne's* in there do they? I *love* Suzanne, my virtual hot babe quick to find and use her vibrators when needed. It has been a long time since you asked me to just sit and listen so I'll dare attempt a metaphysical approach to what I think was a request for an opinion from a really good friend, once lover.

Whatever it is that you are imagining is what you are creating for your life. Imagine yourself Responsible Nurse (RN) but having trouble getting a satisfying relationship happening, and that's likely where you are going to stay if that's where you are right now. Imagine yourself above all *Suzanne*, coming with careless abandon, wild with her hair down, and you are likely to attract something/someone quite different. What do you *really* want? Play pretend, *imagine* what you really want as if it's already in your possession, and that's what Law of Attraction will bring to you. That's how I see it sweetheart. Hope we go to Paris. Your Michael

DeLeon: The scedule sounds great - and very glad we get the time with the realtor/sales agent, surrounding area, etc... to yes get a feel for it. Feel a lot of synergestic thinking is going to be spawning, between us, when out on the land, before, during and after... re the future of Seven Eden.

DeLeon: Stay as long as you want and are comfortable with - don't pinch, go when your ready.... our time is precious and powerful. Love U

DeLeon: This is soooo exciting.... what a gift to have Ashley taking over. Where do we find out what the weather is like - so I'm prepared - clothes wise.... girl thing, ya know.

DeLeon: Glad you went back to the 3 hours as you originally desired. I sent an email out to the other instructor - haven't heard. I like the one you call Tantra Healer..

M: Thank-you for that. I need to be back before the end of April though, I'll be moving Loa then.

DeLeon: thank u - going to bed nity, nite, Darlin...

DeLeon: Well, unless my room-mate kicks both of us out! It's pretty small in here. So 4 days or so - As I said something to Roomy - and don't have a whole bunch more than that..... as I picked up. You know she rules around here. Just noting. Hope all is okay....

Oh, oh, I don't want to be in the middle of that, better book a room at the Inn.

M: (to DeLeon) I send our itinerary from April 12 through April 25, 2014.

M: Our flights are booked Ashley, please proceed with your five night plan, thanks.

M: (to myself) Whew, that's was ONE DAY in the life of Me!!! It's now 10 pm April 3 in Yuma, Arizona, United States of America and we have a quarter of e-book Book 11 written already. Still interested in reading about us? Fantasy or not, we're on the way to Eden Seven and Immortality. And yeah, my guess is that Suzanne my woman in Texas is going to feel the need for sex pretty soon. Like that? What's it going to be like doing twelve days of it with the tall blonde Goddess of Bling in Florida and Costa Rica? Should I bare it all to you? You know I will don't you. Keep in mind that I LIVE my books so YOU can live through me and mine.

Real Estate Agent: Hi Michael, Thank you for contacting us about land in our area. Have you been here before? How long will you be in the area? I can definitely show you this property on April 19th. Where will you be staying? Why don't you tell me more about what you are looking for in a property including location, views, access, and all around usage. Then I can send you a few other options and maybe we will have some other stuff to look at too!!!!

M: (to Agent, cc Suzanne, DeLeon, Ashley, Carrie) This is a message I sent to a real estate agent in Costa Rica on April 4th. The property I am interested in is listed at the following link. I believe that we can do this with suitable solicitations for donations from sponsors and founders. We can probably attract volunteer skilled labor to plan and construct buildings, and applications from people who want to live in Eden Seven once we get the word out about what we are doing. I find this immensely exciting as the vision expands and unfolds and more and more leading edge people are attracted to us. I'll be in Costa Rica in just a few days. Your comments are invited.

M: (to Real Estate Agent) Good morning, it's really nice to communicate with people who check their email often and respond quickly, thank-you. A friend of mine runs tours to Costa Rica. Below is the itinerary she will most likely set up for me and my lady friend, we're only staying five nights. As you can see we'll be staying in a hotel "close to your property" and available to look at land on April 19th. I'll let you know when I have the hotel name. Regarding the use of property at this point in time I'm chasing a dream, but one that could manifest with not much difficulty when funds are available. I want to buy at least 100 acres of treed land with flowing water in a peaceful place with a climate of 'eternal spring'. My friend who does the tours is recommending Costa Rica. Your online presentation of the land I want to see fits that profile.

As a writer of visionary metaphysical fiction books with creative friends and contacts, I want to surround myself with happy creative folk by creating "COWA", a Community of Writers and Artists. I visualize that as a private self-sustaining green community where creative people can rent small cabins for a nominal fee and live next to similar others in peace and tolerance, doing what they want to do, which is create art of all kinds, exchange ideas and pleasant stimulating conversation, and write. As we get established we'll allow tours of COWA during which our residents can display and sell their art and perhaps present dinner theater for the tourists. As our COWA becomes known, we'll attract famous guests such as singers and actors who will perform to invited guests and tourists in exchange for a donation to help maintain the community.

I foresee us having tilapia ponds and beautiful organic gardens of flowers and produce to be as much as possible self-sustaining, each resident contributing labor and skills when not doing art. With the exception of the occasional tour bus, motor vehicles will be at a distance from the residences with silent golf carts prevailing where people live and do art. Small secluded studio and one bedroom cabins will be surrounded by trees with a winding walkway to reach them. There will be a central building for kitchen, dining, and communal gatherings, and a nearby outdoor stage for our performing artists to strut their stuff. We'll try to structure our lifestyle to model the "City of Enoch" written of in the bible where residents lived in peace, harmony, and love to the point where the community was taken to heaven.

Yes, I'm a writer of fiction I'm allowed flights of fancy, but that basically outlines my vision, I believe it to be realistic. As a believer in Law of Attraction (as per Rhonda Byrne's *"The Secret"*) I know that the right people and circumstances will be attracted to build and occupy this community, which I am naming "Eden Seven". We would bring wealthy tourists, famous people, and art and culture to your area. The love and peace emanating from Eden Seven would spill over as we become a new light that attracts leading edge peaceful people to your nearby villages, towns and cities. Your indigenous people would teach us their ways and culture, and we would share ours with them and marvel at each other. Diversity, tolerance, peace, love and harmony would be the order of each new day in Eden. That's how I see it...

M: (to Suzanne) It's surprising to me that you never even mention, let alone write excitedly about my offer to take you to Paris, London, and Las Vegas all expenses paid. Is your woman intuition telling you that it's not going to happen?

Wow, fast response from Suzanne, unusual, delightful.

Suzanne: I'm thinking since I still haven't been approved for vacation that it may not be or it may be only a week, which then would mean maybe just Vegas. So until vacation is approved I'm holding back.

M: Ok, thanks much honey, and yes one week would mean Vegas Baby. We'd have great fun there and there's always another Spring in Paris, I'm known to stretch too far now and again. Enjoy your day sweetheart, I feel great love for you as always. Your Michael

DeLeon: Good Morning. THANK YOU - I so appreciate your "organizing" soul. I was tired last nite - and sad I came on too strong on the time here at home. We can talk about it - I feel it is not necessary to stay in the Inn. We can cook here - or go out, we've a lake to hang out on.... can go to the swimming pool - there are now 2 of them..... and more..... I have to pay someone to walk my dog. Let's just talk about it, when together, okay? I want us both happy..... A Grand Journey.. Thank U for making it happen. Love,,,, DeLeon

M: Good morning sweetie. I've already booked the Inn and don't mind the cost, it will give us privacy, I enjoyed our time there. I don't want a hassle for either of us. If you can assure me that roomy is *absolutely* ok with us being at your place I can cancel the Inn. I like your name DeLeon Goddess of Eternal Spring. Your Lover

DeLeon: I like my names, via my Lover.....they keep changing, expanding, rising... Let's talk more together - and we have time, etc. etc.. My room-mate may be going away on the 23rd to be with family. MAY.... will see how things unfold. mroe later...

Tantra Healer: Let's talk Michael, I don't believe we've had a phone conversation yet. I'd like to explain more about my work. Please call me at your convenience. I don't believe I have your phone number. Mine is in my bi-line below. Love and Light

M: Is it possible that this could be done by email? The reason why I ask is because all I have is an old basic pay per minute cell phone that I never carry, seldom leave on, and use only for unavoidables and emergency type happenings. I'm really looking forward to your instruction. I get more pleasure from giving than receiving and I'm aware of the Tantra teaching that males seldom ejaculate and the reason for that. I'm completely willing, wanting to satisfy my beautiful partner as best I and she are capable of together.

Tantra Healer: Yes, I will write you again tomorrow as I'm having a very busy day. I want to explain a few things about how I work.

DeLeon: Actually now, my room-mate's thinking of running up north (taking the dachshund with her), and hang out with a friend of hers.... while we're back here, after Costa Rica. So, we would have the whole place to our selves. That would be good - will just see how it all unfolds.

M: It still seems uncertain so let me know when you think I should cancel the Inn.

DeLeon: You have such a way with communication - everything was beautifully presented.. Oh, yes, that's right, your a writer. Do you think we need another day looking at land - and being around that particular piece - or others he may want to show us? Just a thought.

M: I exercised that discretion you so generously bestowed upon magnificent me and wrote five days in stone, the flights are booked. But we may not need to look at a lot of places, I'm not prepared to buy just yet I don't think, I just want to get a general feeling about possibly locating Eden Seven in that area. I think I already know but I want to validate that knowing by observing how the two of us react while in Costa Rica, and discussing our feelings in private. (If that's possible, right now I just want to spend every moment learning Tantra together with you and loving you completely - you are my goddess. I think Tantra is now as important to me as it is to you. But I still want to hear you whisper your story detail by detail up to the time you came with me, your most beautiful experience you said. Then there's that matter of wetness. To the extent of my present knowledge, it seems that Tantra is primarily about males treating women as the representatives of Divine Feminine that each woman really is behind the masks Western society forces them to wear. Tantra will be featured prominently in my books for male and female alike to read and marvel at, and hopefully immerse in.

Law of Attraction will be particularly in play during our time in Costa Rica so having leading edge you along as a second observer will make it less likely that I might miss a vital rendezvous that could lead to beneficial synchronicity and a faster manifestation of Eden Seven. I think you understand what I'm saying. But we'll shoot for fun too, you and I seem to have a knack for that. Bestest today my love. Your Michael

DeLeon: Additionally tantra is about taking the energy of God/ Creation/Christ/Source - and learning how to work with that energy in healing self, in controlling the energy, maintaining the energy, etc... And much more. That's why they call it "Sacred Sexuality". My heart says – you writing about tantra is one of the most sacred, incredible gifts you could bring to humanity.... hence literally creating Eden Seven - not just in your Eden Seven community - but EVERYWHERE to every reader. There's my deepest truth for you, dear one. I love the power of participating in synergetic creation.... I love what and how it flows through being the channel. Michael, this journey we are sharing, is SACRED, powerful, and beyond our wildest dreams. Blessings this nite, I'm going to bed. Your DeLeon...

Ashley: That is amazing!!!! I will get all the details finalized quickly. I have to start by contacting the hotel and drivers and get confirmations and prices. Please be a little patient and no worries I will have it all arranged for you! So exciting! My life has become so much more magical since I met you.

M: Magic is what we do together my dear. I have seen so much 'magic' happen daily since I started this project that I have complete faith in it, we're engaged in a whole lot more than merely selling books, important as that is. The entire universe is conspiring for our success. I am moved urgently to going to Costa Rica unprepared, just knowing that the 'magic' is always here/there. DeLeon, Goddess of Bling and Eternal Spring (read the books) will be there with me as a second trained observer to make it less likely that I might miss a vital rendezvous that could lead to beneficial synchronicity and a faster manifestation of Eden Seven. And because she and I do Tantra particularly well together, and we love each other for it.

Ashley: Please proceed to contact the person or agent of the property to set up a showing time.... for April 19th - that one I will leave with you as it is personal business. The best day for the showing would be April 19th. Also ask them about a pick-up and near by hotel. The jungle is not marked with signs... its a different world here.

M: So you're saying it's a jungle out there. I've already contacted the agent, he's expecting us on the 19th and needs to know where to pick us up.

Ashley: Do you need two rooms or are you both ok with sharing a room. And two beds or one?

M: Oh Ashley, Michael and DeLeon are absolutely a one bed family. Someday you'll get to read the books and understand... But thanks for caring and checking, I never thought to mention it to you.

Carrie: hi there... your vision sounds wonderful and i do hope you manifest it in all it's glory! have you ever been to costa rica before? to this part of the country? if not and you have only read about it, i have been there twice, in fact i own a piece of property close to dominical so i can fill you in a little... and, who's the mystery lady? hoping it might be suzanne???

M: I will not be manifesting Eden Seven Carrie, it's WE, leading edge souls, who are co-creating that. There are many who are now being attracted to the project, it's much more than just the books, as important as they are. I have witnessed so much 'magic' happening every day since I became first involved with this that I have faith in what is happening. It's just that as creatures of physicality we choose to not let ourselves remember what's coming next in the grand play we ourselves wrote in the heavens and are now here, real life, acting out our chosen parts.

Thanks for the plug for Suzanne but the "mystery lady" is none other than DeLeon Goddess of Bling and Eternal Spring. You'll eventually be able to read all the books and understand better what's happening, it's quite fascinating really. I love every moment as more and more of the script unfolds, it's truly delicious. We always serve it up bigger and better each time but *this* time it's not a rehearsal, for many of us it will be our final act as we move on to immortality, bigger and better things to do and be. I actually thought of meeting you in Costa Rica but we weren't talking at the time, and DeLeon is a former real estate broker.

Suzanne and I are waiting to see if she can get two weeks leave next month so we can travel together to Paris and London, she's big into culture and I'm right there with her. At this point it's looking doubtful, one of the hospice nurses was in a bad accident and another is on pregnancy leave. Paris gets too hot beyond May so if we can't go this year we may settle for a week in Las Vegas when Suzanne can get time off. So that's where it's at right now.

I really appreciate your help Carrie. It never was a problem with me to pay you what I could for the work Ashley asked of you. You very often read me wrong, not discerning me from book character Michael - you know, that raunchy guy in those soon to be discovered books. When money starts rolling in I will funnel more of it to Ashley and my guess is that you'll get a raise or at least a bonus? Enjoy the day Carrie. Stay in touch sweetie, life's *real* good. I suggest you do some healing of others when you get some free time, even remotely. You'll be amazed at how Source will FLOW through you again even more powerfully than before you took a tumble. You're going to be extra happy because of the contrast, you'll see, you're an ancient soul darling, you came here with us, you're well loved.

Carrie: i really appreciate that you had a change of mind/heart about providing some compensation for my time and effort... and, it's important to me to understand what motivated you to make the change, before i jump back into action so, please take a few minutes to send me a note about this... thanks, carrie

M: I think I did that with my last email Carrie. You set up a straw man, I did not have difficulty paying you money when you asked, it's just that money is all coming from my savings right now so it's limited.

Ashley: Once we have confirmation from the seller that you can look at this property in Uvita on April 19th, I have a contact for a very cute hotel there which I can arrange for you easily. I will probably be able to meet with you in Uvita if the universe allows... as I will be living about 20mins away from there. Are you comfortable getting a taxi on your own from the airport to the hotel which is 10mins away. I always manage on my own and there are tons of taxis waiting outside to help and they will know the hotel. You will also have the contact info if they need it. OR do you require someone to be there to greet you and bring you to the hotel? All is well!

M: Lovely, lovely, I'm thrilled that you might meet with us Ashley, I didn't know you would be there at the time. I love it when a plan comes together! Will you be able to look at property with us on the 19th? If so I'll tell the agent to expect a party of three. "Cute" hotel sounds like exactly what the Goddess of Bling would order up. That's a for sure "yes". Taxi is fine, just provide clear directions, name etc. of the hotel. I used to get around in China with non-English speaking cabbies so I can probably manage Costa Rica with my very clearly pronounced "no hablo" or however that's spelled in Chinese. Indeed, all is exceedingly well my dear friend, all is well...

Ashley: Oh great!!!!!!! Just saw this now. I'll go ahead and make the hotel reservation in Uvita. Its working so perfectly!!!! I love this stuff!!!! I love it so much. Costa Rica is a very magical place.... you will see.

Carrie: to whom should i submit editing changes needed which i find as i read? i found a number on the web site and, i imagine i might find some in the books, as i read them... michael, would you like these to come to you or go to ashley? or neither of you? fyi...i'm a retired english teacher, so it's impossible for me to read without proofing as i go

M: If it's something on the website you are referring to it should go to Ashley, she hasn't told me how to make changes on her pages yet. But please keep in mind that although book "Michael" is careful to write proper English, if it's not a quote from him I always leave grammar up to the writer of the message I'm quoting. So in every book there are a huge number of Engish mistakes. (Yep, did that.) Thanks for the offer though, we'll probably go with frontier English. My attitude is that once a book is published it's best to just forget about it, readers expect mistakes and ignore them unless they are prolific. And I'm not about to start unpublishing books and starting over again, can't keep up with the live manuscript as is right now. I've been typing steady since dark a.m. and still haven't even caught up with emails, and have a date arriving in less than two hours.

Carrie: happy to hear you'll be traveling with deleon...that will be lovely, i'm sure there's only one thing i really wanted to impart based on your desired qualities for eden seven... you said you wanted a climate of "eternal spring" you will not find that type of climate in costa rica, especially not in the dominical region... it's quite hot there all year long...i've been twice and was dripping wet to the core both time... even in the rainy season, near dominical in october, it was 90 degrees and 90% humidity all the time... very muggy, not at all spring like you are going in the dry season, though on the cusp of the other wettest time of the year, which is may, so you may either have very dry hot days or if the rains start, it will be hot and muggy...

interestingly where i live is called "the valley of eternal spring" as it is at 3500 feet above sea level, so the temperatures range from about 65 to 75 all year long...true spring time temps...we do drop down to 60 some nights and up to 80+ on some days, but it's generally about 75 during the day and about 65 at night... but, the only way to get a spring time climate in the tropics is in the mountains... anything close to sea level is going to be typical hot, humid tropical climes... just wanted to prepare you a little for the reality of costa rica... especially along the southern pacific coast... the northern pacific coast is dryer all year, but still quite hot, not spring like... and, if you don't find the perfect place in cr, you might want to check out where I am... my property is quite small and on a hill side, not suited for what you are planning... thank you for the love...

M: Excellent suggestions Carrie. I had read that Costa Rica was real hot except in the highlands. If the feels are not right on there I might take a trip to where you are and scout that out. As I mentioned early on in our virtuality, I was at one time in touch with a man who lived halfway up a mountain in Panama. He described that as "eternal spring". Good, good, thanks much.

Ashley: I should be able to! and I think there is two rooms in your lodge? hahaha so it may just work very well. I could come in the evening of the 18th, the driver can pick me up on the way to Uvita and then be there to go look at the property in the AM. Then probably head out that evening or just play it by the day.

M: Sure, let's work it out so we can spend time with you Ashley. I don't know the travel times there at all so if you can overnight with us that could work well. But I'm wondering now with all the enthusiasm rushing about for Costa Rica if it might be too hot there for what we are planning? Please give me a considered response thanks. The trees of course would be wonderful but we don't want to sweat every minute of every day either. Maybe halfway up a tall mountain somewhere in the tropics where it's eternal spring???? Just wondering, we're for sure going to Costa Rica, I do want to feel the feelings there, a magical place could make up for a lot of not so perfectness if need be.

DeLeon: Yes, my room-mate being away is uncertain. Will probably become apparent before we meet, will advise. However, if doesn't let's talk it thru and make decision.. together.. okay?

M: I would love to make decisions together with The Goddess of Bling and Eternal Spring.

Ok, I don't want another major reaction from DeLeon but I'd better run Ashley being in Costa Rica by her.

M: (to DeLeon) I've been going like crazy since dark a.m. just trying to keep up with arriving emails today and just now at 5 p.m. about caught up. So there's a whole bunch of new stuff re our trip. But surprise, Ashley is going to be in Costa Rica at the same time and may be able to look over the land with us. She has us booked into a "cute" hotel near the land for two nights. I think the real estate agent will pick us up there. Ashley is doing the website and marketing for my books. I've never met her but I know she's a whole lot younger than us, I think in her early thirties, not sure. I hadn't planned this, are you ok with her being there with us? She is major into metaphysics and labels herself a Law of Attraction "Global Specialist". She's a godsend, a referral from Carrie. Your thoughts.

Carrie: good morning…below is a reply from my friend about a piece of property in Panama that fits your description.

M: The price is much less expensive than what we're looking at in Costa Rica. I want to get a feel for Costa Rica but may possibly look near where you live too, thanks much Carrie.

Carrie: my pleasure…

M: For economy, if you're ok with that I might come by myself sometime and just quietly look around with Eden Seven in mind.

Carrie: as long as we are clear about the nature of our relationship (friends *without* benefits) and we are agreed that there will be no attempt on your part to get into my bed, i am open to that at this point…

M: (to myself) How should I respond to *that*? Anyway, all she knows of me is book character Michael and I do like that character a whole lot. So perhaps her comment is appropriate, though Michael loves and respects women and would never deliberately harm anyone. I won't respond…

DeLeon: (re us meeting with Ashley) Sounds all okay for me….. thank you for asking. I would assume she won't be around the entire time in Costa Rica.

M: Here is the thread DeLeon. I would not allow anyone else to be with us our entire time in Costa Rica, this is *our* time, I'm thinking and dreaming of *you*. I really do want to meet Ashley, she is hugely involved with and committed 100% to my project. It looks like she's angling to overnight at the same hotel we are in the night before we view the property, maybe it's a long travel time back to wherever she's living.

Real Estate Agent: I read your vision and it sounds great. Do you have some ideas on how to raise the funds for the project? I know the place you are staying and I can pick you up there and take you to the farm. We can confirm the exact time a little closer to the day.

M: Thanks, I'm looking forward to meeting you and looking over the property. I'm going to assume that us being a party of three will work out ok for you. When I find the right property and the time is right to buy, the funds will be available.

Real Estate Agent: 3 people will be fine!

M: (to DeLeon) You're a former real estate broker DeLeon, will you remember to keep an eye open for any of this stuff that Carrie sent that applies to buying raw land in Costa Rica?

DeLeon: Michael, am sorry I can not find the web site you sent for the weather. What I did see was it's HOT. Well, DeLeon, it's down south, way down south. The Tropics! Won't have to worry about getting cold, except on airline. Please resend. thank u.

Today Roomy danced in an independent competition down in Boca Raton. We were up at 4:30 a.m., getting up, dressed, all stuff gathered, dogs walked in the dark and out to Boca. The competition started at 8:30 a.m. - she danced 23 dances! Someday, someday I am going to be able to do a competition. But, not 23 dances.

M: She dances up a storm. But no storms on the horizon where we're going. Thinking of you tall one...

DeLeon: Thank U - just had another afib episode hit, so took my pill and going to lie down. Had one last night - good news it quit with the one pill! Have talked with my doctor about that and he is giving me an extended amount of the pills, to take on the trip.... it's also what they use for IV's in the ER rooms, so I know what needs to be done. However, all is going to be good. No matter what.

The universe continues to unfold. I'm getting everything I ever wanted. All my deepest desires and dreams from childhood are becoming real as society and religion's myriad thou shalt nots peel away and I become *myself*. What I desire comes as if by magic now that I *expect* what I want and allow it to manifest without allowing contrasting thoughts or fears to stay in my mind. The women in my life who wanted me the Western way (exclusively) are now changing their mind about that. In my fantasy I'm looking for *seven* beautiful women for my immortal Adam and Eve family. Part of why I remain so connected with Suzanne is because she has told me outright that she has no problem with me having sex with other women, in fact she encourages me to be with others. And I encourage her right back, I do not seek to possess her exclusively for myself.

DeLeon was *adamant* that she have me exclusively or not at all (she sent me packing when I told her I am still fond of Suzanne) but that has now changed, what I do when I'm away from her she now says is "my business." And because of that change of attitude we will be trained in Tantra together and will most likely emerge closely connected for a lifetime. I think of DeLeon often now and want to be with her. *Catch and release* ladies, it works wonders with men who yearn for freedom - and you'll probably get what you want anyway.

My books teach immortality, living a thousand years and more, and Adam and Eve families to populate new planets. Such things are new and seldom if ever spoken of. My books make such things *possible* in the imagination, then move along to *expected*. There may be Adam and Eve families organized with just one man and one woman, that is the norm in Western society, it's what most men and women expect. It's just that in my *personal* vision there are at least eight of us in my family. That may not be for everyone but it makes sense to me that a woman would want female companionship too during the eternities, and not just a man to talk with.

Women usually have female friends to interact with in addition to a man. A man's a creature who will never be a mother, never experience giving birth to a child and other events and feelings unique to women. I think too that a family of equal spouses (one man and several women) each in effect 'married' to each other and thus intimacy of whatever kind being welcomed by all, would be appealing once the prevailing norms against bisexual women float away into nothingness. DeLeon wrote that she is not "a fuckin bisexual". That attitude may change as she begins to remember that those who associate with me and my books are most likely ancient souls who love each other, souls with *history* with each other in past lives. (Not special, just unique like everyone is. There's nothing *better* about "an ancient soul", he or she is just someone who started along the way a bit sooner than someone else.) This time around will most likely be our last as we make our present incarnation immortal, some of us wanting to be with each other forever.

That's how I see it, I'm not looking for converts to immortal families of eight, I'm looking in my fantasy for seven beautiful women who share my dream, seven *Eves* then?

Chapter 6

———◈———

Carrie: hope you like your little hide away (she's talking about her guest room photo) and, know that i am happily contemplating your visit, whenever it can work... hope you've had a wonderful day hugs, carrie

M: I still enjoy those hugs Carrie, thx. It was a good day. Two women kidnapped me about 5:30 and took me to a movie at the Marine Corps Air Base, one is a retired Navy officer. Quite a good movie, never read the book. Not sure when I can come Carrie, I'll let you know as far in advance as I can.

Carrie: ya know... you are going to be sooo close when you are in cr, it's a shame to have to come all this way another time... is there any chance you could reroute your return. i know you said this was a tour arrangement, but maybe there's some flexibility? just brainstorming...

M: I thought of it Carrie and then you and DeLeon could have met too, but our flights are all booked non-refundable including my return from Florida to Yuma, so it's not going to work this time. But when I come I'll most likely bring one of my female friends with me because you are so sensitive about me being there on my own. We'll likely stay in a hotel but if you don't mind going with us, the three of us could drive together to see some land in Panama. Would that be better?

Carrie: no... not better... i'd much rather you come alone... i'm quite fine with that... not at all sensitive about you being here alone... just wanted us to be on the same page, that's all. i much prefer that you do not bring another... let's just get to know each other one on one and, please do plan to stay here... i extended the invitation with full conscious awareness and forethought.. things have changed for me in the last week we are now partners and i would very much like to explore and grow our friendship... bringing another will interfere with that, regardless of how wonderful the other is one on one is a certain energy, and bringing a third into that changes the dynamic completely, as i'm sure you know... so... come alone, stay here and let's enjoy getting to know each other... sound good??? 'night, and sweet dreams..

Wow Carrie, that's telling a lot. Spider web woven? What's really motivating this woman who would never allow me to visit her before and suddenly it's me alone even though she knows I have other women in my life?

M: That's nice Carrie, thanks, I'll most likely do that then.

M: (to DeLeon) We'll be limited with what we can take on the flights to and from Costa Rica, they are very strict. I paid $280 extra for each of us to take one carry-on and one checked bag not weighing more than 40 lbs. each. But we'll only be five days and can wear the same clothes twice so that should work out. The only reason for a pant suit or skirt and blouse for you for example is if you want to wear something nicer to dinner at the hotels - I won't expect even that, it's up to you. More importantly, carry comfy shoes/boots for tromping through forest and jungle, a swim suit, sandals, and jeans, shorts and light tops for 90 degree temps, sunscreen and a hat. The min temp will most likely not drop below 65 at night so a couple of long sleeve shirts or a light sweater would be in order. When we're at the hotel in Florida, dress away as you will, I love my gorgeous shiny Goddess of Bling. We'll do Banana Boat again, I want to walk magic with tall beautiful you throwing off delicious pheromones like we did before. Your Michael

DeLeon: Holy Chit! Since it's not a boat - and carousing, struting around... big difference in clothes, jewelry, etc.. I know how to get simple - remember - farm girl and ranch woman. Thank you for the very important notice. Okay - play time..... We can strut down town Delray - in the eves as well. And if you need to leave more "stuff" at the apt. while in Costa Rica - can do. Okay. Your DeLeon.....

Ashley: Hi Michael, I'm back in Costa Rica! My driver is aware of the dates and is working out a price for the driving and availability and will follow up with me soon. I have a Room booked for you in Alajuela 10 minutes from the airport on April 16 and April 20. With private bathroom cost $65 per night. Breakfast and taxes included.

Ashley: Anything up higher is more refreshing that's for sure... or close to the ocean cools off a little at night. You do adjust to the heat in time... but at first... its quite hot! The ocean water here is as warm as a bath. In behind Uvita up from the ocean it goes up into highlands. I will send you a link to another property house in Uvita a friend forwarded to me today. We can potentially make arrangements for the same day to have a look. Anythings possible and for now I recommend going with the flow the universe is offering you... hot or not, I think this first step to exploring the area is a great start!

M: DeLeon, Tantra Healer sent an email last night asking about expectations. I told her I am not shy and to do *whatever* she wants to do to teach us Tantra. We only have three hours and it's private with just her and the two of us. So I think we should take advantage of the time we have and go with whatever she feels inspired to do in the moment with no concern about shyness or asking permissions on our part. By the time we get to her session you and I will be connected lovers anyway, used to seeing each other naked, she'll be like a doctor there to help heal us. But I told her that you will speak for yourself and gave her your email address. I don't know if she'll write you directly, she may just talk when she gets to our room. Here's what she wrote to me when I asked for email instead of a phone call:

> "Michael, I can teach you how to have orgasms without ejaculating, and enable you to choose when to ejaculate. I can also teach you to help your erections last longer. All of this is done with your shorts or underwear still on. An erection is optional, if it happens it's fine but we won't really be doing anything with it because I don't touch men's genitals. I will give you a healing, chakra expanding, Kundalini awakening massage on your spine, teach you how to run energy with and through DeLeon, and teach you powerful breath practices and Taoist techniques to prolong love-making. If you and DeLeon choose, I can do a full body awakening massage on her and teach you how to pleasure, heal and awaken her Goddess spot. Each session is individualized and we will decide together what to do after I spend a few minutes with both of you finding out your history and your intentions for the session. Please let me know if you have any questions or concerns. Love and Light."

I'd love sweetheart to do that "*how to pleasure, heal and awaken her Goddess spot*" with her there to teach my fingers what to do, if you will allow it. Please try to let your hair down my lover and go with careless abandon into this beautiful experience we will share, we'll dream of it for the rest of our lives. I have much love to give you, I want to experience the *wholeness* of you my Tantra Lover. It is my hope that you and I will meet often as the years go by, we're going to *really* like each other and be permanently soul connected after what we have coming for us. But we'll both need to allow the sacred experience to *fully* happen while our expert teacher is there - it's what you wanted I think.

I wrote back to her: *"That sounds good Tantra Healer. DeLeon of course will speak for herself but I would opt for anything I can learn to give my female partner added pleasure, don't hold back on my account at all. I have read about 'dry' orgasms but don't think I have ever experienced one, I would like to. I encourage you to go as far as you feel in the moment to go with us that DeLeon is willing to participate in. I'm not shy, I am eager to learn as much as you can teach us in that time frame. So please know that for me you needn't ask permission for anything you do, you have it, but I don't know about DeLeon.*

As for experience, all I know about Tantra is reading half a book written by a man who lives in your area I think, it was recommended by DeLeon. She has a bit of experience and is very eager for more knowledge and experience of Tantra, I have none. She has read your website and says she likes you. Here is DeLeon's email address (insert) I'm not sure what you mean by "individualized" sessions. It is my hope that we can both be together for the whole experience unless she tells you she needs privacy from me. I want to know the female role also, thanks. I look forward to our meeting. You must have one of the best jobs in the world."

Tantra Healer replied: *"Thanks Michael, I do love my job. In my couples sessions I've never separated couples from each other. "individualized" means it's catered to the two of you and where you are right now in your Sexual/spiritual path and where you both wish to go from here. My pleasure is to guide you joyfully towards your next step. It will be amazing. Your willingness and openness to learning will serve you well. Love and Light"*

I'm so looking forward to this special experience with you my dear DeLeon sweetheart, and our bonding. Your Tantra Lover Panting with the Heart of a Lion

Carrie: glad to hear you accept my invitation… from all reports, the guest bed is very comfy! as is the rest of the house which we can enjoy together but come asap, while i am still in this house! i am going to try to negotiate with my landlords to hold off putting it on the market for at least 6 months, but i think they are quite anxious to sell, so that may not fly... i need to manifest a wonderful new living situation... hold that thought with me, ok? think i'll take that into the creative workshop right away i do plan to have a guest room, no matter where i am

M: (to Suzanne) Hopefully this coming week we'll know if it's Paris or Vegas or more delay for our physical reuniting. I'll be flying from Yuma to Fort Lauderdale, Florida for some time with DeLeon. (April 12 to April 25.) That time will include a 5 day trip to Costa Rica where I may not have internet. But I'll be thinking of you sweetie, I don't ever want to lose my beloved Suzanne, she cannot be replaced. Your Michael

M: I hate to do this Suzanne but it's going to take several days to plan and book our trip to Paris and London and I'm leaving for two weeks. So I'm going to put an arbitrary deadline of April 8th for Paris. If you don't have approval for two weeks vacation in early May by then we'll call it off simply because I won't have time to work out the logistics. If we can't do Paris this Spring hopefully we'll be able to go next year, I really want to do that with you if you're still single. However, Las Vegas is easily arranged, just your flight to book and make it up as we go along. So if you get even one week in May we'll do Vegas for sure. If you get approval for two weeks, from Vegas we can take Loa to the southern California beaches or the redwoods or wherever you'd like to travel, we can fly you home from there. Are you ok with that?

Suzanne: I am absolutely fine with that. Had a crazy weekend with wedding events. My daughter from Chicago was here with her guy since it was her roommate from college. I stayed up way too late too many nights and probably had one too many glasses of wine. Wouldn't change a moment. Your Suzanne

M: I still want to get you drunk in Vegas baby, maybe *two* glasses too many, carry you to bed, lay you down, pull your boots off, lift your skirt all the way up those long lovely legs, hmmm no panties this whole time sexy one, and take big bad advantage of you. And I want to buy you a little black dress to take home with you and wear when you're out for sex so there's a part of me walking with you. I'd love it if it was a woman who took it off of you. Would you tell me about it and her? I'd be so pleased sweetheart, I want that for you for us my earth darling. Glad you had a great weekend, knew you would. Your man wanting you Naked in Vegas gorgeous one

M: (to DeLeon) DeLeon, Maybe you just haven't had time yet to respond to my last email. But if my description of what will take place when we meet with Tantra Healer is beyond where you are prepared to go, please give her a call and discuss what you want at the session with her - I'm sure she will not go further than you want to go. It was my understanding that you already have some experience with Tantra so I thought you'd want some advanced training from an expert. I gave her permission to go as far with *me* as she feels inspired to go, and told her you would speak for yourself. I simply don't know where you are with it DeLeon. Please call her if you have concerns, and let me know how that went, thanks.

DeLeon: Michael - quiet doesn't always mean - what one surmises. I've been dealign with heart & gut issues and been off the charts. All is good with Tantra Healer - I was comfortable with her description of process etc.. In fact, relieved when I saw what she was indicating. No worries. Wanting you...... DeLeon

M: What *me* worry? Makes me want you all the more, won't be long my darling. Your Tantra Lover

Today's musings: In the Bible we read: Matthew 18:3 *"I tell you the truth, unless you change and become like little children, you will never enter the kingdom of heaven."*

Little children have fun and play all the day long if adults don't interfere, they live in imagination. So it's nothing for a child to believe that they CREATE their own world. Little children have not yet learned the myths of scarcity and limitation so they don't go there. We can learn much from the children about what it's like to have faith enough to believe that we are literally *one* with God and everything, and therefore capable of, no, *expected* to generate desires and harness the power that creates worlds to manifest them. For of such desires and manifestations is the universe made.

Adults have much to unlearn along the way to being creator. But that learning can come in an instant along the way to immortality. Should you become immortal and choose to be an Adam and Eve family, how will it be in your worlds? It will be exactly the way you

Adam and your co-equal Eve or Eves imagine it will be! Why is that? Because you Adam and Eve are the god of *your* world and its children! You create all things there, you hold it all in your mind because that kind of holding is the substance the entire universe is created of, and held in place. There will be one exception. (My imagination continues.)

You will love and teach your children the way of love. But there is a universal law that you must abide by, it was from the beginning, and we find no beginning, so it must have always existed. That law is that every individual is free to choose for themselves their desires and expectations.

So, eventually, as your planet circles its sun, there will come a time when one or more of your children will choose another way than the way you taught. Sin will enter your world. The vibrations of your planet will slow, it will darken, it may fall to the state of *this* world as I write these words. Your children will travel from Innocence to Experience, and back to Innocence. (A la William Blake.) You and Eve will have moved on to populate new worlds. That is the way it has always been. You and your Eves may so love what you do that you will be content in that state for enormous chunks of "time." But, should any of you choose differently, of course in a universe that must always expand, there will always be opportunities for newness and added joys. And yes, if what I am writing troubles you because of your religious upbringing, doesn't it make sense that SOMEWHERE SOMETIME there is a Much Greater God in whose mind (male and female/s) is held EVERYTHING.

DeLeon: Evening Michael, My room-mate is warning against mosquitoes. Should we have repellant on us, when we go, or buy there. Also she thought color was an issue on what attracted or didn't? In other words what one wears? Any suggestions or thoughts? I have one request of you, Mighty Michael,..... (except the fact that you *will* show up here as agreed upon. okay, now I'm messin with you......would you, please, please, accompany me to church on Palm Sunday - which is the day after you arrive. Since we are in town - and will be "hangin" with each other for a few laid back days.... I am supposed to usher that sunday.... and would love having you by my side. You don't have to be "super fancy".

M: I would love to accompany you to church sweetheart. In fact I was at a non-denominational church in Yuma yesterday, two women picked me up and took me. I liked the music but the sermon was long and mostly dull. I'm not bringing a suit, do I need a tie for church? I'll ask Ashley about mosquitoes. The forums are saying take repellent but it won't be a problem. I wouldn't be concerned about color, it's never considered in Canada where there are hordes of mossies.

DeLeon: Oh, Great! Yes, don't need a suit - tie might be nice. You will see everything at Unity.

M: (to Ashley) I should have mentioned if you want to spend the night at the same hotel as we do to see the property, go ahead and book a room for yourself, I'll take care of it with my credit card. The three of us can have dinner and maybe a few drinks together, it will be nice to get to know you a bit better, this seems a great opportunity. Tell me how you'd prefer to work it. Do you need two nights and ride back with us, I don't know how far from there you live?

Ashley: The two nights would make it easier because trying to catch the bus can be a pain in the butt... but I may be able to catch a bus later in the day if needed. I'll check to see if there are more rooms available.

Back to the mundane, it seems that my real world kids are planning funerals, not just mine but their mother's too. Here's an excerpt of what I wrote to my daughter today who was inquiring as to where to bury my dead body should I decide to croak.

Actually I'm planning to live forever. However, since it is obviously bothering my children and it's important for them to have some physical place to go and visit the memory of me, sure beside my dad would work well. That way you can remember him too when you gather there, and those whose physical remains if any lie beside him. And just a few miles away are the graves of my father's parents. That area is where your nearest roots are on my side of the family, good idea, excellent.

I don't want any expense on your part, no box, no funeral, no church, nothing formal, just the legals. I never fit in to a community where a formal service would be meaningful to anyone except family, I never felt that I needed to. But if there is a small private gathering of some kind, make it a happy laughing one knowing that I am content with my life, at peace with God and myself, blessed with great treasure - *beautiful children* - no man could ask for more. Talk about me fondly and enjoy each other, I would rejoice at that and fly superbly high with love in my heart and beaming from my countenance, a life well and truly lived. Gravestone too is for the living but maybe model it after my dad's so it fits in better, I don't look for attention, I am just me. Or write: *"He loved much."*

M: (to Suzanne) I need your woman advice on a matter I'm having a difficult time reaching a decision about. Like it was with you, I met Carrie on a singles site a long time ago. We bantered back and forth enough to give me content for a book, raunchy Michael was in full swing in those days. She wouldn't let me visit her on her mountain in Panama because she is doing the western woman thing, demanding a man's body exclusively for herself. But she kept leading me on and I was an easy lead though I always revealed that I would most likely visit more than one woman. I found out later that meanwhile she was chatting with another man and had invited him to visit her without telling me about it. The man came and she found out he wasn't what she expected but had a hard time getting him to leave. Eventually he did, that was about two weeks ago. About then Carrie started getting nasty, writing critical emails to me to the point where each time I saw a message from her I sort of felt like I was going to get a parental spanking, not pleasant.

Then she referred Ashley to me and Ashley is now doing marketing and e-commerce for our website. Last week Ashley met with Carrie in Panama and hired her to help do social media marketing, so indirectly Carrie now works for me. Carrie got wind of me and DeLeon going to Costa Rica to look at land, and meeting with Ashley who happens to be living in Costa Rica right now. And Carrie also got wind that the beautiful house she has been renting in Panama for several years is going to be sold. So, Carrie does an about turn and goes back to the pleasant conversations we used to have, saying it's because we are now business "partners". Carrie starts pushing her country as a better place to buy land than Costa Rica. (It looks like it might actually be quite a bit better.) She invites me to come and stay in her guest room but not to try to get into her bed! I write back that if I come I'll bring one of my female friends and we'll stay in a hotel but she can travel with us to look at land. Carrie comes back strongly wanting me to come alone and stay at her place so we can get to know each other. She says nothing about bedrooms.

I'm tempted to visit Carrie, to meet her, to look over land, and maybe to stay for a while because cost of living is low there and the temperature is eternal spring every day of the year. She wants me to come quickly (probably because her house is going to be sold out from under her and she's real short of money and she thinks I have money.) But if I go it won't be until after you and I have had our vacation together, unless it's put off for months again, in which case maybe you'd come to visit, or I'd come back to be with you. You are my absolute number one priority, I think you know that from the way I write. Regardless of whatever comes for us in the future I will always feel great love for you. You are the only one of the women I know who if you asked me to come to you and we passed the hug test again I would be willing to settle down with long term and keep writing books together. I'd still like to follow you in your hospice work and write those stories first hand.

I know you would not take away my freedom to travel when I wanted where I wanted, with whoever I wanted, then come back to you. And I in turn would expect the same of you. Ironically, we might find that we prefer to be with each other exclusively anyway. But maybe not - especially if you are bisexual in real life, I'd encourage that, and want in on it if you and she were willing. Maybe we'd find a goddess who is willing to live with us and share our bed when there's no company, going to her own room as a "boarder" or "room-mate" when there is. I'd really like that, I don't know for sure if real life you would or not. Would you? (Please answer that question, tell it true, it's important for the health of my fantasy life.) Do you have any advice for me sweetheart? I'll make the decision but I highly value your advice. Do you think I should visit Carrie in Panama or not?

M: (to Tantra Healer) I think I may have neglected to tell you that should you choose to speak to me and DeLeon in metaphysical language, we are likely to understand. We are both familiar with Law of Attraction and Abraham. I'm a writer of visionary metaphysical fiction books. It's just an enjoyable experiment at this time to teach LOA and Abraham between lines of fiction. My website is just being developed (by a young lady who loves Abraham.) It isn't e-commerce enabled yet, but if you're interested in knowing your clients better, here's a link.

M: (to DeLeon) I can't stop thinking about you sweetheart, really wanting us to be private together so I can hold you in my arms and share our bodies completely. I'm so ready for you in so many ways. I wrote

Tantra Healer that both of us are acquainted with Law of Attraction and speak "metaphysical". She wrote back:

> *Dear Michael, That's fantastic. Your website is beautiful, I skimmed it and will go back and read more when time allows. So glad we speak the same language, you're definitely ready for Tantra and will grow with it very quickly! Love and* Light

Your Lover will be with you in Four days my sweet.

Here are some thoughts flowing through my mind right now, especially when I think of someone such as a lady I've been writing to who travels spiritually but travels complexly with spirit company. I have no desire to do that. It seems that I was born to do an 'end run' around programs and systems, born to be unique, to go straight to conclusions and desired results (to leap from A to Z) rather than to have to take the ponderous steps dictated to reach such destinations. I feel as though I have already experienced all the 'stuff' that one must know, in other lives. I am here in this final one to make the transition from an incarnated physical body to an Immortal physical body. I am becoming Adam, headed to a state where I and my (in my case seven) immortal sister wives will create environments (new worlds) in which *others* coming along behind us will be exposed to and ultimately learn the essential stuff.

Are my Sister Wives already a part of me, from the same Non-Physical Entity? Are we all here on this planet, already incarnated, my wives being attracted to me, their 'patrix'? Or, once I am immortal will it then be revealed to me where my Eves are, and I be empowered to gather them home to me? Suzanne and DeLeon are my lovers, Suzanne was first. Are they both among my Eves? I am allowing myself to remember...

Suzanne: Be careful. I don't trust Carrie and she will divide you and DeLeon. What value does that have for you?

M: Thanks sweetie. I will most likely not go to Carrie unless it's to look at land, and if so not for quite a while because I agree with you. By the way, DeLeon and I are only going to be together for 12 days, she's aware of that. What we're doing now is putting closure on that sorry scene we went through the first time. She now says what I do when I'm not with her is "my business". That's a reversal of the attitude she had that sent me packing to overnight alone at the airport. She's planning to move to Colorado where she used to live.

I don't know where I'll be going at the end of the month except it will be to a cooler place than Yuma. If I found a desirable long term situation and a compatible long-term companion (since that woman in Texas won't have me) I'd most likely sell Loa and settle down, buy a car, write books, work my business online, and travel now and then. I'm finding that I don't need to travel for adventure to write books anyway, adventure comes to me. With the motor home I tend to just stay in one spot anyway, I've already been almost everywhere I can travel to in USA and Canada with a motor home.

I guess we're not going to Paris this year. But Vegas for sure if you're willing, I never know for sure with you, much as I love you. I'm really hoping we can get together again soon. Do you think when you sell your house you might move out of the area, or are you likely to rent/buy in the same city? My guess is you could get work anywhere you go in the world, but then who knows how *real* Suzanne really is? Anyway, I love Suzanne and I think I'm in love with her 'mom' too...

Suzanne: I hear a pensive man now. You are predicting the future before it happens. Stop and rest a bit. I hope to have my house on the market in a few months and at the moment not sure where I will go.

M: Are you detecting a bone of responsibility in me who makes everything he wants come true, except those things that other people's freedom to choose for themselves mess with? Rest I could use but it's more of a probing my first choice if it ever was a choice actually. There are new doors opening constantly, any one of which I could choose, none of them would be wrong, just different. Sleep well my love.

Well, I'm way overdue but I think I've finally concluded that Suzanne is for sure not wanting to spend much time with me, most likely the age difference. (Unless I had money to rescue her the "Pretty Woman" way perhaps.) So once again I'm back to the singles sites looking around. Why do I want to give up my delicious freedom and be tied to another? I think it's just that I love women so much and need to be with one full-time. (I know, it's difficult to do when living in a motor home, unless constantly traveling and she's into fresh scenery big time.)

Carrie: just thought i'd stop by for a connection... very busy this week completing something i started in december and wasn't able to finish then... once this is done, i'm all yours and ashley's.. anyway, just thought i'd say hi and see how you're doing tonight? hugs, carrie

M: Hey Carrie, The temps in Yuma are approaching 100 in the days so I'm out a lot in the evening, just beautiful. And since I'm into aviation, my daily walks to the airport where there's a Marine Air Base are enjoyable. Tonight as I was close there was a formation of seven helicopters in the air, two others further, and an F-35 fighter doing a loud vertical landing. Loved it. Enjoy the evening.

Ashley sends the itinerary for our journeys in Costa Rica. I forward it to DeLeon. Speaking of DeLeon, I haven't heard from her for quite some time. If she can't go, should I go on my own and meet Ashley, travel with her as my guide maybe?? What do you think dear reader? How would you like to see this plot unfold? Is Tantra training with DeLeon vital to Michael's progress? Would DeLeon still be able to do the session with Tantra Healer, just not venture so far as Costa Rica? If so, I would take that trip on my own then return to DeLeon for a few days when I get back. That might work out.

DeLeon: Thank you for the ongoing details - I am printing them off, so I will have them with me, including the "topics" of discussion with the agent - that I can study, when we're together - on the plane - etc.. Not distancing self, just kind of in overwhelm and doing all that is necessary to keep myself calm and present. Love

I did notice that DeLeon was signed on to the singles site early this a.m. It's possible that she has found one or more other men who she chats with? And that would be appropriate for her, she knows there is little possibility that she and I will live together even though we may always have a Tantra connection and hopefully will meet together now and again.

M: (to DeLeon) I don't want you in "overwhelm" sweetie, I want you in joy loving life to the fullest. Am I asking too much of you? I'm really hoping you'll go with me but if you are overly concerned about the trip to Costa Rica and let me know soon so I can cancel your flights,

I could go on my own and look at the land, maybe not venture so far as a tourist, that was mainly for you and for us. We'd still have those lovely days before and after that trip, and the session with Tantra Healer together. Please speak it true, you're the only one who really knows if it's wise for you to fly to a foreign country at this time, maybe later would have been better for you? I can handle the trip on my own no problem if you let me know soon so I can put some brakes on. But I sure do want us to have those other days before and after together. We never did take towels to the beach or do the night scene, and I want my Goddess of Bling at the Banana Boat again, you were spectacular darling.

DeLeon: (she forwards the daily Abraham quote and writes) We're taking this one one!!!! Joy ourselves to Joy.

M: Wonderful quote, they all are, I really love what Abraham is doing for us. I take it you're going to Costa Rica with me and we're going to have the time of our lives then?

I'm not sure though if she got my email first, I sent it moments before she sent hers re the Abraham quote. So, I'm still not sure if DeLeon is going to Costa Rica with me. Yes, I'm a bit anxious about her response (unbecoming of a metaphysician, but human.) I've had sudden blasts from her (and Carrie) and don't look for a repeat of that kind of drama, I'm into joy instead. If we must have drama to sell books, let it be how we do sex together.

Chapter 7

DeLeon: Oh, My God - I'm not in an "i'm not going state - HELLLLLLL NOOOOO! I'm great I'm excited and heading back out the door - been at hair dresser - going back tomorrow, as they didn't get it like I wanted it and I want it like I want it - FOR MY LOVER!! So, for heavens sake - Costa Rica is going to get to experience both of us, and I'M SO EXCITED for everything you and I are going to be doing. Love and later..

M: Sounds like the woman I know. You know, the tall gorgeous one I want to get to know a whole lot more of, inside and out. I love your attitude baby, we're going to have incredible fun with each other, soooooon. Remember the last words I said to you at the airport when you dropped me off? *"I don't know what we're doing, but maybe someday we'll know."* I think "someday" has about come for us, and we both know what we're going to be doing. I was reluctant at first, you had to turn me on to the notion of Tantra Sex. Now I'm hugely eager for us to really get into Tantra at *all* levels of our being, and to write about it. It's beautiful to believe that I am not 'pushing' you to learn what Tantra Healer has to teach us. Somehow, way down deep, I know I've always wanted this, and with a tall beautiful blonde goddess too, what man could be more richly blessed? I'm glad too that we have a few days and nights together before she comes to our hotel room to change us for the better. I want to hold and cuddle and make slow delicious naked love with you a whole lot first, just the way we are before we change. I *really* want you darling DeLeon, as you are, and the way we will become. Your Lover

DeLeon: Thank you, so beautiful. Goodnight. Tired. Long Day..

It's April 10th. I had a completely unexpected and incredibly beautiful surprise from my lovely Texan last night. My computer had been shut down since 6 pm because a lady friend had come and we went for dinner at a Mexican restaurant (fried shrimp for me, delicious.) We then came back to Loa to watch a movie. But she started talking metaphysics and later the normal nothings so we never got to the movie and she didn't leave until 10:30 pm. In all that time she never even reached for my hand, and no hug as she left. I think she likes me a lot and is deliberately standing back because she knows she can't take me home and keep me. Today she's picking me up at 3:30 pm for a 'party' at her friend's house that will go until 8 pm or so. I couldn't get out of it because I had already accepted the invitation the last time we went to Mexico and were visiting some of her friends who are dry camped (no hookups) in a 5th wheel RV (recreational vehicle) on a hill near the border.

Of course when she left I instantly turned on my laptop. What a surprise to see a whole bunch of emails from none other than Suzanne! That was unprecedented. And what a lovely surprise when I opened the emails and they turned out to be photos and a video of my beautiful passionate woman taking care of her sexual needs! First thing this morning of course I was back to looking at and listening to my lovely Texan naked in her bathtub and in bed, vibrator throbbing in her hand, busy doing things a woman needs doing sometimes. What a treat it was that she so generously shared with me last night.

You're just going to have to trust me on this but if you're a normal male or a bisexual female (like I think she is) I know you'd come quickly watching this naked born-in-Texas woman taking care of her sexual needs at the end of a busy day! And if you're a normal female past puberty, you may even wish you were her, she's so complete with passion and satisfaction, you'd feel her energy moving through you. Can you feel it now as you read these words and create the image of lovely long-legged Suzanne naked in her bath tub, one hand flicking an erect nipple, another busy moving a throbbing vibrator over and around her bursting pleasure spot, and in, deep deep in, and out of her wide open sopping wet vagina? Oh how I love and treasure my dear Suzanne, she's all woman to me.

I was so excited last night that I couldn't really think what to write to her, words cannot express my delight with the gift she had sent. The only greater gift would have been her knock on Loa's door. (Or a longer video darling, the *whole* of your wondrous experience including the time your panties came off or when your hand first reached for your magical breasts and wet vagina.) So bear with me dearest reader (gosh I'm in love with you too this morning with the feelings Suzanne draws from me – Suzanne for me IS love!) To me, Suzanne represents Divine

Feminine - soul connection that includes deep lust for her delicious hot and swaying naked body, but goes way beyond that, as though she and I are become ONE. Suzanne won't accept the title "goddess" thinking that is reserved for those who walk mountain peaks. But she IS my Earth Goddess, the naked one I saw in vision lying on her back beckoning, legs open, softly, tenderly, lovingly, compellingly calling me home from her valley below, speaking my name when I get too high on my mountain and the air becomes too rare there to sustain life as she knows it.

I hope you too male and female can catch the image that is given me. It's not that Suzanne is unusually beautiful physically, she's of earth not sky, it's it's it's her PRESENCE whether naked in Loa's bed as she once was for a night, or a thousand miles away in Texas that is so compelling. It's her earth energy that like a volcano is dormant most times, you'd never know it was there – Responsible Nurse Real Her. Then suddenly like last night she feels her wondrous woman power like a tractor beam pulling up earth magma and EXPLODES *screaming in delight*, strewing red hot woman stuff all over everything, bursting out into the universe in long glorious waves of raw unbottled unadulterated SEX - awakening and making mellow yearners and lovers on distant planets, renewing and making real once more the legend, the timeless love story, of Michael and Kira.

Oh you'd like Suzanne at all levels of her being. If Michael has become legend, it's because you see Suzanne's woman stuff splashed all over him, I would not be without her. I wish you too could see Suzanne in all her naked glory. But you can't dear one, so strip yourself naked, go look in a tall mirror, and you'll see what she's made of. Suzanne is made of the same stuff YOU are made of! It's just that she through me in words and images and thoughts and imaginings and feelings brings to the surface *your own* glory, your own beauty – because you see, you too are the child of a Greater God, you too are growing up to be like Him and Her. Only *believe* – and live a thousand years and more in that belief - so we can know Eden once more upon this planet. Bear with me now as I bare last night to you in mere inadequate words, the messages I sent to Suzanne most likely long after she had gone to sleep, sweet dreams my dearest darling.

Suzanne: (referring to her getting vacation time to spend with me) I should know by the end of the week dates...

M: You are so incredibly beautiful my glorious Texas Woman. Thank-you so so much for sharing those photos and video with me. Especially your *sounds* darling, what a turn on, I almost came immediately without even a touch. I MUST BE WITH YOU, ABSOLUTELY MUST MUST MUST!!! I've got to hold you my sweetheart and make love with you, you've got me so excited it's almost unbearable. I desperately need to drink from your copious sweet fountain again. Thank-you thank-you thank-you. I'm going to play that video all night and listen to the sounds of your coming over and over again.

We've *got* to make that happen with us together physically my darling. I just can't express enough appreciation to you for what you gave me tonight. I'll dream of you coming for many nights now, wanting only to be *with* you, watching, adding male energy, making it happen. You *could* have me in your bed and bathtub every night you know. I would please and pleasure *every* part and in and out of you night after night after night and always come back for more of you after you'd told me how your day went and I'd brushed your hair and rubbed your shoulders while you were doing so. I am yours completely if you'd only have me Suzanne.

Tonight of all nights while you were coming alone and thinking of me, I was with a local friend, dinner at a Mexican restaurant then back to Loa to watch a movie that ended up being just her wanting to talk and talk, never even held a hand, no hug, nada. But LIFE itself is so worth living, especially tonight to turn on my computer and be turned on immediately by YOU my lover YOU all woman YOU. You'll never know how incredible it was for me to actually *listen* to you coming and to see those naked breasts I've only been able to imagine for so long. I love you Suzanne, I'm so needing you darling, thank-you for that wonderful wonderful surprise my love, I'm totally at a loss for words. Now I am compelled to go back and look at your naked breasts being massaged so nicely, and especially, especially to HEAR you come again, I needed that so much. Your Lover Delightfully Overwhelmed with the Wonder of YOU my beautiful incredible sharing bare naked Texas woman YOU.

M: I watched the video of you in the bathtub over and over and I just can't think of how to describe the feelings that come over me to see you moving the vibrator up and down, in and out of your glorious vagina, and to actually LISTEN to you coming. It's just, it's just overwhelmingly *beautiful!* You've given me an incredible gift tonight dear Suzanne. I deeply want to please and pleasure you and make you come and come and come over and over again, long rolling orgasms and soul connection the Tantra way. The only experience I could imagine that might be better than being naked in bed with you right now is being naked in bed with you and another beautiful woman like you, the three of us equally sharing our loves and wants and desires for a long long time, maybe forever. You're incredible beautiful sexy Suzanne my love my lover Suzanne, Suzanne, Suzanne.

M: It's lovely watching your sweet open vagina being pleasured so expertly, exceedingly beautiful. I connect almost as if it was me in the tub, thank-you for taking such good care of us. But sometimes I close my eyes to focus solely on your sounds. It's those indescribably beautiful sounds that make you REAL as if you are here in Loa with me tonight. You're all woman my love, all glorious Divine Feminine, I love you I love you I love you.

I'll be out for a while from tomorrow afternoon to tomorrow night but not so late this time I hope. Please send whatever you want to share with me anytime, I love it, I am *hopelessly* YOUR male my darling. But then, you already knew that didn't you? Tell me what I can do for you.

M: I love your tits and the way you take such good care of them, massaging and passionately tugging at the nipples when they're hard and needing attention. It's delightful, sometimes I think I feel what you feel Suzanne, when you make love I make love, I am the male in you, you the female in me. You gave me great pleasure tonight my darling, great enduring pleasure. Thank-you so much, I'll always be grateful, I'll always be wanting to feel of you at my side forever.

M: I can't stop watching your beautiful video, it's as if it was me there naked and busy in that tub, feeling the feelings making the sounds, we are so one my love. When you come to Vegas bring your toys. I want to watch you play like you did last night, and to suck your toes and nipples while you do, immersing you in the strength of male energy the whole time, touching where you aren't. Your Lover Wanting the Whole You

As I write and move around inside Loa I have Suzanne's video on auto replay, just the sound. She's so incredibly intuitive, as if she was right here with me the whole time since we met and I felt bonded with our first hug, her panties quickly dropping to the floor, then under the purple pillow where she hid them. She knows I'm going to see DeLeon soon and was focusing my attention on DeLeon's woman parts and functions. Suzanne would be ok with that, it's as if it was she herself taking DeLeon to bed. (Maybe someday it will be?) But being woman she sent me the photos and video at this perfect time, knowing that it would work her magic on me and a big part of me would remain with her. I find Suzanne incredibly attractive, she's much more than just under my skin. Listening to her come over and over right now makes her the wholeness of *me*. But I can't come anywhere near to describing in words what I am experiencing. It could not begin to happen with another woman making those beautiful woman sounds. What I am experiencing comes only because it's SUZANNE/ME breathing, panting, sounding the delightful tones of a woman approaching orgasm. Surely we are destined to live together forever. Will somebody please tell *her* that...

M: (to Suzanne) I expect that it would be much more effective for you to hold and use the vibrator yourself. But if we were in our hotel room in Vegas and I held the vibrator, where would you want me to put it first? And next, etc. Is it important to please your breasts first to get you wet and ready for more? Teach me honey how you like to do sex with a man. What do you *really* want me to do with your body besides obviously get you to orgasm?

M: (to Tantra Healer) In the interests of helping you better prepare for the three hour session you will have with me and DeLeon in our hotel room by better understanding us your clients, I have a few thoughts to run by you. I'd like you to keep this email private between you and me. I have another dear friend besides DeLeon. They both know about each other but DeLeon doesn't want me to speak to her of my other friend Suzanne. I believe myself to be in love with both of these ladies and hope to never have to make a choice between one or the other of them exclusively. My fondest hope would be for the three of us to live harmoniously under the same roof, all content, all equal, all loving each other, all sharing our bodies. Ok, maybe not so unusual, but there is a delightful (to me) complicating factor. Suzanne is bisexual. And DeLeon has expressed strong opinions *opposing* bisexuality in women!

I love that Suzanne is bisexual. I find it exciting, attractive, wonderful that she would freely share her love and sexual activity with other women. In fact our relationship such as it is at present (we don't live together) is completely open, both of us taking delight in the other having safe pleasure with the partner of our choice in the moment, both approving, then coming back to each other once *that* fruit has been tasted and hopefully savored sufficiently, life is meant to be fun. Now, where do you fit into this? I don't know if what I am going to suggest is even a part of Tantra so govern your actions accordingly, as of course you will regardless. You stated that during your sessions you do not touch male genitals. But you didn't say that of females.

Would you be willing to touch DeLeon as much as she will allow, hopefully even to the point of making her climax (as part of your demonstrating Tantra techniques to me perhaps) so she will feel and come to understand that love and sexual pleasure can come just as readily from a woman inside her aura doing wonders to her body as from a man? My objective is to witness and experience the pleasure you would bring to my darling, and to move the three of us (Michael, DeLeon, and Suzanne) closer to living together and perhaps eventually contentedly sharing the same bed. Anyway, I wouldn't share what I just wrote with anyone except such a one as yourself who understands the power of love and sexual energy and relations without restrictions except always the freedom to say "no" and be instantly obeyed.

Please know that it would delight me greatly if during our session you take as much time as you feel good about taking to move DeLeon along towards approving of women acting in a bisexual way. I would take pleasure in watching you make love to DeLeon as much as she and you are willing to do, and as far as such a thing fits into what you do professionally. I object to *nothing* that the two of you are willing to do sexually in my presence. I am completely open to that taking place as a top priority even if there is no time for anything else. I would feel richly rewarded if DeLeon was to pleasantly climax at your hands a few or more times, and feel the fullness of your beautiful female goddess love concurrently. She would want that again, her prejudice against bisexual women would be negated. Perhaps then I could more easily bring my two beloveds together, and let them feel of each other and me. And maybe next time we meet in session, it will be a couple of *three* who await your further instruction Goddess Healer, thank-you for being you. Enjoy the day woman with the bestest job in the world.

Tantra Healer: Michael I appreciate your honesty and openness. However, it's important that I be just as open and honest with you. Even though you're the one paying for the session, it will not be in your best interest to come in with a hidden agenda. I will speak with both of you together and ask each of you in that moment what you envision for the session, what took place in your past, and where you are at that moment in your Tantric experience. You are welcome to speak of your desire for DeLeon to open to bi-sexuality. She, however, is also free to decline. My work with women's bodies is not of a bisexual nature. I am a healer, awakener and source of empowerment for women. If DeLeon wants to be touched for healing and awakening I will do that graciously and with unconditional love yet more as a doula or birth coach than as a sexual partner. I ask you to please ask the Universe for what you want and then let go of the outcome. Allow the session to evolve from what arises in the moment between you.

No need to write me further with more explanations or requests. I read people in person, I read the moment, and I've left enough room in the beginning of the session for both of you to speak your truth about what you want to see happen in the session. Please trust the process and surrender to the Universe and to the guidance I receive from the spirit guides of all three parties present when we come together next week. Love and Light

M: (to Suzanne) I've told you this many times before but I'll tell it again, you are incredibly intuitive Suzanne. And you know you need our connection, the maleness of my energy flowing silently towards you because I love you so completely. A short while ago I concluded from your most recent messages and our history that you will not likely ever allow us more time together physically than a week or two of vacation now and again. And I withdrew, going back with boldness to the singles sites looking for another to focus on. No doubt because we're so connected, and because you're so WOMAN, you quickly detected a disturbance in the flow of maleness towards you and you sent that beautiful surprise last night to take care of it. As you no doubt knew it would be that way, today I cannot even focus on DeLeon who I will meet again in two days time and am instead bursting with a surplus of male sexual energy aimed straight at YOU instead! (Though my guess is that you don't have a problem with DeLeon and I making love in our mountain top way because in your earth way you will be right there with us the whole time anyway, as it was before.)

So again I give you great respect my love my lover Suzanne, you've got everything this man wants and more. I only wish you'd recognize that and the source of much of the earth energy that flows through you today if you'd only believe and accept. I love you darling sweetheart, will there be a time when you will let us BE? Your Man Still Wanting YOU

DeLeon: Went back to the hair salon - was supposed to be an hour procedure at best - three instructors & 1 student and 3 hours later....I walked out. Done for now. Will walk both dogs - then down to rest. Too tired to write. Just sending love. We are going to have to be careful with this body - I simply can't handle a lot of efforting. So, be aware I will probably be resting often.... while lying in your arms, in my arms, with each.. and.... back to resting. My focus is to be all that I can be with the real estate agent - and when we are looking at the property. And being at peace with the rest of the trip - and being with you. Avoiding the heat as much as possible - so out in the morning and evening.

I too, am shocked and yet not.... that this is happening. I can't explain it to anyone, let alone myself. There are things I want to say to you - all good - but I want to be eye to eye with you. As you helped open that door further and further on the journey of experiencing the Divine Energy, in such a beautiful, gentle way - giving me freedom and more undescribable,......more of which is to come. Sent for 3 tantra/ tantric books - the last one arrived today, yeaaa - Will have all 3 with us. The other tantra teacher did not respond to my email - so the heck with her. Besides, I *think* Tantra Healer will be very enlightening and quite fulfilling for this quest, so to speak. If you still desire to see her - I'll effort a connection again.

I misspoke re my room-mate - and having you here. She is very fine on all levels, having you here with me at the aptment. Sounds like she will be here as well, not taking her trip to the west coast of Florida, is going to Nebraska to be with family, but doesn't leave till the 26th. She may try to make her self disappear as much as she can. or whatever. So, it's back to you, if you want to keep the reservations or not - my feeling, on top of the financial part - it would be good to be back home - and at least with the door closed to my bedroom, yes Darlin, you can putt around naked. the lake is such a beautiful presence, you could sit on the patio and write... as we can plug your computer into the wall, just inside the Liv rm.. Ok - now, going to walk the dogs. See you soon - wow. Life is so amazing..

M: I would enjoy staying at your place sweetie but when I booked the Inn at Boynton Beach I chose a rate that does not allow cancellations. So we can come and go to and from your place but we have the hotel room booked anyway so we may as well do our overnights there. Ok?

I have no personal desire to see the other tantra instructor, that was for you if you wanted it. I agree that Tantra Healer is most likely to be very good for us, I'm excited about our session and each of us learning how to do Tantra better. You've got me intrigued about those things you want to tell me but only "eye to eye". I'm glad you noted that they are "all good". I want us to have a perfect time together my sweet lover. I dearly want to hug and hold you and forget about the rest of the world whether we're doing sex or not, I believe that we can find peace and healing in each other's arms. Be happy my darling, we'll soon be together.

DeLeon: Thank for how and what you said - especially your last paragraph - I so needed that to calm myself and relax into... you, finding peace and healing in each others arms! Amen and Amen and be happy Amen and Amen That is the totality of our gathering, My Love....

Suzanne: I have the May 6 through 11th off for Vegas

Suzanne: Actually it's may 5 to 10, I'll be home 11 for Mothers Day

Suzanne: I can't leave the 3rd, I'm on call the weekend, earliest I could leave is Monday. That was the I made to get time off and have to return on Friday May 9th. Have call again on 10th and 11th.

M: Five days is still wonderful Suzanne, anything to be with you again. The non-stop flights below were available when I checked but I need your date of birth to book for you, please send right away thanks.

Suzanne sends her birth info and asks me about last night, she knows I was going to be with the lady in Yuma. Is she probing for possible female competition? And if so, does she in real life want me for herself? Wishful thinking on my part or realistic? I just don't know, but we'll soon be together and then I most likely will know for sure by how it goes with us.

Suzanne: How was your evening?

M: (to Suzanne) My friend was supposed to pick me up at 3:30 yesterday afternoon but she arrived fifteen minutes early and caught me shutting down my computer and in my usual one piece at-home attire. I quickly changed and we drove 12 miles to where her friend lives. Eventually about a dozen people arrived and we sat around chatting, eating, and drinking whatever. I nursed a solitary can of beer and later she gave me a taste from a bottle of tequila I had legally carried across from Mexico for her. I'm catching on to the "snow bird" culture, am among them actually. These are people who live in Yuma for six months and elsewhere for the rest of the year. The couple at the event from furthest away are from Newfoundland Canada, an island province off the east coast. Most snow birds are already gone, the big melt in the rest of America is happening, but it's still the first topic of conversation to find out when the people you are talking to are leaving Yuma. There's almost no traffic in the streets anymore, about one third of the winter population has flown.

When everyone was gone about 6:30 p.m. I helped cleanup, then my friend walked and later drove me around the neighborhood pointing out dozens of empty lots serviced for RV's, obviously encouraging me to come back for the winter season and to settle near her. To rent one of them would be less than half the cost of where I am, but I'd have to buy a vehicle to do shopping. I love Yuma, the winter and present 80 degree night temps and daily sunshine are glorious. If I do another winter in Loa it will most likely be a return to Yuma.

My friend is a teacher of artists. She sees the nearby mountains in colors I hardly knew existed. She pointed out last night as we observed a perfect circle around the moon that it takes most of her art students months to learn how to free hand a circle. Mother Nature does it effortlessly. She came to Loa to chat for a half hour but as usual there was no touch except this time because it will be the last time I see her in Yuma (and maybe forever) we hugged briefly as she left. She is hoping that I will visit her at her rural Oregon home this summer, says I can park Loa in her yard. Her sons will take me fishing and along the forest roads in the night with lights to see bear, elk, deer etc. And she says she and I will hike to, climb, and overnight in a fire watch tower. I feel no sexual attraction for her (strange for me huh?) but depending on how my summer goes I may visit her for a couple of weeks, I like her as a friend and it would be fun there back in the woods.

I'll be with DeLeon tomorrow, getting back from Florida on April 26th after our five day trip to Costa Rica. I will soon after getting back move Loa to Phoenix to visit my son and family. And from there to Las Vegas to have five glorious days of fun with an incredibly sexy woman from the Lone Star State. And you know, I don't know where I'll go from there except it will include visiting my kids sometime within the next few months. But as always, choices will be presented and a goodly direction in which to travel will appear at the right moment as life continues to flow as it should.

I'm loving your video my darling, I listen to your beautiful sounds often and am so longing to hold you again. Thank-you for taking precious vacation days to be with me. I'm so grateful for you in my life Suzanne, you are my hope, my sunshine, my inspiration, my dearest sweetheart. Your Michael

M: Your flights are booked and paid for Suzanne, both non-stop and both at reasonable hours. I will rent a car and meet you at the Las Vegas airport, baggage carousel. If I or you are early or late, wait at the info desk near the carousels. It gets real hot in Vegas and my air conditioners might not be adequate so I'll most likely get us a room at Excalibur where I think I can leave Loa in the parking lot. We're actually going to pull this one off Suzanne, it will be so nice to see you again.

M: The last time we were going to do this you were wanting to mainly just laze around and we can certainly do that if that's what you want. But have a look at the shows and events while you'll be there and let me know if you'd like me to get tickets, or if you'd prefer that we just wait and do whatever feels like the best fun at the time. It's not likely that any of the shows listed below will sell out, but best seats might. I expect to take us out for meals but you mentioned cooking last time and we'll have Loa in the parking lot with a generator, and a car to go grocery shopping. So if you want to cook up any particular homemade dishes we will still have that option even though we'll have a hotel room. I'm real excited with the thought of being with you darling, and tasting whatever it is you cook up for us. Your Michael

Suzanne: I'll look this weekend. Maybe a couple of shows would be fun. Maybe reservations at excellent restaurants, seafood is my favorite.

M: Shoulda known, mine too. I swear we're twins Suzanne.

Chapter 8

———— ◈ ————

M: (to Suzanne) You are so magical Suzanne. Here I am less than 24 hours away from being with another woman for two weeks and as I write a final note to her I'm listening in wrapt awe to the sounds of YOU on the verge of orgasm! *You get me so excited to be with YOU!!*

But writing that note to DeLeon and listening to your wondrous woman sounds at the same time is certain to further refine my expectations so that a part of your energies will be present with us as DeLeon and I walk the mountain peaks and learn Tantra sex together. I'll love DeLeon, I'll hold her and throw myself totally into her. I know I will, that's the way I am, capable of more than one woman, seeing seven in heaven. But YOU will be doing sex with us too on our mountain Suzanne, because part of you resides in me. Your earth presence in me will magnify our Tantra experience and make it much more beautiful for me and DeLeon, thank-you for that my love. It is my hope that some day DeLeon will allow herself to understand that energy mix, and will accept and welcome the loving living *vitalness* of Suzanne in our lives.

I'll do my best to do Tantra with you a few times when we're together, and talk about it if you want. But not every time. I must hotly sway to the beat of jungle too, it's a big part of what is *me*. I find that part of me in *you*, panting, orgasmic in your video, naked, legs open, fingers moving, beckoning, calling my name from your warm inviting valley floor. To me, whether you accept the title or not, you Suzanne are EARTH GODDESS. I cannot wait to hold you and throw myself totally into YOU...

DeLeon: OMGod, tomorrow this time, you will almost be landing in Florida. Actually, you just landed. Would you please call me when the plane lands - to give me an idea if it's on time, etc... so I know how soon to be outside the door, for you. Also, please call, when you're on the airplane in Yuma... bye for now... hi for tomorrow

M: The most important connection is the one in Phoenix. Once I'm on that plane I'm as good as in Fort Lauderdale, and once I'm on it it's too late to call. But I like our plan to meet at the Fort Lauderdale Airport arrivals area at 4:30 p.m. tomorrow Saturday. If either of us is going to be later than 5 p.m. at the arrivals area we'll try to reach each other by phone. Obviously if I'm still in the air we won't be able to connect because they don't allow cell phones. But if my flight is delayed in Phoenix for more than a half hour I'll try to reach you by email or phone, most likely email, you won't have left home yet. It's going to work out honey, we'll have the time of our lives for almost two whole weeks. I'll SEE you at 4:30 tomorrow tall one. This time come to me - I LIKE YOU!

DeLeon: Actually - I can't come to you, as I have to be with my Panther - so, you can come to me.... Panther and I will be quite noticeable. I'm glad you like me! There's a big performance at the dance studio – roomy is dancing in 3 dances.. And I just had another heart episode... have taken my pills, hope to get it stopped in next hour or so.. Will probably pass on pushing my self to go see her - will need to rest... waiting for it to come back to normal rhythm...then rest to let the heart re coop. It's been a sweet heart - no episodes since last Sunday. So, bye for now. I ike you, Michael. I had a cousin that when he was really little and staying with my folks he would say "I ike you daddy", when crying for his daddy.

DeLeon: Just as I sent the email - took note, and checked...yes the heart went back to sinus/normal rhythm. Hallelujah. Nity nite sweetie. Love, DeLeon

M: I ike you darling DeLeon. I wuv your beautiful heart, it beats with mine filled with health and quiet breathing. Hunt with me long Lioness with long flowing Golden Hair - you are Goddess of Eternal Spring. You *cannot* die, you need not tire. I will hold you tomorrow my love my lover DeLeon. And I will hold you CLOSE!! Your Winged Lion Loving You - Us Filling and Healing Holes in Each Other - holes that need no longer exist - we are greater than they.

DeLeon: I WUV U MY LION - IN GRATITUDE AND GRACE.. DeLEON

Suzanne: Of course, teach me tantra sex. I tried to order books to read but have had multiple issues. I had such a sweet experience today, one of my 88 year old patients proposed to me. He has asked me every visit over the last month and when I tell him I am not married he has an impish grin. Today he popped the question. I had to refuse due to ethical issues. It made my day.

M: That was so sweet honey. But quit your job and take him up on it if he's wealthy. I mean, he's already in hospice. Seriously, I understand the ethics, but wouldn't such a thing just CROWN an 88 year old man's life whether or not there was sex involved! *Such dreams as may come to us all...* I didn't know you were much interested in Tantra. Ok, let's look at that then. DeLeon and I are having a three hour session with a well-qualified Tantra instructor, a woman who will come to our hotel room. So I'll know a whole lot more when you and I get together. I'd actually love that even though you and I are already soul connected because it would give you possibly hugely heightened pleasure and fulfillment. Yes my love, we will do Tantra together, I'm very excited about that. I had wanted when we meet in May to do the process I once described to you in detail when we were thinking of meeting in Las Vegas before. But you never responded so I questioned your interest. I'd be very pleased to make long long love to you with you not having to do anything back except as will happen naturally, *share* your female energies, not holding back.

But that would be glorious if both you and DeLeon were deep into Tantra Sacred Sex Suzanne, truly glorious because I'm a natural at much of it and I hugely acknowledge and respect the Divine Feminine aspect in all women. I think you'll like me for a male partner, we're already connected. And it might bring the three of us closer, all speaking the same language? I *yearn* for three of us Suzanne, though with you I'd be content if just the two of us under the same roof or at least meeting often was the way *you* wanted us to be. If you want to, you could try to find a Tantra instructor in Las Vegas who would do a private couples session with us and was not overly expensive. But we don't want a prostitute in disguise, we want to be actually *taught* Tantra by a certified well qualified instructor. But please, if you pick someone, *pick a woman!* Talk to me, tell it true honey, you so often surprise me. (Sure loved that last surprise.) Don't be shy, I want to KNOW you...

M: (to Suzanne) Just in case you can't find the message, here's what I wrote about Tantra Sex when we were first planning to meet in Vegas. Tell me your feelings about this. Is what I describe below what you want me to do to your naked steaming body while you lie on the bed in Las Vegas *feeling* what I'm doing to you, holding off your orgasms until we get to the promised destination? I don't know how well this will work,

I'm a Tantra virgin, I've never tried it before, but I know I can do it. And as always you keep the timing, I'll have to rely on you to tell me exactly when to switch from clit to g-spot back to clit and back again for maximum pleasure and effect. Here's what I wrote several weeks ago.

I have a book about "Tantra Sacred Sex" that DeLeon recommended, she knows the author. I only read a bit of it because I'm a natural, I take more pleasure in giving pleasure than in receiving it. If you are interested in exploring Tantra with me I may read the whole book before we get our bodies naked together and see what comes for us.

Tantra is an ancient Eastern philosophy that covers a lot of disciplines, sex is *everything*. The basic as I grasp it so far is that in normal Western type sex the man ejaculates and loses his sexual energy about the same time that the woman is really *needing* it. So he leaves her far less fulfilled than it *could* be for her. She may not even know that there's a whole lot more available. I mean, *what western woman would ever think it possible to have an orgasm that keeps on going for half an hour?* It's true though, after ejaculation, male energy is diminished. And so is a whole lot of the male desire for more sex just then, even though the woman of course can go on and on and on delighting and energizing her companion as she does. I love the beautiful sounds of a woman's coming, and even more so the sounds of her coming for ME. In my own experience I have observed that very soon after ejaculation my sexual energy is diminished. For me though there remains love and gentleness, a saying of thanks to my companion for giving me pleasure, the female part of me expressing as best it can in a male body.

So in Tantra the male seldom ejaculates. He gets greater pleasure from receiving the fullness of a woman's thanksgiving when he takes her whole and complete to the Valley of Paradise Found. The spiritual connection the woman's body creates between the two is felt by both for days. I experienced that emotional connectedness with DeLeon and she said she was feeling the same for me. It was as if we were ONE for several delicious days.

There is a procedure in the part of the book that I read that I would like to try with you my dearest Suzanne, and see where it leads. I didn't need to do anything of the sort with DeLeon, my body was absolutely *right* for her. She came long and loud almost instantly with no penis anywhere near her vagina. It was the most beautiful experience she had ever had in her life. Yeah, she was our Goddess honey, but she had a broken heart from her birth and couldn't sustain our energies. Maybe we flowed so strong because *you* were there with us too, as you said you'd be. (You're a most remarkable woman Suzanne, I don't think you have any idea how deep you are into this man.)

I could find another Goddess for us so you can share our love and loving whether or not you're physically there. I hope you will be there because we'll be Mountain and Sky our Goddess and I, we'll need Earth to meld our mortal bodies and bring them pleasure. I'd love it if the three of us traveled physically together. Goddess and I would not have the same fullness of pleasure if you were not there in some form or other when we made love. We need you Suzanne, you are Earth, and it is on Earth that we find ourselves right now. For so long as we have mortal bodies we will need you. And having grown accustomed to your feel, we will hope that you will come with us into the eternities when you say it's time for us to go. We could never be whole without you Dear One. Be there for us?

We need to talk about that Suzanne. It's strange but delightful to me how willing you are to share my body with another. Not many women are like that, they want to own a man's body exclusively. I love you for being the way you are my Love my Lover - I love it, I love *you* Special Woman for me, the Female in my Maleness.

Even though by then I may know more from having read the whole Tantra Sacred Sex book, here's what I'd like to try first when we throw our bodies together in Las Vegas. We'll learn of course by *doing* what works best for the two of us, making it up as we go along. Our goal will be long rolling orgasms for you, a fullness of delight and pleasure for me from observing you, knowing my part in your journey, and long emotional connectedness for US.

We'll first strip you bare naked. I want to do that myself, get your blouse open, your bra off, panties on the floor, my fingers caressing your magical points, maybe blowing on them, kisses and gentle suckings to follow, can't wait. But I'll do it much slower this time. There's no rush, we'll have a whole week to make love and content our bodies, we've waited long for this. You can make me naked however you want that to happen, I stand or sit or lie down at your command, take any posture. You can do whatever you want with this male body - it's yours completely, every millimeter, every function, every drop of it. *Take it,* bring toys if you will. I'll lust watching you do what you do upon the maleness of my body. Take the whole week to play with me as I play with you. Play every fantasy you've ever had for yourself and one male. (Another female in our bed with us - that would be heaven, I'd take great pleasure watching and helping you two along. Women are Divine Feminine to me, their bodies are glorious, vaginas are the greatest of all creations. But no other males in our bed thanks, got enough with this one.

Ok, you're naked now lying on the big Las Vegas bed watching me watching you, my out and your in raped by the eyes in this love affair, eager, anticipating, me not sure where to focus, the wetness of your wide open vagina, or your magical pointed breasts, wanting you all at once. I make long slow love to the whole of your body except your vagina, turning you over to lift your hair and taste your nape, inside and behind your ears, the small of your back, behind your knees, and kiss the vulnerable cheeks I find. I'll be sorely tempted to open your valentine, touch and kiss and pleasure you, but waiting, later maybe, *yes* later - *this* is Tantra Sex, not Western, we'll go west another day, I want to travel towards the sunset with you my valentine.

I focus particularly on your breasts, they heat a woman and I want this one heated, hot and panting would be even better. She does her best to hold off her orgasm. Yes, that's right, *hold off* your orgasm as I do mine. It's important, it's not time yet for that pleasure, we haven't arrived at the Valley of Promise, our destination, the Palace of Greatest Pleasure. And then, finally, with your nod of approval I approach the sacred mystery between your legs, gently feel of its soft yielding surface, caressing, learning your moist loveliness. Then slowly explore deeper, moving up, fingers wet, tongue tasting of your waters until your pleasure spot is fully engorged. Your g-spot is now excited and ready for my beckoning call. You tell me it's time to go there, holding off your orgasm as I do mine. My fingers find you deep inside and when you are almost there you tell me quickly to surface and I do, with pleasure. At the clit we repeat until you're almost bursting with a clitoral orgasm but tell me and I go deeper yet again.

And there, then, your bare naked body and long overheated passion are ready for the Valley of Promise. I beckon you there and you come helplessly, impossibly. You come, and you come and come, and come, *imploding*, carelessly spewing woman stuff everywhere, your magnificent nakedness a bow ready to launch its arrow, arching towards the sky where my cupid soul awaits the fullness of your coming. Your body rewards mine and we are content for the moment. Our souls are connected as one, we are ready now for our delicious alone-in-our-own-world walk about the streets, the hotels, the casinos and strip joints of Las Vegas, Nevada, United States of America. Our now clothed bodies are on the street and in the casinos, hands clinging tightly to hands, but our minds are hopelessly back in the hotel room naked where we belong. And that's how it will be when Suzanne and Michael do Tantra Sex in Las Vegas.

Come teach me how to make love to the earth body of a goddess - *you'll be there with us when we do it!* Coming honey?

Suzanne: Get over it Michael, I value myself to much to marry for money. You don't know me well enough to know my life is not about money. I am a bit pissed you would suggest such an avenue. Did you see me flashing money or prestige at you? I was complimented he saw me as desirable but I want much more. Much much more. I am coming to understand my presence challenges a man to be a man because I am earthy feminine. They have the courage to embrace my heat or they run. You have the courage to embrace the hot lava that flows from me... shall see if you survive or burn in my flames.

M: Honey did you miss the humor? I don't want you to marry for money! In fact if you marry again I'm hoping it will be some writer who's hopelessly in love with you and will give you all the love and attention and hot sex you so richly deserve. Yes you are hot, for most men *unbearably* hot, maybe for most women too. Yes I need you for your heat, your tits on my chest and in my mouth, your vagina wrapped around my body parts. No you can't burn me up because you too would perish in the same flame so you'd cool it before that could happen. We're the same body silly, we have the same intensity of need, we think alike, we may even look alike, we're *beautiful* together, complete in each other, like human bodies are meant to be.

I'm watching your video again, listening to your sounds as I write. Please bring your toys with you, I MUST watch you pleasure yourself the same as you are doing in the video. I must see all the ins and outs and depths you plunge to as you travel towards your goal. I must hear the breathlessness of your orgasmic sounds. But this time it will be *me* pulling on your hot tits as you make yourself come. Then I'll drink your lava, it cannot hurt me I am lava too, we are one soul you and I. Bring it on my lover, bring it on as hot as you get, I'll meld with your passion. I am not only capable, it's *exactly* what I WANT!

Suzanne: Such a good dad!

M: Oops, didn't catch that one, please explain.

Suzanne: It was for my brother chasing an armadillo...

M: So I tell you in great detail how I am going to act like an animal and ravish your naked body in Las Vegas and you respond with a comment about somebody chasing an armadillo. Shields up! But then, why should today be any different? I wuv you baby....

Suzanne: Ravish me my Michael. You tell me a man loves a woman as you do but life has taught me a different story. My time with you in Vegas will tell me if a man is capable if truly loving a woman.

DeLeon: If there are any delays - please call - don't email me - as I will be in and out today. See you soon, Darlin...

M: See you soon my love.

DeLeon: Blessings of safe and happy flight, My Love....

M: (to Suzanne) It's 3 a.m. in Yuma as I begin this message to you Suzanne. I went to bed extra early last night after packing a suitcase. I'll stay up now so I don't fall asleep and risk missing the taxi I ordered for 5:45 to take me to the airport. I'm scheduled to arrive in Fort Lauderdale, Florida a 2,000 mile journey at 4:30 p.m. local time. I'm expecting to meet DeLeon on the street outside the airport terminal in the pickup truck she calls "Panther." She has been fussing for days, packing for Costa Rica, getting her long blonde hair done to perfection and all that a woman does to prepare for a special event. She's Goddess of Bling and Eternal Spring making ready for her lover from afar, the man she once called her King Magnificent, then sent packing when she discovered that he was still in love with Suzanne.

Now, weeks later after a long torturing silence, she has exchanged messages with me and says who I'm with when I'm not with her is "my business." We'll hug and kiss and make up and I'll continue to forever love Earth Goddess Suzanne, my twin soul who says she's not of sky so should not be called "goddess". But she *is* goddess to me, I need her,

I'm incomplete without my Lady of the Valley. It is for her that I write books. You who read and enjoy my books owe your enjoyment to my love my lover Lady Suzanne.

You ask sweetheart if a man is truly capable of loving a woman and I say a man is capable of WORSHIPPING a woman! Could your fingers be without the hand, your toes without the feet? Men are oriented toward *power,* their role is to protect and provide for women and children. Life has taught you that many men do not know how to interact with a greater power than theirs other than doing their best to fend and fight it off. The greater power of a woman is a fearsome thing, a power men can choose to join or to fight, but can never overcome. What is that power? Why, it's the greater ability to LOVE of course!

"He that loveth not knoweth not God; for God is love." 1 John 4:8

God, the most powerful of all, IS love. Man with his puny power is confronted by God every single time he faces a woman who loves greater than he does. Sometimes he will bluff and bluster and pretend, strutting away in fear and anger at *himself.* Or if he's a finer man he will stay and reflect that love, needing to feel love in his heart, wanting to hold love in his arms and kiss her gently on the lips until passion rises and they withdraw to the bedroom to express and fulfill each other and make children.

Be gentle with us Divine Feminine, have patience, do not expect us to love as perfectly as you are capable of. We do not conceive and bear and deliver and suckle an infant at our breast and learn love in that manner, we are outside keeping the beasties and bill collectors away. But when we come back in to you we observe and emulate and feel of your love as best we can. *Just love us, that's all we ask of you.* And with that love glowing in our hearts we'll fight strong and true and brave. We'll even give up our lives to protect you because you have taught us by example how it is to love without condition or reason. Yes, a man is capable of truly loving a woman, but not as capable as a woman is capable of loving. Judge us in *that* light. Neither of us is capable of becoming God without the other. God IS love. Teach me how to be God my love...

I *will* ravish your naked body in Las Vegas with great pleasure. And I will continue to love you as best I am capable of loving. I will get much better at loving you when you teach me how to get better by showing me how great is your love for *me*. I fly to DeLeon now. Be with us, we learn Tantra Love for ourselves, and I for you. Your Michael

M: (to Suzanne) In Fort Lauderdale, all is well. I love you. Tantra training session tomorrow. Leave for Costa Rica next day, may not have internet for five days. Hoping you are well.

Tantra Healer: Hello Michael, I look forward to meeting you and DeLeon tomorrow. If possible, I'd like to start at 1:30 or even 2 pm. That will ensure that I'm not arriving rushed from a prior appointment. Please let me know whether that will work for the two of you. My cell phone number is below in case you need to text me tomorrow. Please give me one of your cell phone numbers as well. Love and Light

M: 2 p.m. will work for us. We're in room 405. Looking forward to meeting you. DeLeon's cell phone is (insert).

M: Suzanne, Just a quick update while DeLeon is out running some errands. I arrived in Fort Lauderdale and went outside where DeLeon was supposed to pick me up at 4:30 p.m. I excitedly watched every dark colored pickup looking for a lady with long blonde hair, and almost waved to several. About twenty minutes later I called DeLeon. She was running 45 minutes late. It turned out that she had decided at the last minute instead of meeting me in the pants I had expected, to get all dolled up for me. (Goddess of Bling of course.) So about 5:15 she arrives and steps out of "panther" her pickup truck with pipes and a purring sound at highway speeds. She had on a blue dress that scooped at the front, scooped high. We hugged, loaded my bags and headed to Boca Raton on Interstate 95. The hug established familiarity, we clung quite a while. Then when she sat in the truck, that scoop rode up almost to the destination a man yearns to arrive at, and some women too, maybe you would. She had on mesh stockings that showed a whole lot of tall leg. (She's 5 foot nine inches.) Later, I didn't dare yet to discover it myself, she told me she wasn't wearing panties!

But my hand of course spent a lot of time touching those inviting legs during our 30 minute drive to the hotel. She wore lots of bling as usual, a huge Cleopatra necklace, and later a replica of the blue gem worn by Princess Dianna. I quickly realized that this woman has changed a lot since the night she drove me to that lonely airport, a pleasing pleasant change, a much more open attitude. We checked in, ate, and went back to the hotel.

She went to bed with her blue dress on, lying next to my nakedness. But it wasn't long before she pushed past her boundaries as best she was capable and we became lovers. Ask me about it when we get together in Vegas my love my lover Suzanne. There are some almost unbelievable but beautiful things about our happenings in Boca Raton that I will share only with you, and only whispering into your ear after we've made delicious love and I'm slowly caressing your beautiful body while we pillow talk at the peak of a delightful afterglow. You will be pleasantly surprised at the goings on in Boca Raton of our goddess and your Michael.

Next morning we went to the church DeLeon attends. It was my first time at such a service and I was impressed. I was introduced to many people who know and love our DeLeon, including the pretty (and single) minister. DeLeon told me today that many women at church were looking at me in awe. Maybe it was my grey dress slacks and shiny bright red shirt with matching tie. Or maybe it's because all my life pretty women have done a second or more glance my way, and having a tall blonde goddess on my arm was added incentive to look at the two ancient souls she and I present in our walkabouts. One man at breakfast in the hotel told us that we look "elegant". Our Tantra teacher will be an hour late, arriving at our hotel room at 2 p.m. today. Yes, I'm there/here for DeLeon when I'm with her, but I think she knows (though it's forbidden to talk about) that I'll always crave my beautiful Texas Woman. Your Michael

Suzanne: Thanks for your note and pleased you are experiencing life. You know, women can be so competitive, maybe she's feeling a need to be more... enjoy. As you know Michael, I am earth. I'll never be bling but my glow of jewels lives deep inside my unseen treasures. As you know, you must search deep in my earth to find the glimmer of diamonds and gold. I have been working 12 and 14 hour days and done nothing to plan Vegas. Maybe this weekend... have a beautiful joyful time... Your Suzanne

M: It was lovely to see your message in my inbox. I have a lot to tell you when we get together. I love you.

M: I'm now in San Jose, Costa Rica. Ashley made the arrangements and put us in an old bed and breakfast instead of a hotel. Oh well, life's good. A driver will pick us up tomorrow and we'll travel through the cloud forest. I discovered that DeLeon goes back for another heart surgery soon, but she's doing pretty good. Our three hour session with Tantra Healer yesterday turned out to be four hours when she got involved with healing DeLeon. Lots of interesting stuff to tell you about. It was real nice to see your message yesterday, you have a very demanding job. There was a lot of love around me when your message came in but my heart lit up and the room brightened. I continue to feel close to you sweetheart, I'm really looking forward to our time in Las Vegas. Your Michael

M: (to my ex) I am well, new life is awakened in me and pathways beckon that bring much fulfillment. I believe that it will be so for you as well as you let go of me and the past and sense a fair wind and a following sea moving you forward to fresh destinations and a greatness of love for *everyone*. Maybe you are a healer and being with me kept you from following that path? But whatever, we are climbing to the same mountain peak, just taking different paths and meeting different others along the way, it will be well for us. Enjoy the day.

Suzanne: Are you writing any?

M: April 17th, early a.m. on the balcony of the Vida Tropical a bed and breakfast in San Jose, Costa Rica. A whole lot of birdsong but I get much the same in Loa parked in Yuma, Arizona with mockingbirds and doves in the trees. It's a beautiful sunny morn with some clouds on the mountains I see in the distance. DeLeon is getting ready for the day, quite a process for the Goddess of Bling but she's pretty much on time for whatever needs doing. She still gets heart fibrillations and in fact is having one as I write this. But her new meds take care of that and slow down that hyperactive heart that loves to race and jump about.

Thank-you for asking about me writing, that would be you my love, always wanting me to be Writer. I write a bit but am sensitive to people looking over my shoulder, and most times my laptop is packed away. I continue to feel great love for you, a hope that our real world coming together will be revealing and wonderful for both of us. I feel it will be so, you are where my heart resides continuously. Enjoy the day. Your Michael

M: Suzanne, Just trying to catch up, not sure what I wrote below, going fast, but here's something. April 17th 9 p.m. No internet tonight so I am writing today directly in my word processor and will send this to you next time I'm online. As I write we're in unit 27 of the Arenal Montechiara Hotel after a three hour drive from San Jose with our driver, a friend of Ashley. It's a gloriously beautiful country we're in, the only country in Central America to have no military, a place of peace. We arrived about noon, rested for a couple of hours, completed some miraculous business we had to take care of before taking a taxi for the short drive to Baldi Hot Springs. I wish some day my darling Suzanne to take you there. It's an incredible place that would take much more than a day to fully explore and experience.

It begins at the waterslides and Pyramid Restaurant where we enjoyed a buffet dinner. That restaurant is on the slope of a magnificent smoking volcano. The volcano produces a never ending supply of hot water that some enterprising people have harnessed to create a resort of caves and waterslides and pool after pool and waterfalls of water varying in temperature from cold pools at 68 degrees inside pools of water ranging up to 116 degrees. We soaked long in one pool at 108 degrees with a waterfall of hot water that thunders down allowing you to stand in the buffeting and go behind to rock benches of coolness. It's a must experience again and again everytime I go to that beautiful country.

I write in the dark with DeLeon in bed, I having already cuddled her and napped. I love that tall blonde the image of actress Katherine Hepburn, but there is another that I must be with and DeLeon and I both know our time together, delightful as it is, is brief. I'll write more of our miraculous experiences later. The magic continues for us as vibrations are set for success. As DeLeon lay back on a long lawn chair today near the caves, I explored a bit then returned to her telling her I had waved my hand and created a beautiful green meadow with horses grazing. She came with me to an isolated trail and the setting sun shone brightly over that meadow and the horses as if by magic. But there's too much to write about and it's dark and difficult to write, I don't want to disturb DeLeon's sleep with a light. So, yet another glorious day in Loa Land, today it is Michael and DeLeon. Your Michael's in Costa Rica honey, but much of his heart remains in Texas.

M: (to Suzanne) April 19th. Yesterday a different driver took us on the six hour trip to Uvita, close to the famous "Whale's Tale" land formation in the Pacific Ocean. We made some stops, saw enormous crocodiles in a river, huge, many feet across, and huge iguanas etc. It's a beautiful country but wild. We picked up Ashley at Dominical just a few miles from Uvita. We talked a lot last night, the three of us in our two bedroom unit while howlers and all kinds of birds went about their monkey and birdbrain business outside. Ashley is 31 years old, divorced, has one 11 year old son who lives with her in Dominical.. She's like a daughter, very upbeat, shares many of the same dreams regarding setting up a Community of Writers and Artists in Costa Rica. In fact she was already involved in a similar startup, that one for a healing community. She has now moved to Costa Rica. Everything we hear and experience about Costa Rica is positive and inviting - except the cost of real estate, very expensive!

At noon a real estate agent will pick us up and show us the land we came to see. Then Ashley will go home and DeLeon and I overnight in this rustic place. Tomorrow a.m. our first driver will take us back to San Jose for our Monday flight. I'm outside under an open air roof where there's internet. DeLeon got talking with a man from Haiti then Ohio who just bought some land across the street from here and she has wandered off with him to look at it. I think you'd like it here. Your Michael

Suzanne: Sounds intrequing.

Suzanne: Thank you.

Suzanne: Are you back in Florida? Happy Easter to you.

M: We fly tomorrow Monday April 21st to Florida. I'll stay another four days then return to Yuma. It's such a beautiful country Costa Rica. Hope to bring you here someday.

Suzanne: I find it an adventure as you go between the world of writing and the world of reality. DeLeon then DeLeon. I wonder then more deeply about your heart. Just as I do as you travel between Suzanne and real life you.

M: There is certainly a big difference between virtual reality and real life interactions. If real life you is in love with virtual me then I would have to ask the same question of where your heart is as you ask me. We will soon both know much better. All I know right now is that even while I am in a distant country with another woman and work hard at keeping my mind off you, inside a huge portion of that heart remains with ideal YOU.

DeLeon and Ashley and I and the realtor looked over the 220 acres on the mountain today. It's glorious but it takes a 4x4 to get to it. Much more to say but it's bed time now. See you soon my love. Your Michael

M: (to Suzanne) April 21. We're back in Florida and checked in to room 412 at the Boynton Beach Inn. As I write this I can't get online so will send it to you as soon as I can. The return flight is only 2 hours and 50 minutes from San Jose, Costa Rica to Fort Lauderdale, Florida USA. I seem to be beginning to see myself as a "world citizen" rather than as an American or Canadian. It makes more sense. DeLeon is gone home to walk her dog. I stayed behind to catch up on emails but internet is not going to work and won't be fixed until sometime tomorrow. Not much more to say about today. The plane was full but the guy sitting next to me had bad breath and needed a shower so maybe I sent the signal, I didn't bring that into awareness. Very soon a flight attendant walked all the way to the back of the plane where we were located, asked for a "volunteer" and moved him I think to first class. That left room for me to sit in the aisle seat and DeLeon to lay her head in my lap and stretch almost completely flat. Everything continues to work out as if by magic. M

I have four more nights with DeLeon, then home to Yuma and preparing to be with Suzanne in Las Vegas after a visit with my son and family in Phoenix. I miss not having the means to check for a message from Suzanne tonight. She is never ever far from my mind.

Suzanne: I would like to see Zumanity in Vegas. Looks like the night after I arrive might work. The description sounds like you.

M: (re Zumanity which is the *sensual* Cirque du Soleil production) Ha, sounds like US sweetie. I'll book later, remind me when I'm home in Loa? I'm sure looking forward to being with you. Your Michael

M: Are you still working those really long hours or back to normal now?

Suzanne: Still long hours. I have forgotten what an 8 hour days feels like... And look forward to getting away to play....

M: *Viva Las Vegas!* We will play my darling.

Carrie: (she sends a link to a Costa Rica website) hi...in case you don't know about this, you might want to follow the news in cr with this resource...

M: I wasn't aware of that Carrie, thanks. We had a great trip to Costa Rica and are now back in Florida. Enjoy the day.

Carrie: glad to hear it was a good trip... when do you go back to yuma? and, what was your overall impression of the land there for your purposes? and, please tell deleon i said hi...

M: I'll be back in Yuma three days from now. We loved Costa Rica. The 220 acres we looked at was impressive: magnificent views, waterfalls, swimming holes, hardwood trees ready for harvest, etc. But access was only 4x4 for quite a few miles and that very bad.

M: (to Ashley) We're back in Florida, I'll be returning to Yuma on Friday. It was lovely meeting you. DeLeon and I are both impressed and can hardly wait for you to sign the adoption papers to make you our daughter. Take care sweetie, we love you.

Ashley: I love you guys too!!!!! I really enjoyed our time together. Just send the adoption papers whenever you want.

M: (to Suzanne – I forward an email from Carrie with excellent expat resources for Costa Rica) Going to move to Costa Rica with me?

M: Suzanne, It's 3:45 a.m. April 24 as I write this in room 412 of the Inn at Boynton Beach in Delray Beach, Florida USA. I am wide awake as I ponder the marvels of living in harmony with Source and the Law of Attraction. Yesterday I wrote you asking if you would move to Costa Rica with me. Last night at 6 p.m. we met with two acquaintances of DeLeon who own a property in Costa Rica. We met to discuss that nation as a follow up to my and DeLeon's trip and my vision of creating Eden Seven. We met them at the outdoor portion of the Bellagio Restaurant in West Palm Beach, a beautiful community oozing with money not far from Donald Trump's tower where he apparently spends much of his time.

True to Law of Attraction, we no sooner sat down with them than one of several waiters came to us and we discovered that he is a Costa Rican citizen (a "Tico") working in the USA to save money to buy a house and return home to that "happiest country in the world" as the United Nations or someone apparently classifies Costa Rica. During the course of the conversation, we learned that about ten years ago the lady we were meeting with designed and over the years lovingly built a beautiful home on the side of a mountain a forty-five minute drive from San Jose, Costa Rica. It's on 20 acres with views and a whole lot of room to construct more buildings. They are Europeans and want to live somewhere in Europe. They have a caretaker family to tend their vacant home in Costa Rica and two dogs. The lady has such an emotional attachment to the house she built that she won't rent it out to anyone but will sell to the right party who will love it as she loves it. She hinted strongly that I go there and live a few months while I explore Costa Rica and write books. (And obviously consider buying the property.)

Could this be Eden Seven, not for a Community of Writers and Artists but for my original dream of a place where the founders of Travels with Loa can gather and enjoy each other when they want to? Tell me your thoughts on this my darling Suzanne, it could become real world for us. Would that interest you? Your Michael

Suzanne: I don't have an answer for such a question at this moment. Have you had a blessed time these past days?

M: Your timing of course is impeccable. DeLeon just went out for an hour or so and I was thinking of sending you a message without concern about anyone looking over my shoulder and possibly reacting negatively. My next thought was that I first needed to hear from you re the Costa Rica opportunity before sending you another message. My next thought was writing *"Your timing of course is impeccable..."* You are so in tune with me Suzanne, I love and cherish that, it's like we are twins. It is my deepest desire that all goes well for us when we get our physical bodies together again. I can easily envision us living happily together, maybe in Costa Rica if you have the desire to be with me longer than just a few days.

The days here in Delray Beach, Florida are a little long, I'll discuss that with you when we get together. But I think for DeLeon it was necessary for me to stay the extra days after our return from Costa Rica. She has been doing a whole lot of healing since we've been together, almost miraculous if she can sustain it. But our togetherness can't be long term, there are insurmountable barriers to that much as she may desire it. (I don't know that she does.) My heart is just not in such a venture though I always try to be fully here for her. Even should you my well beloved choose not to be with me long-term I would not choose such a living arrangement with any but a very special as yet unknown other woman. I can instantly picture you and me in that beautiful home on a mountainside in Costa Rica. There are several flat viewpoints on the 20 acres where other homes could be built. Maybe that property would be "Eden Seven" for us and others who believed in my project from the beginning. Any other larger community we may build would be built elsewhere, maybe nearby?

I think you'd love Ashley too. She is moving to Costa Rica permanently from Canada. Who knows, maybe she'd come and live with us after you and I had settled in? She has an eleven year old son who is spiritual and gifted. He is with her in Dominical, Costa Rica, a world famous surfing beach. Anyway, such dreams as may come... We'll be together soon my love. Your Michael

M: (to DeLeon with title "It was a good hunt".) Thank-you for a wonderful two weeks, I thoroughly enjoyed our time together. Please stay in touch.

DeLeon: Michael - It truly, truly was. THANK YOU FOR THE $!! - I didn't realize until after you had disappeared. Something really amazing. As I drove off, I turned on the radio and the song that came on the moment I turned it on was: "You Are My Shining Star". I was smiling all over, how sweet of the universe to let me hear you. We will always be in touch Much, Much Love and Gratitude..... I am so sleepy, can't hardly type this.

M: (to Suzanne) At Phoenix airport, two hour layover on the way home to Loa. Thinking of you.

Suzaane: Tell me about your time as you have the layover...

M: I wasn't plugged so shut down my laptop after I sent the message. I am now home in Loa and it's late, will reply tomorrow. It's lonely though to come home to an empty house, I guess you know all about that. Quite frankly it's the hope of you that keeps me going, you mean so much to me... I did send you a brief outline most days I was away, is there anything specific you'd like me to comment further on?

Chapter 9

DeLeon: Morning Michael, My Love... Didn't hear while you were waiting in Arizona.... so trusting all is well and your home, safe, resting well and moving "forward", this morning I went to Publix, to get my almond milk, made breakfast, and shortly will go to pool with coffee and pad and pen. Hugs for now. DeLeon, your Lioness.

M: Good morning my sweetheart Lioness. I am home in Loa with incredible memories of 13 beautiful days with the lovely Goddess of Bling and Eternal Spring. Much catching up to do. Your Michael

M: Suzanne, Out of respect to DeLeon and the love we share, while I was with her in Florida and Costa Rica I didn't watch the video you sent me of earth you alone taking care of your woman sexual needs with a vibrator in the bathtub. So I thought it rather magnificent of me to refrain from watching it today while I did a long list of priority stuff. I refrained until almost noon but couldn't wait any longer. But now, having seen and heard you do beautiful things, this time on video, I am again fully engaged in deep desire for you and the lovely body that I have only had naked in Loa's bed once before. *My whole soul calls out for you my darling Suzanne!*

Let me tell you a bit about how it was when the goddess I call "Tantra Healer" visited me and DeLeon in our Boca Raton, Florida hotel room by appointment. She texted right on time and we went downstairs to meet her. She stepped out of her car with a bundle of the tools she uses to teach Tantra Sacred Sex to couples. I was immediately attracted to her inner and outer beauty, she's a truly lovely lady in every way. We hugged and went upstairs to our room. There she burned incense to cleanse the room and talked with us about our objectives for the three hour session we had begun. My expressed desire was to prioritize whatever she felt was most beneficial for DeLeon who has had a rather traumatic past.

Tantra Healer taught us how to "move energy" between the two of us, then asked me to strip to my underwear and lie on my stomach on the bed. There she did various things to awaken "Kundalini" energy in my body, touching, massaging, and blowing hot breath from her open mouth up the length of my back. I couldn't see what she was doing as DeLeon looked on but it sounded so loud and felt so hot as she did that I thought she was using a mechanical device. But as I had told her, I think Kundalini was already alive in me from my childhood because I have always been so powerfully filled with life force that I had once required that it be reduced. I felt as that reducing process happened, that energy was being released from my heart center like the slow letting go of air from an inflated balloon.

Tantra Healer's focus then switched to DeLeon. I was proud of DeLeon as she unashamedly stripped naked and agreed to allow Tantra Healer to do whatever she felt she needed to do to heal and fine tune DeLeon's long beautiful body and help her engage more fully in the Tantra Sacred Sex experience. Tantra Healer, dressed in a pretty blouse and flowing skirt that she never removed but allowed to creep very high as I watched, knelt on the bed beside DeLeon and commenced to heal her body of things from her past that negatively affected her present. DeLeon responded wondrously and as she dealt with traumatic experiences from her past, before she spoke the words I was so in tune with her that my own emotions responded with tears and shudders, some so powerful I had to turn away and weep loudly as I too relived DeLeon's sometimes tragic past. Tantra Healer expertly elicited the troubles to awareness, and energetically yanked dark things from DeLeon's naked body, symbolically throwing them over her shoulder and away.

Healer asked me, still in my black briefs and nothing else and not caring, to first kiss and caress DeLeon's face, then kneel on the other side of DeLeon and mirror what she Tantra Healer was doing. Each with two hands on our side of DeLeon's beautiful naked body, we moved energy from just above her knees to her sacred space and along the side, barely touching and up her body, moving slowly to her breasts, gently pressing her firm nipples before lifting our hands and going back to do the same. I came too close once and Tantra Healer said it wasn't time yet to touch DeLeon's vagina, she needed to be opened more. About then the three hours ran out and I said I'd pay for another hour for DeLeon, she needed it.

Then, with my face less than six inches from DeLeon's sacred parts, Tantra Healer taught me how to very lightly and slowly caress DeLeon's pleasure spot with my thumb, very very lightly. She asked for permission and DeLeon allowed Tantra Healer to do whatever she wanted to do, she had already been healed of so much. Tantra Healer said, *"I'm going to enter you now"* and slowly inserted one finger deep inside DeLeon after asking me first to do the same, to locate DeLeon's g-spot. Healer wanted me to insert my finger alongside hers so she could teach me what she was about to do, but that was too physically uncomfortable for DeLeon, so Healer used her own finger, slowly sliding it into DeLeon after lubricating her finger and the vagina. As she moved her finger inside, Tantra Healer exclaimed with delight. I thought she had discovered what I already knew, that DeLeon, after being closed and dry for ten years due to a traumatic experience with her ex, was sopping wet inside. But no, it was more than that, DeLeon's vagina was *wide open and accessible!* Healer moved her finger all around DeLeon's g-spot, telling us like on a clock face where her finger was located as she touched and healed. DeLeon was still, lying naked on her back, eyes closed.

And here was nearly naked male me, once raunchy book character Michael, in bed with a naked woman, my face inches from her wet open vagina, watching closely as another woman in the same bed, skirt pulled up, bare thighs inches from my eyes, moved her finger deep inside the naked woman's vagina! I lightly stroked Healer's arm and she moved her gaze to my eyes comforted when she found there not lust for the second woman but my gratitude for what she was doing to and for my lover, doing it the Tantra Divine Feminine way. Healer asked DeLeon if she wanted to climax, but DeLeon insisted that she wait until she was alone with me. It would have been a good experience for me to watch how Healer brought an orgasm to DeLeon, but she respected my companion's desire. The orgasm came with no difficulty that night when it was just the two of us together.

DeLeon, because of her willingness to learn and grow and be healed, went from expressing disgust at the thought of bisexual females, to allowing a female finger to sink deep into her sacred space and move around therein. I don't know that, but maybe now DeLeon is better prepared to share a bed some day with me and you my beloved Suzanne? And that's how it was when Tantra Healer came to the hotel room of Michael and DeLeon, and stayed there for four hours.

Over the next ten days DeLeon and I traveled far and slept naked in the same bed each night, sometimes in the jungle with howler monkeys roaring in the back yard, who knows what slinking around below them. Cuddles were often, love was evident, sex was slow and not always. But the healing continued and often she and I would weep with joy together as barriers a decade old crumbled and the Goddess of Bling and Eternal Spring discovered that she is in very deed Divine Feminine - ALL WOMAN! Your Michael

Suzanne: A beautiful time, thank you for telling me the story.

M: I keep watching your video, sitting and listening and pleasuring, deeply desiring to be with you. You awaken in me lust and love in copious quantity, I don't think I could ever get enough of all of you. Send me more tonight if you are alone and feel the need to be naked and all woman for your man. I already know you are but I must taste and feel of you again if even still for a few more days only from a distance. Your Man

M: (to DeLeon) It's strange not having you around, we had fun together. I especially enjoyed cuddling you naked all night, our spoons fit. Keep me posted on the proposed May 1st event sweetie. We are not here to learn, we are here to teach. We hunt for the love of joy. ("The joy of love" as you put it.)

M: (to Ex who keeps sending friendly 'let's get together' messages.) I now believe that the same "muse" who inspired my first book in 1984 and inspires me now is of the same group of non-physical entities collectively known in our time as "Abraham". I believe too that the non-physical part of my own being is of Abraham. Knowing now how Law of Attraction works, it is possible that you too are of that group? You would learn much of value from studying at www.abraham-hicks.com. If you do, tell me about it, I can help you with your studies and respond to questions if you are sincere and open-minded. I have a vision of life for me in the eternities and it is almost overwhelming with fullness of joy. I am now preparing for the fulfillment of that vision. It could include you if you so choose and prepare yourself, but it's very different than what we have been socialized and taught by organized religions into believing. I am grateful for my Mormon time but I never really fit in there, as evidenced by my never even becoming a bishop, just a branch president. There was another 'mission' for me outside of that and other churches. I now know what that mission is and am joyfully embarked upon it.

M: (to Suzanne) I have reserved tickets for Zumanity on May 6th in Las Vegas. Should be fun.

M: (to Tantra Healer) My companion and I want to express our gratitude to you for the wonders you performed during our private couples session. It was not just the Tantra teachings but the healing work you did that was almost incredible. That healing continued for the next ten days as each of us took great delight in observing that yet another barrier to the full enjoyment of sexual activity had crumbled. My companion who had endured traumatic experiences in the past is now well on the way to being a fulfilled and capable woman thanks to the work you did with us. You are beautiful.

M: (to Tantra Healer) I am personally delighted that DeLeon was willing and you felt inspired to do what you did with her. It was wonderful to observe and to be so much in tune with DeLeon at the time that I think I was feeling much of what she was feeling. Your love for me and DeLeon was always evident in that room. You are truly beautiful inside and out, I'm sure I fell in love with you too. It was my desire that you focus your attention on DeLeon and you did, thank-you. But a question remains for me about how to have a 'dry' male orgasm? And also, your mention that it is 'ok' for a male to ejaculate. That seems to be contrary to the Tantra teachings I have read in books. Would you care to explain?

I will be meeting with the other woman in my life in Las Vegas between May 5 and May 10. Can you recommend someone comparable to yourself who might be able to meet with me and her in Las Vegas during those days?

DeLeon: It is strange and for me, hard to find a word for it. Good brite morning, as I wore my yellow Pura Vida T shirt when walking my dog this morning. I'm to see my regular cardiologist on Monday - and had set an appointment with the other doc on the 30th to talk to him. However, will call him on Monday, to talk with him about putting the procedure off, to see how it's doing as I haven't had it go into an episode since we've been back. It's had some irregularities. But seems to be gentling down. There is a repercussion from the last one, that I hadn't experienced in prior ablations, in my throat and esophegus - and it comes up when I'm being winded or when an episode hits. Have kept forgetting to ask them about it, when in their presence, so am facing it this week, with them. Will keep you apprised. Thank you for standing with me on this.

Had a long, long talk with Roomy - about the trip, Costa Rica, you and I and what my next move and movement is, etc.. She's settled down and being supportive of it - even apologized for her part in keeping me, another 2 years (her words) here..... because she needed me to get her thru her stuff.... selling the property, etc.. - that was a first. I spent a nice session in the "community" room/meeting place next to office - and loved the open, yet quiet and comfortable setting - for thinking writing, etc.. And that will be my place of abode... to get "the writings" rolling. Got to get ready for church, Have a blessed day, My Love..... DeLeon (In gratitude and love for all you have done to and for me, in my life..body, mind and soul)..

M: Good morning gorgeous. Here's some possible synchronicity you may want to investigate. Just before I went to you the second time, Marcy (a shaman friend) referred to me as a possible match a lady by the name of Corine who currently lives near Las Vegas I think. Corine like you is a dancer and a speaker/author/healer. She is involved with a metaphysical group known as "The Magdalene Order" that promotes Divine Feminine. I left a message for her on singles but she hasn't read it yet so there has been no direct contact between us. Feel free to contact her directly if you want to.

DeLeon: Oh, Oh, Oh! Magdalene - remembering my words with you, rather awakening/startling/interesting/reinforcing... As I said -man/woman had been "split" - THE VERY WORD USED, as they described The Twin Flame. Perhaps describing - our "unknown" known - perhaps best describing us. This shows up a few days after we part. I've listened to all 3 links. Thank You Love... BIG.

A few things..... I wore my black dress to church with the Cleopatra necklace - SHINING - all over the place. Comments galore. I feel new, strong, moving onward and forward, thenyousend these 3 links to continue re-enfocing.

Would you be able to restart my encrypted email? And does it have any monthly fee? As you said - lots of things -would be downloading over the next 4/5 weeks. They are in process. I want that email address. And what is the web site, where I sign in. I want you doing the process, as you know what your doing. BTW - I like the number in the email address. Well, unless you want to do 13. What do you think. As much as I love my 13, I feel your number may be a new energy. I'm on roomy's computer - as mine is scarily stopped – my friend is coming in tomorrow morning to help me. Your DeLeon - In Love...

M: DeLeon, It's a delight that so many powerful 'forces' seem to be able to work through me. No doubt the project is much bigger than even I am aware of at this time as *all* powers that are currently working on this planet play their part to prepare its people for the leap to Eden. I felt your uncertainty other than a desire to write books and get a message out. I think your choice to work almost exclusively on helping restore Divine Feminine is a noble choice and that you will shine *magnificently* on that stage. From now on as you focus on that choice and take inspired action, many 'coincidences' will most likely occur and people and information will be attracted to you when you need them/it.

When that powerful referral (Corine) from Marcy came to me and I checked out her profile on Singles I was a bit baffled because I felt no romantic connection there. Now I know that it was for *you* my love. It seems that you two will work wondrously together, maybe eventually each of you conducting workshops in different parts of the country or together even? Co-authoring books perhaps? I hope you will become great friends if your heart and hers move in that direction, you could make each other shine much more brilliantly both playing harmoniously on the same stage. I feel to *congratulate* you DeLeon!

I just don't want to go there with the image you create of yourself in that little black dress and the long turquoise necklace from the beach at Dominical, Costa Rica. If I picture it too clearly I may find myself on the next plane to Fort Lauderdale. I'll have a look at encrypted mail and see if I can get it back for you. You could then use the business cards I gave you. You delight me Lioness of the Golden Mane, we will hunt long together. Your Michael

M: Oops, I just noticed a little problem with my image of you at church in your little black dress today. I had imagined the turquoise necklace when you said it was Cleopatra's instead. Oh well, either way I'm sure you shone brightly.

Suzanne: I was at a hospice conference last 2 days. Home today, covering my peach trees with netting to keep birds away, planting my tomatoes and then mowing. It's a beautiful day. I am getting more excited about our time together.

M: Good morning sweetie. Me too, it has been a long time since we were together physically. It will be a great delight to be with you again, I'm sure I'll cherish every moment we have. Too bad we have to sleep some of the time away, but at least we already know that our spoons fit. We'll see how it works out for us this time but I'll forever remember what I felt when we first hugged in Loa, a feeling of perfect peace and belonging. You are close to me in so many ways Suzanne, writer me would not exist without you.

I now have ten books published all over the world in several languages, waiting to be discovered among the 8,000 new books published every day. Carrie and Ashley are working on that part, books need to be very heavily promoted to generate sales. It will be exciting once our books start selling well and the money flows smoothly, opening new doors for us.

Suzanne: I am fascinated by tantra sex. I believe pure enjoyment of sex is so much more than the physical. Maybe we can have a session?

M: I've been trying honey, I want that too, but I haven't been able to find anyone that I think would be suitable for us in Las Vegas. I'm waiting for a response from the tantra instructor who was with me and DeLeon in Florida. But I'll keep trying and will let you know if there are any breakthroughs for that brief time period that we have. I don't want it to be just a prostitute in disguise (or a man) but someone who is well qualified to actually teach Tantra techniques. For you and me it would be much better than for me and DeLeon because I very much doubt that you have the intense need for healing that she had and that took almost all of our time, an extra hour even. So it may not happen for us this time, but let's discuss it when we meet. Maybe we can go see Tantra Healer sometime, maybe on the way to Costa Rica? Your Michael

M: But a very big part of a satisfying Tantra experience is simply sharing love and soul connection. We may find that we already have that.

DeLeon: Are you experiencing an awareness of huge shift within and with energy? I CERTAINLY AM. You are my angel, Beloved.. You not only have seen and experienced the depth, the soul of me....You see me probably as no one else has, as you truly SEE ME. As I do you.

DeLeon: The black dress was stunning, so don't want you to miss that image. So many comments - most were about my energy, as many were sensing it. Wuv U.... How did your day go - besides progressing forward. And thank you for paying for a year for my encrypted email..

M: You would be stunning regardless of what you were wearing or not. I wuv you too darling, and I ike you as well. My day, as always was well spent and enjoyable. Sleep well my Lioness.

M: I have grown accustomed to living my life daily with such things as you describe. I EXPECT life to be like that. You too will be there as you focus on your task because you have become enormously *useful* to those non-physical entities who are working with us to prepare for the leap to Eden. Your sacrifice is accepted, you are ready now for inspired action, here to teach not to learn. You are without doubt being watched over carefully, protected, and loved deeply. You cannot die unless you choose to and give up this incarnation. So go forward with boldness ignoring the past and mighty forces will come to your aid. Lift up your eyes unto the hills from whence cometh your help. Your usefulness is that with your writings and energetic speakings that you have been prepared for over the years, you can reach and influence *many others*. You MUST write your books darling, many souls are waiting for them, and for you. Seek your muse and write and act confidently, fearlessly, the universe steps aside to let pass a woman who knows where she is going - and you do.

Keep me posted on your Magdalene dealings, I'm very interested in watching where you go with that. I think you are perfect for that role. I believe that you will do much to help move women towards their true role of Divine Feminine, and men to acknowledging it. You have an incredible personal story to tell - tell it well, tell it powerfully, tell it often. As I have often told you, I see you as perfect and whole because that's who and what you *really* are Lioness. Each moment is the beginning of your new life. Live those golden moments each happy, perfectly confident in WHO you are gorgeous goddess, Divine Feminine. And SMILE sweetheart, it's so beautiful to us who look upon you with love and caring as we always did before. Your Michael Lion Proud of his Lioness with the Golden Mane

M: (to DeLeon) I wonder if the woman I mention below could be of help to you on the technical side of Tantra as you write your books? Maybe she could edit or co-write anything you write about the practical side of *doing* Tantra, or offer suggestions after reading your drafts? She seems to be quite knowledgeable about techniques and is globally minded, planning to do "sacred seminars" and radio shows. Could she travel and speak with you, you on the spiritual side, her on the physical, do demonstrations maybe??? I found her on Singles, I'm calling her "Bliss".

M: (to Bliss) I have a female friend who is planning to write books and do seminars similar to those you are expressing interest in doing yourself. I thought maybe eventually you two could travel and present together, she on the spiritual "Divine Feminine" side of Tantra, you on the physical? Anyway, just a thought after I read your profile. Would you like to have her email address, or give me yours to pass along to her?

DeLeon: I just now saw this, is - very, very interesting. Think I said that I had been told years, years, ago, by several people, that I had the Mary Magdalene energy. Bless you and thank you for your extended efforts to support me on so many levels. My Beloved Angel, there's no end to you.... thank God. And Good Morning to you - Handsome.

M: Mornin babe.

Tantra Healer: Hello Michael, Thanks for the Testimonial. I'm delighted that my work was so powerful for you! For Las Vegas I don't know anyone personally but I recommend two sites. Love and Light.

M: (to DeLeon) I sent photos to your encrypted address. I suggest that you download them to your computer then delete them from both the inbox and the trash to free up space.

DeLeon: Yeaa!! I'm in!! THank U!! My friend just left after spending couple hours working on my computer issues. Bless his heart. He's an awakened being - so was thrilled to hear my new story - done with the old, creating the new and yep, moving forward. He was able to clear some needed space, to give me a bit more time to put it all together. Pura Vita

DeLeon: That was/is a gorgeous load of photos of an incredible journey with US. I've downloaded/saved/deleted all but last 3 emails. Taking a break - thank you again for all of your efforts. The pictures are such a joy. One of my steps forward today, was applying for a credit card that works with challenged credit - to enable my purchasing a new computer! Progress in action. Going to the community room for a break from here - and move into DeLeon. Oh, and today, I called the Dr's office and told them to cancel my May 1st ablation procedure at the hospital.

M: As I wrote earlier, CONGRATULATIONS DeLeon!

M: (to Suzanne) DeLeon has healed to the point of not even needing another scheduled heart procedure. I brought some good into her life, I'm grateful for that. And grateful for your coming to me soon. I feel so close to you, always did since that first hug in Loa. You are my sunshine.

Suzanne: What a blessing. We are such complex creatures. I will pray her healing continues and of course you were a part of that journey for sweet DeLeon. I do believe as our lives touch and intertwine, beautiful moments unfold and love heals.

Ashley: Hey!! I have an idea!! We've been talking about taking a trip to Nicarauga to see something new, but I'd hate to lose my place here. It's only $350/month and maybe you would like to occupy it while we are gone... no obligations or conditions, but it gives you an option. It's secure, a nice spot down the river and has cable and birds sing in the morning... its across from an amazon style river with mountains with wifi. It may give you the time you need to get to know the area. It does not have air conditioning, but you could pick one up or bring a portable one with you. Its only a small room with balcony, so it will cool off quick. Just a thought I had.

M: I'll keep that in mind Ashley, thanks. I'm exploring several possibilities right now and would prefer something long term if I take the leap to Costa Rica. How long will you be away?

I'll start looking around for alternatives to Carrie if you need the help and she isn't providing it. I thought she'd be good at doing it that's why I recommended her, but her time seems devoted to other priorities and I don't think she's sold on creating a legend out of mere me. (A prophet is not without honor except in his own village. *Me a legend? Not a chance, he's too human...*) Will you be able to handle the social media marketing, or do you need to focus on the website and I should find another professional for social media? (I get lots of spam from people wanting to promote my business site on social media, some of them sound like they're knowledgeable.)

DeLeon was concerned about a lot of things too. I've been abandoning my business sense the last few months, putting too much blind trust in others. But it's not working out well so far except for my personal life and writing the books. *I just want to write honey, help me with the other stuff and make it a priority?* I'll love you forever if you do that. (*Most likely will anyway...*)

Enjoy the evening or whatever it is when you read this Ashley. I hate to come down on you like this but there's that sense of urgency that can't be denied. We *must* get this really happening, and we must get it clean and get it right, and get it NOW! cc DeLeon

DeLeon: THERE YOU ARE MICHAEL! THANK GOD. VERY WELL SAID! VERY WELL DONE! EACH.... and EVERY.... WORD !!

M: Your Lion roaring a bit...

M: (to DeLeon) *"As we pick up the thread of my life....I hasten to remind you that I had already begun the process of youthening my body by disengaging from the collective consciousness that believed in aging and dying."* (she lived for 600 years) Anna, Grandmother of Jesus, Claire Heartsong

M: (to DeLeon) I'll be sending you stuff at your encrypted account so please check it now and then, thanks.

DeLeon: Will do.

Suzanne: You know that you will continue to be a significant player in DeLeon's healing. Be wise and gentle.

M: Hi Sweetie, I appreciate your love and concern for DeLeon, she and I communicate daily. I hope you two will meet some day but she still sees you as competition. I never mentioned your name the whole two weeks I was with her, but would have if she had said it first, that was our agreement. I suppose she woman knows that I'm still deeply in love with you Suzanne. No doubt I always will be regardless of what time and choices may bring for us. I hope that we'll move physically together you and I, we can achieve everything we put our minds to, perhaps attract and eventually bring together under the same roof my fantasy, our eternal Adam and Eve family, and become immortal. We'll have such love and joy, our cups running over with goodness and daily delight. *And oh such children as we'll conceive on our planets!*

DeLeon is beginning to write the first book she has in mind, then will go on speaking tours. When I went to her this latest time she was uncertain which of three paths to take. She had dreams/visions about pursuing them all but it was obvious that her focus needed to be exclusive of the others. She has spent years in addictions counseling and is apparently very good at it, sensing spiritually what each individual needs for healing, and providing that. She is tall, graceful and noble in appearance (draws eyes always) and is an excellent natural dancer - she's got the moves built into her.

Yes of course, she demonstrated those moves a few times in our hotel room for my male delight, clothing optional. Also at a dance studio where everyone knew and hugged her. And at a hotel one night where the manager talked with her familiarly and a member of the live band knew her. She used to live nearby, they remembered her. She did a brief solo on the floor in front of the band and as we stood to leave, the band leader asked her to stay and dance for everyone. But it was late at night and we hadn't yet had dinner, so we moved on to the restaurant where in a few inspired sentences I spoke the words she needed to hear to make her choice.

DeLeon loves to dress up and be flashy with bling so every day is bright and shiny, and she loves to dance. So, she was thinking to open a franchise of centers where addicts of all kinds would be exposed to the world of dance and thus be healed through rhythm, physical movement, pleasant association, and an acceptable alternative 'addiction' - dance. That was a path she could take, she felt it a 'mission'. She was also deeply impressed with a book written decades ago which is now public domain. She wants to record the book to revive it, and take it on the road, she felt it a 'mission'. But I looked it over the first time I was with her and wasn't similarly impressed, though I didn't tell her at the time. That was a second path she could take. And more recently, she has become deeply interested in "Tantra Sacred Sensuality" (as she puts it) as an instrument towards freeing the Divine Feminine in women and teaching men how to respect and respond appropriately to that.

We had attended a session at a dance studio earlier before going back to the hotel to change then wandering around downtown. At the dance studio I was just watching and DeLeon danced only twice - once with a handsome instructor in a grey tuxedo, once by herself.

That because she was paying attention to a heart condition that left her breathless when moving energetically. So, while we waited for our meal in one of the few restaurants still open that late at night the conversation got around to where I told her that having just witnessed modern ballroom dancing, I couldn't really see many serious drug addicts voluntarily going into that, and you can't force treatment on anyone. Somehow that comment clicked in her mind, and DeLeon wrote off the idea of combining addiction treatment with dance. (I think.) I told her that each moment in time presents a brand new life and she needn't feel bound to any former 'mission' she may have been dwelling on, she could make a different choice right now *this very moment*. I told her that instead of pushing an old book she could instead use what she had specifically learned from that book in her own books and presentations, telling her personal story and referring to the book if she wanted to. She lit up with that idea and seemed free. She later raved about how important to her our casual conversation had been in that restaurant late that night.

Yes, DeLeon's present choice, her chosen 'mission' is to focus on teaching Divine Feminine. And that choice fits in perfectly with my project whereas the other two might not have. All is well, the universe continues to unfold as it should... I love you Suzanne Darling. Your Michael

Ashley: I don't have a solid plan.... ever! Universe just doesn't let me do that. What I was saying is my place will be available and it could buy you a month or two to look around and get to know different areas and find a more permanent place. There would be no obligation to even keeping it. If I'm not here, you can just choose to leave. Or if you are leaving or find a place you like, maybe then I will come back. It's just hard to find a place that's available here sometimes, so mine may be available to you in mid-June and I wanted to give you first option.

M: Understood, thanks.

M: (to Suzanne) I always appreciate and need your counsel sweetheart. I love DeLeon in a very different manner than I love you. I came away from those 13 days eagerly, feeling somehow that I had completed a 'task' and did it well, not wanting to stay longer, she now had what she needed to "run and not be weary", it might be best to just slowly back away and 'allow' her to do that. But you pull me back to her as you always have, so today I started including her in some of the back and forth between me and Ashley to show that there's some earth grounding here, not just my visionary way of doing things lately, expecting Source to take over - as in *"let go and let God."* Tell me when you feel I need a gentle push in some particular direction, I do need you. And tell me how much if any you want to be involved in the business end of marketing and selling my books. I'll copy you in if that is of interest to you.

DeLeon: I just got the funniest vision - we two lions standing side by side, with our tails coiled together. I know I've seen that when they were standing side by side, connected, yet fully aware of the world around them.

M: Yes, that would be us.

DeLeon: Interesting - my entire body has been at peace, fulfilled, content. No vibrating, Until a little while ago, when the desire began "communicating".

M: And here I thought it was the wind vibrating Loa when it was *you* doing it. Yes, I've been feeling those vibes, wanting to be with you again when before I too was content. If I lived anywhere near you we'd be doing a rendezvous tonight, an inside job most likely. It's wonderful that sex never satisfies for long, we need to keep going back for more, that's the stuff of life. Fond memories dearest...

DeLeon: I'm cleaning off computer - am sharing this photo with you... I created and had on my wall, once upon a time. Putting it back again.

M: The word "sizzle" seems appropriate to the moment.

DeLeon: I see that twinkle in your eye.

M: I would opt for your Halloween photo looking like an English Queen rather than Cleopatra. But that doesn't rule out an Antony somewhere...

DeLeon: Somewhere – absolutely

DeLeon: Entertainment - this was the notice that I sent out to those who were invited to the first gathering. I had completely forgotten about this flyer. My language was so beautiful, would you agree - now????

M: You do have a way with words DeLeon. I like it, it's quite unique requiring an influx and sometimes a deep breath from those you bestow them upon as they dance towards the dawning of your intention. (Don't take me too seriously sweetie, never could dance, just having fun, now go write books will you.)

Carrie: hi there... i'm working on your page and someone just had an instant message chat with me, in fact i just had two chats... but one wanted to see photos of you, so it's time for you to send me some that i can add to your profile... we can use some from your past, but not just childhood photos...we need something women can relate to as the sexy michael that we are presenting... let me know asap what you can come up with... hope your last days with deleon were wonderful...how is the romance going there? or have you two settled into more of a friendship now? whichever, i hope it was lovely... hugs, as always, carrie

M: It's imagination that creates myth and legend so no photos please, I look too human in them. DeLeon and I are old souls with a lot of love in our hearts. That's likely about where we will stay in this incarnation as we dance in close proximity to share and manifest compatible goals. She is focused on releasing the Divine Feminine in women and that's a major theme in my later books.

Carrie: we need some photos on your page... so, at lease send me the childhood ones... otherwise people are going to be suspicious of you...that already happened once tonight...we don't want to create that image... how about some from early adulthood? teens, and childhood... nothing recent, but we do need something... this isn't about being a myth... this is about being a human being others can relate to who then will want to go to your web site and read your books... let's help them like you...

Chapter 10

———— ❧ ————

Actually this IS all about a myth, the legend of Michael and Kira, now incarnated as "Michael and Suzanne". I don't think I'll ever get Carrie to see beyond consensus reality and to accept me for who and what I SAY I am. I think I will refrain from responding to Carrie's email, she seems to be a myth destroyer rather than creator. Had she read my books that might be different. Do we need her for balance? Maybe, just not today. Today we have a drum to beat, a legend to create so I can sell my e-books, they'll never become known otherwise.

M: (to DeLeon) Any chance your room-mate might finance you for something like this? (insert link) It's the best known site for expatriots living in and wanting to live in Costa Rica. Their email list is 25,000 members and it looks like it's a great money maker, especially for real estate. You may recall that realtors in CR don't need to be licensed. Maybe you could go there and make money from the leads pouring in to the website? He says he and his wife made $500,000 in one sale. Not too hard with the prices they add on to what the seller wants... Just a thought, but it's writing, it's real estate, it's travel, it's outreach, it's a money maker, it may only take three or four hours a day online, it's it's...

DeLeon: Very, very Interesting. MUCH to take in. I feel like I'm standing in a continuous rain shower of good.... of/from you. In Gratitude...

DeLeon: Michael, At the moment, am giving a moment, although I want so share much. There is so much coming my way, am in awe. Something huge has happened within me, during and after our April Time. At this time, I really have no one to communicate with, except you, as its' so far beyond "them", there's no concept. The Magdalene - I really haven't responded to you, as it has been stunning for me, re-affirming my "ME". The times we were together and words that came out of my mouth - i.e. the "split", and I kept talking about that. From the beginning when starting, then continuing to read info on Mag. The words I had spoken, were all over their writings. When we were in the restaurant or somewhere in that time, I had written down, as you saw, the name of my book as Resurrection........ and before we left, don't think

160

I said this to you, i wrote Resurrection of Womanity - the name of the book.

Low and Behold, as i continued to read and opening links and re-reading the Mag things you were sending - I saw something very similar to that very wording. IT may have been Womanhood, not sure but another re-enforcer... that I Am a Mag. The synergy was so potent between us at the restaurant - creation just kept flowing. I haven't been able to get in that space, again, yet.

I keep accidently hitting the send thing, so be patient w/me. I do have sincere interest in meeting Corine - my angle and whom and how I'm wanting to touch/reach out - is different than hers. I know she's my breed/tribe. My direction is for those who are asleep, talking their language and opening the doors. Michael, there is such a "Holiness" within me. You have been my Sacred, Powerful Angel. (Okay, so Angel's are often disguised as Lions, MY Lion King.) Who took my hand and wouldn't let go. I AM SO DEEPLY GRATEFUL. Being distracted by a lot around here.

DeLeon: Honey, I need to switch focus and work on stuff about my ex. Anyway, to finish... Today - 21 years ago my life was saved by a beautiful Dr. in Colorado, I actually connected with his front desk, 2 days ago, about sending all of my records to him, for feedback from him, in dealing with CO sealevel - and much more. The gal, became very present with me and was wonderful. Also, went to my regular cardiologist, who agreed with my declining the procedure... as there is an issue I hadnt' told the other dr - which had occured after last procedure. They want me in for some other tests next week. So, that is good. (i feel it is an awarenss that the Universe wants exposed, for me to proceed forward in my healing). HOWEVER, ABOVE ALL ELSE. I have not had any episodes, since they stopped in Costa Rica.

Today – is also, your last day in Yuma with LOA. Blessings of Grace filled Safety and Guidance - which you know is yours. I Love You The Legendary Michael. Hugs and Kisses are yours. DeLeon

M: Your joy is my reward sweetheart. I know you are meant to do much and your time has come. No pillars of salt, it's only *forward* from now on. I very much encourage the Magdalene in you, it runs in my blood too, maybe the feminine part of the Abraham that I am? We'll share much as we go along. Never hesitate to send your deepest thoughts and feelings. I think I'll always understand and I *know* that I'll always respond with love in the best way I am capable. We are entangled a lot you and I, and lovers. Your Michael

M: (to Suzanne – copied the DeLeon messages above) Extracts from today in Book Twelve.

M: (to Suzanne) I kept telling myself all day today that I never get tired and it worked. So I did the many hours of tedious editing etc. and sent Book 10 for e-book formatting. (The box set is effectively book 9.) Book 11 is ready for editing and Book 12 is well on the way. Will this never end? What do you think? I paid my final electric bill here and will leave for Phoenix to visit family tomorrow a.m. I'll probably be in Las Vegas with Loa on Sunday and will rent a car to be ready to pick you up at the airport Monday at noon. We'll meet at the baggage carousel for your flight or if that fails, please wait at the information booth in the middle of the carousels. Wave if I don't recognize you. My cell phone is (insert). Would you care to give me your number? I won't call you unless we miss connecting more than a half hour after your flight shows on the board as having arrived. See you soon.

M: (to Suzanne) I just arrived in Phoenix, Arizona to visit my son and family. It was a nice stay in Yuma since December 29th but is getting real hot there now. I don't mind the heat much but Loa does, she's not dressed for it.

Just in case Suzanne might prevail, I checked Victoria, British Columbia and there are job openings for hospice nurses. Under the North American Free Trade Agreement, you can't be denied residence and a work permit as long as you have a solid job offer in Canada. Thought I'd throw that one out since you are selling your house and I'm trying to persuade you to travel with me real life long term. (Did you notice?) I love Victoria and have often thought of moving back there. Health care is almost free in Canada. Still excited about Vegas on Monday? Your Man

M: Do you like the way Ashley designed our buy books page?

Suzanne: I do like the page. I've been swamped with work. 12 hour days last 2 weeks. So ready to leave town.

M: We'll have loads of fun sweetheart. Nice visit with my son and his family. The littlest one was just a baby when I last saw her at Christmas but she's walking and running and saying a few words, and

'reading' books, they're all such a delight. They just bought their first house, a two story with five bedrooms and a nice pool and waterfall feature in the back yard. But my son is overworked too, they're opening their business in California also and he's driving the 400 miles each way quite often. This is the time of year when they get university students to knock on doors and sell their contracts so they're super busy, but their business is growing amazingly well. My son will be picking me up for the day in a half hour, he's taking today off for me, nice kid you'd like him. I love you darling, can't wait to see you at the airport and and...
Your Michael

M: (to Suzanne) I've been trying not to so the time passes faster but I'm thinking a lot about you tonight, kinda vivid at times...

May 2. I'm parked at a Walmart in Phoenix, Arizona waiting for my son to pick me up for breakfast. Last night I thought it might be helpful to get more people to my website if I wrote a couple of how-two books and sold them on that site as well. I might write a small book called *"Singles Site Success"* about how to use singles sites more effectively to attract a mate. And another one on how to publish an e-book and get it distributed worldwide in less than three weeks. I'll let those ideas percolate a bit then most likely start writing when I get settled somewhere for a few weeks or so.

M: (to DeLeon) Hi Sweetie, I heard from Corine the Magdalene. Hopefully she'll write you. I'm very interested in following your conversations if you'd be willing to forward the emails to me. But of course that is your business, I won't be offended if you don't. I hope you are well and moving forward.

DeLeon: Thank you, much, dear for the info.. & details. Viva LasVegas.

DeLeon: I am sure I am a Magdalene..... there is no question. I just didn't know what it was, nor had I heard of the Magdalene till recently. There has been so much filtered in to me over the years... often would be so big, would just take it in, then let it go - thinking omg, what do I do with that. I was in a seminar in the appellation (sp?) mountains and had a vision. Never told anyone about that one, until now, with you. If you shared her email & phone with me, would you do so again.... so I can log it in. thank you. Will be appreciative to hear about your meeting with her. Thank you for all.....

M: That must have been a powerful vision, thanks for sharing it with me. And thanks again for those wonderful days we shared. Pura Vida.

Suzanne: Beautiful photos. Ashley reminds me of my oldest daughter. Worked the weekend and now packing for the trip. I'm really excited to have the time together, we have so much to talk about. My phone number is (insert). I'll check in to my flight shortly.

M: We do have a whole lot to talk about sweetheart, I can hardly wait to see you tomorrow. We have a room reserved at Excalibur, right on the strip, connected to several other hotels, and just a five minute walk to Zumanity. The most restful thing to do would be for us to stay there the entire five nights. However, there are alternatives that we could consider as we go along. Loa is parked near the South Point Hotel several miles from Excalibur. It's a nice hotel, if you want some variety we could stay at South Point Friday night if I can get a room. There's a movie theater inside South Point and a movie called "insert" is playing. My son saw it and said it's very good. Just a thought. Also, I have a rental car for the week so we're mobile if you want to get out of town. One possibility is to go to Zion National Park (very nice) about a three hour drive each way. If we go Thursday, we could take a hotel there for the night. Anyway, as I wrote, if you need a rest we can do a whole lot of things without straying far from Excalibur the whole five days/nights. See you tomorrow my love. Your Michael

May 5 – today's the day Suzanne and Michael meet again after that one night stand in Loa at San Antonio, Texas months ago. I haven't been allowing myself to get real excited about it, there have been so many false starts along the way, will she really and truly step off that plane? But it's real this time, isn't it? *She's REALLY coming!* I'll be holding her in just a few hours, we'll make love again this day. It's almost unreal. That was a lovely message from her last night, especially the words *"I'm really excited to have the time together, we have so much to talk about."* That lit up my heart because it resonated so much and because she hasn't been saying anything about her love for me the last few weeks. Talk includes planning for the future, maybe we have a real future and not just a virtual one? I don't really know...

What will it *feel* like to hug again? It was other worldly for me the first time, an 'all is well'. She never said how it was for her, but her walking away early in the morning indicated that it wasn't the same for her at the time. Only months later, after a few long silences and an "epilogue" did she first say *"I love you"*. When we first met, we by-passed the talk part and went straight to bra and panties on the floor. That worked at the time, but it didn't last. We need to catch up on talk. If she invited me to go home with her I would go of course, but I can't see that happening, more likely hopes for a future, probably months down the road? And I need to visit my family soon. I'd take her with me if she was willing and not tied to a house and job in Texas.

Yesterday morning I set it up to check in to our room before noon. I want to get everything nicely arranged for her, chocolates etc. Flowers? It's the best room they had available when I booked, for the bestest woman in my life. I love her so. It's a lovely day today. Be with us this week?

DeLeon: (she writes to our private driver in Costa Rica and copies me in) Greetings From DeLeon in Florida: I am slowly recooping from the incredible journey traveled in Costa Rica, of which was dominated by your protective presence, kind/caring/sharing/guiding professional direction and mostly by your safe and always courteous driving and aiding my entrance & exit of the wonderful automobile. The first few days I was experiencing some concerning, painful stomach and heart issues, however with your control of our passage, there was peace everywhere in my heart and soul and eventually towards the end of the stay, gratefully all calmed down. I will never forget, when on Easter Sunday, we stopped at the booths near the sea.... I was looking at jewelry and happened to turn around - there you stood, tall and strong, arms crossed, like an angelic soldier on guard watching for the good of Miss DeLeon.

I appreciated your sharing the journey and incredible efforts you and your wife are doing for yourself and your family. I wish you prosperity, safety, joy, peace, accomplishment of your dreams and reinforcement of the Best and the Most in life, on every level of heart, mind, body and soul. For everything I thank you deeply, as it was such

a peaceful, precious, Blissful time in Costa Rica. I so want to return
to visit - would love to live there part time, as I felt so at home with all
I experienced (especially that fried pork!) Have attached the picture
of you and I near the water fall and just for fun.... Seeing DeLeon in
her Glory on the Red Carpet at a Gala Affair - in Feb. 2014. In Loving
Kindness and Gratitude.... DeLeon (aka DeLeon)

DeLeon: (to Costa Rica driver) Until we meet again.... Grace in
every step you take. DeLeon

I included the above to present another side of DeLeon. While
she was falling in love with our driver and appreciating his stature and
'protection' there was another man standing right at her side protecting
her and paying for the jewelry she wanted. Pause for thought? And then
there was the time in Costa Rica where she got talking with another
man as I sat nearby and then wandered off with him without saying
anything to me, coming back 30 minutes later after apparently looking
over the house he was building. She bowed to him and kissed his hand
in front of me. Where's me in all this??? Do I matter? But at least she
copied me in. Time to get a better grip Michael?

As I write this note early in the a.m. Suzanne is naked, asleep in
a king bed a few feet away from me. Nice change of events yes, lovely,
another miracle that she even came, I'll write more of that later. But
already we both know that we won't be living under the same roof
anytime soon, most likely never. Ok, gotta go, she stirs and I have much
email to catch up on. Talk to you later.

May 1..., Suzanne flies back to Texas, I drop her off at the Las Vegas
airport.

M: (to Suzanne) Thanks so much for coming to Las Vegas.
Regardless of our differences, it is my hope that we will stay in touch
and share much for many years to come. I love you. Michael

Carrie: hi there... i noticed you took a look at my profile recently...
any special reason? how's it going? any new ladies in your world these
days? and have you decided yet what your summer plans are going to
be? hope all is well and you are enjoying writing, writing, writing...
hugs, carrie

M: I was going over some old emails yesterday and clicking on
photos, guess yours was one of them. I am in Las Vegas at this moment,

life is unfolding as it should. Yes, there are several ladies in my life and/or on the horizon as I continue to seek concept "Kira" and stories to write. As for summer plans there are many roads I could follow including invitations to park Loa next to someone's home for as long as I want. So I don't foresee a visit to Panama at this time much as I'd like to meet you and see for myself your beautiful part of the world.

Carrie: glad to hear life is unfolding in a lovely way for you... and, delighted you have that option for a place to park for however long you wish... that must take a bit of pressure off and feel really good... looks as if i'll be here for a while as i am going to oversee the improvements needed on this house before it can go on the market next january, so you still have some time to come for that visit if you wish... meantime, as always, i send you some nice hugs... carrie

M: Hugs back Carrie, enjoy the day.

M: (to Suzanne) I assume you are home sweetheart and hope you are home with fond memories of our five days together, memories similar to those I cherish. I will never forget this morning's events after that not so precious conversation we had that I initiated at 3:30 a.m. long after we'd both fallen asleep. As I write this I am parked at Arizona Charlie's Casino trusting that it will be an uneventful night in a part of Las Vegas that is not so desirable. I have now met and had dinner with Corine. As you know, I mentioned that I did not find her attractive in the singles photo, and although I had hoped that impression to be incorrect and left myself wide open to any possibility, it was not. I knew that at first glance as I opened Loa's door to her knock. I have zero attraction for her but was able during dinner to provide her with some counsel as she was stressed out and came to dinner with a bunch of pills to consume. But she's a writer and I'll most likely keep in touch with her by email, she's a Magdalene and I'm curious about them.

So I'm at a loss as to where to go until my ex returns home about May 22 and we meet so I can arrange another storage unit for what is left of my stuff after the break in. A few moments ago I received an email from my firstborn asking me to visit. So maybe that is how I will fill in the days until my ex returns if I can find a safe and inexpensive place to store Loa while I'm away.

Carrie wrote tonight that she has been retained to supervise alterations to the house she is renting until January next year. She again invited me to visit her in Panama. What do you think now that Corine is out of the picture? My guess is that Carrie and I would become sexually involved. How many lovers do I need, and how many women (not you) to take advantage of me financially and otherwise while I temporarily suspend normal behavior and learn from experience how to effectively "walk by faith"? Will I lose my freedom if I go back with my ex? (I know, I will talk with her, won't leave her on a limb wanting someone who is as you put it "not available" at this time.)

I loved our time together darling, and I love you. But we both know if we tried living under the same roof that I would attempt to change you so you were more like Suzanne and less like Responsible Nurse RN, which you must be at this time to put bread on your table and pay the bills. We are also both well aware that I am quite a bit older than you and you don't want to be burdened after spending your days working hospice with coming home to the same kind of situation with a 'husband'. Our times together will most likely remain brief events such as our days in Las Vegas, if we have any future times together at all. I do hope there will be more for us than just virtual contact. You elicit much love from me regardless of our differences and the very wide disparity in our need for physically expressed affection from the other. You seem not to believe that a man can love you and you tend to completely ignore the one walking or sitting beside you, seldom if ever looking at him or initiating conversation, and never touching (though you generously allowed me to touch you, not shying away from that contact, thank-you for that, I needed it desperately.) This man loves you dearest Suzanne, thank-you so much for spending some time with him, up and down as it turned out to be, similar to our virtual relationship.

M: Happy Mother's Day Suzanne, I hope it is a delightful day for you with your children. I'm missing you today, only with great effort holding off the sadness of you leaving yesterday. Every time I close my eyes a picture of your face is there. And now after writing that sentence it seems as if I *am* you in real life, my lips pursed as if breathing through my mouth, looking like you, aloof, introverted though you may not think you are, thinking your thoughts. It's powerful, almost overwhelming sometimes how connected I feel with you even though that may not be reciprocated because you *choose* to keep a wall between us, trying perhaps to drive me away or keep me at bay because as you say, *"I'm not available"* and I'm older than you. (From my point of view though, during our five days in Vegas it's *you* who was not available to me, giving me the cold shoulder almost the entire time we were out of our room, and much of the time within.) I like though that you'd be willing to share an open relationship, our each being free to spend occasional times with other lovers, then returning having sampled another part of life's great offering for those who are free and pluck with abandon the low hanging fruit within their reach.

As I write this your presence Suzanne is *entirely* here and within me. I cannot hold it off much as I try, and I'm weeping because even though a part of you is here in spirit, our naked physical bodies will not be touching this night, I so want them to. I'd grown confident that they would touch even that last day when I suggested that you do as you will in Las Vegas, free from me, and you went out, returning with tickets to two shows for the two of us. Although you were never comfortable with making public displays of affection and gave me the cold shoulder the last two days when we were in public, we did have some discussions in our room. I'll never cease to be grateful that you came to bed naked every night and were ok with me cuddling you regardless of how the day had gone. That's what I miss the most from our five days, your naked body pressed against mine, spooning, our sometimes doing things intimate, undeniably becoming the fullness of lovers, me feeling great love for you, our energies intertwined deliciously, inexorably, a part of me a part of you.

It's thrilling to me to know now that you *are* bisexual in real life. That's a sexual turn on for me, to think of you being intimate with another woman. Why should it matter unless we were so closely connected? Could we still do a threesome under the same roof do you think?

I overnighted at a casino parking lot after Corine dropped me off following our dinner last night. I had no desire to encourage anything more than that. This a.m. I moved to the RV park at Circus Circus to dump tanks, replenish fresh water, and get Loa showered. When I called the RV wash people they initially said they couldn't be here until tomorrow, but then less than three minutes from my call they were here tending to neglected Loa's need to be clean and lovely looking in public, Law of Attraction had moved their truck to me.

You Suzanne, my dearest of dears, lay in Loa's bed and closed your eyes that time we visited her near the South Point Hotel. Your presence in that bed is revitalized, I'll sleep with that memory of you every night again. Thank-you sweetheart for that, thank-you for making my life richer, it's loveliness increasing because you were near. Loa and I are now ready to depart tomorrow for a time of 'dry' camping with no hookups as an economy measure (it cost me $81 for the single night where I am right now) while I wait in the area for my ex to return and get my stuff from her garage.

I wrote the following for Book Twelve this morning. I am alone as I write this in Loa in the parking lot of a casino, early a.m. cold and a strong wind blowing. I went to bed very early last night, not knowing where I would go from here but confident that by this morning I'd have a plan. And I do have a general outline. Law of Attraction will fill in the details and will most likely present many other richer possibilities as the summer days and Loa roll on. I had planned to stay in Las Vegas for 10 or more days for Corine. But I left after buying dinner at Claim Jumper last night and won't be getting back with her again other than possibly virtually. I have no romantic attraction to her at all. I had hoped to, especially after Suzanne looked at Corine's singles photo and said, quickly turning away, *"She's lovely."* (Singles site pictures can be deceiving!)

There is much I want to tell you about my five days in Las Vegas with Suzanne. They were great and terrible days, exactly as has been our virtual relationship. But my guess is that it will take some time to get that story told. It must dribble with distance because I still do not take pain and heartbreak well from her, though I rejoice in the sometimes great times we shared, the few moments in those five days when she tentatively reached out for me, and I thought that maybe she loved me a little.

The outline of a plan fell into place this morning before I arose to make some hot white tea and write. (With Loa's generator running I have electricity for the microwave and air conditioners.) Tomorrow I may move to Mesquite, Nevada and dry camp at another casino parking lot. Although I program my mind with the expectation of attracting wealth, so far my 'walk by faith' has only been "without purse or scrip" and my credit cards are running. From Mesquite I may move on to a state park I know of in the Virgin River Gorge on the Arizona Strip. The Strip is a tiny slice of Arizona that juts into Utah so Arizona too can tax the commercial traffic along the Interstate 15 'trade route' as has been done all over the world since ancient times. The Strip was once lawless, the abode of criminals on the run, such as Butch Cassidy and the Sundance Kid who are rumored to have often visited Utah.

About May 22 I will meet with my ex and see what develops from there. In the meantime I will hike and write and may meet with Marcy for a chat. Corine told me Marcy came back from the Philippines a week ago.

The tentative general outline that came to mind before I arose from Loa's bed this morning will then move me and Loa to Montana for a visit with family. Then maybe Mount Shasta, California, and maybe a stay with the lady I met in Yuma who summers in Oregon, to fill the warm months. But always looming is the registration renewal for Loa in October which will cost about $7,000 state personal property tax. If my purse is not filled by then I will probably put Loa on consignment for sale (or storage for a wealthier day) and may move to Victoria, British Columbia, Canada to rent and live and have my being until a bigger and better plan surfaces for this strange visionary man.

Suzanne, a threesome??? What will actually come of my fantasy I wonder? It will be enormously exciting to find out, I hope you are excited for us as well, and will continue to buy and read my books. At this point, with my e-books not selling well my plan is to not pay Ashley or Carrie anything more. I'll consider the already published books of value mainly because they are my journal. Some day that may be meaningful enough to others to motivate them to buy the books. But if not, I'm happy anyway, Loa has traveled and Michael has written and *lived* his books.

Corine is living on her book sales but it's obvious that she is not living abundantly and several times she dropped hints about needing money, maybe thinking I would supply some for her? She said she'd call DeLeon soon, she hasn't yet. I haven't heard from DeLeon since she copied me into her love letter to our young driver in Costa Rica. (I have no reason to fault DeLeon, I too look for more, and I too see myself as much younger than the government says I am.)

I'm trying to decide whether or not to move to Circus Circus before I start writing about Suzanne. It's early still but my laptop is running out of juice and I'll need to soon start the generator (push a button) to get it charged. It's not that it takes a lot of gas from the regular gas tank, it's the nuisance of having to get the oil changed on the generator every 150 hours that messes with my often expressed desire: *"I just want to write honey!"* Ok, I think I'll take care of business and move before writing about how it went when Michael and Suzanne spent five days together in Las Vegas, Nevada, United States of America. See you soon dear reader...

Chapter 11

---⊰⊱---

Wow, the following message is a strange one, and out of the blue, I wasn't expecting it. But maybe it's best that DeLeon back out of this series now?

DeLeon: (in huge bold red letters) I decree/require there will be no further communication from you. Also cancel the encrypted account.

M: (cc Suzanne) You are a strange one indeed DeLeon, you've done this before, what happened to spark it this time? I took Corine to dinner two nights ago, she said she'd call you re the Magdalenes, she thinks you are one of them. By the way, Corine makes a living from her books, maybe you could too. Heart of a Lion? Goddess of Bling and Eternal Spring? Divine Feminine? I surely don't understand your message in red. *Who have you become really? Who do you WANT to be?*

M: (to Suzanne) As you know, before change happens often there is a time of destruction such as a flower having lived its fullness fading away or even you selling your home so that the new can emerge. I wasn't expecting that from DeLeon, especially since I invested so much time and emotion and money in her. But I think it's for the best that she voluntarily fade away now to allow the new events I spoke to you about to unfold. She was never mine, I was never hers, we're *very* different people. But you and I are like twins from my point of view, alike in many ways. I love you darling. Your Michael

Here's another interesting matter. What a lovely morning as new ground is being prepared for Michael and Loa to travel upon. *Exciting times...*

Anonymous: If I share some information with you, can you give me your word that it will stay between us? Or if you do anything to follow up on it, you will do so without involving me in any way?

M: Yes of course, tell away.

It didn't turn out to be much at all and she asked for confidence, so I'll not trouble you with it, you're not missing anything.

M: Corine, I want to thank you for a pleasant evening in Las Vegas. You are a very interesting woman, I hope you'll keep in touch. I've now moved to Mesquite, Nevada for a time while I await the big thaw to complete in the northwest states where I'll likely spend the summer. Enjoy the day.

I'll likely be here in Mesquite until about May 22nd to take care of the business with my ex when she returns from visiting her son. If she wants to be friends and get together with me occasionally, I'm ok with that. But I don't want us to get stuck in the same rut again. I miss like crazy having a naked woman in my bed each night, sex happening or not. But I hugely value my freedom and the 'walk by faith' way of life I have embarked upon. I consciously realize that as I allow Law of Attraction to play fully in my life, that my mind is being prepared for immortality - I am becoming Adam.

As I drove from Las Vegas today, my mind thought about the past and I came to realize that although I may not let it surface into full awareness, may even deny it, the women in my life have always given me everything I *truly* desired of them deep within. Even Suzanne played that role almost perfectly in Las Vegas by denying us close *physical* connectedness. I don't think we could live amicably under the same roof at this time, though that could change, I love her so. Suzanne encouraged me strongly to get together with my ex again at whatever level and not leave her wanting me if I'm not wanting her without telling her so. As Suzanne put it, *"You're planning to live a thousand years or more so what's fifty years or so to fulfill your responsibilities to your ex, your children, and your grandchildren?"* She's right about the time, but I pointed out to her that I have not abandoned my children and grandchildren like she seemed to think I had. I will most likely visit with them as often as I did before I embarked on my present path. *Now where's that wretched virtual Texas woman again?*

She did tell me that she wants to keep book character Suzanne going, that Suzanne is who she *really* wants to be, but she has a long way to go to retirement and she's responsible. She also said that she wants to be free to stop responding to me. I told her of course she has the right to do that but to let me know and not just wander off into complete silence like many others have done on me. As far as I know, the eternal love story of Michael and "Kira" continues...

Corine: Hi Michael, I too enjoyed our evening and thank you for paying for dinner. If you ever do read my book you will see how much I appreciate it. Who knows I may run into you sometime in the Northwest as I expect to be there for awhile this summer as well. Thanks again.

Suzanne: Sounds like you are in movement toward change. Hopefully you will find encouragement in transitions. If you get the site redesigned then a visit with your son would definitely be a blessing. Then a trip to Panama sounds in order for the summer after your visit with your ex.

M: Thanks for responding and for the counsel. I'm glad to be in touch with you by email again, especially after once again being suddenly and unexpectedly cruelly (in my opinion) dumped by DeLeon for who knows what if any reason. I wish her well and hope she will write her books and go forward instead of sliding inexorably backwards as it seems she may be doing? As I see it, change is the only constant in a universe that *must* expand. The joy and the fun is in not knowing what is coming, only that it will be good - bigger and better than ever before.

I hope your first day back at work was fun and engaging for you and that you survived the excited responses from four dogs to see 'mom' home again. I hope too that mother's day was wonderful for you sweetheart, I know that you were an excellent mom. Thanks so much again for coming to meet me in Las Vegas, you made "Suzanne" come to life, and come delightfully. (Did I ever tell you that I love that woman?) Today I moved Loa to Mesquite, Nevada, we passed through there on the way to Zion National Park. I'm parked in a gravel lot without hookups behind the Virgin River Casino Hotel. I'll most likely stay here for quite some time because there's free wifi drifting to me from the hotel and they gave me the password.

So it looks at present that I'll be located in Utah (we visited Snow Canyon and lunched at the artist's community in Kayenta on the way to Zion) until my ex returns about May 22nd when I'll meet with her to get my stuff out of her garage and have that talk you've been encouraging me to have with her. Following that I will most likely drive to Montana where a son lives, and rent a car there to visit my other children in Canada. Everything's in flux when your home has wheels of course but at present there is a gathering power (several contacts) drawing me to Mount Shasta, California and a hundred mile radius from there, perhaps for the summer? So, much as I'd like to go to Panama, that's most likely not going to happen anytime soon, but might. (Typical me drifting with the stream huh?) Sleep tight my dearest, I love you much, always will, wish we could spoon naked tonight, such delicious fun that was, let's play it again sometime... Your Michael

M: Suzanne, When we were together you told me that you are bisexual for real (and it thrilled me, really and truly it did. I love you so much, I want only fullness of joy for you.) Since you are not (I don't think) a member of the singles site that I recommended, I did a search of Texas for bisexual and lesbian women about your age who you might want to communicate with. I sent the following email to three or four of those possibilities.

I have a dear 58 year old friend who lives near San Antonio, Texas. She is bisexual and looking for a long term relationship with a compatible female. She's a hospice nurse who lives by herself in her own home at the outskirts of a small city near San Antone. She's not on singles but would you be interested in exchanging messages with her if I swapped email addresses for the two of you? Michael Today I received the following:

> Hi Michael, I tried to send you a response from my smartphone this morning, but it appears that it did not go through. So... It is wonderful that you are thinking of your friend. Since I do not give out my e-mail when I first correspond w/someone from this site, I was wondering if we might try something else. Why don't you send your friend a link to my profile? If she is interested then she could contact me. Have a Beautiful Day! Sandy

She's 53 and pretty honey! I'll copy her profile below as best it comes out but here's a link to it if that works for you: (insert) If you can't contact her directly because you are not a member of that singles site, send me a note for her and I will copy and paste and send it to her via the singles site. If you are interested in communicating directly with her, include your email address and permission for her to contact you.

I only wish I could peek at your exchange of emails if that happens but of course that is your business, I don't expect that. But please keep a copy of them all. If you two get together that would make a wonderful story to tell whether I become any more involved than sending you this email or not. ("Bisexual" as opposed to lesbian of course is extra exciting for me because if it was eventually invited by your companion I expect that Suzanne would share and we might get that threesome after all???) Please let me know how this develops. Your Michael thinking of you as always.

Hmmm, did I stretch too far for the story this time? Just thinking of *you* dear reader...

M: (to Sandy) Wonderful, thank-you so much for responding. I just now sent your message and link to Suzanne, she will of course speak for herself. If she can't get a message to you because she is not a member of singles, I offered to relay a note from her to you. I am older but Suzanne and I are good friends, we met when I was living in San Antonio a few months ago. She's a wonderful woman, I love her intensely, but I sense that she is needing and wanting most of all a long term relationship with a woman who is capable of loving as much as she does. As a devoted hospice nurse I know she sends many of her charges on their way to heaven with a smile on their face from the love they feel as she holds their hand breathing their last breath, some of hers mixed intimately with it. And then, with the exception of the pets she loves and treasures, she goes home each night to an empty house! It is my fondest hope that much goodness will come from this for the two of you. I sometimes wish I was a woman myself. You, Divine Feminine all, are so much more capable of loving without bounds or restrictions than are men.

I will immediately forward any message for you that comes from Suzanne. I'm excited for the two of you, I expect Law of Attraction is in play. Enjoy the day.

M: (to DeLeon) DeLeon, I'll never understand your behavior but I respect your choice to be silent again. I just wanted you to know that I wish you the very best and will always be open to respond to any messages you send to me. It is my hope that you will write your books, find joy, and as you say "Go Forward" with your life and being.

M: (to Suzanne) I am super excited with the possibility of you and Sandy getting to know each other, she seems so sweet. Please follow up with this, I'd dearly love to know that you have a quality female lover such as she seems to be to pair up with at least on perhaps alternating weekends, or maybe getting a room halfway between your cities, or flying to each other. You have much to teach one another. Having found her on the spiritual singles site I can say that she is most likely of considerably better quality than those found on most other sites. I think she may be the gift, the solution to what I observed is lacking in your life right now. And knowing you, you'd be for her what she is for you.

I love you darling, you have so much to give. *Exude* that confidence for it is based on reality, you are her equal or better, you'd be for each other a great 'catch'. I wish that I could see the two of you arm in arm, deliriously in love, bumping hips, proudly swinging along the streets of any city or town like I'd hoped it would be for us, but almost certainly never will happen now given how we interacted in Las Vegas. For me, it's as if I am you presented with this golden opportunity for joy. I continue to think we are twin souls, we are so alike in ways which real you denies but my dear Suzanne would agree with. (Did I ever tell you that I'm in love with Suzanne?) I look forward to hearing from you soon regarding Sandy. Your Michael

P.S. today, right after my matchmaking you and Sandy, feeling great love for the two of you, I received a beautiful message from a lady on singles who has spent the last five years traveling and teaching metaphysics in Europe and elsewhere and now is ready to find a physical home on a warm island from which to write books. We seem quite compatible. She lives very close to Mount Shasta where I am feeling drawn after I visit my family. I'll keep you posted on how that develops.

M: (to Suzanne attached photo of Sandy) Talk to me sweetheart, you're so important to me, I want you in my life even if it's only virtually in. If the idea below looks like it will get going I'll write a short book promoting it called something like: *"How to get Published Worldwide in three weeks for less than $300!* What do you think? Maybe we'll get that house in St. Kitts or Costa Rica or wherever and you (and Sandy?) will move there and live happily ever after surrounded by awesome writer and artist residents and guests and your own gardens?? Am I silly getting excited about the thought of you and Sandy together? I mean *real* excited, as if I was you...

Talk to me darling, share your life and thoughts with me, you know me well. I want to be your confidante and sometimes lover - *anytime* you want actually - just beckon, I'll come to you, we'll get a room. I crave what you have, your flower's so sweet and moist, tasty, petals exuding woman fragrance, exceptionally beautiful. Your spoon fits mine deliciously all the night long, your soft naked willing body pressed tight against the throbbing maleness of me, probing your depths it does not matter where, I love it so, I love *you* so. Your Lover Michael

I walked today to a nearby RV camp just yards from a large grocery store. I inquired if snow birds stayed here for the winter and was told that they come in flocks and stay. So, it's a possibility if I get Loa re-registered that I could stay the winter in Mesquite, it's warm enough for RV's. What would make that attractive to me? Well, if my ex became a part-time lover and came to visit me overnight sometimes… But I'm still looking. I'm missing Suzanne but will have no choice but to let her go if that is what she wants. I think it might be, she came to Las Vegas she said to check out the "love" situation. I don't know if that meant her love for me or my love for her or both of us together? But whatever, the way she acted in public it didn't pan out for her. Is that what I really wanted? Did she simply give me what I really want deep inside like most women do eventually and I deny or only allow myself to become aware of it much later?

It was strange her coming to Vegas right from the beginning. I arrived early at the baggage carousel, there were two flights on the screen to arrive before hers. I watched carefully but never saw her and was surprised when the carousel started dumping bags from her flight on the turntable, obviously the passengers were already there. Getting concerned I walked around the people several times, looking for her. Then, because I'd asked her to meet at the information booth on that level if we missed each other, I walked there and back to the carousel a few times, even had her paged, all to no avail. Finally, because I'd left my cell phone in Loa, I called her from a public phone. What a delight when she picked up. I asked if she had missed her flight but she said in her incredibly cheerful and upbeat way: *"I'm in Vegas!"* I could hardly hear her but asked her to go to the information booth where I was. I said just in case: *"I'm the guy in the red shirt."* Long minutes passed as I looked around staring at female faces, but didn't see her, maybe as long as fifteen minutes when it would have taken her only a few seconds to walk from the carousel had she been there.

Then, like it was with DeLeon the first time we met at the Fort Lauderdale Airport, I sensed Suzanne behind me. I turned and there she was walking towards me, wearing a long billowy skirt, pulling a suitcase. We hugged and it was kind of a so so feeling. I know why, because I was for just a brief moment disappointed in her physical appearance and no doubt she picked up that swiftly fleeting thought!!! (So, my fault really, but that's my truth, my memory said she looked different than the woman my physical eyes were seeing, *I was in love with a myth!*)

So where do we go from here? I try hard to keep my vibrations up but earth intrudes and my source of income is exceedingly shriveled and shriveling. I keep picturing myself wealthy but you know how it is... I'm at this moment vulnerable to a woman with money, even to the point of giving up my dreams and giving up writing these books perhaps?? Weak moment huh? I'll get over it, real fast, I can do that, just wanted to bare it all to you, as I always try to do. I'm so human, so mortal, so dependent.

Suzanne has sent only one brief obviously hurried message since she returned home from Las Vegas. She has not even responded about Sandy. Will she ever? I still feel much love for her, yearn for her even, there was so much more I wanted to do with her before she left. But I'm shaken, Suzanne may be gone, *and I can't do anything about it...*

M: (let's call her "Karen" for now, maybe change that if she responds) I like your profile and your photos. Care to swap some words after you've looked over mine?

I guess all of these singles site connections are potential paths I could walk and none of them would be 'wrong'. But it's true, when I am not focused on higher vibrations which brings a sense of completeness within myself, I am focused almost always on getting one or more women into my space. *I really do love women!*

Today as I walked about outside I thought that I no longer need to seek COWA or even a house for the major characters in these books. The reason is that they have all failed me in some way, or I them. I have provided money and things of value to all of them except the first woman who drew me from San Francisco, California to Texas in the beginning with her life after death story. She was an excellent writer but dropped out completely, won't communicate with me anymore, so I don't write about her. In that way all the major counterpoints in my books have already been paid, I don't owe them anything. Even Carrie got money from me. DeLeon and Suzanne received much more, each thousands of dollars in value. I feel free from those former self-imposed commitments, I'll walk my own paths from now on without obligation to others, I am *free!*

Again no word from Suzanne. Is she playing same old same old, or is she gone for good this time after giving me much cold shoulder in Vegas? We went to the Tournament of Kings dinner show at Excalibur. She sat as far away from me as she could possibly get and half turned her back to me the entire show (yes, *really!*) It seemed that she was with the guy sitting next to her on the other side. She never looked at me once to see how I was reacting to events in the show. In fact, I noticed that she was looking at the guy next to her. (An older gentleman.) At one point that man looked at me with a question in his eye. How could I respond? It was obvious that the woman I'd brought did not want to be with me. Of course I was hurt, but I let on that there was no problem until 3:30 a.m. that night when I woke her to discuss it. She tried to toss it off as if I was wrong to expect different behavior from her. But in truth I doubt that she would have ever treated any other friend like that, would not likely treat any other *human* that way, it was extremely rude of her, like me or not.

I took her on a gondola ride at the Venetian. The man with the pole sang to us making it romantic as it was designed to be. He told us that lovers kiss every time they go under one of the many bridges. At the first two bridges I tried to kiss Suzanne and got only a little peck back. It was obvious by the third bridge that she didn't want me to kiss her and I didn't try again. This man too looked at me, wondering why I was with this woman, trying to love her when she obviously didn't want to be with me. It went on like that the entire five days. In the privacy of our hotel room she was aloof but could be reached. Twice in that entire time she tentatively reached out for me and I lapped that up. But she did come to bed naked every night and she never stopped me from touching her even in public, just never reached out herself.

Once in our room when I told her we'd meet again sometime in Paris she turned away and I heard her subvocalize the word *"shit"*. Did Suzanne do everything she could to discourage me from pursuing her in real life because one or both of us knew that would not work for us? I was assured when she was with me that she is in real life bisexual, she said so. So why is she not responding to Sandy? I even sent her a photo of Sandy, and Sandy's pretty... What's with that Texas woman anyway? I guess I'll not write to her again for a long time if she doesn't make the next move. I think I have the strength to do that now that we've had that experience in Las Vegas. I love her, but I feel zero *obligation* towards her. But don't get me wrong, that babe's naked HOT in bed, even with *me*. I think it's just that she can't handle me being so much older? Nuff said, now you know...

Karen: (lady I wrote to on singles) Thank you for writing. I did read your profile, and it strikes me that we are not well-suited. Wishing you the best........ namaste.

M: All the best to you. I'm curious though, what drove you away so swiftly? Perhaps you can help me plug some holes in my profile, maybe misunderstandings? Photos? Your frank comments are invited, after all, we're all family on the spiritual site as I see it.

M: (to the person who sent me the confidential message about Ashley) You are so right about Ashley unfortunately. She seems to have dropped out of sight, maybe with her sister or "in the jungle with no comm" as you put it, not returning communications.

I notice that DeLeon is often logged in at the singles site, probably chatting with someone. She could very well all along have had other men she was more interested in than me and just went along because I provided free travel and adventures and genuine affection. But I fail to understand why she suddenly (again) won't even *write* to me after all that connection, international travel, tender sex, love, tantra healing at my expense, and much giving on my part? One thing I have learned clearly from DeLeon and Suzanne is that becoming lovers doesn't mean a heck of a lot in today's world! I thought it would be much more meaningful, I had surely hoped so. I told Suzanne before I dropped her off at the Las Vegas airport that she had "matured me". She seemed puzzled at that. But it's true, I was hugely naïve and ill-informed about casual sexual relations. I was expecting a different kind of behavior, even tenderness following, but it wasn't so!

Darn, as I wrote that I was once again seeing myself as Suzanne, the movement of my lips in particular. Will I ever get that woman out of my system? She could of course come back with a message bearing some excuse and of course I'd be right back there for her, she knows that. And so do my feelings – tears are threatening at the thought of maybe not losing her. *Why did she have to be that way in Vegas???* We could have had such fun together...

Should I not be content with the present prospects, maybe my ex becoming a lover and I staying close by? But no, the world's a much larger space than that, maybe I have a few more trails to travel before I settle somewhere and switch to writing more traditional books - as will happen if immortality is held off for too long. Isn't it fun though, the not knowing what's about to come and change your life forever, again and again, and again...

Karen: Hello again... Sure - I'll be happy to give you MY feedback, which might not be anyone else's take on it. And I'd be thrilled if you would "critique" my profile too - or tell me how I come across to you, because I get almost no mail whatsoever.

Anyway, I inwardly cringe when I read descriptions of the ideal woman. Yes, a 100% self-confident woman of 5'4" would not let it bother her, or perhaps not even pick up on it, and I believe you didn't mean to discourage shorter women, but you might have to be a woman to know/feel the effect (on a sensitive and non-100% self-confident woman, anyway) of the American society's pressure on women to "measure up" in so many outward ways. So, to be clear, even if I were tall, it would still give me pause to read that you attach numbers, physical measurements, to your ideal partner. And, by the time you admit the universe might have something else in mind, you've already put it out there, so shorter women will already know they don't quite measure up to your ideal. I'm not saying men aren't visual, appearances don't count, or chemistry is a non-issue. But I think, given that the photo is appealing, and the correspondence goes well, one should assess the visual and the "chemical" in person, and keep quiet about unfulfilled ideals - as long as other good qualities abound, and you decide to give it a try.

Also, the cliche about "the little black dress" is so overdone! You might be shocked at how many men write the very same words. How does it come across to a woman? Well, a woman who looks great in her little black dress and knows it, and loves to party and show off, might consider it a plus. A more sensitive, thoughtful type might wonder why such a superficial criterion needs to be spelled out (is it that important?) in a man's profile, when there are far more essential ingredients for loving, lasting relationship. And then you mention your partner "making you look good". I am not here on this gorgeous planet and in this wondrous life to make a man look good. I want to shine from the inside, to be a person who attracts by the qualities of my heart, not by outward appearances. And, even though I am not at all indifferent to appearances, I hope he has similar aspirations. Another thing many men write is "she is attractive". Some are wise enough to write "she is attractive to me", but even at that, I don't know why they put it in their profile. It doesn't provide useful information for the reader, because what we consider attractive is totally subjective!

I guess what I'm saying is that the drive to find "the perfect package", whether on the part of a man or a woman, lacks depth - to my sensibilities. I hope I'm not offending you! Oh...... and why do people post primary photos of sunglasses on a face? The eyes are the windows to the soul. At least you furnished others that show your full face. Namaste

M: Thank-you so very much, that is extremely valuable advice. I'd never have guessed it on my own and I see myself as being quite 'sensitive' for a male. I'm going to make those changes to my profile and get back to you with a 'critique' of yours as best I can as a male who represents only himself. Just keep in mind that I've already found your profile and photos attractive enough to initiate a hopeful conversation. (I was surprised when you outright rejected me - now I know why - again, thanks hugely, you're a dear soul.) P.S. check my profile again in a while, maybe you'll like my makeover.

M: Your photos are beautiful, that's what drew me (typical male) to your profile in the first instance. I think the astrology will not help your cause from the male point of view, too complex, too analytical, I'd get rid of that and tell it the way you see yourself as simply as you can. You say you are "very open minded" and "embracing of all people". You also say you get very few messages. And yet, from my personal point of view you rejected me even though I am apparently one of only a few men who have written you. And you did it without giving me a chance to clear up misunderstandings for what in my opinion are minor faults in my profile Are you writing sincerely? Maybe looking for an ideal man who most likely does not exist? A bit intolerant rather than open minded perhaps? Blocking your own success? Otherwise I like what you wrote and how you wrote it, that's why I contacted you, I don't write to many. In fact, knowing myself and not just the words in a space-limited singles profile, I am almost exactly the man you described as ideal!

Why really did you reject me? Fear of failure? Lack of confidence? Not recognizing or allowing that which is in your vortex to manifest fully when it is presented to you in real life? Is the search more important to you than the finding? I wish you the very best, it has been nice communicating with you even though you lit only an extremely small candle for us, and let it burn out almost instantly. That's how I see it.

Carrie: sorry to be right about something that's not good for you! and, that your test purchase didn't work as it should have… if you want to work with me directly on daily posts to your pages, we can do that… i haven't done more since the end of april as i couldn't communicate with ashley and then thought better of it when i got your "it's not working" email… did you send her the money for me for may yet?

Ouch, Carrie, did you earn the first $200? Not a whole lotta love or loyalty is there? Time to change my entire cast perhaps? Whole new play maybe? Let's see what comes with ex, could she become a major player? I like the way Karen presents physically and she's a good writer. Maybe she will come back and be the one to replace Suzanne, if Suzanne is gone for real?

How would you advise me dear reader? Let Suzanne slide away now after being with us from the beginning? I couldn't prevent that anyway. But you know, I kind of expect Suzanne to be back, but just short sentences, a paragraph or so now and then like it was before. She won't open her heart to me I'm about certain of that, she built an impenetrable wall between us in Las Vegas, or came with it already there.

Oh, I asked Suzanne if she remembered what was in the heavy bag she brought to Loa that first night we met. She does remember but she didn't tell me. We had much unfinished business (from my point of view) when she left. Being together physically was the same relationship pretty much as being virtuals. Except for the great treat at night, cuddling her naked in our room. She never failed to strip bare naked before she want to bed. I loved it, she's soft and willing, a sexual being under the covers. But out of bed, even DeLeon walked around nude glancing at me where Suzanne did not and kept professional Nurse

Responsible on her face, hiding in her 'toy box' I guess. Except, except, when I glanced at her face in public, it was like watching a child looking with delightful innocence at things new, the constant stimulations of Las Vegas. It was delightful to see that, but she never turned to smile or even glance at me, it was as if I wasn't there. She'd walk away and leave me behind if I wasn't careful to keep up. No joyous bumping of hips there at all, it was not fun being with Suzanne's 'mom' on the streets and in the casinos of Las Vegas.

Why couldn't I reach her? I'd thought it would be such fun. I guess it's best that we didn't go all the way to Paris. What a disaster our time in Vegas turned out to be when we weren't in our private room. I asked her about her once writing to me *"I love you"*. And even that she turned into a comment about there being "different kinds" of love. Secretly I wonder if she really does love me but was reacting to my moment of disappointment in her physical appearance when I first turned and saw her at the Las Vegas airport? She wasn't as I had remembered at all, did she put on a lot of weight? Was she letting me know that it was ok for us to not be together physically? Well, ok, I can always dream that she loves me can't I? I continue to believe that the universe is unfolding as it should.

Chapter 12

—⋅◈⋅—

Karen: Dear Michael, Thank for your critique! I think I'll insert my responses below.

You may well be correct about mentioning astrology in my profile. There are a few but not many men who are interested in this type of thing. Typically they don't know or don't want to share their horoscope, and wonder what is wrong with me that I am so "superstitious". (granted, I am mainly referring to other singles sites). Recently a man told me he regards astrology as entertainment, but nothing more. I'm beginning to realize one should not make assumptions about what that means...

You commented on my writing that I am "very open minded" and "embracing of all people". I meant this in a global way. for example I have all my life gravitated towards people of other nationalities, cultures, belief systems. I treasure diversity and am intensely interested in differences. I wasn't thinking of anything you wrote as a "fault", but as something indicative of different values. Everyone has a right to value what they value, and it's not for me to "correct" them. but, when asked... Of course I am writing sincerely. I'm not interested in wasting time!

Maybe looking for an ideal man who most likely does not exist?

I don't believe so.

A bit intolerant rather than open minded perhaps?

I don't see myself that way.

Blocking your own success?

Perhaps...... like with the mention of astrology and personality profiling, but that's why I asked you to critique my profile. I don't want to block success. I very much want to be in a relationship.

Why really did you reject me? Fear of failure?

No. I don't fear failure, at least not in this area.

Lack of confidence?

I do have a certain lack of confidence, and when attributes I don't possess are spelled out as desired (or even required), the wind goes out of my sails, even though I realize other qualities could overshadow the missing 5 inches or whatever. By the way, many men do this: spell out precisely how the woman should appear (sometimes down to shaven legs), but this is the first time I have commented about it. I recognized from your writing that you are intelligent and interesting, and given that I think it's rude not to respond (although I sometimes don't), I did what I did.

Not recognizing or allowing that which is in your vortex to manifest fully when it is presented to you in real life? is the search more important to you than the finding?

Not at all! I find it very frustrating!

Back to the question of why I 'rejected' you, there is something else. It's much more personal, but I'll share it, briefly, even though it doesn't fall into the category of how you might improve your profile. This is really just about me: two years ago I met (on a singles site) a man I thought to be absolutely ideal. He appeared to share many of the sterling qualities of my former husband (of 30 years), with the addition of qualities I had longed for in my marriage. Like you, I am young in mind and body, and certainly far from conventional and tradition-bound... to a fault, it now seems. I allowed myself to be swept off my feet, and I moved across the country after 8 months to join him in California. When he had me "hooked", he began to show his true colors. He is a psychopath, and it was one of those stories women are warned about with regard to online dating. My therapist (who, by the way, has known him for decades, through the spiritual community) says he has narcissistic personality disorder (very serious - not just a matter of spending time admiring ones reflection in the water, or gazing in a mirror.)

I had never even heard of this illness. I don't want to go into lots of detail, but just to say that I have had much counseling, psychotherapy, and other forms of therapy, recently. My sister is trained as a psychotherapist, although she does not work in the field, so she has been a tremendous help. Anyway, "everyone", my terrified family not the least, has worked hard to convince me that I was not careful enough, I did not put sensible boundaries in place (in the beginning), I did not require him to earn my trust etc. etc. My nature is very trusting, and perhaps a bit naive. I am also unusually spontaneous, fun-loving, adventuresome, enthusiastic, idealistic, and nearly always cheerful. "the perfect victim", he thought...... So I have to take this lesson seriously and not jump into my next relationship before I really know - and thoroughly trust - the other person. It has nothing to do with stuffiness, nor does it reflect one way or the other on the man in question. It is simply what I must do to take care of myself. I am not stuffy - nor am I distrustful. The problem is rather the opposite. That relationship ended early last Oct.

I wish you the very best, it has been nice communicating with you even though you lit only an extremely small candle for us, and let it burn out almost instantly.

I'm sorry that you look at it that way. I think what happened was okay, acceptable. I thought it was impressive that you wanted to know why, and, when I told you, you took it to heart. "A man without a huge ego... how refreshing", I told myself. That's how i see it.

Wow, that lady can write! I think this may be the one to replace Suzanne if she opts out, or even if she doesn't?

M: Thank-you so much for sharing that with me Karen, I appreciate your candor very much. I won't say "I'm sorry" about your experience because it wouldn't do any good, and also because as we go through life we often learn valuable lessons from happenings such as you describe. We needn't dwell on them though, each moment is the beginning of a new life, we are always free to choose happiness going forward. As Esther Hicks/Abraham would say "take a fresh start now" or something like that.

I'm a very prolific writer, having written and published nine visionary metaphysical fiction books in the last six months. I'm pleased to note that you are a prolific writer too. Not many people can or would string together as many meaningful words as you did in the message I am responding to. As a writer myself I admire that. Have you written books, or are thinking about doing so? I enjoy what you write. It is my hope that you will continue to see where this might go for us if only virtually from a distance for now. As I see it, neither of us has much if anything of consequence to lose by being pen pal friends, and possibly a whole lot to eventually gain? By the way, how often do you shave your legs? (just kidding of course) Feel free to respond to my email address if you prefer, or here is fine.

Karen: Wow... I'm so pleased that you didn't slam the door shut! I'm really tired, and have a 2 hour balance test (possible inner ear damage) tomorrow morning early, so I'm going to make more insertions between the lines.

I appreciate your healthy attitude.

That is exactly right: I now have the opp. to learn a major lesson about taking care of myself, and I discovered that I have an amazing amount of compassion, patience, and understanding for people with such impairments as personality disorders. I only ended the relationship because I was in danger. Otherwise I would have, misguidedly, continued to try to help/fix him. But I found the strength to get out, which was necessary! He has all manner of spiritual/healing certifications. He has devoted himself to "self-improvement" for decades, and only worked, free-lance, when he needed to. I now understand he did this because such workshops, courses, and retreats are good places to find idealistic and trusting female souls to prey upon.

Have you written books, or are thinking about doing so?

I am thinking of doing so. I just need to make friends with my newish computer.

As I see it, neither of us has much if anything of consequence to lose by being pen pal friends, and possibly a whole lot to eventually gain.

I agree.

By the way, how often do you shave your legs? (just kidding of course)

Actually, never - as if I ever did. Thanks for asking. I'll write more, but maybe not until Saturday. I have a therapy appointment tomorrow afternoon, after the balance test ordeal, and then I want to go Sufi chanting in the evening, if energy allows. Goodnight.

M: Sleep well.

I may be too complex for her, too easily flowing between fantasy and reality, presenting myself often as if they were the same. She's obviously a woman who needs to be treated with great sensitivity. But she puts herself out there on the singles scene and I *love* this conversation. She's a writer, and she wants to be pen pals. And you know, she's my age but in the photos she looks great. That's very important to keep my interest because the goal will be to meet her eventually even as we write books together from a distance, as I did with that woman from Texas. (What's that Texas woman's name again?) I could go for this Karen.

Well, think I'll go to bed early, it's cool enough. I had the air cons and Loa's generator working hard all day in the 100 plus degree temps today. I actually like it here. What will come of this new woman in my virtual life I wonder? I was getting close to negotiating with my ex to rent a room in the house I once owned, *and sell Loa!* Maybe not???

Do you want more books to read? Karen just might breathe some fresh air into that possibility. I was expecting something of that sort to come along, it always does doesn't it? And I was needing a new crew onstage after DeLeon, maybe Ashley, apparently Carrie, and perhaps even my sweetheart Suzanne failed me. (Yeah, that's her name....)

Oh, I thought a lot today about my stand where I felt I could not ask a woman to live in Loa unless we were traveling most days. She couldn't even watch TV while I was writing, it would trouble me. But you know if that other woman also spent as much time on a computer as I do it just might work out. And Karen says she's a gypsy and wants to write books. Hmmm, what's Law of Attraction up to now? It's possible that Karen and I could 'click' when we meet. Maybe she's the one who will travel with me this summer after I visit family? Anyway, nightie night if it's nightie where you are when you read this.

Karen: Good morning! Just re-read your profile and wanted to tell you I love the notion of frolicking in physicality - and it's such a tasty expression. Now I'm off to find my balance, hopefully (actually I'm fine, but have recently had some dizziness and want to have my inner ear checked).

M: I reread my profile too and made a few more changes to reflect your suggestions. E.g. "pretty woman" becomes "loving woman". And I reread yours. Once again I am struck by the pretty face and words that resonate including our age, likes, desires, and ideals. There are always rough spots of course but from the virtual image I have of you, I think we'd be quite compatible if we ever got our physical bodies into close proximity. Experience shows me though that meeting physically usually shatters ideal virtual images. It's fun discovering however what can be rebuilt from that shattering if both parties are amenable to going forward.

Was that Canada photo of you taken on Vancouver Island? I would like to live in Victoria again as long as I can on occasion get away in the winter to warmer dryer climes. I love that city, and especially nearby Sidney on the Sea. I'd have to sell my motor home to do that but it makes sense because I've found that adventures for my books *come* to me now whether or not I drive physical miles.

As you may have gathered, I am deeply impressed by the teachings of the group of non-physical entities collectively known in our time as "Abraham". Abraham is expressed verbally by Esther Hicks whose home in San Antonio I have been inside by invitation. (No big deal, there were a lot of others invited for beer and barbie too.) I am not an Abraham groupie and don't follow Esther around the country to attend her frequent workshops. In fact I believe my own non-physical part is of that group. Abraham is my muse my inspiration when writing. It's from Abraham that the expression *"frolicking in physicality"* comes. The teaching is that we in physicality are parts of our non-physical entities (as I put it in my books, we ARE the ancient gods.) We are sent into time primarily to have FUN and along the way create new and unique bigger and better desires. That's what the universe which must ever expand feeds upon, desire. But maybe you know all that, it's just not mentioned in your profile that you are acquainted with Abraham.

I hope your events today go well. You are a good writer, I note in particular the phrase *"it's such a tasty expression."* You probably noticed in my profile that I tend to get much too familiar, much too bold, much too quickly. But let me say (with that caution in mind) that I often think I could never invite a woman to live in a motor home unless we were constantly traveling because when I'm writing I wouldn't even want a TV going near me. However, if that woman was also spending about as much time as I do on a computer, writing her own books or whatever, that situation could possibly work?? Anyway, I'm near Las Vegas, Nevada for business and visiting with friends for a couple of weeks. Just thought you might be interested... Enjoy the day Karen.

Here's a note from a woman I'd never heard from before. She seems to have it all figured out for us, except that little part where I think for myself. I thought you might find it funny.

Honey Bunny: Your wait is over. I am here and will meet you on the astral plain. I did read your profile, and I do wish mine could be as good as your. The movies, and music are together. The desires are together. Even the travel will be together. So my little honey bunny when you look at my profile allow your soul to read and see who I am. Look back in time, and you will find me. If you can look forward in time, you will find me. As I sit and write this note to you, I am building the golden thread to you. Take my hand and I will travel with you to many, many galaxies. We will become able to hear the others thoughts. To be able to talk to one another without voice, mind to mind. A light touch will set all of you spinning. Park the RV in the driveway, put your feet up and stay awhile.

May 16th. Ok, here's the message I've been expecting. We now have to say good-bye to Suzanne, it's her choice. It doesn't seem to matter how much you love and spend money and time on and share intimacy with another, they may suddenly dump you for any or no excuse at all. Once again though, in this final matter Suzanne's timing is perfect!

Suzanne: You have no right to match make for me. You seem to function in order to generate stories that you can write. Now as DeLeon, I want to be written out if your books, out of your life.

And thus closes "The Suzanne Chapters" that turned into twelve whole books that she wanted to write with me. It was delightful. I'll miss her like crazy, probably always love her, most likely will never write her again unless she writes first. Strangely I feel little emotion right now. Maybe because I think she'll be back once Suzanne gets relief from Nurse Responsible, and maybe because I knew that writing was already on the wall and prepared for it. And maybe because it was time for a change in the direction this series was taking, and new characters have already poured onto the stage?

Yes, of course my darling Suzanne (if you ever read this) I'm a writer, you knew that. I (and Law of Attraction) DO function "in order to generate stories that I can write". But my feelings for you (and my actions all along) were always loving and always with the purpose of trying to help you live life more fully. I do believe that "Suzanne" wants to escape from the toy box and really and truly live life! To justify leaving me after all these months, you provide only an excuse for an excuse - me referring you to Sandy. The two of you, SUZANNE and

Sandy might have had great fun and enduring love for each other, she seems so sweet and was waiting your response.

But I'm wondering now if becoming Suzanne in real life doesn't fit in with your giving up, your wanting to die like all your patients? Real life you wants to cast away this incarnation and come back refreshed in another body. I saw that dark shadow in your physical appearance, and you did not correct me when I mentioned it. It's true, you want to die, it's written all over you. Should I die too so we can come back perfect for each other?

But you said if you came back in another body you "might" come back as one of my sister wives. Maybe that's why I love you so much regardless of how you treat me. Maybe you'll come back as pure Suzanne? How will we recognize each other if you do? Will your heart leap when you read my books? Will your given name be Suzanne? Will you seek me out or must I find you, the ancient soul I'm so in love with? Much as I love you sweetheart, I can't say that I could live long with solemn Nurse Responsible either, particularly when MY HEART AND SOUL IS SUZANNE! Come back to me my love, come in this incarnation or another, just COME. We have unfinished business including two things I asked of you in our room in Las Vegas the day before you left, and you didn't fulfill. Will you remember those two things, and fulfill when the time is right? Will that be our sign that it's you? Be well my true love, be well…

This may be what I needed - the slate of old characters has taken their final bow, the wings are filled now with a new and promising cast. Bigger and better books await the filling of pages yet kept blank because on earth it's fun to not remember.

My ex - (better give her a name, but she denied permission to write about her so I won't quote her emails, there would be two or three books right there. Let's call her "Ex".) I meet with her soon at her home (formerly mine.) We're friendly, take care of business, she wants to keep me in her life to cuddle etc. sex or not. Do we become casual part-time cuddlers and spooners, maybe 'accidentally' lovers on occasion? Does she travel with me? Am I tempted to move back in with her and give up writing these books? (YES, I will be for sure, real life!)

Karen: Dear Michael, So nice to hear from you so soon again. I hope you don't mind my responding, briefly, in the same form as before. I don't always do this! Assuming it's okay, for now anyway... (She writes in caps between my lines.)

I reread my profile too and made a few more changes to reflect your suggestions. E.g. "pretty woman" becomes "loving woman".

That was wise, in my opinion. the thing is a woman you find pretty might not find herself pretty. Substituting "lovely (as opposed to "loving") might still convey your meaning w/o triggering insecure thoughts in your reader. "Lovely" is so much more all-encompassing and less fraught with high expectations than the word "pretty".

Was that Canada photo of you taken on Vancouver Island?

Yes, somewhere not far from Courtenay. I have only gotten a glimpse of Victoria, but found it so enticing! It's great that you need not drive to access the adventures you write about. I have heard of Abraham, but not read anything. For most of my adult life I have been a student of Rudolf Steiner.

At the ENT's office, I was tested, quite thoroughly, by an audiologist who found that I have no functioning vestibular system at all! Needless to say, I am in shock. I'll have to spend some time reading up on this, online. The audiologist was likewise shocked. She said I am "extremely high functioning" for someone with this impairment. I frankly don't get it. I do have bouts of dizzinezz - some that last a few days - but this is rare. If my vestibular system doesn't work, and I therefore somehow compensate and get along well most of the time, why the occasional dizziness?

You are a good writer, I note in particular the phrase "it's such a tasty expression."

All I know is that I love, love, love to write, and I can often express myself better this way than by speaking... seems strange.

You probably noticed in my singles site profile that I tend to get much too familiar, much too bold, much too quickly.

Same here - assuming I feel comfortable, but I'm trying to change that, although I can already see I'm not too "successful"

But let me say (with that caution in mind) that I often think I could never invite a woman to live in a motor home.

That's right; you never could - at least not me. I "never" watch TV, but I can be quite a chatterbox. As far as my own writing is concerned, I'm with you on the need for quiet, but I have the additional need for my many books, notes, and musical instruments to be close at hand, and I need physical space. I teach music - or have taught - partly through movement, and I need space to be able to choreograph the movement.

However, if that woman was also spending about as much time as I do on a computer, writing her own books or whatever, that situation could possibly work?? Anyway, I'm near Las Vegas, Nevada for business and visiting with friends for a couple of weeks. Just thought you might be interested…

OH YES… I AM.

M: You've kind of got me off balance here (yep intentional) with your statement in response to mine that you might be interested in knowing about my immediate plans. Delightfully 'off balance' because I'm right there with you, wanting to give us a try if that's what you intended to convey. Made even bolder by your confession that you too get too bold "too fast" let me ask you what timing you need? Where are you now? If you are planning a move, when *must* it take place? Would we have time before that deadline to travel together in Loa for a few weeks so I can listen to you chatter and we can get to know if we would likely be LTR compatibles? Could we discuss during those weeks possibly moving to Victoria together, maybe renting a house or an apartment for a while so you can spread your wings much wider than you ever could in a motorhome? I too am more comfortable writing than speaking, except with close family of course; I love that you love writing.

By the way, my 2014 33 foot motorhome has four TV's (and a fireplace) but I never watch them either, except for a couple of DVD's with company a while ago. Talk to me, tell me about your pending move and your plans for the summer. (I'd like to insert a term of endearment such as "honey" here but should probably ask your permission before getting so familiar so fast?)

Karen: Hello, I just woke up from a nap. That's how knocked out of shape I am about having no vestibular system. It feels as if someone just told me I don't have a brain. I'm thinking: "Yikes, how will I manage?" Then: "I'll manage just like I always have". Then: "But maybe I lost my vestibular system recently, like yesterday…."

What I meant was this: When will you have accomplished all your traveling/visiting and be at liberty to allow the Law of Attraction to work its magic? I didn't mean right now, although it must have come across that way. Just 3 days ago I sat down with my neuro feedback therapist and filled my calendar, up to June 13th, w/ as many appointments as could be crammed in. And there are loose ends galore, beyond that. I hardly know how I'll be ready to move soon, but I must - assuming escrow closes as planned (on the 13th). Actually, I am then going to house/dog-sit for 10 days, for friends in the neighborhood. So my departure date is June 24th, although most things will have to be done by June 13th. Then I'll head up to the Seattle area, unless I have to go to eastern Washington first. I won't get into that: I'm hoping to avoid it. Plans beyond this are not concrete. I can stay w/ my sister in August, and possibly at my daughter's cabin on Whidbey Island before that (she and her husband have a hobbit condo in Seattle). It probably would not feel right to take off as soon as I arrive, as I haven't seen some of my relatives for 4 years. But I do think it bodes well that we will both be in the Pacific NW! Something will be workable, if we want it! You may call me whatever you like, WHEN you decide you like me in my frolicsome physicality. I think it can take time, even though we are probably both quite intuitive.

I recently spent weeks with someone from singles who surprised me by being entirely unlike what I had expected - and likewise for him. It wasn't terrible, but we were both disappointed at how our temperaments clashed. And, try as we did, we weren't able to create the desired harmony. This was another lesson for me, as a woman (hence vulnerable), to be a little more cautious. BUT, with all that said, let me add that I really look forward to meeting! And I'm so glad you took your sunglasses off. Ciao, Karen

M: Ok, no rush then. I did grasp from your words that you might have some deadline you were up against and should the two of us hit if off you could possibly move to Victoria with me instead of somewhere else? Just hopeful/wishful thinking I guess, thanks for explaining. (Such things do occasionally happen with Law of Attraction, *everything* works with perfect timing.) Let's keep swapping messages then while we each clear some space on our calendars and keep our minds open to the written word and whatever else Law of Attraction might bring into our lives in the meantime.

Karen: Dear Michael, Thanks for sending the Abraham material. I am familiar with these ideas, but only knew them as "The Law of Attraction". I had a very enlightening and interesting session this afternoon with my neuro therapist (not sure what his official title is), and now I'm sipping on a strawberry/coconut milk/avocado smoothie. Life is good! I would love to hear more about you, when you have the urge to write. I wanted to have a 3rd child after my 2 daughters, but what came my way was the musical instrument import business I started and ran for 19 years. That was clearly my 3rd child, and I never gave the matter another thought.

I attended music schools in the east, played professionally in and around NYC and then got a symphony job in Norway - "on my way to India". I never made it to India. After 4 years with the orchestra, I got pregnant, got married, had my first child, and at the end of that orchestra season decided to be a stay-at-home mom. This lasted through our year in New Zealand, 5 years later, and then we moved to California where we had a mini farm, and I started my business. I think I told you I was married for 30 years. My ex and I parted ways in Germany, 12 years ago.

About my wanderings, I was foot loose in my youth, but don't have quite the same energy level now - naturally. I do, however, have a long list of places I still want to experience, among them Lake Atitlan, where there is a Waldorf school in San Marcos... very inspiring that the people involved have managed to put the school together and attract enough donations that they can offer scholarships to indigenous children. The main thing for me would be to have a center to return to, a place that serves as "home". Oh, it's getting late, and I have to call a couple of people, so I'll bid you good night. Sleep well.

M: I was hoping to hear from you tonight. It's delightful to correspond with someone who writes back soon instead of like some who wait several days and you think they've gone off into the frosty silent night that some seem to relish after they've gotten another's hopes up. Your prompt and frequent response makes me think you are making me a priority. I like that a whole lot, I'm virtually fond of the image of you in such a short time already.

Rhonda Byrne *("The Secret")* got her information while on a cruise with Esther Hicks. Her "Law of Attraction" is of Abraham, though of course it's much older than Rhonda, beginning of time actually, and Abraham says *"we've looked but we cannot find a beginning."* Seems like we ("the ancient gods") created that law to act like the invisible "operating system" in our computers. Work it right while in physicality and LOA must and will *always* deliver! That smoothie sounds delicious. Share?

I too feel the need for a permanent address, this RVing is not all it's cracked up to be when you're on your own and you've already 'done' the fifty states and all of Canada except the Maritimes. I'm thinking Victoria for a number of reasons including I simply like it there. Hope to 'talk' with you tomorrow Karen. Sure you won't share that frostie?

May 17. I walked sidewalks early this a.m. instead of desert and hills and was impressed at how beautiful this community really is. I even inquired at a place that sells condos and the prices are encouraging. So, thoughts of reconciling with my ex are flowing. (I don't even know for sure if the judge has signed the final papers yet or not, so maybe we're still married?) We'd have to move I think but could downsize our beautiful home and perhaps live in a condo for a few years while we saved to build another 'retirement' home. My goal is not to be a gypsy and to write these books. My ultimate goal (my fantasy) is to become immortal and populate planets with seven beautiful sister wives (each of us 'married' to each other, each equal.) I could still await that happening reconciled with my ex. Who knows, maybe she would go along with it, help co-create that eternal family, and be one of them?

Suzanne told me emphatically while we were together in Vegas that I am "not available". One of her pieces of advice to me was that if I am going to live a thousand years and more as I expect to, why not spend fifty of those years closely aligned with wife and family in the traditional manner? Indeed, why not? Suzanne continues to give beyond compare. She is a true friend though at present it doesn't seem like she is. I'll always love Suzanne.

I've learned that the women you think might be your ideal, who even share their bodies with you, are very capable of then turning and rending. I understand Suzanne (in some ways I AM Suzanne) but why did DeLeon so suddenly go? Anyway, it was all for the best, it was time for her to leave the story. Will Suzanne ever come back? Will I reconcile with my ex and stop tilting? Sometimes I wish I knew. But, like telling someone how a movie ends before they've seen it, that would spoil the story. We'll discover what happens together. Ex is looking real good right now!

Chapter 13

———◆◆◆———

M: (to "Ex") I'm still in Mesquite. I'm expecting to meet with some people to talk about promoting my books and don't know when that will happen. But if it's not going to be at the same time, you are welcome to drop in for a chat when you have time to come this way. Let me know.

When an idea comes to me I usually do something about it just in case it's setting the scene for one of Law of Attraction's magnificent schemes. So, to cover another possible base just in case, I sent the following message.

M: (to Carrie) I've decided to get back into business mode Carrie so I'm taking another look at what I'll be doing for marketing my books, it's not working at present. I know the books are unique and experimental but they should still be selling considering the money I've been putting into promoting them, and they aren't. So until I work that out and get a plan that looks more promising I'll be keeping my wallet zipped. Thanks for the offer to continue though.

Now that the frost is about gone in USA and Canada I've started traveling with Loa. I'll likely keep that happening until September or October when it's prudent to scurry back to warmer climes. If your offer to visit you will still be valid at that time, I might consider parking Loa somewhere and flying to your city for a few weeks. If I really like it there, who knows, maybe I'll find a place to rent and stay the USA winter months. Comments?

M: (to Carrie) P.S. I haven't decided yet regarding Ashley and haven't told her about the review I am doing. So please keep to yourself the information I just sent, thanks. Michael

Carrie: i fully understand and fully support your decision to consider other marketing means... have you been in touch with the alternative source that the other author turned you onto? if you would, at some point in the future, like my help let me know and we can discuss that... i do wish you great success in getting the books to fly off the virtual shelves... have you officially ended your relationship with ashley?

regarding coming here, that option will be open for as long as i am here and have the space for guests... so you will be welcome... just know that as we get closer to october/november we also get closer to the heaviest rains... it's often still nice in the mornings and doesn't rain everyday, all day, but those two months along with may are typically the heaviest rains... though this month has been less wet than other mays, so who knows... i have no idea where this will be by then, but i have connected with a man with whom i may want to explore a serious relationship...it's very new... only a few weeks, but there seems to be a connection, meeting of the minds & spirit and an attraction i've yet to experience with anyone else so far... he lives in Hawaii but would not move here full time, as he owns a palm planation there... for the first time, i am opening to the possibility of returning to the US... though Hawaii is one of the very few places i would consider... by the time you would plan to come, my guess is all will be revealed about this connection... and who knows, by then it may be long gone... or i may be... but, i will keep you in my loop as things become clear to me/us...

i had a reading by a clairvoyant in march who told me i would be leaving here... he said i would be going south, though Hawaii of course is far north of here... he said i would be leaving for some sort of protection, though he couldn't see what i needed protection against... i plan to do another reading with him soon, so maybe will be given more insight... i have worked out a plan with my landlords that can include me living here for at least another year... so at this point, anything's possible and everything is up in the air at the same time...

Carrie: ok...i will not discuss anything with her... but, did you send her the 200. for me for may?

M: Carrie that sounds potentially wonderful for you, you must be quite excited about that possibility. Living in the Hawaiian Islands, and on your own plantation at that, doesn't sound too shabby to me. I wish you the very best with it. Re the clairvoyant I'm quite sceptical about such "readings" from personal experience. The last clairvoyant I went to see decades ago asked me why I was coming to him because I'm the same as him! Readings seldom if ever come true unless you throw yourself into it and *expect* it to happen. Nobody can predict your individual future except yourself - you are creator, you make your life up as you go along. Please do keep me in your loop and of course if there are things about that developing relationship that you'd like to run by a male for another point of view, I'm here for you, you know I'll tell it the way I see it.

I'm glad the pressure is off you to be forced to move from your home anytime soon. That must be a huge relief. I could tell you were horrendously concerned about your future and low on cash in addition to having had a not so good recent encounter. You've got to look after yourself honey, just always keep in mind that each moment is the beginning of *"a fresh new start"* as Abraham would put it. No, I did not pay Ashley a second $200 for you.

Carrie: i am containing my enthusiasm... having jumped into other possibilities too soon in the past... it would be a delight to live in Hawaii... he lives close to the beach. he's been there for 24 years and has been growing palm trees for all of that time... he comes from northern california where his mom still lives on the family homestead... she's 91, so looks as if he's got good genes, as i do...

i have a close connection with the man who did my reading... after having read his book, done the reading and also listened to about 15 hours of a seminar he did... i am also going to edit his next book... he is a psychologist of 20 years who had a spiritual awakening in 1989 that gave him his spiritual gifts... his reading of the people in my life was right on, so i do have a verified experience of his accuracy in relationship to some of the men in my past... there are some features of the reading that have a future time line, however, i am not putting any weight on them... it's a wait and see proposition for me... and one that will give me more info as to the validity of all i was told... he is able to read soul contracts, not predict the future... the man from Hawaii was not part of the reading as i had it done in march... i have invited two other men in the last year here and have learned some important lessons about doing that... part of which is why i told you i wouldn't have you in my home without a audio/visual connection, which of course you have refused... he and i have talked and will video soon and certainly there will be lots of those connections before i do invite him, if i do... meantime, i do know he is legit, has a very successful business and beautiful home in Hawaii and is showing up to be very conscious, forthcoming, communicative and vulnerable... BUT... as i said, it's relatively new and time will tell... i may send some of his info to you.

yes, it was a huge relief for me but cash is still an issue, but one that is not affecting me emotionally any longer... at least not right now... as i am believing it will all work out perfectly and that there is an abundance of money and resources flowing into my life all the time now... *You've got to look after yourself honey, just always keep in mind that each moment is the beginning of "a fresh new start" as Abraham would put it.* - yes, this is absolutely true!

M: I should have known that you'd be right on top of every concern I could think of! Carrie you are so THERE!!! You may not agree but I think you dug yourself into a rut a while back. But you are so not there anymore, you are soaring and creating a wonderful life for yourself. It's not just the incredible prospects you have, it's the change in *yourself* you are revealing that is so delightful.

I like your man, he seems sincere and genuine. My only counsel to you is DO NOT CONTAIN YOUR ENTHUSIASM! Let it flow, be overfilled with the joy of *living* every moment of every day - exult in it, be happy, happy, happy. Let others see your light, it will brighten their day. An excess of caution can only breed fears, an excess of happiness can only breed joy. EXPECT the best and that's exactly what you'll get. *You got your groove back girl, congratulations...* I think pretty much everything that comes into your life now will be something you should pay at least a bit of attention to just in case it's the tip of one of Law of Attraction's magnificent schemes to bless and make deliriously happy one Carrie Fisher whose disk is now untethered and flying high. I'm very happy for you Carrie.

Carrie: thanks! the only thing i meant when i said i was curbing my enthusiasm had to do with not getting ahead of myself with him... been there, done that and it wasn't good... twice.. taking it slowly on an emotional level, BUT i am very much enjoying the connection and leaning in all the way in terms of transparency, authenticity and vulnerability in communication and revealing who i am and who i want to partner with... so far, we've met each other everywhere we've each wanted to go, he's kept his word, and he's been more communicative than any other man i've met so far... he's a delight to communicate with on every level... no walls, withholds or limitations... and we keep going deeper with each other... the last thing we need to do now is have a real time visual connection and that will give both of us a taste of our chemistry and show us if it's what we are both hoping for...

he has out of town company right now, so when they are gone, we will have that last piece... then i'll know if either him coming here or me going there is an upcoming step or if we are destined to be friends... we both know until we are actually in each other's presence we won't know the full reality... but i know, from my past experiences, that the audio/ visual connection will tell us a great deal... either way, it's ok...and i trust it...

M: You're for sure doing all the right things Carrie, and doing it smart, you would have overwhelmed me with your wisdom. Personally, I tend to get in waaay too deep way too soon and I think it scares women away. (Maybe that's what deep inside I really want?) But unlike you, I don't seem to learn, can't keep myself from keyboard gushing as if my life depended on it, I live to write.

By way of update, DeLeon, the one I called "DeLeon" went silent not long after our trip to Costa Rica. I think that's just fine actually, she tended to get cranky even in front of Ashley in Costa Rica, I didn't need that. We weren't really close except in moments. It seemed like I had "a job" to do there for my tribe, I think I did it well. But the most disturbing to me and I'm still reeling from it is Suzanne writing a couple of days ago that she wants not only to stop being book character Suzanne but to be "out of my life". Her expressed excuse, after those almost daily (albeit up and down) virtual and a couple of physical encounters over six months, was that I "had no right" to try to match make her with another woman - they're both bisexual. No excuse really from my point of view, I was as usual just trying to help her get out of the "toy box" where she hides and be in real life more like the Suzanne she tells me she wants to become. But out of her life is what she wrote, I must respect that.

She may be back, I hope, I'll always be emotionally entangled with her, like it or not on either or both parts. It's because of Suzanne that I became a fiction writer and wrote twelve books in the "endless" series of e-books I am writing. It may now not be so endless, I've still got my muse, but I've lost my Inspiration. I was deeply in love with Suzanne (still am) but recently spending five days with her real life component in Las Vegas taught me much about professional 'Nurse Responsible' who oversees and overwhelms Suzanne. My precious virtual illusion was shattered by that too close encounter with this world's reality, perhaps shattered forever, pieces having flown off even beyond the restaurant at the end of the universe.

I gave those two women my all, spent a whole lot of time, an ocean of emotion, and much money on and for them. But I've learned from that experience that such things as I gave have little or nothing to do with love and loyalty. I'm not disenchanted or lost: I'm disappointed, I'm saddened, I'm matured. So there's an entirely new cast needed if the series is to continue. And, true to the way Law of Attraction often plays out, now my ex is beckoning me back to a familiar, stable, and comfortable lifestyle. We were together for a couple of hours recently in the former marital home and it seemed as if nothing at all had changed. We hugged and cuddled and intimacy was avoided only because I wouldn't go there. If I heed her beckoning it will most likely be the end of my wild days traveling with Loa. *It's tempting me hugely Carrie!*

I could write traditional 'how to' or whatever books that may actually sell, and I'd go down in history as ordinary, unknown except to my family and a very few others, and nameless. (Unless I become immortal for real because whatever paths I choose to follow from the plethora LOA always announces, I will continue to imagine that I am becoming Adam, and *expect* it to be so.) What do you think about that beckoning from my ex? Would going back with her be retrograde, giving up on my dreams and ideals? Or could it work because I'd continue to imagine what I *really* want and thus create it?

I've witnessed miracle after miracle keeping me and my books alive for six months. Maybe it's best that the series now concludes without a conclusion. In any event, I firmly believe that the universe continues to unfold as it should. I am now much better trained should I be called upon to participate in future events critical to the preparations needed to usher in the Golden Age. Thank-you for being part of my wondrous experience Carrie, it was lovely actually. It's just that Suzanne is gone. I'm going to miss her terribly...

Carrie: i am just about to leave my studio for the night, as it's been a long day, so i will have to wait until tomorrow to give your email the justice it deserves in a response... just wanted to touch in before i go, though, and say how very sorry i am to hear of suzanne's decision...

sounds strange to me that she would not want to stay in touch... but having one of those loves in my life too, i know all too well that the intense connections sometimes have to take a break...

i've been in love with the same man for over 40 years and he's been in and out of my life many times, often taking the last remnants of my shattered heart with him... he may indeed be my twin flame, based on the dynamics of our relationship and all the signs and stages i now know are part of the twin dynamic... doesn't make it any easier to deal with the separation... though i have matured with the knowledge of the twin dynamic and can now allow him more time and space to be who and where he needs to be... so...that said, maybe suzanne is in a similar need to reduce the intensity for a while... maybe she'll come back after she gets a break from it...

regarding your ex, let's save that for tomorrow... i will respond after giving it some thought... if i were you, i'd not rush into anything... let's explore the dynamic and the possibilities tomorrow... meantime, do something really nice to support yourself... a long walk, a great movie, a special dinner... call a local friend to come over... something, anything to give yourself a break and some nurturing... sending hugs, carrie

Karen: Dear Michael, Today was a turning point in the rocky effort to sell my property. Now, unless someone dies, the sale should go through. I had been on pins and needles, because my place is so non-conforming that I figured I'd have to sell it to someone with cash, but a cash buyer didn't show up. Quite recently I learned the buyer's lender is requiring me to make some ridiculous and expensive changes nobody wants. But, today the buyers and I hit upon a compromise to pay for the "improvements". Whew! I absolutely love this place (and so do they), but I need to cut loose. Not only that, but the haggling was taking its toll, even though it was quite civilized. Now the reality of my moving is sinking to a deeper level.

So, you like smoothies? I specialize in making smoothies out of healthy ingredients, many of them "super foods"...... and without sugar, sad to say. Tonight's was concocted from avocado, lemon juice, garlic, arugula, romaine lettuce, and chard. How does that sound? It was delicious! I love to experiment with whatever I have on hand. What do you typically eat? I hope you had a good day. I'm throwing the pins and needles away now and will celebrate tomorrow! Maybe I'll be able to squeeze in a short hike. We are having fabulous weather these days, so it's a shame to be indoors. Goodnight

M: I'm pleased for you that the sale of your property is working Karen. I understand the need to sometimes "cut loose" so we can refresh our lives and allow Law of Attraction to serve up bigger and better events and circumstances and joys, for that's our nature.

Healthy ingredients in smoothies YES, I'll vote for that, I'm just not likely to build it myself. I've always been one who eats to live rather than lives to eat, but I can appreciate good tastes and textures. Please understand that I'm at present a bachelor living in a motor home, always busy at a keyboard that loves to gush. So what's "typical" today may be as plain as a mug of hot white tea and crackers for breakfast, maybe a can of sardines with green olives and crackers for lunch, and since I'm presently located very close to the arches, a Big Mac (almost all the food groups) or a 75 cent hot dog with sauerkraut for dinner, with occasional unhealthy but tasty snacks, cheese puffs etc. in between maybe.

Not impressed? Neither am I but it's fast, it's easy, it's life sustaining, and I can eat while I type. I have a friend coming over for a visit today so I'll probably take her for a real meal somewhere nearby, prime rib, seafood, buffet whatever, it's wonderful to live in a country where we can so easily do that. But I walk a lot, climb hills etc. and meditate/raise vibes a bit most days, so I'm always happy and feeling good, grateful for life and the many simple wondrous bounties of it. I neglected to ask you about that "interesting" I think you said visit with the doc re your newly discovered concern. Was it relief for you? Enjoy the day Karen, keep in touch, I'm enjoying our conversation and still planning my summer with many roads to choose from. Tell me more about the books you want to write.

Carrie: hi there... hope you're feeling a bit better today than last night... not sure how wise i am, but i have learned some lessons and have made a commitment to myself to use those lessons to make my experiences better for me and more authentic for those in my life... i believe you may be correct about getting too familiar too quick, as that's what happened to me when you sent me that first email suggesting you come here... no one wants to be bowled over or pushed too far too soon into connection... connection needs to unfold as a flower... and flow like a gentle stream until it's ready to be a roaring rapid... which, of course, also has it's place... but that's never at the start... of course, it's possible that you're deliberately driving women away... but my gut feeling is that's not really what anyone wants deep down

so what is it about the gushing that seems to give you something? Just because you "live to write" doesn't make for the gushing... writing is an art, not a tidal wave... so when you gush, you are missing the finesse of word play to gently tease open the connection... the playfulness of using your words to open the flower... which would actually give you more sustained pleasure over a longer time period... just allowing a stream of consciousness to flow here... not "thinking" about any of this... allowing the words to come through me... and, now that i think about that, maybe that's where you go wrong... a gently allowing to flow would hold back the gushing...i.e.... if you are *paying attention* as the words come, rather than letting them run away with you, my guess is they would flow more naturally and softly so as to allow that opening to occur...

my ex just reminded me of a phrase i taught a close friend of mine decades ago... a phrase that has been his guiding light all these years... Go Slow - Pay Attention - Tell The Truth... you might adopt this for yourself... my friend tells me it has been golden for him and he still lives by it...

i have to say something here... you've told me on a couple of occasions that DeLeon is the love of your life... now she's a crank and a job... something is amiss here... maybe going back to the getting in too deep too quickly...

i took an online course early on in my online explorations... a course taught by a man who had dated online for over 10 years... 300 women... and, among many great teachings he shared from his experiences was this one: pay attention to the things that stand out that you don't like when you meet someone... most do just the opposite... they glory in all the good stuff and overlook the stuff they don't like... but it's the stuff you don't like that will undoubtedly come up later and make you pull back... if those things are paid attention to in the beginning, and you basically ignore the stuff you like, you get a much more real experience of the person... then, if those things fade in the background over time, you really have someone who could be a good match... i think that's stellar advice and advice i heed... even now, with my ex, there is one thing that has my attention that might be an issue... i have even brought it up to him already as we have agreed on a totally transparent, authentic, vulnerable and honest relationship, no matter what form it takes... so... to put this into a usable format for you... how about if the next time you are attracted to a new woman, you start looking for the places where she is NOT a good match for you, rather than diving in head long ??? just an idea to keep things more real and less in fantasy land for you... we can always go to fantasy land with the right person... but that's after we determine that the person is right...

Suzanne's excuse sounds like BS to me... if the two of you are friends, then you connecting her up with another friend is a gift... if she's not interested, all she has to do is say so... but to run away and tell you you did wrong and badly enough that she wants no more to do with you is ridiculous and sounds to me an excuse she's been looking for... my guess is there's another reason and one she's not courageous enough to share... or maybe doesn't even know herself... and as i said last night, who knows if she will or won't resurface another time... in the meantime, though, you need to decide if she is really someone you want in your life? she may yank your chain over and over if you let her... i can't believe one person is your inspiration... you said you love to write... that's not connected to any one person... that comes from inside... it's a calling... an inner drive... be careful not to give that power away to anyone... especially not someone who would walk out of your life for no good reason...

generally, our ex's are ex's for a good reason... of course, some do need time apart and come back together renewed and recommitted to making the relationship work... but you need to carefully examine if that is the case here or are either or both of you simply wanting to take an easy way out and settle for something familiar though maybe not great??? i think you getting back with your ex is rife with danger, unless the two of you have either done the work needed to make it work this time, or are committed to doing it once you are back together... you left for a reason... what was it and has it changed? has she changed? have you changed? has the ground of the relationship changed? if you go back, will you be going "back" or into something new for both of you? is she capable of meeting you where you want to be? are you capable of meeting her where she wants to be? are you both capable of creating something new? a much higher turn of the spiral? can your dreams and ideals be fostered in her presence? can she imagine what you want and create it with you? do you know what she wants and can you create it with her? do you even want to? does she? or are you both being lazy and taking the easy way out because it's comfortable and less work than creating something new with someone new?

it's a choice...don't forget that... you can miss Suzanne all you want and be miserable or you can let go as easily as opening your hand and be happy and ready for what's new to come... you are in control... you can choose you can be happy, sad, right, wrong, new, old... and on and on... do not give up your power here... grab hold of it and decide what you want Carrie

M: It's all good solid advice Carrie, I deeply appreciate what you have written and the time you have taken to compose and write it. In particular I would stand to gain by heeding the advice to go slow, and to retain my own individual power. I also like the idea of looking for all the *wrong* things in a developing relationship rather than focusing solely on the things about the other that one likes, though that may be contrary to the teachings of Abraham. But I live to write at this time in my life and the book series (my journal actually) is what I am focused on whether anyone else reads it or not. I've found that the *timing* of thoughts, events, and messages received from others is almost always impeccable.

Suzanne in particular seemed to be able to read me like a book, her messages from a thousand miles away invariably, almost uncannily, being *exactly* what I needed *when* I needed it (to the minute often) for inspiration to go forward. It's almost like we are twins in real life, sharing our lives even though it's highly unlikely that we'd function well living under the same roof for any length of time. We must have been close in past lives. I do think she'll be back though, words and wordsmiths are her secret love when Nurse Responsible is not suffocating her need to be her own fun self. But she has worked hospice so intensely now and loved her dying patients so much that she has a perhaps inexorable urge to follow them. I saw the mark of death in her countenance when we were in Las Vegas, and she wouldn't deny it. That's all I'll say about that, it's not tragic, it's life giving, humanity at its finest. If she goes she'll come back very soon fully refreshed, I can live with that.

Two days before getting that final message from Suzanne I sensed that it was coming and as usual Law of Attraction let me know it would work out by bringing to me a fresh face, a lady in California who writes amazingly well and has the appearance and qualities I am looking for. I wrote in my journal then before hearing from Suzanne that Karen could very well be the next Suzanne/Concept Kira if I keep writing the series. We'll see how that develops, she writes ever so long emails ever so well, ever so often. She just sold her home in California and is needing to move within weeks to "cut loose". She's a professional musician.

I took your advice last night and went for a long walk, the kind I usually do in the early mornings. I thought of doing prime rib too but by then it was too late for a heavy meal so I settled for a can of pressed ham with green olives, mayo, and crackers instead. Not unusual for me, sometimes it's sardines. From that walk came the motivation to make some changes to the website and the descriptions of my books. I was at first delighted when Ashley started targeting a younger crowd but that kind don't seem to want to buy! I'll give them more time but I'm also going back to my original intended market, Baby Boomers. You'll see some efforts towards that at the top of the home page on my website. What are your thoughts on what I wrote today on the website? Would such a description draw you at your age into buying a book? If not, what's missing, what would compel you to buy?

I am presently located not far from my ex and will meet with her on Tuesday. My guess is that she'll invite me back to our former lifestyle and living in our beautiful retirement home. My guess is that I'll be open and honest as usual and will invite her to travel with me in Loa for a while if she wants to, and be an occasional companion, cuddler and spooner, possibly lover.

The secret to knowing what motivates me is knowing the power of my dream, my all-encompassing vision of becoming Immortal Adam with beautiful wives, populating new planets. That vision allows me to no longer be psychologically or morally bound to the western notion of monogamy. Suzanne accepts my vision, I don't think you ever could. That's why, much as I value your friendship you and I never met. Each to their own, I respect that.

I think there will be a 13th book published, but first there's that tempting hurdle to go back to where I came from to get behind me, I'll face that in two days.

Sure Suzanne yanked my chain, every single day she tugged at my heart, tugged and tugged and tugged mercilessly. It made for great drama once I learned to live with the pain, Loa would never have traveled without that. Now that she's gone and my heart is more experienced though, perhaps Karen or some other/s will be allowed to enter. *That* story will be in Book 13 if it ever gets published. Enjoy the day Carrie, thanks for being my friend, sometimes confidante and sounding board.

M: (to Ex) I've been given notice to move along from where I am by Tuesday so I'll be moving then. Your son arriving early will make it difficult for us unless we meet when he's working on your rental properties, or unless he doesn't mind seeing me again. But I can wait for you to return from Las Vegas on Tuesday and you could follow me. That way we can talk briefly to update our plans, and you can take me and whatever papers I'm going to need to your place to get the business taken care of. I'll buy lunch before we leave. I'm trying to get my other appointment on Friday, so I'll be available for three days if you are. Does that sound like a plan that will work for you or do you need to be with your son every day all the time from the time he arrives?

Carrie: will take a look at the web site and answer your questions soon... maybe tomorrow... glad the input held some value for you... now remember, karen is an experiment in being, doing and interacting in a new way... no gushing... go slow, pay attention, tell the truth... have a good night... sent with love, carrie

Karen: Hi, Another great expression: : *"........a keyboard that loves to gush"*. I have the same kind of keyboard, albeit not as much time to indulge it as you seem to have at the moment. Maybe we should go into business selling keyboards that love to gush, for people with writers' block. (I hardly know what writers' block is!)

Well, when I reflect on it I guess I'd have to say I live to eat...... not really, although probably more than I eat to live. I can see it both ways. I have always had such a fondness for food, but also such a HUGE interest in food...... how it's grown, foreign cuisines - or anything I haven't tasted before, sustainable agriculture, social justice in terms of the food supply, eating locally grown food, edible landscapes, healing through food ("your food is your medicine"), nutrition, truth in labeling, animals' rights etc. etc. It is simply fascinating to me, and one of my passions. JUST one - not the only one! I would be a classic foodie IF all those great tasting dishes were actually healthy - for us and for the planet. I realize this is only one component of health, but it's one we can control more easily than some, and I find it rewarding.

Yes, I'm happy about my house looking like it will soon fall off my shoulders. It has been both a joy (living in such a gorgeous place, in the mountains yet only 15 minutes from the ocean... palm trees, redwood trees, fresh air, sunshine and quietude) AND a black hole in terms of money. It was a fixer upper, and although I've put a lot into it, it remains a fixer upper. So now I turn my attention to the other house, the one I was financing the loan on. It went into foreclosure recently. It was in pretty good condition when I sold it, but is now another fixer upper. Oh woe... If I didn't have so many books and instruments, I might choose to live in a yurt. But I do need a really good kitchen! Have you seen the Mandala co. round, energy-efficient houses in Nelson, BC? They appeal to me!

I am not able to convey the technical details of my session with the neurofeedback practitioner. I'm not a particularly technically-minded person, but I readily latch onto the big picture, and, in this case, I was able to see, in my brain scan results, that everything I struggle with is right there...... it's real, it's verifiable (I'm not a scientist, but I appreciate science in some ways). Yes, it IS "all in our heads". I had gone to a lecture he gave on the topic on brain maintenance, and I was impressed by his knowlege - especially the fact that he has developed computer brain-training programs that got approved by the FDA... which equates w/ insurance coverage. Come to think of it, I asked him if he works with - and has had success with - personality disorders. He said he has, but only if the person genuinely wants to change. Anyway, I am going to be working on residual trauma from my relationship with the NPD (narcissistic personality disorder) man I have mentioned. He's the reason I have changed my too open, overly enthusiastic and unguarded tune.

Oh yes, my book. I think I'll save that for next time. It's a BIG subject... but not a novel. Maybe I can keep you in suspense for just awhile longer...... Have a great day!

M: Suspense, the very stuff of novels, can't wait. I love the way you write. Maybe we can co-author books instead of pushing gushy keyboards from the door of our yurt when you're not too busy running the grand or whatever other instrument/s you play. Decades ago I was thinking fondly of straw bale or something similar, but never made the move. I do like Fuller domes, I think monster winds would most likely just flow on right by, maybe yurts too?

I was in Costa Rica a few weeks ago and loved it, still have an open invitation to rent/caretake a beautiful home on 20 acres near the capital city. I also have a friend in Panama who keeps inviting me to visit her place high up enough on a mountain to be eternal spring. Would you live in the tropics do you think? Hmmm, tell me about the books you want to write?

M: (to Karen) Just in case you're curious, here's a photo of my "Loa", taken in Yuma, Arizona.

Karen writes back but in all caps and nothing much is relevant to the cause of us being a match. She wouldn't want to live far from her daughter but would enjoy visiting warm countries in the winter. Her book would be about teaching people how to play music, far from the kinds of books I will ever write. She's a good conversationalist online but I'm growing disenchanted with this woman I once thought might be a replacement for Suzanne. I think Suzanne is *irreplaceable.* I pray she will return, at least virtually even if we never again see each other in the flesh.

Also, given my experience with DeLeon's health problems I'm concerned about getting involved once again with a woman who has already mentioned to me two health problems she herself is concerned about. Why *start* with negatives like that already in play? I think I'll get slower and slower responding and see what happens. *Ex is looking good indeed!* We'll see how that plays out. I think if I continue the way I am I'm eventually going to live under the same roof as a woman anyway, that's just the way I am. She may be my already familiar Ex. But whoever my maleness drives me to live with, I can always continue to *expect* to be Immortal Adam in my secret thoughts. But I do value my freedom to go where I want when I want. Maybe Ex is ready to grant me that???? I'm prepared tonight if she is receptive when we meet, to suggest that she travel with me to visit my kids and we'll see how compatible we may be after these six months apart. It may be the end of my book series but I think I'd at least get Book 13 out there, and I'd probably write traditional books from then on. That's how I see it tonight.

Karen: Forgot to thank you for this pic. - pretty spiffy... looks like it might contain a bowling alley. So that is what you are sleeping in tonight!

M: Yes, Loa is my home office, I sleep and dream in Loa Land almost every night. Bowling alley was an option but I opted out to have storage space for keyboards just in case the one I'm using fails to gush properly. Sleep well Karen.

M: Sandy, I just wanted to give you an update. Unfortunately Suzanne was not at all happy that I was "matchmaking" for her and I'm in a world of trouble with her right now. Much as I loved the thought of having a magic wand to wave in her direction and solve all her problems, it looks like my Harry Potter impersonation just wasn't real enough. I wish you the very best, you seem to be a sweet person, I still think you two would have done well meeting each other.

M: (to myself) I'm looking forward to seeing Ex, expecting her to drop in tomorrow a.m. But obviously I'm still trying to cover bases just in case that doesn't work out too well. If it does, I'm thinking of asking Ex to travel with me to visit family in Alberta and British Columbia. By then we'd sure know if we want to get together again. My ideal hope would be that we get together but she allows me to travel where and when I want, accepts my dream of becoming Adam, and is not overly concerned if I visit women friends now and then. Knowing her though *that* would be a miracle! Could she be ready I wonder?? I have in mind Suzanne's counsel in Vegas to spend 50 years with immediate family. If I'm going to live a thousand years and more (as I expect to) that would be just a drop in time.

I just had ham and eggs at the casino where I'm parked now and as I ate I thought of Suzanne. Yes, I have to keep my mind positive and see only love for her regardless of how she treated me and wants me out of her life. But I miss her, it's true. Sure wish Nurse Responsible would unlock the toy box now and then so Suzanne could come out and play with me. But I'm kind of sensing that it won't happen anytime soon if at all, the connection's gone, maybe it's best? Should my books sell like crazy though I might someday be sitting on her doorstep when she comes home from work, as I threatened to do a few times in the past. I'm concerned because she has now disappeared from the singles site where I found her, must have cancelled her account. Has she found her man or woman I wonder? I sure wish that upon her rather than some dire thing that caused her to suddenly withdraw like that. She was drinking very often when I was with her, even a large nightcap every night on top of everything else throughout the day - drowning sorrows or loneliness? The only comfort to me the whole five days was her invariably coming to bed naked each night, and never pushing me away in bed. Does she think that I too failed her like all the other men in her life? I feel somehow that I did fail Suzanne, but I don't know what else I could have done. If I had a lot of money I'd chase after her even now.

My guess regarding us is that I'm simply too old for her, though she did say I'm "not available." Did she mean that I'm still attached to Ex and have responsibilities for children and grandchildren that I'm not fulfilling?? I did tell her that I continue to visit my kids as often as I usually did in the past. But she was already gone when she arrived in Las Vegas I think. She delayed meeting me for a half hour after she got off the plane. (How could she have missed me in a red shirt walking around the carousel several times? And why didn't she come to the information booth as arranged?) Or did it happen in that first small moment when I turned and saw her and secretly questioned her physical appearance, then tried to cover it up? She'd gone downhill, and I suppose she knew that. My darling darling Suzanne, I still love you sweetheart, just the way you are.

I really want to know what's happening with her, but I have no contact to check on her. I noticed that her address was on the luggage tag on her suitcase, but I had too much integrity or foolishness or whatever to even secretly write it down when she was out. I do have her phone number but don't dare call, I must respect her desire for me to be out of her life. What's happening with the deep connection we once had? Is that gone forever or does she miss it too like I do? It's strange that I have more sorrow and sadness to unfocus upon regarding losing

Suzanne than I felt when my wife of 18 years filed for divorce. Or is it because Ex is not really gone? Well, tomorrow will be an important day in our lives, Ex is coming to Loa for the very first time. I have choices and decisions to make based upon how I find her regarding me and a reconciliation.

But sweetheart Suzanne, my darling, even if I get back with Ex we could still swap emails and be virtual friends like we were before. *You'd LIVE then Suzanne, and Loa would continue to travel…*

In meditation I just tried to reach Suzanne but I could not. There was just an absence, an empty space where she used to be all the time. She is deadly serious about getting me out of her life. I don't like it but I must respect it and let her go completely. I hope she is well, I need to face up to the facts and allow her to be as she desires to be.

Sandy: (re my message to her about Suzanne not wanting me to match make for her) No worries. Have a great evening.

Ex: When I leave tomorrow morning I won't have internet. Can we meet at the visitors center across the freeway from the Virgin River Casino.

M: Come to the Casa Blanca park, I'm in site 15. I need to check out by 11 a.m. so come before if you can. Let me know you got this.

Ex: I think I should be back before than. If something happens and I can't is their a second option of were I can meet you.

M: I'll stay at Casa Blanca until eleven. If you're not here yet, I'll move to the free parking place. If all else fails I'll move to the Wal-mart tomorrow leaving Mesquite sometime after 1 p.m. and we'll contact by email. Ok?

Ex: That sounds good. How am I going to know what your RV looks like if you are in the free RV parking place.

M: I sent you a photo of my RV, you must not be getting all my messages. But here's a crazy suggestion. When you leave for Vegas take a swim suit and toothbrush. If you get here before 11 and want to stay the night I'll pay for another night and we can stay in my RV. There's only one bedroom but there's a sofa if that's of concern to you. (You get the sofa.) I have quite a few movies. Anyway, it could be a fun time for us? Let me know your thoughts on this, I'm still fond of you as you know.

In less than 2 hours I am expecting Ex to show up. The way I am thinking right now, if she offers reconciliation I will reconcile! In which case Loa becomes redundant and I'll probably sell her. I'll try to get this Book 13 finished and just hold it on my own computer until there's a demand for it. My wild gypsy days may be over. Once again Suzanne uncannily with perfect timing gave me what I think my inner being needed and wanted, hard as it is to write - *her leaving my life!!!* I must stop thinking of her, it's over now.

Let's see what demeanor Ex shows up with, how forgiving she may be, and how this unfolds from here. Ideally she'll sell the marital home to give us both some space from the past and we'll buy a summer home in Canada and a winter one in southern USA. I'll keep writing *something,* but this series will most likely wrap up unless there's a surge of buyer readers. So, wish me and Ex the very best of outcomes, and Loa a wonderful new owner who will treat her with the great respect she deserves, and will travel often and well.

As I write this on May 21 I am sitting at the huge built-in desk I had constructed for my office when Ex and I built our beautiful retirement home. We spent the night together cuddling in the very bed I slept for many years. It was familiar, it was nice for both of us. We'll probably rendezvous as friends now and then in Loa Land. But we will *not* be playing married couple again, it just can't happen for us. I'll stay in the area a few days and maybe do some stuff with Ex just for fun and old times sake. I spoke to Ex about my selling Loa and getting a summer and winter home instead. As always, with the expression of that desire, Law of Attraction started moving such a thing in my direction.

I sensed two or more days ago that Karen's first impression that she and I were not a match was correct. The last 48 hours or so there has been no message interchange between us, I have no desire for more, and I have zero feeling of connection.

I'm in Loa parked close to Ex. She has visitors for a few days and I am not welcome in her home while they are there. I hate the sneaking around, won't do it much longer. But I'm not in a rush to drive north yet, it's still May and I need to pass through mountains. I did my part with Ex, genuinely offered reconciliation even though we almost immediately fell into the same habit of walking parallel lives under the same roof. I think that Ex even though she still professes love and I feel it, mainly just wants more of my body? I have things to consider because there are (as usual) many paths open to me and none of them are wrong. All paths will lead to joy and fulfillment, they'll just bring different circumstances and different people.

Ex suggested last night that I leave Loa here and fly to visit my family, then come back. Except that there is stuff that I want to leave with my kids that I could not take on the plane. So, the top thoughts re the immediate future are to drive to Great Falls, Montana and visit my son. A daughter from Canada will come get me and lend me her car for the Alberta visits. Pending counsel with my children I may try to sell Loa in Great Falls, fly to Victoria, and stay with my sister until I find a place to buy or rent nearby. Those are just possibilities of course, Law of Attraction may bring bigger and better offers, but that's where I am right now because my darling Suzanne, my *inspiration* for writing is gone. Life as I knew it in Loa Land *must* change.

M: (to my sister) I'm visiting (Ex) right now. We are good friends but there will not be a long-term reconciliation for us, it just wouldn't work for the best interests of either of us. So my tentative plan at the moment is to drive my motor home to Great Falls and visit family there. My daughter will come for me and lend me her car to visit my Alberta crew.

When I bought my motor home I thought I'd be traveling a lot to interview people and write their stories. But I have since found that with the internet the stories come to me and I was just using the motor home as a place to live. So I'll counsel with my kids but it's quite possible that when I get back to Great Falls I will try to sell my RV there. If I do that, my next step may be to move to Victoria or thereabouts, which I have been thinking of doing for quite a while. I think the time has arrived for me to become a genuine Canadian again, maybe even find and marry a Canadian woman? So, my question to you is if you'd allow me to live with you for a while until I find a place to rent or buy on the Island. I'd probably buy an older car to get around with and would of course pay for my share of the food and extra expenses my staying with you would incur. Please understand that these are not fixed plans, just ideas that I am exploring and running by you. What do you think?

M: (to Ex) This entire parking lot is posted as a tow-away zone for RV's so I'm getting out of here. If you still want to visit me today I'll be at the overpass where trucks park at night. I'm feeling pressured now to get my RV on sale as soon as possible, so I'd like to get the paperwork you want done completed right away and be on my way to Great Falls.

I'm disappointed that you are no longer available. I thought you might be but your loyalty has been firmly transferred to others. I understand and don't fault you for it. My way seems clear before me now after pondering your continuing to make others your priority. That's a choice you could have made differently when I outlined what I saw as possible for a future together. I hope that we will continue to be friends, keep in touch, and maybe even see each other occasionally. I will most likely move to Victoria soon after my visit with family in Alberta. I may quite possibly settle there, maybe even get married should the right person come along.

Yes, I thought a lot about my future last night and my former ideas about us being together are not so compelling anymore. I have to face up to that, you are not available for me. My series of books may have reached a conclusion with Book 12 now completed. So my purpose for traveling and living on my own is done as I see it at this moment of writing. What will actually happen remains to be seen but I expect that what I have outlined above will prevail. Keep in touch, I do want to complete that paperwork but I now want to do it as soon as possible. Please make that a priority even if you have visitors, thanks.

Ex: It has been difficult today not seeing you. I wanted to see you. Rentals are a priority when my son is here. This is the first he has been here since Christmas. I can't rent them with some of the problems I am having. Can't afford to hire someone else. Tomorrow, I have to rent a truck and buy items for the rentals and take it up and deliver them. Not sure how long it will take. Most likely will not be back until after 3:00 PM. If you are available I will come by if back early enough. We will get together for sure the next day OK. I will pick you up to come over to the house and we can work on your list of properties. I am sorry about all of this. I would of preferred spending time with you but responsibility is tugging at me.

M: Well written, thanks for explaining. My daughter is planning to pick me up in Great Falls on June 2nd. I need to get the RV sold before October and it may take some time, thus the rush. Sure, come over today if you can. I may do some walks so if there's no response when you knock on the door, call, I'll try to remember to take the phone with me. Enjoy the day.

I'm a bit torn, she's a good woman and seems eager to see me. But she won't allow me to rejoin her in the marital home and take up life where we left off, so Loa *must* travel some more. And that means there will be other women in my life, though right now I'd settle for one and stability. It's just that now that I'm back where I spent a lot of years and my ex is eager to have some time with me, even intimate time, that all the old ways are knocking on the door. I did have an enviable life, our home is beautiful, I love our city, I left to write, *I wrote!!!*

Her visitors will be gone in two or three days. Should I put the rush on hold and spend some more time in her bed? She'd like that, and so would I, playing married again. But this time with the curtains drawn, her hiding the naked man in her bedroom.

I'm getting a pretty good handle on missing Suzanne. I'm thinking now that she will never come back, our connection is severed, long and beautiful and *vital* as it was. But I'll always love her, though virtual she was my dearest sweetheart, my darling, my glorious Suzanne.

As I write that I am sorely tempted to watch her video again and listen to the delicious sounds of her coming in a bathtub, vibrator busy in and out, her panting and moaning as it sunk ever deeper. I confirmed with her verbally that the vibrator was actually inside her vagina the whole time, it's curved. It seemed to be going much too deep, she's quite the woman. She brought it with her but never did show me let alone demonstrate, which is what I had been hoping for. She left with so much undone from my point of view, so much I wanted to do with her and to her, what a crushing disappointment. I still want her naked body pressed tight against mine. I'd meet her in a heartbeat anytime anywhere for days of nothing but raw unfettered sex.

I think it was that careless moment of mine when I first set eyes on her at the airport that cast such a chill on our vacation. She surely knew my disappointment in her physical appearance, she knew my thoughts perfectly at the time. But then, why did she hide from me for so long after her bags arrived at the carousel, I hadn't even seen her yet? It seems fated that we not be together physically?? What awaits me as Loa travels without Suzanne I wonder? Gosh I miss her so...

Yes I confess, I watched her video a moment ago. At least I have that left, her sounds are so compelling, though without the live connection we had and the expectation of being physically with her, not so delicious as they were before. Come back to me Suzanne, even if only virtually, I *need* you darling.

Ok, couldn't help it, I wrote to her.

M: (to Suzanne) Yes you slammed the door, I heard that loud and clear. But did you have to *nail* it shut? I understand about Nurse Responsible not wanting to be with me physically. But doesn't she have it in her to at least let Suzanne out of the toy box now and then so she can play? I'll always love Suzanne, she's welcome in my sandbox anytime, *she deserves a life too.* We have stories to tell together. Even my ex wanted me to tell your hospice stories to her when I spent some time with her offering to reconcile. I'd still like to write and publish that hospice book, at least tell more of your stories in my books. I hope you are well Suzanne. I care about you, always will, stories or not, silence or not. I want to be your friend. Talk to me again?

My Sister: We've been wondering where you had got to especially during those tornados. I have thought over what you are planning to do. If it were me I would keep the motor home as a place to live while searching for a house. I realize you probably cant sell it in Canada, but when the time came, take it back to the us. Unfortunately my place is far too small to have anyone here. I spend a lot of time in the space where the hideabed is and cant move things around, space is just too tight (no storage space either). Maybe your Alberta clan can come up with some other ideas. Let me know what you end up doing. Your other sister and I would love to have you on the island.

M: I understand, thanks. I'll let you know my plans as they evolve over the next few weeks. I'd like to move to Victoria, just not sure of the timing yet. I'm still near where I used to live, my ex wants to talk when her company leaves.

Ex: Had to rent a big truck. Now heading to a rental near here to drop ceiling repair items and rain gutter repair supplies. Then headed to another store to buy two toilets and fascist and taking lawn mower to where my other rentals are, tree brock and is on roof. My son has to cut it of and see what damage. The list goes on and on. If we get the work done then we have renter ready to move in on the first. So sorry this happened when you are here. We had so much more to talk about and do. Hope you can hang around a bit longer.

Guess I shouldn't run away on her, she seems so sincere. But what could ever come of this I wonder? Maybe it is best that I stand back a bit and see where she may go with it? I came sincere, thinking we might reconcile, then she seemed to make me a low priority. But that has been explained even though she didn't seem to think my ideas for us being together were attractive because she never responded. She repeated a number of times that she would rendezvous with me in the future but it would just be cuddles if we're not married, if we're not married, if we're not married. Does she want to be married to me? Ok, yes, it was fun being back in bed with her that one night, not great fun, just fun, cuddling naked all night.

Am I still tilting? I knew visiting Ex in our former marital home would be a difficult hurdle to get over. Maybe Loa won't travel much further?? And maybe Loa will. This potential dilemma shows the difference between consensus reality with all its many moth and rust attractions, and living leading edge, allowing Law of Attraction to constantly bring bigger and better, living not for the manifestation, but for the journey itself. Which one will win out for me? Or can the two be blended and reconciled? If I was absolutely certain that I'd live a thousand years and more I'd follow Suzanne's counsel, my answer would be clear, stay with Ex if she offers. But of course I still walk by faith - *it's more fun that way...*

M: (to Ex) It would be nice if you would visit tonight.

Ex: I will come over as soon as someone gets back to watch the baby. Just got home, very tired but want to see you.

Does this woman want me or what? But how does she want me other than naked in her bed? Right now, though I feel hugely wealthy for the experiences of the past six months and treasure these books, I'd go back to her the way it was before we parted. I don't think she'd go for that though. *Now, exactly what is it that I want from Ex?*

M: (to Ex) Thanks for coming tonight, it's always nice to see you, you are doing your best for your family. I'm undecided but will most likely hang around a few more days so we can get that paperwork done. Then we can both be free to get on with our lives without feeling a need to be connected other than as friends. I believe the universe to be unfolding as it should, it will be well for both of us.

Carrie: hi there... thought i would fill you in on my latest adventures with my friend and those to come... we hit a new place in our connection this week and decided we wanted to meet... he had a camping trip planned for june through northern california, so couldn't come here right now, as the timing is too tight... he knows i'm not a camper, so he offered a road trip as an alternative (though i told him i would do some camping with him too, as i really want him to have the experience he's been planning for for months now... i figure i can deal with a little camping if there are respites along the way) so, as a gift, he is taking me on a road trip from northern california to alaska!!!

i leave here on 6/24 on a one way ticket and we are just going to get on the road and let it take us where it will i LOVE road trips and most of this one will be to places i've never seen, and have always wanted to... i have very close friends in california and washington and he has many friends and family in california, so we are also going to visit with them along the way... once we get to alaska, we'll see what's next... we may drive back, may leave his truck and fly back may go to Hawaii together from there or may come here together...or he may go there and i come back here... we're just going to see what unfolds as we travel together and take it from there...

we spent 9 hours on a video call yesterday and now i know i definitely want to explore a relationship with him and go on this journey with him... he's had the most interesting/amazing spiritual experiences for the last 10 years... so much so that he's wanting to write a movie script of it all and i'd love to help him do that... as he said, the worst that's going to happen is that we have a very pleasant time and become good friends... so... i'm off on a great LOA adventure... maybe i'll even write as i travel... who knows where this journey will lead???

M: That's pure LOA DELIGHT Carrie, MAGNIFICENT, I'm so happy for the two of you! May your fondest dreams *always* come true from now until forever. Enjoy sunny days and fun travels my dear friend and confidante. What's happening with the house you are living in? Need a house sitter to care for it and your furniture etc. for a while rather than sell or move everything just now?

Smile Carrie, knowing how LOA works, I just couldn't resist putting out that feeler. Maybe there's even a lovely expat somewhere near you drifting my way, looking for me, has she visited yet? *Man can dream can't he?* But I'm genuinely happy for you and your new friend, he's getting a choice lady. Thanks for keeping me in your loop Carrie, I hope you always will, hello to your friend from me.

Carrie: interesting ideas... he has a "comfy" truck and likes to travel with it, so i doubt he'd be interested in buying a motor home... his idea is staying in quaint hotels, cabins etc, so i also don't think the motor home experience is his idea of how he wants to experience this trip... regarding my place, i have asked my housekeeper to stay, but i have to pay her, so having a house sitter as a trade, house for care of it and my babies, would be a better alternative for me... especially as we have no idea how long the trip will be... so we can definitely explore that option... would be even more attractive to me if you were willing to pay utilities electric, propane, internet, tv...less than 300. you would have to agree to stay for how ever long i was gone... could be 2 or 3 months if things go really well and we want me to go back to hawaii after alaska... anyway, we can brainstorm it all...

M: Quaint sounds fun, sleeping on the ground in a tent does not, especially with grizzlies around. Yes, I would pay utilities and take good care of everything for you including pets and house plants that came with a detailed list of instructions. But I'd need at least six months to make it worthwhile, especially if leaving in the best of times this part of the world and going to the wetness of times (I think) where you are. Any chance of an agreement for a year with the understanding that if you came back I'd be relegated to the status of "guest" and would leave within 30 days if you asked me to? That should give you the freedom you may feel you need with a new relationship, a place to fall back to if needed, no rush to sell or move your stuff, and would give me time to write books at leisure (maybe try non-fiction or how-to next time.) With such an arrangement I could perhaps save enough money to buy a house when I get back to USA or Canada, or maybe even in your country if I fall in love with the place.

Carrie: have to run to an event, but we'll explore all soon...

Ex showed up with her little grandson today and took me shopping with them. She said she may return tonight but my guess is not. She wants a relationship that may include full reconciliation, just not yet. I'm on my own, Loa *must* travel. Will I wait for Ex? I'll probably be interested when she becomes available, but wait if that means see no other? Not likely.

Ex: Won't be able to see you tonight. Very tired and my body is hurting all over. Two days in a row is to much for me. It has been tough on my son he is suffering also but took his daughter to a move. Will be over tomorrow to see you.

Ex: I will be over with in the hour.

M: Ok, I'm home.

Ex: My visitors are gone for the day. So this is a good time for you to come over.

M: Guess I should put some clothes on then huh?

Spent a few hours with Ex, nothing much happening. She thinks we'll get back together in a year or so but not now. Back home in Loa for the night reconciled to the fact that Loa will continue to travel. Sure hope my books start to sell. Not much point in publishing more than twelve unless that happens. But anyway, it has been a grand adventure even if it turns out to be nothing more than tilting at windmills. Last night I thought that maybe it was time to get back on a better path, perhaps a higher one, leaving the past behind me. The women on this one sure haven't done well by me in the long run have they? Best to focus on becoming Immortal Adam exclusively I think. Got to get the vibes raised to the heights where immortal women dwell, and keep them there.

Ex: It was a good day. Will email you tomorrow about coming over.

M: Yes, a good day today, thanks, sleep well.

Carrie: hi…sorry for the delay in getting back to you… the weekend was very busy, culminating with a birthday dinner party i had for a friend last night… also, been video chatting for many hours, last night was 5 after the party ended… we are 5 hours different in time, so i was up til 3 and 4 the night before and on friday, we did a 9 hour call which was our first video session together…

as to the house, at the moment, everything is up in the air... he was actually talking about buying it last night, but i have no idea if that might materialize... he was also considering coming here sooner than our trip schedule, but again, don't know if that's realistic... we were just exploring options... i have just sent him an email with your offer to housesit and your wishes regarding the timing of that and also the info on your motor home... so, when i get his thoughts back, i'll let you know and we can go from there... at this moment, i have no idea about anything! things are changing daily, in fact, sometimes hourly now...

M: Thanks for the update. Isn't it wonderful not knowing what's going to happen until it does, just knowing it's going to be GREAT!! Enjoy the day.

Carrie: yup... it's pretty fun right now... more so than some other times when i had no idea what was coming... i'm definitely enjoying this ride so far...

Ex: I will be over to pick you up for night if you wish.

M: Yes, that would be nice. I'll try to remember to take my cell phone if I go out, won't be far.

Chapter 14

——◦◦◦◦——

Carrie: hi there... well, first as i suspected, my friend is not a motor home kinda guy... he wants as small a vehicle as possible for travel... second, can't remember if i have told you this already, but he is considering buying my house this will depend upon whether or not the owners are willing to sell wholesale, and so far the offer they have made is above what he would pay... there have been no negotiations so far, but they are far enough off what i know he wants to pay, that it may not work... but, if they get close, he will fly here on 6.16 to look at it and make his final decision... i have a tentative reservation to fly out of here on 6.24 so, one of the most important questions we need to address first is whether or not you could be here a few days before the 24ᵗʰ???

if that's a yes, then we need to address the length of your stay... 6 months to a year just isn't feasible from where we stand right now... i could probably agree to 2 months with a possible extension if i were going to go to Hawaii before coming back here, but the problem is we don't even know how we are going to like each other once we get together... you know that dance... we are clear so far that we will do the trip all the way to alaska together because, even if we end up as friends, we both want to do the trip... but, once we get to alaska, we have no idea where we will want to go from there... we may drive back to california, may leave his truck in alaska and fly somewhere... either both to hawaii, both to california, both here or one here one there... or who knows... he jokingly suggested we just keep driving to mongolia... so, since we have no idea exactly how long the trip will last or where we go once we get to alaska, i can't agree to you staying in my house for 6 months, as i may be burnt out and need to come home to my own space... i would of course, give you notice so you could make plans for your next stop with ease and without pressure, but that would probably mean a few weeks... so, what are your thoughts about all that?

M: It was a lovely idea Carrie and I thank-you for considering it. But right now I feel a need to settle down somewhere for a year or so, most likely in Canada. Please keep in touch and let me know how your trip goes, I'm cheering for the two of you. I feel your excitement - enjoy.

Carrie: ok… i understand… if things change let me know… we still have some time

Ashley: Ya I was having a blond moment. So I added the blog page… go ahead and play around with it and add some comments or posts.

M: (this written on blog) Ashley knows that all I want to do is write so she takes care of a whole lot of the other stuff for me: website design, marketing, social media, metaphysical manifesting, etc.. But since blogging is done with a keyboard and my keyboard loves to gush, I guess she's kinda got me cornered here. Actually I think I'm going to like this Ash, thanks for the idea and for setting up a blog I can contribute to. Now what?

Although she is not wanting to reconcile at this time, Ex said last night that she is "courting" me and wants us to get together often, maybe marry again sometime in the future. She is taking me to Las Vegas today for dinner. I've been investigating the possibilities of taking Loa to Canada and registering her there, then living in her in or near Victoria, British Columbia. It looks like what may be the deal breaker on that notion is the general sales tax payable at the border, which would be thousands of dollars.

I'll be near Ex for several days more, then everything is open to Law of Attraction, the way I like it. But you know, true to women always giving me what I want deep inside, Ex is now saying (as eventually DeLeon said) that she is ok with me having *whatever* experiences I want with other women! I like that.

In one of the first emails Suzanne wrote to me after we discovered each other on a singles site she asked if her dress "size 10" was acceptable to me. I thought at the time that size 10 was slim and slender and when she came to me physically that first night in Loa and we hugged, she was a beautiful angel, I never noticed anything as mundane as dress size. But yesterday in Las Vegas Ex pointed out various women and asked me if I'd be interested in them. As she did so, she told me the dress size each woman would likely wear. I realized then that my personal preference would be about a size 6, not size 10! Was that what Suzanne was feeling during our time in Las Vegas, that I was internally disapproving of the physical form of her *real* body even though she'd told me her dress size? It's true dear reader, I was (still am) in love with a virtual *ideal* by the name of SUZANNE. Oh hang, my heart's on my sleeve again as I write that and think of her! I love Suzanne's *real* self too…

Maybe it's best to just settle somewhere hopefully near Victoria and meet someone local rather than stretching so far all the time. Wonder what Law of Attraction has to say about that thought? Should be fun observing what door opens next. And meanwhile, Ex and I are going to watch a movie in Loa tonight…

(Next day) Ex and I watched a Wayne Dyer movie called *"The Shift"* filmed at Asilomar which I visited the day before picking up Loa. We also watched *"What the Bleep do we Know."* I'm getting some very interesting responses from her, she seems eager to know more about metaphysics. We also watched *"Abraham 101"*. Maybe I'm here for so many unexpected days to teach her a few new possibilities and bring us closer into alignment? But I'm ready to move on and visit family.

It's likely right now with no other women in my life besides Ex, that this will be the last book in my series. I may make it much longer than previous books though if I decide to keep a journal. I still have deep feelings for Suzanne, they surface now and again, not sure if they'll ever go away. I sure hope to at least keep track of her because she's no longer on singles and she is planning to sell her house with no plan in mind where to go after that. I guess the solution to it all is to become an immortal and visit when and where I want. I need to get my vibrations up so I feel joy constantly, then just relax and let come the very best.

June 1st. I am now focused on selling Loa and moving to Victoria, British Columbia Canada. I have so reflected my location on singles sites. It seems fitting that I would now be attracted to the beautiful city on the sea where I first encountered Abraham as Muse, wrote my first book, and first became aware of Kira. (That was in 1984.) Who knows what awaits me there, but whatever, it (and perhaps SHE) will be *very* GOOD! It's interesting that I'm becoming Adam and a few minutes after writing the above I get a message out of the blue from "Eve" who lives in Victoria!

Eve: Hi. I would like to hear from you if you're interested, you must have a lots a stories to tell from your travels, I would love to hear them Eve.

M: Hello Eve, I appreciate your interest in my profile. I have been living in the USA for many years but am ready to move back to Canada, preferably the Greater Victoria area. Although I'm currently visiting family in USA and Alberta, I'm checking ads to find a suitable furnished unit to rent in or near Victoria while I look for something more permanent. I expect to be in Victoria sometime in July. Enjoy the day. Michael

I took Ex to a movie last night, it turned out to be a good movie, made me laugh. We then came to Loa and watched "Starman". She came in pj's and went to bed with me about 1 a.m. when the movie ended. We cuddled, then I awoke soon after 4 a.m. hearing her stumbling around in the dark unfamiliar space. I realized that she was leaving so got up, hugged, and let her out the door. I wasn't ready for her to leave, it was another Suzanne experience though not so traumatic.

Ex: Good morining. Hope this email goes out before you leave. If you want to have breakfast let me know.

M: It would be nice to see you again but I just got this and am eating breakfast catching up on internet stuff. Come over if you want. If I don't answer the door just come in, I'll be in the shower. If the door's locked, out for a short walk with cell phone. I'll email before I leave.

Eve: Good morning Michael. thank you for your reply, may be will meet for a glass of wine when you get back to Victoria. have a safe trip.

Ex: Came home cleaned house a bit then went to bed and got up about half hour ago. Don't know if you are still around. If not have a safe and wonderful journey. Love you

M: Still here at noon but planning to leave soon. Come over right away and I'll buy lunch?

Ex: I also called and didn't get an answer, then when over anyway but you were gone. Take care will miss you. I came back and started taking food storage boxes down stairs.. I will do 10 a day. Also syphoning water out of barrels so I can move them in a better location. Had to do something to fill the void. You might want to look into prepaid phones. I think what you are using now is much higher in cost than most prepaid phones. Yes email works for now.

M: (to lady on singles who lives in Victoria, let's call her "Kris") It seems that my premium subscription had expired so the choice to respond to you was another canned 'hello' or wait until my renewal was processed. I waited. I think you can reply to this now whether or not you are a paid member. Either way please feel free to write to me at my email address below, I'd like to swap messages with you. Oh, I noticed your profile before but you but a maximum age on men you'd be interested in. That's a bit daunting but I'm emboldened by the pretty smile you sent. I look forward to hearing from you.

Kris: Hi Michael, Thanks for responding back and sending me your email. I am in Finland right now but heading home in 2 days. I have family here and it has been wonderful to connect with everyone. I am traveling with 2 friends and we were in Africa first. The whole trip has been amazing. RE: the age.... I set this up awhile ago so thanks for responding regardless. I dont have a subscription to this sight and haven't really been doing much with it. I see you live in Victoria. What area?. I have only been here 3 years but absolutely love it. Look forward to connecting. Much kindness Kris

M: What an adventure you are having, I'm happy for you. Did you get to see the "Big 4" up close and personal? The only part of Africa I have been to so far is Egypt (I think that's Africa?) A safari is on my bucket list, maybe you can be my guide.

I am at present in my motor home on the way to visit family in Montana and Alberta. I was born in Canada but have lived in the US for twenty years. Now that I'm retired and single, I am planning to move back to Canada, preferably Greater Victoria. I've been looking at for rent ads the last few days and found a furnished suite in James Bay that I'm thinking of putting a deposit on any time now. I'm a bit hesitant to sign a one year lease because once I get there I might find something that would suit me better. Though I do like James Bay having lived on Quebec Street for a few months many years ago while writing a little New Age book. I too love Victoria, the City of Victory, for me a 'power spot'. What part of Victoria do you live in?

Kris: Hi Michael, That is great driving around in a motor home. I am an avid camper and usually tent it but I have also done pulling a trailer a way back and it is quite convenient. We did see the big 4 except the rhino. We went to Ngorongoro which is the crater in Tanzania. It was the most amazing site. The animals are every where and close to the vechicle. This is my 3rd trip to Africa last May. I was part of a group that fundtaised to build a school on Maasai land and then my friend and I met 2 little girls at an orphanage and we now have them in a school so they can learn English. We have also been fundraising for the Orphange.

What was your line of work? I too am an author. Would love to read your spiritual book: My book launch for my next book is on this Sunday after we retrun from our trip. It was delayed from last April... so not the most convenient...but it is what it is so will make it the best I can. Sounds like we have many similarities... I look forward to chatting if that works while you are on the road. When are you planning to be back in the area? If you are interested.... I do have a Web site. (insert) Enjoy your travels!! Much kindness

M: Kris, I haven't traveled far this a.m. but am in no rush to get to Great Falls to visit my son and family, they'll be there whenever I arrive. (Then on to visit my other kids and grandkids in Alberta.) But I just felt that the next rest stop would be a good place to pull over and check emails. Glad I did...

You have me excited Kris! It was a joyous experience to look over your website and the photo of beautiful you. I would dearly love to spend some time with you so we can get to know each other. Six months ago I bought a motor home and set out to write a modern version of John Steinbeck's *"Travels with Charley"*. By the time I got to San Antonio, Texas I realized that I didn't need to travel, via the internet adventures came *to* me wherever I was. So I wintered in Yuma, Arizona and flew out from there to Florida, Costa Rica, etc and kept a journal. Rather than be a real writer like you are, I fictionalized true stories and published them as e-books mainly just for fun and experimentation to see if that style of writing might find a market. (It hasn't yet - if it does I could write and publish one or more e-books every month.)

I'll bet you are excited about the launch of your new book. If I was already there, I'd want to be in the audience. I love your charity project, will you be going back to Africa soon? It would be nice to have a hands on project such as you are involved with. Law of Attraction has functioned daily for me since I embarked on my adventure to the point where daily miracles have become a way of life for me. So, I'm a bit bold and vastly premature but I thought I'd run the following by you for your comments (no commitment) just in case.

1. Just before I sign a long-term lease on a rental pad in Victoria is there any chance that you rent rooms in your own condo???

2. Before I sell my comfy foot motor home (see photo attached) is there any chance that you might be interested in doing and able to get away to do some road trips in it for the summer months? Alaska maybe? Dutch on the gas perhaps? I buy the food, you cook? I do dishes, drive, and sewer hookups. We both watch for kodiaks and rhinos? (Saw a movie a few days ago where two rhinos were doing their version of multiply and replenish the earth - good movie - not just the rhinos.) Anyway, juuust wondering..... and holding my breath. Enjoy the day.

So, just before hitting the road again (Interstate 15 in Idaho) I take a quick walk, see a woman about my age sitting by herself and scribbling in a notepad. I ask her if she's writing "the great American novel". She says she is and the conversation flows. She's an academic from Virginia driving from Salt Lake City to Montana. She's writing non-fiction but on a topic that lends itself to fiction. And she's stopping at all the rest stops (like I am) to jot down notes from her muse (though she doesn't know that yet.) She writes down my pen name and I know she's in good hands, she'll find my website. So I walk away, time to move on up the road, I'm on a schedule...

Kris: Hmmmm...this is very interesting! Glad you enjoyed the web site it is brand new to go along with the book launch and still needs some work. We had a wonderful day at my cousins house and then went to the cemetery... I buried both my parents here. It has been joyous spending time with family and going over old photos. Fun also to share it with my friends. I have been on a spiritual path since the early 90s and listened to allot of Abraham cds and read their book. I too find life is full of miracles when one is open to receive and connected to the source of all that is. Its just the ego that tricks us into thinking we are seperate from divine consciousness. That is one of the reasons I wrote this book.. to help people get out of their own way and recognize that we are all God sparks and magnificence personified when we just own it. My work in Africa has been a true gift and would love to share more about it when we connect. Our next project is to work on crowd funding and get a well dug on the orphanage property. I will send you a pic if the little girls we fell in love with.

That is really cool about your motor home adventures. It looks like a gorgeous motor home. I look forward to checking out your website. I have always loved Road trips and used to drive down to key west by myself every year for 5 years when I lived in ontario. I was also in costa ricca this year. Loved it. As for your questions. Lots to explore for sure and look forward to chatting about options. I agree that when we are open to spirit anything is possible. I do own my condo in Victoria and it is a 2 bedroom. Do You have a smart phone and do you text? Well best get off to bed. Look forward to more email and hopefully chatting when I get back to Canada.

M: We certainly do have a lot in common Kris. I'm particularly encouraged by your knowledge of Abraham. I wrote my 1984 book in one sitting (not automatic writing) but find now that I have been exposed to Abraham some thirty years later that Abraham is all over that book, almost certainly the same muse I have today. That plus a number of other happenings lead me to conclude that my non-physical entity is among that group of beings known collectively in our time as Abraham. My guess is that you may be also, or perhaps your affiliation (if any) is among the group called "Magdalenes"?

I have an old basic cell phone on a pay as you go plan but it ran out of funds two days ago. Since I am moving to Canada I think I'll just hold off, then maybe get something there that will make me look more intelligent. I'm glad that you were able to return to your roots. It's always a reconnection to visit the graves of one's parents.

I have a virtual friend who counseled me when meeting people on singles sites to focus first on the things that are negative in that other person rather than getting too carried away with the thrill of the *ideal* images we create prior to that first physical meeting. So, here goes because I've never seen a full-body photo of you. My two ex's were slim and slender when I married them but after a few years they both put on a lot of weight and I lost much of my sexual attraction for them. So it's important to me that my next LTR is preferably not a whole lot overweight. Comments? Pura Vida (did you get to the Arenal hot springs?)

Yes, I'm thinking of Kris a bit. My only concern at this time is if she is tall enough and slim enough for me? If so I'm even thinking of asking her if she is adventurous enough and free enough to go to Carrie's with me for a couple of months to house sit, or maybe with Ashley in Costa Rica, or maybe that beautiful home on 20 acres in Costa Rica is still available and she'd go half on the rental? Etc. But, as I drove today I've been realizing that my mind goes from woman to woman when it should instead be focused on my higher self, for only there is my strength. Trying…

M: (to Ex) Overnighting at a rest stop near Lima, Montana and it's pouring rain. That's the first rain I've experienced in six months! That was quite a dramatic flare, you waking me in the pitch of night after only being naked in my bed for three hours then leaving! Who knows when we'll see each other again but I'll always remember that unique way you have of saying goodbye…

Ex: Sorry, WOW! you are blunt. Must be the writer in you. I could not sleep. I was expecting to see you before you left. Sorry I missed you. Have a safe journey.

Kris: Intersting about the group of beings. I do beleive there are soul groups that come and incarnate to support each other on this journey.. and are of course connected to other non visable entities. It is all so very fascinating. Would love to learn more about Magdalenes!

How many times have you been married? I have been on my own now for a long time. Smart phones are very handy and its great to text and do email when on the road. As for your quiry RE weight. Being a Leo the physical aspect of our presense here as humans is a typical focus. I dated a Leo a while back… we are still very good friends. So i get it. I am not slender and weight has been a bit if an issue… However I love all aspects of myself and staying healthy is my focus. Beauty to me… radiates from within. I am a beautiful person inside and out. So all this said…. I may not be what you are looking for. However I would love to connect when you are in Victoria. It is always lovely to have like minded souls to share this adventure with…even if it is just as friends. I have sent a photo from November…my hair is short. Still would like to stay in touch and it would be great to chat once you get a phone. My smart phone # is (insert) I do also have a land line….. thus is the best number to reach me. Enjoy your travels. Much kindness

M: Thank-you so much for the photo and suggesting that we keep in touch and meet as friends when I settle in Victoria. I am certain that you are beautiful inside and out Kris, but you know how Leo's are. I hope we can continue as pen pals and eventually friends, it would be nice to walk and talk with you now and again. Safe travels home today (tomorrow?)

She sent a photo that shows she is quite a bit overweight, just wouldn't be satisfying to me. So, back to the drawing board. Perhaps after I move to Victoria I'll meet someone who is not on a singles site.

I published Book Eleven today. One more to go then I'll wait to see if there will be a Book Thirteen. That will depend on people buying my books, book 12 in particular. I'm still struggling with the notion that I have to travel in the direction of a woman! Now that Kris is out there's a void. I need to get back to meditation and follow my own higher self. It's so danged cold at this high elevation that I'm not even going to shave or wash up, just get traveling down the road until the sunshine warms things up. Am I sure I want to move back to Canada? Maybe I should take Carrie up on that offer? But what would I do with Loa?

Kris: Thanks for the link....I will check it out. We had a wonderful day walking around Helsinki today and now packing up and getting ready to go home. Enjoy the rest of your travels. Hopefully we will touch base when you are on Victoria.

June 10. The magic continues. As I write this I am in room 311 at 412 Quebec Street James Bay, Victoria, British Columbia Canada. Decades ago I lived here in a suite I was renting. Today it is a Best Western hotel. I'm looking for a place to rent in James Bay preferably. Last night I was at a hotel in Sidney by the Sea, the night before in Kelowna, driving my daughter's car filled with stuff from Loa who is parked at my son's home near Great Falls, Montana.

In Sidney I have been wondering for some time what happened to a woman who collects bottles. I had a long conversation with her about religion last August and gave her a hundred dollar bill. She was probably homeless. As I drove to the pier in Sidney I saw her, parked, and followed her in to a grocery store where she was cashing in bottles. I didn't talk to her, would have given her money if I had, but thought maybe she was bringing me luck and bought two lottery tickets with her standing just a few feet away, her back turned to me. If they are big winners, I'll make sure she's taken care of financially for a year or more.

Another woman, I think she owns a restaurant, I had fantasized about for months. I walked to that restaurant and she was there, as usual in a form fitting tight black dress with more than just cleavage showing. All I could think of to ask her was what time they open for breakfast. She's beautiful, I didn't see a ring on her finger, but she's much younger than me. So I now have closure on the two women in Sidney, I needn't go there anymore. But if I do and I see the homeless lady I'll give her some money. What will the morrow bring I wonder? I walked and sat at Victoria's Inner Harbor just one block from where I am now and love it here. But it's time to start accumulating money so I can advance my experiences, make everything bigger and better... And I'm tired of writing this journal, it's not selling anyway, my series of books will most likely conclude soon.

The magic continues. After looking for a place to rent for several days, today it all fell into place assuming my credit check etc. work out, a one bedroom suite in a high rise across the street from James Bay Square, exactly where I wanted to be. So I headed back to Sidney and went into a restaurant to use their restroom, parked in a 15 minute limit. I knew I still had to talk to the bag lady I gave $100 to last August to give her money. On the way back to my car on impulse I took a detour and she appeared out of nowhere. I talked with her for a few minutes. She's from a Slovak country, came to Canada at age 22 with only a grade 5 education. Worked in factories etc. She has a place to sleep in a house somewhere but needs to collect and sell bottles for a living, no pension. I gave her another $100 USA bill. As I walked away she said not to forget her when I get the "tickets". I guess it means the lottery tickets I bought in her presence a few days ago and my plan to give her some of the proceeds, she must read my mind, possibly clairvoyant, that's what they do I think. What a life I'm having as I surrender myself more and more to 'the force" or whatever you want to call it! I'm happy, not even thinking much of Suzanne anymore. But I love her...

Today as I left Sidney to go to an appointment to sign a lease I stopped at a bank then took some side streets to avoid the one way. I'd never seen the lady I gave the money to anywhere on those side streets before and there's no reason for her to be there, unless she lives nearby? Anyway I took the last turn to get back to Beacon Street and there she was. She seemed to be looking right at me as she pulled a hood on her face lower even though it was not a cold morning. I won't forget her, I now accept that she's magic and I don't have a problem with that, my life has been magic for months. I'd like to give her the pension she never got to take care of her for the rest of her life. That will depend on winning the lottery with the tickets I bought when she was near, the tickets she muttered about as I walked away from her.

I should be with my brother and his wife tomorrow night, am stopped in the middle of the Rocky Mountains tonight.

Carrie: hi there… getting ready to leave on tuesday, but i thought i'd check in to see how all is going in your life these days??? any new marketing in place? still working with ashley? where are you these days and any special lady filling your thoughts??? hope all is well… i'm starting to get excited for this adventure into the complete unknown… we have no reservations, plans or have to's just getting in his truck and heading north… will most likely have a detour to hawaii in the middle of the trip for 2 to 4 weeks, so i'm really looking forward to that… we are still in a place of good friends, without expectations, but we are both hoping it will be explosive chemistry and a lover dynamic… either way, we'll have a great trip and i'm really loving jumping off into the unknown and allowing spirit to guide the whole experience… sending hugs, as always carrie

M: It's nice to hear from you Carrie. I'm wishing for the two of you the very best of chemistry. You should both enjoy the itinerary very much, and hopefully each other just as well. As for my series of books, I've now published the twelfth book. It will most likely be the last one because of the lack of sales. I am not planning to put more money into it. It was an experimental venture all along, just a running journal that I was publishing. But I had great fun doing it, it is my hope that everyone else involved enjoyed the ride as well.

I'm in the process of moving to Victoria, a new life where I will use my real name again and forget that for a time I was the "famous" Michael who knew Carrie Fisher. Loa will be going into a rental pool in southern California until I decide to RV again. I'm currently sorting through the 60 or so ladies who almost instantly responded when I changed my address to Victoria. It seems almost that I'm the only male on Vancouver Island. So life goes on, exciting, wonderful, full of goodness. Please keep in touch Carrie, I value your friendship.

Well, I could go on and on with other women from singles who have already written to me and who no doubt will. But this journal is just not working for anyone else, books are not selling. So I've decided to not be a writer, at least for a while, take the pressure off, be a retired gentleman again, one who is moving to Victoria on July 1st. But in the secret parts of me where I find myself one with my Higher Self, there are thoughts like: *"I love our women."* I want to be made immortal and find and gather my sister wives so we can have great joy on this planet, move on to others, and populate them.

June 25, 2014. Ashley, I greatly appreciate your help with my project and am pleased that we were able to meet. It was great fun but I've decided not to put any more money into promotions. It was a good run but the miles are behind now and other ventures beckon. So please do not send more invoices, thanks. I wish you the very best. Michael

Ashley: Hi Michael, Good luck with everything!! I'm always going to be available if you do need anything done. Keep me posted in the future how things are going. Keeping up with the changes in life truly is a skill. I'm in Canada now enjoying some summer and visiting family. Take care, thank you and it was a pleasure to meet you. Never stop being who you are. You are a beautiful person!

Now, in Loa parked behind the Casa Blanca in Mesquite, Nevada on June 27th, 2014 as I read my daughter's first novel I have become aware that I am not the writer in the family, it is she! My hope is to become immortal, to find the women who are a part of myself, to gather them, and eventually to populate planets. I desire a billion dollars to give them everything they want on this planet even before they become immortal. I know in writing that sentence that I present still as a very strange man even though I am no longer Michael and my book project has reached its end - unless I write as an immortal someday. Doing that would be the only hope for my books to become popular. Adieu dear reader, should you ever come to this place where Michael has been buried, only the phoenix of who he had become would bring him back. Yet I am happy and grateful for my freedom, life is so fun...

July 1, 2014. I'm in California about to leave Loa in good hands where she'll be rented by interesting people and have many wonderful adventures without me. She served me well.

Oresha: Hi Michael Here's my "test" message.... lol Please let me know that you got it... I am SO looking forward to spending some time with you, in getting to know one another a bit better... and chatting about some of our life experiences etc. I'll have to save my "Moorea" stories for our "face-to-face" conversations... lol I've been there 3 times, so far... and it would take a while to tell you about that part of my "journey"... I get the sense that you have many wonderful stories to share with me as well. Thank you for sharing the piece about your explorations in the Mexican jungle! I can't wait to hear more about that! How exciting! I also have some incredible things to share about my adventures in The Yucatan from a spiritual workshop that I attended a few yrs ago! SO many "stories"/insights to share...lol This could take a while!...lol I get excited about connecting with authentic Souls who are on their Spiritual Path, "walking their talk".. and "living" their lives on the upward spiral...raising their vibrational frequencies.... and "Living from The Heart"..... Have a wonderful rest of your day! Ttyl...... Oresha

M: Well Oresha, you look just as purty on email as you do on the singles site, you passed the "test". Attached photo is me with a Mayan boy at one of the villages along Lake Atitlan, Guatemala. That was a few years ago. I've been to Tulum a few times, once went in a side gate for a private tour with the prof and his Mexican sidekick, love that beach. You summed up in one sentence exactly what I have concluded after a lifetime of spiritual exploration, women seem to 'get it' a whole lot sooner than men. *It's all about raising one's vibrations!* In that raising we experience not only intimate contact with our non-physical entities, but *happiness*, the greatest experience of all.

But the journey's real fun and we're never done. Isn't it grand that we choose to hide from ourselves that it's really we ourselves who are creating our lives. Life would be so boring (the greatest of pains) if we allowed into consciousness what's going to happen tomorrow and the day after and the day after. Why *live* if we already know the future? I love life. Let's meet soon...

M: Just broke open the last of the dark chocolate bars I had in my fridge, had to give some away to visiting grandkids from Phoenix who stopped by on the way to Alberta with my youngest son and his wife two days ago. After deciding to move back to Canada about three weeks ago, I left my motorhome in Great Falls and rode to Alberta with a daughter, arriving there Saturday night. Early Sunday morning I felt an impulse to rush to Victoria to look at a furnished suite in James Bay where I wanted to locate. My daughter generously offered me her car and I was soon looking over the advertised suite, but was disappointed to find it not up to my standards. Over the following three days I started at James Bay Square and walked around from there looking for something suitable and available in the near future. A second floor suite in a high rise became available and I quickly grabbed it, signing a one year lease. It's a perfect location, across the street from a 24 hour grocery store, three blocks to Inner Harbor, and three blocks the other way to Dallas Rd., couldn't be better from my point of view. What part of Victoria do you live in? Did you move to Victoria from....? Retired?

Oresha: Good Evening Michael Thanks for the complement... Whew! Glad I passed the "Test"...lol (lol means laughing out loud) I really enjoyed experiencing Tulum.... and many of the Sacred Mayan sites. I had an Incredible experience at Kabah!...and at Coba, I "met" a Shaman who "REMEMBERED" Me!... and so much more..... My camera picked up things that I can not rationally explain!... It has a tendency to do that!... Perhaps you'd like to see some of my "Woo...Woo" pics some day? I've got plenty of them!... from many different countries. Are you familiar with "Orbs"? I attended an "Orb Conference" in Palms Springs a few yrs ago...it was a Blast!

I've never been to Guatemala..however I would love to experience some of the Mayan sites there. It's wonderful to be conversing with a man who has had "Spiritual Experiences" and traveled to/appreciates so many "magical" places upon this magnificent earth!... and who is willing to share some of those with me(?)... lol Australia and new Zealand are still on my "bucket list"... as is Bali.... and many more of the Pacific Islands. I almost went to The Cook Islands.... That's an area that I really resonate with. I've also had "past life remembrances" at Stonehendge, a sacred cave in Majorca, Caracas Venezuela, Mexico, Hawaii and Tahiti.. so far...lol Have you had any of those "memories"?

Yes, I do believe that it's all about raising one's Vibrations..on an ongoing basis... There's always something wonderful to "learn/

remember" and experience...if we just remain "open" to the Magical Possibilities! I totally agree with you... Happiness is The Greatest experience.. along with True LOVE, of course... You got me... with the Dark chocolate bars!!!... lol I Love good dark chocolate!... mmmmmmmmm..... I also LOVE LIFE!.. I see you just sent me another message...so I'll head on over there now.... Ciao.... Oresha

Oresha: Well, I'm glad that you went with Your "impulse" to rush to Victoria and explore the possibilities!...lol Like I just said, I almost moved in to that same building...lol However, I was called to another place.... so we're pretty well going to be neighbours... just across the park from one another... I walk over to the James Bay Thrifty's for groceries a few times a week... ha! ha! I'm so glad that you found your "niche" in James Bay! It is a great location! I do LOVE it here in Victoria! I'm looking forward to exploring more of the province and our Beautiful island! Have you ever been to Tofino, Ueclulet, Cathederal Grove etc.? SO many Wonderous places to explore out here! I had a friend living on Salt Spring Island and a friend in Vancouver.. so I came out to visit... and when my marriage went down the tubes...I decided to relocate out here... and the rest is history!... here I AM.... lol This is where "Spirit" dropped me to start the next chapter of My Life! Yes, I'm retired... lol and... Lovin' Life!.... So please tell me a bit more about yourself.... Looking forward to it...... Night.... Oresha

M: Most of my travel experience has been brief cruise ship stops, including 800 miles up the Amazon in Brazil, quite the adventure. I've done about 20 cruises now and am cruised out. I visited Bali for a few hours and almost missed the ship when our guide kept us inland three hours longer than he was supposed to. They brought the "Bali Hai" to take us back out to the ship. Cook Islanders love Americans, their only road around the island I stopped at was built by Americans during WWII. Places like that would be great to spend a year or so living native and saving for a world cruise or a new bicycle or whatever. Costa Rica is very nice too but a tad expensive, I was there a few weeks ago. Pura Vida, Life, Happiness, True Love, Dark Chocolate - what could be better than that?

Chapter 15

———◈◈◈———

M: (to Oresha) Lovely, we could meet along Dallas Rd for morning walks, who needs a car... Yes, I've been to the places on Vancouver Island you mention, in fact I took my sister from the prairies to Ucluelet etc. and overnighted last summer so we could walk beaches and trails next day. I'd better get some sleep too, need to drive this big RV 350 miles tomorrow and want to miss the afternoon LA rush hour. Two more sleeps and I'll be in Victoria...

Oresha: Sounds like you've had some wonderful experiences...in living/traveling to some awesome destinations. Funny, I got cruised-out after 8 cruises!...Ya got me beat on that one!... lol I've been through most of the Carribbean...either on ships.. or staying on the different islands.... I'm pretty well over that right now... lol Like you, I resonate much more with the S. Pacific and would LOVE to spend time exploring more of their islands and connecting with the wonderful souls who reside there.... and experience their cultures. You'll have to tell me all about your few hrs on Bali sometime... Did you see the movie with Julia Roberts... Eat, Love, Pray? That's when I decided I wanted to experience Bali... pretty darned Romantic in the movie!... lol

Costa Rica has been on my list.... Belize is somewhere I might like to go... have you been there? Have you ever heard of Iguazu Falls in S. America? Phenomenally, Breath-takingly Beautiful!!! That's somewhere else I'd love to take in some day... as are other parts of S. America.... I've been to Venezuela and Colombia so far.... through the Panama Canal.... as far as Central America goes.... I'd love to hear about your Amazon adventure! That's a trip I unsuccessfully tried to talk my ex into doing... lol I've done a Mediteranean Cruise (spelling?)....to Rome, Florence, Pizza, Elba, Monte Carlo, Monaco, Majorca, Barcelona etc. on the cruise ship mostly... And I spent a week in London England and surroundings... There's SUCH a wonderful, great big world out there to explore... as well as the Incredible "Inner Worlds"!... So Much to share!... lol Yes, time for you to get your beauty sleep... safe drive tomorrow.... please bring back some of that warmth and sunshine with you to Victoria! Good Night Michael Sweet Dreams.....

Oresha: I trust you've had a pleasant day.... reached your destination... and are now sitting with your feet up...relaxing.... contemplating the next leg of Your Journey Back "Home".... Just a quick and warm Hello to you. I'll write more a bit later when I have more time to engage in a "conversation" with you... lol Sending Smiles across the Miles.....

M: I can feel those smiles and your warmth "across the miles." I feel already that I have found a friend in you Oresha whether or not we discover/create 'chemistry' as time goes on. Can't wait to meet you, let's do it soon shall we? Even though I'll remain totally disorganized for a while, I expect that I will eventually wash up reasonably well once I get some furniture and find appropriate places to squirrel away stuff in the tiny piece of the high rise that is allotted to me.

Today I went straight to the place that will be renting my RV out and just finished taking care of the paperwork a day early. One more sleep (in my coach at the back of their lot) then tomorrow night at The Waddling Dog in Saanich because my flight doesn't get in until late. Wednesday a.m. I will rent a car and pick up some stuff I left at my sister's) then pickup the keys to my apartment. Then it's decision time figuring out what furniture etc. I'll need, go shopping for it, pick up a Canadian phone, and I expect you know the drill moving into an unfurnished place. At least in this case it's just a tiny one bedroom suite instead of an entire house. Perhaps my first stop should be for an air mattress in case they don't deliver a bed same day. If I'm not responsive to emails for a few days it's only because I don't yet have internet happening when I get there, even though I ordered it ahead of time.

My daughter is sending some of the stuff from my RV by bus to arrive Victoria on July 3rd. I don't remember all that she took across the border with her so I'll just have to wait to see what I'm going to need to buy new. When my ex and I separated I gave her the marital home and furnishings and some income property in exchange for most of our jointly held land holdings. I moved my personal stuff to a storage unit. As I wintered in Yuma, Arizona the storage unit was broken into and everything was stolen. So the plus side is that I have almost nothing by way of material goods to move. I kind of like that though it was a shock at first and took a bit of mental gymnastics to see the positive side of sharing contentedly with those who kindly took possession of my surplus worldly goods, without even troubling me by asking if they could. I'll watch for your "conversation" tonight.

Oresha: How nice that you are a day ahead of "plan"... I have been feeling the same... as you stated... that we already have a "special" friendship in the making... I am very much looking forward to meeting You too!... As a dear friend and I "kid" around... we say "Ya don't know... til ya KNOW"... I sense that you and I are looking for many of the same attributes/characteristics in a "Possible Partner"... I know that a deep friendship is something that I appreciate/desire with a Man that I would like to have a Loving/Authentic/Longterm "Real"ationship" with...... I'm going with the Flow... and would like to enjoy the unfoldment of Possibilities... and in getting to truly know" one another...over time... if both people would like to explore those possibilities... I remember reading an article once that said that most people put more thought in to buying a vehicle... than into choosing a Partner!... How crazzee is THAT!... lol

I appreciate the fact that you have lots on your mind/plate right now.. with your move, buying the furniture that will make you comfortable in your new home...and placing things to your liking... etc.... I also understand if your internet provider misses the scheduled delivery of service... although we can hope for the best!... or perhaps send "smoke signals" to one another... lol You'll be well on your way when you touch down at The Waddling Dog.. lol How nice to have your sister's kind and loving support along the way! It'll be like Christmas when you get the package from your daughter!... ha! ha! I also downsized considerably when I moved out here.... However I had part of an 18 Wheeler with my personal belongings and my car in the trailer... as I flew over the Beautiful Rockies.. all the way to Vancouver!

I'm sorry to hear about your "involuntary" give away of your "stuff"! Isn't it amazing how The Universe functions at times... I guess it decided, in it's Infinite Wisdom, that you truly needed a "Fresh Start"! Where were you born, and where did you grow up? So when you joined the RCAF... were you a pilot by any chance? I'm so looking forward to learning much more about YOU and your life up until Victoria!... Wishing You a restful night's sleep...and a pleasant Journey tomorrow.... Looking forward to connecting after you "touch down" in Victoria Town!... lol Night Michael..... Warm Hugs....

M: I'm fine with smoke signals as long as you're in the hallway outside my suite when they emanate from your direction. I am convinced that I was supposed to have been born on a tropical island where all I had to do was command one of my subjects to crack open a coconut for me and reach for another banana while watching beautiful island girls skinny dip in a warm lagoon. But someone somewhere had a strange sense of humor not and dropped me in Saskatchewan instead. Talk about contrast! Notta pilot in the Air Force but did have a private pilot's license. Life has been and continues to be wonderful. Moving to Victoria marks the beginning of (another) new life, it's going to be great fun watching it unfold before my eyes day after exciting day. Aloha Nui Loa

M: I kind of got carried away last night Oresha, smoke signals might have been better, hope you're ok with all that stuff I laid on you before we'd even met. None of it is important anyway, it's just pleasant to become acquainted with a friend's past, makes one feel more at home in the company of the other. We are always free to choose a new life, a new moment, and happiness therein. We create our lives as we go along, there's much fun in doing that. But here I am before the sun has even risen over the City of Angels penning personal philosophy to a lady I want to meet in person real soon. Gosh what feelings Law of Attraction can bring regardless of distance, we'd better serve this one up grand Oresha, best of friends at least.

I hope we make it to Moorea together so you can show me around your special island, maybe next January. Then the Cook Islands perhaps, get lost among the natives for a while and forget where we came from until a ship comes along looking for castaways and mistakes our smoke signals for signs of intelligent life. Don't forget to bring along a soccer ball just in case we stop talking to each other somewhere along the way. (If you remember that movie, we could of course order one by Fedex if need be, I hear they deliver to the South Pacific.) Are you *that* adventuresome Oresha, a smidgeon at least of careless abandon in you when the timing's right and the man's looking good? I love the tallness of you Yet Unseen One. Got heels too? Promise I'll look up to you if you wear them when you're not standing on a sandy beach.

Note to myself, get dark choc bars just in case Oresha makes it past the park headed my way. Maybe she'll like choc with sea salt if I can get that kind at Thrifty's. Willing to share your most prized possessions Michael? Yeah sure, with *her,* oh yeah...

Better get shaved and showered just in case someone bangs on the door prematurely. The owner said he'll come at 10:30 to take me to the John Wayne airport for the flight to SFO and a three hour layover in that strange but fascinating city. Speaking of strange, sometimes I think I'm a lesbian because I love women so much. (Attempt at humor, chuckle hoped for from tall goddess you. Yes, I'm a *creative* writer, the kind who when present provides hand signals over your shoulder so you get to laugh at the right paragraphs, cry at some maybe, and not get the two mixed up.) I love that image of leaning down and looking over your shoulder dear one, brushing against your hair, *feeling* the nearness of you, you turning, eyes fluttering, looking up, wondering what he's going to do next. I hope it's a romantic encounter for us, a lasting fulfilling one for each, completely comfortable from the beginning - that's what I want to create for us, you? Your Friend "Possible Partner" about to make an appearance on your other special island. Aloha Nui Loa, enjoy the day Oresha as I fly to you, where and when shall we meet?

Oresha: OMG Michael..... What a Beautiful, Divinely Inspiring message to receive this morning! Thank You! I totally appreciate the Sharing that you are so kindly bestowing upon me!.. I promise to get back to You a bit later when I can sit down and drink in the delightful images you've placed in my mind!... I heard my "Dream Time" calling me last night... so didn't get a chance to reply to the previous message... I don't think you got carried away last night... I always appreciate sharing of words, emotions, feelings from depths of an Authentic Heart... YES... I do still want to MEET!. lol Enjoy Your Day...... Ttyl.....

Oresha: You've certainly given me much food for thought!... lol I'm not quite sure where to start... Ha! Ha! Thanks again for sharing about Your Life. (How DID You manage to cram all that Living into the few yrs. that You've been on this Planet!...???) I feel that we just may have volumes to share..and possibly "write" together over time!... if The Universe Smiles upon Us Thank You for the complements.... I want to stay grounded and not let my ego pull me out of The Vortex, so that when we meet, I am in the Best possible Vibrational Alignment. I am really, so excited, about Our Meeting!

How about I give you a couple of days to get your needs met, with your furniture shopping, internet/phone... and setting up "house"... and that we meet at The James Bay Tea Room..... then go for a leisurely stroll along the Ocean? How does that sound to You? How about meeting on Fri. or Sat. for our tea and a walk? Then we can spend some time in getting to know one another a bit better... and share some of those Warm Smiles.... Wishing You a pleasant day's travels.... Welcome "Home" PS... Happy Canada Day! EH?..... lol

Oresha: I just reread this message from You... It made me SMILE... I appreciate your thoughts on "becoming acquainted with a friend's past".. and "making one feel more at home in the company of the other"... I like what you share from the Spirit of Your Heart... and the thought of sharing of the dark chocolate!...mmmmmmmm... O Yeah!... lol I'm so glad to hear that You "Love Women"!... since I happen to be one.... lol I'm looking forward to Your appearance on This Island.... and in getting to spend some quality time with You.... seeing where we may "go from there"... I hope things go well and according to "plan" for You when you get to your new Home.... I'll be looking forward to hearing from You... and to Our Time in exchanging thoughts... insights...and... more...???...lol No Pressure!... just time for Sharing..... from The Heart..... Big Smiles to YOU! Night...... Sweet Dream Scene Aloha.....

M: I made it to The Waddling Dog tonight, quaint, thanks for the messages. Let's keep in touch but Saturday would most likely be best for me because I have a car rented until Friday night and may take my sister to Nanaimo on Friday if I'm caught up with the moving in more or less. So, in case we don't make other arrangements prior, let's plan on meeting this coming Saturday at 11 a.m. at the James Bay Tea Room. Just so neither of us is left standing outside waiting while the other is already inside, would it be best that we meet on the sidewalk and walk in together as near as we can to 11 a.m.? What do you think? I'm really looking forward to meeting and walking and talking with you Oresha. Michael Needing Sleep Good night.

Oresha: Thanks for dropping me a note... I can only imagine how long a day it's been for You! Sat. at 11:00 AM... in front of the James Bay Tea Room sounds delightful.... If you need to reschedule... due to all the "stuff" you've got going on.... you can email me.... or.... my cell is... I only use it for texting, emergencies and "hi....I'm going to be a bit late" type of calls.... If Sun.... or a bit later works out better for You then I understand... I know you've got a lot to deal with in setting up your new place... and in spending time with your family. May things go with The Flow..... Ciao... Night Now

M: It should be a fun few days for me. Are you any good at picking out furniture? Most likely the most prudent first stop for me is somewhere I can buy a tape measure. Hopefully it will come with a handbook of instructions. Enjoy the day Oresha, I'm about to break the night's fast then be off to the games.

Oresha: Have you had a productively Happy Day?...lol Did you get your internet access on time? Guess you won't be reading this message if you didn't...lol Ciao...... Smiles....

M: I finally got hold of the man after being without internet and lo and behold the solution was as simple as plugging their modem into the new cable outlet I had not noticed close to the old one! So I'm back online though still standing in the kitchen to work the keyboard. Another busy day ahead, find and pickup tons of essentials and get four boxes my daughter is sending via Greyhound, hopefully here today. Unpack as best I can with no furniture to put things into yet, etc. It took two hours yesterday to get basic furniture picked out and ordered. It will be delivered tomorrow Friday. Slept on an air mattress last night. Loving my location.

By Friday night I should be reasonably well enough organized for you to drop in for a while and help make a list of what else I need, if you'd like to do that. (Dark chocolate and white tea is on me but I couldn't find the sea salt chocolate bars I favor.) Let me know if you'd like to do that and about when you'll arrive, I'll meet you at the door. There is visitor parking in the back or I'll walk you home through the park if you come without your ride. Here's my new cell number. I may not yet have door buzzer capability so call or set a time of arrival by email and I'll be downstairs waiting for you. Let me know if you'll be driving and I'll meet you near visitor parking at the back.

Oresha: Hope your day is going wonderfully well! Glad to hear that things are falling into place for you.... O the Joys of Moving, Eh?...lol I'm surprised you're getting your furniture delivered so quickly... now that's some fancy manifesting! Would you like to pick a time that you might be ready for a visit on Fri.?..... (since you've got so much to do)... What time do you think you might be ready for a "breather"...and a visit?.... In the afternoon..... or...sometime just after dinner perhaps? Then we can decide if I'm driving or walking over..... P.S.....I don't walk through the park after dark..... since the homeless folks are allowed to camp out there overnight. Since I "sense" that You are a "Gentleman".... I will accept your invitation to drop over to your place (for our 1st "meeting")... and I would gladly share some time with You... and suggestions in making that "list of what else you may need". (Be forewarned.. I always have a "Plan "B"..... if needed...lol...) Looking forward to sharing those SMILES... and getting to know one another a bit better.... and... your kind offer of "tea'n'chocolate..... yummmmmmmm....Ciao....

M: If yer havin yer doots we can sit in the lobby and talk first so you can decide if this Lord is gentleman enough for you Lady Oresha. How be you arrive here at 7 p.m. tomorrow Friday? I'll have the rental car returned by then and can meet you outside the Lord Simcoe. If you walk, I'll meet you at the front entrance and walk you home when you go. If you drive, pull into the driveway on Simcoe Street. If all else fails call me. Will that work for you?

Oresha: Good Evenin' to ya, Lord Michael Are you goin to serenade this Lass a wee bit, wi' the pipes? or perhaps a bit o' Highland Fling?... lol I'll leave Me Doots in my car... as I'm havin' the faith in Your Gentlemaness.... My Laird. My arrival for 7:00P.M. sounds purrrrfect... Since the weatherman doesn't seem to be quite sure where his darts are going to land on his "handy-dandy-weather-prediction-wheel" for tomorrow... I will be driving. I could text you when I find my Guest Spot.. and wait for you there? I'll be looking forward to those SMILES. "til we "meet" on the "morrow".... Wishing You a Very Pleasant Eve'...

M: You talk so purty! I'll be at visitor parking tomorrow at 7 p.m. but don't expect me to be wearin me kilt at that hour, specially if the wind's blowin. Just heading out the door to see if anyone's selling hot dogs or quick eats at Inner Harbor. Good night Oresha, til tomorrow then.

Oresha: What! No Kilt!!!...Dang! Enjoy your evening..... See You tomorrow at 7:00ish! Ciao....

M: My sister was married to a Scot. He's deceased now but did have his own kilt though I don't think he played pipes. That's about as close as you're going to get to me wearing a kilt, unless you're looking for a cross-dresser and you supply the skirt.

My furniture is scheduled to be delivered today between 1 and 3 p.m. But Greyhound with the four boxes from my daughter that were scheduled to arrive yesterday are still on the road. However, I expect that too to work out so I can return the car today. Everything has worked out perfectly for me for the last six or seven months, it's a daily expectation, I love Law of Attraction. Even the last leg of my flight from Los Angeles. It was a tiny airplane and I knew that my carry on computer bag wouldn't fit in the overhead bins. It's not comfy with it under my feet but there was one seat unoccupied on the airplane and of course it was the one next to me. So my bag found a comfy home of it's own.

I'm thinking of making a routine of walking Dallas each morning and enjoying Inner Harbor in the evenings. But 6 a.m. on Dallas this morning did not feel like the sunshine I love to feel all over me so if it becomes a routine I'm going to take advantage of being retired and take the luxury of 'sleeping' in until sunshine's a few degrees higher and warmer. Last night I walked to Inner Harbor hungry and almost settled for poutine. But music was heavy near the Visitor's Center so I checked that out and grabbed a Greek donair or gyro or whatever. It was tasty, the tourists were plentiful, a young man tied a note to the branch of a tree near me then walked off hoping I suppose that I didn't notice, and the music was grand. Until I walked back that is and got too close to a man in a kilt with bags under his arm and a distinct wheeze. (Actually I like the skirl - that word ended with an "L" Oresha, not a t.) See you tonight tall one.

Oresha: Kilts, I can handle... cross-dressing.... not so much!... ha! ha! Glad things are moving forward for you according to "plan".. lol YES, I LOVE Synchronicities!... It's like a "Giant Smile" sent to us from the Universe, assuring us we're on the right track.. and "Doin' Good"!... Isn't it Wonderful how smoothly things go, when we're in The Flow!.. There's that Law of Attraction-Thing!... lol When I moved here... for the first few yrs. I wondered if summer would EVER come!.. lol I have adjusted to our Pacific-Nor'West climate... I think... lol This ain't Southern California... however...it sure beats Ontario's climate!... I was so thrilled to leave Ont.... for the sunnier/warmer/not so humid clime of

Denver. Now, here we are... Blessed to be living in the Canuck Riviera!... lol Although, a Lotto winning could entice me to spend a few months in a warmer/sunnier haven, such as, Hawaii..

Speaking of food offerings in The Inner Harbour, have you heard of the fish and chip place next to the float plane dock.... their fare is Yummmm- O!... It's a shipping container, come kitchen... right on the dock. last time I was there a few weeks ago... the 50 or so folks lined up in front of me, had me put my quest for seafood on hold for a while... lol I especially like the lightly breaded halibut for a treat every now and then. SO Much to explore.... and... Enjoy! Wishing You a Pleasant "in The Flow-kinda-Day".... See You at 7:00.... Ciao...

M: I love seafood (except octopus variations) and I love airplanes. So if we're still talking by then and you're not busy I'll treat us to lunch or dinner there tomorrow, we could walk over? Just had a peanut butter and banana sandwich. I don't cook so I'm quite proud of myself for putting in all that prep time. Had my microwave already arrived it would most likely have been warmed up content of can. And the only cans in the house at the moment are spaghetti and meatballs, so that would have been an easy choice. Ah, piece of dark chocolate for dessert, you're going to *have* to get over here sweetie, it's not going to last.

I understand about warm sunshine, I doubt that I'll last here much past December without a week or so in Hawaii, or Moorea or some such place. I'd love to move around this island more than I have, haven't been much further north than Nanaimo except on passing cruise ships. I don't think I've even been to Sooke. CU Soon

Oresha: You're in for a treat!... fish and chips it is!... ("if" we're still talking by this time tomorrow"... lol") It's an easy walk..just past the Visitor's Centre... Michael..... I am open to spending time with people of "like Mind/Heart".... Let's just allow Our Authentic Selves to come out and "play"..... and see where it may take us???.... no pressure.... Bye the way..... I DO cook!... if you like to eat and can do dishes... it may just be a "match made in heaven"...ha! ha!... lol and I enjoy eating yummmy, good quality food.... (most of the time!.. I do give in to some "weaknesses" every now and then, in my food selections...ha! ha! Good thing that dark chocolate is a food bestowed upon us by from The Gods!... ahhhhhhhh!... Yes, there's a great Big Beautiful Island under our feet to explore!...... as well as Warm, Restful Havens such as Hawaii and Tahiti....gotta Love it!... CU Soon...

M: I had the naive notion that when they delivered my furniture they'd assemble it too. (Thought I had paid for that but it was a misunderstanding.) So there are unopened boxes in all my rooms. But the sofa and reclining chair are ready for use so please come anyway, we can at least chat and get into the chocolate. I also picked up the four packages my daughter sent by bus. Trust her to send some of the stuff in a huge *neon pink* suitcase! What does she think her dad's going to do with that item when it's emptied I wonder? And the car is returned, so it's an inside job from here on in, at least until July 8 when they'll bring the undelivered rails and put the head and end board on my bed. Anyway, I'll get a start on the boxes before you get here, meet you at the top of the ramp. You can park in my spot next to the visitor parking if you like, it's empty now. And yes, I do like to eat, and I do do dishes, and I was just kidding about us not talking.

Oresha: So they "dropped & ran" did they!... lol Amazing how some businesses work... I bought my bed at the same chain before I moved here.. and was amazed that they charged extra for delivery in Victoria! They actually "assembled" the bed for me though... very quickly threw it together onto the frame (box spring and mattress...while saying. "we're really not supposed to do this"... HUH?.... They expected me to assemble it myself!).... There's no head or foot board....When I looked into moving here from the US... the Can. gov't prohibits bringing a bed into the country unless one can PROVE that it's been FUMIGATED!... UGH!... I don't THINK SO!... There's NO way I'm going to be sleeping on a fumigated mattress!.... So I left my bed in Denver.... and am still looking for a suitable headboard that's to my liking... lol..

They dropped off my new TV.. and left it in the box for me.... I had a really nice young cable guy offer to put it together/set it up for me when he came to do my cable hook up! Yay! I couldn't even lift that thing by myself without the aid of a forklift...lol O The Joys of Moving!... lol I don't mind the view of a few boxes... Looking forward to the chat'n'chocolate... I'll look for your parking spot and "break it in" for ya... lol See You Soon.... Ttfn.....

M: I enjoyed last night Oresha, wonderful walk in a beautiful city, good company. Come over when you want. If I notice you parking I'll meet you at the servants entrance. If you go to the front door, my suite code is (insert) but I'm not sure if that works, if it does I'll buzz you in, or go down and meet you. If all else fails there's my cell which has been known to work. See you today sometime tall one.

Oresha: How are you doing this morning? I'm running kinda slow this morning... lol Just now having breakfast after a phone chat.. Kathy called... How about I come over around mid afternoon? I'll pick a time a bit later and email it to you.... then we can plan on trying to assemble some of your stuff... and maybe get around to that "list" of things that you may still need... And... decide when to head over for our Yummmmy Fish for dinner?... What do you think? I enjoyed our time together last night... and look forward to getting to know one another better...

M: Sounds like a plan but I've decided to find a handyman to assemble the furniture. And judging by the stuff I've already unpacked that my daughter sent I'm not going to have room for anything more unless I get some hooks and suspend stuff from the ceiling. It's pouring rain so we're going to have to drive for food if that container hasn't floated away already. I'm ready to eat when you are.

Oresha: Ok.. I'll put my handy-dandy screw driver and pliers away... lol As far as the fish we'll have to stand outside in the rain to place our order and wait for it.... so... do you feel up for that?.. or perhaps we could just venture out to the Inner Harbour or somewhere near to your place to find some late lunch.. or early dinner for today... and do the Fish Thing on a nicer day? Maybe we could just run across the st. from you to check out that cool little Bistro?....

M: Let's dash to the bistro today, I'll provide a rain check for the fish.

Oresha: OK...that sounds good to me. Looking forward to Our Dash... lol What time would you like me to make my appearance?...

M: I'm expecting a handyman to come to the door any minute but I'm starving so come over when you're ready. If he starts assembling we'll just leave him to it.

Oresha: OK...will do... Hopefully I can be there in about 30-45 min...tops please don't starve before I get there!..

M: Handy man just came, he'll be assembling Monday a.m. so the day's ours if you want to spend it with me.

Oresha: I'm getting ready to come over..... see you in a few.

Oresha: Going out the door in a few minutes... you'll see my car in a bit... lol

Oresha: Thank You for another Lovely Day! I am enjoying your company and our sharing.... from Our Hearts.... It is a Joy to spend time with You... You are a Sweet Soul Good Night.... Sweet Dreams.....

M: Thanks for sharing some of your special spaces and photos and stories Oresha. Enjoy the day.

Chapter 16

—◦◆◦—

Yeah I know, this conversation with Oresha is getting booooring lol. I'm not sure if my editor is going to leave it in or not, I don't care much either way, it's all for you. You think I'm just inventing the lol laughing out louds? Nope, wouldn't impose that on you or on me, that's how she writes. But it took me ages to edit out the :) smiles in between the lol's. That's just the way she writes, we'll love her anyway eh? Let's see what DeLeon in Florida aka "DeLeon Goddess of Bling and Eternal Spring" has to say after a long silence. Sure, we'll get to Michael and Jen before the end of this book, promise. I'm not lost, just want to catch you up on where I'm coming from pre Victoria, thought you'd be interested. By the end of Book 3 we'll be caught up and living it all *live* real time for you. Excited? What's your guess, Suzanne going to show again? Is Michael still in love with her? Will she send hospice stories? Will they ever get to Paris together? Do sex? Will Elaine drop out? Does Michael ever sleep with her? Is Jen Michael's Eve or his greatest temptation? Is, is… oh hang, you know the drill…

DeLeon: Michael, There is much I want to say to you….as it is important to me, that I do so.:

First Things First: It has taken a long time - as I was hit with another shock from you, after you left… just like I had been when you were here for the first time with me. After you left - you headed to Las Vegas… and dropped me on all levels - no communication - of any type for 8 or 11 days. When regardless, before, there was always something - and done in a sweet way. And unfortunately my heart was shattered. And it had now happened twice with you. As best as I can describe, what I had experienced with you on that incredible trip…. and before we left and after we came back….. opened by body, my mind, my heart, my soul, perhaps, like never before. Perhaps it's called "falling in love"?? I didn't realize that was happening, I just know, that may have been one of the most extraordinary times of my life, because of you. It was an extraordinary movie - and then the movie ended. It has taken a long time to settle in to all, accept all and go on - go "forward".

I cancelled the Ablation Procedure, scheduled May 1st, as I just could not handle another hospital stay, another..... all of what one goes thru. Have finally come strong enuff to take it on, one more time - and that will be July 18th. You'll get a kick out of this.... For some wild reason, (am sure we both get it) I am being pursued by several YOUNG men. I mean young, not younger. My girl friends are having fun, calling me "the Cougar" - one gal said, we've got to put a harness on you. I hadn't even heard of that before. It's a fun muse.

Am working on my Contempt of Court Case - Universe is stunningly inspiring me with a friend from church who is a law professor and another friend who lives in the complex who is an expert witness in courts - and with an incredible personal story.... is such a wizard in the court system. Both spending hours helping me. Hoping all is good with you. See you are still in British Columbia - and wishing you well. Showers of Blessings.... DeLeon

DeLeon: I said all of that, but didn't say....what I was really wanting to say... THANK YOU, THANK YOU, THANK YOU - - - FOR EVERYTHING YOU DID WITH ME... AND TO ME... AND FOR ME.. ON THAT TRIP. IT WAS TRULY......... A JOY, A GIFT, A BLESSING, A HEALING, AN EVOLVING, AN AWAKENING, A KNOWING. YOU WERE MY LORD, MY SAVIOR, MY ONENESS WITH MAN AND GOD IN LOVE, ALWAYS........... DeLeon

M: We did have some wonderful times together DeLeon, it is my hope that we will both remember them with fondness and appreciation. I am indeed settled in British Columbia having gone Canadian again and living in beautiful Victoria on the sea, I love it here. Re your emerging "Cougar" days, I always knew you were of the cat family but took you for lion. I wish you the very best with your court case and other events of the present moment, I expect that you will succeed with it all. You were and are dear to me DeLeon, be well sweetie. P.S. I like your photo on singles, very nice.

Oresha: G'D Eventide Lord Simcoe.... How is your Sunday going? Hope you're enjoying yet another Day in Paradise. I've been enjoying my sun-time on my balcony... reading Abraham... I'm getting into the "Process of Pivoting".... I'd love to discuss more about the teachings of Abraham with you, sometime soon... I was in Sidney By The Sea today to meet a friend for lunch... and lo and behold... for the 1st time ever... I encountered your "Bottle-Lady" friend... And thought about you and your generosity.... It was wonderful sharing "time and space" with you on our stroll through the Magical Beacon Hill.... Sharing that "Energy of Place".... times 2... Wouldst thou like to partake of dinner with me... at my home on the weekend? Perhaps sat. night? Do you like lasagne?..... with a fresh green salad and a crisp glass of Chardonnay ? Good food, Great company, Smiles to go 'round..... O and maybe something sweet for dessert?.... Maybe.. even something chocolatey???...lol Life is Good!.... Ciao....

M: (to Oresha) I'd be delighted to park my humble self at your table Saturday eve m'Lady, the menu evokes reveries of sweet deliciousness. And sometime during the week I'm hoping you will cash in that rain check and play fish and chip with me before I forget the taste of flying otter and can't compare the two. Today I took a sluff day, didn't even shave, went back to bed several times in the a.m. just because I could. I then set out for a walk in the early afternoon, discovered the consignment store across the street was open and bought a used toaster. (Had toast and cheese slices with my customary content of can for dinner, a great improvement.)

Tried the walk again and ended up not getting home for five hours, it was a glorious day. I started at Inner Harbor and spent quite some time listening to an extremely animated man sing beside his teenage daughter with a lovely face and a winning voice, and his tiny son maybe ten years old balancing a huge bass guitar that towered over him, singing along, creating deep sounds, and beating acoustics on the wooden parts of it. They were great, had good crowd. Then headed past the guy with the bag and skirl, along St. Anne's Academy and into Beacon Hill Park. I looked at the map, wandered past the baseball field and walked the (entire - you'd be proud of me) length of your one block street listening for a call from a balcony somewhere. Then along the Village, back into the park, lakes, streams, birds, the hill, along Dallas etc. an almost perfect day except I was (already) missing the touch of tall you at my side, you're fun.

It seems that 'my' bag/bottle lady is appearing to you in Sidney as well. Next time, talk with her and ask her impressions of the American with the hundred dollar bills. But don't talk religion, you'll never get away. Hope to see you soon.

Oresha: I would be honoured to have you "parking Your humble self at my table" on Sat. eve.... We will have to decide upon a time for your arrival, later in the week. I would Love to take you up on your generous offer of sharing a blue fish dining delight one night this week. Good for you, taking a day off for Yourself today... and chillin'... lol So funny... I just didn't feel like much dinner tonight... so went and got a loaf of yummy flax and whole wheat bread along with some incredible balsamic cheese... Yummmmmmm... and that was my dinner! I'm so glad you found your toaster essential... lol

WOW! I AM proud of you!.... trekking that distance again today! Good for You! I did a short stroll through the park. Did you know that every Fri, Sat, Sun. and Holiday Mondays... there are different groups playing at the bandshell in the park from mid June til Sept. 12th... and some evenings they roll out the Big Screen to view the Oldies Movies?... I'm afraid I wouldn't have seen you pass by my humble abode since my apt. faces the back of the building... otherwise I would have "called" to you from yon balcony!... lol How sweet!... I missed You and Your Touch/Smile as well... Another Day.... We shall see each other again... SOON!... let's talk!... lol Just let me know when you'd like to get together again.... And a Blue Fishin' we shall a go!... lol Night to You....

M: Furniture assembler hasn't showed up yet so I'm stuck in the house waiting. I'm interested in the concert in the park etc., be bold suggest away... I have some Abraham videos that you might be interested in seeing...

Oresha: Good Morning "Neighbour-of-Mine"... lol Funny, I was just composing a message to say "Hi" and wish you a Happy Monday.... along with my mentioning that you must be getting your furniture assembled at this moment in time... lol Since we are "almost-neighbours"... I'd like to say that you'll never find me just dropping by unannounced and buzzing your door... lol I like to connect with friends and get together at a planned time etc.... and I appreciate the same in return. So any time that you feel the desire to get together and share some time and space....please just drop me a line or give me a buzz on my landline if you'd like.... or a text on my cell would be great.... or maybe even those smoke signals we previously talked about....ha! ha! Bye the way is the handy man going to figure out what's up with your door buzzer/phone not working?

I would love to watch some of your Abraham videos sometime, thanks... Looking forward to our upcoming Blue Fish Adventure. Next time I see your place, you'll have traded in all those "Boxes"... for "real" furniture...lol Enjoy Your Day!..... Hugz.....

M: I too value privacy, I will not materialize at your home without first sending a messenger and getting an appointed time, email preferred, Scotty optional. The handy man just arrived, I have yet to talk to the manager about the door buzzer, slow drain etc. Love those hugz tall one, save me some more..

M: I tend to think a whole lot into the future, considering possibilities, always have, and I have a question for you. Should you and I ever decide to become travel companions, would you be willing and able to split the expenses? E.g. economy flights to and from Moorea, hotels, meals etc. Or do you subscribe to the tradition that the man should take care of things like that? Or am I waaay too far ahead of myself here and assuming much too much? I'm thinking at this time of staying on the island until after Christmas, though I'm quite interested in exploring beyond Victoria should the opportunity arise. In such a case I would pay the gasoline should my companion provide the vehicle and share other expenses. Just being open, as you were about the smoke signals, I appreciate that.

Oresha: As to your "possible-future?" question"... right now it seems like the "cart-before-the-horse" to me... lol I think this is a good place to open the door to a "face-time" dialogue... lol So could you hold that thought please... til we are conversing in real time ?... I am enjoying our time spent together.... and in getting to know one another better.... Perhaps we should share our individual desires, as to what it is, that we're each looking for in a "real"ationship".... then we can proceed from there. The answers to your query will be addressed then. Are you enjoying your 1st meal-at-your-round table tonight? I hope the furniture assembly went smoothly... and that it's all coming together for your comfort. Enjoy your eve My Laird

M: It came together well, I love my house! Tomorrow they'll be by to finish the bed otherwise it's done, even to assembling and using my vacuum cleaner first time. Oh, still can't persuade DVD to play with Monitor but I'll get that worked out too. Indeed I did dine at the round table tonight. My knights failed to show though so they'll be eating with the maids in the kitchen tomorrow night. Sometimes I get a nagging suspicion that they actually *enjoy* the punishments I mete out.

To celebrate today's successes I fried up three eggs and two smokies with one toast liberally coated with processed cheese. Nada for you I'm sure but believe me, for me that's HUGE! I haven't been able to get out for a walk yet today so if you're reading this before 9 p.m. and would like to join me (and see my place furnished), you're very welcome to come over. Shoot me an email if you're coming, I'll check until 9 when I'll most likely head to Inner Harbor for a bit of a stretch.

Oresha: Too bad The Knights missed out!... as long as you're getting sustenance... that's a Good Thing!...Sure I'd like to POP over for a bit... I've got to grab a bite... and then I'll head on over to the "other side"... I'll be hoofin it...so I might have to text you when I get there... if the door buzzer still isn't working? I'll send an email as I'm going out the door.... in a few.... maybe around 8:30/40..... Hugz...

M: Shall we meet at Simcoe and Douglas between 8:45 and 9?

Oresha: I'll start walking through the park as soon as I finish eating.... I'll send ya a message... before I go out the door..... then we can "find" one another on Simcoe St...... I'll have my phone with me in case we need to text... hopefully there will be no alien abductions along the way!..

M: K, but I've never used text on my phone before and almost never carry it. I'll hang along Simcoe though and watch for smoke and UFO's, leaving in a few minutes.

Oresha: OK... I'll be leaving in maybe 15 min..... if we stay the course on Simcoe St... we should be OK... May The Force be with US!... If for some unknown reason we "Miss" each other I'll head for your front door.... and we can hook up there.... lol

M: "Hook up" eh? Hold that thought....

Oresha: TEE....HEEEEEE!... I'm going out the door in about 7 min.!...lol

She came down Toronto Street instead of Simcoe but we finally met up and walked to Inner Harbor. At my place she never did say anything about going Dutch on travel (so I assume that she won't) but brought up the subject of my email and said she didn't want just a travel companion but a monogamous marriage type of relationship. (Yep, typical.) I said: *"I don't think I can be that for you Oresha, but I can be your friend."* She ducked her head and I felt that I was released because I don't find her all that attractive, there's another/others for me I'm sure. But she talked then about my coming over for dinner on Saturday (still haven't been inside her place, haven't been invited even though I walked her home late last night) so I guess we're still on. She touches me a lot, we walk arm around each other, hold hands, etc. re physical contact and I like that, but nothing sexual. Ok, I'm looking around…

Oresha: Good Night Michael… as always… I enjoyed our time together…… Sweet Dreams

M: Good night Oresha, I enjoyed our time together once again.

Oresha: Good Mornin to ya Michael Thanks for inviting me to stroll The Inner Harbour with You…. That was Fun…. as always. You must be thoroughly enjoying your new found comfort in having Assembled furniture… lol Your place is feeling more like "home" now? Especially since you purveyed a Toaster!… If you'd like to do a store run one day soon, let me know…. then you can pick another pillow for yourself, to your liking… and find the rest of the things on your "list". If you don't mind I'd like to borrow the Abraham CD/DVD(?) on THIN… lol and perhaps another one… after all I'm now craving My Abraham "fix"…ha! ha! SO much Wonderful info to study! Have a Wonderful Day!… Many Hugz… to You!

M: The guys just left leaving a real bed behind, and the door buzzer/opener has started working of it's own accord. It just keeps getting better and better. Sure, I'd like to pick up another cushion for the sofa and need some printer paper if you're going that way. Just say when, I'll be ready. Maybe we can go color some fish before or after that run. (I haven't had lunch yet as of noon today, sooo…??) You are welcome to borrow any of my dvd's and cd's anytime. I'd love to discuss Abraham with you should you want another perspective on this or that, I'm not busy at all now that this nest is feathered well enough.

Oresha: I have to get my "crown" installed… lol so off to the dentist at 2:00 today….. I can see how I feel after the event… and drop you a line when I get home… Then perhaps a trek to Uptown and with a stop for Blue Fishes? Sorry can't make it any sooner…. lol I would love to discuss the Abraham teachings with You! Yes, you nest is nicely feathered now. Time to enjoy…. I'll let you know how I feel after the dentist.. it shouldn't be too bad... maybe I'll even be able to enjoy some yummmmy seafood today!...

M: A few decades ago the 'Abraham' attitude would have been labelled "cock-eyed optimist". But ok, whatever, *enjoy* your visit to the dentist sweetie, seafood's waiting. I wonder what kind of orbs are going to emanate from that newly adjusted crown of yours this time...

Oresha: Are ya ready for our Uptown Run???? I have a bit of a dribble-lip right now while waiting for the freezing to subside...lol I sound like a Canajan!... Ha! Ha! Drop me a line and I'll come and gettcha...

M: Estimate when you'll arrive and I'll meet you out front on the street.

Oresha: Heading out the door.. NOW!...lol See ya in a few in front of your place...

I need to stop seeing this lady so much because I'm addicted to her tallness and her readiness to see me and to touch me (not sexually, I wish) and I'm not otherwise attracted to her. She is concerned about being overweight and that's a huge no no for me. Let's see what else comes...

Oresha: How are things going for you? Have you been taking in more "sights of the city"? Thanks again for kindly lending me the CD/DVDs.... Kathy and I will be intently watching/listening to them over the next little while.... so that I can get them back to you. We just may have to go to Esther's site and purchase some of them for ourselves! Do you still have room on your dance card for Lasagne and some company on Sat. night?... lol Wishing You a Wondrous Day!... Hugz.....

M: Saturday is written in stone Oresha, just let me know what time to buzz your door. Glad you're enjoying the DVD's, you are welcome to borrow the others too. Keeping busy, enjoying this beautiful city.

Oresha: I'm glad that we'll be sharing an evening of fine conversation... Great company... and..some yummy food as well.. lol Do you usually have dinner at a certain time? I'll have the lasagne "prepped" and ready to pop into the oven when you get here.... The chardonnay will be chilled... and salad and garlic bread at the ready for our "feast"... lol I'll head out and get the ingredients needed today or tomorrow... So please let me know if arriving around 5:30-ish sounds good to you? The lasagne takes about 45 min. in the oven. YES.. the Abraham teachings are wonderful! Kathy and I are getting a lot out of them! Perhaps, a bit down the road, if you'd like..... I would love to have you and Kathy over for maybe some appies and a glass of wine... and a conversation about "everything- Abraham"...lol Ttyl...

M: I'll buzz your door about 5:30 p.m. on Saturday then, should be fun, looking forward to some home cooking and fine company. Sure, as you know I'm checking out all the eligible females in town, still a few left on the list and Kathy's one of them, so let's get together with her sometime for that conversation.

M: (to Ex) You're welcome to come and visit you know, it's beautiful here and I still care about you. I don't know if we can ever stay together again for long but I'd like us to remain friends. You'd have to pay for your flights, I could rent a car to pick you up at the Victoria airport.

Ex: I think I can get a flight for less than $300 or so I could come up around the 26 of July for one or two weeks. Let me know right away.

M: I should let you know that although when you are here I will spend my time with you of course, I do see other women. (Single men my age are in short supply almost everywhere it seems, but especially so here.) So you'd be coming here just for fun, not because I'm lonely or needy. Does that change things for you?

Ex: I never thought for a moment you were spending time alone. Glad you have met some interesting women. You are mine exclusively when I visit as you said other than family visitors. I am waiting to find out when I need to go to California to baby set in August. That way I may be able to push my visit date up.

Oresha: Wishing You Luck in the "gathering of Your "Harem"... and in sorting out your" list"... I'm sure you'll be led to make the right choices for you.... after all there are lots of women in Victoria who are on a Spiritual Path of some sort... I guess it's all about the "Vibrational Alignment"... and in the details that we're both looking for... and in "Allowing" the right person for us, to be a part of our lives... Here's to connecting with "Our Best Vibrational Matches" And here's to Happiness, Balance and Joy, Harmony, and Ultimately, LOVE!.... (or at least that's what I'm looking for... I'm looking to connect with "Mr.-Right-For-Me" who is my Divine Complement).... I appreciate

Your Friendship...and..wish You The Very Best in what it is that You are looking for... I hope we can continue to be friends and truly enjoy one another's company. See You on Sat. night.... bring your appetite.... Cheers!.... Hugz....

M: Thanks Oresha, I appreciate your comments and your best wishes. I do want to be your friend and to have fun together even if I can't be the man you really want - I wish you the very best finding him. I thoroughly enjoy our carefree swinging down the street hand in hand, arm in arm. I do love that you accept public displays of affection and that you touch. If I was ever to write a book on how to be a winner on singles sites I'd most likely suggest to women that they write on their profile in all caps something like *"I'M A CATCH AND RELEASE WOMAN!"*

Ultimately I think everyone male and female is *hoping* for forever love, an ideal perfect companion they'd love to spend always with. The problem is that most women even those beyond child bearing age want (and advertise that they want) *exclusive* possession of a man's body, a monogamous form of "marriage", right from the get go. You too are in that category, that's normal for most women on singles. But many if not most men want to retain their FREEDOM, or at least the perception that they are free to be with just one woman, or not, the freedom that organized religions forbid in western culture.

As you know, there is a shortage of "good" men on singles sites, it's a very competitive environment for women. So, what I'm suggesting is that a woman could have a huge advantage over other women if she let it be known that she's willing to "catch and release" should her man want to sample more than one of this world's delights as he exercises individual free will and *lives* the moments of his incarnation. The magic of that catch and release attitude is that it is most likely once the man has grown accustomed to her he's going to give her exactly what she wants anyway, while still cherishing the notion that he's not tied down to marriage like he was before the last divorce, he's *"free"*.

But it is my experience that most women will spend years even decades alone and lonely rather than accept into their arms if even for a short time a man who enjoys her but has not committed to a monogamous relationship. Had she advertised "catch and release" she could most likely have had at least one and perhaps over time several companions to enjoy for as long as it lasted instead of soaking in loneliness pining for a "true love", an *ideal* that may not even exist on this planet except perhaps for a very very few. So, loneliness because of tradition and an inflexible attitude, or imperfect love and lots of fun along the way with one or several short or long-term companions? What do you think of that theory?

Oresha: Thank you for sharing your thoughts on your "Catch & Release" Theory.... I believe you are entitled to your thoughts and opinions, however..... I know it's not My "Truth"... That being said, I do enjoy Your Friendship.... and.... do wish You The Very Best in meeting Your "Match"... lol See ya on Sat..... for our get together.... Enjoy your day! Hugz...

M: Hey it's Friday hon, wanna walk some today/tonight? Take me to a pub and I'll buy you a beer.

Oresha: I'd have some time late afternoon... if ya'd like to get together then?.... (I have a phone call at 9:00 tonight, so need to be home then... I have some errands to run 1st... how does around 4:00 -ish sound. for a bit? I also am doing the vacuuming/spiffin up and needing to pick up a few more things etc. before my "Guest" arrives for tomorrow's Dinner... lol We could meet walking towards each other on Simcoe/ Toronto St.?

M: I'll leave home at 4 p.m. and head down Toronto, won't go into the park. I suggest we walk through the Park to Dallas, to the end of the breakwater, then take the trail at the side of the Ogden Point Cafe to the (Laurel Point) hotel where you want to sit outside, I'll buy you a beer and we'll make it up from there?? I'll walk you home before 9 p.m. Good plan?

Oresha: That sounds like Fun... I'll also leave home at 4..... You take the "high road..and.. I'll take..the low road"..... meetcha in the Middle... lol.. or there abouts... ha! ha!

M: 'Cept I'll get to Scotland afore ye. And darned if I'm going to wear me kilt!

Oresha: No Doot!... lol

M: But ok, I'll compromise, I know you just can't wait to see my hairy legs so I'll wear shorts today. Will that do the trick for you? I'm done my chores, move it up to 3:30 maybe? Give us a bit more time before I start to freeze when the sun turns green.

Oresha: Ok...I'll start out at 3:30... after all... we don't want to see the hair on your legs freeze.. lol

We met at the park and it was awkward because an older man from her apartment was right behind her and she whispered not to show too much affection, plus the exchange of emails re being friends only. But after twenty minutes or so we were back to strolling arm in arm hand in hand. But this woman's expensive! Appetizers and a glass of wine on the outdoor patio with tip cost $110. She did offer to help with the cost but I declined. I'll be at her place at 5:30 today for dinner. Meanwhile, there's Ex wanting to know when she can come and a lady from Anacortes Island breathing down my neck!!! Wonder where that one's going – I've cooled off a lot, too much happening on that scene right now but she seems real interested in me. She makes her presence felt on the Internet, writing product reviews many places. She has certainly moved around the USA.

Oresha: If you happen to be home, on this gorgeous day.... and read this... I am running a bit behind... so would you kindly arrive at my door at 6:00 PM instead of 5:30? Thanx.... please let me know if you read this in time.... Hugz...

M: I'll arrive about 6 Oresha, I really appreciate your invitation.

Oresha: Looking forward to your arrival.... A Fun time to be had.. by All... Bring Your "Hungry" with You!... lol

M: Thanks for a great dinner, the doggy bag, the walk, your friendship, the ride home, the the... Anyway, enjoy the day Oresha.

Oresha: As always, I also enjoyed your company.. and very much appreciate Our Friendship... You're very welcome..it's nice to share a meal... and chat... I LOVE getting out and walking... Have a great day!... Enjoy the sunshiney/warmth... Hugz...

Oresha: PS.... When I got back home last night...I started rinsing the dishes.. and thought.. what the heck... so about a 1/2 hr. later...they were done... lol Thanks for offering to help with doing them... I just wasn't in the mood to tackle them til later... so No... dirty dishes to wake up to this morning... Yay!. lol.... Ciao...

Let's move on. I'll introduce an exceptionally knowledgeable lady who plays a brief but significant role in this story. Her involvement with me results in my sending Jen home from a visit in Victoria a week early. That 'rejection' eventually becomes a life-changing event for her and Jen becomes a stranger to me. She aggressively goes after other men, a man on her second date picking her up, laying her down on her own sofa and lying hard on top of her, his hand on her breast. Yes, JEN!! And I spend a couple of nights in Jackie's bed. Mmmm, like that? Ready for it lol?

Jackie: (a lady on singles) Just received your profile so quickly scanned through it. Not much time to send a note now but felt resonance in your words. If you feel the same resonance, perhaps another, expanded note is in order?? Namaste, Jackie

M: We have a great deal in common Jackie, maybe too much, I think we're siblings.

M: P.S. I have seen you on the spiritual singles site too.

Jackie: It appears that you have been ingesting and digesting much of the Abraham (Esther Hicks) material while exploring and enjoying who you are. Good news for the planet, humankind and you: Yahhhhhh Yes, I was on spiritual singles.... and still am... I think! Initially disappointing since there were very few.... actually non-existent... spiritual men listed in this area. Most are in the U.S and a few scattered throughout Canada. So, here I am... exploring another arm of the river. LOL Perhaps you're an aspect of my soul.... twin soul, soul mate, sibling soul?? Now those are loaded words which ultimately means... yep, we are connected. Isn't that called Quantum Entanglement?? If you would like to create a greater connection.... let me know. Choices are infinite. With Love, As Love, Jackie

M: Pen pals for a while Jackie? Tell me about "sibling souls" as you understand the concept.

Jackie: Michael, Are you (insert my handle) on Spiritual Singles?? I received a "view" from him and went in to see who it was.... had forgotten my password! Sure looks like you my soul friend. I didn't resonate with anyone initially so did not complete my profile. Had been writing a fellow in Washington for a couple months although reasons kept presenting themselves as to why we couldn't meet. So I let it go... "if it doesn't flow, let it go" (smile) I'm not a paid member on that site. Does that make a difference? Perhaps I should go back and complete the profile and upgrade? These are just questions I'm contemplating...not waiting for answers from you...just from me.

And, what I can ascertain regarding soul "siblings" is that all potentials and possibilities exist since we are part of the all... not confined personal souls in a body, or even surrounding a body. We all exist in this Quantum soup of energy. Our souls contain aspects of all past lives and future lives which includes ancestors, soul groups, our star families, guides, angels, and, of course the All That Is. We also have aspects of our soul living in other dimensions and here on earth. The most difficult person in your life can be a soul mate pushing you into a recognition or awareness of your Self. Or, a person who resonates the same kind of energetic frequency can be a best friend, sibling or other close relationship. There is purpose in all of them and no thing is separate from another... just different agreements made with each other... between souls. So, that's the short explanation of "soul"!

Michael, there was a fellow I met online a number of years ago that was, by his definition, very spiritual. He was very interested in what I had to say and kept asking questions without really responding. I wrote long emails trying to explain what I knew. And then he began calling me to have long spiritual discussions. I really enjoyed these times but felt that I was giving much more than what I was receiving. When it came to meeting.... after several months of this... he admitted that he was in a relationship with someone who wasn't spiritual and just wanted to talk to someone about it. That hurt!! All along, I thought there was a possibility for us and he wasn't clear on that from the beginning. I am, after all, human, and deserve authentic, honest communication. I was providing him with what he wanted... which is wonderful... although I was not receiving in return what I was authentically giving. Just to let you know, I had some incredible experiences... too many and too incredible to give words to it here... and later had a long conversation with my guides about such scenario.

My lesson in this life has been... since I tended to give and found it difficult to receive... that's what I had attracted into my life. OMG... there is so much more here... but that will do for contemplation. I have a website that explains more about me... in the process of changing it. Not sure if this address will get to you through here...guess we'll find out. Be well, be Love, Jackie

M: I'm about to walk to the park for an outdoor folk concert and may do a long walk after. But your message deserves an equally comprehensive response, which I will attempt to compose and get to you hopefully before midnight tonight. My handle on spiritual singles is (insert). I have found it to be a very productive singles site but it may be different for women, there seems to be a shortage of eligible males in our age and interest group. Enjoy the day Jackie.

M: If we lived in the same city we would walk and talk and most likely become good friends. But we don't and I don't have a car having dropped off my motor home at a rental pool in Los Angeles and flown to Victoria from there in my recent move to this city. Should we become pen pals I think you would find that I can get along quite well in writing, giving as well as appreciating the returns. But I think you'd be wise to slot me right away into a similar category as the man who wanted to chat. I say that because in the last three or so weeks my singles inboxes have been inundated and the flow of expressions of interest has not ceased. So, like possibly most single males our age on this island, I am in the happy for me not so for the ladies position of needing to wait and see what/who finally settles out. But I'd like to meet you sometime Jackie.

Thank-you for your thoughts regarding soul relationships. Abraham makes it so easy, too easy sometimes because it's alluring to relax, observe, and simply BE, accepting that everyone is here doing a journey their own inner selves are creating so are not in need of healing or modification of any kind. Our place as individuals becomes to be happy and have fun, and nothing else because along the way we're making choices and thus creating newness in a universe that must constantly expand or collapse and rewind back to the primordial swamp. There we'd wait for the Greater God part of us to awaken and start the clock again because some part of us somewhere had an original thought. Or maybe something like that.

Granted that we are all part and parcel of the eternal intelligence that permeates everything everywhere everywhen, what though do you really think about the concept of soul siblings? My good friend Abe (that's me and you too) speaks through Esther Hicks of we who are presently here "banging around in physicality" being part of a non-physical entity, our higher self. Assuming space time and individuality, do you think that such non-physical entities expand by sending to earths like this one more than one 'soul' at a time? And if so, that such incarnated souls might meet their literal siblings in this physical setting?

That's what I was getting at with my question, though I suppose you did address it with the words: "We also have aspects of our soul living in other dimensions and here on earth." But gosh darn, could you be my sister, attached to the same non-physical entity? What say you at that level? Reply in this venue if you wish, or directly to my email address.

Chapter 17

---·◆◆·---

Jackie: Hi Michael; There certainly are lots "ifs" regarding the opportunities for connection, although, 3D reality and freedom of choice dictates the outcomes of any opportunity. Like you, my desire was to form some sort of relationship within close enough proximity to impulsively share a spectacular sunset, a full moon, or maybe to share an interesting video. Becoming good friends is part of that scenario. I have a car and the possibility of me coming to Victoria wouldn't be so much of a problem, except...... the spaces between the trips with the lack of walking, talking and experiencing the energy of two humans be-ings would be lacking. There is so much more to all of us then we can possibly describe with words alone, that it would be necessary to also be in physical presence. So, I agree with your thoughts.

You mentioned just moving to Victoria recently. How long ago and from where? It appears that you've done quite a bit of traveling.

Your ability to write and express yourself makes me think that you're a professional writer?? You have a wonderful way with words.

I'm not sure that I want a pen pal as I spend too much time on my computer as it is. Being a pen pal, or writing a lot, is not a fulfilling agenda for me but will send a few emails for now if you don't mind. No way can I slot you into the same category as the man I had previously mentioned. As yet, there is no category for you and categories are so limiting and could include many for any personality.

I'm thrilled for you receiving so many emails in your inbox.... so very many possibilities attached to each day of sorting and reading. Such an interesting and joy filled dilemma!! Yep, I would say from my personal experience that you are a sought after species in the spiritual arena ...or... any at this age! With that thought, I think my ego is going through a crisis now: Que sera sera... what will be will be! Actually, I don't feel a need, just a desire to share experiences and expand the soul. And, I do have some possibilities as well... some interesting "tea" dates! Ha. Doesn't it make sense that more women are involved in the spiritual due to their ability to be more intuitive and heart centered?? Only in general of course! Also, there needs to be many more women opened and aware to create the balance of the feminine energy which is pummelling the earth with love, nurturing and the desire for peace. At least that's my thought for now... may change in the next minute or two. Actually, to believe anything automatically limits and separates our- selves from each other.

Abraham certainly provides the opportunities for many to become more aware of their own internal creative abilities and direct them more appropriately. Some are ready, most are not... but getting there. Easy for some, not so much for others. I find some "new agers" still stuck in judgment and self -righteousness... sounds like religion to me! Those are things we definitely need to overcome and transform in order to push on the veil of consciousness to expand who we are. Ultimately, no one needs to be healed or fixed as they are already whole and complete. However, if you were the human dieing of cancer or some other disease or illness, you would definitely want some answers as to how to heal your body! That's part of our creative process as well, whether it's through someone else who gives hope in a pill or someone who offers the loving space required for self healing. Either way, healing... all healing... begins in the mind through the creation of thought and emotion.... as does illness and age! And, sometimes, healing takes place at the time of transition. All healing is self healing. And blah, blah, blah... whew, that can go on and on!!

I like the way you described "a universe that must constantly expand or collapse and rewind back to the primordial swamp waiting for the Greater God part of us to awaken and start the clock again because some part of us somewhere had an original thought. Or maybe something like that". I suspect, that to be very close to truth! I seems to me that we've destroyed and eliminated ourselves many times on our way to full consciousness on this planet of free choice.

Ok, I'll try my best to explain what my thoughts are on "soul siblings"! Some of my thoughts come from reading the "Kryon" material and past conversations with my own guides which all totally resonates as truth for me. That which we call Creative Source, is comprised of pieces of all that is. It's responsible for all that ever existed and all that exists now, including the universes that existed before ours and the ones that co-exist with ours now. That's the Quantum soup of energy. Makes me laugh, if we could see who we are, we wouldn't stick around being who we think we are. I don't see how the soup of God could slip into human bodies and be compartmentalized with names and personalities. The soul is not singular. The soul is not limited to humans and is not "learning". Human's learn, souls do not. Human's have a human reality. A soul has a God reality. There is no level of learning or advancement with souls... only with humans.

We can "share souls". Like "soul mates". Example: One person meets another person and they have a connection. It doesn't matter if it's outside of romance, although that's there too. It may be from a past life (actually everything is now which also complicates things as a brother, sister, mother or dad, but they know each other. They think like one person. They can have conversations just looking in each other's eyes and they are amazed. They must have spent lifetimes together in order to have this similarity of thought and thinking of ideas and passions. There's an attraction to be with that person, to just stay with that person, because they represent something that is so special - and we call it soul mate.

What if that you just met a portion of yourself? What if soul sharing or soul mates or soul siblings is simply an attribute where you meet a piece of yourself in another Human Being? Could that then be called a "sibling soul"?? If God is not singular and you are a piece of the whole, and everybody is in you and you are in everybody, then why would that be so difficult to understand? It's simply part of the way soul sharing works. Instead of seeing God in that person, you're seeing you in them! Did you know that aspects of a grandparent's soul... even still alive... can also be part of your soul? Not just chemically or biologically, but also as a soul? Perhaps you have been together as a walk-in during the past, sharing one Human body? Now you are in two bodies again. That's what a soul mate is. No wonder you're attracted to them and they're attracted to you! It seems to me that those who are closest in conscious awareness have often completed many journeys together as both separate and joined souls. Sometimes it gets difficult to explain or cognize in many ways as we'll never be able to really "get it" on a human level.

Have you heard that in quantum physics, light can be in two places at the same time? Welcome to a new reality! The theme here is about us meeting our soul selves within our-selves and each other.....

that's awakening. Basically, it's you journeying to meet yourself. Your soul has been involved in other places, on other planets and in other constellations. It has experienced life that is ancient in this galaxy, compared to ours on Earth. So old! Do you remember?? Love it all!!! Namaste, Jackie

M: *"Do you remember?"* you ask, and present a dissertation deserving of a PhD! I think this particular portion of it all is going to unlax, put on an airy bower filled with happiness and fun, and simply BE for a while. Wanna play careless abandon and co-create my reverie for a few days?

I was born in Saskatchewan, raised in Manitoba, someone's joke, I was supposed to have appeared on a tropical island with nothing better to do than watch beautiful maidens skinny dip in the lagoon while one of my subjects broke open coconuts and peeled bananas for me. Ha, I'll eventually find who's responsible for that switch and send her (gotta be a she) to Siberia when it's my turn to oversee. I lived in the USA for the last twenty years, did investing mainly. But I always wanted to be a writer and saw an opportunity about ten months ago to buy a motor home, travel Interstate 10 for the winter and rewrite John Steinbeck's *"Travels with Charley"* sans Charley. I started in San Francisco and got as far as San Antonio, Texas when I realized that I didn't need to travel - internet, singles sites, and a good imagination brought the adventures to me. So I turned about and wintered in Yuma, Arizona where I kept a journal and eventually Indie published several books of it. But nobody wants to read them let alone buy.

A few weeks ago, after receiving promptings to move to the City of Victory where I was spiritually initiated in 1984, I completed family visits, deposited my motor home at a rental place in Los Angeles, and flew to Victoria arriving Canada Day. I had been here a short time earlier and signed a one year lease on a one bedroom suite across the street from James Bay Square, exactly where I wanted to be. So, this is two weeks for me and I'm exceedingly happy with my move...

I think I'm done with the incarnations Jackie, I wanna be Immortal Adam with a harem of those beautiful island babes and populate new planets. (Do I need to be a Muslim to get the harem do you think?) When the reverie bursts maybe that's where I will find 'myself' and maybe not. Wish me well, or join me if you love swimming in lagoons, we'll co-create such a thang as that - *somebody's* got to populate those planets. Weird huh?

M: (to my kids) After ten days of warm sunshine and calm seas the wind picked up a bit this evening, the waves not crashing but smacking hard enough to wet the walk on top of the Ogden Point Breakwater which I just returned from walking. I don't carry a camera because I've learned that every moment in this James Bay part of Victoria is a photo moment. But what a fascinating sight greeted me this evening on the inner side of the breakwater only twenty feet away, the Carnival Miracle docked close behind. I watched a seal eat a huge pink octopus chunk by chunk! The seal would take a bite of meat, drop the octopus, raise its head above the water, lean back, and swallow. Then go back down for the rest of the octopus, bring it back to the surface and repeat. I doubt that many people see that often, though the divers in our family may have.

I'm thoroughly enjoying Victoria, it's incredibly beautiful, alive with happy people including tourists from the often three cruise ships docked six blocks from me. I walk miles along the sea every day, a fairy tale difference from the hot deserts I've been living in for years. But yes, it takes some acclimatizing, I've learned (again) to carry a jacket after 8 p.m. even in the midst of summer.

I'm happy here, it was the right move. I'll likely stay in Victoria a long time, I'm meeting people, making friends already. My motor home is on consignment with a dealer in Los Angeles who rents out RV's. Mine has several weeks rental booked already so it's actually making money for me. I'll be catching a city bus (first time) to go to my sister's condo tomorrow for afternoon and dinner. My other sister will be there too. I hope everyone is well, keep in touch, I love you all. Dad

Oresha: Here's a pic of my friend's son doing his "job"!.. WOWEEEE! This is somewhere in B.C. the second oldest tree of it's kind..named "Lonely Doug".... He must feel like he's Flying.... and just Touched Heaven!... Happy Monday!.... Hugssss....

M: That is amazing. Does he zip line after work to relax? I walked the breakwater this evening and about twenty feet from me, on the inside where the pilot boats dock watched a seal eat an octopus bite by bite. Fascinating city we live in.

Oresha: YEAH!... Isn't that INCREDIBLE! Sure beats 9-5!... lol How cool that you got to experience the seal having it's dinner... I LOVE this City!!!... I did a couple of walks today... 1 to James Bay Thrifty's... and the other through the park and up to the Overlook..... Wonderful Day in Paradise!... Night..... SMILES....

M: I never think to watch for you at the grocery store, I'm in and out of there often. Made a mistake with the ice-cream today, bought tin roof sundae and tried it, not near as good as track of moose. I was at the band concert in the park on Sunday for a brief time, supposed to be folk but a long ways from the Joan Baez stuff I was hoping for so I wandered the beach to Finlayson Point. Sunday a.m. I went to the church on Superior. They feed each other well but other than a brief time of silent meditation it was not for me at all, especially when they all started free dancing. I walked away early, glad to feel the sunshine again, won't go back.

My ex will be here from July 30th to August 13. A lot longer than I expected but she booked the flights. We'll have fun enough I expect. Not sure if any of my kids are planning to be here at the same time. Might complicate matters a tad but such is life.

Hope your search for the right man is coming along well. I continue to get invites, most of them the kind you know would never click but some interesting enough to write about. I'm swapping emails with a healer in Nanaimo among others right now. She made the first move, but with me not having a car where could that possibly go? Here's her website, she's extremely knowledgeable, you might like some of Jackie's stuff.

I'll be visiting both sisters tomorrow in Saanich, my first venture on a city bus in Victoria, wish me luck. Do you have to hang on real tight when you're inside them? Good night Oresha.

Jackie: Hi Michael; I wanted to let you know that I'm off to Vancouver until Friday evening. I began writing to you but was interrupted. Isn't that like life! I really enjoyed your information and share a similar story. Also raised in Saskatchewan and then went the wrong direction to Winnipeg! UGH! Have to get up very early so off for now. Will write again when I return.

Yes, you populated the planets and then they populated you! I'm returning to the New Earth in my next incarnation. I really want to see all the changes we made! Not weird, just wise. Namaste, Jackie

M: Stranger yet, I was in the midst of composing a note for you when this arrived, think I'll send my note anyway. I lived in Winnipeg too. Instead of returning why not just stay eh? Might be more fun that way... Travel safe Jackie, I'm wiking you.

M: I received advice a while back from a lady friend that instead of boldly flaunting my eccentricities by writing such strange stuff as I am wont to keyboard, and thus driving singles site ladies into silence, I should instead write only mundanely while thrusting roots deep into this planet's soils. And true enough, I observe that when my inner being makes a decision based on things it doesn't allow into conscious awareness just yet (because it's more fun that way) I do write what must come off as highly peculiar, and thus sabotage an otherwise possibly promising virtual relationship. Did I do that today by writing to a lady about harems?? Or is this one different?

In 1984 in the beautiful City of Victoria I encountered mystically a woman of great power, a goddess of some type standing in the air close to but above me. I knew I was being invited to go with her. But tempting as it was (for she was beautiful) somewhere inside of me a decision was made that following the goddess was not in the script for this particular incarnation. A way to take care of what was then perceived as a 'problem' was presented and the outer part of me went along with it, maybe just for fun. She was a she no doubt whatsoever, but in silent prayer to her a goddess I called her "Father"!! It was a brilliant coup, she instantly left in a great huff trailing anything but glory and never returned. I think she's the one who knew what was about to happen and sent me to Saskatchewan. Such dreams as may come...

Weirder huh? Am I sabotaging the potential of us?

Oresha: Sounds like you're havin a fun time wandering around town... lol Too bad about the Church. I've never been for a service.... hmmmm... sounds kinda "flakey"...lol You'll be able to show your ex around town... nice. Has she ever been here before? Yeah... her visit could put a bit of a "damper" on your social life!... There's always the Greyhound bus to Nanaimo... lol

I wrote to the guy who "Blew me off" on Fri. night, after asking me to call so we could chat..... I told him that I was out having a very enjoyable visit with a friend... and that I cut our evening short to get home and call him at the time we had agreed upon, only to have him

Blow me Off!... I suggested that if he was actually looking to meet any authentic women... that he might "show up"... and consider the value of their time and feelings. He actually responded to my message today. He said he had NO excuses for his behaviour... and asked me to Please accept his apology.... which I did.... now he's a done deal!... lol

There seems to be a lot of that goin around these days!... lol Another guy I met shortly before you and I met... treated me very poorly... til I let him have it with "both barrels"!.. Ha! ha!.... Then he apologized.... a few times... and actually came over to the island to make a peace offering of treating me to a nice lunch and to apologize in person... so I accepted... and we're on friendly terms now.... Go Figure! It amazes me how some people are so disrespectful to others! I'll check out the healer's website.. thanks...

So, an adventure on a Victoria Bus!... lol yeah... they're "speed-demons" those Victoria Bus drivers!... have a wonderful visit with your dear sisters.... Ttyl...... Ciao.... Sweet Dreams

M: (to Jackie) I'm out of line sending this without first getting your response to my former, but somehow I sense that you are not one to adhere rigidly to someone else's rules and will most likely read it anyway. I hope your presentation or whatever it is if business across the Strait is going well and meeting or exceeding all expectations.

I love the words you wrote: *"Yes, you populated the planets and then they populated you!"* There is great meaning in that sentence as you know, associations at many levels, I like all that come to mind. We create with a mere thought whatever we will of course, so all things are possible, but even the world acknowledges that there are an infinite number of planets, many of them undoubtedly populated with the human species. So the question I ask is, *"Where did all those Adam and Eves come from?"* And I want to be Adam.

You say that I AM Adam and I love that. Beyond space and time of course it is so, but it's not so fun to remember such things. As non-physical entities that's why we cast barely aware parts of ourselves into time because there in non-physical we have it all, perfection. And as the song goes *"after you've been having steak a long time, beans beans taste fine."* Having it all can eventually get exceedingly boring, boredom being the greatest of pains. Without contrast, opposites, there is only Innocence, not knowing without the absence of one: light from darkness, pleasure from pain, health from sickness, it goes on, the fullness being only Innocence again, *after* having passed through Experience. (A la William Blake's Songs of Innocence and Experience etc. etc. But I ramble, and your time is precious dear one.

So this day I am only *Becoming* Adam, that's the funnest way to do it, not knowing yet what's 'ahead', simply *observing* Law of Attraction work through its mind-boggling plan, loving the awesome intelligence that moves upon mortals causing choices to be made sometimes years even decades in advance to bring it all together when the plan is executed, the desire fullfilled, not a hair on the head lost. (*"I love it when a plan comes together"* - John Hannibal Smith - *The A Team*.)

You write, *"...and they populated you."* Ah such wisdom, such depth coming out from Nanaimo! But when I glance at your website I understand where it's coming from, thank-you for becoming being you. I wike you, I think we could make good music together you and I, unique music that some others may be waiting to hear played because that's their cue to come out from the wings and speak their own lines, effortlessly create synchronous events, gentle new waves to lap upon the shores of a planet newly made Golden because its time had come, its people had been prepared.

One of my favorite authors writes of an experience where all the children he would ever have swarmed from his heart center in a joyous cloud that he then sensed moving away from him laughing, giggling, headed for delightful preparatory innocent experiences. In that sense (all truth being circumscribed into one great whole) no beginning no end, the circle of life 'began' where it will return endlessly, in the heart of an ancient god. For aren't we all the ancient gods, here in physicality like a finger on the hand of our non-physical self, merely playing, having fun, taking delight on planets like these, pretending to forget that it's we ourselves who create the lives we take so seriously as mortals?

"Yes, you populated the planets and then they populated you!" For that author *they, the children,* populated Adam - as you dear one correctly discerned.

Oresha: Hope you're Bus-adventure has been a pleasant one... lol and that You had a Wonderful time with Your Sisters. I'd like to clarify something from my previous message... when I said that I "let him have it with both barrels".... I didn't say anything mean, or nasty to him... I just spoke my truth and told him how I felt about the way that he had treated me... Finding my "Voice"... and speaking "My Truth" (with men) is something fairly "new" and very liberating for me!... It's only taken me 60 yrs to get to this point in my life!...Ha! Ha!... (I guess you *can* "teach an "old" dog...new tricks!...) Have a great rest of your day, My Friend.... Hugsssss...

Jackie: Hi Michael; Another quick note to let you know that I received and read your notes. Decided that I couldn't live without my computer for a couple days! Stupidity of the human brain! Or, perhaps I'm just re-wiring my brain and creating plasticity in areas metaphysically appealing. And, of course your notes were delightful to read and not at all "out of line". No linear thinking! You are an exceptional writer and seem to write from an authentic place of expressed thought.

You've written much that also deserves a response with much more thought than what I'm capable of providing at this time. However, my eyes keep trying to shut and brain fog is overcoming my ability to think! We, (meaning my younger daughter and myself) were up at 5:00 this morning to catch the 6:20 ferry. Up again tomorrow morning by 6:00 am for an early hospital visit and more tests... for her. There is so much to say here but our very few, short visits online just haven't provided the opportunity to become more open and vulnerable in depth. There is still much about me you don't know, and we, as humans, usually reveal parts of ourselves through time and trust. That's where the walking and talking provide such a wonderful opportunity to explore the human mind and heart in real time. As you are aware, 60+ years is difficult to place in such a small box on a single's site! My wish is to be completely transparent with all aspects of self in this incarnation. I've had some of the most incredible and profound spiritual experiences which have also been coupled with a life of challenge, heartache and immense joy!! As you so adequately pointed out...CONTRAST!! I'm sure that you're life has also been filled with tragedy and triumph as well... or perhaps you chose a life of relative ease in order to integrate all elements of all time frames for soul expansion. I don't know and would not like to add more stories to my imagination without providing the opportunity for heart to heart in real time.

Michael, if you would like to meet with me and explore further, I may have the opportunity to come to Victoria this weekend and see where the exploration of time together takes us. I'm not in a rush to find someone but think it's important to touch minds and hearts without creating mind stories. Of course, time online and/or by phone would also create the opportunity at a slower pace over time. Please let me know how you would feel about a real time meeting. By the way, I was intrigued about your "Goddess" story and would love to hear more about it!! Was it a dream or an altered state that created that scenario? Will go for now. Infinite Love and Blessings

M: (to Oresha) I never figured you to be the kind of person who is acquainted with double barrel shotguns Oresha. Survived the double decker both ways and had a good afternoon and evening with my two sibs. Way too stuffed to sleep now though. Think it was that huge bowl of rhubarb pie and ice-cream about an hour ago that finally did me in. Sleep well for me.

Oresha: I'm glad to hear you had a Fun time with Your "Sibs"... lol Too bad about The Pie-thing! What.. No Moose Tracks tonight!... I will try to sleep well for you!...lol Hoping your tummy full of pie'n'ice cream let's you get some shut eye... Night Now.... Hugsss...

M: (to Jackie) Being a Leo I contentedly bask in all compliments wafted my way, so I appreciate your comments on my wordsmithing, and your continued interest in me. I hope all is well for you and your daughter.

Yes, I would like to meet you. Several family members will be visiting me, arriving between July 29 and August 15th, maybe beyond. (Even my ex is wanting to come and be shown around this beautiful city, we're still friends.) But if you're content to make the drive to Victoria, this weekend would work well for me. You are welcome to come straight to my modest one bedroom apartment across the street from James Bay Square, I make a mean cup of white tea and we can converse without interruption. But if you'd prefer to meet first in a public place, the Breakwater Cafe at Ogden Point where the cruise ships dock is a short walk for me, or Mile One at Dallas and Douglas, or Inner Harbor, even the front lawn of the legislative building. Let me know when and where would be best for you and I'll be there Friday, Saturday or Sunday this week, your choice, I have opportunities but nothing scheduled just yet.

I did not see the "goddess" with physical eyes, could have done that with them shut. I was standing, had just walked into a room of New Age people at the time. That was a long time ago it's not important anymore, we'd most likely laugh to tears about my ploy and her huff should we ever meet again. (I think she's hiding though she's welcome back, maybe a tropical island next time.)

Oresha: How's the Fishin' Goin' at your end of The Pond????... lol I imagine it's keeping you pretty busy.... all those Ms. Fishes to "Ponder"... I just got back from a nice stroll around The "Hood".... I think I heard some music coming from yon James Bay? If you have some time to spare, I was thinking perhaps we might wander over to the Inner Harbour, one day this weekend, and take in the entertainment of the Buskers.? I would also like to chat with you about some of the Abraham teachings sometime. I'm missing my "Male Friend Energy Fix"... lol Wishing You a Wonderful rest of your evening, Laird Michael. Night.... Oresha P.S.... The name of the white wine we had at laurel Point the other day is Platinum Chardonnay from Cedar Creek Kelowna BC.... if you're interested.... I will get out and try to search for a bottle one day...

M: (to Oresha) When the stream's flowing fast as it is wont to always do with me, it carries plenty of fish. You are the third to invite me along this coming weekend so let me check my watch and give you a time. I haven't yet heard from the other two what day and times this weekend they want to get together (hopefully no conflict there) so I'm going to hold off for a bit on promising to meet you Saturday or Sunday. But I'd like to get together with you before my company arrives so we can hold hands, swap some energy, and maybe talk Abe a bit. Perhaps during the week would be better, I think the buskers are on for a whole week. But I'll let you know how it shapes up for the weekend if there's time and you're not too busy yourself by then.

I'm about wined out right now, my sister brought along some of her husband's home made wine and plied it relentlessly when I was visiting. You'd have been proud of me, I hung on real tight when I double deckered home. He's been making wine for fifty or more years and he's really got it nailed, wonderful stuff and the price is right... Good night Oresha, see you soon.

Oresha: No Worries....

DeLeon: Tomorrow 7:00 am will check into hospital for another ablation to begin at 8:30. FYI - again, I thank you for being by my side in the last one. For the first time in all of these hospital journey's... anxiety/ out right fear is attempting to rule... something I don't ever remember feeling, about anything. So, it is taking continuous efforting to keep on track. In order to do the ultimate they can, in making this a success, they will only put me half way under... in order to activate the cells that are "activating" the SVT episodes. Needing to rest, so thank you, Michael. My main computer has shut down on me, so didn't have your email.... but as we speak, I'm now remembering. I now have my lap top, just don't use it that much, as still love the other one.

M: I wish you and your doctors the very best of results DeLeon. Please let me know how it went as soon as you are able to. (Or ask roomy to send me a note?)

DeLeon: Thank-you. There truly is nothing I regret..... Thank you for the beautiful Abraham.. Going forth in Joy

Jackie: Hi Michael; Another late night note to you. I think time and space are folding in on themselves.... last two days have seemed exhaustingly long and yet being home seems like I never left. Having company when living in such a beautiful city is a naturally occurring event. I also have company but will be free this weekend.

Wow, I'm impressed! Staying friends with your ex says a lot about who you are regarding the ability to allow the past to be and accept the gift of the present. Wonderful for both of you, particularly where kids are concerned.

How about if I meet you late Saturday morning or early afternoon at the Breakwater Cafe at Ogden Park? I'm not sure where it's located yet but will be able to find it. I'll be returning to Nanaimo sometime that evening so we'll have plenty of time to walk, talk and share parts of ourselves. Oh yes, I'm sure your goddess was upset about you being in the wrong place at the wrong time!! No wonder you have thoughts/ dreams/desires about being on a tropical island waiting for the goddess to return. It'll happen within some time frame and hopefully the outcome will be much different. It sounds like an incredible experience despite her huffiness... and likely never to be forgotten! Looking forward to sharing time and conversation with you Michael. Namaste

M: Here's a suggestion. We meet near the entrance to the Ogden Point Breakwater Café at 11 a.m. on Saturday. You should be able to find parking nearby. If you bring some walking shoes or sandals and are ok with walking about a half hour at a time, we could walk to the end of the breakwater and back to the cafe where we can have a light lunch. We can make it up as we go along from there, maybe walk to Fisherman's Wharf and Inner Harbor. There's a busker event happening at Inner Harbor so should be lots of fun. At any point we can walk back for your car, or after lunch move it to my parking spot which is only three blocks from Inner Harbor. There's always nearby Beacon Hill Park too where we can find a pleasant place to sit and talk if the weather cooperates. If it's raining, let's still meet at 11 a.m. at the Breakwater and maybe go straight inside for an early lunch and decide where to go from there, or walk with umbrellas. Sound like a plan? Other ideas?

M: (to Oresha) The Fates have given me the entire day off tomorrow Friday. So if you are available and want to, we could meet somewhere early afternoon and wander the busker event at Inner Harbor. Let me know if you'd like to do that and the when and where to meet. Have you walked any of the 60 km Galloping Goose trail to Sooke? I had some difficulty today trying to find the trailhead. It was supposed to be near the Johnson Street bridge and I naively assumed there would be signs. Not so, and following directions from passersby got me back tracking a whole lot. But find it I eventually did, well into the afternoon already. By the time I had crossed the trestle bridge I was ready for some Extreme Moose Tracks so chickened out and waited for a water taxi to take me back to Inner Harbor. Hope you had an enjoyable day today and that we can meet up tomorrow.

Oresha: Lucky You...lol A whole day off from The Ladies of The Pond... Could you please see what time the Buskers are underway with their entertainment? I've misplaced my Monday magazine. Then we can decide upon a time to connect. I've done a bit of The Goose..... on different parts of the trail. I used to stay at the Red Lion Hotel on Douglas when I 1st started visiting here... the trail goes right behind the hotel. I've also walked the trestle you speak of.... and much farther north. Good for you braving the "un-signs" and going for it!... lol You'll have lot's of places/activities to share with Your Ex when she comes to visit. I had a very chillin'-kinda-enjoyable-day thanks... Please let me know about the times for tomorrow.. if you can't find it... I'll try going online to see.... Ciao.... Hugzzz....

M: Oops, it looks like Friday doesn't begin until 5 p.m.

Oresha: Here's what I found on The Busker Fest... They didn't tell us much about the times for the various entertainers... So I guess we can just head out in the late afternoon/early evening... and hope for the best... lol What do you think? It says they start Fri... just not exactly when for each location... I guess we could just wander... and see what's happening. I've seen them in front of The Empress before. How about I meet you at your place.... after dinner.... maybe around 7:00-ish.... or would you like to venture out earlier? I have a feeling that for the most part, the entertainment will be within walking distance of the Inner Harbour... we can always stop off for a cold brew somewhere along the way, if we're early for the show... lol ???.... Cheers...

Oresha: Thanks for the info. I just printed out the map of all the stage locations... so I guess we can meet and just wander... lol What time would you like to begin our Busker Adventure?...

Oresha: Are there any acts in particular that you'd like to take in tomorrow night?

M: How about ladies choice starting from the 7 p.m. Friday lineup? Have your dinner except dessert and come over about 6:30. We'll consume Extreme Moose Tracks until we leave. That should give us time to get to the first venue you choose. I don't want to be out too late, I have an appointment Saturday a.m. But should be fun until midnightish if the busker partay goes that long. If you want a glass of Shiraz to wash away the moose tracks, come earlier. Eat your dinner early and come at 6?? Let me know.

Oresha: Shiraz and Ex-treme Mooses sounds like fun!... lol Don't worry... I'll get you home in time to get your Beauty Sleep... and be fresh as a Daisy for your date on Sat. morn... lol I'll see you @ 6:00PM tomorrow evening... looking forward to our excellent busker adventure!... HUGZZZZZZZZ.

M: It's off to see the buskers and 6 p.m. it is, sleep well sweetie.

Oresha: Thanx.... You too!... See ya tomorrow for Shiraz'n'Ex-treme Mooses.... lol See you at 6:00.... SMILES..

Oresha: I just sent you a message on singles...... Please let me know you got it?...... Thanks..... I'm going to just chill..... hopefully be able to eat something later..... Shiraz/Xtreme Mooses... perhaps another day!... lol I'll miss your company tonight... Sorry that I'm not feeling well enough to get out with you tonight.... sigh.... Ttyl....Hugz...

M: Got it Oresha, be well, thanks for letting me know.

She left two messages on singles and phoned too, just as I got in. What's happening, is she genuinely sick, or ticked because she knows I'm meeting other women this weekend? But although I feel an *obligation* to her as a friend and it's genuinely pleasant to hold hands while walking with her, I'm ready to move on. There's no sexual spark for me, she never dresses sexy, covers her body up, most likely has a hangup about a few pounds overweight? Still no word from Jackie, will she stand me up tomorrow too? It doesn't matter a whole lot to me. And I'm not excited about meeting Marianne on Sunday, she's covering something up too by never sending me a photo, I'm just curious, need to read over our emails before meeting her. As for sex, yes that's always a want/need, but Ex is coming in a few days and I'm expecting her to share my bed. I still don't know for sure if we're divorced or not but I expect that we are, the lawyer just never got around to telling us. Perhaps Ex is using that to advantage to quench her religious beliefs that sex is only for married people? Whatever, if it's mutually fun... Looks like Oresha just sent me another message on singles.

Oresha: Thanx.... Looking forward to our next-get-2-gether-n-Smiles.... Have a n Enjoyable weekend..... Hugssss......

Here's comes a catch up of the emails Jackie and I swapped recently that are still in my inbox.

M: I haven't heard back from you Jackie, will you be coming tomorrow?

Jackie: Hi Michael; My intent for a return message was taken over by more unexpected company last night with a mixture of slight chaos today. That full moon definitely brought some surprises and adjustments to plans. However, my intent is still to meet with you tomorrow. Through all the hustle and bustle, I had thought that a note had been sent to you to confirm our meeting tomorrow so looked on my sent messages just now. Aha, there it was! I'll just copy and paste the message here and the only change is the time. Have to see a friend of mine off in the morning but will be leaving here about 11:00 am. Should be there about 12:30 pm. I'm not sure if you have a cell phone but will give you my cell number in case I get stuck in traffic. Please feel free to call if I don't arrive by 12:30 –1:00 pm. Look forward to our meeting tomorrow. Namaste, Jackie

M: Tomorrow about 12:30ish at the breakwater then, thanks for confirming Jackie.

M: I almost never carry a cell but I'll try to remember to take it with me tomorrow because I don't want you to rush or get anxious. Take your time, I really appreciate you making the trip. I'll be at the breakwater by 12:30 and don't mind waiting for you. Call me if you'll be later than 1:30 so I know you're still on the way, or if you can't pick me out in the crowd when you get there. My cell is (insert number.)

Jackie: I thought it would be best for you to have a description of what I'll likely be wearing tomorrow. And since I'm a bit eccentric and out of the norm (smile) the seat covers in my car are black with the outline of big hearts. Also have a little flower waving and smiling at me on the front window.... reminds me to not take life too seriously! Always on a path less travelled. I'll be wearing 3/4 jeans and blue top. Hair will likely be up and back in a bit of a pony tail. You'll recognize me as I'm the same as my pictures. Gosh, I hope the rain saves itself for another day. Thanks for providing your cell number... it helps if I get lost! Will hopefully see you about 12:30...

M: All is well Jackie. As Abraham would say through Esther: *"There is great love for you here."* I think we are both people who have given more than received and thus have in a way willingly 'robbed' ourselves and fallen short of where who we could be. Perhaps we will find that we can accept what the other has to give to us, get lost wholly in each other for a time, renew, heal, be children again, come forth wholer when it's not so fun anymore to toss sand around in the sandboxes we co-create, grow up and be adults again, serve others bigger and better because we learned how to become as a little child and play. But I'm on 'vacation' right now, hiding as best I am able, not among the ancient gods. All I want is to love and be loved and to have fun, perhaps for a whole year. I'm searching for a companion to help facilitate that vacation, maybe with a bit of careless abandon for a while, shun responsibility for anyone except ourselves, immerse each moment in joyous selfish fun. Perhaps we can do be that together, we'll see how the energy flows when we're just being our down to earth selves undercover in blue jeans and pony tail, laughing, holding hands, little flower waving merrily.

New life begins with each moment - I choose happiness in each new moment that my life begins, you? Others have called me "Magnificent", "King", and "Lord". None other has called me "Adam". I choose Adam and look forward to your coming little flower.

Jackie: Awe, such beautiful sweetness, incredible truth and joy filled words! Yes, all is ultimately well when judgment is left behind giving life with grace and joyous abandon. Company up and mulling about.... may be there sooner....will call when I get close to the Breakwater Cafe. In Joy As Love

Jackie: Michael, for some reason the Breakwater Cafe comes up as located in Sidney – not on Dallas Road! So, I'll come to Dallas Road anyway and call when I get there. Sounds like a plan eh?? LOL

M: If you have GPS, it's 199 Dallas Road, Victoria. Drive to the south end of Douglas Street (Mile Zero of the TransCanada Hwy) and turn right on Dallas Rd. You'll soon see the breakwater jutting out into the sea. We'll meet where that breakwater starts, that's where the Cafe is. When you park your car and walk from the sidewalk on Dallas Rd. to the breakwater (it's just a few yards) you will step on a sun clock, a bronze circle in the sidewalk with embedded footprints to stand on. On a cloudy day like today it's a virtual time machine; as you fill those footprints you can imagine/create whatever time you want it to be. So you won't be 'late' Jackie, unless you choose to be. Guess I'd better get shaved and showered if you're planning earlier than 12:30. My guess is that I'll leave home about noon to walk to the rendezvous so you can email anytime before then, I'm always monitoring this email address when I'm home and not asleep.

M: I thoroughly enjoyed our time together today Jackie. Especially that way you have of saying good-bye for a while. Your kisses are sweet and packed with promise. It is my hope that we can get together again soon. As you know, I'm tied up with family visits from July 30 through August 15th, including my ex arriving and wanting me to show her around Victoria. But I do have this coming week available if you want to come for a few days and explore this beautiful city with me. Also, I could rent a car for a day or two and drive to Nanaimo if you need to be home but want to see me. Just sayin...

DeLeon: OMG - Soooo glad that is over. Everyone was sooo sweet to me - and sad to see me again. And yet, Michael, only DeLeon, would be aware of this.... there were several people, that I know I was there to "Encourage" their life. When ever I'm there, I think - I need to volunteer and be in that environment... Then I think I need money and what energy I have needs to go in that direction - damned I want both. What do you think? Good news: Only had to stay overnight... was released yesterday p.m.. Good news no bleeding, like before. Also dr's were pleased they were able to activate 2 cells that "race" - and are hopeful, that they have them all. They have historically been able to ablate the a-Fib's but not the ones that "race" between 160 and 200 pulse. Also by putting me only partially "under" - those cells were activated - as when completely under - they too were "sleeping". It was difficult being partially under - enuff said. It's done. Thank God.. Dr said would give me a month - for things to settle in, then come into office - and see what is next. I asked when could I start weaning off the meds, as I know they have been holding me down and affecting brain... so want that out of my system. Was encouraged by the response, provided all is smooth, will start weaning me off! They had other info, but am leaving that out... for both of us.

So I am living in "immortality" mentality, that all is accomplished for me to move forward in this gift of glorious life. Thank you for your caring... and again, thank you for being with me before... such a Blessing. Showers of Blessings for Both of Us. DeLeon

M: That's so wonderful DeLeon, thank-you for letting me know. Yes, I think when you are off meds you will find new life and the clarity of thought that will allow you to once more manifest the beautiful leading soul everyone knows you are. And yes, I think you should volunteer time where you think you would help bring joy to the life of others, if even only because of your presence and caring at their side. Money in sufficient amounts has always come to you dear one, think about it, and it always shall. But pretend abundance if that's what you want, and it *must* manifest. Enjoy the new life that is granted you because that's what you want. *And write some books girl!*

M: (to Suzanne) I just thought you might appreciate an update on DeLeon, you once cared for her. She had surgery again two days ago but it was successful, she seems to be doing well. I hope you are well too dear one, take care, we'll most likely never see each other again in this life time but I'll never forget you.

Jackie: You simply amazed me this afternoon with your depth of perception, kindness, stories of experiences, and so much synchronicity and resonance within all of it! And that's not even mentioning all the physical aspects of you that was so attractive to me! Wow!! I too thoroughly enjoyed sharing time together and felt totally at ease within your energy. Thank you for providing the space for me to just be who I am. I could go on about this incredible afternoon and add to the wonder-full-ness of all but want to honour both of us by being totally up front and transparent right now. Michael, Before we go any further within possibility, there is more I need to share that you should know about me. Before you make any decision about us being together overnight or for a weekend, you need to know more about me. As I said before, we reveal parts of ourselves through time, although I'm feeling the time is now for total transparency and honesty regardless of consequences.

First of all, although I can walk, hike and do many things, my health is in "question", which only means occasional doubt regarding some areas, probably why my passionate reaction about the possibility of healing being simple but not always so easy. Years of emotional pain and guilt over my daughter's well being has caused some spinal stenosis and arthritis. I've healed much through the transformation of guilt, however, there remains some subconscious areas that require more introspection and I just can't seem to quite "get it"... whatever "it" is! And, there would be absolute joy in transcending and ascending all of it!!!!!! And, knowing that of course the absolute love and joy of self comes first. I'm heading in that direction... just not always there yet!

Also, I haven't had sex for several years now and am just not sure if it can become a reality. Yes, yes, the answer of course is always yes.... leave no room for doubt! Oh how I love to mess things up with doubt!!! The desire is still there, although with a past surgical procedure (like an episiotomy) and scar tissue build up... I've become...ummmmm "smaller"! Which may be great for my partner... just not sure about me.

That would have to be experimental! OMG... can't believe I said all that in such a matter of fact way, and through email... but really felt the need to get this out of the way!! So sorry to be so blunt but feel it's in the best interest for both of us.

Now, knowing these things, you'll have to decide for yourself. And, Michael, I will totally honour your choice of direction regardless of where that goes. There will be absolutely no judgment.... well maybe just a little sorrow for awhile. There is no doubt in my mind that your ability to find a wonderful match is more than possible and highly probable. It would please me immensely to know you are in your joy and sharing that joy with another. And, there's a little more...maybe tomorrow!! Will leave you now wondering "what the @&$*" now!!! Be well, be joy, be love, ^i^

M: But do you think we could have *fun* together as opportunity presents, a gentle open relationship with no commitment, no obligation beyond the next planned meeting, each of us continuing the search for that perfect ideal human everyone seems to think is 'out there' but is most likely already 'in there' being our own beautiful eternal soul, the acre of diamonds in our own back yard? Or do you insist, like most western women do, on a form of 'marriage' with monogamy, capturing a man's body and time for themselves exclusively? If it's the former, I would really like to meet with you again with enough time given ourselves to ever so gently explore and get to know each other at all levels granted a degree of joyful awareness, desire, and willingness. I believe that we could have fun together if we would each allow such a thing to flow moment by moment when we're together, loving the deliciousness of it, taking no thought for what else Law of Attraction may bring in time to add to our individual joy and abundance. (For that is the way of life, that all things must expand, the only constant being change.)

I believe that I too am capable of the level of love that you already expressed with your beautiful soul, hardly even remembering me, just knowing that it is good: *"It would please me immensely to know you are in your joy and sharing that joy with another."* I could never hold you captive little flower, your petals are always free to flutter and remind you not to take mortal life so seriously. Co-create fun with me? Allow it to flow freely with careless abandon, no regrets, for as long or as short or as frequent or infrequent as it may be? I'd like that.

You're human honey. The healer's power is in never seeing the complaint, only the perfection of each soul beneath the clay. And in that seeing a message of wholeness is relayed to the complainer, giving rise to relief, empowerment to self-heal or ignore, focus shifted suddenly to that which is beautiful and wanted. So I color you beautiful dear one, I will not discuss your complaint. My interest is in you as you are and as the way we may once have been, taking it up from there for as long as it lasts. I think we could make good music together. But I'm on vacation right now, just looking for gentle fun, with you. We can face the music later... Your Man in Victoria

Jackie: "Michael", we can certainly have fun together and enjoy each other's company as long as the alignment is sweet, true and in harmony with each other. I would not want to change your reality... and know that would be a form of control not desired. And, I fully realize, there is no ideal "other" outside the self except for how we align with desire for self. Agree that the diamonds are in our own backyard, or more applicable, within our own hearts. And then, I've found other diamonds on my path to show the way.

When I first received your note, there was the initial fear of rejection which quickly turned to relief intermittently tinged with trepidation. What an opportunity presented for me to experience and express myself within different relationships on this journey. In the past, I've always had one focus with one relationship at a time and felt quite fragmented otherwise. I've recently stayed clear of relationships while becoming more centered on the reality presented to myself from self. That too has changed vibrationally within the last few weeks, and I too feel the opportunity to express myself within different relationships in order to experience/test this new found freedom within. I have some great male friendships and others of differing interests, and like you, feel free in exploring all until my focus is birthed from the desire to be all I am within one relationship without distraction. I am a very sensually expressive being and want to explore the possibility of again adding sexuality to the sensuality and the depth of love that lies within.... within sensibility! Ha ha. Each one of us is exploring our contrast with another and I just can't judge why or why not monogamy is credible or not within relationships. Each person needs to decide for themselves whether it's right for them without forcing themselves or another to become what they desire.

And dear sweet soul brother (smile), we were attracted to each other for the purpose of discovering self.... whatever direction that takes. I was willing to become completely vulnerable and transparent in my reply to you last night... although the lack of time may have resulted in my description being a bit blunt and not expressed with emotional clarity! Still, the enlightened part of me required the physical be expressed. I want to live from all parts of me, vulnerable, all knowing, expressive, enlightened, human, afraid, relieved, joyous, tenuous, blah, blah, blah. You get the picture, to become all of it without hiding it, fixing it, ignoring it, repressing it, denying it, and with absolutely no pretence of how it should be, just with total acceptance of what it is. All of it!! Physical, mental, emotional, and spiritual.... that is the true definition of myself... all inclusive.

My main purpose on earth is to experience all aspects of this life from the depths of sorrow to the vortex of bliss. It's all relevant since we live in an experiential world. Of course, I would prefer to stay in the vortex of bliss but to me that would be negating other aspects of my humanness. What say you??? I've experienced so much and continue to add to my soul through all my expressions of love... only LOVE exists through all of it. So, I can only ask myself; is this adding to my soul? Is this loving myself? Is this in my best and highest interest? No one likes the feeling of going along with something they don't want to do. And whatever the experience, it'll be felt through my heart first.... out of love for myself... and I will decide for me only! And, I also have no doubt that an all encompassing relationship is most probable for me as well.

So, yes, for now it would be a pleasurable experience to co-create a further exploration of ourselves within the mystical acceptance of who we are. I once wrote for one of my CDs that I felt that I was on the edge of creation and then realized I Am Creation, there is nothing outside of me. So let it all be in love, with love and as love. Yes, change can be beautiful... and of course, constant and always on course regardless of how we perceive it on the outside! Let's co-create until the creation changes or one of us feels less than soul filled within the creation. I'm presenting a workshop on Wednesday the 23rd and would like to see you again on the 24th and 25th... preferably your place if ok. I'll need to return for the 26th as I have another friend visiting. It then sounds as though you'll have company from the 30th to 15th??

Michael, there is one thing that I request out of respect for each other. I don't expect monogamy but do wish to be informed if others are involved sexually in order to make a conscious, healthy choice to continue sexually or not. Whatever each of us decides is then out of respect for each other through choice and transparency. Neither of us needs to be tied to monogamy but we both have a right to choose how to respond from there. This is new for me... something like throwing the keys in the middle of the room... and definitely not something I would've considered previously! Although it's something I've recently considered... so will explore a little! I may quickly decide it's not for me or vice versa... but that will be what it'll be without regret. So, lets explore and expand within the possibilites!!?? Okey dokey?? LOL In Love and Light. Namaste, Jackie

M: *"Let's co-create until the creation changes or one of us feels less than soul filled within the creation."* Yes, I invite you to my home (modest as it is) anytime this coming week and to stay as long as you want until July 30th when my ex will be arriving, and others concurrently soon after. Please bear in mind that ex and I were spouses for 18 years, so it's likely that we will occasionally engage at least to some extent in sexual relations, that seems important for you to know about, it would be natural for us. Please understand too that if you have the impression that I am some kind of promiscuous 'player', that I have always been faithful to each of the three women I was married to, for the duration of that marriage. So I am not opposed to monogamy, just want to never again commit to the point where I feel that I must disallow experiences presented that would be fulfilling and good for my eternal progression and/or that of another. Nor would I want my lover to be so bound either.

I am willing to let my present lover know should I engage in sexual relations with another, and let her choose for herself whether or not to continue with our relationship from that point on. I'm with you there, I understand, and would expect reciprocation. For me it's not a matter of monogamy, it's a matter of freedom to choose moment by moment how to live one's life fully and without guilt. I simply will not *commit* to monogamy, perhaps ever again. So, having never before 'cheated', I may never again be in a position where I *could*. Should you and I become lovers, as I think you are consenting to explore when the timing is right, you have my word that I will tell you after the fact but before we make love again if I have sexual intercourse with another woman, and I expect the same of you with another man. Is that helpful sweetie?

What I *really* want right now is to have sufficient time and privacy to hold you in my arms and caress your body while we talk and unwind, getting to know each other, finding the love we both already know is there for we have felt it. You'll find that I have a great depth of love and gentle caring for the right woman, I'm hoping she is you. I need especially to touch and be touched, do you? So, July 24th and 25th at my place then, but come after your workshop on the 23rd if you like, I want as much time with you as you will allow. Oh: *"Of course, I would prefer to stay in the vortex of bliss but to me that would be negating other aspects of my humanness. What say you???"*

I say that emotions are our infallible guide through life. If it *feels* good/right do it or look for an even happier thought. If the thing contemplated does not feel happy, choose another thought, focus only on the happy, the beautiful. We *exist* to know love and fullness of joy. Being fully human is all about being fully happy. You've already passed through experience and are like the gods, knowing good and evil and the difference between. Now, you are free to choose *only* happiness my love.

DeLeon: Greetings Michael, Things went well - was able to come home Saturday... have been sleeping a lot - getting "drugs" out of system. Good News: they were able to activate 2 areas of cells that were doing the "racing" episodes - and ablate them. Was in surgery room 3.5 hours - was difficult, as often experienced the pain involved. However, so grateful it's OVER!! And no complications of bleeding, like I had the last time – Yeaaa! If no episodes,,, will start weaning me off the heart meds that keep me so weary/sleepy/tired, etc.. Very excited to hear that.. If there are still issues - he said, "there is another alternative, but we will discuss it then"... So??

My focus, truth, is there will be no more episodes... THAT'S OVER. Lordy, I just remembered, I already sent you an email. Ugh. And am remembering your reassurances and support - and get to writing. I've actually met with an editor/publisher.... He's infatuated by me...

can tell. And he wants to have another meeting, in guiding me on what to do, etc.. He also wants a big check.. So, will listen to his info, and (put my 40 years of selling real estate to work).. He has come highly recommended by a gal at church. At the time when I had met with him, was writing every day.. Then heart issues... and... kept getting in the way. My attention of recent has gone towards going after the Ex - in Colorado and filing a contempt of court, for non payment of everything. Have gotten strong enuff to start the efforting and actually doing good. An angel - appeared to me where I live - he's a professional "expert witness" and has dealt with the legal profession a lot with family issues - Millions $$ of family issues. For what ever reasons - he has met 3 times with me - 3 hours each, in guiding and going thru this stuff from head to toe.. And it keeps expanding - with 3 legal approaches. And between all three of them - put that family in a position to step forward and negotiate me out of their lives! So, that's where my attention and energy has gone. Healing is first for now, will start flirting with the case after this week.

Speaking of flirting - know how you were noticing how men were looking at me.... as that energy kept rising. It has become unbelievable. A 39 year old - yes 39 year old... tall, good looking - professional golfer, spotted me down at Seagate (remember where we went and I danced)... and has been on a courting benge. What the heck does one do with that - I told him "study tantra" then I smiled, turned and walked away. He still texts and calls.. A muse. I learning, Michael. He texted me, "how old are you" and I texted back "you first", He texted back 39. And I responded... Immortal! Thank you for that awakening, as that has become my truth. Have to re-remind often. Bye for now... DeLeon

M: I love it DeLeon - IMMORTAL - what a comeback!!!! With that attitude and spirit you're going to do it too, maybe we'll be in the same transition class. There's always self-publishing e-books you know. For less than $300 you can get an e-book on virtual shelves all over the world in several languages. That doesn't mean it will sell though, the competition's fierce, 8,000 new books a day. Live well sweetie and keep in touch, you'll always be dear to me.

Chapter 18

Jackie: Michael, your thoughts and words were deeply appreciated – thanks so much! I'm wondering if it would be possible for you to come to Nanaimo rather than me returning to Victoria? I thought perhaps you would like to see my small space and share some time here, although, I'm not sure how that would happen without a car! So, maybe it's best I come back to Victoria after all? Just writing as I'm thinking now. Of course, I do understand how an 18 year relationship can continue in many ways after a breakup. That type of continuation can take place between any two people who have shared a significant bond regardless of the time involved. As long as they remain mutually supportive in their enjoyment of each other! I experienced that with my first husband for awhile and found that it can help with adjustments to being single.

Well, have to admit that you being a promiscuous player had crossed my mind and had me a bit confused for a short while after receiving your note. What was really confusing is that I didn't have any intuitive sense or idea of you as a player and instead felt such a genuine presence from you during our visit. Actually, after hearing that you were only in Victoria for 17 days, my immediate thought was that you needed to date and explore possibilities in order to find a sense of place there. I wasn't sure how that would affect me if we had a sexual relationship but was willing to stretch my perceived boundaries and feel it out! It's my understanding that any partnership/relationship that revolves around a sincere desire to expand consciousness would likely include good communication of expressed and implied expectations with unconditional love and respect being the key to freedom from all things that restrict, bind and suffocate.

Monogamy is just a human word that can be defined in terms of love or fear depending on past experiences and expectations. It can be felt in positive terms of co-creation and expansion with two humans joining souls to focus and expand together, or, it can mean two humans coming together with expectations of binding one to the other out of fear of losing control or love or support. We all give the word definition based on our reality of what it means for each of us. My guess is that you may have felt the latter. There is no judgment there! Yes, absolutely reciprocal regarding truth and genuine transparency if we should continue as lovers down the road. The reflection works both ways and if I can't be in my truth with another, how could I possibly be in truth to myself! Again, thanks again for clarifying your expectations and desires! I do respect and appreciate your greater explanation which continues to enhance my idea of who you are.

"What I really want right now is to have sufficient time and privacy to hold you in my arms and caress your body while we talk and unwind, getting to know each other, finding the love we both already know is there for we have felt it."

Michael, I am so pleased that you expressed this desire... it's precisely what I've felt since we met!! Thank you for saying it so beautifully! Touch is deeply and sensually satisfying to my heart and soul. I love it!! My guide once said that we are here to feel everything with the senses... the taste of food, touch, sex, scents...all of it is for our enjoyment. Yes, agreed that we are here to know love and the joy of life in being fully human. I love your words!! If I didn't have the meetup/ workshop Wednesday evening, you would find me on your doorstep that day! Sweet Dreams.

M: I love your messages Jackie, you're a woman after my own heart. (Take that however you will.) I could rent a car and drive to you even today, I'm available all week. You wouldn't need to entertain me, I'd bring my laptop and give you all the time/space you need. Just save your nights and early a.m.'s for me, I want to cuddle and pretend there's nobody else in the world. But I need to know when to arrive at your place, your street address for my GPS, and how many days to rent the car for. Could I attend your workshop or is it experiential rather than a lecture, something I'd not likely easily get into in the company of others? Or just wait elsewhere while you do the presentation, maybe visit my sister? Let me know, this week suddenly seems so short, the moments so swiftly fleeing. I want to be with you to discover how deep or how shallow this pool is that beckons right now so deliciously. What are we going to co-create for US I wonder? Don't you just love the not knowing when the promise of good is certain but how good's the mystery...

M: Or I could catch a greyhound, haven't done that in decades, might be fun, the depot's an easy walk from here. Getting that down pat and you picking me up at the depot in Nanaimo would make it very economical for me when it's my turn to visit. (Should we settle into a long-term relationship and Nanaimo's where you want us to be.) Otherwise I was seriously thinking about checking into leasing a car for two or three years today. What do you think? Wow, all that surmise from a walk in the park!!! It's your parting kisses that did it dear - had to pull back, hey it was public eh. But it proves to myself that I really am hoping to settle down for a while when the right one comes along, as she inevitably must, hoping it's you...

Jackie: I was going to mention Greyhound and think that would be an awesome experience. I've taken Greyhound many times and have met some amazing people in amazingly synchronistic ways. About 12 years ago, I took the Greyhound from Richmond, BC to Spearfish, South Dakota to visit my friend. On the return met several people across from me, behind me and in front of me that were describing themselves as "Lightworkers". Amazing! We ended up talking about all things spiritual for the entire night of travel until we reached our destinations one by one. We were all deeply enriched by our experience and it has not been forgotten. I would be more than happy to pick you up at the depot! Practicality trumps most things while in human bodies.

Michael, I've been on the phone and making arrangements with friends for coming together as well. This will be the first time in the last three years that the house has been empty and would like to make use of it. My daughter is leaving tomorrow, and my meetup group is Wednesday evening. I have something planned but haven't yet put it together... waiting until the last minute for the excitement perhaps! Not a lot of people will be there... probably 6 or 7... and I would certainly love for you to attend...but please.... at a later date when I feel a little more sure footed. Am planning for speakers and workshop presentations for this fall.... then you can attend... if you feel so inclined and are in this area?? My friend also wants to do another sharing of sessions and has sent a couple clients my way to set up appointments. Anyway, the point is that it'll have to be Thursday before we see each other but you can stay until Saturday if you wish. I do have a client Sunday morning. I'm so sorry it can't be longer but you know that everything flows in perfect harmony if allowed.

As well, unlike you, I haven't been with a partner for a long time and may take time to adjust to having someone beside me. As I keep reiterating, my life has not been normal! LOL. Living in a group home atmosphere has also had an effect! I get the sense that your cycle is to sleep well and wake early. Mine, again has been different! Seem to go to bed late, often have difficulty sleeping with waking often.... probably from years of disrupted sleep, moving around, working nights/ weekends and simply not having set times for anything!! So these again are just some of the practical, ordinary differences in human physiology/cycles! You'll also find my space smaller and definitely more cluttered than yours. Nothing is new but works well and does what it needs to. I've become very adaptable over the years. We'll also be upstairs in my daughter's space for cooking and eating but promise I'll make you some good meals... hopefully, if I can find a cook book! Ha ha. Just very much looking forward to basking in your energy for awhile and feeling the closeness of body and soul. Surrounding you Infinite Love and Well Being, Jackie PS.. will write again later....

M: Thursday it is then, we'll arrange the details by Wednesday. I hear your concerns but it's all small stuff, might be fun talking the night away. You'll find that I have great respect for women, we won't do anything that you don't choose to do as long as you always let me know verbally. Just talking and cuddling will work perfectly for me until/ unless you want to move our relationship deeper, and even then it will be slow, gentle, loving, pleasant. My company will be gone by August 15th, we have months ahead of us if we so choose, there is no need to rush anything. Due to my divorce, this year I did not save up as I usually do during the year to pay the annual property taxes on my investment holdings and I lost quite a bit of income with the splitting of assets due to the marital breakup. So I need to be on a budget for a year while I pay that and other abnormal expenses off. By the end of that year I will likely be able to start accumulating some extra cash for travel again.

But while you are making up your schedule, please keep in mind if you foresee long-term possibilities for us that my desire is to explore Vancouver Island and have fun, hopefully with the right woman at my side; maybe a trip or two or more to the B.C. mainland, and probably a couple of weeks or more during the winter in Cabo San Lucas, I can budget for that. So it would be nice if you can leave two or three week chunks of time open for us to do whatever we want to do at the time.

I love that already you are showing signs of not being 'high maintenance'. You paid for the drinks at the breakwater and the tip at the Flying Otter. That was very impressive to me, as are your humble beginnings and unsettled life, similar to mine. The lady I walk with sometimes here in Victoria took us to a waterfront hotel where we had only appetizers (four small shrimp with brown rice) and a glass of wine each. It was pleasant sitting on the patio next to the water, but the bill with tip was $110. I was a bit (silently) ticked because she had been there before and knew what the tab would most likely amount to. But the next evening she invited me to her place for home cooked lasagna and provided a doggy bag, so I guess we're even. She and I are just budding friends, there's no spark of passion there, just someone to talk and walk with. It will be different with us, I know that already. I've tasted your lips and found them sweet and desirable, your passion quick and discernible, your willingness wonderful. We will take our time discovering our mutual desires and capacities, I'm expecting it to be great fun getting to know you Jackie. Enjoy the day.

Jackie: Thanks again for being so understanding...are you for real?? I'll be waiting patiently to hear from you and feeling joyful anticipation of your arrival. It'll be one wonder-filled step at a time while getting to know each other on deeper levels. I felt your great respect and consideration while at your apartment, which was quietly and greatly appreciated! Can't believe you're the age you say you are as you look much younger in years. But then what is one supposed to look like when age is defined in numbers and expectations?? Depending on your birthday, I could be older than you! I'm so glad to hear that you'll be ok with cuddling for now as actual intercourse would be difficult for me until I can get a minor "fix"! No problem with mechanical stimulation and orgasm but that's the best I can do for now it seems. I have no doubt that you would be an excellent lover in all respects and anticipate the time when that will occur....hopefully with you. Gosh, I feel like a virgin all over again! I love your description! Rushing anything doesn't serve anyone and can often impede the flow of energy creating dissonance rather than resonance. A gentle flow of higher vibrational, loving energy, can create miracles. Sounds a bit like Tantra!

Michael, although money can create some sense of security, it really is insignificant in terms of living a joy filled life. In the short term it can buy happiness but in the long term true joy must be sourced from within. So, let it be what it is and enjoy the moments... the rest will take care of itself in time. I'm not really concerned about money... probably because I've never had any...but have found great joy in a second hand store. lol... I try not to have great expectations about anything... even us... but do have to be practical with my work since it provides me with extras in life. I certainly don't want to be overworked and want to save time for enjoying life on the Island. It would be a real plus to share much of my free time with you exploring this beautiful Island together. The workshops and speakers would be a couple times a month only, with clients in between any plans made. It's all good.

All I can say about your appys and wine is WOW!! Do you discuss the expectation of who pays and what the return would be before you order??? If that were me, I would be doing a stack of dishes for sure! Good thing that there was some reciprocation the next day although the initial shock would shake me from complacency around the discussion of who pays for what. The expectation usually is a product of ignorance (not a bad word, just an unrecognized truth) and a sense of entitlement. However, I'm happy that you have someone to keep you company. And, have to admit, happy there is no spark of passion between you! Would not want to put out this spark before it had a chance to grow into a full fledged fire. I'm really liking what you say Michael. There is great love for you here, and there, and everywhere. Good old Abe stuff. (BIG smile) Off to bed now. Wish you were here!

M: Aha, I have discovered you lurking at your keyboard in the middle of my night, thought it was you all along, there's a tiny squeek each time you urge on your mouse. Bit o brie will usually cure that, though process can do it just as well and is cheaper. I'll leave off a proper missive until my own a.m. which begins about 4:30 but hasn't arrived just yet. Yes dear one I am real, we're going to wike me and you we are, just don't blow my cover, I'm on vacation. I wuv the thought of virgin you at last. And just so you know, my fingers are keyboard strengthened and goal oriented - choose your destination and we'll eventually arrive.

I do have a tiny bit of Tantra experience, it comes natural to me. I'll tell you about it some moment my goddess. Let's explore US, what greater fun could there be... I too wish to be in your bed this this this, yes, it is still night at 1:10 a.m.

M: Good morning my love. Yes, we are getting to know each other by the written word, I think I can get away with that opening appellation. I love and appreciate your willingness to explore this promising relationship and look forward eagerly to our time together this week. Let me respond a bit to your last message.

I think I arrived on this planet a few months before you did. It is my belief that immortality is becoming much more common - as you wrote, age is a matter of expectation. Our bodies are mere vibration so it shouldn't be much of a problem to shape them as we will, the trick being to believe that and to ignore past programming that insists on imposing limits on that born limitless. But you know all that, faith dissipates as validation and knowledge arrive. I hear you about money, but I like the stuff and what it can buy, I *expect* abundance. I've already explored subsistence, it's a lack in a universe that is overflowing, filled to the brim with goodness for the taking. Why settle on earth for pennies when we OWN planets? Wealth is created for US, we need only to allow it into existence. That's an attitude.

Shall we co-create with our mutual thoughts and desires abundance and immortality, and leave off thinking life is serious? I think that would be fun to watch unfold while we love each other and are deliriously happy that we came together, ancient gods with purpose. Play with me? Be my goddess? Share my dream? That's all I'm looking for...

Oresha: How are you doing these days? Are ya havin' Fun surfin' The Pond? I'm just starting to feel almost back to "normal" today.... It was a very quiet weekend for me...just chillin'.. lol Have you been taking in the Busker-Fest much? I have still to get down there...lol Kathy and I would like to extend an invitation to you... to meet at The Bent Mast (over by your place) on Thur. at 3:00p.m. Chug a couple of brews, enjoy one another's company and chat about everything Abraham... lol Please let me know if that works for you?.... or if we need to make it another day? Have an IN-Joyable Day! Hugsssss....

M: I'm glad that you are getting better Oresha. I'd love to accept your Thursday invitation but I'll be out of town for several days this week, leaving early Thursday a.m. And I'll have company from July 30th through August 15th so I'm not sure if we can meet soon. But I'll let you know when I get back to Victoria, maybe we could meet on Sunday or Monday if I'm back and you and Kathy can? I walked by several of the busker stages several times but never saw anything happening at any of them that held my attention for longer than a few minutes. So I've given up on it, I don't think you're missing much. Be well.

Oresha: Have fun on your outta-town-adventure... Let me know if you have time before your Ex comes to visit.... otherwise we'll get together.... next month... lol Cheers.... Take Care...

I send a message to Jackie that I won't quote here, it's just too indepth for a book that purports to be something other than a text on metaphysics, as this one does. I can get away with it with her because we are learned in the same field, we speak the same mystical language.

Jackie: You write so many beautiful words lined up in perfect order describing an imagery of love's perfection, innocence, contrast and return to love through eons of time/space. My guess is that your descriptive words flowed through time frames and dimensions forgotten on this earthly sojourn. And, maybe not so forgotten as your story indicates! This may sound so contrite for all that was given... but it was simply AWESOME! Thanks for sharing your truth, your heart, your beauty and the beauty of love's magical journey into time/space dear "star being".

In a world with a little more enlightenment spread over the earth, people will love, love immensely, but their love will transform into a relating, not a relationship. And I am not saying that love will be only momentary. There is every possibility that love may go deeper, may have a higher quality of intimacy, may have something more of poetry and more of divinity in it. And there is every possibility love may last longer than our relationship ever lasts... except for yours (had to recognize that one).....but without binding, limiting or controlling. Relationship means something complete, finished, closed. Love is never a relationship; love is relating. It is always a river, flowing, unending. Love knows no full stop; the honeymoon begins but never ends. It is not like a novel that starts at a certain point and ends at a certain point. It is an ongoing phenomenon. Lovers end, love continues. YES! Will we pave the way with the all encompassing light of love igniting the flame within humanity??

I would like to respond more completely, more intimately, and with much more passion but time is limited for now. My daughter and her "adopted son" left late this morning and I'm cleaning up remnants of their hurried leaving. Also need to make some phone calls, emails and prepare and organize my "stuff" for tomorrows little workshop. Will respond more this evening while having a cuppa and re-reading your exquisite words and beautiful poetry.... Shine your light beautiful star being.

M: You are such a delight dear one. Maybe one day (after vacation) we'll write some non-fiction together for a metaphysically-aware market, perhaps teach the possibility/probability of immortality in our time, find a following to help co-create that vibration for all who seek and choose to tap in and add to, give this planet's light workers a new desire and focus so they'll always be around. Audio books especially would be marvelous with you and your golden voice doing the reading, maybe beautiful sounds lighting the background in places. I love the music on your cd's it feeds the soul and leaves it better, approaches playing you as does the Music of the Spheres which I have been played by on occasion, as may have been you. There is so much about you Jackie that I really really like, but right now it's your love, your touch, your eagerness, and your body that I'm craving virgin you.

When would it be best for you that I arrive at the Nanaimo Greyhound depot on Thursday? Please let me know today so I can reserve a seat online, thx.

Jackie: Yes, doesn't the mundane take up time... what's a vacation anyway?? Ha ha Just going out the door for a walk to stretch the legs and calm the mind. Ended up re-writing an old script for tomorrow night's meetup.. How about the 2 pm? It then gives me a little more time to plan meals which I haven't done yet! Light and Love

M: I have ticket in hand. Please pick me up at 2:05 p.m. Thursday July 24th. I'll probably not bring my cell phone so if we're late check with the dog people. I haven't booked a return yet but I promise to catch the next bus or taxi after you tell me it's time to go. We're really going to do this aren't we. Can hardly wait to see you again - was it all a dream? Nope, there's the water glass, now washed waiting for you to come again. When your daughter gets back we'll most likely visit mostly at my place? I'd like that, it's such a beautiful city to walk around and I'm well located for that. I know, I'm a dreamer, an optimist, an idealist. *But most of my dreams do come true...* Sleep well sweetie, I'll be thinking of you.

Jackie: (she attaches a text about alien beings with two toes) Sending you a short description of your possible, and probable, relationships with Tish and I in "far away" places and on the other side of the veil that separates ourselves from other parts of our Selves. For some reason, my email is not working properly so will send this and try again later....

M: All things of course are possible because we are a part of all. But as for me personally, I like my ten toes! I am so comfortable to be "made in the image and likeness of God" as the bible puts it that it is my desire and my will to always have an unbroken stream of consciousness in human form evolving within that form to become the highest and best that I can eventually become before it all begins again, if it ever does. Let others do as they will, I will go my own way and love my wives and children completely when such a time comes, as it must for it is my desire and I will allow it to be.

That is why I desire immortality, for this present incarnation when the time is right to become Adam, the male in a family of immortal spouses, and populate planets. I really like male and female, that creation is brilliance on a universal scale. I choose to be male henceforth and until being Adam becomes boring and another step 'upward' becomes apparent and wanted. My guess is that will be a very very long 'time' if ever because each child born to my wives is unique and as the father of each child in my worlds I will be intensely interested in their eternal progress, eventually casting them into time as was done with me and with you. In that manner there is no end to desire, so no desire for an end, we will go on and on forever, knowing always fullness of love and joy, our increase being our myriad children on many planets, as it was and as it is with our own Eternal Parents who started out a bit sooner than we did. It is in THEIR image and likeness that we are made. I like that, I need no other, I have seen myself and I am beautiful.

Share my dream? And if not, let's just have fun together for as long as we make it so. I'd like that...

Michael Demers

Well, I don't know if I'm still writing my series of books or not. But at least I'm keeping a journal and if some miracle should occur and the books start selling, I can publish this manuscript and go forward from there.

Chapter 19

M: (to Jackie) Further to my note about choosing to have ten toes, it is my belief that we can scatter parts of our awareness all over the sum total of everything anytime because we are all part of that primeval soup I call "Intelligence" that has always existed and permeates *everything*. We are all co-eternal and co-equal with the greatest of Gods that have or ever will exist. So, by our choice of where and when to center our awareness we actually become everything that has been or ever will be created from Intelligence, the "Cloud of Unknowing."

"And look that nothing remain in thy working mind but a naked intent stretching unto God; not clothed in any special thought of God in himself or any of his works, but only that He is as He is...Forsake good thoughts as well as evil thoughts. He asks no help but only thyself. He will thou do but look upon Him and let him alone." The Cloud of Unknowing, 14th Century

"Not by speech, not by mind; not by sight can He be apprehended. How can He be comprehended otherwise than by one's saying "He Is"?" Upanishads, B.C. 800

"I am the taste in the water, the light of the sun and the moon, the sound in the ether, the ability in man, the fragrance of the earth, the heat in the fire, the life of all that lives, the strength of the strong, the intelligence of the intelligent, and the original seed of all existences." Bhagavad Gita, B.C. 400

The present concern I have for many who wander off in strange paths such as communion with species alien to us is that they do so not just to seek knowledge of what's 'out there' in the universe but to use that 'knowledge' to influence their own thinking and desires. Desires influenced by such alien thinking could keep the person generating those desires from manifesting his/her own highest and best 'destiny', subordinating that to the desire of the intelligence that currently exists in other than or in human form, benign and well-meaning as that external form of intelligence may be.

For me, a human, it seems so simple: Formulate *my own* desires - decide what I really really want for myself, *then create it*. In that manner I become a god unto myself, create my own reality, my own worlds. And, together with those women who freely choose to join me as equal spouses, sister wives each 'married' to the other and to me and I to them, co-create *our own* worlds and children and lovingly watch over our creations with fullness of joy forever. We become The Most Ancient of Gods within our own creations, a family of spouses who love each other completely, all powerful, all knowing, Eternal Parents, Father/Mother/God to *our own* children only, loving caretakers, rulers over our own creations only. For *that* is the way of Truth as I know it, each to their own, all being Love.

I simply don't care about worlds outside of my own present awareness other than to believe that they exist. I already know they are a part of me, just not a focused part - let them be as they will, as for me and my house, we will go our own way. I like it better that way, it's the highest and best that I can think of.

Share my dream? Help co-create my dream? And if not, shall we just have fun together for as long as we make it so? I'd like that dear one.

Jackie: Michael, you have written so much, so deeply, so succinctly, and I'm having a very difficult time wanting to answer with the same intent. However, I do have an appointment in 1/2 hour and then need to run out for awhile. I do want you to know that I've read everything thoroughly enjoying the mind stretching with some introspection, and would love to discuss all of this with you while you're here. Unless I have oodles of time... yes that too can be created to be more malleable... but right now am having difficulty keeping up with everything. I have so much to tell you, share with you, and listen to when you arrive. The quotes were beautiful, understandable and spoke of truth to me. Much more to explore and create within the near future. Co-creation must be present and impeccable. Will save all so we can go through them together....

M: I understand Jackie, your response as is works for me and is much appreciated. It's just that I enjoy writing, have the time to do it, and I know you read what I have to say, agree or not. That's all I ask of you. Enjoy the day sweetie.

M: I'm wishing you the very best with your presentation tonight. Thinking about you a lot, all sweet thoughts.

Jackie: Awe, so sweet Michael!! Thanks so much for your best wishes. It was a wonderful, intimate and cozy evening with just four of us there. Did some shopping and lots of running today... thank you to the stores for creating tomorrow nights dinner! Will meet you at 2:00 with daisy smiling and flowers in my hair. Off to bed now.

M: Aha, I'm on to you now, flower power works wonders with a man! Looks like it's going to be a rainy walk to the bus depot leaving home about 11, so by the time I get to you you're going to wonder what the dog dragged in. But if it's the same as the last time, your steamy hugs will warm me up promptly. See you soon Jackie, rain and all it's a wonderful day.

M: (to Jackie with title "Wow Just Wow") I think you know what I mean by the subject line! Thank-you for such a wonderful time Jackie, I hope we get to see each other again as soon as our schedules permit. I'll be dreaming of you tonight for sure, be well sweetheart.

Jackie: YES!!! I FEEL the meaning of WOW and have been mulling over this incredible dream!!! Thanks so much for the opportunity to see me through you with such a beautiful reflection. You are tucked safely and lovingly within my heart and mind. And definitely thinking of you while I lay in my bed reaching out to feel your body. Now it's time for you to catch up on your writing and I've been doing some laundry and phone calls. Take good care of yourself.... knowing you will.... and be joy in every moment. With Love as Love, Jackie

Yes, it was a wonderful experience being with Jackie, incredible actually. We bonded on so many levels, it felt wonderful at so many levels, it felt right at so many levels. Her kisses are the most delicious I have ever experienced. We walked much and slept naked together in the nights. We will meet again soon after Ex leaves, probably drive to the north of Vancouver Island together and have much fun. Jackie and I are an incredibly good fit, we both blend beautifully... Wow just wow. Thank-you thank-you thank-you.

M: (to Jackie) What did you do to me woman? I tried doing my usual routine of looking over the messages etc. from singles and savoring some of the sights, pondering the possibilities, but you took the fun out of it. All I could think of was YOU, wonderful magical lovely YOU!!!! (Especially you sitting on the sofa in panties and nothing but.) Oh you do something to me all right! I thought it nice of you to stay and wait almost until my bus left, I felt a wonderful connection across the yards that separated us physically. But I'm baffled for an explanation of what went on when you walked up to a man with a beard and a guitar on his back (I think it was) sitting on a bench, then led him a few yards and pointed somewhere behind my bus. My head is still trying to figure that one out... I hope your session went well Jackie and wish you much fun with your friend.

M: (to Oresha) I'm back in Victoria. I have today and tomorrow available if you want to get together with or without your friend.

Oresha: Hi Stranger... lol Nice to hear from You... Hope you had a great time out of town. I just spoke with Kathy, she'd still like to have an "Abraham" chat.... lol so how does meeting at 3:30 or 4:00 today sound at The Bent Mast over by you? Who ever gets there 1st could save an outdoor table for 3..... Ciao...

M: Sure, I'll be at the Bent Mast at 4 p.m. today, should be able to walk that far. Just so there's no misunderstanding, I'd prefer that we each pay our own bill if that will work for you. See you there.

Oresha: Great... see you then... Hugz... This isn't a "date"... Friends getting together-mode... lol

M: You know, for that type of conversation we may want to have more privacy than the crooked mast would afford, so here's a suggestion. You are both welcome to come to my place and share what I have in the cellar, being at the moment only a small bottle of Shiraz and several bottles of amber hard cider. And however much white tea anyone wants to consume of course, though be warned that my help is off today and I don't normally don white gloves for a pouring. If we get hungry, we can walk across the street where pizza can be bought by the slice, or I make a wicked toast with peanut butter. You're also welcome to come earlier, I have nothing else planned for today, just let me know about when you'll be buzzing or calling to get through Lord Simcoe's front door without troubling the servants on a Sunday or creating a public disturbance. If you arrive by carriage I spect there'll be a man available to assist your driver with the hayburners, or just go to the stall that is reserved for my own exclusive use. What do you think?

Oresha: You're right... it would be a more suitable venue for our conversation... lol Kathy and I will arrive in her carriage at 3:30-ish and park in your stall.... If you don't see us... then I'll call you on my cell to get us through the servant's entrance...lol P.S. Kathy and I do have plans for later on.... Thanks for your invitation..... see you then...

This one's clever. She phoned and said she'd be a few minutes late because she had to go across the street from me and buy some beer! Of course I said I'd go get some myself. She offered to reimburse me then commented that I'd "probably remember" what she looks like in the parking lot. I suppose Kathy was with her when she called...

Later: The visit went well, I'm sure I've read Kathy's profile on a singles site but couldn't find it again, she's a poet and writer. She brought me some lovely flowers and some Spanish beer.

M: (to Jackie) Shall we visit Avatar Grove in our travels? Does this appeal to you? I'm not suggesting that we backpack anywhere...

M: (to Oresha) Thanks for the visit, it was an enjoyable conversation. Please tell Kathy I really appreciate the flowers, they are perfect and were totally unexpected, a lovely surprise.

M: (to Jackie) I know you are with a friend today so I'm not expecting a response right away. But I thought I'd send along some thoughts I'm having this a.m. even if only to create content for my journal. The lady I'm friends with who lives within walking distance of me came over yesterday for a few hours and brought a friend who is an accomplished poet and author/writer and deep into Abraham. Surprisingly she (the friend) brought me flowers and some Spanish beer. We had an enjoyable three way conversation sipping beer and eating pistachios in my apartment, talking metaphysical. And with the absence of you I'm again browsing the plethora of photos and profiles that are instantly available on singles sites. And of course responding to messages and "so and so wants to meet you" "I love your photo" types of expressions of interest that arrive daily. Sure, I'd be interested in meeting some of the women, their photos and profiles are interesting, some compelling. But then what?

My thoughts this a.m. are that for every man there will always be a prettier woman looking, and for every woman a more interesting man. And Law of Attraction isn't shy about bringing us choices either. But then what?

For me and you us came easily, I've never experienced such a thing before. Your kisses are the sweetest I have ever tasted. You wear your whole soul on your lips for me, give it all willingly in the stillness of the touch of mine. I could pause in such a moment and find eternity in my feelings - or are they yours - or are they ours? It's as though we could morph into salt or stone, lips pressed together while worlds come and go, unaware of the passing of time, content in our BEING, delicious well forever and ever. But if not forever, then what?

Yes there are others, others for each of us. But it's so easy my darling to melt into YOU, nothing guarded nothing guarding, just BEING as if you were me, imperfect, my love, my sister, my soul. I want to unlax and let go with you because I can, we were brought together for that purpose should we choose us for a while. I want to vacation with you, to co-create delicious moments or nothing at all as we go along, taking fun refreshment nourishment from not each other but from the combination of US twin souls as we are. But then what?

Then, then, then, we'll know then better how and where to forever find each other. We'll always know we can rush to the other any time anywhere should our matrix feel for a moment foreign within us, and find again an instant grounding, a melding in each other's thoughts, each other's arms if the moment allows. I hope they all do. I want your body too, the femaleness of you pressed against me, the peace that dwells within as a big part of us disappears and we rest in our stillness, joined at all levels of our being. We may work together after vacation, help prepare this present people for the Golden Age, the leap yet to come into awareness immortality and eternal life. And maybe not, that will be our choice, our discussion.

But we'll always be there/here for each other from then on. It cannot be any other way for though we are individuals you and I, we cast the same shadow. Come back to me soon my love my sister my soul, I need more moments of us entangled at *all* levels. Your M

M: (to Jackie) So I find myself hopelessly immersed in a steamy long distance love affair and decide that it's only fair that I have a car too. I make a deal on the internet for a 1998 Honda, get a good price, and the salesman says to come pick up my car. So I go by cab, but when I get there they've had a power outage on their block and in those moments after two weeks for sale on the lot someone sold my car to someone, irreversible, money has changed hands. Aha I think, Law of Attraction never fails, but sometimes upgrades beyond our expectations, the universe is full to overflowing.

So I get the salesman to drive me to another dealer where in a brief time I drive away owner of an Acura, top of the line, the car LOA was holding for me, confirmed silently several times as I waited and negotiated the price. Mine yes, mine yes, mine with plates and insurance yes, now in my parking spot at Lord Simcoe yes. So we'll drive my car on our travels my love, it's comfy and automatic so one hand is free to do with as I will, if you still want to travel with me when it's time, I hope you do, let me know.

Enjoy today as always, I'm always thinking of you fondly dearest Jackie. I want to be with you, now it will be easier when my company and your stream of friends and clients are come and gone. Save some weeks for us... Your M

It's July 28 and Jackie should be finished now with her two day get together with a former boyfriend. She says she's not interested in him anymore but agreed to get together with him before she met me. If he slept in the bed I slept in (hers) a few days ago, I guess I shouldn't complain because she has a slate to clean and maybe for her that would be a good comparison of feelings she feels for the man in her bed. But I was on singles a few minutes ago and it shows that she has been "active within 24 hours". That could mean that she was responding to messages already sent to her instead of actively searching for another man. But if she has time to do that, why not send a message or more to me in response to my several as yet unanswered ones to her?

Am I pushing too hard again because I love writing and sharing what I write? Is this going to be another Suzanne situation where I'm always wondering if what I feel is mutual? I wonder... But I know this, if she claims me eagerly, she's got me for at least several months. I'd most likely suspend all my singles profiles and focus exclusively on her because I fall in love too easily and am too loyal, and because even though she's not perfect, she *feels* right. It was for her and for us that I bought a car today.

Oresha: Thank you for being such a gracious Host yesterday. It was fun chatting with you.... I LOVE learning about anything Abraham.... lol I will message you to see when you're free.. (since I know you're going to be bus-Y in the next while... so I can get your DVD's back to you... and

borrow some more, if that's still ok...? Enjoy the rest of your evening....
Ciao...

M: (to Jackie) My ex is not arriving until 1 p.m. tomorrow so if you're not doing much today (July 29) and would like that, I'd drive to you, overnight, and leave about 10 a.m. Wednesday. Crazy about you, or just crazy period?

Oresha: I was just thinking about your flowers... lol Since I'm not sure how much of a green thumb you may have... It would be best to water your little plant away from your beautiful new furniture... as you wouldn't want to possibly get any water spots on the furniture.. As you probably already know, some furniture finishes don't do well with liquids on them... as I've had accidental spills on my coffee table (which is solid oak.. unfinished)... and now there are white spots in the wood.... some day I'll get it professionally finished... Hope your week is off to a Magnificent start!...and that you're getting out to enjoy the glorious sunshine.... Hugzzzzz...

M: How did you know I'm a bachelor and need advice on things like that? Thanks much. I've been running errands all a.m. so caught a few welcome rays. Will walk to the driver's license place shortly and take care of biz there in addition to the exercise tooing and frooing. Loving it here... Company arriving tomorrow and need to get a few more things in order, but if you want to drop in right away to swap DVD's I'll not likely be going out until 12:30. Let me know. Enjoy the day you...

Oresha: I just wanted to offer the advise about your new "visitor" (plant.. lol) so as to keep your furniture looking grand!.. Thanx for the invite... but I'm not quite through with the DVD's.... do you mind if I keep them for a while longer? I know you have company coming.. is there a break between the kids..and your ex coming to visit when I might be able to get them back to you? Or are you OK if I get them back after your ex leaves? I REALLY appreciate you lending them to me!... and I'll try to get through them in the next few days.... Hugsssss...

M: No problem with keeping them for now, I can get them later.

Oresha: Thanks Michael! I will continue taking excellent care of your DVD's... Have a Wonderful time with your visitors. Drop me a line when things are less busy for you..... Enjoy ! Ciao...

Jackie: Lord!! I arrived home last night, read your emails, saw the picture of siblings (beautiful family),watched the incredible videos which made my eyes leak, love the idea of Avatar Grove, and so happy that you manifested a car!! Wow!! Also very happy that you had some company and enjoyed the time with your neighbour and friend. You seemed very busy compared to me! I went camping for a couple days.. no computer.. and then visited a friend for a day before coming home. Nothing to rant or rave about! So sorry your plan for today didn't work out for us seeing each other but I know you'll enjoy the car and it'll be handy for later when your ex leaves again.

Michael, we barely know each other and yet there was such a powerful connection between us. But, please don't be in too much of a rush as we'll have lots of time later this summer. It seems that those that push relationship too quickly become disappointed just as quickly. After your ex leaves, we'll have more time to explore the journey for each of us in an easy, free flowing manner. I've decided to spend some time... about a week... with my daughter and will leave on Thursday. It's very hot in that area but wanted to take this time to visit before you're totally free. I won't be writing you much while I'm there except to say hi, I'm still here and thinking of you. Although, just remembered that your ex may be reading over your shoulder! So, I'm wondering if I should just wait until after she leaves? It's been so incredibly hot these last couple of days but spent some time in the ocean... not enough.

I hope all is well with you and you're continuing to enjoy your friendships, the car (an excellent deal!! Great manifesting!!), and your time with the ex. Please enjoy the moments you have and we'll connect again later. Take good care of yourself. With "Good Vibrations") Namaste, Jackie

M: It's nice to hear from you Jackie and to know that in the silence you weren't abducted by two-toed aliens or whatevers. I disagree that *"we barely know each other"* but I'm willing to play along with that and will try to not "push" too hard though I am wont to do that and do drive away some who walk to the beat of a slower drummer. (Though I do not think you are such an one.) I tend to rush through life, craving a fast moving stream, savoring each moment in passing, lingering in the finer ones, going back even. It's just that you are wiser than me when it comes to such things as relationships and what women want and need - I hear and respect your counsel dear one.

As I walked along the breakwater this afternoon where you and I once walked way back when, all I wanted to do was hold you, *silly unbelieving you*. Please don't stop writing, frequent short notes are fine, tells me you're still thinking about me, I'd like that. Be well Jackie, write soon, enjoy. P.S. say hello to daisy for me tomorrow.

The reference to daisy was because I'm sending her a bouquet of daisies tomorrow and also because she has a plastic daisy on the dash of her car that is solar powered, smiles, and flutters its petals, it reminds her not to take life too seriously. She'll think I was referring to that. Mmmm, my bod wants to be with her even though Ex is arriving in a few hours.

M: (to Ex) Are you getting excited about your vacation? I expect that we'll have loads of fun, there is so much to see and do here. But be prepared for lots of walking, that's the best way to do it.

Ex: Yes it will be great. I am in Las Vegas not going home.

M: Enjoy your night out in the big town. See you tomorrow.

Jackie: scents and colors arrived at my door yesterday. They now sit on my table reminding me of my friend and confidant... Blessed be dear friend

M: I thought you'd like them sweetie, glad that it was so. Travel safe today. Driving?

M: (to Jackie) It's not that I think of you all the time, not at all, I do get some sleep now and again. It's possible that my company will all be gone by about Wednesday or Thursday next week, not sure though. So if you are still wanting to travel the Island with me and have the time, we could possibly get away a bit earlier than expected??

M: (to Ex) I want you to know that I'm enjoying your visit, your touch, and your attentiveness and gentle caring. I'm delighted with the 'new' Jen, she pleases me hugely, you're a special lady when you choose to be. I'm glad that we were able to share so much of our lives in the past and hope we will continue to visit and perhaps share some special dreams as time unfolds and you make choices for your life. But know this, whatever choices you make and however frequent or infrequent our contacts may become, I will always love you for the sweet soul you are and wish upon you the greatest of happiness and well being - you deserve it dear one. Take care my sweetie, it is my hope that you will choose happiness in each new moment of your life, and that you will choose freely for *your own* best interests, it's good to love yourself first so you can love others better. I'll always be here for you by email regardless of my situation or loves, you are a top priority in my life, I love you. Your Michael

Ex: (asking me to help her write a singles profile – sending her ideas) I did some jewelry making and various crafts over time. Love gardening, travel. I am at a time in my life I want to enjoy my partner for most, then my family and travel on the side. If you need me I will be there. If you want to travel I will get up in the middle of the night and go. To be there for my partner first then my family. Share a mutual love for life. My goal is to travel roads I have not traveled before. Show respect to our creature everyday. Fulfill our bucket list. Be spontaneous in finding joy and laughter. Lift my partner to the highest and best self. To take care of my good health so I will be able to enjoy my golden years to the fullest.

What makes me unique: I am a stabling force, that love to be spontaneous with my significant other, When I come to a turn in the road I only expect the best. Many times I have jumped for joy when I went around that corner and saw what was in store in spite of the bumps in the road. Want a companion that is willing to work with me and go down that road and smooth those bumps. This has happened many times in my life. When I love I love very deeply. But respect the love of another and let if be free as a butterfly must be, to only love it more when it returns to me.

Why does she write: *"I am at a time in my life I want to enjoy my partner for most, then my family"*? She always puts her family before me. Guess she doesn't see me as her "partner".

Ex: Michael, Enjoy and find happiness. I realized after being with you and intently listening to your dreams and reading so far half your book. This is a journey only you can take. The time we spent was well special and enlightening and..... yes it was way to long of a vacation. I am glade to be going home. I hope all works out well for you and Jackie and all the others that you want to tuck under your wings. I wish you happiness and joy. This is your life choice and dream unfolding. I didn't know you were planning and wanting Adam to emerge long before we separated or possibly you kept it tucked down deep since 1984. Ok I am not judging your wants. It is a direction different from mine. I go home with much to think about. Will always love you, Jen

PS: I hope I never meet a "Michael" on any single sights. As you put it he is a raunchy fictional character. If any of him is in you, wow unto thee! Please tell me he is not. Even though I know he would never physically hurt any of his virtual friends, He very much in trigs, confuses, and frightens these virtual friends. And with great pressure they kept returning for more (on light side) abuse. So far the three I read about that he fell in love with were first raunchy as him, We have miss alcoholic nurse, then miss Queen gold digger and one that loved to put in in his place and go for tat to tat. My heart weeps for such desperate women. Doing and saying anything for attention. Oh sweet heart what road is Michael taking rid yourself of his.

As I read the writing is much much better. The story telling is much better. It held my interest much longer. Kept me up most of the night, The book really bothers me not sure why yet. Need to finish it. So glade I got a glance of who Micahel is. I think you should rid your self of him in any other books or plan to write a book called the Redemption of Michael. Or Michael sees the light.

M: Thank-you for telling it the way you see it and for giving me permission to publish your emails should I choose to do so. There are many nice things about your visit but I concur, it's best that you leave on Wednesday after a one week visit rather than the two weeks you had planned. We slip all too easily you and I back into the destructive stuckness where we dwelt for many years. We both have beautiful lives to unfold as we moment by moment allow the past to fade away into a delicious dance we once had, and in the next moment choose a new life, and happiness in it. Be well dear one, *enjoy* your new life of freedom and choice, delight in it moment by delicious moment.

Carrie: hi there… just thought i would touch in to see how life has been going for you lately??? my trip was amazing, transformative and is going to have long lasting life changing effects, though most are not even evident yet… My friend and i will be lifelong friends, though we are not a lover match… at least not now and i don't really see that happening in the future based on some big differences but we did have a great time traveling together. how is your new life up north? will send out a travel update and photo album once i get the over 1500 photos i took culled and edited… sending hugs again, carrie

M: It's nice to hear from you Carrie, I've been wondering how your trip was working out. I'm sure you're disappointed in a way but maybe refreshed and glad to be home? My move to Victoria and the absence of book sales gave me an opportunity to bury book character "Michael" and once again become just retired me in my native country, thoroughly enjoying life, much more experienced and better honed than I used to be. All is well. Thank-you so much dear friend for helping me become the tempered man I now am. Please stay in touch.

Carrie: is there a lady in your life these days? seems there is always one at least on your horizon, so i'm guessing something's up anything with suzanne or deleon happening lately??? are you writing? doing anything else to earn income now? and, most of all, i'm intrigued as you call yourself tempered… please tell me how i assisted in that transformation and who the new you is these days? sent with love, as always

M: Good grief Carrie, I am trying to take a vacation and bury the writer and you ask questions that demand a fullness of response and I find myself helpless not to do so. As I write this, my ex is asleep in my bed having come to visit a few days ago, leaving on Wednesday. Surprised? Just friends, we won't move in with each other most likely ever again, but the habits of 18 years are still strong. My daughter and her husband are arriving tonight for a few days. They'll sleep on an air mattress, my suite has only one bedroom.

When I changed my address on singles sites from USA to Victoria I was almost immediately swamped by expressions of interest (hundreds) and desires to meet me - it seems there is a shortage of men in my age group on Vancouver Island, Canada's premier retirement location. And the barrage continues, a dozen or more messages etc. arrive daily. My heart goes out to all these lonely hopeful sometimes lovely in appearance women any one of whom I could become wonderful for in real life because to me women are goddesses and I malleable to their touch, that's just the way I am.

There is one who lives so close that we walk to meet each other and stroll Victoria's natural delights hand in hand, arm in arm. But there's no spark of passion, we will remain friends only. There's another though, one called "Jackie" who when we met we connected at many levels instantly. Her kisses are sweeter than any I have ever touched, for me she wears her soul there on her lips. She fascinates me totally. When my summer company leaves, Jackie and I will explore Vancouver Island and flow with each other for a time, as much as we allot for us.

My name is still Michael, but I'm an evolved happy contented undriven Michael, a new man thanks to the incredibly wonderful virtual and real experiences I shared with a small number of people, including one Carrie Fisher who became my friend and sometimes confidante, never lover most likely ever in this lifetime.

DeLeon "Goddess of Bling" rejected Michael 'permanently' yet again but recently started writing to him, thanking him profusely and with wonder for being for her "Magnificent King" and healer. She recently survived another heart operation and seems to be healed/ healing more capable now of writing the books she wants to write, embarking upon the missions she feels destined to serve. Michael will almost certainly never return to the side of the Goddess of Bling but will always respond to her mails for she despite what she had become is an old and familiar soul, one of Michael's 'people' for whom he in this present lifetime feels an obligation like that of a king for his queen.

Suzanne, dear dear Suzanne my great love has gone permanently of her own volition. Responsible Nurse overcame the Suzanne she really wants to be and she is become immersed in hospice and silence, removed from singles sites, wanting I think to follow her dying people all the way home to start again, more satisfied next time to be who she will come to be. Maybe her *real* name next time will be "Suzanne". I'd be hugely delighted if she broke her self-imposed silence but I think this time she's gone for good. I probe for her mystically, she was once so easy to find, only to find a wall, a wall I could break through but will never do, I respect her wishes and desires, she's gone.

I told Ashley to never again send an invoice, I will sink no more money into that venture. She is silent now, living in the jungles of Nicaragua with her son and her lover, content for the moment.

See Carrie, the writer's gone, buried, I'm on vacation for at least a year, can't hardly find a word to write anymore. Take care my friend, enjoy each moment, choosing happiness in each one, it's better that way.

Carrie: this is the email i sent to some other friends when i got home... thought you might also like to see it... i've been back home for about 5 days now and am finally getting to editing over 1500 photos i took on my "trip of a lifetime" and thought this was the perfect shot to show you who my friend is and the energy with which he showered me with more generosity than i can express... we spent 3 glorious days at the Oregon County Fair and this shot was taken at the end of the 3rd day at a wonderful restaurant in where we connected with and befriended everyone there... we must have brought the fair energy with us as the whole staff and all the clients were up dancing with my friend within a few minutes of us getting there, even though there was no dance music playing when we got there... a trip update and photo album are forthcoming, but wanted to share this with you as my heart swells in appreciation for the gift given to me by my very special friend...

M: I hope you don't mind that I showed the photo of your friend to my ex. She said "he's my perfect man, I really want to meet him." He looks wonderful Carrie, congrats on meeting such a man.

Carrie: of course, i don't mind at all... though right now, he's no one's perfect man as he is in a transition that will probably keep him single for quite a while... that said, he is wonderful in so very many ways and i love him dearly... always will and the gift he gave me is priceless...

Ex: Michael, Thank you for the wonderful visit and for being so honest about your path and desire for a future family of wives.. My trip home was without hiccups. As I arrived at my car and started to drive away I felt the tears building up and knew it would be a whooper. I changed my attitude, said a little prayer and sang all the way home. Do you still pray as your father did? I think you meditate. I plan to work on my spirituality and getting closer to God. I think it will fill the holes in my heart. Love you and miss you, man of mine.

M: It was a lovely visit, I'm so glad you came. Yes, I still kneel and pray but only occasionally and I find that in formal prayer I'm still reciting the Mormon way. That's ok, but my life as you know is now very different and for me much more satisfying and happy. My daughter and family just left for Tofino and the rest of their vacation. I'm real glad they came, it was a pleasant visit. Take care and stay in touch woman of mine.

Carrie: interestingly, i have some friends who have connected with lovers on this site and i've looked at it before myself... just never got into it… have recently decided to check it out, but then when i was just in ca, a friend connected me up with a friend of hers, so i am going to see where this goes before i put the effort into any other sites… but thanks much for the heads up and i will let you know if i decide to use it how it goes… i was also thinking of putting myself back on another singles site but will hold off on all of it now til i see where this new connection goes…

Ex: I thought you might be interested in this for yourself. When I was flying home the airline offered a visa card. They offered 27,500 miles that will fly you anywhere they go and you get to take a companion for $99. So I signed up. Were you also offered this and took advantage. I thought it was great. I almost forgot. I get a $99 companion ticket every year. Now if just have to find a companion.

M: Are you offering me an all expenses paid trip with you?

Ex: Maybe, Can't think of anyone that would be more fun with.

M: For you, I'm for hire.

Ex: Yea baby, Wait a few months and show you the real me.

Ex: Thanks for the kind return. Just read a message from an old friend from more than 30 years ago. She is and has been going through trials of letting of the love of her life go. I will share a bit of what she said since I can relate. I always prayed for compassion for others and I think it has arrived. Everyone will go through some hard times at some point. Life isn't easy. Just something to think about… did you know the people that are the strongest are usually the most sensitive? Did you know the people who exhibit the most kindness are the first to get mistreated? Did you know the ones who take care of others all the time are usually the ones who need it the most? Did you know the three hardest things to say are I love you, I'm sorry, and help me? Sometimes just because a person looks happy, you have to look past their smile and see how much pain they may be in"

I am curious how you would respond to this. I know from what you said you were very happy but experienced tremendous loneliness in Taxes and Yuma. Then I had an opportunity to spent time with you. I could see those tender eyes reaching toward those people experience sing the same as you did. Then by your glance or a few words you leave them a bit better. I commend you for that kind heart that is reaching out to those that pass by you each day. Have a great day my love PS: Did you used the word "touch" mm.... mm..... mm

M: I did write "touch" and yes I do very much like the touch of you. It's just that we cannot be at this time, we each have other roads to travel. Who knows, maybe they'll all lead to the same mountain top? I cannot respond to your friend's comments because I am no longer caught in playing sadness and sorrow and how beautiful it is to 'overcome'. For me at this point life is simply creating whatever we desire to have and to experience, living in the moment and choosing happiness for it. Happiness comes not by fighting or overcoming anything, simply by choosing happy thoughts and starting a new life in the next moment should we ever be disappointed in the one before. Mystical maybe, non-traditional certainly, but it *works*!

Ex: Michael. Please understand I am well aware and never for a moment have I shifted from my responsibility toward my family. My family needs repairing. I will not cope out on my duties as a mother, being that I know I was a unknowing instrument in those happening as you were a knowing instrument of those happenings. So in contrary to Abrahams belief of just moving forward is for those that our of a selfish heart. Some things you can not walk away from and should. As far as you go. Yes you must move forward. There is little at this time you could or should do. It is a must that you do as Abrahams teachings suggest to move forward. How happy I am for you. I do love you!!! I hope all works out well for you and Jackie. I am so pleased. It is important to have a stable partner in life. God Bless.

My turn will come when I am ready and unfold just as I want it to. Always has. Timing is of the up most. For now it is teaching and loving my grandchildren and I do, I do, I do! Aba huh! Below in your writing, what did you mean by *"For me at this point,"*.....Obviously now but I read more into it. Are you expecting another change or shift in your life. I felt there was one when you moved to Victoria. And another is soon to follow. I am curious if you are aware before it happens. If you are comfortable let me know. Yes I agree your prayers are. *Re: Mystical maybe, non-traditional certainly...* Jen (please call me this name.)

PS: If you ever want to suggest any ideas of better penmanship please let me know my mistakes if so incline. Don't know done a better teacher.

M: I do understand how you feel about your family and your obligations towards them. I was surprised when you sent suggestions for a singles profile and laid it out as if you would abandon everything and everyone and instantly rush off even in the middle of the night with your new man. It seemed to me then and remains my thinking that you would not do that, at least most likely not for several years yet. You have a wish (as did Suzanne) to be someone you are not allowing to live in real life. That would be deceitful to a man who would want to meet you because of what you wrote on your singles profile would it not?

Ex: (Let's call her "Jen" from now on) No! I won't run off with a stranger. BUT, It will be the right timing and situation. Maybe with someone new I can make them part of both worlds. With you it would be two separate worlds but good worlds. My family does not have such a hold or do they want such a hold. I would run off in the middle of the night with the man I love with the understanding we would need to return if need be but unlikely that would happen except for emergency.

M: But your neighbor I think would allow you to continue with your family and also to continue with the beautiful Mormon Dream. If he reaches out to you, you could be the friend he needs, the hope for him that there would be life after his wife dies. I encourage you to not aggressively pursue him but to allow him to reach you when he wants to, be there for him if he seeks you out even while his dying wife is alive, be seen over the fence in your backyard. I see nothing at all wrong in that, just let him take the lead and go where he wants to go except of course 'all the way' because you're both Mormon and you both accept the promise of the Dream.

Jen: (formerly "Ex" but Jen from now on.) I am willing to be a good friend and time will tell.

M: Your sexual needs you are going to have to take care of yourself for now. Get some toys, I think that is permitted even as you remain a faithful Mormon. Have fun with yourself, your body will reward you profusely. You also have a willing lover in Canada but if/when you two get together you'll have to set the limits and boundaries yourself to stay within the Dream - he doesn't seem to have many boundaries of his own anymore and he loves what you do to him. He's occupied with others as you know, so you'll have to take the lead in arranging the secret rendezvous you crave, I expect that he'll be willing if able.

Jen: I understand.

M: *"For me at this point"* means now, and for me there's only now. The only constant in life is change, the universe must always unfold, expand, getting bigger and better, including the games the people play to entertain their higher (non-physical) selves, the ancient gods, and keep them from boredom. Sure, my life will change and is changing, it must be so when one allows life to flow freely without the constraints of tradition and religion. Even though I could, I don't often allow myself to become consciously aware of how my life is going to change in the immediate future. It's more fun that way, to pretend that we ourselves are not actually creating our own lives with our thoughts, choices, and expectations.

Enjoy my love. Regarding penmanship, I suggest that you take much more time writing before sending. Use a dictionary, an encyclopedia, and a thesaurus - it's so easy now that everything's online and instant. For example, I am taking almost an hour to compose this message to you and before that took about two hours composing a message for Jackie before sending it. Surprised? Famous authors are famous because they took the time to write right every time.

Jen: Yes, I am surprised. I thought you just spit those emails out like nothing. I was jealous. Thank you for the advice. It is good advice. Thank you for feeling I am worth spending that much time on. I am crying.

M: Take care Jen, I admire the changes that you have made recently to make yourself an even better and lovelier person than the choice woman you already were. I'm thrilled at your potential as you allow your life to unfold more freely. I love you sweetie and out of that love and circumstance I as best I can give you freedom to choose freely without regard for me your former spouse of 18 years, as you have done for me in return. It's better that way...

Jen: I will always cherish those eighteen years plus the beautiful gift of time spent in each others company just yesterday. Hopefully repeats are designed for our future my love.

M: (to Jen) Winds up and the ocean's wild today. As I brave the breakwater, spray erupts above me like fireworks exploding in the night. It's a magnificent place and time to be, a glorious planet, may there be many more created just like this one. A woman approaches on the arm of her man, looks closely at me, breaks into a never ending smile and my body hums as we exchange pure love, energy swirling between us as it does in the worlds of spirit. I tingle for long moments as she walks away. I stop at the breakwater cafe on the way back, buy a huge slice of carrot cake with mounds of cream cheese icing, take it home, and as I eat it I think of you.

Jen: Oh, I wish I was with you enjoying that spray of water as it came up over my head and dripped down my body. How it would of invigorated me to pull you to me. As we embrace in a kiss your magic took its course. As we returned home with the carrot cake I know exactly how I would of enjoyed that cream cheese icing.

Thank you for sharing that with me. I just came in from out side I must have been feeling your enjoyment. As the warmth of the evening breeze touched my skin I put my arms in the air and felt like the sexiest women alive. Then looked up at your hill and came in the house to put tennis shoes on to walk your path and enjoy what you saw along that path so many times. I will making sure a few stones are pushed aside for when you may once walk it again with me hand in hand. Keep giving those women big smiles.

Jackie: Hi dream maker. I just returned from a camping trip and am currently washing and cleaning again... that good old 3D stuff. Didn't have any connections to computer or even cell phone for messages so, again, catching up. Although it sounds as though your company may be gone within the next day or two, another couple girlfriends want to visit for a couple days before my daughter returns. They'll probably be here Thursday and Friday. Also, just accepted a client for an hour for Thursday evening and am invited to a friend's house Friday evening. So, it appears that next week sometime is the earliest I can get away. There is much to tell you about my journey Michael and I do look forward to seeing you again! Until then, take good care and dream of ever expanding love and beauty in this earthly realm. Be well, be blessed and be love PS... will write more later.....hopefully...

M: It's great to hear from you, I suspected that you might be somewhere without internet, hope you had fun. My company will for sure all be gone by Thursday a.m., so let me know when and where you'd like to meet. You're invited to come and stay with me as long as you want, there's a whole lot to do in Victoria, many lovely walks holding hands and linking arms as we will. Although it seems that we are already entangled, maybe a three or four or five night stay here before we travel would help us be better acquainted with and confident of each other before we begin to fold 3D space around us?

But if we're going to travel the Island we should make plans soon while the weather is optimum. My thinking for road travel is that we'll use my car, I'll pay the gas and hotels, we'll go Dutch on food, and you'll plan when and where we'll go and stay. (Though we'll always leave room for spontaneity.) Would that work for you?

I too am really looking forward to being with you again, especially when we can be alone together with no pressure to be somewhere or somebody other than where and who we choose to be in each moment. It's time for US if you will Jackie, I want to get to know you, I sense a whole lot of fun in our immediate future if we will each but allow it. Your Dream Maker

Jackie: Another "Hey You" Had a great time simply enjoying nature although feeling a bit "beached out" right now. My Egyptian friend who now lives in Port Alberni came for the day so we went to the beaches again. She left early this evening. It sounds as though your ex changed her mind about her time in Victoria. Although, I thought you also had children or other relatives coming to see you? I like the idea of spending a bit more time with you before setting out on a journey into la la land. My daughter will return on Friday and I have an event to attend Friday evening with a friend here. And then, finally catching up with my daughter and just relaxing into the flow of slowing down would be my desire for the weekend. Perhaps me coming down to Victoria from Tuesday to Thursday would work? That would give us a couple days to be together and explore our "entanglement" further.

Can't help but like your generosity for gas and hotels and would agree to go Dutch on food. Well Michael, since I've camped or stayed with a friend when traveling around the Island, I'm not familiar with hotels/motels anywhere but that can easily be worked out. There are some nice areas depending on your perception of a good experience. You must know by now that I've always lived quite simply. Travel to me has been camping in nature..... simple! We can discuss different possibilities while enjoying quiet times together after I get there.

It seems like months have passed since last seeing you! It'll be great to re-connect again and feel the resonance within the togetherness. This has been absolutely the busiest summer I've ever had regarding my re-connection to old friends, making new friends, and constant changes in general. Haven't even had the time to go into singles since meeting you!!! I'm now yearning for a bit more boredom in life but also realize my little business needs to be re-worked and built on before the end of August. Will also require time for that as well. Tomorrow... today now.... will be my own for a time until tomorrow evening when I have a client. In Time Eternal

Jackie: Michael, I'll respond to your letter in between with green lettering to insure that you receive all answers you may be searching for in truth and hopefully with love.

M: Aw shucks Jackie, here I thought we were identical twins but you don't seem to have inherited the gene that compels you to jump all the way in with reckless abandon when you've found something that inexorably triggers your curiosity.

Jackie: I may be curious about you and interested in who you portray yourself to be but identical we are not... only our souls contain the true identity of our inheritance.

M: Or maybe you do have that gene but the trigger has not been squeezed?

Jackie: Sometimes it feels suffocating rather than squeezed.

M: I was ready to get together with you today and set off for a two or three or four or or month adventure, just the two of us, nobody else in our world, and see what comes out at the other end.

Jackie: That was not my plan, only yours. and, although it sounds beautiful, it's something that I neither could not do or want to do at this point.

M: But I'm pleased that you are allowing us a couple of days next week before you plunge back into your routine, that will help me better plan the rest of the summer, and my one year vacation.

Jackie: Michael, I would not take your plans away from you if you wish to have a one year vacation you are free to do so. I love my work, it sustains me from the inside and provides a little financial security on the outside. I've been growing and changing in leaps and bounds and hold no one accountable for my growth except me. My service to others is most compelling and I know that I'm living completely from my heart with providing and sharing my gifts with others to help them out of the dark places they conjured up for themselves. In doing so, i also raise the frequency of myself, the earth and the Universe. And, it gives me great joy to know I've helped someone touch the light and transform their own darkness.

M: Perhaps it's best that way... I do gather from your comments though that you are willing to travel Vancouver Island with me a bit in between work and friends.

Jackie: Yes, I was willing.

M: As for traditional camping, I don't have camping gear and much prefer a bed and WiFi to a sleeping bag on the ground.

Jackie: me too but it was the least expensive way to travel and one I could afford.

M: though cuddling away the night with only stars above (assuming no rain, no insects, no bears or cougars, warm enough, and no stones or tree roots below) can be fun.

Jackie: Not at my age with my body! Cuddling yes, ground, NO.

M: I wasn't asking you to choose hotels to stay in but to pick out a chunk of road with a B&B or motel at the end of it for each day we drive, taking time always to stop and experience the whatevers along the way, not caring where we are most of the time, no fixed schedule or gotta be back bys, simply timeless lost in each other, nothing else being more important.

Jackie: There are so many things that are important to me and how I feel about what I'm doing, where I am, who I'm with, what I'm leaving behind, what I'm giving up to be where I am... all play a role in my journey to/from/with/at the present moment. My daughter won't be home until Saturday sometime. I'm currently taking care of her pets and will need to talk to her when she arrives home. She did this trip even though she is ill and I haven't heard much from her. I have responsibility to my children and to myself and to my clients in order to feel at peace with choices made, and to come from a place of love, honouring and respect for all.... including me. Your reckless abandon would make me abandon my daughter and her animals before she even arrives home. In doing so, I would be abandoning my Self, my respect, and all I feel love for just to be with you because??? that's what you want/need/expect??? My heart, intuition and soul tells me not to do this. I think you need to find someone who is in the position to just go, travel, no responsibility, has money (I don't), and is totally free for your life style needs. Michael, I just don't fit the mold!! Neither of us is right or wrong... just different realities that fit our personal journeys. Perhaps with my next incarnation, I'll choose the wild abandon path but for this one I've chosen to help raise the frequency of myself and the earth by reflecting and enhancing the light.

M: Can you be like that? With me?? Wanna try just for the fun? Would such a thing be fun for you? Would you allow yourself to unwind that way, let go completely, find out who you are when it concludes, not caring until then? I think you'd be pleased with me in many ways.

Jackie: It all sounds so beautiful and yet my heart says to abandon what is here for me would be to abandon myself because that is simply not who I am. And, Michael, my discovery of Self, of who I am, is through the reflection of others... those to whom I love. I do know who I am and am very quickly expanding this journey to ascension for all of us.

M: Jen (my ex) flew home yesterday. She too realized that two weeks was too long and that what I really wanted was to travel with you. (Yes, I told her all about you, she's wishing us well.)

Jackie: I feel so very honoured that you told her about us.... you must've had a sureness about us... or perhaps the understanding that we would come together soon.

M: She has grandchildren to tend to at and near home as well. We had our ups and downs, went back to the way we were a few times, but departed good friends each grateful for the days we had together including walks and an all day adventure with my daughter and her husband.

Jackie: I'm so happy to know that there was joy mixed in with your meeting.

M: We drove to Port Renfrew, walked miles through forest trails and trying to find forest trails, strolling stony beaches, searching sometimes slip sliding along tide pools, watching a river otter in the ocean etc.

Jackie: Hmmmm, that's very interesting since that's where we went camping!! I wanted to see Botanical Beach and Botony Bay again. Also walked around the tidal pools and watched an Ottor playing in a pool. You must've been there close to the same day and time!! Wow!!

M: They left this a.m. leaving me with mounds of towels, sheets etc. to wash, it's happening in full 3D as I write. Are you having great doubts about us Jackie, or just being womanly cautious? Fearful? Hopeful? Wanna talk about it?

Jackie: Yes, I'm having doubts about us. As I've said before, we really don't know each other that well and we seem to be on different paths to our own enlightenment. The more we communicate, the more I feel the differences between us. No fear here, just trusting my heart and soul and allowing the flow to happen regardless of direction.

M: What do YOU want for YOU for the next few months? What are your priorities?

Jackie: I am looking to build my business a little more, change my website, do some workshops, get more clients, finish an E-book, and whatever I can do to emotionally support my daughter through some of her challenges. And, I would like a relationship with someone in this area who doesn't demand my time but allows me to travel my path while he travels his and to share magical moments, evenings, days, nights together while adding to each other's energetic frequencies with love, compassion and understanding rather than taking from each other through demands, expectations and controlling behaviour.

M: What do you think you would look back on with the fondest of memories, the work and routine you would do at home, or the careless abandon adventure you had with the mystical man you met in Victoria?

Jackie: I would definitely look back on the work I do and all the love given and received from those around me with joy and gratitude, knowing fully that this beautiful earth has been served, and that what I do for others, i also do for my Self which adds to my soul.

M: What are you needing right now Jackie?

Jackie: My Self!!!

M: What are you wanting?

Jackie: To add to my Self.

M: What are you hoping for that you and I do not have the potential to fulfill together?

Jackie: Time and space for expansion without the needs of one overriding the desires of the other.

M: Are you afraid that you might fall in love and that it might not last forever?

Jackie: No. I am love and it will last forever. Being "in love" is different, and for now, I'm learning to fall in love with my Self.

M: What would be the worst thing that could happen should that be? Could you handle it? What would be the worst thing that could happen should you not be bold and brave enough to expose yourself to such a possibility?

Jackie: I'm not sure what you mean here! I have incredible bravery and courage just to expose and open with gratefulness to the life I have with all it's challenges and rewards because I see them all as gifts given to myself from my self.

M: I hope I'm not coming across as too harsh, I surely do not want to drive you away. It's just that although my present choice is to be with you, you must come freely, willing, wanting to be with me to share and co-create for us a great adventure.

Jackie: Yes, I allow myself the freedom to do what I also wish without judgment or condemnation and with respect. Your adventure is different from mine and as I said before, there is no right or wrong... just different paths to the same Source.

M: And it's that Summer is swiftly fleeing and selfish me has many doors open right now, many roads I could choose to travel. The season for choosing for me is right now, all roads beckon, none of them are wrong.

Jackie: I hope you choose with your heart and enjoy each precious moment.

M: I have other friends to share time with and I will wait for you to travel outside Victoria if it must be so, but waiting another five days to be with you is like, as you expressed, waiting for months. Can we get together sooner?

Jackie: Again, my daughter will be home Saturday, I just found out that I have a minor surgery on Monday, and I'm not sure how I'll even feel after that!! And, I have so many things I desire to do and explore with my passion. I can't make promises but will try to come on Tuesday or Wednesday depending on how I'm feeling.

M: Could we just drop everything and go for fun inseparably together for at least a month? (After three to five nights here in Victoria to be sure it's what we want - you bringing your laptop and working as you will as if you were home.) Then maybe getting together often after our first adventure, staying a week here a week there or wherever, lovers and friends for as long as we will, each free to make individual or mutual course corrections along the way to live our lives even more fully?

Jackie: It sounds magical and promising although, as I've repeated, my work is here, my responsibility is here, my life is here, my love is here.

M: Talk to me about it Jackie, what are you feeling about us?

Jackie: I feel a little discontent about "us" and unsure that your path is also mine. When I first met you, I thought you were wonderful, handsome, and perfectly suited to me spiritually and physically. However, I've also noticed some differing thoughts, beliefs, values and desires, that I felt at the time, would converge and progress further into possibilities and potentials for both of us. Now I'm not so sure! While doing a session yesterday with a 14 year old client, his grandparents came in from the other side giving him so many messages of love... it was truly overwhelming for both of us. When his mother came to pick him up, we all talked and hugged each other and the room shifted so intensely into LOVE.... tears flowed and I knew completely that this was my path, that I must stay here and provide a service to those who are struggling with emotional, physical, psychological and spiritual challenges.

What I do for others, I also do for myself. And, there is no way I can abandon them, my daughter, or my Self to be with you regardless of how magical and joyous it sounds. It just wouldn't be in my best and highest interest. I KNOW that Michael!! That isn't saying that there is anything wrong with you, me or the situation at hand. It just doesn't resonate or fit at this particular time for the "careless abandon" as it truly would mean me abandoning Self and everyone else connected to me. Sorry, I just won't do that. So, you must come from your own Source of internal knowing and do what you feel is in YOUR best and highest interest.

M: Michael Available Now and Wanting to be with YOU.

Jackie: Big apology Michael, it just doesn't feel right for me! Sending you joyfilled thoughts and bountiful love to fill your days...and nights. Jackie

M: (This message was sent before I received Jackie's responses above.) I know you are busy but I miss you Jackie. All I want is to be in your presence, to hug and to hold you, look into your eyes, kiss your sweet lips ever so gently, feel for you, and discover if what we had so effortlessly is still there, ripe low hanging fruit, easy pickings. Can we make that happen soon sweetheart? I'll come to you if it's best that way, but when I do I want us to spend at least one night in the same bed, not just a walk and talk and a hurried good-bye. You slept so soundly the second night we were together that I could have taken big bad advantage of you and you'd never have known unless you found yourself pregnant and no other man could have been the father. Talk to me, tell me you'll come sooner and stay longer, or beckon me to you. Saturday maybe?

What/who else could be more important than us? Or are you somewhere else with your thoughts and feelings and that's why you delay and allow us only two short days together next week? Tell it true Jackie, we both need to know where you are with us. I will not be offended if I misread you or if you find me too peculiar, or if there's another love in your life, or you're simply too busy this Summer for a love affair. If it is so I will respect your choice and move on - maybe there will be time for us another season? Just tell me, tell me true Jackie...

Chapter 20

Oresha: I thought I'd pass this info along for this Global peace meditation.. in case you're interested. Sorry it's such short notice...I just got it..... Night...

M: Thanks, sleep well.

Jackie: Another answer. Yes, Michael, the truth is there is another love in my life.... ME! I just don't have the desire or need to be together as you do and am looking forward to completing my work in so many ways. I'm on the road to self discovery, and I love what I'm finding out about me... truly loving myself and not requiring anything outside of myself. Also recognizing and honouring that voice inside that has been silenced for much too long with denying myself true freedom to be and do all that I want without restrictions or anyone telling me I should only do/be what they want or need. This is truth!! The whole truth, and nothing but the truth.

I truly wish you the best. Explore your life there in Victoria, travel with a friend, be all you can be. And, later, if you would like to re-connect, let me know and we'll go from there. The winters are long and rainy here... usually... so spread your wings and fly. I'll be flying internally and walking to the beat of my own drummer for awhile. So let be what is. I'll always be here and will be your friend to call upon when you desire to re-connect. I truly don't know what else to say.... could fill books.... but is that needed?? Always be the love that you are and tread softly in this world of 3D illusion. With love, as love, Jackie

M: I was about to respond to your first message after a quick shave and shower but this one is even lovelier. Thank-you so much dear one for validating what I have been feeling and knowing all along, that in addition to your disclosures (which are completely understandable and acceptable to me) my year-long 'vacation' was never to be anyway. There is a book percolating inside me, a non-fiction condensation of the twelve fictional books I wrote and published and this a.m. before getting your messages unpublished them all. They were only ideas for something better, something I need to get on with, a journal describing my journey to what I really want to write, and where I want to write it. Much as I love you dear heart, I too love ME the best, and what I do. There's no competing, no contest, we're very much alike in that way too.

A metaphysical lady friend in Victoria last night and early this a.m. sent me links to a bunch of stuff happening on the world's stage as we speak. Here's one of her messages.

> *Did you participate in the Global Peace Meditation? Awesome!... Here's an something I thought you might like to read/listen to... Another "tool" to assist us in raising our Vibration... Cheers..... (More links and stuff attached)*

And my response:

Raising vibrations for me is as simple as imagining my body vibrating more rapidly. Can't get much simpler than that. We exist to know fullness of joy - chronic happiness. Many people seek the warm fuzzy feelings that come with fighting and overcoming 'adversity' personally or vicariously. But we can step outside that addictive ancient game and bypass the whole world if we stop fighting and choose a new life the moment we are disappointed in the moment before, and in that new moment choose to be happy. Try imagining your body vibrating faster or rising - you'll find happiness and self confidence as you do that, you don't need anyone or anything else. You are creator of your own life - what is it that you want? That's how I see it - for me life is ever so simple. I don't need busy systems such as those you link to and describe, I only need me to be me...

I won't give you up Jackie, I don't think you want me to. I want you just as you are (gorgeous delightful mystical you) whenever you schedule time for the two of us and my already arranged schedule doesn't conflict. I'll even come and get you if you don't want to drive to Victoria where we can have privacy at my place, and I'll drive you home each time you say it's time to go. Can you live with that? If you are still willing to come on Tuesday I'll understand about the surgical procedure. Just *always* tell me verbally what you want and don't want in all aspects of what I am hoping will be a delightsome mutually fulfilling long term relationship: friends and lovers, confidantes, travel companions when we comfortably can. I want to be with you Jackie, I accept you the way you want to be. Your Michael if you will have Him

M: (to Jackie) That was a pleasant surprise, to be talking with you just moments after I sent you my last email, thank-you for calling. As you asked me how it would be with me if Jen (my ex) became attached to another man, it was with a bit of uncertainty and confusion that I responded that it would be ok. Confusion because inside my paradigm for the post mortal worlds I want to create there is allowance for immortal 'Adam' to have more than one wife, a family of immortal equal spouses who choose to populate planets. (Not all need to be literal mothers, there are worlds and children to tend and mold and guide.) So, even if Jen chose another man for mortality, in my mind she could still choose to be part of the post mortal family in my (fantasy) dream should she so desire to be.

During my 1984 spiritual initiation in Victoria I was offered a large and beautifully decorated cake. I was asked if I wanted to keep the cake, or if I wanted to eat it. My choice was to ask a question of my own: *"Can I have it both ways?"* The answer was, *"we'll see"* and the vision closed. So, in that respect, I can 'have' my ex and have others as well. And that's why your sense of discernment was triggered each time you asked about my relationship with my ex and received a rather confused response. My natural response of course (because I want you and know you have been socialized to monogamy) would be to deny a desire to be with my ex, and that played in my mind - you sensed all that.

I really care about you Jackie, I am so looking forward to being with you again. It was heartening that you wrote about a possible "reconnect" in our future if I roared off with another woman for the summer. As Jen and I kissed, the feelings that kiss elicited were like night and day compared to the touch of *your* lips. I want to discover if those feelings are still there the next time you allow our lips to press. I've never felt such a thing in my lifetime until our first parting near the cruise ships. You are *awesome* magical mystical woman - *you do something to me!*

Jen: Walked your trail this morning. Enjoyed it. Some places have washed out. Took the time to take in the view. Your not answering emails so I assume you must be with Jackie or preparing for that visit. Enjoy your time with her. Love Jen

M: It's nice to know that you are now walking 'my path'. You are making incredible changes with your life, I hope you continue to be so successful moving towards that which you truly desire. It turns out that

Jackie and I will not be getting together until Tuesday next week. I did feel that you should go home early and I'm glad that you went in such a positive manner. Perhaps it would have been different had we had more time together, we may have fallen back into our old ways?

M: Powerful forces continue to connect me and Jackie. I misunderstood, it turns out that she didn't go to where a second daughter lives. She was actually camped at the same beach we were at, same day, watching a river otter in the ocean! We'll not likely stay long with each other at any given time, but we will see each other, maybe often. That leaves us both with the freedom we crave to be ourselves and do what we want when we want. All is well...

Jen: That's is increasable. No wonder you were thinking of her when we were out there. Gives me hope you might sneak me into your plans once in awhile. It is nice to have fun with someone you are comfortable with and can be yourself. Guess what I purchased. Must keep myself fit. I was pleased to see I dropped a few pounds today. I am doing visualization of how I want to look. Thinking of going out shopping and buying myself something two sizes smaller. Just to look at and see my self in it. So it has to be classy and sexy. My lovely friend.

M: You haven't ceased to amaze me since you revealed when you were here that you were ok with me having several wives in my post mortal world and you might choose to be one of them. Enjoy your purchase, have fun, do a few for me - Suzanne did. Wish I could watch and participate with that now classy sexy lady I once knew as someone very different. You'd never have guessed that I watched Jackie do the same would you? And that she then put her toy aside, reached for me, and was successful... You know that although I will continue to have friends and sleep with some, my door will always be open to you if want to step through. You did things to me that I've never experienced to that level before. I really liked that, absolutely a winner for *any* man, keep it in mind when you practice solo.

Jen: Interesting. I haven't thought of playing any games today. I like that.

M: Wish I could play with you, have fun.

Jen: We could never fall back into our old ways. We have both been awakened. As a man you went first and then you reached for my hand and I stepped forward. Just sad I had to step back. When I lay in bed I feel the warmth of your arms around me and I am pleased. It would have been lovely. We create so well together. We understand and except each other in away it will take years for another to understand. We removed so many barriers in such a short time. Take time each day to think of me for a few moments and I will do the same. I send you my love. Enjoy the connection (twin) you have with Jackie. I know it must be a disappoint that she is not available sooner. Absence can cause the heart to grow fonder.

Jen: I am sensing something different today about you. Is all well.

I responded to this but will copy it below with Jen's responses to mine between the lines included.

M: Jackie, A few weeks ago Esther Hicks held a week long Abraham seminar in Cancun. A new analogy called "clogged pipes" referring to old recurring life issues resulted from the questions asked at the seminar. Today I received a two DVD set titled *"Laying New Pipes"* that was taped during that seminar in Cancun. Would you like me to hold off watching it so we can watch it together (snuggling of course) when you come?

M: (to Jackie) Good morning you, hope you enjoy today. And pistachios, I replenished my depleted dish of them getting ready for your coming. I'm missing you Jackie, life's on hold, think I'm going to have to force myself to rewrite some books to keep busy. *You do some....* right, you know the drill. Could we go to the beach and watch supermoon together tomorrow night? I'd drive myself back to Victoria when you need to go - just want to feel the touch of you again sweetheart, you're precious to me.

Jen: I just read your email again and I am crying.

I sent my part of the following conversation to Jen earlier but she didn't respond until I was in the midst of writing my supermoon message to Jackie while consciously lifting my vibes to all positive regarding that mystical lady from Nanaimo – I want it to be well with us.

M: (to Jen) I thought I had lost Jackie just like I lost others I loved and I began to question myself. She will only grant us limited time together while she tends to her own responsibilities, not long travels etc. as I had hoped, that was just my own wantings.

Jen: Yes, it was your wanting's. I don't know how to respond. I feel as you feel. hurt as you hurt! Not all is lost. You just don't know. How could she not want the sweetest man I know. A man that feels my need to be loved so completely when I am with him. Its not you. It is. Most likely, Her life is a priority and not with a man. I feel that is true with many women this age. They like their independence. Its not you. A inexperienced man like you is a great catch, but they want it for a night or two. Women use men as men once used women. I would say pull back or you might lose her. But, you already realize that. Move on and invite others you just began. Its not an easy world to be single in when you are seeking the right love and companionship. Stay on your vacation for a couple of months and continue enjoying the summer before thinking of writing another book. The virtual world won't give you a warm soft body next to you.

M: I'm still needing to focus only on the positive but it seems that she and I will be getting together next week but only for a couple of days. I will know better then what really attracts me to her and her to me because there is much about her that doesn't fit my ideal physical profile. I expect it will be best that way for each of us, our only being together at times. I might try writing a serious book in between those times, I'm adjusting.

Jen: No one is going to have that perfect profile. The connection is much more important in the long run. Expect to see even more of what you don't like when you see her again. It comes with that age.

M: It's difficult for me to think of you because I know how powerful thoughts are and I want you to be free to make your own choices. I guess what it all boils down to is that even though I hugely treasure freedom, what I am seeking is one woman to love and be loved and treasured by, each of us actively helping the other to realize their own potential.

Jen: We both want the same thing. and so foolishly gave it up. Because of pride. How foolish it makes us and we can't even see what we are doing to someone we love. I am sorry that my pride got in the way of making you happy. Because I have such a deep love for you.

M: But that flies against my post mortal dream where Adam has more than one spouse. So time and Law of Attraction opening even more doors concurrently will tell. For example, last night a woman from Duncan (half way to Nanaimo) messaged me out of the blue. Not bad looking, wants to meet me, and she's familiar with Abraham. What will be my choice??

Jen: Go for it.

I noticed that DeLeon was logged in at Singles and sent her the following note in that venue.

M: (to DeLeon) I really do like your new photo sweetie, hope it's bringing you a lot of attention from the maler part of our species. Enjoy the day.

DeLeon: Oooohh, I like yours too. You mean the one where I'm leaning into the Palm Tree? GREAT NEWS: Thus far, have had NO EPISODES since procedure.. Am taking things gentle and slow. Giving me hope.... had no idea how controlling that was in/of my life - and the anxiety it was causing.. I had saved every email you had ever sent to me - and the day before procedure, computer crashed - and destroyed all email addresses and saved/archieved messages. Must have been time to let "everything" go. You look great - and glad that you are in a happy state of mind, remember that being on your last message. If you feel like sharing, would like your take of Corine. Lately...I've started receiving emails -referencing her seminars... Don't remember signing up for them...m ay have. Showers of Blessings..... DeLeon

M: Yes, the photo of you in the much softer colors than your previous main photo, you look lovely. That is indeed great news DeLeon, I am happy for you. And you may be right about letting "everything" go - hope I'm not intruding. I'll always remember you and that we were once lovers sweetheart - we had some really good times together, those were magical moments with the Tantra healer in our hotel room.

Regarding Corine, you may recall that I once swapped email addresses between the two of you re the Magdalenes. So she may have your address on her regular mailing list to promote her seminars and books. I took her for dinner once in Las Vegas but we don't even write to each other, there wasn't much of a connection in real life. That of course doesn't mean that there wouldn't be with you and her, you expressed interest in the Magdalenes.

Feel free to write me anytime, you will always get a priority response from me even though we both know it's highly unlikely that we'll ever meet in real life again. Be well sweetie, I care about you.

M: (to Jen) Let me know when you have finished the ebooks I sent you. As I think about it, much of the repetition you commented on is that I just strung individual books together for the box set of eight books and didn't take the time to erase the repetitious headings each time you start a new book.

You and I seem to be in sharing mode right now and I'm delighted with that. So when you finish the books you have, if you want me to I will send more. The book I'm working live with right now is 14. I thought I had finished the series but I see that it is still progressing as I copy new emails into the file. You seem to have taken over the role of "Suzanne", the timing flows around that.... For example, I recorded the following in "Book 14" this morning, each message coming in as I was recording the one just before, the timing (as usual) was perfect as it always was when I am in tune with Muse and feeling that I'm writing a book. It used to be Suzanne who kept that timing and moved things along without even knowing she was doing it. I think you too are doing that. (Just noticed two new messages from you arrived as I pen this.) Enjoy the day Jen, I do love you.

Jen: I went out into the desert for a sauna walk. Waited to long but loved it and feel good. Now I will shower and get your papers notarized and in the mail. Then go shopping for that classy sexy out fit two sizes smaller.

Jen: Hang on and take it slow with her. I like the fact she is not rushing things. If it was another woman she might rush things and take advantage of you financially and be on her way. Jackie sounds solid. Down the road you just might have your dream woman in Jackie as far as companionship goes. I would be happier for you to be in that type of relationship. These women are not Mormon women wanting long term meaningful relationships. Women particularly on the spiritual sites don't need it or want it. They are making their own way with an occasional man moving in and out of their lives, this path makes life more pleasant for them but not permanent. With my ex's friends I saw many weekend romances with people coming and going. I think that is the reality of that world. They love the one they are with, for a short time. Then move on. I am sorry if this is not something you don't want to hear. Its just the way I see it. I don't want to be a part of those type of men other than you. I am not judging them. Its about what I want.

My daughter warns me to be careful on the site you referred me to. Being a free sight. To many men with out money looking for a woman to financially take care of them, this has been her experience. I might still try it to get some experience in communication. She also warned me against long virtual relationships because they are mostly not what you picture. So she would communicate a bit then make a date if she is interested. Then decide and move on if its not a fit. She has a sight in mind that will better fit me and my age. We will see. I am not in a hurry. I have two sizes to loose.

M: Thanks for the counsel. You would better understand Jackie if I copied you into some of her emails, she is not after my money at all. I don't think I am betraying her trust by sending the following. It was greatly heartening to me that she in effect 'released' me to another woman for the summer but was available to "reconnect" after that if I wanted. We have since exchanged more messages and I expect her to come to my place next week for a couple of days. I also asked her if we could go to the beach tomorrow (Sunday) night and watch the supermoon rise. I'd then go home. She hasn't responded yet. So if things unfold the way they are at present, I will 'have' my Jackie and still be able to meet with others and with you in between our times together - *perfect!* The following singles site is for people over age 50, I get a whole lot of contacts from that site, women who are interested in me. (insert link)

Jackie: Greetings Michael; The DVD Laying New Pipes by Abraham and Esther sounds awesome.... so glad to hear you sent for the DVD's from Cancun. I've heard her talk about "laying new pipes", it would be great to see it with you. However, I'm sure your anxious to watch it so go ahead. There's plenty of days ahead for us to watch it together and I'm sure you could easily watch again..and again..and again. Of course the pistachios and Super Moon would be great together but have to pass on that. I'll be seeing it from here and connecting with you through the moon beams shining brightly upon us. The energy building has been quite phenomenal and very palpable. My daughter will be arriving home in a couple hours and we'll have much to talk about in the next couple of days.

Went to see a mystic speak at the University last night with my friend. He's from Zimbabwe and is travelling different countries spreading his word about changing the human heart from hate to love through forgiveness in order to bring peace and unity to humankind.

He was amazing, very well educated, and a Shaman who is consciously awake. My friend and I talked until late last night about the changes happening within us and outside of us.

Michael, I realize that you may be disappointed by my inability to connect in the way you do, or as quickly as you do. And, my internal sense says that there may be more desperation and expectation attached within your desire for me rather than the true potentials of heart and soul. I don't know for sure but am beginning to feel uncomfortable with your continued insistence. This is not meant to put you down in any way but to just let you know that I do have boundaries and trust my inner knowing or sensing. So, another meeting will have to take place in my time frame and when I feel able to do so. You are totally free to make choices and create what you desire. Let go of where you feel resistance... and allow it to flow where it will. Infinite Love

M: Thanks for being upfront and open Jackie, I do tend to write too much and too openly and thus be perceived as 'pushy'. I'm very loyal and thought if we got together physically we'd each know then if we wanted to push an apparently needed reset and start over again or not. That can still happen, you are welcome to come next week if you choose to cuddle and talk it out, but it seems that you are already tired of at least my messaging and my invitations to be together so I'll understand if you don't.

I'll go silent now and wait to hear from you hoping you'll some day desire to pick up where we left off when I caught the bus in Nanaimo to return home. All was well then, we were both alive with our connection, *very* alive with hope and promise I thought, until doubts began to be dwelt upon, the flow resisted. Can we return to that aliveness and build upon it, friends and lovers from different cities do you think, or have we already burned out our candle for this incarnation? I just wanted to find that out. Take care, you are welcome back anytime Jackie.

Well, after her rejecting what should have been a wonderfully romantic invitation to watch a super moon rise over the ocean, I am trying my best to not think of Jackie at all, to remove all of my energy from her, to feel free, and to find someone else as she suggests that I do. Did I sabotage another potential long term love?

Jen: How much do your really want to pull DeLeon in? Or is it your disappointment and loneliness calling out. Get out and walk and look at those faces and smile ear to ear at them and enjoy the tender glances that come back. Make life real.

Jen: I don't think Jackie is that much different than many women her age. Women generally adjust to single life better than men. Her priority is not a man but herself as she stated. Maybe in a year or two I will feel as Jackie does. Enjoying life with an occasional friend to go out to dinner with. I am sure there is a woman out there that wants you as much as you want her. It is written in the stars.

M: You may be right, she rejected what should have been a very romantic invitation to watch a super moon rise over the ocean with me. So I'm trying to remove her from my mind completely and am looking for another. Don't feel sorry for me, I'm not hurting, these kinds of things have a way of working out very well from the perspective of looking back in time.

Am I hurting? Naw, skin's much too thick now??? Always focus on thoughts that bring joy...

Jen: The single world is not all that we think sometimes. I will be very much surprised if she sees you on Tuesday. Hope she does. I much prefer marriage. Just the little you have gone thru has sent me up and then down again with you. It seems I feel as you feel. And now I have tears for what could have been for you. You see dear the kind of love I have for you does not appear over a short time and yet it can not be. Carry on. I am truly your friend. Be careful.

M: Thanks for being my friend (and recently my lover) I really appreciate that. Life goes on and Law of Attraction never tires. Already another woman has come to my attention in Victoria. I wrote to her but haven't heard back yet. I can easily imagine myself being with her as I put Jackie out of mind. I'll keep you posted if anything develops there, her profile is wonderful but there are no photos posted.

Jen: Protect your heart my dear and go forth. Please don't call me your recent love. Lets move away from that. My love for you is on a much higher plain. I do want to hold you and cress you don't get me wrong. What I feel for you is much more than a lover.

M: I'm glad somebody feels that way.

But am I allowing my ex to take over again? E.g. although she does it innocently, her suggestions almost appear to be commands – a problem I had with her for years, denying she was trying to control me but doing the very thing. Or is that just the way she expresses her desires?

M: (to Jen) It was a lovely evening for a walk along the breakwater. There were three cruise ships docked, Holland America Amsterdam (I think we've sailed on that one maybe more than once), Norwegian Pearl, and Grand Princess. The Grand Princess made the other two look tiny. There were lots of people out walking Dallas Rd and the breakwater, a glorious time and place. Over the ocean hung a huge moon that tomorrow will turn into a "Super Moon", much larger than it usually is because it's so close to the earth, be sure to see it.

And Victoria being the magical city that it is for me I found myself behind the lady and her daughter that I pointed out to you and spoke about seeing her often on the beach and in Thrifty's and being somehow attracted to her. I meditated once, desiring to heal the daughter but felt impressed that the daughter was here for the mother, I told you about that. We walked beside each other for a bit at the end of the breakwater and talked. The attraction turns out to be that she too like me is metaphysical, she is a clairvoyant and gives psychic readings for a living. Her name is Lynne. Lynne picks up glass and stones on the beach and makes things from them. I like her, she seemed eager to talk to me.

Jackie: Hi Michael. Here is a video of the beautiful soul I went to see last night at the University. A wise and soul filled man.

I won't respond because I'm waiting for a personal message from her and hopefully an indication if she will be coming to Victoria next week to stay with me a night or more.

M: (to Lynne) Hello Lynne, It was nice chatting briefly with you and your daughter on the breakwater tonight. I took the liberty of looking up your site and found this email address in a search. I'd like to communicate with you a bit if you don't mind. I live in the Lord Simcoe Apartments and see you and your daughter on the beach often, and sometimes at Thriftys. Perhaps I could pay you for a clairvoyant reading? Anyway, please contact me at your leisure, thanks.

Jen: It was good to hear you are out and enjoyed being amongst people. I miss those enjoyable walks we took along the breakwater. The blessing is. With my memories, and your beautiful description I experienced that walk with you. I will look for that super moon tonight and think may be we are gazing at the same time. Wow! The timing was perfect for you to meet Lynne and her daughter. From her picture Lynne looks like she is a North American native. Are you open to having her do a psychic reading for you?

Interesting Jackie sent you to this site after she went to the seminar and no invite to tag along. She walks her own path. The video is interesting. Do you think he has a message, since Jackie sent it to you. He said, don't send love get involved with love. He said human bings need healing not nature. You can see he is in tune and part of nature. Most of us don't set in the womb of a tree as he did. I took a minute and leaned up against the womb of a tree when we walked in the park. It drew me in. Should of stayed longer I might of learned something about nature. Is it true people in the metaphysical world seems to manifest its self in as many ways as sand on a beach. Is it true metaphysical people travel many different paths. The word is the same but the each individual chosen path is very different or maybe the same in some situations? Because of this one can not lump them into one group as I once did....

M: Nice, I'm enjoying your thoughtful intelligent emails lately and am putting them in "Book 14". And yes you can keep a man like me going by asking him questions. Law of Attraction always creates rendezvous with the people we are attracted to and attract to us, but sometimes we make last minute decisions and miss them. It's best though not to dwell on that and become a slave to impulse, just relax and go with the flow. It will all work out well with little or no conscious effort on our part other than hoping and expecting it to. Law of Attraction is associated with the combined intelligence of all the intelligences in the universe, it can work out *anything*.

I did listen to the interview Jackie sent but for me where I am now there was little or nothing of any significance, just another sincere man on a mission to inspire and teach others his beliefs. I need not follow another because once you are certain that you are creating your own life and can consciously control it, *nothing else matters.* "Metaphysical" people are the same as everyone else except that most are more aware of themselves and their own role in creating better worlds for themselves and others. So of course they are all individuals who follow the myriad paths that come with mortal life. Generalizing is usually faulty because every individual lives in their own 'fantasy' world when not occupied with the things of mortality and each of those worlds is unique and in many ways different. It is my belief that we *are* the ancient gods...

I sent an email to Lynne suggesting that I get a reading from her. It's not that I am wanting someone else to predict my future (I create that myself) it's just that I'm curious about her and feel that she too may be one of "my people" to whom I perhaps have a responsibility like I did with DeLeon? Seeing Lynne for a reading would get us in close touch with each other.

But last night as I was coming back on the breakwater, right near the cafe I unexpectedly (because I lingered at the end of the breakwater) saw her ahead of me. I slowed down because I liked the way we had parted with me giving her a pat on the arm, exchanging some nice vibes, and I knew that we would be inexorably attracted together again, most likely soon. I followed (it was on the way home) and think I may have alarmed her because she walked rapidly not stopping even though she knew I was behind. Did she fear that a man was stalking her I wondered? They missed their tun and kept walking along the path.

She knows my first name so if she responds to my email I will know that if it was indeed fears that were moving her away from me last night on the way home, she has overcome them. Clairvoyants are extremely sensitive but are still subject of course to mortal doubts and conditioned fears. I did show love to her when we walked together near the end of the breakwater, and touched her arm. That would have been unusual from most people. I hope to meet with her again and expect that meeting to happen one way or the other, it must because we traverse the same orbit right now. She does not appear to be Native American. Enjoy the day as you walk your own metaphysical path Jen.

Jen: I was wondering what Jackie meant when she said "*Always be the love that you are and tread softly in this world of 3D illusion.*". Was she referring to your dreams you shared or your infatuation with her or both. Curious if you know.

Did I understand you when you once said your path is unfolding with out a conscious direction. What is different now? A week later you are adding to the same series of book when I thought you were going to take it off line because no one was buying them. I would suggest you take the rest of the summer off and enjoy the delightful surroundings then settle into writing a personal journal in the fall if that's your desire.

I think this course of searching for women is addicting, consuming, and cutting the life out of you. You are not cut out for this type of life. You are a one woman man.

Now lets talk about me. Pride is something one must let go of to move forward. I think about myself and not sure if I know much about how it is affecting me in my life. Where is my pride stumbling me. This would be a good topic for a series of self help books. Or/ Maybe I need to check online. I sure could use the help. Kathy said she could see some pride in me yet I feel I must be mostly blind to it.

M: Jackie sees herself (and all others) as *being* love. She is counseling/reminding me to always be me and to go gently as I walk in the 'real' world of physical senses. (That world being a three dimensional illusion that people keep telling themselves is reality.)

I unpublished twelve of the thirteen e-books that had been published. My plan is to rewrite them at my leisure, condensing them into just one book. I have started doing that and am really enjoying it. I can't be out walking etc. all the time (just got back from a two hour walk along the ocean and Beacon Hill Park) so writing occupies my time inside my apartment wonderfully.

Please try to be more considerate and accepting instead of bulldozing ahead with your own ideas for what I should be doing. Your "suggestions" often come across as 'commands' like they always did, a serious mistake on your part, men don't like to be controlled. I am extremely capable of living *my own* life the way I want to moment by moment, and I'm happy in it. You are caught up in thinking there is something wrong with you that you must fight. Forget all that, you are unique, you are worthy, you are capable, you should be *proud* of who you are. Just get on with creating the life you want for yourself by dwelling on the expectation of it becoming real and *allowing* it to happen. To keep happy, try that little trick I suggested of imagining your body vibrating faster (or rising). Doesn't that bring you instant happiness?

Jen: The way you interpreted what Jackie meant is beautiful and very good advice for you. You seem to think I just command. Sorry if I offended you. I will have to remember not to be so honest. I really didn't mean to sound like a bulldozer.

M: Oresha, I hesitate to contact you because as you know we both have different goals, there are others in my life, and I don't want to appear to be 'leading you on'. But if you're still ok with us just being friends and getting together occasionally for the fun of it, I don't have plans for tonight, my company is gone. If you are available, would you like to walk to Clover Point with me to watch the super moon rise? Unless that is happening in daylight, in which case we can stroll the breakwater or elsewhere, enjoy the risen moon, and maybe have a glass of wine and conversation at my place after?? Let me know.

Oresha: I would hope that you have no "hesitation" in contacting me... I still consider you and I as Good Friends..even though we have "different "goals"... lol I thoroughly enjoy your company.... and would love to chat with you.... I do, however have plans for tonight, so perhaps we can take a rain cheque for another day? The stroll under the Super Moon would have been Fun!...

Please do.... let us stay in touch... and let's spend some time together every now and then... I highly value All my Friends..... and I especially enjoy conversations from The Heart... I've been busy and still haven't quite gotten through all the Abraham DVD's.... I'll drop you a line soon when I do get through them... and get them back to you.. thanks you for your understanding.... Have a wonderful rest of your evening..... Happy Super Moon to You!.. Hugsssss...

M: Understood, thanks Oresha, enjoy.

Lynne: Hello Michael, Thank you for your message..it was nice meeting you too. I am available for readings Mon - Fri between 10:00 am - 2:00 pm. I don't do readings once my daughter gets home or on the weekends so I hope that this will work for you. You can message me here with preferred day and times or call to book in. Have a nice evening...

M: Thanks for the response Lynne, I wasn't positive that my message would get to you. I'm quite curious to hear what you have to say because a friend took me along with him to see a Dutch clairvoyant who had a degree of fame in Sydney, Australia where I was living when about 22 years old. After my friend's session when I appeared at the doorway to the room where the clairvoyant was, he looked at me and said: *"Why are you coming to me? You're the same as I am."* Anyway, a whole lot of water has passed under the bridge since then but let's see what happens, the price is fine, how about 10 a.m. tomorrow? If nothing else, maybe you'll get me busy looking for glass and stones along the beach.

Enjoy super moon tonight. If you are out strolling Dallas or Breakwater we might bump into each other again, I walk there often. I was behind you last night but you seemed to be in a rush to get somewhere so I didn't try to catch up and chat some more.

Lynne: Hi Michael, That sounds interesting about the psychic that you were mentioning. Usually psychics are aware of others 'intuitive' abilities. 10:00 am tomorrow works for me. It's a good idea to make a list of questions you may have and if you have someone who has passed on who you would like to have some communication with, I suggest that you 'think of them' and invite them to the reading. It is also very helpful if you can bring a ring, watch or necklace that you wear often but keys are also fine if you don't wear jewellery. I hold the objects during the reading to help tune into your energies. Please make sure that it was not previously owned or I will probably tune into that energy. We may be out walking tonight but not sure yet. Enjoy your evening!

M: Tomorrow at 10 a.m. then. But I don't have a thing with me in Victoria that I've worn for any amount of time and even my keys are to a used vehicle I bought only two weeks ago. And, and, I can't think of a deceased person I am particularly wanting to communicate with other than I suppose personal guides who might want to reach my conscious awareness more fully. And I don't have a list of questions though some may come to mind. I'm mainly interested in the experience itself Lynne, perhaps in discovering what results from the combination of our unique energies for a period of time in a meditative state? So, I'm hoping you can compensate for that and are ok with just seeing what happens. Ok? Oops, just remembered, I do have a watch but I only wear it occasionally, maybe that will do, I'll put it on now and try to remember to wear it all night tonight.

Lynne: No problemo Michael, I can read without the objects but it does help.. the watch sounds good... good idea to wear it tonight! Guides can definately come through as well as deceased individuals whether you 'invite' them or not! Every reading is unique. Often times people come without questions and again...no problemo! I'm looking forward to your reading!

Jen: I reread what I wrote and "Cutting the life out of you" is not what I meant it is a nasty statement. I meant consuming your thoughts. The women are addictive and consuming your time is true. Much of what you think and write about is the women in your life mixed with a little self beliefs. Where ever you go it is about women you see. OK Should I just disappear. First I am going to look at the moon.

M: No, I don't want you to "disappear" you are very welcome in my life. Yes, my life is consumed with my love for the women I imagine to be my wives in the world/s I am creating, a family of equal spouses all 'married' to each other, the mothers of my children. To me there is nothing more important than them and us immortal, empowered to populate planets, that's all I want. I have always loved women, that love only increases as I gain experience in the world outside organized religion, it's very different, and delightful. Enjoy super moon. It's still sunlight here, I'll walk again nearer sunset, probably sit at the end of breakwater and absorb the fullness of the moon over the ocean waters.

Jen: Do you talk to other women the way you talk to me in emails?

M: I don't understand what you mean by "the way". Have I offended you?

M: Suzanne, I recently unpublished the twelve e-books and am rewriting, condensing them into one book that may sell better. As I reread our early adventures in Texas it endears you to me even more strongly. From my point of view it was a lovely romance we shared from a distance, worthy of telling. I was in love with the virtual image of you, though at the time unclear where you were with that. My conditioned preference for a female companion in real life is slim and slender to average. But as I rewrite the books and notice your frequent emphasis on "size 10" at the very beginning of our virtual conversation, I know now that you were giving me a warning and a question. My first wife gained more than 150 lbs. at one time so when she got down to a size 10 I was delighted and kept that number in positive memory. So in my mind you were 'slim and slender' and the first night you came I saw nothing else, being delighted that you had come to me. That first hug at Loa's door elicited feelings I'd never felt before. It was my great mistake to undress you before we had time to walk and talk and get to know each other a bit. But that cannot be changed, I've learned from that experience, it showed book character Michael at his raunchiest when inside he (soaked all his life in religion) was not really that kind of man at all, maybe comparable to Responsible Nurse you in real life and your secret desire to be book character Suzanne. I so loved Suzanne, still do...

We never saw each other again after that first night and your stomping away in the morning. Until Las Vegas when those strange (to me) events took place with you disappearing sight unseen for a half hour after your plane landed. Then my phone call to your cell, you gushing that you were indeed in Vegas, and an agonizing ten minutes before I sensed you behind, turned and looked, saw real you and in a tenth of a second you sensed my disappointment that size 10 was not what I was looking for. You told me you came to Vegas (I was delighted) to see if the love I had expressed so often was real. It was (and is) still there for you dear one, but yes, I could not contain the disappointment I felt when I knew in that 10th of a second that we would not be living together because I was not seeing the ideal image of you I had created.

So, woman you knowing, and perhaps your own disappointment in the way I looked as well, we did not 'click' in Vegas. Times in public were frosty cool, it seemed you did not want to be seen with me much as I tried to focus your attention on the man at your side. But regardless of that, I will always remember and thrill that each night you came to bed naked and willing. It was a taste of paradise to cuddle and spoon the all too short nights away with you. The memory of those nights we had at Excalibur will always remain precious to me, especially that gift we were given, a moment in the night when I was able to share with you the essence of me, and you said that the giving was "good". It is my hope that you too will remember that moment with fondness, the brief time when all was well with us. Take care Suzanne dear one, I hope you are well and have perhaps found the companion you were seeking. It would be wonderful to hear from you now and again.

M: (to Lynne) I really enjoyed our time together today Lynne, I feel that I have found a dear friend if you will. It is my hope that we will be able to walk and talk now and again, we have so much we could share with each other. (Without being fearful that the belts on our compulsory new jackets might be fastened too tightly. You are a lovely lady and a seer, you nailed "the book" down perfectly with no prompting on my part at all. I was hugely impressed, be confident in your gifts. Let me know when you have the time and the desire to walk Dallas or wherever with me, I'd love that. I do check email very often so that's probably an easier way to communicate with me than the cell I almost always leave behind.

M: (to Jen) I went to see Lynne this morning. It was a one hour appointment for a psychic reading but became a 2 1/2 hour chat as if we were old friends. I was not surprised, she's my 'people' I may be her teacher. She looks much younger but is in her 50's and single, the 'black sheep' in an accomplished family. And yes, Lynne has Indian blood, you sensed it, her mother's mother was Lakota Sioux, the very tribe I identify with and even today could sing in their language the Vision Quest.

I spoke from memory a sentence from my 1984 book: *"Taku wakan scan scan"*, told her it was the Sioux way of saying *"something holy moving among the stars."* I then told her that the Sioux trace their origins to the Pleides. She instantly put her hands over her face and was obviously deeply moved. She'd often felt a connection with the Pleides, can see them from her James Bay balcony, and often stares up at that group of stars. She once asked silently as she gazed upon them if anyone was up there who knew her, and was instantly informed by a beautiful manifestation of colored circles that seemed to take place way up among the stars that form the Pleides. She and her ex once saw a spaceship and walked almost right up to the "little people" that come from the stars. She has that connection, similar to me awaking when I usually sleep and quickly going out my bedroom door to watch a silent spaceship pass by low overhead.

Lynne remained in 'reading' mode for only a few minutes before it became apparent that I could be the one giving the reading, I expected that. But she quickly detected "a book" in my life even though I hadn't mentioned anything about being a writer. I wrote down one sentence she said: *"I am tuning into your energy and I'm feeling that it's super huge."* She went on about it being "time" for my book, that it was hugely important, but it might take a while - exactly what I was feeling about it, my time and place is yet to come, but it will come in Victoria, and it will be "super huge". I asked her about you, telling her your name and that you had recently visited. I wrote down the following word for word: *"You are a teacher for Jen, she trusts you. She has had paranormal experiences she hasn't told you about. She is more open to those ideas now."* I encourage you to continue your exploration into the metaphysical if you are comfortable with that. You don't need to study books, you need to study *yourself!* Learn to quiet your mind and lift your vibrations.

You can keep your interest to yourself and still be Mormon, like I was for decades. I have often observed that you too are highly sensitive, a good mind reader, most likely clairvoyant (seeing images.) But you remain on the outside of your community or soul group, just looking in, fascinated, instead of immersing yourself among your own kind and being who you are. That was why perhaps that I was never able to reveal my true self to you, I tried often but you wouldn't listen, just wanted to speak. I felt that you were critical and wanting to have control over me, never accepting me as teacher, knowing maybe that we would one day separate and wanting to do what you could to delay the inevitable because you truly love me? I love you too, but I don't think we are ready to live together again in mortality, at least not longer than two or so weeks at a time, at least not at the present moment. (Though parts of my body would most eagerly welcome you for a visit anytime. I only wish you lived around the corner and I could sneak to your bed in the night.

My dream allows the two of us to remain closely connected, even eternal spouses if that becomes your choice, you know what I am creating. But you must be free now to go with another man and keep the Mormon Dream if that for you is a happier thought. And it may be that way, the choice is yours, there is happiness for you with others too, not just with me. Whatever your choice, I will be well, you know that. Loyalty has its usefulness, and its bounds. FLY dear one, fly to your own music and discover with glee over and over again the lovely places it takes you. It's only 3 p.m. and already I've had (yet another) beautiful day in the magical city of Victoria, British Columbia, my womb.

Jen: I appreciate your words. At the moment I feel graduate. Glade you had such a wonderful time with Lynne. Your family seem to keep growing. She sounds like one of your people. Will she dance in your garden? If I had know you felt I hung onto you to long, I would of let you go long ago. Why did you wait so long to tell me? I am sorry I was so undesirable. I am sorry you felt it was me that kept you from becoming who you want to be. Maybe my New York way of communicating is not appealing but I never meant to be critical of you most of the time. I also had needs not meet, I thrust and had no drink, and I hungered and was not feed, I cried and had no comfort, but I loved, I loved. Was it you or was it another that came into my sleep before I knew you and said I was the one he chose to impregnate because he knew I would have his child.

I knew it was a significant experience. Then took me to heights I knew not before. Such an innocent girl I was. Who is my teacher?

I have been frantically preparing all day to leave. Very very tired. I know where I am going but feeling I might not come back for awhile. I cleaned my house changed the sheets on my bed and went out and made sure all my bills and responsibilities are taken care of. Had a beautiful conversation with my daughter last night as I sat at the top of the hill and waited for the super moon to appear. Took a few pictures as I sat alone. I made sure her children have new school clothes. Was going to ship them but ran out of time. They will get them they are hanging in the guest closet.

I feel the presence of three male spiritual beings. I hope they stay with me for awhile. I just asked them to. Wish I could see them clearer. Maybe I will. I might know them. They seem to know me. Don't be concerned. I am not foolish. Just need to go where my heart can mend. I think, I know who can do it. The car is ready and I am on my way out the door. I might see the seven sisters in the unpolluted skies to night. Love you sweet heart with all my heart. Fly free and enjoy. PS: When I count my blessings I count you twice.

M: Where are going Jen? Have you made arrangements with him if it's to a man you are on the way? You seem to have spirit guides with you, they are your friends but you yourself must always stay in charge of your life, make your own choices and decisions. Tell me where you are going and to whom? My heart is still with you you know, though it's in other places too as I explained and I'm concerned for you. You got dressed one middle of the night here and were going to walk off a cliff you said. Would it not be better to become immortal and populate planets with me than that? I invite you. Come back here if you absolutely must, I'll protect you... Please don't just go silent on me now, I need to hear from you, be well.

Lynne: Good morning Michael I enjoyed our time together too and I look forward to walkin' and talkin' with you and learning more about you and your ideas. I'm glad that I was able to receive the messages that you were hoping to hear and thanks again for your validation of my abilities... it's very encouraging and I really appreciate your comments. Thanks for the ebook info, your book sounds facinating! I'll see you soon!

M: Dearest Jackie, I fail to understand your behavior lately and am seeking the enlightenment only you can provide. You virtually meet a man on a singles site, meet him physically, experience a powerful mutual connection, invite him to your bed for two nights, tell him you'll visit him in his home for two or more nights; then when he expresses burning desire to see you again, even invites you to walk on the beach for an hour or so as a super moon is rising over the sea (that should have been a compelling romantic invitation for *any* woman) *and then you freeze him out,* criticizing him for being himself and for wanting to be with you!

He wasn't asking you to marry him Jackie, just to have some fun together! Why are you on singles sites? What is it that you want? Maybe that's what I want too... I still hope you'll come to my home and overnight so we can talk this over and see if we can at least be friends, maybe travel companions when you can get away, maybe lovers when the moments are right? Do you no longer want a man's arms around you, his male energy, conversation, and occasional companionship? If you do but have another man, please just let me know, *that* I can understand. You've got me baffled.

Jen: Don't worry. I have much to tell you when I have time.

M: Ok, thanks for that assurance. I realize that much as I care about you, that care and love should be sufficient to release you so you can fly where you know you need to go. I'm trying to put you out of mind so my thoughts don't overly influence you perhaps against your own inner knowing of what you should be doing, where you should be going. I'm 'secretly' hoping that you will return to me, but should you not I will accept and joy for you that it's to another who is capable of giving you what you most want. This is hard sweetheart, hard on you, hard on me, I'm weeping now too. I so love you, but it was wrong for us to be together now. I felt that in your kisses, maybe you did also in mine as you did your best to please me. Go where you need to go and do what you know you need to do to heal and be reborn. It will be well for both of us whatever paths we choose for ourselves, you already know mine. Please stay in touch as often as you can.

Jen: As I said I had three spiritual beings came to comfort me in my sorrow in our home for a short time and I asked them to travel with me and two stayed for a short while one stayed to the end of my journey.

To answer questions.... I can only tell you and no one else..... for now. When I have time, and time to think clearly I will put it into proper perspective and detail of how it unfolded. You are right when you said time is speeding up. I think this is a stepping stone of progression soon to arrive. You are invited if you choose. I started to write more but felt best to stop need to do other things. Please don stop thinking of me. I am becoming. Love you so very much.

She wrote more but it was a sacred experience for her, I'll leave it at that.

M: Wow, just wow, I am so happy for you and maybe for US if it is me you choose for your Adam and not another. I am hoping that it is me... I'm curious to know where you are Jen and why you are so busy? I never stopped thinking of you, just tried that's all. I love you too sweetheart. What do you mean by *"You are invited if you choose?"*

M: (to Lynne) Here's another validation of your gifts Lynne. As you may recall, you asked me who was Chris and said that I would settle down with her for a while. I communicate with a whole lot of people online but didn't recall a lady named Chris. But as I was going through some emails this evening I realized that before I came to Victoria I had swapped quite a few messages with a lady from Victoria by the name of Kris! Kris is a writer and has a degree of fame in spiritual things. But my preference for female companions is physically slender to average and I discovered that Kris is a whole lot overweight. So I broke off that seemingly promising conversation and won't renew it. So you were right on with the names. Do you think you were mind reading?

Also, you detected my desire to not marry but to 'settle down' with only one attractive compatible woman. There are a few weeks left in the summer and I had hoped to explore Vancouver Island with a lovely lady, then maybe a week or so in Cabo San Lucas in January. I thought I had found a travel companion in a woman by the name of Jackie and I even bought a car so I could travel back and forth and all over the Island with her. But she doesn't seem to have time for me anymore, was supposed to have visited today, and never even responded to my messages. That means that exploring the Island is out for now for lack of a companion, and summer is fast fleeing. So dear Lynne my clairvoyant friend, *do you have another name for me?*

Chapter 21

————◆◈◆————

Yes of course I'd travel with Lynne, she's attractive and sexy in the fashionable short skirt she wore and has never been to Europe, wants to go. She talked to me about wanting to travel but not having the money to do so. She said with money she could hire a caregiver for her daughter and get away. It might be tons of fun to travel with a clairvoyant. But she's 16 years younger than me! Worth a try though eh? Hmmm, the thought of that body of hers pressed even closer to me than the tight hug she gave me at parting is quite stimulating...

The voice that spoke to me a few days ago said I had already "met" two of the women who would be my post mortal wives. I continue to think one is my ex Jen and thought at the time that the other might be Jackie. But where's Jackie now? She has turned out to be inconsiderate and unavailable. She was supposed to be here overnighting with me tonight but hasn't even responded to my messages let alone shown up. Obviously I am way down her list of priorities, in effect dumped. Maybe it's best that way, and maybe as usual I subconsciously set that up with too many 'pushy' emails then leave it up to the woman to do the right thing to move us apart so something/someone even better can walk through my door?

Jen: "You are invited if you choose" Deep down you know the direction to reach what you always wanted. Its between you and God. It was what you wanted and choose before you were born. Many are waiting for you. There are many worlds make sure it is the one you want and the people you want to draw. It will be like unto like. Light unto light.

Thank you for asking me to visit. My visit with you was a transition of direction and I hope for you also. I experienced unconditional love for you that moved me to higher heights and found myself deeply in love with you. I was taught much to see the love a daughter has for her father. I was taught much to see the unconditional love your daughter's husband has for his wife. I am very connected and love your children. It is as I am also their mother of a distance.

You were aware we needed to separate to shift and move ahead but not apart in like heart. There is still much for me to learn. Your knowledge far surpasses mine in many ways. We are very connected always will be. Keep lifting people with your smile. keep sending them love.... it is healing. Enjoy Victoria for now. Deep down I yarn for the time we are together.

M: This is beautiful Jen, you are a new woman in so many ways. I want you, we could co-create much that is beautiful and enduring together even before immortality. Come back soon, but only when you feel that you yourself are ready, there are loves for me to attract and gather too. It's encouraging that you say you yearn for the time when we will be together again. You must still be moving towards a final choice for ME your Adam. I'd like that a whole lot sweetheart, my door will always be open for you. Much as I give you as best I can the freedom to choose another, I cannot accept the thought of possibly permanently losing you, we're just too close for that. But have fun as you will dear one, be free, *fly* but stay safe for me.

And keep me informed, I want to share your new life, it's *exciting*, especially so if it's a beautiful woman and not a man you take to your bed. You could attract her to you (and thus to us if you choose me) if that's your choice. I would like a whole lot to hear the details of that, and maybe to come and live with you and her someday if you will. I thrill with the thought if she loves me too, my love for you would double. I would be so *alive!* It's what I've always secretly wanted but felt compelled by the demands of religion to deny myself me. If you accept my dream of Adam with multiple wives, keep your eyes open for and attract to you beautiful women we'd both want for our sister wives. Tell them about US, invite them HOME, and let's buy or build a happy place for us somewhere if there's time yet for that, it would be heaven already. Tell me what you are creating for our worlds so I'm ready for them too and can join in the co-creation.

I love you Gorgeous Gal Becoming Eve - I need you to be who I am. Are you going to keep me in suspense as to where you are then? I wish you'd tell, secrets only come *between* us. Your Michael

M: (unsent to Jackie – still nothing from her so I composed the following) You accuse me of wanting everything my way. But as I see it you are describing yourself. And regardless, my way is inclusive, your way is exclusive. I wish you the very best Jackie, I thought we had potential to have at least a lovely summer and fall together. But you have made your choice and we'll walk separate paths unless you change your mind and let me know somewhere in time, and I'm available for you when that moment arrives. Enjoy life.

Lynne: I wasn't 'mind reading' but I was responding to your direct questions. When you asked me the name of a 'compattable woman' who you might have a relationship with, a name that had a definate 'Kris, Kristen, Kristina? sound came to me. I also remember that it seemed to begin with a K. This may have been the woman you were communicating with as you felt drawn to her initially but now that you know that you are not physically attracted to her this is a bit doubtful. The name could be a coincidence and a 'new' Kris may be on the horizon. It's very interesting that I was given the word 'sceptre' along with a visual of the object. I feel that it was symbolic as opposed to being a past life indicator since you thought of asking me about that but we didn't dealve into it in a way that might answer your question at the time. As you can probably see now, it is very helpful to keep asking specific questions during readings.

I'm sorry to hear that the woman that you were interested in didn't even respond to your messages. It seems very rude and immature of her but perhaps she was intimidated by the fact that your 'ex' came to visit and she had a fear of being 'rejected again' causing her to behave in that manner. Good Luck in your search for your soul mate and travel companion and summer isn't over yet!

M: Thanks Lynne. I'd love to talk with you sometime, get to know you as a person outside of your professional role. Maybe we'd become friends if you can find the time, we live so close to each other. Just throwing that out there should you feel so inclined. But you must of course follow your own inner guidance and likes and dislikes. I'm much older in years than you are and you most likely already have many friends in Victoria... Enjoy this (rare so far) rainy day.

Jen: Did Jackie come to see you as you hoped. I hope she did I don't want you to be alone. Love sweety

M: Jackie was supposed to have come yesterday but she didn't and I haven't heard from her for several days. Unless there is a good excuse for that I am now considering our once budding 'relationship' to be over. I'll keep you posted if I ever hear from her again. I liked her a lot but there were things about her that were not what I was hoping for, but that I could have adapted to. Gosh Jen, she just wasn't *perfect!*

I receive expressions of interest from a lot of women (several new ones every day) but I'm very selective especially by their physical appearance. I could meet with many women today who want to meet me, but I am not so inclined, always looking for someone more promising or perhaps some inner urging. I have found that invariably I 'sabotage' (with too many seemingly 'pushy' emails) anything developing that I know inside will not move me closer to my dream. That 'sabotage' results in the women themselves rejecting me because inside they too know that it is for my best good not to become too attached to them. (As I am wont to do, I 'fall in love' much too easily.) So there are always several levels of activity taking place between me and women as the universe moves on and we enjoy our mortal experiences whether or not we think at the time they are beneficial.

At present the only woman I am thinking of fondly (besides you) is Lynne who I hope will become a friend even though I am 16 years older than she is. I find her attractive at many levels (and I think it would be great fun to travel with a clairvoyant) but I don't know where she is with that except for a really nice hug she gave me as we parted following my appointment with her. Are you at your daughter's? Why keep me guessing?

I did a check of where Jen's email came from and it was the Los Angeles area. She used to live in Riverside so she may have a friend there from many years ago who can help her "heal her heart". But then again, she may simply be at her son's helping care for his new son, or at his daughter's apartment. The night trip to California would have taken her through the "unpolluted" skies she mentioned but I don't know why she was in such a hurry to get away from her home when she was already "exhausted" and why she felt she needed a spirit guide to make the journey with her, she has driven that many times before. I'm curious to know the details of her leaving her home in that manner. Maybe she'll eventually share.

Jen: I am glade you share with me the happening with women. I feel Jackie does not share your dream. She still want that perfect man. Don't be concerned were I am. I am where I am totally excepted. No lovers.

M: Ok, I once thought it wasn't your business where I was too but that was before you astonished me by accepting my being with other women. Be well, enjoy your adventure, keep in touch.

M: (to Jen) I bought a piece of that fresh sockeye salmon. Do I just melt some butter in a fry pan and let the fish cook slowly for a while? Cover the pan? Could I microwave the salmon instead? Wanna come back and do cooking and cleaning for a living, be a friend with benefits?

Jen: Would love to come and cook that salmon for you. Just put some melt butter in a pan start out medium hi heat and then low heat. After you turn the salmon you could put a lid on it. About 10 minutes total. If you have a lemon squeeze a bit on the salmon. Do not microwave it. Would love to come back and stay awhile but would be in the way of your search for women. Lets see what the future will bring.

I am now at my son's, took my grandon for a three hour walk along the ocean then walked out to the end of the pier. We put our feet in the water. The ocean here smells much fresher and cleaner looking. Beautiful worm day with cool ocean breezes. But loved the charm of Victoria. It's a city made for walking.

M: Too late, I already ate the salmon. But I cooked it pretty much the way you described, tasted ok with tartar sauce, needed something besides toast and cheese slices.

Will you able to make your changes while at your son's and in the old routine, or are you just visiting him today and staying with someone else nearby? I'm wondering about the mystery you created and the rush to leave your home apparently late at night and exhausted, wanting a spirit guide to travel with you. Care to enlighten me what that was all about? It sounded exciting.

Today was the first rainy day in weeks but I walked to the end of the breakwater and back in fog so thick you could only see a few yards ahead, fun, almost comforting like a blanket pulled around you.

I agree, much as I'd love to wake up with you beside me tomorrow morning it's best I think for us if you do what you need to do, especially please, lose some of that extra weight. (No offense meant, I think that's what you want for yourself too.) If all you do is accept an open relationship and are down to a weight you and I are both comfortable with, my guess is that we could live together for longer periods of time. I think I'd like that, maybe we could do some co-creating of a future lifestyle that we both want, hopefully extending into immortality. I try to compare consensus "reality" with my dream and when you really think about it, my dream is just as valid and just as real and enormously better. I am convinced that it is not only possible but is actually probable.

Sure, I'm missing having a woman with me this week, *really* missing that, I'd been expecting Jackie to be with me yesterday and today. Hopefully I'll find out what happened to her. Her daughter was on the road the last time I heard from Jackie so hopefully she was not in an accident or something else happened so serious that it took me completely out of Jackie's mind or she became too busy to contact me. She was going in for a minor surgical procedure on Monday, I never heard anything about it, it would have taken care of the physical problem she had. I hope it went well for her, I wish her the very best.

But my guess is that Jackie has another man who lives a lot closer than I do so they can conveniently drop in and out of each other's homes and stay as long or as short as they want any time they want. She stayed quite a while at the bus terminal when I last saw her, waiting for my bus to pull away. Meanwhile as she waited, a ferry arrived and unloaded. We had a wonderful connection until I saw her walk over to a man seated on a bench with a guitar on his back, he had probably just got off the ferry. He looked at her as if he knew her but was distrustful. She talked to him and lead him a few yards so my bus was not in the line of sight, and pointed in the direction her car was parked. He walked away. She blew me a kiss, signed "Namaste" and left soon after even though my bus hadn't left yet and she had already waited quite a while. (I hadn't expected her to do that, thought it was real nice of her, now not so sure, maybe she was waiting for another man coming on the ferry?)

I asked her in an email about the man with the guitar but even though I received several emails from her after asking about him, she never responded. So I'm not sure what's up with her, I know I'm much too trusting and vulnerable when it comes to women. And I still need to dump the idea that if a woman takes a man to her bed or climbs into his it's a big deal, that's just not so outside of the world most Mormons live in. Having sex is not cause for loyalty even the next morning, just something consenting adults routinely do for mutual pleasure, no big deal when there's no fear of burning in hell forever for having fun with our bodies. Hang in there with me if you will, I'm human but I do have a beautiful dream... Tell me about your spiritual experiences?

M: (to Karen) I haven't forgotten you, we swapped quite a few candid messages some time ago. It was fun, I made changes to my profile several times in an attempt to redo myself in your image and likeness. If you ever come this way, let me know and plan to stay a few days, I'll show you around if you're not yet familiar with Victoria's sites. Take care, enjoy the day.

M: Suzanne, I know you have built a strong wall between us and I respect that, it's your choice. But I want you to know that as I'm condensing twelve books into one and reading again the way it was for us before Las Vegas, my love for you has not faltered. We could be friends, pen pals, maybe confidantes if you so chose. And who knows, one day we may meet again for a brief time to tak a cup and renew auld lang syne, maybe cuddle a bit if you will? I'm full of questions, wanting to know how you've been.

Jen: You need to know what you really want. Often the onion needs some pealing to get down to what we really want and what makes sense. The surface stuff can be what stumbles us. Its just how long do we want to linger with the first peal that we think we want but does not make sense. That may be the reason we can not get out of the way of it. Peal your wants to get to the pure heart of what matters most to you. Then get out of the way and it will happen.

M: The way I see it, Law of Attraction is impersonal, it does not judge, it knows that we are *always* worthy of receiving everything we want. Like typing in a password, Law of Attraction ALWAYS delivers when we get it right - it *must*, just like the operating system of a computer. My take is that you are making it much too complicated, you already know what you want. As Abraham would say, it's *already* in your "Vortex" it was created the very moment you desired it. Law of Attraction is simply waiting for you to *allow* it to manifest on the physical plane. Contrary to what we are taught about the world and how things manifest (hard work for long hours etc.) we don't have to do a single thing, the entire universe is here to serve the race of man, the leading edge CREATORS of desire. There could not be a universe without a constant flow of new desire.

Just relax and let go, your fondest desires will come true when you allow it to happen. *"But ok"*, you say, *"then why are you always asking me to decide what I really want?"* Because, as a Russian poet put it: *"I'm just a young god, I don't always get it right?"* Or maybe because you are not really needing to decide, it's already decided, you are merely allowing yourself moment by moment to become aware of the incredibly wonderful life ahead that is now manifesting as you let go and let God/Source/Spirit/Law of Attraction bring it (effortlessly) to you.

But having said that, I think it important to take inspired action when the thought to do so is a happy one. For example, if it feels a happy thought that you win a lottery and you feel inspired to buy a ticket - *buy the ticket* - and expect to win. If you feel it a happy thought to weigh less than you do and feel inspired to eat less, *eat less!* I'm still working on better manifesting myself, but it's coming along well. A happy relaxed state of mind without any negative thinking I think is needful for the best manifesting. That way you'll almost invariably receive much more than you thought you would get, like my driving home a top of the line newer car instead of the old lesser model I had set out to buy that day. TRUST TRUST TRUST and always expect the best. That's how I see it today, tomorrow may be different...

Jen: Yesterday evening I became Ill. The girls have been sick also. I went to bed early woke about 1:30 very week had a hard time getting to the bathroom I was nausea and dizzy. Ran bathwater and laded in the tub for over an hour afraid if I got out that I would pass out. Finally did and kept my head level with my heart and managed to get into bed. Slept for over 12 hours. Took medicine for my migraine headache and feel much better now. I am enjoying my grandson. He is setting on my foot. Always a big smile. Love's to be rocked. I am enjoying my self with the family. My granddaughter said "Grandma you are losing weight" Made me feel good. She's the first to knowtice. Love Jen

M: Glad you're better - and losing weight. Although I hadn't really planned it, I realize that I'm still writing books the same as I used to. But I feel that the time is *now* to rewrite and get the condensed book published. Lynne affirms that it's time for *some* book to emerge, maybe it's the condensed one. Also keeping busy writing occupies the time I thought I'd have 'on vacation' exploring the Island with a lovely lady. Maybe the condensed book is more important?? I could be wrong of course but I felt as I showered today that Jackie most likely has a younger man who won't complicate her life and take her time like I would have, and would give her younger energy in bed. And now with that surgical procedure behind her, she may be wanting to see first if a younger local man will work for her better than hanging with me?

But that's mere surmise, I still find it hard to understand that such a spiritual lady could seemingly be so inconsiderate as to leave me hanging like she did, my expecting her to overnight with me this week. Maybe she will write back with an excuse that will move my feelings right back to her. And maybe I'll never hear from her again. Our feelings ran deep, there could be as much emotion if her thoughts of me became negative, maybe she's not ready to face that. I thought of phoning to see if she's ok, it's possible that her computer broke down, but I don't do phone well and she could phone me, she has my number and called before. It's best I think that I just be patient, get on with contacting other women, keep writing, and see what comes.

Jen: Sweet baby, you are punishing your self with your thoughts of her. I've been there. You told me many times to let go. Let her go.

M: I won't let Jackie "go" until there is either some closure by a message from her, or until I have found another to explore Vancouver Island with this summer. Thanks for your sincere concern though, I appreciate that, you're a dear soul Jen, I love you lots.

Jen wrote between the lines in an older message I sent her. Here are a few quote/paraphrases from what she wrote today.

Routine is the same and delightful. The spirit guide or comforter is now abiding within me. I did rush to leave home and it took till about 9:00 or later to leave. I will write about it more someday. Just not the time.

Jackie's daughter is just fine. Its something else she is not comfortable with and for that reason she did not show up??? I believe Jackie has other men. If you were willing to be friends as they are you would be seeing her from time to time. They also love her.

Welcome to the world you choose. I am becoming and still am a one man woman. I am becoming without judgment.

I liked what I saw of Lynne down on the beach. Tender caring soul to take care of her daughter all these years. She will continue. Her daughter is her first priority. If you send sexual or relationship vibes you are risking losing her. It is to early for that. I hope you and Lynne become *friends,* I know no reason why not.

So do I have a beautiful dream. In time I will tell you about my spiritual experience.

Below is another message I sent to Jen that she responded to between the lines.

M: In my opinion if we are going to co-create together we need to be completely open with each other and not keep secrets. For example, how am I going to co-create with you the dream I have told you about when you secretly are creating a dream where we live on earth during the Millennium and have children here rather than on other planets as I visualize we do? It just won't work Jen, it seems yet again that by keeping secrets you are wanting to control, to be 'above' me, and have everything *your* way rather than us creating the worlds we want *together*.

Jen: I admit I don't know everything or how it will really work. But I do believe we will go thru a Millennium or why would we be translated instead of resurrected. I always thought translated beings were for this world. So do we not need to experience it and help other spirits come to this earth. in a perfect world ???

M: That's how your keeping secrets is coming across to me. Wouldn't it be better to tell me the whole truth, discuss, and decide what WE want? It's US, not your spirit guides who are creating OUR worlds if you choose me for your husband. But you could choose of course to give up agency and become slavish to others who come in brighter clothing than I am presently wearing. Is that what's happening? Tell it whole and tell it true Jen. It's much better that way, the way you are doing it with bits and pieces and secrets and allusions to mysteries only serves yourself and the cause of confusion, it does not serve US. Are you thinking that I'm going to come back to Mormonism and we'll live happily ever after during the Millennium, having children on this planet? Is that your belief, your desire, your dream?

Jen: Maybe I should go silent and think things out. Other wise lets just talk about other subjects and not let this one consume us for now.

Karen: Nice to hear from you. I can well imagine your being happy in Victoria. Without seeing much of it at all, I "fell in love" w/ the city in 2009. And to have walking trails right there.......I wonder how your weather compares with that of the area I've moved to. I've been staying on north Whidbey Island, but just today found a house I might want to purchase. It's in Sedro Woolley, just east of I 5, and half an hour south of Bellingham. The weather has been so sunny since I arrived, mid-July, that the misty past two days have actually felt like a relief. There is soooooo much natural beauty here, and I'm happy to be near my family. Ciao

M: It's nice to hear from you too Karen. I saw your smile and pretty face while browsing SS and thought it was about time for us to do a bit of an update. As I recall we exchanged a lot of (very candid) messages not too long ago. I found it a fascinating conversation maybe because neither of us really cared a whole lot, you had already written me off as a lost cause. Now tell YOUR version of the story...

I've read that Victoria has far more sunshine and fewer rainy days than Vancouver but although I have been there briefly in the past I am not familiar with Whidbey Island's weather. My guess is that it would be similar to Victoria, we've had oodles of sunshine since I arrived July 1st, and yesterday and today with a bit of rain and some fog. But we're getting off to an excellent start again should you choose to continue swapping messages for a bit, it's so inspiring to discuss weather don't you agree? Maybe that was why you wrote me off in the big inning? Good luck with your house purchase, as for me although I'm just renting a one bedroom suite in James Bay right now, I've promised myself I'd remain in my native land for the foreseeable future rather than go back to USA after 20 years there.

M: I was fixated on your pretty face but just reread your profile and now I remember why I contacted you in the first place! Wonderful Karen, I love what you wrote and who you are, you are indeed a choice soul. (Not sure about the goat cheese though...) Talk to me?

Karen: There is nothing on this earth like goat's cheese..... truly! I can hardly bear to walk by the cheese bin w/o purchasing some, and then it magically disappears before I get home. I just wrote you a longish letter, but when I clicked "reply", nothing happened, and I don't see it in my "sent" folder. Did you receive it? Please tell me you did!

M: Whoa, your message came through, same one, eight times! Ok, give, should we ever get together we'll have goat cheese in our lives. No, I didn't get a different message but I really want to read what you had to say, hope you kept a copy. I suggest that we bypass this venue and continue our conversation at my direct mail. Hope to see you there.

Karen: (she replies to my email address) Whew! Much better to bypass singles!! I had the same problem w/ the last email, as you can tell. I clicked on "reply", and nothing happened.... again and again and again. But, apparently, that one did not get lost...... Now I am really tired. I have so many computer problems - whether it be the site, or my piece of equipment. It drains me, and my passion for writing instantly disappears. I'll write more later.... tomorrow, that is; there's no WI FI at my daughter's cabin. Oh, I think it might bother you not to know why I stopped writing. It was because I am a lowly 5'4" (or even less by now), and of course I knew you wanted a tall woman..... and men are soooooooooo visual... and I'm not getting any taller. (AND, I have always yearned to be tall.... maybe in my next life. Might you be able to wait? Goodnight

M: Sorry Karen, can't wait, just going to have to 'make do' with beautiful you as you are. I'll watch for your message tomorrow. Goodnite, sweet dreams.

I'm really liking this woman, she may be my travel companion for the summer? She's a "gypsy" too she says – she's my age - and her family live within 50 miles of Victoria so this could be a good place for her to come and stay awhile now and again if we survive that all important first day or two or three. I think it won't be long before I suggest that to her, we've already got history so it's not waaay out of line I don't think.

Jen: Why does there need to be a replacement for Jackie before you move on to another? Why not just Michael? Do I dare say more?

M: That's a question that I keep working on the solution to. Almost every time I walk I keep telling myself that I'm ok with just me. But it's a lie, I'm not, I'm only part "me" without a loving woman I can often hold in my arms and converse with. That's just the way I am, and for one who professes to be "Becoming Adam" that should be understandable. I cannot be Adam without one or more wives, the same as a Mormon man cannot be exalted without (at least) one wife. (According to Brigham

Young, a man who does not have *more than* one wife cannot progress in the eternities. That's not taught in Sunday School anymore.

I love you sweetheart but there are more loves for me concurrent with my love for you. I hope you can continue to accept that, it's vital to fulfilling my dream and my lifelong desires. But hard as it is on both of us you must make your own choice, you could almost certainly find a faithful Mormon man if you are stuck on monogamy and can't share me with others. That's just the way it is. But miracles always happen around me and today the spiritual woman I mentioned who lives in the USA but just a ferry ride from Victoria sent several promising messages to me, her name is "Karen". I feel really good about her, maybe she'll be my travel companion for the summer? That's the hope that I need right now to banish Jackie from my thoughts, be happy for me. (And if you choose US, be happy for us should she prove to be one of our immortal family - as you wrote *"like attracts like, light attracts light"* she could very well be.

By the way, you asked about being translated (physical body made immortal) versus resurrected. I don't really know but Mormon doctrine would make out that resurrected beings who are exalted create *spirit* children, not the physical ones that I want as Adam to create with my immortal wives. We need to be immortal to survive travel to other planets and the prospect of aging and dying, so that's a given. I have no problem living on this planet for the Millennium (and having children) as long as we can go at the right time to populate other planets as immortal Adam and Eves, that's the fullness of my dream, there's no rush at all once we become immortal. Sleep well my love, there will always be a place at my side for you once we are immortal.

Jen: (she attaches references from Mormon sources) Michael, Thank you for wanting to know more of my personal of late experience. I felt I needed to understand to a fuller level what I had emailed to you. So I decided to do some research. I am now most comfortable with what I learned from the comforter and shared with you thus far. Most likely you know these things already but I needed reassurance of what I understood. Would be interesting to hear your take. Love Jen

M: I am pleased to know that you are researching, I did this kind of thing often over the last 45 years since becoming a Mormon, it's much easier now with internet. If you are finding some conflict with my dream or between my dream and yours, let's discuss it shall we? There is no need for secrets between us, they only cause misunderstandings, frustration, confusion, lack of harmony, and lack of co-creating the worlds we both want. I repeat that I have no problem with remaining on this planet for the Millennium and having children, as long as we can go on and populate other planets with physical bodies also, and as long as we have sister wives. We can choose to die and resurrect anytime in the eternities and start creating spiritual instead of physical bodies, as I understand eternal progression, and if the Mormons got it right.

It is my burning desire right now (my fantasy) to populate planets with *physical* bodies, as did Adam and Eve on this one. It is not clear to me if resurrected bodies can do that, Adam and Eve were not resurrected when they left the Garden of Eden and started having children, they hadn't died yet. There is much that is not taught in the Mormon doctrine that is available to ordinary members. Who knows what is in the secret vaults, especially those accessible only by the First Presidency? It's obviously things that would shake up the members (even the apostles) or they wouldn't be kept secret. So advanced souls are left to find out such things for themselves, and God help them if it's anything that includes polygamy because they'll be swiftly and mercilessly cut off from the Church that is supposed to be the pathway to 'heaven' meaning exaltation, meaning being able to create spirit children. That doesn't ring true to me anymore than did the old Catholic doctrine of condemning their members to burn in hell forever if they ate meat on Friday. It's just a mass of confusion that leads to slavish obedience to doctrines that are constantly changing to reflect the times and the whims and politics of church leaders.

We've got to find out for *ourselves*, or alternatively simply bypass everything and create *our own* worlds the way *we* want them to be. That seems a fitting thing for God's children to do when they grow up and become like Him/Her don't you think?

Define "comforter'. Do you mean the spirit guide/s you refer to mysteriously, or the "Holy Ghost" as taught by Mormons? It would be most helpful if you would tell me your secrets so we can discuss. Why not? I am *completely* open with you. That's the only way co-creation can work. Keeping secrets from aspiring co-creators can only lead to *"an uncertain sound"* and the accomplishment of nothing.

Jen: We could video to each other and talk without it costing anything plus I could see your hansom face.

M: I'm a writer Jen, we may video someday when you want to show me the real you that you are now in the process of manifesting.

Jen: Michael, I think you want me to be honest with you. As much as I love you and totally accept you for the wonderful qualities I know you possess. I do not fit in the life style you desire at this time. I have decided I could never invite a woman into my bed to please me or you. Because of age I may never have another man in my bed in this life time and yet their might be. Once I loose my weight I might look, just not sure. If someone comes along I can deeply love and is a good fit I would consider marriage again. Your Adam seems to feel the women that come into his world have to see things just as he wants. Where is the women's point of view and dreams. Now you know where I position myself... It has been very painful and heart breaking to loose you and yet I feel blessed to have you as a close friend once again. You have helped me realize your search for women is a number one all consuming priority in your life.

I think, you will most likely settle for one woman for the rest of your life even though you want it to be an open relationship. I realize you do not want it to me. I am a safety net on the side just in case it does not work out the way you thought it would with other women. Not sure if I can be that person or is it fair to use me that way. I am a number 1 not a number 2 or 3 down the road. I believe, you are afraid of us settling into the past as it once was. I could not settle for that either. I don't believe either of us could be those two very dull people again. It was so much fun when I visited and sorry you could not see it continuing to be great fun but glad I went home early. Seeing that you finally emerged was invigorating. For the first time in many years I felt I could be free to let myself out and be me once again without offending you. In other wise, in our marriage, in many ways I became you and it was not appealing for you to see yourself being reflected back. There is so much of me left to emerge.

Our potential is to be teachers, interesting people and sharing people that which lifts others. I suppose if we wanted we could continue teaching each other and have fun doing so. It is all there to be but your pride about some things still exists as a stumbling block that is effecting your relationships. God Bless and go for your dreams and keep me posted every day as a trusted friend that has unconditional love for you. Thanks for being so open with me.

The following is a compilation of several emails exchanged between me and Jen over several days, with writings between the lines.

M: And thank-you for being so open as well, I appreciate that very much. I just didn't know how committed you were after that sudden totally unexpected announcement when you were here that you were ok with me being with other women concurrent with you. I guess you've changed your mind about that.

Jen: I have no hold on you. I have no problem with you being with other women. That is your choice. We still remain very close friends. I will respond to comments below as time permits. I just wanted to clear this up. The future is not here yet.

M: That's good to hear, I read too much into your message. I like that, *"The future is not here yet"*, well said.

M: Regarding your statement: *"Your Adam seems to feel the women that come into his world have to see things just as he wants. Where is the women's point of view and dreams."* That is simply a misunderstanding, it is completely false, that is not at all the way I am. I value and treasure above all freedom for *everyone* to be as they will be.

Jen: This is good to hear. But what if the majority of women want a man to join in?

M: Then the majority of women will have chosen to leave my world/s and go to those of another immortal. They are free to do so and to have him be the father of their children from then on. In such an unlikely scenario, I would attract other women to me. Remember, ONE man and several wives is the true order of heaven as taught by Mormon prophets Joseph Smith and Brigham Young, and that's the way I see it too, it is my greatest desire.

M: The way I see it, every single human being is a creator unto themselves.

Jen: I see, but how do you keep "being a creator unto themselves" make it possible for a large group to want the exact same thing for eons of time. When everyone is a creator unto themselves Thus giving to themselves to benefit themselves. What about creating to benefit all people.

M: This could be explained by your "bubble" analogy. Everyone already *wants* to be in the larger bubble/world we'd co-create to have fun in and on which to raise our children or they would not be with us. And yet, as it is with human beings on this planet, everyone creates their own smaller 'bubbles' on/within the large bubble called Earth. If we co-create our own worlds, one of us who so desires could be responsible for plants, another for bodies of water, another for mountains, another for etc. etc. to make the whole glorious and beautiful. I assure you there is room for everyone to create what they want within our world/s forever as along as it harmonizes with the whole. And if not, they can create unpopulated Venus's, Pluto's, etc. to do their thing on where it won't interfere with our primary task of raising our children. And if not, they are free to withdraw to some other dimension or some other immortal's world/s.

M: The women in my dream are all equal with me and equal with each other. Of course we all create (as you put it) a "bubble" within the greater bubble of the world/planet we live in, it's our nature to do that. And of course in my dream and in my everyday reality nobody is forced into having or expected to have sexual relations they do not desire, far from it. I spoke only of *ideals* from the point of view of where I am now, which of course is flexible and evolving as it should be.

Jen: Yes there is so much left. I know there will be a time when man can become (A God) My understanding is there is no disharmony within the Godhead. These men are. They think the same because they know the beginning to the end... They have been at both ends of a never ending circle they connected. It is an earthly man's pride that creates the fear of another man being in the midst of women he feels is his.... I believe.

M: You are big on "pride" as if that was something wrong when in fact it is something beautiful, an expression of the love one has for oneself. There will of course be many men in our worlds, males born to you and your/our sister wives and eventually millions of others descended from them. We are all perfectly free to interact with our children and their descendants, possibly even have sex with them. It is recorded in the bible that there was once a time on this planet when: *"There were giants in the earth in those days; and also after that, when the sons of God came in unto the daughters of men, and they bare children to*

them, the same became mighty men which were of old, men of renown."
Genesis 6:4.

But I maintain that an optimum *Adam and Eve* family (creators of *physical* bodies) consists of ONE man and several women. It works much better that way because when females are present males compete and fight with each other to prove that they are the strongest in the 'herd' and so they are the one most deserving to be father of the children. Prides of lions, deer, elk, moose, most beasts allow only one adult male to remain with the females. But a man can seldom fight or even want to fight a woman. One Adam per family would greatly help increase the chance for enduring harmony and success the way I see it. The members of the Godhead you write of get along perfectly but that is not a family organized to produce children, it's a governing body, something very different.

M: In my desire to be completely open with you, I told you about my *ideal* desires. But you haven't really told me about yours and how they might fit into mine, or how they might possibly *modify* my dream (as I see it today) if we had become co-creators of the world/s (the greater bubble) we mutually want to play on. I am disappointed that you changed your mind and have decided to opt out of my dream and to try to fit yourself into another man's bubble. You are attractive and will certainly find another man if that's what you want. He will be different, he will come with strengths and gifts and also with weaknesses and faults that you will discover as you live together, just as we did. You may find that even though it's exciting in the beginning, he may not be better than me. But the choice to be with another man, as I have been frequently telling you, is *your own* individual choice, it *must* be that way.

Jen: I never opted in or out but have been exploring to understand as much as I am capable of. I am sealed to you for eternity. That happens to mean a lot to me. I want to make sure I am on the right path.

M: I thought that you had opted *in* when you accepted my being with other women. But ok, I'll allow now that you've said it that you are neutral on the matter, waiting for a future time to make a choice for me or for another man. As a matter of Mormon doctrine your forever "sealing" to me who have opted out of the doctrine is valid only to ensure that you get to be with *someone* for all eternity, assuming that I understand correctly, and that today's Mormons got that right. The way I see it today, you can never get it wrong if you create it yourself. "Wrong" in the sense you use it could only be if you failed to obey *someone else's* notion of reality when the truth is that you are grown up and capable of creating whatever you want for yourself. (Allowing of course for the freedom of choice that all others have. You might create your own worlds but not attract to them the exact people you want because those people could choose not to join you.) But from the highest perspective, we are all part of EVERYTHING and EVERYONE anyway, so it all equals out.

M: It's different for me because it's the man's responsibility (as per Joseph Smith and Brigham Young) to attract more than one woman, but not the woman's to choose more than one man. That's just the way it is for wise purposes we don't at present allow ourselves to be aware of, but I am coming to understand much better as I search myself and bring to awareness my own deepest desires, they are my true compass.

Jen: I hope we are able to continue exploring your deepest desires. Yes and find your true compass.

M: My compass is my deepest desires, those are my dream to become Adam populating planets with the physical bodies of human beings together with sister wives who are equal to me and to each other, all of us knowing a fullness of joy and love, a family of spouses.

M: Sure we can remain pen pals, I had hope for more, but that will just have to do unless you change your mind again. If you would have been completely open with me as I have been urging you to be and to dump the secrets, we could have discussed what it is you want. I think (with the exception of the western notion of monogamy) we could have found a mutually acceptable foundation to build upon. From that firm foundation we would have known where we are each going and could have actively and consciously co-created *everything* we mutually desire, helping each other to become who we really are as individuals without needing to come back (if reincarnation is true) and do it all over again, and again, and again until we finally get it right. This *could* be our final incarnation, we have a lovely enduring dream in full awareness and the power to manifest it if we will. We are both ancient souls already, we just need to ALLOW the dream to be and it will be ours...

Jen: I feel no need for reincarnation because I will be moving forward to my next level of destination not back. Where is our common ground?

M: I am not certain of reincarnation but most of the people in the world believe in it in some form or another and I am leaning towards it being true. As I see it, there can never be a movement "back" because after the death of a physical body there is no judgment, mortal life was just for fun and learning. I think the churches deliberately got it wrong to put fear into the hearts of people so they can better control and take their money. The soul always remembers its former experiences and learns from them even though it commonly does not allow most of those experiences to come into mortal awareness. *It's more fun that way...*

M: You ask *"is it fair to use me"*. What I am offering is very far from what you seem to think I am offering. I am offering you an *equal* place at my side for eternity, populating planets with the physical bodies of human beings. And should we ever tire of that, perhaps going on to create *spirit* children for some other Adam and Eve's physical children, or maybe our own?

Jen: I was referring to this life (being now) of me being one of many you seek after. Like there are at least three or four or more women in front of me before you would even consider me as a partner in your life again. I want to be the number one person in the arms of my man.

M: Ok, I can understand that, it's the western teaching of monogamy that drives that in you. Looking more expansively, you could choose to see other sister wives as being additions to you, increases, people you LOVE more than anyone else, conscious parts of YOU, more arms to enfold and comfort you. But I have not ruled out living with you Jen, especially if you would be accepting of an open relationship this time. But at this point in my life I think it best that I have several lovers instead of just one woman who I live with exclusively because several would be more in keeping with my dream of one man and several wives. And I would have more time to write - and make my own meals.

M: How could that possibly be my *using* you? Think about it....

Jen: Yes think about it. if I told you I was involved with several other men that are good candid's to being my husband here and the next life. And if they don't work out I might make my way back to you, if that is if you change your thinking or lose your stomach. No disrespect just making a point.

M: Your point is not valid because the role of women is different than the role of men. According to Brigham Young a man cannot be exalted (allowed to create spirit children) if he does not have more than one wife. What you are suggesting is that one woman should have more than one husband. Fine, if that's what you want you can most likely find the men and who knows maybe create such a world as that. But really, do you need the love of more than one man, or the seed of several males to create children? That's the purpose of Adam and Eve families, to populate worlds. No doubt there are an infinite number of other types of organizations, but the way I see it, the best organization for an Adam and Eve family is one Adam and one or more Eves, never two or more 'Adams' and one Eve. It has likely been tried though. It's up to YOU to choose for yourself what you want.

By the way, in a typical open *mortal* relationship the female has just as much right to have sex with other men (or women) as the male does, they don't have to first ask permission of their spouse to go off with another person after the party. But in most successful open relationships both would most likely be courteous enough to tell the other that they'll be away for such and such a time while they experience what pleasures other bodies have to offer.

M: You write, *"it is all there to be but your pride about some things."* Please explain that point of view, I would very much like to understand and to be able to discuss the 'weakness' you see in me that you think is affecting my relationships. Be completely open and honest with me, never hold back and keep secrets regardless of what it is that is motivating you to be secretive and thus cause distrust and confusion between us. You can't hurt me Jen, I know where I am going and I will get there, I am 'there' already in the dimensions where time and space cease to be. I welcome you as "a trusted friend" who perhaps has "unconditional love" for me. We could still have more, but for that we'd have to freely discuss every one of your concerns about potentially being US.

Jen: What do you mean by more. I feel you toy'ee with me.

M: By "more" in that sentence I was assuming when I wrote it that you had opted out of my dream and I was suggesting that we could have more than mere friendship. If you opted in and discussed everything openly with no secrets kept between us we could become active co-creators of the things and world/s we mutually want to manifest. That would be doubly powerful and like it is with this present exchange of emails, it would help each of us to better understand what is driving our desires from deep within and what we really want. I do not toy with you. Why would I?

M: Or, you are free to fit yourself into another man's bubble. He will welcome you there, he will love you, it could be as equally desirable inside his bubble as in mine. Or, you could find along the way that your new man doesn't even have a dream, just moves towards someone *else's* notion of reality. You could find that your 'other' marriage (the one with me) would have been a better bubble for you to create your own smaller bubbles within forever. (And have many children.)

Jen: How about you fitting into my large bubble and I give you a smaller one. Are we not then equal in our thinking.

M: Possibly, tell me about the "large bubble" you want to manifest.

M: I love you unconditionally, that will always be there, but of course in this world there are things I'm hoping you'll do to make yourself more compatible to my dream, just as I'm sure there are things about me you'd like to change as well, and I might be willing.

Jen: As I *might* be willing.

M: Except that I will never change my desire - similar to that of Joseph and Brigham - to have more than one wife in the eternities. To me one man with several wives is the true order of heaven - as difficult as it is for western women trained to monogamy to accept.

Jen: No as much as you think. Many Mormon women are aware to this day their husbands are temple sealed forever to more than one woman. You happen to be one of those men that have more than one woman sealed to you.

M: And I will never change from my desire that each of my wives be equal with me and with each other, and each be free to do as they will except have another man father their children while they remain on our planet/s. They are free anytime to go to another man's 'bubble' if that is their choice, but they must then leave mine, my planets will have only one Adam who hopefully will be the first father of all the children thereon.

Jen: What are these women allowed to take with them when they are no longer welcome. Their bubble, their children? What makes this equal with you when you can choose who you want in this bubble but they cannot. Why does just you have this privilege. I would be interested in your answer.

M: Assuming conditions as they are in this world today, mortals cannot go to another world until they become immortal, unless of course they invent a space ship to do that. So no mother going to another Adam's world could take "her" children with her. There would be nothing else to take, none needed, *stuff exists everywhere!* I can say that because I know I would not go with any sister wife who abandoned my world/s to live with another man in his bubble world. I would remain and be Adam/Father to my children, and would attract other sister wives and/or create a new planet to begin populating, hoping that I'd be more successful next time in keeping my sister wives. That's the role of an immortal male as I see it, equal, but different.

M: And that is why my logical mind thinks that if my wives were lesbians except with me the one male exception, it would be easier for all of our children to have a single father.

Jen: A true lesbian would not want you!!!

M: Such a woman who would not want me would not be attracted to me in the first place, it would be like attracting unlike, doesn't happen. I'm speaking of an *ideal* world for my dream as I am now aware of it. In such a world if all the women were lesbians with the one exception they would not be tempted and be forced to struggle with desire for a different immortal Adam. I believe that there are women who would love to share my dream and that Law of Attraction will eventually bring us together.

Jen: Many men secretly would like that.

M: Yes, many men secretly desire to have more than one woman in bed with them at the same time. That's very helpful in creating eternal families of one man and several women, as seems to be the true order of heaven. Your point is?

Jen: Not so, would be much more interesting to have different fathers.

M: Not to a man it would not be, and it would eventually result in division, tribes and wars among the children. But ok, let's discuss this.

Assuming you want to become part of an Adam and Eve family, is it your desire to have more than one husband in the family?

M: I place high value on that for many reasons. We must all love each other unconditionally on 'Mount Olympus', at least in the beginning of our creating.

Jen: Are your lesbian wives going to only have female children? I would think you would want baby boys. They do grow up to be men and men have needs and the women (your wives) will love them. Blood of their blood. Blood of your blood. They will not want to lose them. Since age is not an issue in that immortal state, do you not believe your sons will have children with their mothers and sisters? Did you think of this possibility?

M: As it was in the beginning of this world, the mortal blood was pure, brothers and sisters *had* to have children together, there was nobody else to choose from. And keep in mind that we "the ancient gods" create the rules, the 'commandments' for our children. Sexual attraction and interaction is incredibly wonderful, why would we want to prevent anyone from having sex with any consenting other? Let the churches that will almost certainly come along much later invent such a commandment, it's for *their own* benefit, it makes lives miserable and people malleable.

Of course we'll have male and female children. How else could we populate worlds? We ourselves may only birth a few children on each planet. It is they, the children who will multiply and increase exponentially as we watch over and teach and guide them in the ways of love and happiness, and have fun doing it. I don't understand fully at this time but it may be that gods can have sex with mortals and the mortals will bear children, but can a goddess be impregnated by a mortal man? I don't know. We'd have to consider children who are half god half human maybe, maybe not. I don't think it would work well but everyone in our immortal family must be free to do as they choose, including having sex with the mortals if that is their and the mortal's desire. Greek mythology records such happenings, and so does the bible with the conception of Jesus. Do we need a fall of Adam and Eve experience on each planet so our children by disobedience lose the immortality that comes with having been born of a god and a goddess, and in that loss of innocence become capable of knowing good and evil? That seems to be how it was done on this earth.

Jen: Tell me why do we talk about this when I wish and hope you would feel a need to concentrate on getting it right in this life and let the next take its given path. Are you interested in planning and doing what is most important in your life now. Such as helping your families and friends to be a better self. Being true to your selves. Staying grounded enough, to make earthly dreams come into focus. Is it worth spinning your wheels on what you only had a glimpse of in the next life. I want to enjoy the balance of time I have here with those I love and not seeking after dreams that are not for this earthly season. But let that be said it would make a great science fiction novel. I could really get into that. How fun it would be to let your imagination travel to a world you seek to create. We did a bit of that when I visited and it was fun. I could even play that part to a greater depth. Don't you think?

M: I can interact with my children and friends in mortality (and do) and still concurrently be actively (and secretly if wanted) desiring and creating my own dream for a future world. That would be *"being in the world but not of it"*- a good thing actually. If you settle in this life for letting *"the next (world) take its given path"* then you are giving up control of your post mortal destination and are accepting instead someone else's world as your destination. If reincarnation is true, then such people I think would be back for another round until they get it right that they themselves have the power and the obligation to CREATE their own worlds and be independent in them. In effect they become gods themselves. If you can't do that yet then you are not yet ready to become a god the way I see it.

Jen: From now on I want to talk about what you want now and your plans for next week or next year. The ups and downs of your life. The smiles you received as you walked. Who your next love is. Plus your new novel. I will finish your book and we can talk about it. If you have some spiritual experiences I want to hear about them. OK sweety?

M: Sure, I can get down-to-earth and talk dirty too. My "new novel" is a condensed version of the twelve books I have now unpublished. It will remove all the repetitions, and will hugely reduce extraneous material that crept in to the twelve books. For example, I am leaving "Bonnie" out entirely, her views were just too different, she has nothing to teach about immortality or Adam and Eve families which is my focus in between the entertainment. I am presently working on that one single book which will most likely turn out to be a series, but a series of much longer books than the original twelve were when first published.

If "spiritual experiences" include Law of Attraction events I would never have time to write them all, it's a way of life to me. And since I'm creating my own world/s there is no need for people in bright clothing to teach me about theirs. Except for those who come to teach me about the Mormon concept of immortality called "translation". I may need some help with that. But then again, maybe not, I just don't know yet, still (and always will be) moving *forward*.

M: Enjoy the day, I'm glad you are at your son's. I still don't understand your drama and mystery about getting there this time though, you've been there many times before, why should this time be so different?

Jen: I don't understand this question.

M: The answer is to tell me about the spiritual experiences you had that caused you to leave for California exhausted late at night and wanting a spirit guide to travel with you so you could heal your "broken heart." You leave that hanging as a secret mystery. I am suggesting that we do not keep secrets from each other if we are going to become co-creators of my/our dream.

M: Yes indeed, I'm still writing books, and you if you will are the new 'Suzanne' who draws from me my many musings, I feel the rhythm of Muse as I write.

M: I heard from Jackie today.

Karen: EXCELLENT RESPONSE! After reading your current profile, I'm sorry I dropped you as I did. You seem both sincere and playful...... the perfect combo. In the first version of my online dating profile, years ago, I stated my wish for a playmate..... until I realized it often created the wrong impression. But it's actually true. I want someone to *play* with! All other ingredients could be there, in good measure, but I would not be happy w/o playfulness.

So, what was I writing yesterday? Something about Seattle.... My daughter and her husband think I should live in Seattle. They see me as an "out and about" type, who loves to be around people and loves city culture. True enough, sometimes, but Seattle has horrendous traffic, too many cars, long distances to drive, and not enough parking spaces. I prefer to play the country girl, given that I work for myself, want to grow my own veggies, berries, herbs and nuts (maybe chickens too, and maybe even a dwarf goat - for the cheese), and relish "small, slow and quiet". It would be nice to have both, but one has to get far from Seattle before the rat race fades, and real countryside emerges. Also, here I am nearer the high (still snow-capped!) mountains - another fav. of mine. Of course there's water absolutely everywhere!

I guess I've lost the thread. Can we say the ball is in your court? I'm sure that would get me back on a roll. However, please remember I don't have WI FI back at the cabin. Looking forward to more words, and standing up a little straighter.

M: Your altitude works just fine for me Karen. It's all relative, my ex was only 5'2" and we're still friends even though I suppose I must have 'stooped to conquer' a time or two too many over the married years from her perspective. (Did that come out as "tutu", where's my mind at around you?) I too need to play and am hoping for someone lovely like you who will throw sand around in my sandbox with careless even reckless abandon. That would be exceedingly delicious after having been turned from poet to businessman for too many years by said ex, she only being the responsible gal she is, it worked while it did.

Let me run the following idea by you, I think it's within protocol because we already have (virtual) history you and I. Summer is swiftly fleeing and my desire is to explore Vancouver Island while the weather is optimum, including going as far north as the highway does. I would very much like to have a fun companion along with me for that adventure. You know how Law of Attraction works, you no sooner get the desire than several roads open up to choose from, most likely all of them good. So there are already several women in my mind, including one very specific message that came in yesterday from someone I'd never heard from before, her very first message:

> *"Hello! You get around! My kind of man.... I'd love to do more traveling, but most of my friends are either married or otherwise engaged... LOL. Are you into road trips on our fair Island? Care to meet for a coffee halfway... say Duncan?".* And others.

But I'm particularly interested in you Karen, we speak the same language, and your mischievous photo on the beach makes me think you would be great fun, exactly what I am longing for right now, and so it seems are you. Interested in traveling with me? Bold enough to come to Victoria where we'd stay (my place, or you could get a hotel if you prefer) three or four days walking and talking and deciding if we are compatible enough and want to go the distance for a few weeks with my car? (Maybe a week or so at a time, several days back in Victoria in between when you could visit family if you want, then on an Island road together again until weather sets in or we tire of the journey and decide to play house now and then, or not. Cabo in January maybe?)

Candidly, I don't want to marry again but who knows what might come for us by way of friendship or a lovely long term relationship during such an adventure? Victoria is so close to your family that you'd be ideally poised to see them anytime when you come to Victoria for visits. (I think it's only 2 1/2 hours by ferry between Anacortes and Sidney.) Anyway Karen, summer is fleeing fast and all the metaphysical people are saying (as I'm experiencing too) that time is now sped up, we live a week in a day. So I'm bold to ask for your candid comments and questions on the above idea. Enjoy the day sweetie.

Karen: Oh... of course I didn't realize you had other women in the wings. You are certainly handsome enough... and obviously intelligent, and adventuresome. I did wonder.... I'm sorry to say I can't take off from my house-hunting. I need to find a place while the weather is mild enough for me to live in the unheated cabin on Whidbey. I think you should travel with the lady who wrote to you out of the blue. She sounds great. And if you develop "a relationship", she'll be within much easier reach. I am sad, but you need not be! My best wishes.

M: Thanks Karen. I'm disappointed of course, you were my first choice. I even thought if it 'clicked' for us you might want to live here for the winter and wait to buy a house. But maybe when you are better settled we could meet. Enjoy the summer, keep in touch.

Back to the drawing board.... And rewriting/condensing the book which today August 15th, 2014 I named *"Becoming Adam"* a series.

Chapter 22

Jackie (yes, Jackie!) Dearest Michael; Yes, we met and had a beautiful, powerful connection and I thoroughly enjoyed our time together Michael. You were kind, considerate, gentle, a great communicator, intelligent, and good looking! I did not find anything "wrong" with you in my estimation. There is just a disconnect with expectations and needs. That certainly doesn't make either one of us wrong or right.... just not workable for each other.

If you had lived closer, perhaps I would've gone to the beach with you Sunday evening to watch the full moon... it was spectacular! However, I didn't feel it was fair for you to come all the way to Nanaimo only to then return to Victoria a couple hours later. Also, I began to feel "squeezed" into seeing you which would've left me feeling a need to please you rather than pleasing myself. My daughter had her three nephews and a niece staying over at the house since they were experiencing some very difficult situations at home. So, we decided to take them to the beach and spend that evening with them.... something I felt was important for all of us. Also, you must remember that I was then going to have a small surgical procedure the next day and had to be prepared. I was at the hospital all of Monday with my daughter bringing me home Monday evening. My reaction to the anesthetic was not good at all and I was very sick Monday night and all day Tuesday going into Wednesday. There was no way I wanted to come to Victoria or deal with your notes to me. Only yesterday did I begin feeling better again.

It wasn't my intention to be silent but I do have a life here and many other things take priority at times. I felt nauseated by my surgery and even more nauseated by your need to have me respond to you in a manner you felt you needed. I felt a disconnect from you within your words of what you needed from me. Michael, I'm truly not the one who can give up myself in wild abandon for what you want life to be for you. I am truly devoted to my spirituality and that includes all of life... responsibilities here and giving as much love as I can to these children who are suffering. Whatever your beliefs are around that doesn't matter to me, only how I feel about myself and my life here. I'm not looking very hard for a relationship and am not in need of anyone at this time. I would like someone close by to hang out and with whom I can discover self on a reflective basis, but I don't want to make someone my be all and end all for his sake! A nice balance would do. Whether I find that person or not is not mandatory for me since there are plenty of relationships in my life to reflect on.

And that's why I'm letting go of our budding relationship as I know there is not a balance there that would suit either one of us. We would only make each other miserable and unhappy in trying to fill needs and expectations as requirements for each other. I've given up myself in relationships before and am not interested in doing it again! I know there are plenty of women out there who are spiritual, capable and able to have a relationship with you in the way you desire. I truly wish you the best in life and hope you write your book someday! That is pure creative talent. Take good care. Namaste. Jackie

M: Thank-you so much for your thoughtful message Jackie. I had a great hope with you, it will always be with fondness that I think of the brief time we had together. For me it was like magic sometimes. Sure there were things we didn't like in each other but I've never before experienced such feelings as I did when we kissed. I think you misunderstood me a lot, I was driven by your lack of communication having no idea what you were going through when you had told me you'd be coming to Victoria to be with me, and then nothing.

You speak so seriously about me as if I was trying to claim you for myself forever when it was not so, I never want to marry again. I thought we were going to travel the Island a bit, have fun, maybe meet now and again after that. I don't mean to make you feel negative about this but as evidence of my sincerity I even bought a car with you in mind. Except for an outing with family it has been sitting unused while I waited to hear from you. (Amazing that we were even at the same beach same time, in addition to all the other 'twin-like' things we observed about each other.) I deliberately stopped thinking of and feeling for you quite some time ago, thinking (correctly it seems) that you did not want to be with me. But just now my soul went out to you again for a brief moment. What we had I think could come back swiftly for us if misunderstandings were discussed and cleared away.

Should you ever think you'd enjoy a few days with me with no commitments beyond that, please let me know, I'd like that. If I was available in your schedule I'd come to you instantly, or my time and place would be yours for the duration you had in mind. But your absence thrust me right back into writing mode. I am currently condensing twelve now unpublished books into one and enjoying it. I met a clairvoyant a few days ago, she did a 'reading' and almost instantly, without me even telling her I was a writer asked about "the book". She went on about it being time now for the book to emerge and that in time it would be "super huge" her words, she was deeply impressed. So "vacation's" off, but a few days or a week now and again with a lovely one I connect with would be wonderful should it ever become a mutual desire. I think we'd strengthen and renew each other to better travel the individual paths that are uniquely ours. I am not wanting to possess you and monopolize your time as you seem to think I am, just to have fun and renewal with you when you have the time and the desire. Take care dear heart, love life, we really don't *have* to end like this, please reconsider if you will...

I am thinking now that it would be much to my advantage to have just one or two lovers that I'd get together with now and again rather than a live-in such as I was thinking of for Karen. That way I'd still have time to be a writer, I'd be retaining the vision of several wives, and I'd still be free... Regarding Karen, I don't think she is ready to be with a man, she may have some health problems, maybe just wants a pen pal? Whatever, I feel calm about it all right now. It would be lovely if Jackie and I would be occasional lovers, as I suggested in my response to her. Ready for one or two more Michael? Especially one lovely one I could walk to who would welcome my soft knock on her door anytime of the night? Best of all become immortal Michael, then you can have your pick of the world and would know which ones would be yours almost forever! But now, in real time, with the thought of having two or more lovers in the area, of course Law of Attraction responds.

Carrie: did you have good visits with all your family??? anything new and exciting? sending a hug, carrie

M: Good visits thanks. I was hoping to take a break but felt prompted a few days ago to unpublish the twelve e-books and edit/ rewrite to make them into one book. That should pleasantly occupy the next few months... Did you get to Victoria in your recent travels? It's such a beautiful city but it does take a bit of getting used to the much colder temps after living in the south for so many years. Are you still pressured about the house you are living in being sold or you otherwise needing to move? Hopes? Dreams? Plans?

Carrie: glad to hear all went well with your family and also that you have a new direction for the book… keep me posted on how that's going… since we were last in touch, there's been a wonderful new man who's come into my life… can't remember if i told you anything about him yet and too lazy right now to go back through old emails… but, i am in serious like and both our comparative astrological chart (which he ran) and a tarot reading i did point to a special connection and very possible future… almost a destined one… so we'll see… having a great time so far as we are sooo aligned, have so much in common and are really appreciating the connection and conversations…

my house is officially on the market, though not listed yet… i have a potential buyer in a neighbor who already has 3 houses on our road and i'm hoping he will be the answer... he's "very" interested, though in toronto where he's selling his 5 million dollar house there after the recent loss of his partner... going to send his contractor over to see what need to be repaired/improved but we priced the house to seel quickly, so it looks good… then there will be a 60 to 90 day closing, giving me time to find another place if need be… or who knows, i may end up leaving here altogether... my new friend will be starting a new job in belize and i wouldn't be opposed to moving there… even starting to think of just letting go of all my furniture… sacred possessions until before the trip... now everything is open and on the table… a whole new beginning has great appeal and all this stuff is emotionally tied to my ex anyway...

i've been to victoria before but not on this trip… remember i lived in WA for 20 years… the weather there is no biggie for me… i love the cooler climes… keeps me more awake… so… all in all, things are wonderful, exciting, expanding and unknown for me… all good hugs, carrie

M: That *is* hopeful Carrie, thanks for sharing. I'll expect along with you for everything to work out wonderfully for you from now until forever, *I wish that upon you.* It's strange but wondrous how sometimes we allow a tiny something to move in our brain or attitude or whatever and instantly the past is done, done brilliantly from the new perspective, and Spring has arrived, we breathe again. We're designed for chronic happiness, it's just that sometimes we let ego get in the way for a little while, thinking that we can serve it up better than our higher selves can. When we relax, trust and let go it invariably comes along, was there waiting all along, just around that corner we hadn't yet turned, paused too long looking back over our shoulder for something that never was there.

Time to brush up on your Belizean 'English' do you think? There's a whole lot of American standard development going on there should that appeal to you, not a shabby place to be at all. Create something new and unique for the tourists to share perhaps? Last time I was there on a cruise ship there wasn't much choice. Stay in touch my good friend, you are destined for joy - with your name on it that's already written in the stars. But enjoy your unknowns too, that's the funnest part of life, to forget that it's we ourselves who are creating it, and observe what the best part of us dishes up next, it's always good. Mmm, loving my dark chocolate with touch of sea salt. Can you get such delights where you are?

M: Jackie, I'm not planning to bug you with emails but since we have some (delightful) history in our beginnings I wanted to reach out and let you know that I realize now that my task for the next several months is to write a book. So the lengthy road trips etc. I talked about are out for this year, maybe Cabo in January. But with busyness comes a need for times of refreshing and I'm wondering if you too need those and would like to occasionally share two or three or so days at a time with me in Victoria? We'd forget the world for a while, walk and talk, hold hands and cuddle the nights away, have fun just the two of us, no commitments beyond that given time. I'd even come and get you each time and return you the moment you decide it's time to get back to your home and family and your chosen work. Does that appeal to you?

M: Jen, All those colored sentences between the lines are confusing at times but with long emails it's sometimes necessary. If you are going to respond between the lines again, please use the message below, it's the way I wrote it up in my journal, I did some editing and made some additional remarks.

Jen: You said you heard from Jackie. What did she say about not visiting for a couple of days.

M: In our new spirit of openness sharing and trust I am copying Jackie and my messages below. Please treat our words well, don't share them with anyone else, and don't criticize either of us for being who we are.

Carrie: yes...hope is on the rise and strong, though the hope is tempered... it really doesn't matter as i know it's as is should be and all will be revealed in good time no matter what, my changes support me and my growth... and, thanks for standing with me for the best... i don't know anything yet about belize except there are some expats here who left there because of crime... i doubt that will be much of an issue with this new school... my guess is that will be covered by the plans and cooperation with the local officials... but again who knows... the school is designed to train at risk kids into entrepreneurs... business focus but also the arts... the kids will come from the court system... those who have committed one or two minor infractions can be sent here instead of to juvie... it's the first of a number of campuses that will be built all over the world... long term project with a huge focus and very big vision... my friend has been hired as the director of photography for the whole project... anyway, i'm having fun and am excited by the prospects, though staying away from expectations at the same time... just in appreciation... have a great rest of your weekend... hugs, carrie

M: It seems like a great project Carrie. Get them working on something exciting for cruise ship tourists to do?? Anyway, just wanted you to know that those "hugs" from you still excite me even though I know you say that to all the guys. Sometimes I wish we had taken the time to meet if only for a few days. But I know I'd be outclassed intellectually so it's probably best that we didn't. Take care Carrie.

Carrie: you would NOT be outclassed in any way in my presence... just appreciated... where the hell did that come from anyway, mister LOA!

M: Much as I might want to be, I can't BE everything for everyone. But I can sure try to please... Bestest today Carrie.

Carrie: sounds as if you are in a bit of a funk... you don't need to be anything to anyone... all you need is to be just who you are... that will be more than enough for anyone who you draw in and who loves you! consider yourself hugged with a hug that's just for you today!

M: Thanks sweetie, er, you're the one who doesn't like terms of endearment aren't you... No funk, just trying to be clever with words as always, hugs back.

Carrie: i LOVE terms of endearment, just not babe! that's a pig i know and love...

Jen: The following words are something for you to think about. Maybe there is something I can say to help you in future relationships. Even my pain might open your eyes and again maybe not. You do want me to he honest and open. The comments do not include any references to your Adam dream.

Thank you for sharing this with me. For your sake I am sorry it did not work out with Jackie. I truly want you to find happiness. You just admitted to Jackie you never felt this way for any one else and you only knew her for less than three days. Of course it hurt me a little that i never heard those words in 18 years. So of course I realize I can not compete with your need for continual fancy loves. I think in time you will settle for one person but continue in your heart searching for a more perfect virtual fancy loves. I knew you were cautiously involved in having those in our marriage from time to time. Now be honest.

In your loneliness you found a place to put me under the title of comfortable to be around some times and a distant friend. I am the past of reality. I now serve a place as a back up plan. You are a bit forceful in virtual relationships you seek after. I don't see your personality being that way in real life but I haven't heard your conversations with the women you spent time with and have loved this past year. Can you believe it has been a year. You wasted no time. It must hurt to continue to be hopeful even though you say you put her out of your mind, when you really haven't given up. In our relationship you would tell me you did not think of me when I was gone and it hurt me so much. Yet I dared not tell you. You never apologize for your lack in the relationship. Maybe you blamed me. (Sorry I get a little emotional when I think of what I missed in our relationship that I desperately wanted.) You mostly expressed if I lost weight it would make our marriage for you. Is that really true. Would it of made me a different person? Maybe I am saying these things to keep me grounded. I want a man to say to me what you wrote to her. I don't expect it to happen over night it would require time well spent together. And I will play my part well to make it happen. A love of a life time is what I want. It will be everything I missed in my marriages. Even I can fantasize and dream and yearn.

Jackie hit it on the nail. *Michael, I'm truly not the one who can give up myself in wild abandon for what you want life to be for you.* That is a powerful statement. What does she mean "give up myself in wild abandon". She sees a bigger picture than just a two week trip. I will have to admit she is a very intelligent women to see clearly what she wants in her life. How kind she is in her responses to you in the manner she did. How could she be any clear in her position without being nasty.

You asked me to be honest. This is it. I will continue to be your good friend but you will never have me as a wife, lover or companion ever again. Why! because it has to be your way or not at all. I am not up to open relationships. I want one man that deeply loves me in this life. That does not mean I don't love you or want to be your dear friend. That does not mean I judge your relationships and I truly want you to be in a happy state and again thank you for sharing with me. I also am learning much about me. When you hurt deeply I hurt deeply. There must come a day this no long is. How do you relate me to Suzanne. What does Suzanne represent?

Below is another compilation with Jen responding to my message later and me including her responses below my original paragraphs as if the conversation had happened in real time.

M: Interesting comments Jen, and not unusual that a few words I write could have so much power as to turn you from lover to NEVER AGAIN meaning we will most likely never even see each other ever again. I seem to have a way of doing that to women, that's exactly what happened with Jackie, she rejected me because of words that I wrote to her in my burning desire to be with her again. It's a familiar pattern.

Jen: What have you learned about the way you go after romances?

M: But those words of yours will dampen my enthusiasm for what I thought was the new you too. Men are driven by sexual desire, it's hugely enormously motivating, exceedingly useful, I would never have traveled or written my books without it. And western women are driven by the notion of a woman possessing a man exclusively for herself, as you wish to do even though I explained over and over why I must be as I am to be "Adam." And I thought you understood.

Jen: Yes I understood you want to be Adam. Did you forget, Adam is not a reality for you in this dispensation. I was never asking you to be my one and only. I was being honest with you and letting you know what my heart desires. I listened with a open mind and entertain your thoughts and desires to be with many women. Now I know you don't want my honesty.

M: But ok, it's your choice to never be with me ever again, that's clear and I must respect it.

Jen: If I repulse you so why would it matter to you.

M: I wish you the very best becoming who you want to be and who you want to be that with.

Jen: Thank you.

M: "Suzanne", the real life hospice nurse in Texas, was the woman who turned me into a fiction writer, and almost devastated me in the process. Because of her frequent rejection I had to learn how to grow a thicker skin, a better protected heart. She it was who with a few words or sentences would elicit from me long 'rampages' of philosophical thought, thought that may someday be found important by some. And you, as you should have observed from the lengthiness and the serious content of what I wrote in response to your messages, were becoming the replacement for Suzanne in my ongoing writing.

Jen: The book does not read as fiction.

M: Now I don't think we can continue, I cannot trust you with my words anymore. And I *must* have the thought of you being sexually desirable and within the realm of possibility that we'd share the same bed again. Now you have shattered that dream so I don't know where I am with "Suzanne." But right now it doesn't matter much anyway because I'll be busy for many weeks rewriting what was already written, just too long. I'm sure Law of Attraction will come up with another "Suzanne" when the time is ripe for that.

Jen: Suzanne was a virtual reality woman you fell in love with that sent you into long rampages. As you quoted. Then when you meet each other in reality neither of you like what you saw. I am not a replacement for Suzanne. I am Jen. Anything she has to offer you in your writings is hopefully to help lift your thoughts and help put the puzzle back together solidly. To not trust me with words is your choice. I have not betrayed your words or shared your writings with anyone.

How could I share a bed with you when I know how undesirable you felt I was. Why would that change just because I am thin. I really don't understand. Even though I am finally loosing the weight I desire to loose. How could I trust such trivial thinking that I am loved and desired. The adventure we had together in Victoria I thought once was a joyous time for us has now become a painful memory now that I know I was so unappealing and embarrassed you. I think deep inside I knew and did not want to believe it. Please strike out all phrase of me thinking it was a fun and joyous time. Enjoy your search for a new Suzanne. I am not her, I am Jen.

M: When you say you were "hurt" because I would tell you I did not think of you when you were gone, that was because I was actually doing you a favor in a way. I know the power of the mind and I wanted you to be free of my mental influence so you could freely make your own choices for or against me. But of course I still thought of you, it was just a (from my point of view) 'noble' gesture on my part. *All along I was hoping you'd choose ME* even though you knew there must be others too in the eternities, just as there are for Joseph Smith and Brigham Young. (As I keep repeating because I know you still cling to the Mormon dream - I am trying to speak to you in a language you understand.)

Jen: Why would anyone think that. When people love each other they want their love ones to be thinking of them. I was referring to when we were married. I did choose you almost 20 years ago. That is when we meet and started our life together. I did choose you. (I also secretly want to be back into your life as soon as I possibly could but not now that I know my kisses were not welcomed.)

M: You ask if you lost weight if it would have made a difference. YES, I told you over and over and over again during our marriage that it would have been so. It remains extremely important to me that the women in my life romantically not be greatly overweight. I love a shapely slim to average woman in jeans, my eyes would follow her around unceasingly, admiring her form, pleased and proud to be loved by her, to be seen with her. YES Jen, it was extremely important to me that you take care of your body and make it pleasing to me, you knew what would do that. And yes, that's what I 'sent' you home from Victoria to do, to lose weight mainly. I was unable to fulfill your sexual wants while you were here primarily because of that, your physical body had not changed, your kisses were not so promising as Jackie's were, the feelings were not so tender. Much as I loved what the new you did to me I did not see you as sexy. Sorry if that 'hurts' you again but it's the truth, that's just the way I am, you knew that.

Jen: I already look good in jeans. So you invite me to Victoria and found me repulsive and sent me home because of that. Oh great, that's really feel good. Yes it brings great pain to my heart. It makes me feel really bad. What hole did you climb out of. Why did you lead me on in word and action, like you wanted me but inside you were rejecting me because I have a overweight body that you were well aware of for many years. What a fool I played, what a fool you made of me. I have never regretted and been so ashamed of us as I am now. You played your part well and made me the fool". No wonder your daughter told me to go home and enjoy my grandchildren. Could she see your intent. Then to tell me my kisses were not so promising as Jackie's. When you rub something in you rub it deep. I hope you enjoy the pain you sent.

M: You can't seem to understand that you will never be a "back up" for me because you have an open invitation to be a part of my Adam and Eve family. Regardless of how many or how few other women will also be sister wives, you are included among them if you choose to be, that's not a "back up". And in this lifetime, if you had been ok with me being with other women occasionally and concurrently, and if you took better care of your physical body, it is possible that we could have lived together again had you wanted to. Now you have shattered that hope.

Jen: You shattered that as ever being a possibility for me also now that I know my visit was not real.

M: You ask what Jackie means by saying *"give myself up in wild abandon"*. My desire when I met her was to travel and vacation for a year, I told her that. I told her that I was deeply spent, physically and emotionally drained, worn right out from many months on the road alone with constantly pressing unfulfilled needs, divorce, loneliness, financial concerns, frequently rejected by the women I reached out to for love and relief, writing 18 hours a day. I told her that I wanted to just forget the world and asked her to with careless abandon let go and be with me as if we were little children playing in a sandbox, our only purpose being to have *fun* together. (She told me that was what she wanted/needed too - to have fun - I was making it possible.)

Jen: What scared her off? There had to be something more to this.

M: Since then responsibilities have crowded in upon me again and I am back writing, thinking of myself as being 'a man on a mission', the mission being to produce a book that will in time become 'super huge' in its impact on contemporary thinking, specifically teaching people that they can become immortal and live a thousand years or more, as it will be during the Millennium - even Mormons know that. I believe that it could be that way right now. *Why not?*

Jen: Don't forget it was my information that reminded you of what you once knew.

M: I didn't think when I sent you a copy of my and Jackie's emails that you would judge me so harshly and allow that foolishness on my part (I trusted you when I sent it) to influence you so strongly that because of that single email I sent you you have now decided that "I WILL NEVER HAVE YOU AS A WIFE, LOVER OR COMPANION EVER AGAIN!!!"

Jen: I did not judge you harshly for either emails. This not about those emails. You did not like my decision of realizing I was undesirable to you in this life. I also secretly wanted to be back in your life as soon as I possibly and now know it was a pipe dream when one is called undesirable.

M: Then so be it Jen, you have chosen - you can never be the strong devoted one behind this writer, the woman who makes him so great...

Jen: That I did want. That is to be the woman behind the writer, that makes him so great..... and still do but can not bear knowing what you said is not true. I am not on equal grounds in your eyes with Jackie. You stated she was much more desirable. If Jackie and I were both your wives you Adam would be a living liar.

M: So, understand clearly that your choice means that you have opted out of my dream of us and beloved others living together forever and populating planets with our dear children, and also that we will never again be together in this lifetime.

Jen: If this is your wish. How could I trust you again. My heart is so broken from the lie I found out you were being with me in Victoria I don't care. Should of known you could not stand being near me and that was why you sent me home. Yearning for a woman about to reject you. I am sorry you had to experience that pain. I understand, it is called karma.

M: Quite a powerful email I sent you today wasn't it.... I wish you the very best Jen, take care sweetheart, I wanted you, let me know if you ever change your mind.

The following is a second email from Jen. I did not respond to it, it came in as I was sleeping.

Jen: I shattered your hopes of me and You shattered my heart. I realize you think you need to search for women. Also I am aware I am no where as equal in your eyes as Jackie. What I can not handle. First you sending me home because you see me as being so undesirable and embarrassing. Second, I spent a week in a lie. Now that I realize how you felt when you looked at me. Leaves me with almost unbearable feelings of shame and hurt that I would be with such a man.

Why does your earthly Adam tell this lie of equality. I am glade that the women thus far you got involved with saw you clearer than I. The next two you thought were going to be your sister wives are gone. None of this is about the email Jackie sent you or the one you sent her. it is what you said to me. When you can stop loving yourself so much and start loving those around you *more* there might just be a mighty change in your world and the real Adam might rise into being. I now need time to mend my heart is really hurting tonight.

I recall being impressed with a phrase I read in my youth that went something like this: *"The Universe steps aside to let pass a man who knows where he is going."* I must never be swayed by the influence of any other who tries to make my world into their own image and likeness. Jen sees my world only through her own Jen-tinted glasses. That's normal. BUT I AM BECOMING ADAM!

"It matters not where my consciousness centers in this life or the next, or what anyone teaches differently, or however I may be challenged and criticized by others who see it differently and want to sway me to their way of seeing it, or who say my dream is impossible. As my soul roams the universe it will always be with the utmost thought and fixed determination that I am becoming or that I AM Adam!

Only in that manner can I create the reality I want for myself. Only with that strength can I attract the Woman to me who shares my dream exactly.

That's what I want, that's what I am becoming regardless of any other soul who would tempt and beckon me into worlds of their own choosing. I am not theirs, they are not mine. The gods keep the timing, when the time is right for me, my well-beloved Eve will appear, and we will be ONE..."

So let it be written, so let it be done!

Jen: May be we are not done yet. Friends

I send her the following and then send her the quote from my journal about my absolute determination to become Adam. She responds between the lines and I add those responses to my email.

M: (to Jen) You misinterpret what I write and judge me wrong yet again. I think you *want* to be "hurt" so your "poor heart" can "mend." You invent meanings in my words that are not intended but that can be loosely construed into them so that I come out as villain and you come out as victim with a delicious story to tell about how you were wronged by the man you were married to for almost two decades. I say it the way it is for me and you say *"no, you meant something else."* (My first wife was an expert at the very same thing.)

Jen: Why are the two women whom you spent 95% of your adult life with in your mind this way. Why so much miss communication from your point of view? Why did the other women quickly disappear. I might experience the same when I start dating. Why do you think I have a desire to be a victim with a delicious story to tell? That's your point of view not mine. I avoid that like the plague. Sorry, but my self pity seems to all comes down on you.

M: I loved you sincerely when you were here. I loved every moment of you when you were in bed with me. But because your body is so overweight I stayed in the past where we had been for many years, loving to make love with you but not even wanting to glance at your vagina because I knew there'd be an unsightly mass of flesh between me and where that was. I was absolutely delighted however in everything else.

Jen: I believe you love me as long as I fit into your mold. After the comments you just made above. How could you expect any women to have passion for you after those comments. I would feel way to self conscious of my body now. We are both old and nothing between the two of us looks very good and never will in this life. Your skin sags also. I will lose weight for me not you. I am a dress size down now and will look great when I go down one more I will feel great, than another size. The man I marry will love me enough that my old sagging body won't matter.

M: I compared you to Jackie because I am open and honest and because you told me you didn't have a problem with me being with her, in fact you seemed at times to be encouraging that. At the time she was new and exciting so your kisses couldn't compare. But that doesn't mean I didn't enjoy your kisses, I did. I was hugely encouraged because you had become 'good' in bed, I wanted you.

Jen: I have no problems with Jackie. But I am a sensitive woman. Thanks for clearing that up a bit.

M: You are welcome to come back here and try it all over again if you want to, but my guess is that much as you keep disregarding it and finding blame in everything but that, for me to be right back with you the way we were when we were courting in the beginning, you'll have to lose that excess weight and make your body look physically good to me. Like it or not that's just a fact, that's the way it is with me and I'm not likely to change that attitude, I'm happy with me the way I am.

Jen: I also want to try again but have fears. Yes sweet heart the problem is you liking yourself the way you are. It is a unhealthy attitude you held onto most of you're life. This has effect all the women in your life. When are you going to get out of this immature boyish faze and begin to see as a mature man sees. My heavens you are getting on in years now. The universe is going to keep sending you fat women until you get it right. They will never have a thin woman for very long. It is part of your karma. This could be changed just like that. It is your thinking that gets in the way of your relationships. Your actions with money is another Karma that is coming back to bit you.

M: But I've learned again and again that it is not good to be open and honest with you because you twist my words to make me into something that I am not. You most likely do that now so you can justify being overweight and so you can play poor hurting victim. Keep in mind that it was YOU who filed for divorce, not me. That's an undeniable fact regardless of how you want to change the story to you being victim of a heartless man, a man you now say you never want to see again.

Jen: I did not have to tell any stories to any one. They could see for themselves. Even some of your kids are glade you are not in my life because of the path they see you have taken. Don't get me wrong they love you and want you to be happy but are waiting for you to come back. I wonder what stories you have told. First of all you wanted out of the marriage and that's why you left. You considered your self a single man the moment you walked out the door. Don't forget you left first, cut me out of the company that I co founded and financed, and then ran off to hid while creating great amounts of debt to finance your dabbling in virtual fantasies. Is that the making of a mature sounded man. Any women in her right wind would file for divorce unless she also wanted to be a victim and reap his consequences. We were far from being financially sound for retirement. We both have and will suffer from your decision for the rest of our lives. Ok it is over and I will adjust to a better place. Will you.

M: Lose the weight my darling, then come back to me if I'm still available and you've changed your mind, and let's see what we can become together then.

Jen: My heart says yes, yes, yes I want to come back and I will be thin that is if I am available. We can create so much together. Or, stick to your stated choice and stay away from me forever. That's what you said you wanted, *but I'm not so sure...*

Jen: That's not a bad choice either. There is so much in my world to desire. We spent many year in the same world mostly good and some not so good. That's the world of being a couple. We grow, learned from each other's mistakes. It seems we are not done with each other yet. Let make sure we are leading each other to a higher state and help smooth those bumps in the road..... Remembering along the way we will be picking up the pieces of each others hurts. Even now we are helping each other see things clearer.

We like being around each other. I now see my world much improved. It will be sometime before we let go completely of each other or become whole with in each other's world. I am sorry that it did not work out for you with Jackie and I will try to remember where I see my self fitting or not. I will learn to work on my own quest and not try to fit my emotions into yours wants. Found they shoot me down after time. They must be my wants just as Jackie explained her wants that are a priority. Her wants are much more admirable than a trip to please a man. All though it could of still been if she wanted it. She is following her destiny and who she is becoming. It is not unusual for people our age to realize their family relationships are the most important gift they can leave this earth.

M: Meanwhile, forget the "hurt" it doesn't move me, you bring it on yourself, you can remove it with a little click of your mind. Life is meant to be happy, entertain only happy thoughts, tell the story the way you really *want* it to be, you are not a victim except of yourself. I've told you often that your fight is not with me, it's with *yourself*.

Jen: You are right but do you have to add the negative part over and over.

M: Enjoy the day sweetie, be happy, life's hugely worth living, it's even fun, *enjoy, enjoy, enjoy...*

Jen: I really do wish you the same... Enjoy... enjoy.... enjoy I will enjoy this day, my son always plans a exciting day each Sunday for the women in his life plus his new son. It always starts with a big breakfast he cooks for us.

M: You continue to judge me 'wrong' and put me down, trying to mold me into the image you think is 'right'. But that's the way you and most people are. I do not believe in "karma", in my opinion it's a hugely destructive notion that most likely causes enormous numbers of believers to think they are unworthy of receiving the good things in life because of something somebody thinks they have done wrong in this life or in some previous lifetime. And because they think they are 'unworthy' and are just getting back what they 'deserve' they give up creating a happy life for themselves moment by moment, each new moment potentially being the beginning of a new life for them if they should choose for that to be. Each human being is empowered and entitled to forget the past and choose a new life each moment they are disappointed in the moment that came before, and in that choosing choose HAPPINESS for the rest of their life.

That's how I see it, and as for me, I will always choose to focus only on happy thoughts each new moment because I believe (as did Joseph Smith) that we *exist* to know fullness of joy. So be *happy* Jen, that's what I wish upon you, and upon myself and my family forever.

I send her the quote mentioned above and wait, not anxiously because I can let go the past and everyone/everything in it if need be to become Adam. (Yeah, right, good story, working on it....)

Jen: I started to make corrections to my last email meaning, I did not make my self clear. I made the changes in a darker black. Oh I do not have time to correct my other mistakes and make myself clearer. With out a proper desk or mouse. My curser popes around and I find I am writing in the wrong place way to often. Don't always catch it.

Jen: Yes, you told me you were going to tell me like it is and be honest with me, You did so I responded back like wise.

M: So all is 'forgiven' then and we're even, but does it remain your desire never to be with me again?

Jen: The truth is I will probliblly always have a side to me that desires to be with you. At this time in my life it is way way way to strong. I want to be with you so bad and jump into your arms and smoother you with kisses. Hold your hand and walk beside you. But also scared to be with you in fear of disappointing you and not being the one that can fill your cup. Being thin is not a fix it all. You found that to be true with your second wife.

M: Lovely, my door is open to you, you could have what you want for the choosing if you'd give up feeding your fears and in your imagination create instead life the way you really want it to be. However, you misunderstand because you are immersed in the western notion of monogamy. There is not ONE woman who fills my cup, there are several, always will be, and we're all equal. And yes, my becoming Adam *is* for this "dispensation". It's just that current Mormon leaders do not accept the principle of one man and several wives that was taught by both Joseph Smith and Brigham Young. They don't because monogamy is politically correct. The 'commandment' to live polygamously was never retracted by the Giver, just set aside because of destructive force threatened by the crop of politicians then reigning in the USA. My guess is that polygamy would be accepted by today's politicians. I'm really not so 'far out' as you seem to think I am, just a bit ahead of the times, as visionaries always are. My second wife and I had other issues, it had nothing to do with overweight, with you and me it does.

I'm really hoping to find an occasional (not live in) lover friend to settle down with exclusively in between writing books. I'm guessing that

I insulted Jackie with my last email. She's not wanting sex or a lover right now I don't think, so that final email of mine most likely didn't settle well with her at all. If nothing else it should provide the justification (if any is needed) to never contact me again. The way I see it, yes I'm looking after my own interests, but I also thought it would have been a *mutually* beneficial arrangement for us to have with each other and should have fit into her expressed desires, especially when I was willing to do all the driving between Nanaimo and Victoria. It really doesn't matter to non-Mormons does it, for a woman to take a man to her bed for a couple of nights, part as friends, and then never want to see him again. But in a way I'm pleased because there was a lot about Jackie that I would have preferred different if she was to be my exclusive lover. Sure wanted to taste those kisses again, and feel what finer feelings came as we hugged. I guess she's gone....

Jen: Questions about choice of road to travel and obstacles that keep us stuck. OR "Will all roads lead to Rome?" Regarding what you said about the quote and what you want: Being said, Women are from Venus and Men from Mars. Do you really think the intelligent women will travel only your road and think just as you do in the beginning of this journey. Even your thinking is going to change and has changed as you progress to becoming an Adam. Moving toward making your worlds a reality. Would you consider including strong women that have their own thoughts that take a different road that would be more satisfying to them with a mutual purpose. As a result reaching the same end that would allow pure harmony. These desires would allow some of the most supreme of women to follow, including me. Is that not the type of women you want to attract. Those that co-create at the highest level. An evolution of changes for better understanding until it becomes a knowing. Meaning the pure love (light) of Christ. Meaning live in a manner that allows that light to shine so bright an average man could not look at it. Yet those of like will be drawn. We are told all really good people will be ushered into the Millennium with many types of beliefs and religions. Free agency will be in place. All will see the truth and eventually be of one mind.

We all have obstacles that hold us in one way or another. Sometimes to long of a delay. When we are ready to move forward the obstacles will move aside. So what position are we in now that is holding us back from future knowledge that moves us forward. How much new light do we want or are ready to receive. My logical mind starts from the beginning learning what is necessary to make the end complete. Learning the lessons that reassure you are on the right path. That gives the right answers. To me this chosen path is a creation inside our selves necessary to form wisdom beyond measure. One of the requirement to be a God. Thus this will show the path for others to follow that desire it. Have you ever felt you needed guidance. My question to you is are you or me, and others putting the ox before the carte? I believe to much talk of the end often frightens to many wonderful candidates off. Maybe start with just attracting like light to like light. Let it flow one step at a time.

Let us discuss more in the future "what gifts we think a God possesses that make him a God." For now what lessons and obstacles are keeping us stuck in present time. I believe it is an individual journey but there are teachers along the way. "When the student is ready the teacher will appear" I have always loved this quote. How does one know if he is stuck and keeping the teacher away? What are the signs? Will a time come that issues trials for our benefit that will help us see the direction we are headed in order to dismiss those obstacles. Then more light will flow. Stay grounded.

M: Very well written Jen, I'm impressed, bet you took your time doing it, I always do with mine. And well thought out too, deserving of comment. I am not asking anyone to follow me. I'm not asking for that because like attracts like, or as you aptly put it: *"like light attracts like light"*. There is no need for all of us in our immortal family to cling together in mortality. Though we *could* if we found each other. We could discuss and co-create as mortals the world/s we mutually want when we become immortal. But regardless of our individual paths, we WILL be together when the moment is right because like automatically attracts its own when choices are made and allowed to be.

I am male and have a different role than you do, I don't want you to be like me. My sister wives are each becoming Eve, I am becoming Adam, we're equal but different, parts of the same body. There is no doubt that we will each travel different paths as we climb to the same mountain peak. We are individual souls with different preparations to make to become ready for our own unique part in the harmony that will be ours. I can hardly wait to get to know each of you when we are immortal. I know you are all beautiful and that you'll each love each other and your Adam. We are going to delight and marvel in each other's unique talents and skills, perfection and beauty. We'll praise God for the magnificent plan that prepared us, brought us together, and made us ONE.

In my emerging role as "Becoming Adam", my light, my strength, the beat of my drum calling, must be sufficient that each of you can hear that mystic throb and come to me your mountain peak when the moment is ripe. I must be *myself* as I become your Adam Jen, don't try to change me from my path or thrust imagined weakness upon me, it only harms yourself. Your struggle is with yourself, you could instead of fight and wonder simply grasp the next moment as the beginning of a new life of your own creating, forgetting that which came before. *What do you want?*

You are still hung up I think on power and control when it's really all about love and light and BEING. I am not seeking to control anyone, I am seeking to attract to me those who are like me the way I am and the way I am becoming. I am seeking to attract those lovely ones who are sure of *themselves*, not needing to cling to or control any other. Think upon that because you tend to make a 'straw man' out of me, then tear that down when it never was me in the first place, just your own image of me and your desire to shape and mold me instead of yourself. I am not "stuck" Jen, nor should you be. I flow with each new moment, loving life, who I am, and who I am becoming without effort other than to *allow* it to happen and rejoice as it does, giving thanks always.

I will not "stay grounded" as you suggest. I am *in* the world yes, but not of it. Grounded is the useless clinging to somebody else's notion of reality. Those who are becoming gods reject such consensus notions and create *their own* reality, their own worlds. They *"render unto Caesar"* because as mortals they must, but they also secretly render unto themselves, the god they are becoming as they grow up, spread their wings, and fly independently. Then God too is happy - one less soul to nudge along the way, one new world to add to His/Her glory.

You don't need a "teacher" Jen. I suggest that you go your own way, meditate daily (quiet your mind, use imagination to lift your vibrations) and teach YOURSELF. That would be the best way, otherwise you'd get lost in other people's words and programs and worlds and miss out on creating your own. You could also pay some attention to what this man writes to you, especially if you feel already that your final decision will be for him rather than for another man. He is not asking you to follow. He is not asking you to lead. He is asking you to be Beautiful You, fitting in *equally* with his other immortal wives when that time has come, should that be your choice. You are *loved* Jen - just be yourself, that's all we're asking of you.

You write: *"Let us discuss more in the future what gifts we think a God possesses that make him a God."* A god is God to His/Her own children and their descendants. A God is God because He/She learned somewhere in time how to be independent, how to create their OWN worlds exactly the way they wanted, with no heed to the worlds others create for themselves. Other of course than to LOVE because ultimately we are each an intimate part of the biggest 'bubble' of all - EVERYTHING! So love yourself, you are everything. Enjoy the moments and be grateful for them, relax, be happy, you are worthy, you are where you should be right now. *Then more light will flow...*

Jen: Please be always totally honest with me. That's the only way I can stay grounded myself.

M: I am always honest Jen (I do not tell lies) and lately I have been open with you too. However, now that you tell me you'll never be with me again I may not keep you in the loop so much. What would you think if I told *you* that? Would you even want me for a friend anymore? What makes you think I'm telling lies anyway? I never have and never will, that's just another 'straw man' that you create of me, "my ex *the Liar!*" Not real, not true...

Or is it that instead of "totally honest" you mean totally open, telling you everything I do? You still haven't told me why you wanted a spirit guide with you that night you left your home and made a big mystery about it. You left at 9 p.m. you said so that would have put you at your son's about 4 a.m. I'm sure that did not happen. Where did you stop along the way? How much missing time is there in your story? When did you actually get to California, was it days later? Why do you speak of stars in the desert skies? You were exhausted when you left, you felt you had to hurry somewhere. There were three spirit men with you when you left, only one when you arrived, wherever that was. Did you stop in

Las Vegas that night? Openness must work both ways, secrets always cause distrust.

Jen: Totally open. When you are ready to see me again and really want to be with me. I will do what I can to meet with you. I do want to be in the loop. I want to know about your lady friends and happening. For some reason it helps me to understand this age of dating. It keeps me on tract to loose and look better than any of them. When I am done loosing weight and if I can afford it. I may have some procedures done. I do want to look good for you and the men I date.

M: Great attitude Jen, winning attitude. And ok, you're off the hook, I'll now consider your door propped open for me should the right moment arrive. I like that, I can start thinking of you sexually again, it would be pretty much incredible for me to see you slim and slender. Already I'm thinking of inviting you back, but you've still got some home work to do I'm sure, let me know when you're ready, I hope you'll come. Take care my love, be happy, good luck with dating, your pretty face will hook them every time.

Here's some news from the last 24 hours.

I saw Lynne on the beach today, first time since I was at her home for the reading. I spoke briefly with her but she didn't seem warm so I kept on walking saying, *"I hope to see you again"*, and I do. Yes of course I find her sexually attractive. Women in Victoria are dressed the same now as when I was here in 1984, short skirts, long bare sexy legs. I like it a lot, not suppressed anymore by stern religion and fear. Lynne hasn't invited me to walk with her like she said she wanted to do when we parted at her home several days ago. Maybe she was expecting more money from me for another 'reading'? And maybe I misinterpret her, she was by herself today. I spotted her from a long ways away, just knew it was her, and I think she looked my way too at the same time, she's very sensitive and attuned, has to be to be clairvoyant. Too bad there's such an age difference or such an attitude about age, I'd love to travel with her, it would be mutually beneficial.

I walked by the second chance store in the mall across the street two days ago and instantly bought three items somebody left there exactly for me, dirt cheap. A rocking chair, a perfect desk with drawers for my printer, and a fan the perfect height and size for the living room. More Law of Attraction in action, and an easy carry back to my place, three trips. Yeah, saw Lynne today, thrilled, feel love for her sweet sensitive soul, and want for what's beneath that short sexy skirt... (Open and honest right?) You be too, please... I washed those king size sheets today, the ones you put on my bed and slept on while you made delicious love to my body, and put them back on the bed all by myself. Proud of me growing up a bit? Want to be back in bed with me? I'd like that...

A tall slim gorgeous (but wrinkled) one my age emailed her phone number to me today, wanted me to meet her at her "club". But I didn't call, suggested instead by email familiar territory for me, walk the breakwater like I always do now when meeting a woman first time. She didn't respond, not yet anyway. Not sure if I really want to meet her, could be complicated, she may walk higher social circles than I'm familiar with. I'm not wanting to learn new social protocols and conversation, will stay away from clubs and golf courses, don't need them. Another woman from Duncan, pretty blonde wants to meet me. I suggested tomorrow but she came back from exercise class today with a pulled something, so that's on hold. It's true I'm looking for a steady (not live in) lover to be exclusive with from time to time so I can get on with writing my book and still have my need fulfilled to touch and be touched, and to love and be loved.

The book's lovely, coming along real well, but will take months to get it to where I'll be really proud to publish it, it deserves my and Muse's time. I continue to go to bed early, before eleven usually, and get up about 5ish. Good night my love Jen.

Chapter 23

M: Suzanne Dear One. The new (condensed) book is coming along well and it's beautiful, the love story of Michael and Suzanne shines ever so brightly on almost each page. I've come to know that you played your part perfectly, even Las Vegas and your sudden silence was perfect though it didn't seem so at the time, at least not to me, we had to go our separate ways. You always possessed an uncanny knack for timing, knowing what was next in Michael's script as our play in time unfolds. Here's the part I'm rewriting this beautiful Victoria a.m. beside the sea.

A writer must have the freedom to *become* the characters in his book, good or bad as they may be, to LIVE their story. It's like actors and actresses, you've got to get so deep in character that you actually *believe* you are that person. Only then can you feel every emotion they feel as deeply as they do when you finally step aside and allow them to take over and write their own story. All the world's a stage and mere illusion. We're the gods who made this world to play on. We come to physicality for a time forgetting who and what we are because we love the feelings, the drama, the bigger and better games we play each time we're here. We invariably surprise ourselves with the magnificence of our performance every time we come. Yes, we love ourselves – and in that loving we *are* love.

When someone returns from physicality they come with fresh stories to tell, bring chuckles and weeping to do as we slip away from the sticky illusion of physicality and join fellow gods and goddesses around a warm campfire somewhere. There around the flames, sharing who we are we forget there's such a thing as time and space – *until we run out of stories and feelings.* At such times there's always a pause as we covertly look for each other's demeanor and higher Gods wind again their pocket watches, relishing the thought of bigger and better to come, chattering amongst themselves maybe, sharing the excitement of a new beginning. (The Gods *always* keep the timing to themselves, that's their job, it's in the contract.)

Sometimes it's a long pause at the campfires, even a very long pause, as the Gods allow our sands to run out completely and we are drained, nothing more to tell. Existence becomes stale. We have a close encounter with the thought that *an eternity of nothingness would be an eternity of boredom, and boredom is the greatest of pains.* We must play again, a bigger and better game this time. There must always be *expansion*. We can never go back, that has been the Law since the beginning of time – *and we can't find a beginning!* The seventh day has waned and gone all too soon, another day arrived already. Once again (was there ever another time?) we thrust eager willing screaming parts of ourselves into time, down to a lower world, tie ourselves to the ancient wheel within a wheel, find parts of ourselves actors and actresses on some lonely distant planet somewhere in time. But before we go, the Gods always secretly slip a forgotten penny into someone's pocket so we can get back to our campfire in the night and tell our new stories. We're stars again, stars on a stage of our own creating. We write a new play, cast new roles, learn scripts, and sign a contract to participate in time. We forget when we're there that we *are* the ancient gods, it's *delicious* that way...

> *But it hurts, it hurts a whole lot in time to be a writer deep in character.* Who could ever love Michael unless they know him as themselves?
>
> *If you give me a name, your eyes may see me with that feeling.*
> *If you give me an age, your mind may know me with that much energy.*
> *If you give me a personality; you may think you know me.*
> *Allow me to be nameless, and to be ever changing.*
> *Allow me to be ageless, and to live in this moment.*
> *Allow me to be nondescript, and to melt into your needs.*
> *If you feel you must age me, let my age be forever.*
> *If you feel you must name me, let my name be Love.*
> *If you feel you must know me, know me as Yourself.*
> Anonymous

I write almost all day and much of the night Suzanne. Creative writing brings me happiness and fulfillment. I'm free, I've got my muse and life's purpose back. I should have always been a writer but I allowed myself to get trapped in the thought that I could make money and status being *"responsible"* the thing harsh consensus reality demands of its slaves. But I've found no freedom there, only shadows of the life we *could* have had, the person we came here to be. *What, settle for a penny when we OWN planets!*

Sorry, my fingers on a keyboard slip so easily into Writer, that's who I really am now, it's in my contract, I'm cast for the character. There's not an ounce of normality in me anymore – *I like that*. But it's hard on those who once loved me, and those I fall in love with; confusing for them I suppose, never knowing for sure if I'm Writer or me. (Can I myself tell what's *myself* anymore?)

I've been working long and hard plying my new wordsmith trade dear one. I need my playmate *real* in Loa. And it seems that she too needs times of refreshing. Loa's sandbox is always ready for *you* my love. *I stand at the door waiting eagerly for you to knock.* Would it be possible someday do you think for me to watch over your shoulder as you play your hospice nurse role? I think I'd like that. I want to see who you are then, and who we'd be together. (Maybe you could pass me off as a writer doing research for a novel he wants to write?)

I was once an ordained lay minister of religion. I've performed weddings, conducted funerals, counseled, blessed, sometimes healed, visited the sick and the dying. Much compassion and love lives within me yet, I don't think I'd be much out of place. (Might have to find something other than blue jeans and a holey t-shirt sans collar to wear though – that *could* be a deal breaker.)

I love you dear Suzanne. Or at least I love the thought and the feeling of you, great and compassionate woman as you are. I don't know you yet, though I'm learning with each message you send. Please gift us some time to become familiar in each other's arms my love. I'd like that. I'd like it a lot. Still your hopeful lover. Enjoy your day today my love. It's in our contract this time I think to romance and love but never to live together. *That doesn't mean we can't enjoy each other from a distance....*

I'm thinking if I ever hear back from Suzanne, I might start my response to her message something like this:

What a glorious and beautiful day this has turned out to be! The lost is found, and she's been to Texas, knows how to prepare delicious savory meats from the fatted calf, so let it be done....

Silly? that's what was running through my mind as I prepared to wash dishes. Oh well, back to the kitchen I go... But I'm thinking today as I rewrite the Twelve Books and make them one that what I am writing could create a whole new way of looking at life. Like the "Star Wars" movies, it could open imaginative minds to unique thoughts, endless desires, new playwrights emerge. Oh yes, oh yes, this could be *SUPER HUGE!* (Thanks for that Lynne, I love you dear sweetie, we're not done yet you and I.) Oops, dishes to wash, Ms. Responsibility hums her ever cloying siren song.

Jen: The selection of women seem to be very different people but interesting. It sounds like Lynne might be concerned of giving you the wrong impression. Where is Duncan? If you find a woman to settle down with occasional visits and cuddles. Would you tell her it is an open relationship with the same considerations you agreed on with Jackie? Have fun in the hunt.

I tried to set myself on a dating site but had trouble finishing. Gave up. Guess I not ready yet but will try another day. I talked to a couple of older men in the park, nothing of interest. I went to an art festival around the corner and talked to a couple of men behind the booth that I could of been interested in but came to find out they are married. I love artists. I guess that is one of the reasons I married my first husband, he was a talented artist. The happiest well adjusted men I am attracted to seem to be married. And I will not date a married man. Still thinking of my neighbor with the dying wife.

M: Duncan is a town about 50 miles north of Victoria. She actually lives in another community she calls "Hicksville" but it's not far from Duncan. I don't know if I'll hear from her again or not. She told me she couldn't meet today because of her injury at exercise class. But she also didn't suggest another day to meet, so it could be a polite brush off. I won't contact her again if I don't hear from her, it's just that she looked slim and cute in that one photo, and she lives closer than Nanaimo where I was prepared to commute if it had worked out with Jackie. And regarding her that may be just as well because travelling 50 or so miles each way is still a long commute for a lover type relationship. What if one or the other wants last minute to meet just for a few hours in the night?? Now Lynne, being only a short walk from me... Yeah, I know, 16 years difference in age does take a toll on expectations.

Yes of course, I am looking for an open relationship. It is not my desire to control or to be controlled, especially when it comes to who someone can choose to have sex with. Every adult should have that freedom, but I understand the importance of marriage and stability when young children are involved. Thanks for sharing your thoughts about and interaction with other men. I'm glad that you are now able to think of other men that way, and are checking fingers for wedding rings. You're exuding pheromones now, men know instinctively that you're available. Even married men will be subtly prompted to pay attention to you simply because they're male. Take notice and you'll observe that.

It's still kind of scary to me to think that I might lose you to another man. But you having the freedom to consider and to choose for yourself is of great importance to me. I do think your neighbor is well worth considering, he would most likely give you the Mormon Dream if you two get together after his wife dies. He'd probably take you to the temple to be sealed for eternity if that is your choice. *But then you'd be sister wife to your neighbor's dying wife forever!* And in the Mormon way as I understand it, SHE would be "First Wife." Is that what you really want for you for forever? You see, when you think of it that way, my own dream isn't so far out. And *my* dream does not allow for the ranking of sister wives unless that's how *all* of them want it to be, they/we are a family of equal spouses as I see it at present. Get yourself in the shape you want to be to please men my darling. Then if you still want to and can accept an open relationship, you and I may live together again in mortality. I know I'd love you because I already do, and I know you love me too... Enjoy the day.

M: (To woman from Duncan. So what if I said I wouldn't?) Are you still interested in meeting? If so, please suggest a time and place, thanks.

Woman from Duncan: Sorry about that. As I mentioned my friend is in hospice and has just days left and I am feeling quite sad. But I could meet you in Duncan on Thursday afternoon if you wish. Are you a coffee person? I am flexible for time so let me know what works for you.

M: I'll understand if you want to wait. If you were comfy with me I'd visit your friend with you. I was once (lots of years ago) a lay minister and fairly often visited the sick and dying, conducted marriages, funerals etc. Rusty and no longer into organized religion, but the heart's still in the same place... But sure Thursday afternoon would work for me. I'm not familiar with Duncan so if you can give me a street address for my GPS that should work. Say 1 p.m.? (I'm totally flexible but would prefer early than late so we have lots of time to talk if we find that we enjoy each other's company.) Do you know a nature or seaside trail in or near Duncan we could walk, or maybe a park to sit and talk? I'm much more of a nature lover than urban, but I want you to feel comfortable with the venue wherever it is we meet. Did your strain or whatever the ice pack was for heal already? Cheer up a bit?

There, that worked, as in I think we'll be meeting on Thursday.

Jen: Went for a walk today and saw a older man walking his small dog. coming toward us. So I smiled at him and he smiled back. He stopped for a moment and talked then went across the road and unlocked a gate to go into his beach front condo. It was nice to have someone respond back like that. He had a pleasant look about him I liked. Would love to have a male friend here. As I looked out over the beautiful sandy southern California beach and on to the blue waters, I thought Michael is looking at the same ocean every day just like me. Except our part of the ocean smells much better than yours. We don't have cruse boats but we have a loud train. Victoria has more foot traffic, I think we are just spread out more. Anything new happening with possible lady friends.

M: It seems like you are in the perfect place right now, much better than being tossed around by your daughter's needy little ones. I hope you do find a friend if you'll be staying in California awhile. I'm sure that would be as enjoyable for you as it is for me to have female companionship, even if only for a walk and maybe hold hands a bit. Did you tell your son you are looking? He might find a friend for you quite easily. Older people tend to be creatures of habit, so do your walk about the same time of day and you may run into the same men. (But then miss others of course.)

Nothing on the woman front today until a few minutes ago. I drove around exploring Victoria a bit, then walked to the end of the breakwater after that. About twenty minutes ago I got a message from the woman in Duncan. She'll meet me there on Thursday afternoon.

She's kind of hesitant because she has a friend in hospice who will only last a few days and she's sad. I picked her out not only for the pretty face and youthful look (essential to get on my list) but because in her profile she bills herself as "class clown" and says she has a "quirky" sense of humor. I think I'd like that a lot after always being the one who tries to be clever enough with words to make people laugh. We'll see what happens Thursday but I'll most likely know if I'm interested or not in the first ten minutes. That doesn't mean it can't evolve, there are always ways to make your mind more receptive and to allow your heart to open to those you at first thought were not going to work out for you. I really do want to get this settled though. I'm tired of the singles sites, just want a steady exclusive friend/lover to be with occasionally, an arrangement that is beneficial and rewarding for *both* of us.

I'd still like to travel the island before the cold weather comes but even today wasn't enjoying the drive because it was by myself, seemed like a waste of gas, I need a travel companion. Wish to me a lovely friend and lover for me and I for her while I write my book.

M: Jackie, I guess from your silence that it's completely over with us then. I'm sad that it worked out that way after we were given such a beautiful gift with the powerful connection we both felt for a few days and our finding out that we had so much in common. Please don't be offended with my suggesting that we be occasional lovers. I always tell it open and honest and yes, I wanted more of your body than the two limited nights we had together. I thought it would be a mutually beneficial arrangement for us, so I made the offer. I wish upon you happiness and joy Jackie, perhaps you called it right for both of us, women usually do, I will always remember you. I respect your choice and will not write you again unless you contact me first. Take care sweetie.

Woman from Duncan: Hi: Interesting about your spiritual background. What religious affiliation? My background was very strict and my father was an ordained minister. Unfortunately most of the time I get sad thinking about back then. Maybe share sometime. We can pick up a hot or cold drink and then go to the park and walk and talk. There's a coffee place in the parking lot where we can grab a beverage. It's just after you cross the bridge, turn left at traffic light after bridge.

M: I was a Mormon for a lot of years, hope that's not a deal breaker, am not into any organized religion anymore and much happier. We're going to have to work on that sadness sweetie, life's meant to be fun and happy. In fact it is my belief that human beings *exist* to know fullness of joy. You'll find if we get to know each other that I am completely honest and open, I hold nothing back even though my life too like everyone else's had moments of trial and sadness. But no need to go there, each new moment is the potential beginning of a brand new life if we choose it to be so. And if we do, we can choose *happiness* in it, moment by moment. One p.m. then at that location on Thursday? I seldom carry my cell but will try to remember to take it with me, my number is (insert.) I drive a grey sedan. (You know, the cars that just sitting there minding their own business persuade entire squadrons of seagulls to do at least one bombing run every day.) My daughter and her husband visited me last week from Calgary. They're both high school teachers, he in science. He explained to me that seagulls eat stones, the stones interact with lime in their intestines, and voila, a perfect recipe for *concrete!* Yep, my car's got some of that. So you'll know it's me when a grey car drives up disguised as a cement truck. (Just kidding - maybe - it's not Thursday yet.)

Woman from Duncan: OMG I had a feeling you were Mormon. When you mentioned your children Alberta I kinda suspected. It is a definite red flag for me unfortunately. For a few reasons I don't want to get into so please understand when I say that I am not comfortable with meeting you.

M: Oh no, is it really that bad? I'm not Mormon anymore. Tell me it's not so and you'll meet me anyway?

I can't believe this – is she serious?

M: Now it's my turn to feel sad. I know that Mormons are indoctrinated but someone *really* messed with the "class clown" it seems. Active Mormons who live their religion are among the nicest sincerest caring loving people in the world when you come to know them for yourself instead of listening to the hateful stories some people like to tell about others. But ok, I have to respect your decision and will not be going to Duncan on Thursday unless I hear back from you with an invitation. I was beginning to feel fond of you already, just from our swapping of messages. I truly wish you the very best with everything, and much happiness. Take care.

I send the gist of the above to Jen for her comments and ponder this wonder to myself. However, I also suggested changing her, most likely a huge red flag even though it was a suggestion to move her in the direction of happiness.

Woman from Duncan: All the best to you.

Yep, she was serious – can't believe it, but very glad we worked this one out before anyone turned a wheel towards the other. It's better this way, thank-you, thank-you, thank-you.

Jen: Sorry she has it in for the Mormons! You can't take her rejection personal. You did not even meet her. You can just keep moving.

Jen: Did you know getting your emails and writing you is one of my high lights of the day.

M: Yeah, you're hopelessly in love with this irresistible man. I like that.

Jen: You just might be right!

M: Writing a longer update, stand by....

Jen: Good attitude. Hopes of any body else in the horizon. What about the lady you were walking with that wore layers of clothing.... Have you walked with her lately or are you hopping Lynne will have a change of heart and give you a chance. Maybe take a break from lady hunting and visit your sisters again or your kids. Maybe you can fly your other sister out to visit. Just some ideas so your not lonely. I know your writing is keeping you busy but I hate to think of you alone. I am.

I am a size down hope by the end of the month it will be another size down. It is really hard when you're a women and older to lose weight but it can and does happen. Just not as easy or as fast as when I was younger. Well it wasn't a problem until I got into my late 40's. The old metabolism needs kick start. The cliffs keep calling for me to climb back and forth to the beach. Wish I brought my tennis shoes feel like I could walk further if I had them. Interesting even if I had a busy day I still walk at bedtime just before dark. Seems like I just have to walk.

M: I know the feeling about needing to walk, I'm addicted too, I go to the end of the breakwater at least once a day busy or not. I want you to know that I am highly encouraged with what you are doing. Of course my preference for someone to live with in mortality would be slimmed down newly emerged good attitude co-creating loving me YOU! As you mentioned, everyone our age comes with a whole lot of baggage. And much of *our* baggage has the same name tags on it already, including that hugely formidable one of already knowing and loving the 'in-laws'.

The lady who "wore layers of clothing" was too busy to walk with me last time I checked but we're probably still friends. To me she's a prude but we swap male and female energy while we walk hand in hand arm in arm conversing about nothing. I like her touch, she likes mine, we feed each other that way in a limited way. Sure, I'd walk with her again.

No, I don't think Lynne and I will ever be lovers because I'm much too old for her. If I was a zillionaire she'd most likely travel to Europe with me (she told me she'd never been there and wants to go) if I paid all her expenses. But if I was a zillionaire I could also 'hire' much younger travel companions than Lynne. I'll most likely stop and talk with Lynne briefly when I see her during my walks.

I can't take a break from "hunting" women. It's women who motivate me to be *alive* and who I am, I love love love love women!!! When a healthy man is 30 he looks at the 20 year old girls. When he's 50 he has 30 years worth of women passing by to enjoy the sight of. At 70 he has *fifty* years worth of women to enjoy looking over in his travels. *It just keeps getting better and better.* Yes, I am alone right now, that's gotta change at least for a few hours each week, I must have the frequent touch of a woman. Working on it...

Why not buy some new tennis shoes? That would be a good investment... I have been real busy online this a.m. and there are still messages coming in that I haven't even glanced at yet. Below are my journal entries for today and it's not even noon yet. Please don't criticize, just accept it as me who and what and where I am in this moment, and that includes being a writer of fiction books. I'm already aware that I sabotage most of the virtual contacts I have with women. But I've concluded that I do it for a purpose (even Jackie) because inside I already know that such and such a woman is not good for me at the present time, she would keep me from being a writer and/or would take my focus off my goal for immortality and populating new planets. But new stories are vital for fiction writers to retain a lifeline of readers, so I indulge daily in what motivates me the most – *the prospect of romance, love, and sex with one or more beautiful women.* So please don't judge, just accept and enjoy my journal as I share it with you.

Jen: It is a beautiful day. Just made some homemade salsa. Guess what I had for lunch.

M: Easy guess. You had *food* for lunch today silly.

Jen: Yeah it was food.

M: You dig at me about your going home a week early but I continue to think that was for the best, I felt very strongly about it. And it seems to be working out well too. You will be such a delight to me when you've accomplished the things you list that you want to do to become attractive to men, especially if you are still so madly in love with this handsome irresistible man. When you were here, because of the past I wasn't giving you back in like proportion the love (and sex) you were pouring out to me so copiously. But now should we get together and you have an open mind about my dream and what I want to do while still here in mortality, we'd never look back. We'd be happy people you and I, free to each do what we want to do at any given moment. If you decide to give up the Mormon dream we could live together without marrying again, that would be much less complicated given the hassle and disagreements we had about our temporal assets. We could even spread the word that we'd never really divorced in the first place, and give the appearance in polite society of being married. What do you think of that idea? (Yeah, I know, monogamy reigns huge among women in western society so maybe that would not be attractive to you.)

Today I felt over a twenty minute period that I should go down to the sea near the beach where Lynne picks stones and glass for the huge collection in her home. But I hadn't had lunch yet so I lingered at home, even took a nap. Then I went down to the sea in my own time and sat on a bench where I could see Lynne's beach. She wasn't there but a powerful comforting feeling came over me, very powerful, somebody was invisible there with me, we swapped a lot of love. I thought it might have been Jackie because she is capable of tuning me in like that (as can Lynne) and there'd be a message from Jackie waiting for me. But there wasn't a message, so now I think if it wasn't Lynne then it might have been you, you could do it too.

425

I'm still wondering too about the voice that spoke to me saying that I had "met" two of my post-mortal wives. I continue to think you are one of them. I had thought Jackie too at the time, but don't anymore. Who's the other? Want to help me find out? Are you keeping an eye open for sister wives for US? It's a beautiful day today in the sunny City of Victory. I'll most likely do the breakwater walk again this evening, went earlier than usual today.

M: Lynne, I suppose you know from your psychometry and clairvoyant reading that I am unusually honest and open, telling it like it is the way I see it at that moment. So here goes.

I'm a bit confused about you. And since we live so close and walk the same paths by the same beach almost daily, you aren't going to go away (thank goodness), we'll keep running into each other. So I'm going to have to understand you better if you don't mind, or ignore you as we pass in close physical proximity. When I left your home you gave me a wonderful hug, I wish I had held it longer, I felt in that moment that I could love and 'protect' you forever even though we'd just met. You said you wanted to walk and talk with me and I wanted that, for us to become friends. But you never responded to my last email and I am all too aware that I'm single, male, and although much older than you am powerfully attracted to the possibilities hidden within that fashionable short skirt that you wear, and the gorgeous legs I couldn't help but keep glancing at through the glass table top as you tuned in with me. You were right on with the reading. I hadn't even told you I was a writer but you quickly asked me about "the book" and said my energies (and I assume the book) were "super huge." I agreed, I believe they are, and are for a purpose that will soon unfold. I am working on the book, a condensation of twelve books I had previously published that weren't selling, it will be a series.

I surely hope you don't mind my sending this message to you Lynne, I'm much better at expressing myself in writing than in speech, I'm counting on your clairvoyance for understanding. When I came down to the beach a couple of days ago and spoke with you briefly you were about to walk off and I was confused, misunderstanding, wondering why you didn't want to talk with me. So I muttered that I hoped to see you again and you walked off to get some bags for your abundance of stones and glass from the sea. Instead of walking away I should have stayed to guard your treasure and chatted when you came back with the bags. But I didn't, and when I discovered a piece of sea glass right beside me on the log I was sitting on and wanted to give it to you, you stood at the same moment I did, and left. I still carry the glass in my pocket, there's nothing special about it except that it was meant to be given to you.

I'm not sure if you want to speak with me, or if you are even comfortable in my physical presence? Please tell me candidly how it is with you Lynne. Are you frightened of me, my male energies flowing even though you are so much younger? Should I be a 'father' figure to you perhaps, quench those energies? (I could be that, or just friend or acquaintance if that would please you, but I must know what you want from me if anything at all.)

Early this afternoon for about twenty minutes I felt someone 'calling' me to go to your beach. But I set aside that beckoning because I hadn't yet had lunch and wanted first to get that taken care of before I went out for my daily walk. When I went down to the sea you were not there. I sat on a bench that overlooks your beach just in case you came along, and while there felt a powerful comforting delightful presence. Someone was there with me, someone who chose to cloak with invisible robes, someone lovely, someone female. I thought it was you but was not sure because there are others who could reach me in that manner, it could have been one of them. Where are you with me Lynne? Could we be good friends and confidantes who walk and talk with each other, maybe hold hands now and then to share our unique blend of energies? Could I sometimes drive you to different beaches to gather your treasures, sit beside you as you do, we at peace in our warm silence? Would you like that? Or should I pass by with just a casual 'hello' from now on? Tell me please.

I copy and send to Jen my message to Lynne. Jen has become my confidante, as Suzanne once was. But I miss Suzanne, I'd love to have a few more nights with her. Does she read my messages? Will she ever write back to me?

Jen: I am concerned about any sexual reference you have written about you and me. Would you please delete them from your journal or soften them. I don't want your family or mine to read what is very private and secret between you and I. Sexual counters for me are just that. Present me as a very close friend or/and x wife, that loves you very much and cares greatly about you and sometimes gets upset if you choose to say that. But ever growing closer and at more peace. I did a lot of thinking about you today. Two nights ago, around two or three in the morning I woke having a powerful experience. You were cuddling me just as if you were really next to me. It felt so real. I had no doubt it was you. Even after you left the warm loving feeling lingered with me for a long time. I could not sleep for the longest time after that. Were you aware you were traveling. You are welcome to come back any time and cuddle with me in the night. I think most people dismiss these premonitions. I don't.

M: I am aware that I 'travel' at night, always did. And I am aware that I want to cuddle and have sex with you. We are close on many levels, enjoy!

M: Suzanne. Muse is creating a fine rewrite that I think is destined to be "super huge" as the clairvoyant said. I'll most likely have it printed in hard and soft cover as well as e-book format after I've published and tweaked the e-book a bit. Are there any more hospice stories that you'd like to have inserted in the book? If so, now would be a good time to send them to me so I can find appropriate places to put them. Sure hope you are well Suzanne, I think about you a lot, wish we could have a few more nights together somewhere...

Jen: Just me thinking after looking at your website. As you know I'm not very experienced but would think the female reader would like but not sure. I think its good writing. Is there a way to turning more of the (email conversations) yummy lines into physical conversations.. Take them to various places around Victoria or Texas. Give them a more exciting life, talents to show off. Like as you walk with your scuba gear toward the break waters you look down and see Lynne on the beach. Or as you walk the brake waters you look across the inlet and visualize the beautiful woman you been in contact with and create a imaginary friendship, relationship then encounter with either ladies or both. Women like to take their time in the build up and more build up just like they do in having sex. It pulls them in hoping and waiting and wanting and then and then and and wow - your at the end of the book! I know I know nothing about writing so hope you don't mind if I share some thoughts. I may be way off base.

M: You're not way off base at all, normal writers do exactly what you suggest I do. But I'm just not that kind of writer.

Jen: That was not my intention to criticize you. I thought I was sharing ideas.

M: No problem, your emails are important to me. Yes, I'm lonely and have no prospects in the works at present. I was hoping to have a relaxed travel the Island summer with a close friend/lover but instead I'm right back into being alone and writing. Maybe that's for the best, don't know. But I do know that I really need the frequent touch of a woman. *Hurry up and get ready to come back for a while will you....*

Jen: It takes time and I have a lot of work to do. Wish I could reach out and hug you from a distance. Be reassured you are loved.

Linda: (lady on singles) Is the "Law of Attraction" a belief system?

M: When you become consciously aware of the power of Law of Attraction you can take conscious control of your life and attract into it theoretically everything you want. Personally I live by it, it works for me the same as does the operating system in a computer, quiet, unseen, but WORKS every time you get it right. E.g. try typing in the wrong password, won't work, type the right sequence of keys and it MUST work.

Linda: So, seriously, it is a belief system. When were you first attracted to it and how has it worked for you?

M: I was a fan of Rhonda Byrne ("The Secret") for a year or so, really immersed myself into her published media of all types. Then I found out that her ideas originated during a cruise when she was filming Esther Hicks speaking for Abraham. So I checked out the Abraham website and that worked very well for me. The secret to Law of Attraction is to simply always expect good things to happen to you, and to be chronically happy. That puts you in a frame of mind where you ALLOW what you really want to manifest without putting up resistance one way or the other. It works for me daily. Becoming chronically happy can be as simple as every day for a few minutes imagining your body vibrating faster than it normally does. Try it, and let me know how it works for you.

Jen: Did Lynne ever reply to your last email. If she hasn't and you want to know what I think you could of chased her off from possibly even being a friend. Might help you with future emails to other possible women.

M: Yes, I know that but I wanted to be open and honest, especially with her, you can't hide things from a clairvoyant. I'm just telling it the way it is with me and am willing to accept the consequences. No, she has not responded to my last two emails so I will most likely just consider her another person on the beach or say a polite 'hello' should we pass close. Or later, I may pay for another formal 'reading' and see where that goes. I do like her and would have appreciated walking and talking with her like she said when I was in her home she wanted to do, I was following up. But no problem either way, life goes on...

What follows is an email I sent to Jen with her later comments inserted between mine, and then my response to her comments.

M: (to Jen) You write from the western female monogamous point of view, which is normal. I am a single man with needs (not just sex) and am looking around for those needs to be filled, which is normal.

Jen: Of course I understand its more than hopeful sex. But you wrote to be complete it needs to be with more than one woman. Not one woman could fill all your needs.

M: It's possible that one woman (you maybe) could fill most of my needs for the rest of my mortal life. But the original Mormon way is one man, several wives.

M: Please show me where I told you that I'm looking for a semi-steady for sex so I can continue looking to "conquer" others. I don't believe I would ever say or write something so untrue as that! But I can understand that you would make a 'straw man' in my image who might say something like that, then proceed to tear it down. *That's not how I am at all...*

Jen: Maybe it does not sound so good when it comes back to read or in different words. The result is the same. That's exactly how it sounds to a woman's ears. You said you do not want a woman to live with (a girlfriend) just to walk with, cuddle, with hopeful sex. Spending several hours a week fulfilling needs. But must be open to include others that appear.

M: An open relationship for me is more a matter of *freedom* than anything else. Should I want to sleep with another woman I wouldn't have to feel like I need to ask anyone's permission other than that woman's, and I wouldn't have to feel that I was 'cheating' or being 'unfaithful'. Which to western women it would be except in an open type of marital-like relationship.

Jen: You have said over and over you want to have a homosexual relationship with you and two women. You even asked me to find another woman to join in. Even if you are involved with one woman you want to be free to have sex with other women you meet when out and about if opportunity arises. Reread your emails.

M: I was only being open and honest with you about my fantasies instead of being like most people and hiding them. Yes it's true, I would like to have two attractive loving women in my bed at the same time, especially if I was in effect 'married' to them and they loved each other as much as they loved me. You see, for me right now I live in a (delightful) blend of the world of consensus reality and the fantasy world of my dreams. Which latter world I believe that I am creating. It's not so uncommon a desire I don't think, even Mormons were once polygamous and who knows how often several were in the same bed at the same time behind closed doors. And it's not at all uncommon for women to love women intimately whether or not male energies are present. My desires are natural and most likely normal, they are just not within the tight boxes that organized religion likes to keep people.

M: As I mentioned to you several times (even Lynne picked that up in the reading) I am by habit a one woman man even though that goes against my dream. Once I am together with the right woman who takes care of my needs as I take care of hers, I will most likely stop looking for another woman for anything other than friendship, walks and talks perhaps. For me at this point in my life that would be ideal, not a live in, but a close and intimate relationship when we both have time and the desire to be together for a while.

Jen: I am glad you have considered and will let go of that dream. That would be so much better for you and me. I would do my best to fill all your needs and more. So why did you tell me all that other stuff. Even with Jackie, you talked about it being a open relationship. In my heart I could not see you being that way but that is not who you told me you are now.

M: I haven't "considered and let go" of anything. I have always been a one woman man until now that I find myself single and wanting to date several to find out the degree of compatibility that would allow each of us to retain our freedom yet be by choice most likely almost always exclusive to the other when it comes to sexual relations. If you fill most of my needs and I yours then we wouldn't have much to be concerned about would we? And as for "why did I tell" please keep in mind that I have been living the character of the somewhat raunchy book character "Michael" who lives in my books for almost a year now and I have a 'reputation' to keep. It's a bit difficult to get out of character when I find myself still writing (journal keeping) the same as I did before I came to Victoria. I wanted a vacation from that but it's not happening and I'm growing tired of it. Even as I write these notes to you, I am in fact writing a possible future book, exactly that!

Jen: So why did you tell Lynne you wanted to get under her skirt and explore? If a man I just met wrote that to me I would run as far away as I could from him. You must of really frighten her and that's why she was cool with you.

M: I actually regret doing that even though I certainly did not put it as crudely as you just did. I was just being open and honest and telling her my feelings which I won't deny. I'm male and I'm normal. (But I could do a better job of hiding my feelings if that would be more pleasing to women who want to pretend that they are the one and only desirable female in the world.) Women want to make it impossible for men, they want their man to desire them sexually but also want him to not desire other women sexually. That's just not how it works, males are 'hard wired' to have sex with females, period, like it or not, get used to it... I hoped that Lynne would realize that I am in character writing a book to entertain (and teach) others. But most likely not, and true, I may have frightened her. I wish her well, I could have easily become her friend and would have loved her well enough without sex.

M: It would be nice if once you complete your self-improvement plans you and I get together often, maybe eventually even live together full time. It would be easy to do, we've already done that, our bags are labelled, same names.

Jen: Yes it would be very easy to do.

M: Regarding my Eves, I have expressed to you that I don't know yet if any of them are here in mortality right now, with the exception of the two that a voice told me I have already "met". My best guess is that you are one of those two. But the choice to be so of course is entirely up to you. So, yes, it would be hugely ideal if I ran into one or more of those women who are already my eternal companions in a dimension beyond space and time, and we established a loving relationship in mortality. The finding of my Eves though could easily be taken care of *after* I become immortal. Until then I'll just have to trust Law of Attraction to bring my Eves to me when the time is right. There is no "competition" for my Eves, we and they are already one, we are perfect for and *want* to be with each other in the eternities. In the meantime I'll continue being a single man with needs, doing what a single man with needs does to attract one or more single women with needs that can be mutually fulfilled by the two establishing a close relationship.

Jen: I know your universe is totally your creation but women have their own ideas about what they want. You just might be out voted in a equal setting. To have your perfect universe the women must not have a mind of their own thinking. That will leave you to tell them what to do. You will then be the creator of all and they obey at your command because all think equal with you. Don't know if I am making myself clear. I know there is a solution but neither of us are there yet or I don't understand your thinking of the subject. That's why I keep writing about all this stuff over and over.

M: Even though I have explained my position on that before, you continue to be hung up on self-created issues of power and control. I simply do not see such a thing as you describe. In heaven there is perfection, peace and order without coercion. And if not, keep in mind that everyone is free to leave whenever they find they can't tolerate our heaven or think there's a better one somewhere else. Maybe they'd have better 'luck' in another man's world, or in a world of their own. But no, we're together because like attracts like, we are perfect for each other, there is no possibility of tyranny, certainly not on my part.

Jen: I care about you more than just thinking.

M: I care about you too sweetheart. Do what you need to do and all will be well. Just keep in mind that my wives in the next world are all *equal*, not even you will rule over them unless they *all* want and set it up that way.

But ok, Jen made some good points. And I'm tired of being book character Michael, time to be me again (if I can find me.) Enough of *sharing* raunchy thoughts and feelings even though I might have them. It's time to get back into normal consensus reality with the women I come in contact with. Yes, that means competitive dating, but with the goal of a monogamous relationship of some type - friendship first, as many of the women write in their singles profiles. Might be difficult because I'm reading Michael daily as I edit to make my new book, but it's best that I try, I'm really tired of being lonely and on the edge all the time. And if Jen really does do what she says she plans to do to make herself "attractive to men", and really does fulfill my needs and I hers when we're together, well, why not make it long term living together? Sure would be easy...

I've arranged to spend tomorrow afternoon and evening with my sister, tea at my place then a walk in the park. If she feels up to a long walk maybe on from there to Cook Street, Dallas, and to the end of the breakwater. Carrot cake maybe, then I'll take her home.

The following is a message from Jen that I just found in my inbox. I think it is the message I was responding first to above but I didn't include it. So here it is.

Jen: After 20 years we have similar, love and concerns for our family luggage. We know the history of both families and lived it together. That says a lot about who you want to be with in the future. At our age most likely, who ever we may end up with have family that won't be happy with our intrusion. At best we can expect politeness. Of course your desired relationship does not include your woman's family because you won't be living together. Is that what you really prefer having a steady but no live in. Many fish but few land in the nets. Even though most of them are thrown or jump back into the waters to float away in their dreams.

It seems you have a desire to connect easily with most thin women for sex. I think my search will be much more difficult. I defiantly want a strong connection, free loving loyal steady responsible man to enjoy travel and have adventures with. Other wise I will choose to stay single. That probliblly leaves the door open for you. Oh, except the faithful part. Please understand and don't take it personal. We each have our wants and understanding. I am expressing....

What I don't want is... to be walking down the street watching my mans eyes going up and down another woman's long thin legs and wanting what is under their skirts. You always see in the movies a woman hitting her man for this obvious gesture. Hoping and dreaming for the opportunity. I never felt you discrased me this way. But now you are free to look as you please as a single male. I think you see yourself clearly and that's what you want. I think you need at least a couple more years to get this out of your system since it became a want for your eyes. You say you want a semi-steady for cuddles, hugs and sex so you can continue to looking, hope and conquer. Do you think in your heart you will ever want to settle with one woman and find happy and satisfaction? I am using you as a example but mean any man which is in the progress and moving forward toward their next leg of the journey.

Thought: Why do you feel your Eve's need to be searched out. (mostly now). Some were born thousands of years ago and some yet to be born. Of course a few are now. Have you considered they might be watching from afar your conduct, your progress, and commitment to those you love. Does not your Adam, being the only male God in your world.... be of the highest order and in harmony with the universe. Surely you have considered you already knew these women as they knew you before coming to earth. You were not the only male, others are in competitions for these Eves. Your conduct here will tell if this man has the making of a God. Thus their watching to see. It is their decision. When will they make the final choice. Which leg of the journey will that happen. Surely not now. To many disruptions. Surely not now? Still watching and worth the wait? PS: Have you ever wondered why men ask a woman to marry them. Then she says yes or no. It is the woman's choice whom she follows.

Linda: Does life not intervene at times in one's happiness? How can that be avoided or overcome? I work with Native Americans, some in the far north. A trapping people. Life is so basic, down to earth there.

M: Basic down to earth is much easier to live with. Like it most likely is with animals, there is no fear until a realistic fear presents itself. And then you deal with it in that moment. But complex societies and environments come with unrealistic fear as our constant companion. And that means stress. And that means sometimes short nasty lives if we get too carried away with it and create out of this beautiful planet a world to fear. My personal way of dealing with life's negative interventions is to create the rest of my life in the next moment, start all over again - and choose happiness. It's a simple little mind trick but it works. If you're not happy with the present moment, mentally start a new life all over again. Set aside the old one (don't fight or criticize or regret it, just accept and ignore it) and choose only happy thoughts from that time on. And on, and on until it becomes such a habit that you do it automatically and you become chronically happy, brimming with internal joy that's hard to hide, people keep smiling at you for no apparent reason at all - it's great fun! Anyway, it works for me.

I appreciate your emails Linda, I'm a bit of a pedant and love to pass along information that I think others may not already know. But you know the secret of 'keeping' a man - just keep asking him questions, pretend you didn't already know the answer, and gush with thankfulness for the pleasure of associating with such a brilliant being as he is. Enjoy the evening or whatever it is out there when you read this.

Oops, this is becoming complicated. She seems sincere with her questions. Why? Am I going to have to meet this woman even though she's not one I would normally put on my short list from just glancing at photos?

Jen: Walked along beach and all the way to the end of the pier and back. Then made my way up the hill pushing as hard and fast as I can to get my heart rate up. Then slow down for the balance of the walk. If it was not so late I would of taken a longer route home. I think I am seeing curves around my waist. My jeans were slipping down from my waste. Good sign. I am on my way. Love ya.

M: I'll keep an eye on those jeans for you then, glad you're getting it done.

Jen: I'd like you to keep an eye on those jeans.

Mmm, that was nice. As I used to say about Suzanne, "Vivid thought..." *My ex!!!*

True enough though, if she loses the excess weight that has plagued her (and me) for years and comes with that newly emerging attitude of hers, there's a very good chance that we'll live together again in mortality. Live *somewhere* that is, not sure that I'd want to go back to the same neighborhood much as I loved the retirement home we had built for ourselves. Life's so exciting, thank-you thank-you thank-you.

Linda: I ask questions because I am curious - chronically curious I suppose. Yes, that is a photo of me.

M: That photo of you by the sea is hugely appealing to a man, begs for finding out more about the mysterious woman in it. Looks like your hair was longer then? Me too, always been curious, tend to jump right into things that interest me greatly, in for the duration, full plunge, deep end, don't remember (or care) if I can swim kinda thing. I'm wondering what you are doing among the people in the great white north. Tell me more about you, you've got me curious, still shy of the deep end but edging closer. Enjoy the day, I'll be spending some of it with my older sister. White tea at my apartment in James Bay then Beacon Hill and maybe Cook Street from there, Dallas and Breakwater, she's good for it. Should be a walk in the park...

Jen: You know we could really really really make each other very happy. The other women don't bother me that much. You are single and I want you to enjoy your time being single. Experience what you feel you need to. I still like you sharing your experiences with me. I have no negative feelings. Although I have expressed my thoughts quite strongly at times that did not set well with you... You know it is nice to not have negative feelings for anyone else. You just want it to turn out well for all. I think that's why I enjoy being at my son's, there is very little negativity going on here.

Cooked a great roast today. Had enough left overs for tomorrow also. Wish I was with you to cook you some yummy healthy food. My daughter is looking for a couple renters to live with me in the house. So far they have been men. I told her I don't want male room mates. She said she agreed. This should help keep my finances from going into the red every single month.

M: Save me some of that roast, sounds yummy indeed. I miss your cuddles and ers all night sweetie, am looking forward to much more of that some day when we're both better prepared. Airplanes still fly, maybe we'll find us a warm place to live in the Bahamas or Cabo or wherever, I'd sooner not move back to USA. House prices are so high in Victoria that it makes much more economic sense to rent. We've both owned houses before, we don't need to buy one just for the sake of ownership, maybe rent a house so you have a garden. We could continue to sell investment land for many years wherever we happen to be living as long as there's reliable internet.

That's my tentative thinking today, a life ahead with newly emerged delightful you. It's exciting to think of you willing and loving, sexy slim in jeans, little black dress or nightie, or even better, nothing at all. Your visit with me was hugely important Jen, it showed me the potentials of a new you, a new me, we needed that to plan a fresh start. We just have to work on that conversation part a bit more. Should we actively plan and co-create my immortal dream together, we'd have much that is new to discuss and share daily. But we can't do that unless your heart is in it too. Your continued assurance of love and longing for me puts a different perspective on my search for the female attention I need right now. I don't need to be looking for a stable long term relationship when my primary desire is you and we're moving in that direction. But I do want a close friend and lover in Victoria, so I'll continue to seek and meet prospects. I love you babe, I'm thinking of those jeans you look so good in, always did think tight jeans were sexy on a lady.

Yesterday as I walked the seaside path I saw two women approaching, a bit younger than me, engaged in conversation. One I instantly took my attention from but the other intrigued me. She was tall and slim with long blonde hair. She wore a long skirt that moved just right as she walked. But her face, though pretty enough, didn't fit my ideal pattern, there was something there I didn't like. She noticed me coming, turned her head and focus and boldly fixed her sun glassed gaze on me never wavering. I looked back but didn't put emotion into that looking, my internals I suppose saying it wasn't right, would never be. But as I stood at Lynne's beach a few minutes later I realized that she was better looking than many of the women I'd choose from a photo to look over on singles sites. And she was tall and slim, and she was bold, a potential lover for sure. So I wandered back along the path a bit hoping she'd return, but she didn't. Just another potential rendezvous missed, I may never again see her, don't feel like I should.

Jen: You do tempt me.

Jen: A couple photo's from yesterday. I took the picture so I could not get any further away to show you more.

M: Those are lovely photos Jen, my heart goes out to you, you look so happy. I never did appreciate you enough when we lived together, you're such a pretty woman, exactly like the one I'm looking for. You've got me excited again, sure you can't come tomorrow?

Jen: (she attaches older photos of the two of us) We did like each other and look good together.

M: Yeah, it shows. I do love you my darling, we had great times together, just needed a jolt to make them even better.

M: But I won't likely ever be Mormon again, so take that into consideration when you're thinking of me. It's just too much of a hassle and there are better dreams than the Mormons offer. Kind of tongue in cheek, but the way I see it every church has the same game plan: Live by our rules, give us money, and if you do that all your life MAYBE when you die you'll go to a better heaven (or avoid going to hell forever.) It's as simple as that when you stand back and really look at the perils and promises of organized religion. I much prefer to create *my own* reality. So that's where I am with that. Still with me?

M: What follows is just a crazy idea, don't hold me to it, but you've really got me going today with those beautiful photos you sent, my heart is truly softened. How long will you be at your daughter's? There's still a bit of summer left in this part of the world and I haven't yet done that Vancouver Island exploring I've been wanting to do. (Because I haven't yet found a travel companion.) So, if the following conditions were met, would you come back soon and travel the Island with me?

1. You tell your daughter I've invited you to come visit me and she's ok with that. (You needn't mention the first trip.)
2. You think you will be able to continue your self-improvement program while you're with me and not just go back to the way it was.
3. You pay your own flights (leave the return date open if you can.) We'll use my car, I'll pay the gas and budget hotels along the way, and we'll go Dutch on food.
4. You give me lots of love and touch and try to talk more about the present and the future than the past, and I'll do the same with and for you. We both do our best to avoid sinking into the old behavior patterns that caused us so much turmoil, starting a new life moment by moment if need be so we remain delicious to each other, a bright beckoning future together assured when the time is right.

Please be completely honest if you don't think this is a good idea, we can meet later when you're better prepared if you think it's wiser to wait. This suggested visit is optional, I'll still love and hope for you even if you don't come just yet. It's just that even though I have appointments to meet other women, right now today I'm truly YOURS. Crazy huh?

Linda: Well - you have led an interesting life. I prepare Ethno-history reports which are used to substantiate the use and occupation of an area by Native Americans. Useful in bringing a corporation or government to the negotiating table. (I negotiate as well at times) I have a few young people who work for me on them. I am cutting back - or at least trying to. The great white north is beautiful. It is at its best in the winter. And yes, I am also impetuous but oddly shy. Have a good evening.

M: You do sound busy, a full interesting life for sure. I cruised to Alaska twice, one of them as far as Anchorage. It's beautiful but I much prefer the tropics.

M: (to Jen) Please let me know asap if you coming here soon to travel the Island with me is a good possibility or not. I'm meeting someone new tomorrow and possibly another woman today. Depending on how that first meeting goes, each of them is a potential travel companion. So I need to know whether or not to even discuss it with them, thanks.

Jen: Just can't see it happening yet. As much as I want it and it has been tormenting me. I would really like to be with you. Love you

M: Ok, thanks for letting me know. Let's get together again when we can then. The more I think about having to get to know someone else's kids and grandkids etc. and how easy it would be for you and I to get together again instead, the more I am liking the thought of us together. We've already got everything in place except the same roof over our heads. And we already love each other. Even if it's just you coming to Victoria for a couple of weeks at a time every two or three months, that might work for both of us and your family until we find that common roof? What do you think?

Chapter 24

———⬦⬦⬦———

M: Oresha, Are you busy this afternoon? I've been hearing about "Willows Beach" being sandy and real nice so I'm planning to drive around Oak Bay until I find it. Would you like to come with me? If so and you're available, let me know what time to pick you up in front of your apartment.

Oresha: Good day Michael. Funny..I was just thinking of you!... lol Wondering how you're doing.... and... the fact that I need to get through ALL your DVD's this weekend.. so I may return them to their "Home".. It's a beautiful day... I would like to join you upon Willow's Beach. When are you thinking of going?... I have a couple of things to do... and must wash my hair.. lol I could be ready in about 1 hr.....

Oresha: Hello again... I just reread your message... lol How does ringing my buzzer at around 1:30-ish sound?... Please drop me a line and let me know if that works for you.

M: Let's make it 2 p.m. today then, I'll buzz you. Ok?

Oresha: 2:00 is Purrrfect!... see you then.

M: I don't remember your apartment number so just come down at 2 p.m.

Oresha: Hey... OK... be down at 2:00.

Jen: Yes, I feel I need to take things slow. With my daughter deciding to divorce I am concerned about some of her discussion at this time. She feels she always needs to be doing something. Once she is settled I think it will be different. I will then approach her. Need to go visit her and help her realize some of the moves she thinks need to be done are not the right timing. To me that is what got them in trouble in the past. Just need to be there to guild actually with a strong hand but come off as a gentle nudge. I Love you sweet heart. Yesterday was an emotionally difficult day for me trying to see away to be with you..... plus computer problems...... knowing I shouldn't at this time. I am happy with my progress but I am not where I want to be in losing weight. I want you to grin from ear to ear when you see me. So don't get to serious with those women. Let me know how it goes.

M: I understand, it's not a problem, I just needed to know for sure if you'd be coming soon or not. I walked with Oresha today (just friends.) Tomorrow I am meeting a woman for the first time, just a pretty face maybe nothing there at all. Then on Wednesday I have an appointment with the tall slim one I sent you a photo of. But I'm not sure if I even want to meet her. She phoned this a.m. and sounds like a wealthy lady used to taking charge of everything and everyone, asked a lot of probing questions. She lives in the country. I found a long sandy beach right in Victoria, took Oresha there for a walk, real nice, real sand. Yes, take care of your daughter and her family and yourself. My guess is that we will be together again, it's inevitable if we both want it and right now we both do. I love you sweetie. Looking forward to that ear to ear grin.

Oresha: Thanks again for inviting me to spend time with you... I really enjoyed our walk at Willow's Beach.. and the sea wall.... Ttyl... Hugsss...

M: Thanks, sleep well.

Oresha: Sweet dreams to You.

Linda: Your sister sounds intrepid, you must take after her given your photos. Yes, I am as busy as I choose to be, or not to be. I am in the process of cutting back on work although I want to keep my hand in to keep my mind active. At least for a bit. I have sailed in the Caribbean three times. It was heavenly. I agree, warmth is wonderful - and sun during the winter months. The north is nice to visit and experience. People braver than I actually live there.

M: We most likely did the same Caribbean cruises though maybe on different lines: east, west, south. I've toyed with the idea of moving to Bahamas someday, nice and warm and just a quick flight to Miami. But I'm loving Victoria right now. I used to be interested in the Mayans and traveled Mexico and Guatemala a bit climbing pyramids etc. As an anthropologist were you exposed to that culture at all? By way of travel companions I'm looking for someone to explore Vancouver Island with for a few weeks before summer's done: my car, budget hotels. I suppose you've done all that already have you?

Jen: I took the leap today. I signed up on a dating site. Wanted to find out for my self. A little scary. One man my age. Good looking, young looking and good health. He is a construction engineer. I think we look a lot a like in our features as a brother and sister would. He has a masters degree.. Meaning he is most likely very intelligent. Surprise one contact and he is asking to meet me. He wants to have breakfast next week when he gets back from Oregon. I told him I might be in Utah if he's not in town early enough. If he is back in town early we might meet at the pier for breakfast. Most likely I will be gone before he gets back. He has a large sail boat, likes the out doors and camping in a tent. Not sure about the tent or the fact he is looking for a life partner. I don't think that means marriage. Another man says he is my age but looks older than that. He has been sending messages. He is so funny. He said he was the class clown. I wonder how many women he contacts to share a few laughs each day.

Then a man from San Diego contacted me. He is a serious down to earth type that puts all his ducks in a row. I found in his writing that I could appreciate that side of him that is like me. He is older but looks a lot younger. His wife died and he raised his two daughter alone. Just bought a house in Redondo Beach and is renovating it. He has no debt, drives a truck and plays the stock market. He doesn't say anything about wanting to travel. Looking for a wife. I miss you sweety, Love Jen

M: I knew with your pretty face that if you signed up with a large singles site you'd quickly get tons of attention, you're an exceptionally pretty woman, you are desirable. (Makes me want to rush to you and claim my own, but you're not "my own" anymore.) Just please keep some time to write to me too every day. Singles sites can be highly addictive and time consuming, they will steal you away, mating is the greatest of games. The dances sometimes are beautiful, and there are men who really know how to dance. They'll make you look lovely on the floor as they effortlessly twirl you about, a soft and tender butterfly with wings wide open to catch the moist wonders of the night. You'll feel safe in their arms until daylight, and echo again with some. But you'll hear the beat of another drum and that of your wings as they lift you up for a better look around. You are free my love to flit and flutter as you will, I release you, I let you go. I must, you are not mine right now, you may never be.

Yes, you will be meeting men in the physical world, it's inevitable, it will be soon, your heart will flutter. Stay safe sweetheart, you'll fall in love with some for a while (maybe even as much as you are with me) and it will be exciting when they offer to carry you away, pay for your travel to exotic places, and protect you from all the world's perils and responsibilities. That's just the way men are with pretty women, especially those who have warm willing eager bodies. You will have choices to make, hearts to conquer, new feels to feel, new baggage to unpack. It will be refreshing and exhilarating. Just remember to look out the window now and then as you fly about, to see where you are and if it's really where you want to be. Let's meet again sometime, I hope we will.

Have fun of course, you are single, you deserve it, you have chosen it, but right now I want you back soon if you will come. I must get used to letting you go knowing there's a good chance that you will not come back, there are better men than me. Be free my love, dance your dance, but fly back to me too sometimes. Let's rendezvous now and then, check in with me, see if I am where you want to be. I can wait for you, for me there are others too, but you will be making a different choice. Money will lure you, perhaps to happiness. Stay safe, please keep in touch, I'll be thinking of you. Don't worry about me, my life flows, I'm already grateful for the years we had together, I shouldn't ask for more. You have a new life calling you now, play it well, play it full, do yourself right. And meanwhile try not to get pregnant with another man's child. Sweet dreams sweetheart, you will find what you are looking for in the end.

I am not going to allow myself to get emotionally upset about Jen's venture onto singles sites, but it's very tempting to do so. I see this as her having struggled with it but decided to explore other men. She said some time ago that I needed two years to work the stuff (other women) out of my system. I think now that was her telling me subtly (hiding it from herself) that she herself wanted time to explore the singles scene. I'm a little surprised that she's already ready and willing to meet men in the real world. I'm wondering if she has been on singles sites for some time and just didn't tell me? She says one man has been sending messages (plural) and yet yesterday she had computer problems, and she has been letting on all along that she's real busy. So, did she only sign up for the first time yesterday? I wonder if maybe instead it was when she sent me beautiful photos of herself a few days earlier? (She'd need those to post on singles sites.)

The last few days I had moved all the way to Jen. Had she come and traveled with me, I would most likely have suspended my singles site profiles and just waited for her (hopefully frequent) visits. But now it seems that I am no longer her exclusive, much as she professes great love for me. It is now me who has become the 'backup' for her, though I never did see her as a backup for me like she said I did. I didn't because it's different for me a male. I am looking for more than one wife, she will only look for one man to commit to.

That's how I see it. Jen's message about the men now coming into her life is a game changer. I will no longer be so open with her and my guess is that she too will not be open with me after reading the (above) message that I sent to her at 2 a.m. this morning. (If she ever was open, she still hasn't told me why she wanted a spirit guide to travel with her to her son's in California that night, or about her being visited by three spirit guides while standing or sitting on the hill I used to walk every day. She obviously had a spiritual experience, and is keeping it from me. What else does she keep secret? Even Lynne said that Jen has had spiritual experiences that she hasn't told me about.) Yes, she may move to and fro for a few days, trying to get back her exclusive feelings for me, but they have flown, meeting other men is what she has chosen to do, I'm convinced of that. And she'll fall in love, find her 'one and only' maybe several times and be disappointed before she settles, I expect that too. It could be a happy road for her, there's no need for the game of 'heart break' at her age, perhaps she and I have finished our mortal course together.

And now that I know what choice Jen has made, I am free again to look for a long term relationship with the right woman. But to be true to my dream I think I should mimic it as best I can in mortality and hold in mind not monogamy, but me and several wives concurrently. Yes, that will drive many women from me, most want a man's body and thoughts exclusively for themselves, calling such men as me "players" and shunning them. But not all, Law of Attraction will bring the right ones to me once I get polygamy firmly fixed in my mind and expect and allow it to happen. *I thrill at the thought…*

I had hoped Jen would make her changes, we would soon live under the same roof again, and she would love and co-create my immortal dream with me. So it is with some sadness (not retained) that I know

now I must let her go. She has as much right as I do to make her own choices and explore this world and its people. I'll still always have a place for her in the immortal eternities, but my guess is that she will attract a man to her who will be much better than I am for mortal life. (More money, good dancer, actively plans outings, takes her all over the world, showers her with flowers and expensive gifts, good at conversation, etc.) She deserves all that, I (reluctantly) let her go - I *must!* I think this all stems from my sending her home early because I was at the time infatuated with Jackie. She felt rejected and most likely has been probing me since then for justification to do what she is now doing, chasing other men. Is her objective friendship, sex, marriage? I don't know.

My time with Oresha yesterday was acceptable but not close like it once was. She turned her cheek to my greeting as I picked her up at her apartment building, me expecting to give her a light kiss on the lips. And holding hands was by my initiative. She left early, I walked her home after pizza carrot cake and a beer at my place. We did not swap much energy or satisfaction and she often mentions expensive places to go. It's time to back away completely I think, friendship has its limits, this one's with a practiced prude - that doesn't work for me. This afternoon I will pick up a woman in front of her apartment building and probably drive her to the breakwater for walk talk. She seems eager to meet me but we have exchanged very few messages and her profile is slim. We'll not meet until 3 p.m. because she has to get back from church and change. I know nothing about her and have no feelings in advance other than neutral. I expect little to come from this.

And I may have driven Linda away with my comments about looking for a travel companion. Most western women are like that, sexual activity is not something to even infer until after friendship is earned with outings and gifts. In effect, western women want to be bought. But my task right now as I see it (other than to write books) is to take the time to focus on my dream, one man, several women. That may take some time to get firmly in place. But then again, it doesn't have to, I know what I want, I know where I am going, I just need to find Eve to get there...

M: (to Jen) I just saw a clever message on singles: *"If we meet offline and you're nothing like your pics, you're buying me drinks until you do."*

Also interesting is the word "sapiophile" defined as: Sapiophile (noun) means someone who is sexually attracted to intelligent people. Monica is a sapiophile, she gets turned on by intelligent men and cannot resist to end up having sex with them. Bit of that in you do you think?

Jen: Thanks, I have seen that word. I would say I am a Sapiophile. More than muscles. Has always been important to me. Now how do you pronounce the word.

M: say pee oh file

Linda: Yes - I know a bit of Vancouver Island. I do not stay in budget hotels and motels. I prefer to stay in three or four star hotels at budget rates, or funky historic hotels. Having said that, I enjoy travel, but would really need to know a person well enough to feel comfortable with them before I ventured out on a road, plane or boat trip. I have my sister and my cousin, and a friend that I travel easily with. Right now I am looking for a long-term relationship, not just a travel companion. I have never been on a cruise ship. I really did sail the Caribbean. It was and is a relaxing way to travel. My friends tell me that cruises are even more relaxing - and that the food is marvellous. Someday I will take a cruise - maybe the new one in the south of France. A new adventure. My youngest son has spent time in Mexico and Guatemala and visited the Mayan ruins. I have yet to, but hope to someday. Where would you like to travel to next after VI? Enjoy the day, it is beautiful out there.

M: I'm thinking of exploring VI a bit this summer before the rains set in so I just tossed that out in case you might be amenable to such a thing as that. But I understand about not traveling with someone you don't know. And I understand about budget hotels too, I just thought there might not be much else available in the northern parts of VI. A long term relationship with a compatible companion would be most desirable for anyone I would think, especially in western society where monogamy reigns and women in particular have a driving need for that. I'm looking for a LTR primarily as well, but I'm practical enough and realistic enough to know that sometimes settling for a short term travel companion keeps life and fun flowing in the present while you plan for more. So with that, I'll say that I've enjoyed our conversation and will continue to swap messages if you choose to, but I'll certainly understand if conversing with a man who at this very moment is looking for a travel companion is not to your liking. Just say so and I won't trouble you further. Enjoy this beautiful day "out there" Linda; however this turns out, I wish you the very best.

Jen: Well, most likely nothing will come from any of this. I am not going to push for it. Might meet the one man for breakfast. Don't know yet. Just to get my feet wet with the dating game. Not looking forward to the game. I have not lost as much weight as I want to and that might chase him away. I do look much better. Will wear my smaller size jeans now. I have lost almost 20 lbs. But still have 25 or maybe 30 more to go. Plan on leaving to go back to Utah hopefully this weekend. That will put a hold on things down here. I certainly won't be looking for anyone when I'm visiting my daughter and tending her kids. You are by far the number one in the running. I will keep my feet on the ground and the fantasies to a minimum. I will email you every day as long as I have reliable internet.

Hmm, she's not signing off with a term of endearment anymore, that shows a change of attitude – a healthy independent one for her if she's really wanting to break away from me, as it may be best she do? At least she now acknowledges that being overweight might chase a man away. Why don't women (generally speaking) pay attention to the need to look good for their husband so they don't chase *him* away I wonder?

M: Even 20 lbs and a couple of dress sizes down must feel wonderful for you as you gain confidence in who you really are and begin to look like her. I'm pleased to be your number one, I still want you sweetheart. But being "number one" when there's not even a number two let alone three and four in the works yet is not a huge accomplishment. Enjoy the day.

Jen: In my eyes it is. That means number two and three have a strong completer that will be hard to beat. It can be a big step from two to one.

M: Keep your skirt fashionably short and sexy, but keep it tight so you can't take big steps and get away from me.

Jen: I think I have that skirt. Do you remember the red suit I had for my son's wedding. I should be able to fit into it soon. It had a tight red skirt with it.

M: Wow Jen, the thought of you being....

M: I keep your photos in my inbox so I can look at your pretty face several times a day and keep in mind whose roof I want to live under right now.

Linda: Tough to respond to your reasoning. Yes, women prefer long term, monogamous relationships. We love feeling protected and taken care of - it is in our genes. At least that is true for most of us. We feel secure in loving, tender, supportive, fun relationships - and it takes time to develop that sense of security. I can see that short term relationships would work for men in the short term as they often do not form the close friendships that women do. Women have a more difficult time moving from one relationship to the other. A short term relationship can and does get in the way of developing a more fulfilling long term relationship. It takes patience in getting to an "LTR". Communicating with you is fun. So - let's keep doing that. At least we can start out as friends that way and see where it leads. I am not in a hurry.

M: That's the best explanation of the difference between Venus and Mars that I have ever read, well done. I'm going to post that somewhere so I don't get the two planets mixed up and arrive at one when all along I thought I was headed to the other. Thank-you, I would love to continue swapping messages with you Linda. And you're right, there's no rush doing it this way. But someday we'll have to meet physically and see what can be remade from the shattered pieces of the virtual images we create in our minds while working these singles site venues (wearing hope, romance, and love on our sleeves.) Speaking of which (venue that is), conversation here is fine if you prefer it this way, but we'd each have more room to expound if you contacted me at my email address: (insert)

M: (to Jen) Here's a message I received from Linda today. I find her comments about the differences between men and women very interesting. She lives in Victoria. We haven't met yet but have swapped quite a few messages. I'll most likely meet her someday but won't set that up just yet, she's looking for something serious and I'm not there yet. "LTR" in her message means long term relationship. You'll see that on singles sites a whole lot, it's basically a marital type of relationship that follows friendship but doesn't have to include living under the same roof. It normally infers that both parties are monogamous, exclusive to each other. Like the old teenage concept of "going steady" and the old adult concept of being "engaged to be married."

Jen: I also forgot to tell you I bought a classy cream colored suit I purchased awhile back. Have not worn it yet. I should be able to fit into it.... It has a short skirt just above my knees.... Have to get used to feeling it is good to look sexy.

M: Even though her singles site profile was very skimpy, I agreed to pick up the lady I mentioned and drive to the breakwater for a walk. My agreement was based on the pretty face that is posted with her profile. Well, I'd heard that some people post older photos on singles sites and was a bit concerned because some of mine are two or three years old. But my goodness Jen, this woman's photo that drew me in must have been *thirty* years old! There was no resemblance. But she was nice and it was a pleasant enough walk to the end of breakwater and back, I'm getting much more comfortable with casual conversation. And along the way back, for the second time in three weeks I watched a seal eat an octopus. It was directly below the rail on the breakwater so it was a perfect view just a few feet away and the water was clear. A sea gull tried to get some of the octopus and when the seal wouldn't give anything up, the seagull pecked the seal's back. It gave a roar and lunged for the bird unsuccessfully, quite funny to watch.

As we got back to the Breakwater Cafe part of me said out of courtesy I should buy some refreshments for my walking companion. But I resisted that, figuring she had cheated me with that very old photo of her, so I took her straight home. She appreciated the afternoon out and thanked me for it. That's the end of my contact with her, another lesson learned, photos can't be relied on.

M: (to Jen) I'm going to Nanaimo tomorrow to meet Luchia and look over her art, hoping I can afford to buy a copy of one for my wall. I'll take a small suitcase just in case I decide while I'm there to keep going to Long Beach or stay at a hotel and explore the local beaches that I didn't see when with Jackie. And I won't likely take my computer, so if you don't hear from me for a couple or three days or so, that's why. No, I'm not planning to drop in on Jackie, that's over and done with, she never wrote back, doesn't want me, most likely for the best.

Luchia is much younger than me, we have virtual history from months ago. I love all of her incredible art, there are photos posted on singles. She's a beautiful woman so it really hit her hard a while ago when she was running along the beach and fell, going into a concussion with nobody finding her for 45 minutes. But worst, getting a huge gouge in one of her cheeks from landing on a sharp stone, marring the perfection of her features. At the time we'd only exchanged a few messages but she's extremely spiritual, uncanny, her abilities far beyond those of Lynne, she *knows* you from a distance. By email she turned to *me* for healing. I just happened to know right then that 24 "powerful women" were gathered in Los Angeles for a special cruise together. They were all metaphysical people. So I called them in to help Luchia from a distance, and also Marcy, the healer in your city who I went to for massage once while you and I were living together. (Marcy is now a psychic surgeon, she was trained recently in the caves of the Philippines, then right after she returned her mentor died.) Everyone helped Luchia from a distance, each in their own way. I assured Luchia that she was loved and not alone.

Luchia expressed her thankfulness on singles as follows:

> *"My friends here arrived like a chorus of angels. I can't describe the depth and the power with which I was held throughout this experience. Friends, friends of friends, I truly know now that I have never been alone and have always been well loved."* She additionally writes in her profile:

> *"Like everybody else on the planet I have been on the path forever. Lately I have returned to the gnostic path and three questions keep coming up – where am I right now? In the story... What am I doing right now... being in the story... Is there a chance I'm not in my physical body? Oh Yeah."*

I'm really looking forward to meeting her tomorrow morning and discovering how our energies blend when we're physically in the same room. Life for me continues to be like a beautiful dream unfolding...

Jen: I wrote the man I am suppose to meet for breakfast and told him I was not skinny and reassured him my pictures were current and gave him a out. He reassured me he was looking for more than a thin lady. So it is still on. I watched a man frantically walking around early yesterday evening expecting a date to show up. He was well dressed. You could tell how nerves he walked and looked. He gave up and got in his car and left. Saw the same thing tonight at the pier a tall man well dressed walking back and forth looking all around also nervous. I wondered if he was going to leave then saw a beautiful tall lady walk up to him. then they walked toward where I sat. I could see he was still very nervous. He put his hand on her shoulder then thin waste but she moved away and he dropped his hand. I got up and continued my walk pushing my little grandson in his stroller. Just interesting watching people. I also saw a wedding on the beach yesterday.

M: It will be nice for you to have proof that you are still lovely and desirable just the way you are. So, you know that he is looking for a relationship with you, he's serious. What are you going to do if your heart flutters and you like him a lot? What are you wanting?

Jen: Just not there yet. I don't really know anything about him. You just never really know if you are compatible. So far the only heart I had flutters for in 20 years is you. We will see. The look of older men is not very appealing to me in pictures. Hopefully more in person. If my heart flutters, I will take it real slow. I might see him one more time before I leave to see if it is a real flutter. I am leaving for Utah shortly after that. I will shut the singles sight down when I leave. I am in no hurry. I have you.

M: When are you meeting the man for breakfast? It would be helpful if you give your men a name (any name, just stick to it) the same as I tell you names. It would make it easier for me to know which it is among the possibly many men you will eventually write me about should you continue to want to share your life with me virtually. Law of Attraction will bring to you what you want, and will bring in abundance. You will have choices to make, many men will want to meet you. Your cheerful personality and good looks, your tight jeans, short skirts, and hint of cleavage, your penetrating pheromones, your dreams and fantasies on the surface, and your desire and eagerness to love fully and freely and be loved back will bring them back wanting more of you. They can't help it, they're male and you are available. They will swarm to you until you're caught by one (or more) and lose your pleasing new 'virginity', the pheromones that served you well when you were in heat, needing a male, desperately needing a male because that's just the way you are. Yes, the one (or more) you choose to mate with will be intellectuals or artists, they must be, that's what you want.

Though I can't really see you dating a lot of men, I think with your sense of loyalty it is more likely that you will fall in love with one man soon, write to him daily, see him every chance you get, give yourself to him wholly, travel with him, and eventually move in together. I expect that he will take good care of you sweetheart, at least for a while. It will be a new life for you. You and I will slowly drift further apart much as you have deep feelings for me (and I for you) right now. You have chosen to look for another, that's normal, I don't blame you for that, I even encouraged it not knowing how I would feel when you're in the arms of another. I know now, I'd sooner it be these arms that wrap around you, but we already had that, maybe it's time for another's to take their place. Fly, be safe, take joy in your freedom Madam Butterfly.

Strangely, now it is me who is the "backup" for you. Though you were never a backup for me, that was just your own invention. It is very different for me a male because I am *supposed* to have more than one wife, but you are supposed to have only one husband. So I don't need a backup, but I'm sure it is comforting to you to have me for one for you. And that I'll be for you, for as long as you need me to be. I won't desert you though you could easily desert me for another man, it is your present wish to explore that possibility. You agonized about it, but that was your choice, your decision, all is well.

There will always be a place for you in my post-mortal planets with my other wives should that be your choice and we both become immortals. It's not likely however that you will ever find another man with a similar dream, and thus with your mind focused elsewhere, you are not likely to become immortal in the sense of "translated". You will abandon and forget that desire because you will sooner be with the man of your mortal dreams for mortality. If he's Mormon (unlikely now that you are exploring and your body's available) then you would have a hope for the Mormon Dream. And I would wish the fullness of that upon you and your chosen man. (Though in the eternities if Joseph Smith and Brigham Young were correct, your chosen Mormon will also eventually have more wives than you.) I suppose in the Mormon Dream as I understand it, instead of you populating planets with physical bodies as it will be in *my* dream, you will be creating spirits for those physical bodies. That may follow for me too, but I can't imagine not being content forever with several beautiful loving wives and us populating planets with *physical* children. *I love the children so...*

Jen: Luchia looks like a very nice woman. Hope you find a painting that speaks to you. Wish I had bought more works of art in the past. I can't help but think you are hoping she will ask you to stay at her place. Best to stay in a hotel. She may be willing to walk with you on the beaches and have lunch. Have a nice trip. Hope you take your computer. Would love to hear how things are going and you are safe. Yes I agree it would be in bad taste to try to see Jackie.

M: (to Jen) Luchia writes about my complimenting her on how talented she is: *"Well thank you, and yes, as a 'human' work in progress, I have many projects if you know what I mean...... Yes I have a print of the beautiful water maidens..... that was a glorious day."* Adamani

I'll find out how much the print and framing will cost then decide, *"Water Maidens"* is my favorite of the photos of her work she posted on singles. As usual (you are highly psychic) she has already suggested lunch, and of course I'll be packing an overnight bag just in case, you would too.

She writes: "Awesome, of course I have time for you the address is (insert). Stay to the right I'm the little shack on the beach and you have to cross a little footbridge to get in. Why don't you try for around 1130 and maybe will drive to Parksville or Qualicum for lunch totally looking forward to it see you tomorrow." She wrote earlier when I was going to visit her with Jackie but she was on the way to Vancouver: "hi Michael I'm disappointed but I would definitely look up your friend Jackie and look forward to seeing you soon.. ciao for now Luchia... have very fond memories of your extreme kindness."

It will be a good visit Jen.

Linda: I do believe that men and women approach things differently because they are born that way - although socialization obviously plays a large role in it. Grey sold many books by exaggerating the differences - but he managed to get the basics down in writing so that the average person grasped them. Of coarse - there are also cultural and generational differences, which must play a role in the law of attraction. Yes, we should meet in person, maybe for coffee in a few weeks or so once the holidays are over. For now, swapping emails is good.

M: Yes, let's take our time, I'm content to swap the written word for now. It's most likely that our continued interest in the other will eventually result in that all important sometimes image-shattering first sip of coffee, eyes locked or eyes averted across a table, which it is depending on the first quarter second whole body impression. (Though eyes once averted can eventually lock fondly with time and familiarity.) I will be traveling tomorrow and may be delayed so please write but understand if you don't get a fast response. Enjoy the evening Linda.

Jen: His name is Jerry. I am meeting him on Thursday. He gets back from Oregon on Wed. I only have time for this one person right now. I still want to loss more weight. Most likely I will shut it down at the end of the week. Not enjoying it that much. Most of the men are not appealing to me. I saw a lot of people use a app on their I phones. I suppose that's how he is contacting me while traveling. I'll have to ask him.

M: Oh yes, almost every singles site member uses their cell phone to communicate while at work or wherever whenever they are not otherwise occupied. Even Suzanne always used her iphone to message me. That's the kind of thing that's happening as you look around and realize that almost everyone is staring at a small screen, smiling, and pressing little keys instead of enjoying the moment of where they are when.

All the best with Jerry Jen, I expect that you will find him sincere and wanting to know more about you when you part because you're a lovely woman, among the few who have not aged. He will want to stay in touch with you even when you're in Utah, you can expect that, and to be fair to him you should probably allow it if it seems a happy thought to do so. If it's not happy, then let him go, slip off into your own silence and look for another.

I'm missing you darling, not ready yet to give you up to another man. But I know it's inevitable now that you've opened yourself up to exploring the choices this world has to offer in abundance. The mating game is great and grand, all the emotions become engaged and you feel *alive* with exciting new possibilities, a brand new sunset to ride off into, a new dream to make and share and follow with another. I'm here for you for as long as you want me to be, I'm backup, I'll support you in your choices and decisions, be happy when you are happy, wish you only success and fullness of joy, you deserve it. Take care my dearest love.

Luchia: Hi Michael, thank you so much for your visit today..... an angel turning up with chocolate!!! Lunch was wonderful as was the walk and of course I am utilizing your spiritual suggestions as we speak! To be truthful, I feel blessed and hopeful that you felt called to my aid and of course, how could it be any other way. What interesting beings we are, immortal and beautiful. Thank you and I will soon be looking into the two water maidens for you, what a lovely compliment! Take care dear one

M: I enjoyed the time we had together today Luchia, it was nice and much too short, perhaps another day we'll visit longer, please stay in touch. I feel your great aloneness sweetheart, your confusion where you are right now, your disappointment today perhaps. It is my hope that the next moments will bring you the happiness that will make your heart sing as you flit about your home and yard like the butterfly newly emerged: humming, singing, breathing *life* into your surroundings and your art. Even your dogs and cat will respond as you lift your vibrations, put on beautiful garments, and let your light and love shine. You have a perfect home for an artist like yourself, and you are well loved. Could it be time to let go of pain and discontent, find your matrix within yourself, always be *home* wherever you are, choose happiness moment by lovely new moment?

Sweet dreams tonight dearest Luchia, awaken refreshed I hope, new life pulsing within you, the urge to *live* and love life because it's full with *joy*, low hanging fruit, ripe for the choosing, moment by *exciting* moment, the way life is meant to be, it is your destiny.

I care about you Luchia, I look to see a new art form from you. It has begun already with the butterfly because butterflies are free. They only crawled in the dirt so they'd appreciate their wings and daily give gratitude and thanksgiving for being who they really are. Not everybody can be an artist, be glad that you are and buy some fresh canvas, a colorful skirt for your rebirth. That's who I want to see and hear when I come back. *Sing* for me dear one, I would hear your beautiful songs, the ones you used to sing so well, we loved that about you. Your new works will sell because they're happy, and that's what people want. Portray the transition if you will, but I suggest you not linger too long there lest it become sticky and hold you back. Move forward to fullness of joy, songs of innocence found *after* experience, so you know the difference. Joy's a much happier place to be, that's where you belong beautiful Luchia.

Jen: Don't you want me. I miss and want you to. Hope you have an enjoyable lunch and short vacation with Luchia.

M: *Yes I want you!* But we're not together right now and you are looking for another man so it makes it more difficult for me, it introduces uncertainty between us where before I felt certain that we'd be together again. (I invited you to come back, remember.) I want you to be free, so I'm not going to say anything negative about you dating others and will support you in whatever your choices are. And I *will* be a backup for you should that not work out well for you. Maybe it's best that you do gain experience with other men, maybe even sex if that's what you want? (I'm not encouraging it, I'm encouraging you to be *free* to choose for yourself.) I'd still be your backup, you must make your own choices without me holding you back. You already know what *my* choices are and why. What do you *really* want Jen? I think for now you want to run around a bit and try to find a better man than me, or maybe just a lover for a while to see what it feels like to be with another? If so, now is a good time to do that, much as I'd miss you. You're single and uncommitted, go for it *if that's what you want.*

I visited with Luchia for a few hours. I drove her bright yellow 150 mph capable sports car (stick shift) with the top down to a nice place along a beach where we had lunch. Then walked along the sandy beach together, the ocean was warm there. For about a half hour when we first met I felt a connection with her but nowhere near as powerful as that with Jackie. Then I realized in my mind after that half hour that I had been assessing and making a decision. The decision was that I was not going to get further involved with her. At that exact moment she said, *"I feel a separation from you."*

I became (as usual) just another woman's angel teacher, and I did. She made a decision right there that she had been needing to make for quite some time, I provided the key for her, I had come with the message she needed. She feels that she is an immortal, but doesn't know that for sure, just that she has always felt alone, not fitting in. (Heard that one before?) Luchia and I could be friends if we lived closer together, I could have stayed the night, moved in whatever, she invited me back even with a girl friend along, but it's not right for us to be lovers, that I know, at least not now.

I drove by Jackie's on the way home, if her car had been there I might have stopped to say hello but it wasn't in the driveway and I wasn't feeling a connection with her, nothing at all. That's over I think, and most likely for the best even though I can very quickly find feelings for her. I hate the way it ended so suddenly, there was no closure at all, no final talk and hug. If she contacts me in the future of course I will try again. The women in my life always seem to do the right thing in the end, meaning they drop me and go their own way, leaving me free to go my own way as well, though my way so far sure is a lonely one. I so miss the frequent touch of a loving woman, especially in my bed at night whether there's sex or not. So I'm home alone as usual, waiting now until Wednesday to meet the woman I'm not even sure I want to meet and see what if anything develops there.

Talk to me more if you miss me and want me, tell it true and whole so I know where I am with you, it's hard to know right now. Why are you looking for another man when you know darn well how quickly you would attach to someone who made your heart flutter even just a little bit, and you'd stay there out of loyalty? That's perfectly ok if that's what you want sweetheart, I'll remain your backup. But it would be nice to be with you for a couple of weeks say every three months or so with the possibility anytime of maybe working out a more long-term arrangement, I think that's what you wanted when you left Victoria. Talk to me, tell me the way it is with you, with us, tell it true and complete Jen, don't keep secrets from me please, I need to trust you. Why are you looking for another man?

Jen: I realize even before meeting Jerry that it most likely will not go anywhere. I can't see myself making a commitment toward a man when I have family that needs me. I will be free someday. Hopefully after the first of the year. Maybe we can get together then. I am OK but also dealing with you dating and searching for other women. If you find one better than me you will go for her and commit to her. That leaves me out. I am not even looking 1/10 of what you are doing. I only looked for one day and gave it up. I would say you are in the number one running. Its just the timing isn't hear yet. You are still the only one I want to cuddle up to.

M: Ok, thanks for that, glad I'm still the only one you want to cuddle up with, let me know if that changes. I understand your fear about me committing long term to another. It would be normal for the immortal phase of my life to be with more than one woman. But I understand you wanting me exclusively for the mortal part, that's the western way, and the way of religion. Let's see how that works out. I would still where I am today favor us living under the same roof but with an open type of relationship. As time goes on I may choose not to have sex with anyone other than you anyway, I value the freedom to choose for myself, and would grant you the same. Do what you have to do, have fun, be happy, keep reminding me that you still want me more than any other man, and don't be away too long.

Linda: I look forward to that image-(earth?) shattering cup of coffee! Have a great trip.

M: Hopefully after that experience of first meeting we'll be able to retrieve some of the better pieces and together fashion them into a co-creation made more in the image and likeness of us. (Admittedly, getting too serious here, a romantic at heart for sure, tank of hope not yet drained, still actively working on stemming the flow but running out of fingers to plug the widening holes, help please...)

I like what we are doing, this is much more comfortable than the experience I had meeting a lady a few days ago whose singles site photo turned out to have been taken at least twenty years ago. It was pleasant enough but short, I felt that I'd been tricked into the meeting, guess it worked for her. I visited with a friend who is a great artist yesterday. She lives in a little cottage on the sea, we walked the beach and talked much. I seem to be slotted as angel friend with a message from God kind of thing, it happens a lot even as I'm looking instead for romance and love. But the latter is hugely motivating, moves me around, and I'll be buying one of her lovely art creations for my bare apartment wall. Enjoy the day Linda.

M: (to Jen) Ok, maybe you being First Wife would work in my dream. Maybe we'd live together more than I with any other. Maybe your love for our sister wives would not be as intimate as theirs for each other, unless you chose it to be moment by moment. I'm willing to explore that possibility, maybe co-create it with you if you will, it seems to be what you want. Would you help me pick out our wives?

Jen: I have really tried to understand your position of why it seems so important now to be in search of these women. I can't help you pick out these women. Let the next life or realm care for your wants of many wives. *Truth is I want one man and for him to want one woman.* Then dream together our wants, our connection, our love and create joy each day, bring some excitement, and accomplishments into our lives. Plus bless the lives of our children. What I want is very simple. I think this is what would make you also the happiest if you could set aside your desires in your mind. Otherwise I wish you the best in your search for your wives.

Ok, that's plain and simple and right down to earth where she lives. Am I sabotaging that relationship too with my one line message about helping pick out my wives? And if so is it because I'm so not of earth, or at least think I'm not? I do get carried away, I thought she had changed when she told me when she was here that in the night she had learned to accept my being with other women and to love my dream. But then, she knows now from apparently only one day on a singles site that her pretty face and *"I'm available"* pheromones can attract men like flies to the promise of honey. She doesn't really *need* me anymore... But then I look at the photos of pretty her, think of her slim and loving me fully, and I'm so very tempted to be that man she wants. I *could* have a normal life with her. But then, should I not hold in my mind as the highest ideal my dream of forever? Should I not mimic that dream as best I can while still in mortality, like some native tribes do to create on earth what they see in their dreams? Am I in the world but not of it, or am I in the world and of it?

But she's so pretty. I knew she would be my greatest temptation. Can I have both worlds, keep my cake and eat it? Would she allow that, down to earth her as I press footprints in the soils of this planet, go shopping with her, take her to movies, yet in the secretness of my mind *be* my fantasy? But she'd know and she says she wants "one man and for him to *want* one woman." With that one revealing sentence of where she stands she makes it impossible for me, for us, she has not changed. She demands not only exclusive possession of my body but also wants possession of my thoughts, my desires, my fantasies, my dream, wants it made in *her own* image and likeness. That's just not me is it? How can it be? Can she not see that even the Mormon way for eternity is one man and several women? Or does she just want to suspend that for now while she lives out responsible world mortal her? She *is* caught up with her family right now. There's potential yet, but it seems we may need to let each other go for the best interests of each other.

I know I can choose my own wives without her, they'll be attracted to me, and it doesn't have to be now. It's just that I'd hoped they'd be OURS. It's not looking right now that that's the way it will be. I may need to continue my search for one more compatible with eternity in mind. Or just a lover for now? Maybe that's all I need as I write my books, the frequent touch of and sex from a willing woman who cares for me, and cares enough to let me go the moment I choose it to be that way. I love me, but it's lonely being me most times.

I met my next door neighbor a few days ago, rode the elevator, she's from Liverpool, tending a grandchild, worried that his sounds last night (I never heard them) would be bothering me, the "poor man" who lives with only a wall between us. She's attractive enough. Would it be foolhardy to make her my lover when we live only inches apart? Or would it take care of my immediate needs and wants as I write without having to take the time to search for a lover? Tell me what's best someone? Anyone? Who can I turn to but myself? Even Linda or other promising ones would want me to want only them, that's the normal responsible down to earth way for a long term western style relationship. So if that, why not Jen instead, and keep our luggage tags?

I think I have lost my blooming confidante, my new 'Suzanne'. I can no longer share myself fully when what she wants is a man to think only of her. And I will, I *must* think of others too, she should know that, why did she sabotage what we had going? It's not that she wants to share my life with other women by proxy as I thought it might be. I think now it's that she wants me to share my stories so she can constantly assess the validity of her hope to live with me full-time again. She asks herself with each new story, how close am I to making a long term commitment and then not want her? And should her desire for me wane, or even anyway, she will explore the possibility of other men whether or not she tells me about them. (I can't trust her to tell me, she keeps secrets.)

Of that I think I am certain, but it's based only on her short paragraph last written. Like the woman in Texas, I think inside Jen is a WILD ONE wanting to be loosed. Maybe that's how it is with most women, especially those caught in the snares fears and guilts of religion?

Jen: Hi Michael, Haven't heard from you all day. Hope this email gets to you. still friends. Love you Jen

Jen: Hi, I could not sleep thinking about you. Hope you are alright. Please let me know. I do love you and very concerned about you. I know you are lonely but I don't think that's going to last much longer. I am having so many issues with my computer that I don't even want to use it. Love Jen

M: Jen, You wrote: *"Truth is I want one man and for him to want one woman."* And you seem to write me off and send me on my way if I continue to want to follow my dream and live my life *my* way: *"Otherwise I wish you the best in your search for your wives."* Yes we can be friends Jen but your statements make it difficult to imagine us being anything more than that. I understand your desire to possess my body exclusively for yourself, that's the monogamy and religion way, normal in western society. But you even want me to give up my dream and desires, you know what they are.

That's a very long way from the woman who woke up in my bed in Victoria and surprised the heck out of me by saying she had had a spiritual experience in the night and was now ok with me being with other women. And if I recall correctly she was ok with my dream as well. I was happy and hopeful for us. But it seems what you told me was either not sincere or you have changed your mind since then and want to go back to the way we were. I understand now what you really want with me and I think you understand what I want with you. Is there a way to reach a happy compromise do you think? What parts of my dream and desires could you live with if we decided to live under the same roof again but do it differently this time so it's not boring and blah? Where could we live?

Linda: I have met a few men for coffee and had a similar experience - but they had also subtracted a decade or so from the age that they had posted on the site. You write beautifully - or maybe I am just intrigued with what you have to say. Your friend sounds interesting, maybe, if our souls do connect, I can meet her someday. And yes, I am a hopeless romantic at heart. I like what we are doing as well. We should feel more comfortable and familiar with each other by the time we meet than we would meeting as strangers. That will help. I have been moving my office this week - my downsizing effort. Tough with such a large library. So many decisions to make about what to keep and what to let go of. Have a wonderful evening,

M: Sure, I expect that my artist friend would enjoy meeting you, in fact she invited me to come back anytime, even bring my girl friend with me. Hey, you might buy some of her art eh? She's single and pretty but as I mentioned before I seem to have slotted myself in with her in the role of angel/teacher. We're both spiritually/metaphysically inclined, we speak that common language. It sounds that you have arranged a most enjoyable weekend, the littleuns are precious and adorable. Anytime a child is in a room with adults socializing, invariably all eyes are on the child, all lips are smiling. Little children as the poet wrote come trailing clouds of glory. They settle in and teach us if we will but listen and observe, the things of heaven we have forgotten. I'm glad there are other hopeless romantics in this world, there's hope for this one yet. Enjoy the day Linda.

Jen: I do not write you off and send you on your way. This adventure is a two way street. Like I said I did embrace your way of thinking and really wanted to understand where you are coming from without judgment. Still don't judge. I also needed to get my head straight enough to think about what I really want. Maybe sooner than later we can come to a comfortable place for both of us to be happy. I am being honest to what I really want as you have been honest to what you want. Being together takes giving on both sides. Even if I am not comfortable with some of your desires. That does not mean I don't understand his desires and love the man. If we were together I would want to be monogamous. You would be free to be faithful or not just like any man in a marriage that chooses to be faithful or steps out on his wife. All men and women have that freedom. Its just a matter what is most important to you. Any monogamous woman that has a husband of many wives or knowingly knows her husband is sleeping with other woman are NOT in a marriage for love.

With some cultures it is to bear children with the right name or family, and/or to be well taken care of. Its an arrangement often they have no say about. If the man is good to her and shows kindness then maybe she will come to respect him and yet always reserve her love for her children. Her dreams are based on what he can provide for her. With some cultures men and women each cheat. the man openly the woman quietly. It is excepted. The middle east. Woman have very little choice. There marriages have nothing to do with love. Just don't see any of it being very desirable. Its just never really worked in this life. Even the prophets of old had problems with the women being jealous. Those were the good stories.

I just don't think it should consume our future outlook in this life when it is not going to happen here. Maybe its us western women and men that put so much emphases on love. I am not saying people in other countries don't love each other. I am saying that's not what it is based on when choosing wives. I know you have your dream and beliefs. To me, the time is not here. Someday it may be. It is prophesied to be. When that time comes I think I am one of the few women that will accept it and help other women come to grips with it. Because the times will be such that it has to be. My problem I have is the intensity you are going about it. I am not sure that's how I want to spend the rest of my life helping you find more wives. I still have dreams and desires to be filled also. I believe most women our age will choose to be single over helping a man find other women to bring into his fold. We are not made that way. Women have been forced into those relationships because of the fear the men put into them. Most play the part to survive in that culture. Love Jen

M: Well written Jen, good clear thinking, thanks for that. I love you and want to be with you. I wish you were here while it's still such lovely weather for walking and for exploring Vancouver Island. I do want to work this out for us to be together again, but not together the way we were. We need to find exciting things to plan and talk about or we'll go back to the silence. I was hoping co-creating my dream would do that. But I understand your desire to be 'normal'. It just troubled me a whole lot when it seemed you wanted me to let go my dream and go back to what we had and nothing more, or else you'd write me off. Though with your new body and newly expressed sexual desire for me, and me improving my attitude towards you it could possibly work without us getting intensely into my wanting to manifest my dream right now.

In fact, if I only *wrote* about my dream imaginatively, instead of *living* it like I have been doing for almost a year now, maybe that would be sufficient for me and it wouldn't trouble you a whole lot? I do need real world stability now, you would bring that to me, you're good at that. You might even enjoy being my "Suzanne" writing me messages from your office, me responding from mine as we co-author books of fiction, maybe even move into writing romance novels for Baby Boomers just for fun and to show that there's *life* (and sex) after 55?

I drove the Texas hospice nurse I call "Suzanne" to your city on the way to Zion National Park when she visited with me in Las Vegas. I drove by our house and showed her some of the sights: Snow Canyon, lunch at the artists' place in Kayenta, she's big into art and culture. Later she told me she watched me closely as I toured her about and spoke so fondly of your city. She told me that I was "not available" that I was still attached to YOU! I think she was right, and that's the main reason why she left me. I haven't heard from her for months, she's gone, I miss her, she was my virtual sweetheart and my tormentor both in one. Real life shattered our illusions, destroyed what we thought we had, there were no pieces left big enough to pick up and fashion something better from. We'll see what comes for us. But please give me a chance to be the man you want when the time is right for you. Should you fall in love with another man, come see me first and let's talk about it before you make a long term commitment. Chances are we'll still love each other a heck of a lot even though we've both moved on. We still have the same name on our baggage tags, it would be easy to move our suitcases into the same closet again, easier than to rewrite the tags with another's name on them.

I fear the thought of losing you permanently, I don't want that to happen, you were good for me. But I'm realistic enough to know that with time and neglect to what we have right now that we'll both find happy matches in others, and will give the fullness of our hearts to them, that's for certain. So don't be away too long, I'm inviting you back to me right now. I'm still single but there are others closing in, some of them carefully working their woman magic, spinning their compelling web in all the right ways. I feel their presence and I'm drawn because I'm lonely and I'm needy and I'm vulnerable. In my dream that would be acceptable, but it won't fit yours, I know that now. *What can we do about it?* I felt much love for you today as I walked the breakwater. You're in my head for sure, and it's not just flashbacks and memory, it's now. Where could we live, will you plan it for us? Or do you want to first explore being slim and single, lovely and in demand, and take the chance of new baggage tags for one or both of us? If you do I will surely understand. I have no hold on you, you have no obligation, no strings are attached, the choices are all yours and mine. The mating game is exciting, *it's calling and calling and calling...* Who will it be for us?

Wow, maybe I really do have Suzanne back. Look at what she is eliciting from me and Muse. And her words are wise as well. Only time can tell...

Uncharacteristically I haven't heard from Jen for a while as I rise from the queen bed in my one bedroom apartment and warm the keyboard this Thursday the 28th day of August in Victoria, British Columbia Canada. And she has a long message oozing commitment yet to respond to, she should have by now. But her mind's elsewhere I think, I'm not her priority yesterday and today, she's taking care of herself, I'm backup. Today she meets Jerry and I realize too that she has been swapping messages with males and not commenting except that bit several days ago about Jerry. She has her own life, new confidence gained from posting her pretty face on a singles site and instantly getting expressions of interest from males, *she doesn't need me.* Maybe it's for the best the all-is-well-always part of me keeps repeating. She may not be responding yet to my last message because she wants first to see how it is with Jerry. If her heart flutters for him she will respond to my message colder than if it hadn't. At least that seems logical. It may simply be that her computer or internet connection isn't working.

It will hurt to let her go I know but I need not just to be prepared for that to happen but to be better prepared to invite another woman into my life, long term. I'll meet with the women I'm not sure I want to meet with tomorrow I think, haven't heard from her after her saying she'd phone yesterday and didn't. It doesn't seem to matter much either way anymore if I meet her or not, I think I'd sooner not. I like messaging with Linda but don't feel emotions, it's an intellectual exchange that feeds something each of us needs, we pretending that romance is in the works, we're becoming friends first we say. Linda's not in my head,

I've created no fond image of her, no image at all, she's just on hold. I would quickly forget her if she didn't message back. Am I growing stale and jaded with the singles scene, just needing sex when not working a keyboard plying my wordsmith trade?

I put a "skip" into Heather's step she says. And she phoned me, her parting words filled with the sound and feel of deep affection. She has imagined an ideal in younger me, and she won't be disappointed. If I like her a lot, with this one I need to stand back and let *her* do the chasing - if I can, I'm so impulsive. She owns a waterfront condo. So she could most likely travel Dutch if we do and I ask. But what will she look like when we meet on Tuesday? Will she look old and wrinkled like most but not all women that age do? I don't know, and it's important to me to know. She says she's blonde and slender so she takes care of herself, maybe touch of class, used to having some means and status perhaps, she's a widow. At this point, setting Jen aside, she's my number one prospect. Time will tell, the chase can be exciting.

Ok, as I write that, feelings arise for Heather, dear dear one. Why do I feel like that for you? We've never met, I've never even seen a photo of you. Is it because you are feeling like that for me and I sense you feeling? She'll feel good when we hug, her heart and yearnings are already there, she's woman soft. But what will she look like? I want so to throw myself into a beautiful woman, a fullness of careless abandon, allow life to *sweep* us away, sunrise sunset together forever. I want it, I want it, *I want YOU...*

I still think sometimes of knocking on my next door neighbor's door (the woman from Liverpool) just to see what might develop from that tapping, lovers maybe? It would be so convenient – two taps on the wall that separates us: come over, three taps, I'm coming... I realize that when we rode the elevator my sister was with me and Liverpool might have took my sister for my wife, so I'm feeling no vibes from behind the wall and LOA is not moving us together in the hallway.

Ok, no connection felt with Jen right now, she prepares herself carefully to meet another man, a man with money and a large sailboat. He'd bring her great excitement for several years if he kept her. *I wish her well, I love her, God be with her and keep her safe...* May she have the very best that life has to offer, even if it is not with me, I wish it upon her. Perhaps it is *freedom* from her that I most need right now to attract the right other into my life? I could so easily feel nervous today about Jen meeting her first man from a singles site: sadness, sorrow, loneliness, loss of hope. But I don't go there anymore do I? Even if Jerry doesn't cause her heart to flutter, I feel certain that Jen will look for more, most likely without telling me, that's one reason why she wants six months apart. She agonized about it because she's so loyal and she genuinely loves me, but I believe that's what she has decided to do. With me looking at other women, it's in her own best interests to look around herself, that's understandable.

However it is, I must now stop thinking of Jen as a confidante and sharing everything with her. She didn't even ask about the woman she knew I was meeting yesterday. I think she sees me sometimes as a child she loves and feels responsible for guiding, like my first wife did. There's not much coming back from Jen, she keeps her life to herself. I must do that more too, it would be wise. Jen's on the look for another man, I may suddenly hear that she's got one and nothing before. It will be interesting what she reports about breakfast with Jerry. If it's very little then it's likely that it went well, her heart fluttered, she felt excitement, the hope of promises to come. I'm dreading, but kind of wishing it is so easy for her. If it's negative then she still clings to me and I to her, for now. Until a better one arrives?

That's how I see it in this moment of my longing. We'll see what comes through my doorway, it's open, wide wide open right now. My body is craving, my heart and brain are mush, my soul is yearning.

Chapter 25

———— ✦ ————

M: (to Jen) It's my turn waiting now, what's happening?

I look at her photos again since she has lost some weight. *She's so beautiful!* But is that smile and happy look because her pheromones are flowing free, she's now available for *any* man who makes her heart flutter, and not just for me? I'll answer that myself: *She's single and wanting, why wouldn't it be so?* This moment I want her so much and she's most likely at this very moment with another man… I can't wait to hear how it went with Jerry, I hope she tells me and tells me true, and tells me soon. My guess is that it went very well, she's pretty, and she's eager for the love and protection of a man. But she's not committed yet I don't think because she needs to get back to Utah to tend her grandkids there. She and Jerry will stay in touch and meet again unless perhaps I myself commit soon and completely to her, *her* way. *I just might do that!*

Heather? Haven't even met her yet, might not work out for us right from the beginning, only time and our physical meeting will tell. I've been there several times before, it didn't work out well, even with Jackie who I had so much hope for, yes Jackie made my heart flutter. Or with Jackie was it just my intense NEED again I wonder, now that she's gone? I want you *right now* Jen, I need your newly tight body wrapped around mine, your lips full upon me. Will you come home to me and share my bed again? I'll be better next time, not holding back like I did because I clung to the past. I did not satisfy you, but you did me.

It's noon now, she may have gone back to her responsibilities for the other grandson, she and Jerry parted. They may meet again for dinner at the pier, hold hands, hug and kiss on the beach as darkness falls. I did that with her and more when we were courting 18 years ago, it was good. I hope they don't go as far as we did, but I think she's capable of doing that if Jerry's real good with her, she's got to be lonely and needing with me so up and down and far away. And if dinner or evening sail is on for them, I may not hear from her. She's off to Utah tomorrow I think, unless Jerry delays her parting, and he may, she'll be eager for the newness of life that he can give her. Where are you with US my love right now? *Please don't forget me…*

469

As it works with Law of Attraction, many roads are always offered. I had no sooner finished writing the sentence above than I got a phone call. We'll be meeting at her golf club for lunch at noon tomorrow then going to her place to talk, hmmm. She lives quite a few miles away from me so I'll need to research and get my timing organized for tomorrow a.m. She's a tall slim blonde, hugely attractive from a distance, to die for, but a close up shows her face has not survived the test of time, leaving wrinkles appropriate to her age, which is the same age as mine. If it wasn't for the possibilities told above, I might think long term with her, but just lovers for now would be my thinking. My guess though is that she'll have a huge say in that herself. (I hope you're assuming a whole lot of smiles, I deliberately take them out of my and other people's emails, wouldn't likely look good in a printed book.) But whatever, at her home we'll have all doors open that we mutually consent to walk through, including her bedroom door. (I'll take a toothbrush.) I would most likely be her lover if she offered, much as that could complicate all of the above. I'm just too needy right now to pass up a tall slim gorgeous blonde who beckoned me to her bed.

There, forgot Jen for a few minutes real quick. I'll try not to dwell on her today, hope she writes soon, maybe it's just computer problems and everything else is just a story coming from my mind. Except as far as I know she was in real life planning to meet Jerry for breakfast today. Oops, the feelings are back, *I want you Jen.*

Good stories happening dear reader? Want more like these? Give me a moment to live some more then, they're always coming, Law of Attraction never rests. I just received notice that Carrie was looking at my profile on singles a moment ago – nope, not about to head for South America anytime soon...

2 p.m. and I'm trying real hard not to think of Jen and Jerry, but I'm not successful. If she leaves me for who and what I am I'll understand, but I really don't want to lose her to another man she has chosen instead of me while I'm still available. I expect she's having computer problems, but *please write to me soon Jen.* I love you darling, other women are calling, calling skillfully, compellingly, I'm needy, I'm falling for their siren song, *tell me you still want me?* Jerry, Jerry, what hast thou inadvertently wrought upon this man who's still in love with his ex,

the woman you are with today? Can you not sense that SHE'S NOT AVAILABLE??????

Well, it's best that I just go about my business and leave her to hers. It doesn't mean yet that we can't get together in a few months and have that talk that I'm wanting to have this very moment. Linda, Samantha, Heather, JEN!!! Which one will it be or none? Is there another yet to come?

I was just about to change to go out to drive by Heather's place but felt I should wait longer. At 2:12 the following arrived:

Jen: Had a nice breakfast. He is kind and pleasant. He talked a lot. Was in the navy special forces when young. It took him to more than 50 countries. He has a sail boat. Plus restoring another sail boat. We sat, walked and talked a bit. Never touched except to say Hello and good by. He asked me to go to a movie sometime. Just to be friends. No connection. But neither of us was seeking that. I think he is lonely. Just wanting someone to hang out with. Would work well for me. Been divorced 10 years. It was a pleasant visit. He's nice enough looking and in good shape. I can see we are both alike in some ways. So nothing very exciting. Don't like the hunt. Don't like the dating sites. He figured out I was Mormon. Jen PS. Just about to the point that I can't wear my old clothing. I did buy some smaller sizes. But not enough. If keep losing weight I won't fit into them either.

Just in case she's still online I quickly sent the following:

M: Thank-you so much for the update, I was thinking I'd maybe lost you to a man who can give you much more than I can in terms of material things and excitement. So where do you see yourself with me now that you have that experience behind you?

She obviously knew I was stewing because she instantly went into telling me about Jerry even though I hadn't mentioned him recently. I do think because she has told me so little, just the facts, that indeed he did make her heart flutter and there's a whole lot more went on internally than she's saying. And he did invite her back to him. So she'll be thrilled, will meet him again, and I honestly don't know where she is with me for sure anymore, or how close I need to keep my heart from another. Even taking her to a movie connotes at least hand holding along the path to intimacy, and knowing her loyalty, my loss. Yeah, I know, I'm doing more than hold hands with other women, Jen knows that, I must accept her and her new freedom to be who and what she wants to be. I should be thrilled that she had that experience today. Maybe I'll write her.

M: I sent that last note in haste, thinking you might still be online. Maybe it was not in order, I should be thrilled for you Jen and should have congratulated you. It was a wonderful experience, and just your first date since going on singles, there may be even better to come. What a thrill it must be for you to be shopping for smaller size clothing. (Thrilling to me too to think of you, I'm still in love with you you know, or do you?) I've been doing a whole lot of journal writing today about a lot of things, reshaping my priorities. But I'm not sure of anything, life is thrust upon me so quickly and with such abundance in the Law of Attraction fast lane that about all I can do is observe rather than absorb and think rationally. And maybe that's the way life is supposed to be on the leading edge of thought, someone's got to be there... It would be nice if you would respond thoughtfully to the last long email I sent, the one that begins: *"I love you and want to be with you."* I love you sweetie, I'm pleased that life is working out well for you.

Jen: (she sent this just as I sent the above so she hadn't read that yet) You are still in the number one spot but don't know who's in number two. Oh, no one. Not much competition. Haven't followed up with anyone else. Will not most likely. The site is overwhelming. There are hundreds of men to look at. Being LA area. They are announcing single activities going on all the time. Might go to one of those if close by. Otherwise just doing my family stuff. *You're the only man I love.*

So with that, what do I do? For Samantha and I to become casual lovers would be normal I should think, we're both single. But with Heather it's very different, she was widowed only 15 months ago from a man she loved dearly and lived with for 19 years. He was prominent in the community. I must be extra gentle with her, maybe just listen to her tale would be the best, try not to fall in love with her and play replacement for the deceased. Maybe become good friends to give her time to grieve, and a shoulder to lean on while she does. *But I can't imagine a woman like I think Heather is ever wrapping her mind around becoming Eve.* Though maybe she could, I'd want to see what she writes, she says it's novels, maybe she's imaginative. *I can however imagine Jen working on becoming Eve!*

There, I've thought that one through as usual with my fingers on a keyboard. Jen it is, but I'll meet with the other women and take what comes, maybe not even tell Jen about them for her own feeling of security in me being her backup? She's obviously expecting to stay on the singles scene, meet Jerry again, attend singles events, she's not devoted to me like I think she once was. I just wish we could get together within the next two or three weeks she and I.

M: (to Jen) Well, if I'm the only man you love, how be you come as soon as you've done your tour in Utah and if you come soon enough for the weather, we'll explore Vancouver Island together? Where are you now with that? It's an invitation.

M: I'm going out for my walk to the end of Breakwater, back in about two hours most likely. I do want to continue our conversation today, especially if you're headed to Utah tomorrow. Are you? I'm having strong feelings about you today, thank Jerry for that. Please be as open with me as you are capable of being, especially about the strength of your desire to actively *look* for another man. It does seem like you are expecting to meet Jerry again and to start going to singles events etc. Maybe that's what you really want. I may be the only man you love right now, but that could change if we don't soon make some concrete plans for US and start co-creating that future. Sure wish you'd come right away even though you haven't yet done all the physical improvements you want to make on your body. You could continue those here, at least the weight loss, we'd sure do a whole lot of walking (and talking about a possible future for us.)

Your photos sure are beautiful, and that was only a 20 pound loss. Maybe it's the newly released *"I'm available"* pheromones playing on your face. You got *me* humming that's for sure. Talk to me please, I'm wanting you, I think I'm deeply in love with you, and ready to do something about it. *Will you come back?*

That should be plain and simple enough. If she writes back and says she wants me, she's coming soon, then my heart is not free to give to another. But if she makes excuses and doesn't see herself coming here anytime soon then I will feel free of that self-imposed commitment. It will mean to me that she wants to enjoy single life and play with other men, at least for now, with me as backup. She has been 'warned' she knows my present willingness for her and my need, and she knows too the fickleness of this present heart, it's longing to be given away real soon. Her answer, hopefully tonight, is very important to me, whether she senses that or not. She could lose me tonight to another, because if she doesn't come real soon I will feel that she is lost to me already anyway, all ties severed by her longing to play with others.

For years I've had dreams of Jen gone. I'd look for her in strange cities, know she's there or had been there, but never able to find her, or if I did she'd walk away. Was that just fear or was it prophecy that eternity with her was never meant to be? She dreamt vividly of having sex with a man who impregnated her, of seeing him in a Mormon temple, a voice telling her that was her husband. *It was not me!* I gave it my best shot, as the sign on the side of a bus spoke loudly when I walked today, my eyes pulled to see and read it. How will she respond? However it is I am accepting. It will conclude with this test of her willingness to come to me within the next few weeks or not. If not, my heart is available and I will share little about my comings and goings with Jen from that time on. Although we may have a brief surge or two, she and I will drift further and further apart until I can no longer find her even if I wanted to, it will not matter, she belongs to another.

There could be others presently unknown of course but I feel good about Heather sight unseen, we could get serious real quick if she looks good to me the moment I first set eyes on her, like Jackie did. And I *can* keep my dream secret for a while until we know each other better. Maybe she would *want* to become Eve, if she can give up her deceased husband and catch that vision. That would be a toughie, maybe impossible to overcome. But I feel that it will not be so, my focus still is on Jen. She and I *could* make it happen, together become Adam and Eve regardless of all else and others. All we'd need do is to in unison and harmony put the *fullness* of our minds into it. I do love her, she's still my number one choice for Eve.

Jackie, Jackie, I'm beginning already to forget Jackie – she must be in some strange city somewhere, lost to me forever by her own choice, as Jen may be as well... Ok, 7:15 p.m. and I have my answer, it's not to be Jen.

Jen: As much as I would like to come see you I have much to do. My family is first. Walk with your walking buddies and I will do the same and when I am down to the size I want to be. Love you Jen

M: I understand your priorities. It's unfortunate because today was a very important day for me, I felt that I had decisions to make. But this is not the first time you have chosen others over me (as you have every right to do) when I made my desire to reunite abundantly clear. I was asking you to spend the week or so you had planned to be with your daughter first, and then come. I will stay in touch but I am disappointed, my heart is soft and wanting to be given away. It most likely will be soon. Here is an excerpt from my journal early a.m. August 28th, 2014 before you wrote me about Jerry.

Suddenly a moment later the sun has risen behind my curtains and I feel a great love coming into my life, I'd give all else away for *her* whoever she is. No, I cannot give up my dream, but I could keep it secret. What I'd give away is my present lifestyle, running here and there disguised as a self-made angel, teaching my tale to women who are not really my own, just imagined from the desperate wants I have, my foolishness and loyalty, the tenderness of my heart. If Jen and Jerry click and I know that, then I have my answer, my heart is free again to give away. And I will, I will, *she's coming!* But isn't what I just wrote exactly what Jen *wants*, just her and me and nobody else? MAYBE THERE *IS* ONLY ONE EVE?

Suddenly Jerry and Heather whom I have not yet met but have long term expectations for are exceedingly important to this story. Will Jen be Michael's Eve? Or will it be another? And if only one Eve, will Adam and Eve rotate sister wives through their immortal family to help populate planets, to create ever freshness in their lives and that of their children, and to give the temps experience they will need to become Eve themselves on some planet somewhere in time?

Hmm, that seems just as acceptable as the story I've been unfolding so far, the story that Jen cannot accept, the story of multiple wives at this time.

Jen seems to know the end from the beginning, all women do in near awareness. Wouldn't it be so much simpler if weeks ago she had told me about this new thought, *just one Eve*?

Hmm, she DID didn't she?

It was *me* who was not yet ready...

Please keep in touch even though our trust and confidence is shaken, perhaps irrevocably, I will always love you.

The only thing that would change my mind now is if she wrote back tonight and said she was coming to me real soon. Otherwise, I may not even respond to her messages for a while, she is not mine, we do not work together in harmony. Eve's *first* priority would instinctively be to Adam and to no other, she would rush to him when he called. This clears my path exactly when it needed to be cleared. Who knows, maybe *Samantha* will be the one I am looking for long term, we meet tomorrow, Heather not for five days, Linda nothing scheduled yet.

Life's so good. I will miss Jen, but in some ways it's a relief, it was just going back to the past, though her new body is exactly what I needed many years ago, it might have made the difference in itself. But then, had she slimmed down years ago I'd not likely be a writer today, and you'd not be reading this delicious true life story... What's to come next?

Linda: Lucia sounds interesting. The role of angel/ teacher should be an honour - unless you were anticipating a different role. I am presuming that she is a bit younger than you given her the slot that she chose for you. Yes I would like to meet her someday - even if we choose simply to be friends after meeting for coffee. At this age friends are important. Moving a library is exhausting and great exercise. Downsizing is a challenge, but I am ever the optimist. There may be hope for both of us yet. Have a lovely evening.

M: There you are, surviving the move and the decision making. I still have boxes of books from my undergrad days tucked away somewhere, maybe in a son or daughter's garage, never opened and most likely never will be because everything's now in e-book format and on my Kindle.

It was fun to see outside on my artist friend's deck an "old" painting of a Siberian tiger with the first line or two of William Blake's "Tyger Tyger". And even more fun to recognize that my English 101 prof had taught me well, sunk Blake deep into my mind. Of course in this case, having a young son who loved all things tiger, even his blanket, helped remember that I had once memorized that poem to quote to my little son's delight. There's much meaning in Blake's Songs of Innocence and Songs of Experience, I like his work a lot.

Re my role with Luchia, I'm a hopeless romantic at heart, always hoping for that one solitary perfect soul mate to ride off into a glorious sunset with forever, become Adam and Eve maybe, populate new planets, what else is there to do in the sunset anyway? But it was not Luchia, so I turned into an angel instead, I mean, what else could I have done?

Jen: Oh Michael, Your writing is so beautiful. My heart swells as I read your words. It creates a want in me to run into your arms and never let go. The sadness is I can't be with you at this time. Jerry will never be you nor any other man. I have no desire to find another man to replace you. It baffles me that I don't have a yearning to explore for the comfort of another. I guess my heart knows there is no other. Until then I will have friends not lovers. I know what I risk. I understand your needs as a man. I understand the needs of your heart. Until then my sweet love.

Did she *have* to come back with that brilliant return? It seems she still thinks we'll be together in the end regardless of what I do or do not do. She says she'll not have sex with another, but she also includes others as "friends" so she's for sure going to continue her search to be with other men (including Jerry of course.) *That's* what she wants, I called it right. And knowing her, she *will* forget her love for me when another flutters her heart. And she *will* have sex when it's right in her mind to do so, unless she sticks faithfully to her Mormon faith that forbids sex outside of marriage. Or, of course, unless she marries again. But I *must* give her up, she will not make me a priority. I'm asking for two weeks of her time when she's done tending her Utah grandkids and she will not give me even that, finds it acceptable risk to lose me to another instead. She has powerful priorities, or maybe was shown in vision in that experience she will not share with me the way it will be for her and me? My present belief though is that we create *our own* lives, that nothing else is written in stone for anyone.

She does not even comment that *I changed my dream for her!* ONE Eve, not me and several others, but allowing for temporary sister wives to rotate through our family. No mention at all that I've cleared the way for US to be together, eliminated all her given reasons for needing us to be apart, gave her monogamy for mortality, that's what she wanted most I thought. But no, it was her freedom to do what single people do I guess that was her priority. And that I understand. She also seems to be ok with us not even communicating anymore. At least I read that into her: *"Until then my sweet love."* Meaning I suppose six months or so as she stated a while ago when suddenly everything will be all right for us? Though she does acknowledge taking a risk that she might lose me, *and accepting it* for whatever her agenda is for the next several months before she's willing to come to me. I'll respond to her messages if she sends more, but I will not tell her my personal details, she has not earned that confidence and trust. Jen releases me, gives me her blessing to be what I must be right now, and takes the risk that I will never again be hers.

Well, 'Suzanne's' gone for sure, yet again. Will there be another, or am I now to just rewrite what I've got and make two beautiful books that will sell? Perhaps I should go back to Lynne, pay her to learn more about what my book/s are all about? Lynne, was I forgetting you? Actually not, just thought that fit in well with my comments above about forgetting Jackie, which is true. I pass by Lynne's apartment every day and notice if her balcony door is open or not. If open she's there, if not, maybe at the beach, and I watch for her, can't forget her that way. I have many interests, many desires, many loves, *who am I?* And with that, I'm going to put it to bed for the rest of the night. It was a busy day today along the way to becoming Adam. Did you enjoy our day together? Tomorrow *Samantha* – and in her home, real life! See you there?

Oh what the hay, I never gave up on Suzanne, why give up on Jen, here goes another try, the best I can give right now.

M: (to Jen) Given the very real risk that you and I will never again be together because of your choice today, I fail to understand why you will not come for two weeks after you've been with your Utah grandkids for a while. What is your *real* agenda? Just to be single and free to be with other men again for a while, Jerry and your neighbor maybe? If so, I can understand that. Surely it's not so that your body is perfect when you return should that ever happen, for that is not what I want, I want you here with me for a while just as you are and as you are becoming. Why really will you not grant us that especially when *I even changed my dream* to give you everything you said you wanted. You never even commented on that. You are a strange one indeed Jen. What is motivating you to be like that when you profess undying love for me and could have me but refuse? *What are you hiding from me that is so powerful?* I think you owe me an honest explanation why you won't give us two weeks between Salt Lake City and California, it would be so easy for you to do.

Whatever, I'm now considering Jen gone so I'm going back to my original dream, one man, several wives in the heavens. That one's much better, just thought that Jen needed some encouraging and we'd co-create our immortality side by side while living in the world of normal.

M: (to Suzanne) I don't know why I'm bothering to send you emails, you may not even read them for all I know. But here's something I wrote in my journal early today as I prepare to drive the distance and meet Samantha for the first time, we've been virtual friends for weeks. Then I'll meet Heather next week, we've talked on the phone (yeah really.) She breathes affection, I'm going to like her a lot. Jen's my ex, she visited me in Victoria two weeks ago. It was pleasant enough but she didn't stay long and there are no plans for her return. I don't know where we are if anywhere and I'm well ok with that. Wanting to settle down with one though, to know sweet love's looking over my shoulder each day. I thought you might be pleased to know that even without real world you, Suzanne lives on in my burgeoning books of the real life adventures of Michael. I do miss hearing from you sweetheart, I hope you are well. A short note now and again would be hugely appreciated. I can never forget you, don't even want to try.

From my journal then:

I awake this a.m. feeling good all over, Samantha's beautiful body discovered delicious in the night, her long legs wrapped tight around me. Will it be real like that for us today? In her I want a burning love, bodies sweaty entangled, bed sheets twisted, panties on the floor, vagina sore from hard and frequent use. I feel comfy with her, merged already, our naked bodies are earthy one. We may spend many nights together shacked up in passion, travel perhaps. She's Rock.

With Heather it's different. I want with Heather a tender long lasting spiritual love filled with gentle kindness and caress. I want with her a mountain peak of slow burning desire ever cooled by the snows of altitude. Bodies fulfilled or not our heavenly souls are one. She's Bach.

With Jen it's I don't know what. Like Suzanne Jen keeps the timing, and keeps it to herself. Jen's in between. She's Rolling Hills and Valley Streams, pleasant to look upon and dream, wonder what's real and what is not, is she even in life's plot? There may be others I'll discover, Linda's not between the cover. Some day I may even bother to find out why we feed each other Linda and I.

What's with this rhyme Muse? Are you seeking to amuse bemuse dear reader today? Are you succeeding do you think? Or are we just being playful, feeling great, waiting for Samantha to reveal the fullness of her glory? Hmm, vivid vivid, I want that sight that feel this night. Yes, I'll pack a bag and leave it hidden. Suzanne brought a heavy bag when she came to Loa's door, but never told me what was in it. Wretched Texas woman, silent to this day, why ever for? What will it *really* be like in the privacy of Samantha's golf course home this day? What color will she choose for her panties? Will I find out? Suzanne came with purple, I found those out... *Who's Suzanne?*

Linda: I haven't heard that poem for a very long time. My grandmother used to read it to me. It is so beautiful and yet so ominous in tone. An aeteological poem. And all children thrilled to hear it. It sparks the imagination - I will read it to my grandson Soarin' this weekend. You write so beautifully. Have you published anything? Are you a poet? An author of novels or plays? Better go, get dressed and enter that busy world.

M: Good morning Linda. Yes, I fancy myself a writer now in my retirement, just for fun. I published twelve ebooks but they didn't sell so I recently unpublished them and am condensing them into one book, enjoying the task really. Who knows where if anywhere that one may go with some 8,000 new books now being published daily, Indies taking over from traditional publishers. It matters not how well a writer plies his wordsmith trade, if his works never come to the attention of potential readers they will not be read. I write what I call 'visionary metaphysical fiction'. If you've never heard of that genre it's just as well. It's kind of like science fiction except the target audience tends to believe that what you write is true. (Like new Adam and Eve's being chosen from worlds like this one to populate the planets the gods can't resist making daily just for fun.) Scary huh? Enjoy the day.

Sam: Hi Michael Really nice meeting you today. Enjoyed our time together, thank you for lunch, hope we can do that again, since we are still speaking.

M: Sure, still speaking. It was nice chatting with you Sam, thx for the wine.

I really do look young for my age don't I.... Sam's renting a house and it has been sold, doesn't know where she's moving to yet but doesn't like Vancouver Island, a bit lost right now. She asked if I have a two bedroom place, maybe she's just looking for a man to take her in? Some serious health concerns. I hope Heather looks a whole lot younger than Sam. But this meeting women is giving me experience I need and I'm becoming a reasonably good conversationalist. Better prepared for Heather, hope that works out. I'm still missing Jen a lot but must stop thinking about her, I think she has written me out of her life for a while, she's not responding to my emails. She has a life of her own and is not willing to share it with me.

Linda: Wasn't that how Scientology began - with Ron hubbard and a novel and a following of true-believers?

M: Except I say that my books are fiction. Hmm, Hubbard's rich right?

M: (to Heather) Still practicing that skip? Looking forward to meeting you, enjoy the weekend.

Heather: Hi Michael: No need to practice my skip. I have it down pat. Anyway, looking forward to meeting you as well. I'm heading to Victoria tomorrow morning accompanied by my younger son. It's always nice to be in Victoria and to visit friends and family. Enjoy the long weekend and will see you Tuesday.

I must take it real slow with this lady, it could pay off with much shared love and happy times for both of us. IF we pass the physical test on Tuesday that is. That's so important for me, especially because I haven't even seen a photo of Heather. I'll know when she comes up to me at breakwater if it will be easy or hard for me to want to be with her; not that I can't overcome first impressions, I can, I did with DeLeon. At Heather's age, two years older than me, I can expect wrinkles and aging, that has been my experience meeting women about my age.

Jen is a beautiful exception, no wrinkles and she's not much younger than me. We'd make a cute couple if we got back together again, her with her gorgeous new body. I hope we do but I'm not going to wait for her if another right one comes along first, she was warned and she accepted the risk. I need to love, to love deeply, and to have it returned. I need to touch and to be touched freely back in return. *And I need that NOW!* I have much to give.

The physical test didn't work with Samantha. I knew there was a problem for me as soon as I spotted her getting out of her car, and that even though she's tall and slim. She's aged and looking it. But we went to her home after lunch at the club and when we relaxed into it, I found that I enjoyed talking with her. I'll even confess to having two or three stray thoughts about taking it further if she was willing, but I quickly quenched those thoughts. It would have been too much like my affair with DeLeon. Sam's a cancer survivor, and it's coming back, I do not want to get into that.

Now that she's lost some weight, Jen is sooo pretty compared to the women I've been meeting. But she's playing real cool with me now, might even be out with Jerry tonight, she didn't go to Utah. That's her business, I must discipline myself to wait for her next message to arrive before sending anything more to her, I must respect her choice for privacy. I wish her well, I love her so. And yet, I know that my heart is on my sleeve right now and could be very easily rubbed off and stolen by someone like Heather if she's pretty. I wish Jen would have come, my falling in love with someone else will make it complicated for us to get together again. Maybe it's best that way, I've often had those dreams of her walking away and never coming back to me. We could create something different of course, we have that power, but it's not looking good for us right now. I'm looking forward to Heather, she's my latest and greatest hope now that Jen has withdrawn.

Linda: This downsizing is for the strong of heart, or maybe just the strong. I once scribbled a verse in a notebook: I used to be able to turn mountains into molehills, But now, This mountain won't shrink, And I, I don't know how to climb mountains. Well, that was after I left my ex and had three small sons to raise. I climbed that mountain, and downsizing really is a molehill by comparison, but there is a lot of letting go. Good thing I am an optimist, I always look forward to the future.

M: May your mountains always be molehills, may there be stacks of green for the bills, may your futures always be sunny, may your cares vanish with song, and if you think this verse is funny, you wouldn't be far from wrong. Cheer up Lady Linda, mountains look real purty from a distance. And the view's spectacular from the top too.

Linda: You did make me laugh. Is that an Irish poem? Abraham sounds very wise - although I might regret carrying all of those boxes of binders tomorrow when I pick up my two year old grandson! But - maybe I am stronger for it. It should be fun spending the next four days with my grandsons - I love children. How old are your grandchildren? Do you get to see them much? Sleep well.

M: The only Irish blood in me would come from a grandmother so no, that verse is not Irish, it's just something I threw together especially for you. Enjoy your grandkids. I see mine occasionally, usually only when I visit my kids or they visit me. You too, sweet dreams.

In a weak and wanting moment I wavered from my dream of having more than one immortal wife when I was trying to address Jen's reasons for not wanting to be with me. (She never even commented on my changing my dream to accommodate her, her mind was already firmly fixed against returning to me anytime soon – most likely to experiment with other men first now that she's single, can't blame her.)

But anyway, along the lines of monogamy or not I need to get my head on straight (correct thought = correct vibrations.) Whether it includes Jen or not, I *will* attract the women I need to co-create my dream of immortality and the way it will be for us. We *will* have fullness of joy in each other and populate planets. So let it be written, so let it be done. I want *multiple* wives in the eternities, *they are coming to me now...* I like that thought, I like it a lot.

Linda: Well, I loved it and it did make me feel better. My ancestry is mostly Irish. And those stacks of green might be better than that pot of gold at the end of the rainbow. I do believe that positive thinking not only keeps a person happy, it also causes positive things to happen. I have always believed that. Anthropologically, religions are an organizing principal that is almost Jungian in nature - universal. All nations went from tribal governments to nation states - and those were theocracies. They then moved on to being simply nations - but unfortunately few have dropped the theocratic component of governance. That may be because we all need belief systems in order to make sense of the world. Or it may be because mankind uses belief systems as a vehicle to control people or as an excuse for war. I had better get ready to catch the ferry.

M: It is my belief that a belief is just a thought that we keep repeating. Speaking of the latter, it is my belief that a belief is just a thought that we keep repeating. All churches impose oft repeated rituals upon their members, keeps them believing. The way I see it, the operating system of most organized religions regardless of label can be summed up with the following sentence: *"Do as we tell you to do, give us money, and MAYBE when you die you'll either go to a better heaven, or you'll escape eternal torment."* Not so compelling when you think about it that way. Now, having said that, all I have to do is repeat it often enough and it will be true. Enjoy today.

Carrie: sorry, but i can't get this into a link, so you'll have to copy and paste it into your browser...but it seems right up your alley... hope all is well... hugs

M: The man you quote has been teaching that for several years. Maybe now the info's free, or maybe it's just a come on to upsell videos and cd's. It's quite an industry, a lot of people have gotten wealthy teaching ancient knowledge in modern context. I'll stick with Abraham, that's a unique response to today's questions asked at each seminar, and it's evolving as leading edge souls ask bigger and better questions. The wheel within a wheel is being reinvented in our time, should make for a highly advanced but never complete vehicle to drive around in the future. As I see it, the leading edge of all edges are the seminars Esther Hicks puts on. With the exception of course of finding God/Abraham within oneself, and drinking daily from that pure source. Enjoy the day Carrie.

Carrie: it is a promo for his full course, but still will probably have some good info... most promo's these days have good content, even if only partial... and, i like the last one below best too... right now my preference is for monogamy... maybe someday that will change... it's interesting that you view monogamy as an "unyielding addiction"... one could say the position for non-monogamy could also be an addiction... two sides of the same coin... for me, what is wanted is the depth and vulnerability that monogamy can allow... in order for most women to be completely vulnerable the connection has to be deep and very safe...

and, it's hard to feel that safety with someone who is sleeping with others… i'd say it's more about how women are wired, rather than an addiction…being a man, it might be hard for you to see and appreciate that about women… thanks for the link… will check it out… i always enjoy listening to abraham! i love their sense of humor along with such great info… have a wonderful weekend… hugs, carrie

Carrie: i just went to the link you sent, thinking it was abraham, but of course, found another… will watch each one of his 11 forgotten law clips and skip the tuesday night thing… thanks… sometimes i forget that so much is available online!

M: (to Jen) I tried to send you a message and a rose on singles but it won't allow me to because you have blocked all messages and gifts sent from men who live more than 75 miles from your son's. Anyway, you seem to have gone into silence with me and I must respect that, but for all it's worth, here is the message I tried to send to you on the singles site, I thought you might be interested. I've edited the message now that I know it will not be delivered insecurely on a singles site, but it's almost the same one I tried to send you there.

You are glorious and beautiful, every one of your photos would be one I would pick out of thousands and want to meet you in person. I seem to recognize the writing in your "About Me', I could have written it myself. (Did actually!) It's beautiful writing, compelling, pulling ANY male your age to you, you are exactly what he's been looking for all these years.

I am weeping now as I write this note to you, lips shuddering, wanting YOU with me before I give my lonely uncertain broken heart to another, perhaps irrevocably. I feel its approach, it's very near, I am drawing it in. It's what I need, what I *must* have right now even though you may think you know better. It's we ourselves who create our own lives, we cannot rely on advice and prophesy from others, even spirit guides who come with pure intent. It's not their life you live it's *yours*, and you alone create it the way you want it, choosing each moment a new life if need be to give you the greatest happiness and the fulfillment of your deepest desires. Do not be swayed by others regardless of how shiny their clothing may be at the moment, yours will be shinier still some day. YOU ARE MY FIRST CHOICE, my dearest and deepest love of all. Come home to me my sweetest heart, let's co-create our life the way we want it, dream our dream together...

The men you'll meet here on this singles site will be exciting for a while, like the women I've met. But it wears thin when you KNOW your heart's already given. But I should not impose, I must respect your desire for privacy, your choice to explore the world of singles while you can, it's your right to do so, I cannot fault you for that at all, it's what I am doing too. But I've been there done it already, it's not so much fun, just exciting never knowing who might show up, hoping always that one of them might be the soul mate you'll ride off into the sunset with forever. That's what we all seem to be searching for on singles sites, regardless if it's just "friends" we tentatively say we are looking for.

You write in your profile: *"I will give him all the time he needs and wants. If you need me at your side, I will be there"* so you are obviously looking for much more than just a friend, a lover at least, husband maybe. Combine your stated desire for "friends" with your statement that you are "an adventurer" and looking for "a relationship", and your About Me comments, and ALL males will conclude that you are their dream, a beautiful woman who will travel and adventure with them at a moment's notice, be totally devoted to them exclusively, available for sex, maybe really really good sex judging by the photos. ("Willingness, spontaneity, eagerness, and love" you write - that does not leave out intimacy at all, in fact it *invites* the fullness of you.)

AND YOU DO NOT EVEN REQUIRE A COMMITMENT ON THE PART OF THE MALE!!!!

Just "friends" you say, even though you express that you are willing to give your all to him, the strongest one, the man you choose as you ooze availability and heated woman pheromones all over the men who chance upon your profile. It's just not fair at all. Men *must* come to you, they're hard wired for that, hard with the thought of you. They'll drool over your photos, needing you in their bed right now. You are naive in some ways - just *"friends"* indeed - it can start but cannot stop with that.

Men will play along with you for a while, walk and talk and dine and entertain you. But they'll work towards meeting you in private: the darkness along the beach, your home or theirs. They have more than mere friendship in mind regardless of what you in your innocence think it might be. Your man of the moment was in special forces you say, so he is trained to kill and to get his will by force in many ways. I suggest that you be cautious about private moments with him, be sure he knows each time that someone knows who you're with, and where you are likely to be. He's sweet, but he almost certainly has the blood of men on his hands (maybe many.) You've been there before you told me, his kiss too may not be so sweet as you thought it would be. *So why be with him at all?*

I'm male, I've written the above from one man's point of view. Not every male is the same as me, but is what I've written what you are searching for? Is that what you are wanting to attract? What I've written (being male and experienced) is what men reading your profile will *think* you are asking for, I'm pretty certain of that. Is spirituality important to you? If so, maybe a Mormon singles site would be better (and safer) for you? You'd have a much better chance of meeting a forever man there, if that is what you want to do. And if not, what do you *really* WANT Jen?

If it's *me*, as you seem to indicate it is (or was) then you must pay more attention to what I'm telling you, or you will never have me again, much as you might think *your* way is the only way - it's not, not for me it isn't, and not for anyone else. That's not a threat, that's a *fact*, a fact that I'm telling you maybe one final time. I think it's worth this try, I'm doing the very best I can to get you back. You've strayed so far this time, broken the connection we had not so long ago, *can't you feel its absence?* Enjoy the day, I wish upon you the freedom to choose, and that your choices will always bring you the great happiness you so richly deserve after all those years with this man who writes you today from a distant land - this man who failed so often to acknowledge that YOU ARE BEAUTIFUL! *Please forgive me if you can, I did without doubt wrong you in the past.* I think we have much in common. Will you at least write to me?

I so wish that you would relent and come to me for two weeks so we can walk, talk, cuddle, and maybe plan a possible future for us, exchange promises, make a commitment even. I think it very important that you do that *real soon*. I need to talk with you in person, no other way will do, and it will take that much time. The choice is yours, I'm inviting you to come back to Victoria right away, or at least right after you've been with your daughter. You were easily able to delay that, you *could* have rushed to me when I called, but I guess your heart was not in it. *Where is it now?*

Take good care sweetheart, make right choices, the *happiest* feeling ones you can think of, let your emotions be your guide. If it feels happy to come to me, come. If it does not, don't come, we are not meant for each other. But if you come, come for YOU. *It's just that right now, maybe you could come for US?*

From my journal today:

I just found Jen's profile on singles. She looks glorious and beautiful, I would pick her out of thousands and want to meet her. I'm weeping right now, lips shuddering with deep emotion, tears flowing, *I want her back!* But she's not writing to me and she was on singles today, so it's not computer problems, she's just too busy for me. Contrary to what she said about not liking the singles scene, she is obviously busy on a singles site. It will be exciting and deeply encouraging for her to have such a response from available men as she must be getting, she knows now that she does not need me. *I miss her, I miss her, I miss her!*

Come back to me my dearest love before my lonely uncertain heart is lost to another. I fear it may happen soon, my needs are just too great. I will attract one to me who will fill the holes life has thrust into my soul, I in hers. I am desperately needing those holes filled right now, there is only part of me here, I cannot bear it alone any longer.

Jen says in her singles profile that she's looking for "a relationship" and "friends" and that she's "an adventurer". That connotes to a man that she is available for sex, just not for a long-term commitment, *exactly* what most men on singles sites are looking for! This woman as she presents herself would travel with another man for sure. And she'll attract them like flies to honey with those beautiful photos. Am I lost forever without her? Where is my resolve gone that I would cease to think of her? Maybe she'll start writing to me again soon... And I've made it so easy for her too! It was me who wrote the following for her. It's so compelling, those words will elicit the intense interest of any available male her age, even some much younger, that will flatter and entice her, she's not experienced on singles sites. Here's part of her profile, the part that I wrote myself, and now regret doing so:

> *"I am at a time in my life when I want to find and enjoy my significant other as a priority, I will give him all the time he needs and wants. If you need me at your side, I*

will be there. If you get a sudden urge to travel I will get up in the middle of the night and go with you gladly, that's just how I am. Love me completely and when you look in my eyes you'll see looking back at you not only yourself but a glint of mischief, willingness, spontaneity, eagerness, and love. I expect that we'll have tons of fun together, I'll help a whole lot with that part, I love life.

I want to be there for my partner and to share a mutual love for life and having fun together. My goal is to travel roads I have not traveled before, show respect to everyone and everything, fulfill our bucket list, be spontaneous in finding joy and laughter, help lift my partner to his highest and best self, and to take care of my health so I will be able to enjoy my golden years to the fullest.

What makes me unique: I am a stabilizing force, one who loves to be spontaneous. When I come to a turn in the road I only expect the best. Many times I have jumped for joy when I went around a corner and saw what was in store for me in spite of the bumps in the road. I want a companion who is willing and able to walk beside me as we go down that road and smooth out those bumps."

I'm such a good writer but: WHY DID I HAVE TO WRITE THAT FOR HER AND MAKE IT EASIER FOR HER TO GET ANOTHER MAN???????

In her singles profile under "First Date" Jen writes: *"Looking for tips on dating. Been enjoyably busy and now ready. Please share your ideals!"* Much as I wanted it to be different, and kept telling myself that she had other reasons for not coming to see me when I invited her, she says she's "NOW READY" to date other men. (And to risk losing me forever, as she wrote earlier.) It's her choice for sure, to explore other men, that's why she's not coming to me. She says I'm her first choice and the only one she loves, but meanwhile she's *actively* looking for another. Why can I not accept such a thing? All other women have done the same while urging me on as a possible alternative or backup. It's all over my books, that's just the way it is. I do it myself as I search for the right woman for me, keeping in touch with several others concurrently. But at least I tell Jen about it, she left me confused and wondering why she would not come.

The message I just sent to Jen *must* be my final one inviting her back to me. If she comes very soon I am prepared to commit to her forever, she will be my Eve, I will close down my singles profiles and stop looking. If she does not come I will actively do everything in my power to attract to myself a compatible good looking woman who wants me NOW and who wants me long term. With such a relationship in place, the writing is on the wall, Jen and I will never again live for long if ever at all under the same roof. She's willing to risk that to try to find a better man, keeping me as a hopeful backup. However it works out, I expect that we will BOTH live happily ever after with our sweethearts. *I wish that upon us.*

Ok, a few more thoughts. She knows if she comes here that we will have sex. She now says (in her singles profile, she never told me) that she is "divorced" whereas when she was here she was telling herself (and me) that we were not yet divorced, so sex was acceptable. She's still Mormon and knows she can't have sex outside of marriage and still go to Mormon temples. And she naively thinks that all she is wanting (and all she will get) from men on singles sites is platonic friendship. Deep inside she must know better - get hormones raging on a dark beach at night or in some other private place and the deed is as good as already done. She's been there before, over the eighteen years of our marriage I have heard her stories. By doing what she's doing she's got to be deep inside looking for or willing to have sex with another man outside of marriage.

She told me she was going to suspend her singles profile but she's hard at it, signed in to singles today, that information is shown when I log in. Looking for another is a higher priority to her than to even send a brief message to me, her supposed one and only true love. So, I conclude it reasonable to think that her primary motivation for not coming to see me right now is possibly that she still clings to being a faithful Mormon. (In addition to wanting to have her self-improvements done before she comes so she can knock my socks off with her new body.) But that same reasoning would apply to her coming to see me *anytime*, even after the many months she seems to think she needs apart from me. So her choice to visit me is a choice to no longer be a faithful Mormon, a huge decision for her to make. Try as I want to conclude differently, *this woman is on the make for another man!*

If she was only completely open with me and voluntarily shared the fullness of her thoughts, sending me daily love notes of assurance the whole time, actively planning a future for us, maybe I would wait for her?? (I asked her twice where we could live, hoping she would engage and plan, but she didn't, just ignored my messages.) I just don't know if I would wait for her, my needs are so great right now, and not just for a casual lover. And others like possibly Heather will always be coming to me as long as I have those desires, that's just the way Law of Attraction works.

What do you think Dear Reader? How would you advise me if you could? Write down your counsel and date it, maybe someday I'll blog and give you a chance to tell me what you thought when you got to this point in my book. But enough, I'm so tired of this. Final decision: if she comes to me real soon, I will commit to her and her dream of monogamy. If not, I will look for and be prepared to commit long term to another. I feel that I already know what's going to happen even though she may respond with excuses, declarations of love and hopes for the future even as she says she can't come right now, but maybe later. *I don't think she will come, she will look for another...* And so must I, my greatest temptation finally behind me, my Eves await.

And thus, ironically, you and I at this very moment have come to a fullness of understanding. With my original dream restored (one man several wives), from the point of view of immortality I can *still* be Jen's backup. There will always be room at my immortal table for her, an equal sister wife. So thus, if she has the desire, even though she denies the visit I asked of her, I have good reason to stay in touch from a distance, and keep a cordial relationship with my former wife, we were much in love.

And in that spirit I wrote:

M: (to Jen) I think you should remove all mention on singles sites of you being an entrepreneur with your own business. Just put in "tell you later" or something like that. Otherwise people will think you are wealthy, you will be swamped with men who secretly only want a free ride, and you will get flattering messages from men much younger than you are who are just looking for information to sell to those who would steal your personal information, your identity, and your money even as they seem to be sincerely interested in you, looking for friendship, romance and love.

I don't think you realize the power of those photos of beautiful you. But I do, they're exactly the kind of photos I've been looking for over the months. I think, although you're not immune there either, that you'd be much safer using only Mormon singles sites. I love you darling, I'm deeply hurt that you have gone into silence with this man who you say (or said) is the only one you love. I had hoped that we would be open and honest with each other, discuss everything, best of friends if that's still possible. Enjoy the long weekend.

M: (to Suzanne) Michael hasn't changed a bit has he? He's still generating real life stories to spice up his books. And he's good at it too... Samantha turned out to be 20 years older than her photo. It was a pleasant enough visit but she may be headed your way, cancer. Now Heather, who I'll be meeting blind (not even a photo) on Tuesday, that will be a different story, I might even fall in love with Heather.

Should you need a vacation anytime you are invited to visit me in my new home on the sea. Victoria is a destination, I often see three cruise ships at a time docked just a ten minute walk from where I live. There would be no commitment or obligation of any kind of course, just friends, maybe lovers if you will - you get yourself here and back, I'll take care of expenses while you're here. Smile dear one, I know Suzanne's alive and well, sitting right beside you in your toy box - hope you two have some toys in there with you, could be boring if not. Enjoy the long weekend. Mere Michael aka Michael the Great, Survivor of Months of Suzanne.

Jen: Hi Sweaty, Sorry, I didn't get back with you. I was so busy yesterday. I cleaned carpet and cooked all day. I was so tired last night I just dropped into bed. Still tired to day. The three girls are here now. Tried to get on the internet but fail asleep. I took your advice and blocked my site. I find I don't even like looking at those pictures of men. Most are not very appealing. I guess I am not ready to date yet but would have a friend. I love you and in no hurry to find someone else. My heart goes out to you. I am still tied to you. I love you and miss you. That makes it hard for me to see or feel the need or want of other man.

I know you want me now but at the same time you sent me home for another woman. (Jackie) If she contacted you.... You would be on her door step as soon as you could. I need some time. I need time to see my life more clearly. I think you need time also to see things clearer and prepare for reality of what is going on and where you want to head. Watched a movie last night where a couple divorced and the man marred a beautiful younger woman. Cutting the story short. He realized he still loved his first wife and they had a hot affair. The issues that caused the divorce now forgotten. He realized her life style was much more attractive and satisfying than with a much younger woman. I could relate to what they were going thru. I need to spend more time rereading your most resent emails so I can respond in kind. Love you sweety.

M: Thanks for this, a crumb from your table. I look forward to your response to my other emails. You give me some hope again, just a tiny bit. Don't hold past history against me, I learn from that, as do you. We now have a new moment to create whatever we want going forward, I won't be meeting anyone until Tuesday. But I really mean what I wrote, you've got to take me seriously. It's not true that I would run to another woman if you were here. I am/was ready to make a commitment appropriate to our discussions over the two week time period I've been asking for. The way I see it, you have no valid excuses it doesn't matter what you come up with, just a choice to make. Though we could remain friends at a distance if you choose not to come and talk, I'll never forget you, but I *am* capable of not needing you.

By the way, regarding your statement: *"I think you need time also to see things clearer and prepare for reality of what is going on and where you want to head."* Do not ever presume that you can think for me and know what's 'best' for me or what I need or where I should go. I'm perfectly capable of taking care of that myself, and do, thank-you.

There, I gave her an out (to remain friends), I think she will take it, she will not come. And I checked her singles site, it's still up. As I walked a few minutes ago I realized how much fun I'm having and rejoiced in it, joyous energy bursting suddenly from my chest, causing a woman approaching on the sidewalk to smile hugely and say "hello". What a great trip it is to be living these stories. Focus on *that* instead of what is not, and *life's really really good!*

Jen: Oh you are funny! I will be writing when I have time and not so many people around. From your comments you see I am not perfect and I see you are not perfect. AND WE STILL LOVE EACH OTHER. That sounds like an old married couple that's comfortable with each other. That's a good sign.

M: Hey, careful with that "old" bit, I keep thinking I'm only 35. Yeah sweetheart, we do love each other, it's a good sign...

M: Unless we were living under the same roof with the understanding that it was to be monogamous, if I found a casual lover (or more than one) would you want to know about it or not? Would knowing I have a lover affect your decision to commit to a long term relationship with me? How are you with the Mormons now? Still temple faithful, unable to have sex with me if you visited soon? And if you visited two or three months from now as you seem to want to wait to do (for reasons I don't understand unless it's to be with one or more other men and I just be a backup), would that have changed so we could put our bodies together completely by then?

Please respond to each of those questions honestly and fully, it's important to me to know as I make my decisions about where to go with my life right now. There are opportunities all around, many roads to choose from, you among them. Help me decide the you part. What do you *really* want for us?

Don't beat around the bush much do I?

M: (to Jen) In your singles site profile you state emphatically that you are "divorced" and yet when you were here you were saying you didn't think we are. Has something changed since you left here? Do you now know for sure that we are divorced? If you have a divorce certificate, please send me a copy, thanks.

I went to bed early last night thinking to get up during the night and check for messages from Jen. I did but there were none, and there are still none as the morning slips away this holiday weekend. I am not an exciting priority for Jen anymore, she's not doing as I am doing for her and did for Suzanne, waiting anxiously for the next message to arrive. I'm thinking it's best that she not come now, so I am free and uncommitted. Being woman, perhaps she senses that too and that's the main 'reason' why she won't come and visit me. I feel that I need some high powered help with my writing, power that it is not within Jen's assets to give. Perhaps I need to relax and lay off the strong sex drive that motivates and moves me about so much, and yet maybe has now become detrimental to my progress as a writer, the future that could be mine, the influence my books could have on this world's people?

Here's a vitally important message from Jen, a life changer, and my response. I'll start with my response, her message follows.

M: (to Jen) I wonder what other messages you "sent" to me that I never received? The one below is dated 21 days ago but I don't recall ever receiving it. I'm glad you sent it, it helps me understand what's happening in your life much better. Had I received it (or had I given it the attention it deserves if I did), the last few days of unpleasantness and strong emotion might not have happened. You needn't respond to my earlier emails, that's already over and done with, there's no need for more intense emotion. Let's take a fresh moment, a fresh start with our communications. We now know much better where the other stands, at least I do of you. I accept your need to hold the hand of other men, that's what I've been writing in my journal all along that you want, and that you *will* do that. It's mainly because of your yearning for true and everlasting love (that you didn't get with me) that it didn't matter what I wrote to you, *you will not come back to visit me!*

I also wrote in my journal about you being Mormon and that if you visited me we would have sex, and that would make you unworthy of attending Mormon temples. So it was a huge consequence you'd face to come and visit me. You want the Mormon dream and I am no longer capable of giving it to you. Maybe your neighbor or some other good Mormon man you meet can do that for you. (If you are willing to share his other wives in the eternities - that's part of that particular dream - my own dream that I offered to you was really not so strange if you'd think about it.) I understand your need to experience other men after divorce, it's normal, I think it's the right thing for you to do much as I wanted you with me and am going to miss you terribly. That's what was driving me, the thought of losing you forever was unbearable at times. But I too (as you already did) can now accept that risk. Who knows what and who we'll eventually each attract into our lives, it was most likely foolish of us (me actually) to try to reconcile just yet.

I loved the already partially new you who came to visit, I wanted much more of that. And of the new slimness of your body, it already shows in your singles site photos. *I really really wanted that, oh how I wanted that, still do!* Had you stayed with me that extra week we might have foolishly committed back to what we had, and you'd never have the opportunity to hold another man's hand, a man you might keep for all eternity if the Mormon dream is true. But such is life, I'm sure we'll both know happiness with or without the other physically in our lives. Let's walk our separate paths then and individually serve life up well. You are much stronger and wiser than I am, you already knew it had to be that way. I wasn't ready yet to let go, I am now. I now think that it's best this way for both of us, thank-you so much for being open and honest about your need to date. I needn't have put so much pressure on you to come back to me but I don't recall getting that email, maybe I was just busy when it came and filed it away somewhere.

I thought the last few days that there was imminent hope for us if only you'd come and talk with me about a future together. I was ready to commit to you, even to abandon my singles site profiles and stop seeing other women. But I believe now that you were right, not just treating me like a child thinking of what's best for me as you saw it, not wanting to hurt me but smart enough to put yourself first as you should. I was already ready to commit to you when I first visited you in your home and thought nothing had changed, it was pleasant and good. But you wisely sent me away, we would have quickly fallen back into our winters of discontent. So, given all that, I now see clearly that our being together anytime soon will not be. *I understand and I accept.* I will continue to love you but there can be no promise of our ever again living under the same roof, or even meeting in this lifetime. We must both be free of the other to attract to us what we both know deep down is best for our own individual interests.

Please stay friends and keep writing to me dear one, I will always be interested in your life. I won't interfere or think badly of you whatever you do from now on, you are completely free of me as I am of you even though we'll be tied by emotion for quite some time yet. Go back on singles sites if you will, they're productive. But if it's a Mormon you want, you'd be much safer on Mormon singles sites. Use the profile I wrote for you there on those sites if you want to, you'd be much less vulnerable. It's *exactly* the type of commitment a good single Mormon man is looking for in a mortal and eternal companion - *I wish it could have been thus for me.* Your beautiful face will draw them in to read your profile. There are probably many interesting men online in Utah right now who would respond to you, date you, walk and talk with you, give you affection, *and hold your hand.*

Take good care of yourself sweetheart, the best is yet to come for both of us, I'm convinced of that. P.S. I wrote the following in my journal yesterday before getting your message today:

> "And thus, ironically, you and I dear reader at this very moment have come to a fullness of understanding. With my original dream restored (one man several wives), from the point of view of immortality I can still be Jen's backup. There will always be room at my immortal table for her, an equal Sister Wife. So thus, if she has the desire even though she denies the visit I asked of her, I have good reason to stay in touch from a distance, and keep a cordial relationship with my former wife, we were much in love."

Jen: On 8/31/2014 at 10:22 AM, "Jen" wrote: Michael, I sent this to you awhile back regarding the divorce. We both have suffered tremendously from the loss of each other. I think there is a place in each of our hearts hoping the other will not find or choose another love. We both now know we have the makings of a far superior relationship then most people. We do work well together in so many ways. Most often it takes time to put a relationship back together and ours has complications to consider. Two people in love need to be patient with each other. We also need to use our heads about getting back together. Emotionally I am still married to you. Thus far I have not even held the hand of another man. I think I should at least do that. I am trying to act and feel divorced but don't really like it. Need to experience a bit of what you have so fully done.

When I am emotionally able I will respond to your two other emails. I know you were sharing deep emotions. I do not take your words lightly. We both are on this ride of ups and downs. I miss you and I Love you sweetie, Jen

Jen: On 8/10/2014 at 3:47 PM, "Jen" wrote: Went to church today. Had a young man speak going on a mission. I really felt the spirit and it felt so good. Talked about temples today. Then a relief society sister that is teaching the lesson told me she wanted me to share a few words about what makes a good marriage. I quietly said, *"Don't you know I am divorced?"* She said, *"Yes"*. She is a widow. I started crying and have not stopped. I left and missed Relief Society. Could not handle what a good marriage is when I failed so miserably. The pain that I have keep down so deep for so long started a river flowing. I sit here crying as I face the facts that I lost the love of my life. Realizing I can not go down the road you are going. I AM MORMON. I WANT MY MORMON HUSBAND BACK!

But realize we don't always get what we want and for me that was you. The attorney finally sent me the divorce decree after I called to ask about it the other day. Spent the last couple of days trying to accept it. You are totally free. You are totally free of me. Nothing, no obligations, nothing is owed in either direction except our friendship. Hope we always keep that. Sorry, my heart hurts and feels like it is broken. I have tried to be so brave. The tomorrows will bring a better day. I think I will go to the temple. I truly thought we were still married. I will miss that so much so very much. Thanks for the wonderful time in Victoria. It was a wonderful reunion. It was like being a young woman again with the love of my life. I love you so much and except you fully as you are. Live your dream as you desire. I just need to remember why you didn't want me and the other reasons it cannot be. I feel so alone. If I could stop existing I would it hurts so deep. Oh, please forgive me I hate this one person pity party. Sweet love Jen

Jen: I disabled the single site. Just don't enjoy that right now.

M: It's still online Jen.

Chapter 26

———⟡———

Jen and I were married for 18 years. In some ways she protected and 'raised' me all that time, keeping me safe, preparing me for the time I was to write these books that will become "super huge" if the clairvoyant saw it right. As it is with parents, you can never repay them sufficiently for what they did for you. All you can do is go forward as the new adult you are, and *live* your life to the fullest. Thank-you Jen for that.

Jen: It says profile is hidden. Don't know how to remove it.

M: I can still access your singles profile but that may be because I have the link already, maybe it's hidden to everyone else. But you may want to delete all of your photos, they identify a beautiful woman, and where she walks every day. Someday you may be ready to go back to that site and enjoy it. Right now you and I are still too emotionally involved, feeling the feelings we should have felt before but didn't because we were both in denial, thinking that we were still married and had a future together. When I visited you in Utah and hugged you at the door nothing had changed: still you, still felt good hugging you, same beautiful retirement home that you created for us. I must now program my mind for your absence, but wow *what a blow that was today!* I was having so much hope for us recently even though you had backed off a whole lot the last few days.

You called it right though, we walk very different paths, I will almost certainly never again be Mormon, I wish you well with that. You will *easily* find a good Mormon man who will take you to the temple and tell you sincerely that you are the best thing that has ever happened to him. You will be loved and treasured, protected, and provided for all the remaining days of your life, as it is with your friend. Keep me posted on your family. In memory your son's kids will always be my kids too, I loved and treasured them. Take care, the emotions will slowly fade away for both of us and we'll emerge much better for having shared them.

Jen: There is a party going on right now across the street with a live band. They are really good. People gathering from everywhere. With food and the works. I guess I should go out. Of course it has extended into my son's drive way.

M: Yes for sure, get out there and really *enjoy* life. I'm about to do that too...

Jen: I had some man post on my site. Will you have sex on the first date. Of course I told him no and blocked him. He had just posted his message just before you posted your beautiful message. Love Jen

Ok, decision time, I was hoping she'd show some emotion over my last message and she didn't, just friendly. Should I or should I not send her what's written below that I've been composing for several hours? I will.

M: (to Jen) I don't give up easy, learned that from Suzanne. So here's one final try for us and if you don't respond positively to it, I'll try my best to stay away from the subject of us ever getting together again, unless you bring it up. Here goes.

From my Journal – one final time:

I'm really struggling right now. I thought she and I had escaped the pangs of divorce after 18 years of marriage, but it is not so. I'm hurting, *I want her back!* But for her it's a choice between me and the Mormon dream of maybe going to the highest of heavens after death if you live just right, don't drink coffee or smoke, and pay them 10% of your income while you're still here. She "agonized" over that choice between me and organized religion. So, it was Mormonism and her desire to meet men while she's still single that swayed her. I can't see her staying single for long, she will quickly attract all the men she could ever want to hold hands with, many of them good Mormon men like I once was. I can't compete with that while she's still Mormon, and that's what she has made her choice to be.

Why that choice over me, the only man she says she loves? I don't know anymore, I've backed so far away that the dream the Mormons teach today doesn't even make sense anymore. I liked it much better with the early prophets who taught one man and several wives, and bet their life and salvation on it - *that's* the commitment, *that's* the dream for me. But if she came to me now while I'm still hurting I'd commit to her anew. Or would I? Am I ready to drop to my knee and propose marriage again, put a ring on her finger? I don't think so, just live with and enjoy her, co-create the reality we mutually desire for as long as we desire, it could be forever.

Yes, I'd give up singles sites and other women, I wouldn't need them in mortality. I thought not long ago that my doing that was all she wanted and she'd rush back to me when I told her I'd give that up. But today she complicated it all by telling me she wants a *Mormon* man – that's not me. Does she *really* know what it is that she wants? What makes a Mormon man better than this one except that the faithful Mormon adheres to *somebody else's* dream, and I choose to create my own? It's all *her* choice isn't it? I've made myself abundantly clear, she's invited back, she *could* come to me and talk it over, even if we (somehow) refrained from having sex to take that pressure off. But I know she won't come, it's much deeper than that for her, she'll never tell me, I'll never understand. Maybe it's her memory of another man in the temple, a voice telling her that he was her husband to be, another man making love to her in a dream. We *could* create a different future, it's *our* lives we live, we're all powerful in that, *everything's* our choice, nothing for us is written in stone that we don't write there ourselves.

So, it's *her* choice to make, ours to reap the consequences. My choice is for her, she knows that, so what else can I feel when she refuses to come to me but sadness, sorrow, and REJECTION!!!! Crazy crazy me, watching anxiously for her next email while she's out having fun like she should be, enjoying the Labor Day street party. DID I EVER LOVE HER AS MUCH AS I LOVE HER THIS VERY MOMENT?

Why does she agonize and think she was a failure because she "lost" the man she loved? It's *still* a simple choice for her to make because I'm still available to her. Her choice is either *me*, or Mormonism with another man who can promise her only what I promise, that she's invited to be one of his several wives in the heavens *if* the dream is true, and if it's Mormonism that she chooses, *if* she and he both qualify under rules and judgments made by other people. She knows she can't have both. Which is it that she *really* wants? If she does not come to me soon we'll both know for sure, and almost certainly irrevocably so because I'm seriously looking for stability right now, and that's what will be offered to me, whether it's with Jen or with another, doors are already opening to manifest that very thing so I can write and publish properly. She could still be the rock solid woman, the unshakeable *believer* behind the writer, the one who kept him going when all others were failing and deriding him. SHE COULD STILL BE ADAM'S EVE!

Here I am Jen, come get me, low hanging fruit, ripe for the picking – if you want it.

You can't say you weren't offered *me* Jen. If there is any "failure" on your part that cost you the man you loved the most, it will be only because you refused to give him and you the time to talk it over face to face when he asked you *one final time* to come to him for two weeks and do just that. Come talk with me?

There, I've sent it and I feel peace come over me, I've done my part. I accept whatever comes, I did my very best to invite Jen to be my Eve. I think now that perhaps she will be, but it might take some time. I must allow her to do what she wants to do, to be who she wants to be, and in the meantime I must keep living, enjoying life, being happy, AND WRITING BOOKS!

My best guess is that she will still want three months before she comes. (For reasons I will never completely understand.) And if so, I am willing to grant her that and do my best to not permanently close any doors that are between us. I am also willing to allow her do whatever she wants to do in that time, date men, have sex, whatever she chooses to do, my door will remain open for her return. And I will allow myself similar freedoms. Maybe it should always be that way, except western women want *monogamy* so I must be prepared to grant that to her if she insists on that being a condition of our living together again. But if she gives up Mormonism she may go wild and want to sleep around instead of just with me anyway? I think what I would want as a minimum until we play house under the same roof is that we get together for at least two weeks in every three calendar month period. And when we're not together, that we are both free to do as we will. When we do start living together then perhaps monogamy is in order.

Free agency must prevail, everyone must have the freedom to choose for themselves that which they will do, believe and think, and who they will be. Let Jen do what she wants, including having sex with other men (and women) if she freely chooses that for herself, and she grants the same freedom to me. Whether we actually do that or not isn't the point, it's that we both feel free to do as we want without first having to ask another's permission. My guess though is that she would not be so liberal and I am prepared to accept monogamy if need be to keep my beautiful Eve. Yeah, peaceful feelings, all is well….

Except that I just checked the singles site, and *she's on there right now,* even after I sent the above! And after she said (again) that she had closed down her site and was not interested in looking at photos of men. And after I suggested that she delete her photos.

Regardless of what she tells me to the contrary for whatever woman reasons she may have or none at all, I think she may have the singles bug big time, maybe hopelessly addicted, and *that* maybe even more than Mormonism is why she won't come to me? She used to play computer games all night every night (she moved out of my bed many years ago because I wouldn't allow her to watch TV all night when I was trying to sleep.) So the mating game, the excitement of the chase, the image of holding hands with a man who was a stranger the day before, with the thought of maybe, just maybe more that night if the moment's right, has got to be hugely more exciting. She does like sex a lot, but never told me that until a couple of weeks ago when she visited me in Victoria! Here I thought all along during the rare times we had sex in the last years that I was imposing myself on her. We didn't communicate well did we? Oh well, at least she's home on her computer tonight, and not out in some private place with ex special forces operator Jerry. I've got to stop thinking that I am her protector, I'm not.

I miss her so. I guess the peaceful feelings were not a prediction that she and I would be together soon but a reward for doing my best to make it happen. I've always been an idealist, it seemed ideal that she would share my dream and become my Eve, she knows all about it. Is there another ideal woman for me, or no such ideal to be realized in mortality maybe? Whatever, it seems at this moment that Jen will not be Eve, and that I need to adjust to that reality once again. Oh well, life's good, Law of Attraction's in play, I may as well go to bed and sleep the day off, no point in waiting just in case she sends a message. She became such a stranger in such a short time – starting the day before she met Jerry I think, or maybe when she registered on a singles site and started getting messages from men, found out she didn't *need* me. She has been cool and unresponsive since then. I have seen that behavior before with other women I was fond of and it didn't end well. Unless it did, the woman not being best for me, a better yet to come.

> *But this is the woman I lived with for 18 years!!!*

And I suppose in my desperate yearning for her as I watched her inexorably slip away, I have become in my messages to her more and more demanding and possessive. Face it, it doesn't matter what I write or how logical my arguments may be, for her own internal woman reasons she doesn't want to be with me right now, *and that is not going to change.* Yeah, much as I speak of freedom, I'm jealous that she wants to be with other men, holding their hands, getting closer to intimacy whether she allows herself to think so or not, falling in love. It could have been *my* hand she was holding, *my* love she was feeling, I wanted that. Was it my wanting to be with Jackie and sending Jen home a week early the final straw that moved her far away from me perhaps forever? But I felt good about that choice, it was a happy thought. Perhaps all is working out the way it should. Time will tell, I'm meeting Heather tomorrow. Will she be pretty to me?

Yeah sure, no sooner decide to hit the sack then the following conversation takes place.

Deanna: (lady from Nanaimo on singles, no photos, asks to be called "babe") Hey there.

M: Hey you, where's your photos babe? That's kind of essential on a singles site I thought.

Deanna: Hey! back... well at least you called me "babe"! Hopefully, photo is attached.

M: Nice, you needn't hide that bod, if it's a recent photo it's a great asset. But what do you do about getting to know men from a distance? Has that worked well for you in the past? You'd think with that much distance between you and a man from Victoria to make it worthwhile you'd want to spend a couple or more days and nights together each time. Is that how you work it?

Hardly obvious that this man wants to check out what's under that slim woman's clingy dress is it? Nanaimo – shades of Jackie from Nanaimo who took me to her bed for two nights then while Jen was here, dumped me cold, total silence, I had great expectations for the two of us. I still think Jackie has one or more local men, may even have been with one right after she dropped me off to catch the bus, I saw her go to a man while I was inside the bus watching. I asked her about him and she never responded. I sure don't like the singles scene, my heart and reason flee all too quickly. It would have been simple getting back with Jen, not even baggage tags to change, and we loved each other. I'm disappointed in you Jen, we're sure not on the same page anymore – maybe never were even though we lived together for 18 years? Yeah, I think we *were* actually, we genuinely loved each other. Jen is just wanting to explore the exciting new world of strange men now that she's single and it's allowed within her religious beliefs, can't blame her for that. I'm doing my part with the women, why shouldn't she with the men too? Wish it was women she was playing with, maybe we could check out the singles photos together.

Should I be searching for a bisexual woman? Not really, I wanted to go straight this time, would have given my all to Jen had she come. I don't regret having sex with Suzanne, I would sleep with her again. But now with Jen gone, I'm wild again, ready to meet a stranger in her hotel room, eager to meet another woman from Nanaimo, this one easy with sex, that's all it would be. It could be enough!

Deanna: Thank you for the compliment. Distance hasn't been an issue if we're talking Victoria or Vancouver. I currently drive to Victoria frequently to visit longtime friends & do some shopping. If I'm getting on well with someone & we enjoy each others company, then to your point, we tend to spend a couple of days together each time & take turns driving. Where there's a will, there's a way. Being with a person you enjoy makes it worthwhile. Bye for now.

M: That's interesting, guess you know where I was going with that and bold enough to do it because you invited the "babe" babe. Though that may mean something different to you than it does to me. If that photo's recent, I'm interested. What do you suggest?

See what you did Jen? It's all your fault. If you had come to me I wouldn't be looking for women to sleep with, I wanted to go straight, don't want to be a player, just have needs. I've always been a one woman man, don't like it being otherwise, all I want is the right woman to THROW myself into completely.

This Deanna who just showed up will not be such a woman as that. But she might be fun for casual sex, better than nothing at all? I must keep Heather in mind though, I'm pretty much determined if she's pretty or not to give her every chance with me and at least be friends.

If she's pretty I might risk giving her my heart along with my body if it comes to that. I'm vulnerable and uncertain right now, never want to be without the love and touch of a woman who is attractive to me and I to her. It should have been *you* Jen my former love and recent lover. You were real good at that when you visited, like never before. Was it just that you were trying your very best to get me back, *before I sent you away?*

Did I do right by being raunchy with Deanna tonight? What if she's serious and doesn't need a long 'friendship' first like some women do? Am I prepared to sleep with her? Yeah, probably, except Heather will be a priority. I guess the woman from Vancouver who will be staying at the Empress for three nights has fizzled out, haven't heard back from her following my suggestion of wine in her hotel room. I would have preferred her to Deanna. What was with that three day at the Empress woman anyway? What was she after? Here I was hoping it was my body.

Deanna: Photo is from my nephew's wedding last year in Aug, but trust me, you will still recognize me! And if you're still interested, I suggest that I could meet you for coffee/wine in Victoria on Sun Sept 7 between 1 - 3 pm as I will be in the city attending my friend's grandson's christening earlier in the day. Nothing ventured, nothing gained. Cheers

M: Let me get back to you a bit closer to Sunday Deanna, I do have some commitments coming up but Sunday might work out. Remind me if you haven't heard back by Friday? Good night.

Deanna's obviously not a priority, it's Heather I was thinking of as I wrote that. Or maybe another yet unknown who would give promise of getting my heart along with my body. Looking at her photo, though Deanna's attractive enough and sexy (yeah, I'd sleep with her, her photo arouses me with the thought of that) I don't think I'd want Deanna moving in with me or I with her more than two or three days at a time. Heather? I'll find out tomorrow, I have hopes there, sight unseen. But maybe because she owns a couple of condos and seems well to do?

Ok, it's not so early in the day anymore, sun's been up a while and nothing from Jen. But beneath the turmoil I easily find that peaceful feeling. Yes, I feel happy about my dearest sweetheart, my long-time love, my Jen. This moment I feel almost certain of her again, and my eyes well with the thought, she's beautiful. Yes, there it is again, the peace, the sweet assurance, we're solid yet that dear woman of mine, my Eve to be. She and I together can co-create my dream, live happily ever after, forever. But maybe not for a while, she's not completely back, she chooses I think to first pass through experience, hold hands with other men, until with time she tires of that game and comes to me again, her Adam - or marries another. What will this day bring for us I wonder?

Deanna: Will do, Michael. Hope your week goes well. Deanna

I just noticed that although she hasn't signed into singles since last night, Jen hasn't even taken the time to look at my profile on the same site. Not exactly oozing curiosity and interest for this man anymore is she? But I must think positive, I still feel that all is well even though it's almost noon already and no sign of her after that long poignant message I sent her last night. Surely she will not just ignore it and go into silence like Suzanne would do? Maybe she's struggling to keep her mind and heart away from the turmoil that thoughts of me must still bring to her, especially when I won't let rest her refusal to visit me? I must have patience and watch for a response from her. Once again, whatever it is she writes, it will be for me a life-changing message.

And today's a holiday, she may be gone to Disneyland or a theme park or surfing until late tonight with her son and his family, they're very active people. It's a valid excuse if she feels she needs one for delaying her response - children and grandchildren are more important than an ex. I may not hear from her until tomorrow, maybe not even until *after* I've met Heather at 10 a.m. I was hoping to have a clearer understanding, a clearer mind about Jen before I had that meeting. Why is Heather so important to me? Do I sense a possible long term commitment there? Yes, I think we will like each other and I think both of us are looking for that. A whole lot will depend on whether or not I like the way she looks and feels in the first hour of our meeting. If it goes well I may not even meet with Deanna even though it's likely that sex with Heather would only come after a lengthy friendship. I will leave the timing to her, sex can wait as long as hope for future intimacy is desired and is promising. I can take care of myself in the meantime.

M: (to Heather) The forecast for tomorrow is cold and wet. So look for a handsome man hanging around the park bench between the Breakwater Cafe and the entrance to the breakwater at Ogden Point. He plans to walk from his apartment near James Bay Square so will most likely be wearing blue jeans and a warm light blue long sleeve pullover. He may possibly be carrying (or using) an umbrella, and maybe wearing or carrying a blue windbreaker. He'll provide a big smile and look the speaker in the eyes when he hears the name "Michael" spoken by a pretty lady. And he'll most likely want to hug her but will refrain for decorum's sake unless she makes the first move - which is invited. Will that work for you, 10 a.m. tomorrow Heather?

After reading your profile and messages, it is my hope dear one that you will make no attempt to compare me to your deceased husband. It is my guess that he was a far better man than I will ever be. You will never be able to find a replacement for your lost love, but maybe in time you will win a consolation prize. I look forward to meeting you.

M: Lynne, When we parted after my session with you, you expressed an interest in us becoming friends. Based on that I sent you two candid emails in which I expressed my feelings openly to you. I figured I couldn't hide anything from you anyway. You never responded so I assume that I offended you and that any additional contact we might have with each other would be strictly on a professional/client basis. And I'm ok with that if that's the way you want it to be. I did not mean to offend you, I do sometimes get carried away with what I write when still in character with my main book man who does tend to be a bit raunchy at times, all the better to entertain my readers. But I don't want either of us to feel awkward should we meet along the breakwater or on the beach so I'm hoping this present email will help clear the tension that I think has developed between us - maybe it's just me.

But you were right in everything you told me during the reading so I'm hoping that if you ever feel prompted to tell me more, particularly about my book, that you will contact me. I will then pay you for another session by appointment. What you have to say is important to me, you are very talented, perhaps I need your help to bring forth this "super huge" book properly? I hope you are enjoying the long weekend.

Jen: I can't see things being over with us. We are two connected. I am here for you please don't stop sharing what is in your heart and the happenings around you. Hope it is a good connection tomorrow. Don't settle for less than what you want because of loneliness. Be patient and you will have what you desire. I will be going to Utah in a couple of weeks. Need to be back in California before the middle of Oct. My family back east are getting wind that we are no longer together. I told them we are really good friends and still love each other. I can except you not being Mormon you would not have to be Mormon for us to be together. Mostly because you understand the Mormon ways. Busy house today. Everyone is here and so lots of activity. I am taking a break in my room. Sometime I need a bit of alone time. Kind of have a headache today. Love you Sweetie.

M: Thanks for responding, please stay in touch.

Well, that settles that. Like Suzanne was, Jen is willing to share me with other women even though she could easily have me for herself. Unlike Suzanne, Jen hints at a future for us. She has changed enormously in the last week but she seems grounded and knowing what she wants. It's just that it's not me that she wants right now. So get a grip I say to myself, seize the day and get on with your life without any further thought of Jen being in it. I still feel peaceful about her even though I know she will be dating other men and quite possibly settling for one of them instead of me. But I'm not done with her.

M: (to Jen) You ask me to share with you and I would, I'd like you to live my life by proxy if that interests you, right down to the intimate thoughts and details I record in my journal and you know you will someday read in my books, except that you'd have it long before anyone else does, and you could ask questions and get detailed answers in real time.

And I would love to live *your* life by proxy, it's of great interest to me. It's sexually stimulating as I think of what you are now embarking upon with your new found freedom, as I did with mine. A part of me would be there in bed (or on the beach at night) with you and another man if it came to that. If you were bisexual we could pick out photos of women on singles sites together. (Just kidding sweetie, I know you're not going there, just thought that was a good line.) But I can't trust you to share fully with me, your history of doing that is not good, you keep secrets. You know I am meeting with Heather for the first time tomorrow for example, and that she's important to me. But I have no idea if you plan to meet with Jerry or with other men over the next two weeks. (Or have already met again with Jerry or any other man and how that went.) I miss that kind of sharing, I want to keep on *knowing* you, never judging what you think or do, just *absorbing* your life into mine. Share your life completely, openly, honestly, *fully* with me and I will share with you likewise, but not unless.

I want to read how you feel and what you think about each man and each time you meet; what it felt like to hold the hand and look into the eyes of a man who was a stranger the day before; how you noticed his arousal and when, and what you did with your woman ways to feed and sustain it. I want to feel the sexual feelings you are feeling as you describe them, and be aroused myself as I read. I want to know what you do about those feelings to satisfy them. I want to know the fullness of life from a woman's perspective, especially the romance, the love, and the sex in particular. What does it feel like to be a woman immersed in a warm perfumed bath, candles casting soft shadows, vibrator moving in and out of her wet vagina, eyes unfocused, making mounting sounds as she moves towards her climax? Suzanne shared that with me in a video with delicious audio. I still treasure it, but she did not write about the feelings, I could only imagine that they were good.

If I can't see you in person, I want to see photos of you naked, your newly slim body taunting and arousing me from a distance; close ups of your tight but open vagina, making me salivate with desperate desire for the woman who once was mine. You're my only hope to know such things, we're so connected already. Sharing intimately with me as I share with you could make us great co-writers, and great lovers, maybe sharing the same bed again someday. You were already tight and satisfying from having exercised certain muscles the last time I plunged into your eager willing body here in Victoria. *I was so thrilled sweetheart, you can't begin to imagine how that felt!* Sharing your life intimately is hugely interesting to me especially because I too think that you and I are not yet done. *And then we'd not be strangers when we meet again.* Will you share *everything* with me, holding back nothing until the day you marry another or come home to me? Do that and I will share *me* with you.

Oresha: How is your long weekend going? Have you been to anymore "Octopus vs Seal" matches lately?... lol Hope you're enjoying these last days of Summer.... Kathy has been having "Abraham_Withdrawl" symptoms... lol and asked me to see if you would kindly loan out the rest of your Abraham DVD's.... so that she could get her "Fix"!... ha! ha!... I have a couple that I've finally finished watching/"taking in".... that I could get back to you. Hope you're having a Mahvelous Day !.... Hugsssss....

M: Hey you. Sure come over and get the DVD's you want. Just let me know when you want to come and wait until I confirm by email so you'll know I'll be here.

Oresha: Hi Michael. Just got in the door... lol I spoke with Kathy.... Does tomorrow afternoon, say around 3:00-ish work for us to drop in to see you and borrow your wonderful DVD's? Looking forward to seeing Your Smiley Face. Ciao....

M: I'll get back with you on that tomorrow afternoon. I have a commitment in the a.m. that may extend into the afternoon. I'll let you know by 2 p.m. if I'll be available. If you don't hear from me by then, I'm not.

Oresha: Fair enough... lol Hope it's a "Fun Commitment"... Ttyl...

M: If you don't hear from me by 2 you'll know it was.

M: (to Jen) I wish you would have shared more with me, you just suddenly switched seemingly overnight from courting me to outright rejecting me. That happened I think when you registered on singles and found that you didn't need me anymore and wanted to try on other men. Or maybe it was the day before you met Jerry, I never heard from you that day. It was astonishing how quickly you dumped me. (Though admittedly you left a door open to let in some hope for the future.) I love you lots, I want to remain in your life, and you in mine. Let me know what you think of my suggestion about sharing. I think that would be great fun, maybe make that rejection I'm feeling worthwhile.

Yes, she has logged into singles several times today, she's working it for sure, didn't shut it down like she said she had. She has done what all the other significant women have done to me: say they are interested in me, lead me on, sleep with me maybe, then suddenly dump me. I had hoped for better from her, she pushed a huge number of buttons by doing that. She no longer puts any emotion into her messages to me, seems indifferent, calculated, cold. In three or four days she has become a different person than the one I was communicating with before. Yes, she invites me to share my thoughts and feelings and happenings with her, like Carrie maybe, leading me on as a potential backup ("there for me") but not allowing me to visit her because meanwhile she (Carrie) was secretly conversing with and inviting another man to her bed.

Jen has two weeks before needing to go to Utah, she's not far away, she *could* come to me if even only for a few days. But something has changed, *incredibly changed*, she's genuinely not interested in seeing me anymore, gives her blessing to another woman instead, hoping that it goes well for us. She's got her own life to live and it doesn't include me right now. I understand that, *but how could it possibly have changed so quickly from boiling hot to freezing cold?* Is this Source working through a grand plan for me, hoping that I'll enjoy the adventure along the way and be happy with it? Should Jen join whole heartedly in my sharing plan and do it, we could get some great stories for the books. Is that what this is all about? I'm feeling this moment *exactly* as I felt when Suzanne began rejecting me - that it's just not worth the pain that comes when you're a writer who *lives* his stories. *I feel that I should quit!*

Had it been anyone but Jen, I think my skin would have been thick enough by now, my heart well enough protected to not weep out loud and pace the floor heartbroken with this latest rejection. BUT IT'S THE WOMAN I'VE LOVED FOR 18 YEARS WHO IS REJECTING ME!!!! I need an abundance of fresh air in my life *right now.* Like maybe a pretty woman who truly wants and loves and needs me long term, I'd be faithful to that one I think. Could that be Heather? I'm going to give her every benefit of the doubt tomorrow even if she doesn't look pretty to me. Nobody but the promise of Heather and Jen are looking like there might be a future there for me. And the way I'm feeling right now, I'm prepared this very moment to let go all thought of Jen my ex.

Chapter 27

It's almost my bedtime and I must be a glutton for punishment because there's still no response from Jen to my last emails, and I just checked and found that she is online at the singles site. I am sick at heart that she dumped me so quickly and dumped me so conclusively. I'm just not of interest to her anymore after such great professions of love as she rendered just a few days before. Fickle fickle woman? Or just addicted now to her new all night computer game, the exciting one called *"The Mating Game"*?

No, I'll not reach her easily if at all from now on, she's gone, she's gone, she's gone... And not even on a Mormon site. She's living dangerously, wonder if she's aware of that, that she could easily dump her Mormon beliefs in such a venue as she is frequenting, be invited to an interesting man's bed and find it too compelling to resist. She'd quite possibly be excommunicated from her church for fornication, though they don't go after women as much as the men. Could it be that unknowingly she's doing everything she needs to do to become Adam's Eve? Would it be easier for her to accept me and my dream if she was no longer Mormon? *Grasping at straws Michael? What else do I have?*

Yes, I know, I'm on singles sites all the time too, but *she* is my top priority, I drop everything to instantly respond to every message she sends. (Very few now.) Shades of Suzanne. Pains of Suzanne. I've gotta get a life without her, hopefully tomorrow with Heather will be promising, if not or maybe even if so, I think I'll explore Deanna. I feel sexuality oozing from the photo she sent even in a modest dress, just the way she stands, the way she tilts her head, and my needy imagination. Plus, the messages she sent are suggestive, wanting to be called "babe" and writing about us staying overnight at each other's home. I think that she too will be like Suzanne and DeLeon who were in bed with me the first night, and Jackie the second time we were together. And like those three, the candle we light together will waver and not be long. Maybe Deanna's what I need right now. *BUT IT'S JEN I WANT IN MY BED TONIGHT!!!*

Yes, it's confirmed, I checked again and Jen's back and forth working the singles site with no regard to my unanswered messages, responding instead to emails from men she's never met, men looking for a rendezvous and sex with a beautiful willing woman. (Just as I am.) Why did she have to reject and leave me *so abruptly?* With her it was much worse than the others because we have 18 years of history, a recent week in bed, and her many professions of love and a future together since then. She may just be addicted to all night computer games again. But *this* game can quickly lead to a real man's bed! Maybe that's what she's secret maybe even to herself wanting to explore. With my recent history in mind and her knowing it, I can't blame her can I? Maybe we both need the experiences we are having to become Adam, to become Eve. It's just that it hurts right now, to share Eve with other men. Is it that way with her, to share Adam with other women? Good night my darling Jen, play the games you must, just save some life for me – *PLEASE!*

I think if I'm going to have a strategy of sorts, the best one is to simply stop writing to her other than to respond to each message she sends. Am I disciplined enough to do that? Dunno, but better try, that's my only hope, to try to get her chasing me again, rather than the other way around. It could backfire by her thinking it is me rather than her who has lost interest in the other? But what else can I do? I've given it all I've got to get her back and it hasn't worked, she's gone…

This morning, September 2, the day I meet Heather, there's no email in my inbox but there is a message from Jen on the singles site.

Jen: I would love to come walking with a good looking man like you.

M: Let's get together then and do that, you're not far away, airplanes still fly. I'm really missing you, you don't even respond to my messages anymore. I'm suddenly a very low priority as you respond to strangers instead, not used to that, don't like it. You've gone from boiling hot to freezing cold in just three or four days the same as other women have done, pushed a whole lot of buttons. But if that's what you need then enjoy your life that way sweetheart until the excitement (and uncertainty) of the mating game gets too disturbing, as it will, I know. Thank-you for the note, enjoy the day, be who you want to be, you are free, you deserve that, dance and fly. I'll always love you, it was a wonderful 18 years, you are beautiful.

I'm clinging to that note I just wrote and sent to Jen on singles, reading it over and over again compulsively at 4:30 a.m., it's my only connection with her. I love her, I want her back, I can't stand the cold, not from her I can't. How will she respond? Or will she even bother? She signed in to singles many times last night. (I don't think she knows that information is shown to me as a paid member, she can't get away with the pretense that she's busy offline.) That kind of activity can only mean that she's responding to messages from strangers as they arrive and she gets a notice in her email inbox that there's a message waiting for her on the singles site. Meanwhile as she rushes to write to strangers, my heartfelt emails to her grow cold and stale. It may be just one man who has particularly captured her interest that she's rushing to swap messages with, his singles handle will be shown to her in the notice she gets, she can screen that from the many others who are writing to court that beautiful woman with the compelling "about me" comments that I wrote for her myself, wish I hadn't. Why was I like that when she was here? I sure didn't think I was about to lose her, she tried so hard to get me back but my mind was on Jackie, and Jackie's mind was *not* on me.

WHY sweetheart? Why are you now the same as the others who roared into my life like fireworks exploding, showering heat and light upon me, then moving suddenly from hope to darkness, only quickly fading sparks left as prelude to complete and utter silence, a tiny trace of memory left of their having once been there. You are better than that, don't freeze me out Jen, I'm hurting here. What will *this* day bring for us? I want her heart, and her attention…

As I go back to bed to nap and meditate, the vision floats into awareness of my glorious immortal wives. They are beautiful, real, as if already manifest. And I am home again, centered, becoming Adam. I become aware that if Jen would join me with her whole heart and mind as co-creator, live with me full-time, faithful monogamy for mortality would be fine, then she and I would become Adam and Eve. We'd have ten sister wives to help us know fullness of joy and populate planets, the twelve of us together as one, ancient gods on Mount Olympus. *I WANT THAT, THAT'S MY DREAM!*

But so she can know that she wants only me does Jen first need to explore other men, do to them what she did to me deliciously with her vaginal tightness, her skills and talents, her newly educated mouth and tongue? She'd been preparing before she came to Victoria, why didn't I keep her then? She tried so hard, even said she accepted my dream, but it didn't feel right. Can I give her up to other men for now and still be Becoming Adam? I don't want to, I'd avoid it if she would, it doesn't have to be, her flight to Victoria would be less than two hours, we'd talk it over. But I'd have no choice if that was her yearning first desire, to be with other men as I think it is. I'd wait for her, but I'd be with others too. Could I break away from them?

We have the power she and I to create our lives going forward from this moment the way we want them to be. Choose me Jen, choose me, you don't need those other men, it doesn't have to be. I'd be a writer, you'd be my wife again. We'd focus on family, exactly the way you said you want us to be. This moment I'm ready to marry you again sweet love, somewhere, anywhere, quietly. I see an *eternal* future beckoning for us, together we'd make it happen. We'd have a common goal and topic of discussion, no longer bored with life and each other, excited, jointly creating our immortal family, your newly trim body resting lightly on my knee, my arms wrapped securely about you, me carrying you like a child even, laughing, having fun. New life, the way it was meant to be. But I must wait for her to come back to me so we can talk about this and make decisions. I would that she would come this day, this day of Heather, this week of Deanna, I want to go straight instead. I would marry Jen again today, a Mormon bishop would do. We could keep it secret, meet together often for sex and companionship until we find a better way to be together. But I can't tell her that, she must come wanting me as much as I am wanting her if she is to be Adam's Eve. She must come and discover for herself that Adam's waiting eagerly in the garden of his desire. Come today my darling? Come *today*?

But today in her absence, for such it will be, I am completely vulnerable. I wear my wounded heart on my sleeve for all to see and touch. If it feels right, I'm ready to give my all to Heather or another for the duration of whatever it is we start and sustain together, maybe a mortal lifetime, I will be true to my new love. Jen was warned, she knew that I sought stability, and chose to let me go. So I let Jen go as well, I *must*, I release her to the strange men she craves now to know, it was her choice. May God go with her, and with me...

Instead of Jen abandoning her singles site she has added her Utah town to it. This lady's determined, she has made her choice, her course is fixed, she's in it for the long haul. I've lost her, she has lost me. I feel right about what I wrote above. But I must have stability, for me the singles game is done. I put great hope in Heather now that Jen's gone. I will surely be blind as we meet two hours from now. *If* we meet, I haven't heard from her for a while. But I'll be there at the meeting place with smiles and hopes, watching for her light and heat exploding. I hope for me and her it's the grand finale. But I must remember to go slow with her, women keep the timing to themselves, they will *not* be rushed. I know that now. I must go and prepare for HER.

Quick note before I leave to hopefully meet Heather, still no word from her even though she read my last message. She's into fashion and society and I am not, never owned a tux, maybe a deal breaker? But if she's there, in my own best interests maybe I need to not appear too eager to see her again? Let her chase me, if she will.

Jen was on singles a half hour ago, she read my message and didn't respond. On purpose she left a dress and a few things with me when she left Victoria. I accepted the medal with chain that she probably made for me, but told her to take the dress. She hid it instead. Must be a woman thing, I found it later. I need to get rid of the dress at least, it reminds me of her. I *must* forget her...

M: (to Oresha) I'm back, so 3 p.m. today works for me, please confirm. If I see you in the parking lot I'll come down and let you in the servant's entrance. If I'm not there, walk around to the front and buzz and I'll unlatch the gate. Come on up, see you.

Oresha: We shall be arriving by carriage... around 3-"ish" this afternoon... Looking forward to dropping in to say "Hi"... hugzzzzz....

Suffice it to say that I met Heather and although she's not a bad looker, I soon realized that I am looking for much younger energy to match mine, someone who is still climbing, has not given up and started down the hill like she has. She said I am handsome and look younger than my singles site photos. But shucks, they *all* say that. I'm content for now, still happy, loving life and my great adventure. No word from Jen Who. I still can't believe that she dumped me like that. There's something wrong with that picture. What can it be? Are we done? I think not... There is one more thing that I need to try, just in case she thinks I have not changed and that's what's keeping her away.

M: (to Jen) You might be very pleasantly surprised if you came and talked to me face to face. Maybe I'm willing now to give you everything you want (except other men.) You could come for just a few days. We wouldn't need to have sex if that would trouble you. I think you owe us one more effort at reconciliation, if even only because of our long history together. I'd send you funds to refund your tickets, you could be here just a few hours from now if you were willing to give us a try. We could continue to live apart if need be for a while, just meet often until we can come up with a better plan, a place to live together. I'm wanting you and stability real badly right now. You could make it happen, but we need to talk it through while looking each other in the eye, find out what will work for both of us long-term, I'm willing if you are.

Please talk to me, your hurtful silence is exactly what I got from the other women who were significant to me during the last few months. I thought you were better than them, you've suddenly changed and locked me out. What happened? Please know that I will not discuss this further from a distance, you should come to me now.

If that does not bring her to me, or at least elicit a candid and open discussion by email, then I think I will cease to respond to her emails for at least one month, and then evaluate my feelings. I simply cannot allow this to hang any more, it's too unsettling, I cannot get on with life as long as I have the hope of her.

Jen: Let me think about this. The emotional ups and downs are a bit to much sometimes. Maybe I can come for a few days next week. Before I go to Utah. I can not make a commitment to you but I can come to be with you for this moment and because I care about you.

Note the absence of her usual affectionate "Jen"- nothing more than the above – *I've lost this woman's love most likely irrevocably.* I'm not sure how to read that note, I think she might come for two or three days because I am buying her tickets. But it seems that she will come cold and suspicious, not wanting to commit to anything with me. *Has she ever changed!* It's incredible how she has changed in the last few days, she is just not the same person I ever knew before, as if she is on drugs. Maybe I was just not noticing and she actually made the change beginning when she left Victoria, giving up on me, and I continued all too familiar fully open as usual when she was actually reading my comments as outlandish, not at all what she wants with her life? There's a good chance that she will come for a brief time of discussion out of a feeling of obligation to me. There is a good chance that *whatever* I tell her, the commitments I am prepared to make to her that would give her everything she told me she wanted will no longer be meaningful. Nothing will work because SHE SIMPLY DOESN'T WANT ME ANYMORE – SHE HAS CHANGED COMPLETELY, SHE HAS LOST HER LOVE AND DESIRE FOR ME.

Kathleen: (Oresha's friend, the one who brought me flowers) Dear Michael, Thank you so much for allowing me the opportunity to experience such a wonderful piece of art. It is a movie I will cherish. A significant personal moment in the movie... when I first started competing in Figure Skating Rachaminoff Rapsody Paganint was the very first piece of slow music incorporated into my solo. That music is cellular for me. I felt that music and skated to it for years. Please let me know a time that is convenient to drop off the movie. Thank you again.

M: Wow, you are fast! I knew you'd enjoy that movie. Hang on to it until you are finished with the Abraham DVD's then either you or Oresha could arrange a time to drop them off. Enjoy the evening Kathy, it was nice visiting with the two of you today.

Looking back on this, I think Kathy was wanting time with me without Oresha around?

M: Oresha, I thrill with your new hope for the man from Courtney. I know this is uncalled for but I care about you, we had some fun times together, I just wanted to candidly share with you a suggestion for when you meet him. I hope I don't offend you, I'm just telling it the way I see it from the male point of view, I thought you might want to hear that. My experience with you is that although I enjoyed your touch immensely, the way we held hands and put our arms around each other when we walked was delicious, there were times when I craved that. But there was always something starkly missing, *a spark of passion!* Males need that, it's very important when a male is thinking of marriage or a long term relationship that he anticipate many hot nights entwined under the sheets with his chosen one, she willing and wanting to share male/

female sexual energy. I have never even seen a *hint* of cleavage with you Oresha, you always cover your feminine self completely as if you were ashamed of your body. I suggest that you buy new clothes if you must but give that hint the first time you meet your prospective man, and undo another button or two the next day. That's important Oresha, it's normal, it's beautiful, I hope it works well for you. I enjoyed our visit today. Your friend, Michael

M: (to Jen) Thanks for at least responding Jen, I appreciate that, even a short note is infinitely better than the sudden silence and coldness from you over the last few days. I don't think I deserve that, I have always made it a top priority to respond to your messages and did, writing you before I wrote to strangers. But what you wrote is not at all encouraging, you didn't even sign your note with the usual affectionate "Jen" let alone the expressions of love that used to come with each of your messages just a few days ago. You are suddenly stiff and formal, not even friendly anymore. *What happened?*

Although after you think about it you *may* be willing to come for a couple of days, I interpret your note as saying that if you come it would only be out of a sense of obligation, and because I'm buying the tickets. You loved me when you left Victoria and I assumed I was still in your heart so I kept writing to you openly, sharing my feelings and desires which must in that new context for you have come across as strange and unwanted. My feelings and desires have changed enormously in the last few days as I saw you drifting away and wanted you back. I saw in you a companion who would work closely and effectively with me to co-create what we mutually want, even making family visits a priority as you said you wanted to do. But I now think that I have lost you forever, I was blind to that, it came suddenly without warning. I don't think you love me anymore Jen, you have hardened your heart against me. But I accept that you "care" out of empathy/sympathy, as you would for an old friend. I think you have changed almost overnight (for all I know it might have happened weeks ago, you keep secrets.) I think now that it doesn't matter what I offered you in the way of giving you everything you told me only days ago that you wanted, it would not change you back to the way you were. Is that correct? *You no longer want to be with me, you no longer love me, that's where I think you are now. Is that correct?*

I regret enormously sending you away a week early. I apologize profusely for how I treated you when you were here trying so hard to please me and win me back. I had no idea that I was losing you, I thought you'd go home and make the changes to your body you and I both wanted you to make, that we'd keep in touch lovingly, and then you'd be back with a fullness of love and desire for me. I thought we would ride off into the sunset together and live happily ever after, eventually becoming immortals, that was my dream. Now I know it was not *your* dream, though you seem to have accepted it temporarily when you were here, it gave me great hope. I can live with your loss of love and desire for me. I will adjust, as I adjusted to other divorces, so please don't do 'obligation' with me, I hold you to no obligation whatsoever, you are free to do as you will, you know that. But as you say *"the emotional ups and downs are a bit too much sometimes."*

Please confirm that what I am thinking now is true, that it matters not what I offered if you came, you would reject it and go your own way anyway, your final decision is *already* made. I think you have already decided to find and marry another man and settle down with him. I think you have already decided that I am not the man for you anymore, you no longer want a reconciliation. Is that correct? I need to know. I cannot stand the thought of you walking through my door with arms open wide but a stone cold heart inside. If that's the way it would be and you know it, please don't come. If you no longer wanting me is true and you tell me it is, we will simply move further and further apart until it is the same with us as it is with our former spouses, no emotion left, just, just, *NOTHING!* We've both been there before, we could handle it.

Once you confirm that I'm not wanted, I will no longer bother you except that we can still do business together if you will. I'd like that, I'd like us to remain friends, we just can't be confidantes because you won't share like I am willing to share, it's just not the way you are. Knowing what I believe to be true now, that you have lost your love for me, I would not have sent you that message about sharing. In the context of today it was out of line, too gross for normal life, normal people don't talk about sex, that's stuff for books of fiction. If you don't want me, I will get on with my life and you will get on with yours, some happy memories perhaps but no chance of us ever getting together again because we've hurt each other too badly and won't want to take that risk again, better to keep our hearts tightly closed. It would be better instead to find another and take on their baggage, tough as that task can be. I wish you well with that. I hope you go knowing that when you find another the honeymoon will not last, faults will appear when the courting's concluded.

You may quickly realize with a throb of pain and regret that you would have been much better off with your last husband, and that you could have been with him because he had invited you back!

It would have been easy for us to blend again, we've already shared so much for 18 years, we have the same baggage. And with the adventure of a new dream we're secretly creating together, and your new body, we could have had as much excitement as you'd get with a new man. I pictured your newly slim body sitting lightly on my knee, my arms wrapped securely around you, our lips pressed close as always. Maybe you'd even be light enough that I could have carried you like a child, laughing, having fun, headed for the bedroom, another precious night with our bodies pressed together under the sheets, content with each other and our love making. You have no idea how important it was to me for you to be slim. Now that you've lost me and want to attract another man, you are quickly on the way to what I your husband wanted from you all those years, how ironic.

I'm sad and sorrowing that it came to this after we came (I thought) so close to healing our wounds and being together again. I loved you like crazy and I think you loved me too. I still want to hold and cuddle you all night, for many nights my darling lost one. Is there no chance at all that you can open up your heart again so we can sing our lovely song in unison, care for our children and grandchildren in mortality, and bring new children into new worlds when we're made immortal? *What happened sweetheart to suddenly destroy what we had?* I want to understand. Are you in love with another man already? In love with the chase perhaps, the knowing that you are beautiful and desirable to other men not just this one? Addicted to a dangerous all night long computer game called "Mating" that can only end with you in bed with another man? Have you thought it through? Or is it simply that you don't want *me* anymore?

I might even have married you again had you come back to me fully. I was thinking that a Mormon bishop in Victoria might do that, we'd keep it a secret if you wanted to. I think I would have been faithful to you like I always was before, I'm really a one woman man, just didn't have one woman around this past year. I might have lived monogamously with you for mortality, I thought just a few days ago that that was what you really wanted. I was wanting to surprise you when you came to talk, to help you be deliriously happy with the man you were saying you were deeply in love with. I was hoping you'd co-create my dream of immortality, us having children to populate new planets, you said you wanted children. But then, there are other men who have seed as well, you now know they will flock to your beauty, your availability, your invitation, your pheromones. *Do those men on singles sites have as big a dream as mine?* Or is it something else they have that may be bigger and you secretly lust for that? If so, that would be normal, you are single, you've engaged in the thrilling (for a while then disappointing) mating game.

The possibility of marriage (even if secret for now) is one thing I wanted to discuss with you when you came. But now, with your continuing coldness I think I have already found your answer: marriage yes, but with another man. Is that correct, or should I still have imminent hope without having to wait for months while you explore other men first and make your final choice then? I can take it, just let me know where you truly are, tell me your final decisions. There's no point in you coming if you come cold out of a sense of obligation or duty because we once loved each other. I need to know, please tell it true, thank-you.

But if you think the two of us together for a few days could talk and hug and cuddle and rekindle your love and desire for me and a long-term relationship, then tell that true too and give us some time to see if we can make that happen. It's *vitally* important forever (if there's hope) that you give us as much time as you possibly can right now, nothing should be more important to you if you are sincere. There may even now be millions even billions of spirits waiting breathlessly to see if Jen will be Adam's Eve. Is there any hope for that or are you already too far gone from me? Tell it like it really is for you. Were you just leading me on the last few weeks, telling me you loved me when it was already lost? I must know.

You could phone your kids and simply ask what they would think if you and I got together again because we still love each other. You *could* work it out and quickly for us to be together again if your heart was set on doing so. Until we find a proper place to live together, we could just meet a few weeks every couple of months, it could be a year or more if needed before we play house again. If you think there's hope worth exploring, then come sooner and stay extra days, make the two of us together right now your *top* priority, even if we can't live under the same roof just yet. We need to either open the door of US wide right now, or close it permanently. And we need to do that as soon as possible (why not come tomorrow?) I can't stand not knowing if there's hope for you or not. Tell me one way or the other. There's life and love to get on with for both of us, either together or with another. We *must* make a final choice either way and we *must* make it now, the pain is too great not knowing which way it is.

Wow Jen, you took me so by surprise! (Like the divorce.) I still can't believe you loved me like you kept telling me you did, then dumped me so suddenly and so conclusively, boiling hot to freezing cold in a day. Was it Jerry or another man you're already in touch with who triggered that? Please don't lead me on anymore, tell it openly and fully right away, let's get this behind us one way or the other. Where really are you with us? Is there hope or none, or somewhere in between? Is it worth you coming and finding out for sure? Don't come unless you come with hope and come with IMMINENT hope, not just the vague uncertainty of maybe months down the road if you haven't yet found a better man, you might come for backup me. I still love you Jen, but it must wane fast, it can't remain the same with this uncertainty, it hurts too much this way. I must soon harden my heart to you the way you have done to me...

Yes, you guessed it, she's logged into singles, looking for other men to play with, or more likely responding to one or two interesting others she wants to meet. That's so hard for me to accept. Just getting my own back maybe? I wonder if she'll respond to the above, or even read it? I took hours composing that, thought it might we worth it, that will be entirely up to her. I must very soon harden my heart to Jen, if I can. I think she has already broken it in tiny pieces, maybe there's nothing left to harden. I must constantly keep my immortal wives in mind, and the fact that it is for them that I am becoming Adam.

M: (to Jen) Please don't ignore the long email I just sent to you, read it carefully, and respond very soon, I need that. I thought it was important enough that I took five hours composing it for you, give me a bit of your time too. I am asking if only for old times sake that instead of rushing to respond to strangers on a singles site tonight that you respond honestly and fully to me instead. There will be time enough for those men to woo you into their life and bed, that's what they seek. Have you thought that whole game through? There is nothing else they want regardless of what they may say to get you there, they want that beautiful willing woman in their bed. (I do too.)

Is she ready for that? Maybe she is, I don't know her anymore...

Please respond to me tonight, I'll stay up a while watching for your message, thank-you.

M: (to Jen) Please remove from your singles site profile the words I wrote. They are untrue and very misleading from someone who just wants "a friend". I don't want to be responsible for what those words may do, it might not turn out to be a happy ending for you and I'd feel responsible, I know the power of words. Just write your own profile, you can do it, I taught you well. Saying it your own way will first cause you to think about what you are really wanting and will represent the real you much more accurately. Good luck with it, I hope you enjoy the game while it lasts, it can be exciting to think of a new body in your bed, that's what the mating game is all about. For me, I was gathering stories for books that I was writing. It wasn't fun at all, it was hugely painful, filled with false hope then rejection over and over again. If I was not writing books I would have left that mad game a long time ago. I feel for those lovely longing women whose hearts and hopes are on their sleeves. For most of them it will not turn out well, they will remain lonely and unfulfilled.

Should you and I reconcile soon, I'd suspend my singles profiles right away and cling only to you, that's what I really want, I need that stability right now. I crave *genuine* proven love, the kind you used to give me abundantly, I'm heartbroken with its loss, never before knew what it was I had. I met Heather today and as usual with my careful choices found her to be a wonderful woman, we had a good conversation. (I'm getting pretty good at that.) She said I am handsome and younger looking than my photos. (They all say that.) I found out that for every man in Victoria there are nine women. But I quickly realized with Heather, as I did with others that it is a much younger energy that I am seeking to match mine. Someone who is still climbing up the hill (like you are), not someone who has already given up and is headed back down, believing in and playing the aging game, I won't go there.

Take care my once sweet love. Please respond soon, I'll be going to bed now, having heard nothing from you, as usual the last few days. I continue to love you and hope for us. But that's entirely up to you, I'm inviting you back into my life. I hope you never regret that you turned down your last husband when he invited you back, he might have been by far the best you will ever have. I wish you a life of happiness with your new man, and much innocent fun with the others along the way. Be careful, stay safe, they're not all temple going Mormons out there. You may be out of your depth right now, innocent as the game may seem to be right now until you get hurt, as I think must inevitably happen, it sure did for me. Think carefully about what you want, and what you're likely to get going the direction you are headed. That might be a startling eye opener for you, it's not the same as the other computer games you played all night. Don't be deceived, there are real and lasting consequences with this one, life changing events will happen. Good night Jen.

It's now 3:30 a.m. I got up to see if she had written back but no she hasn't. So I checked singles and she's online there, last logged in at 2:49 a.m. So it's an easy call, she will not be mine again. It's just that I don't want to accept that, no more than (much more than) I still cannot accept Suzanne being gone forever either. I am still baffled at how suddenly Jen left me, from deep love declared in every message to in a day *nothing, nothing at all...* What more could I have done than I have done? I offered her everything, even marriage, thinking she would be my Eve. Deep down I guess her woman-knowing tells her firmly that she will not be, that there is another for this man and others, it's one man several wives for me. How could I have missed that? She was so wanting me when she was here. But it didn't *feel* right! All is well Michael. Just take a lover until Kira comes? Deanna's looking good at 4 a.m. today...

So even if Jen does write back and offers to come, would I even *want* her back in my life knowing she can reverse her love the next moment? She's hooked on computer games like she was for years, playing mindlessly all the night long, guiltily shutting them down should she hear my soft early a.m. footfall coming down the hallway to check on her. If we got together again she'd almost certainly go back to that instead of being where she belongs, in bed cuddling me. How could she avoid it? What would she do when I am writing books? Jen is an online gaming addict, this time with a dangerous new game. She might with time give it up but why should I get involved with that again now that I am free? I want her to be someone she's not wanting to be. I fear for her if she gives up the Mormon faith with its moral constraints, she'd go wild I think, who knows what would come out of that? But she must be free to live her own life, and so must I. I can still be her *immortal* backup, she could be one of my sister wives yet, just not mine for mortality. I have to harden my heart to her once and for all, let her go, open the door for another to step in, *Jen's just not mine!*

Law of Attraction will bring me another, a beautiful bride to be, a Kira, an Eve, that's who I am looking for. But how long will it be when my soul cries out NOW for immortality? Just press forward Michael, there's a very bright light ahead, see, *Kira comes already...*

As I lay in my bed at now 5 a.m. September 3, 2014, Victoria, British Columbia Canada, I realize where I have gone wrong and am thus myself inviting all this present turmoil. My mind has been focused on the things of mortality, looking for Kira in *this* world when she is of another. My goal, what I am seeking is plain before my eyes – it's *immortality*. I've been writing that all along, but pushing it into some distant future, dragging these books out endlessly when it doesn't have to be that way. Only in that state of immortality can I find what I am looking for - my family of spouses to populate new worlds. Every time I agonize over an earthly need, including my need for sex and the frequent touch of a beautiful woman, I am closing the door to the entire solution – THAT I AM IMMORTAL NOW!!! In that pleasant state of immorality none of the things I concern about now matter anymore. I flit and fly about at will, the greatest adventure of all, to be *superman* on a planet such as this. That is the only fitting end to a book like these I am presently writing, for Michael to spread his fledgling wings and *fly*. And with that knowing, can I now close down my singles profiles and be just who and what I am instead of slogging through the muds of mortality? *Should* I? Can I give up a lover? *Should* I? What do I want?

Did Jackie leave because she sensed that I wanted her forever and she was not ready for forever, had things to do here first? Is that where Jen is right now? Does she sense that I am not of the same world she is and she thinks it's helping me to abandon me? Everything, *everything*, every single concern and struggle that I have had for the year of my becoming is fled with the thought that I am already among the immortals. Here in this happy state of immortality, just a simple change of attitude and focus, I can find those who will be my sister wives and gather them, *wherever* they are right now, in whatever state of being. If there is a need for that, I can go too to certain women on this planet and if they so desire, impregnate them with the seed of a new race of beings, half god half man, the way it needs to be to complete our Mother Earth for another thousand years. I would love doing that and the joy of being father again, watching carefully over and loving the mothers too full time. I'm spectacularly well prepared for that role already, *wanting* it, but was denying it, setting it aside for some future time.

And when the time is right for us, my immortal wives and I (there are twelve of us I think) will fly to our new planet and there be Adam and Eve in all our fullness, joys and function. *Yes Michael, you are IMMORTAL - get on with it!!!* Now all I have to do is *prove* it to myself and others. No problem for an immortal. *Now where's that first woman who wants my seed?* And with that, at 5:30 a.m. another door has closed, there's room now for a better one to open.

Jen: I am trying to see if I can come for a short visit next week. I am very busy. My comments below are regards to the reality of my everyday life decisions. Later we can talk about where you are in your thinking and what are you wanting. I am trying see if I can come next week. But before that can happen I want to say. We can not get back together at this time. I don't know when it might be possible and do not want to set a deadline. If I come it is to comfort you and be your best friend. I know we will want to cuddle but need to be careful. This causes me to be iffy about coming. This is what I am dealing with. (She lists her "busy" things.) Could spend more time with you if I came toward the end of October. When we were married I would most likely not run off to help family unless you approved. But being single just like your first wife. I found I can fully and freely help my family. I really like helping. I need and want to do this. I think this will change with a bit of time and I will be available to spend much of my time with my man (hopefully you) and doing what we desire.

As far as us planning on a place to settle together is a bit early for that type of planning. For me I still have to decide what to do with the house I rarely seem to be living in. The work to prepare it for sale seems overwhelming to do by myself. I know I can't afford to keep it much longer. I don't know your financial situation and it is none of my business. If we were to get back together again at that time I would need to know your situation as you would need to know mine. Don't you think. These are the facts as I see them. Love you sweetie Jen

M: Please don't come, it would be like meeting a stranger for the first time. I have no idea who you are anymore, it's as if you are on drugs or haven't been sleeping for ages, it's much more than being "busy". Are you hooked on all night computer games again and can't think clearly? I don't want the person you have become in my life except at a distance. You can continue to write me if you want, we can continue to do business and possibly be friends, though I don't know how we can be that because friends tell each other their secrets and help each other through life - you're not there anymore. I don't need you, I don't want you, you have lost me. I will not marry you again. How could I? I'd never know from one day to the next if you loved me or if you had suddenly and inexplicably thrown me away. I gave you my heart and offered my soul and you rejected both. I think you need help with your addiction, you need to sleep. I could have given you so much but that's destroyed now. I retract all offers, they were for someone who has disappeared, probably forever, I don't know where she went. I wish you the very best.

And please take down the profile on singles that I wrote, it's not the real you, nothing in it is you anymore, there is no resemblance. Your photos are beautiful but your words are fake, it's a lie, you are deceiving people, take them down. I hope you enjoy who you have become, I sure don't, good-bye.

Linda: It is not that simple. Life is made up of little rituals - from coffee in the morning to how we prepare for bed at night. Religions use music, art and magical thinking to embellish their rituals. Organized religions were developed by people - and corrupted by people. They are what we (human beings) make of them. We seem to need to believe in something - hence the formation of cults, all organized religions began as cults. The anthropology of religion 101. Our beliefs and rituals and how they evolve is what makes people so interesting. Although extremists in any religion make them terrifying at times. But then, there are extremists in many aspects of life including extreme sports.

M: Our messages are becoming academic Linda. Should we meet and take whatever comes from there do you think?

Gonna do just fine without Jen aren't I…. Wish her well though, would have been nice to be with her slim and willing. But this very moment she seems so shallow and uninviting, I'm much better off without her.

Jen: I don't understand you either. I was just telling you the facts of what is going on. I kept the emotions out of it, feeling it would be a clearer message of responsibilities that life brings. I do love you very much, but very cautious to not miss lead you. I also am very venerable when It comes to you. I am like the other woman in one way you lost and that is I have responsibilities beyond you. I know you want it now and I am not ready yet. If our relationship is not worth waiting for a new start than we most likely are making a mistake. You choose your road and it left me for adventure, sex book, and other women. You just can't expect me to jump back in when you say so. I was willing to come see you because I love you and yes be your friend.

A man in St George wants me to call him tonight. Can't decide what to do. I don't think I would like him much. Most people have so much baggage. You and I have a lot of the same baggage. Are we not worth giving us more time. I am not asking you to stop dating. It would be much harder for me to let myself get involved with another man. Particularly when I am in love with you and I have always been a one man woman. I know you want to sleep with other women but would be faithful if together. Yes we both are taking a risk the other might find someone else, that causes insecurity. I was willing to come see you because I love you in spite of the risk and timing. Maybe in a couple months or so you will change your mind and ask me again.

Who do you think I have become? I feel I am the same person with the same beliefs with a wider understanding and acceptance of the people I love. Who have you become? I see a better person in many ways and other areas are questionable because of your new beliefs. I was willing to let be because I know you at a much deeper level than others do. Don't have time to reread my message. My grandson requires much more care now and is crying for me to pick him up. Love Jen

Suddenly it doesn't matter what she does on singles sites or with other men. Suddenly I want to live her life by proxy again, her physical senses and feelings taking life in as if they were mine.

M: I'm completely confused Jen. I thought from your unusual silence and lack of expressed emotion, ignoring my messages over the last few days, that you had rejected me - that's how it was with other women as they dumped me from a distance. Now I'm not so sure, you come right out and say you still love me, I can't argue with that. I think I'm still in love with you too, it's just that I don't *want* to be in love with you right now. Ok, come if you want, but only come if you are coming because you sincerely *want* to be with me, not because you think it's your duty or that I need your advice or sympathy, I don't. And keep in mind that everything I offered is retracted, don't come expecting any of that. Just come because you like being with this handsome guy, and you know he'll share his bed with you. It will be nice to hold you again even if it's only for a brief time. If we can get together often enough, maybe we *can* sustain something to look forward to, we'll see. You know as far as sex goes that I *will* go as far as you allow. I'm hoping that your limits will be similar to what we had before we married, but that's up to you.

I do still want your body sweetheart. I'm eager to see the changes you are making, it's real exciting for me. Please don't go into silence again, I so want to share your life with you and intimately know what's happening all the time, I would like to live your life by proxy if you will. I won't judge you regardless of what you may do with other men, or how you take care of your sexual needs, I understand now, just tell me about it and how it was, I hate secrets between us. But I *will* judge and disapprove if you ignore me, that I cannot handle.

If you are not willing to share real time, please keep a daily journal like I do, and copy into it every message you send and receive. Someday we may co-write an exciting book from that, or merge it into mine. But it would be nice if we'd both share fully and openly every day - then each time we meet we're not meeting a stranger and starting all over again, we'd *know* each other. Do you want to know about me and other women? Please tell me what you want to accomplish by visiting, when you'll come, and when you'll leave. You *will* be my top priority, but let me know as soon as you can so I can be better organized. I'm getting excited about seeing you now, please come, I need to touch you and to feel you touch me. I love you.

M: (to Deanna) I've been thinking about your invitation to meet in Victoria. There is a Starbucks right across the street from the apartment where I live. We could meet for coffee there then go to my place to talk in private if we're still talking after the coffee's drained. Would that interest you? Or we could walk the breakwater at Ogden Point if you'd be more comfortable doing that. Just suggestions, let me know.

That should flush her out and give me a much better idea if this woman will make a casual lover for me while I wait for Jen or another longer term to come into my life. I'm up and down but now with the possibility of Jen restored, I'm again in the market for someone casual to take care of my sexual needs, as I take care of hers. It could be good with Deanna, her photo arouses me, I can easily picture us making love.

Jen: I have not seen any other men since that two hour breakfast. Just not wanting to date just now. I will let you know if I do. My life outside my family is almost nonexistent. Once I am back in Utah I will then be able to let you know when I am free to come. Love Jen

M: You have given me hope for us, thank-you for that. Though I have concerns that if we get together we might fall back into old patterns (computer games all night instead of cuddling, etc.) it might be worth it when the alternative is to have to get to know a whole new set of in-laws and still have to take the chance that after a while the marriage (or other arrangement) wouldn't work out any better anyway. It would be easy for us to reconcile and take our chances. I think with your new body (if you maintained it, that would be *very* important to me) it would be like starting all over again. You've got me excited that I might have you in my bed again sometime soon. You were so good with your new skills, I hope that's within the bounds you set for us, though it's likely that I will have to miss out this time on the results of those muscle exercises, too bad, you were fabulous, mmm.

Does it excite you to think of sharing my bed again? (Be honest with me always.) If you will allow it I'll do much more for *you* this time, can't wait to hear your woman sounds, I'm hard as I think about it. A big problem in the past was that I think you had a yeast infection and the smell was unpleasant for many years, I just didn't want to go there.

I've since learned with great delight that not all women are like that, the normal smell (and taste) of a woman are pleasant and highly arousing. Do you like me to talk like this, or would you sooner I don't?

Re your comment about calling a man in Utah, I think you should always first ask yourself what you want to *accomplish* by meeting or dating a man. In your case it's probably not to get laid, so what is it you really want? If you think the prospects of getting what you want are pretty good, then go for it. If not, why bother? Are you using your new toy much? Going to bring it/them with you? I like to watch, and it works on me too. How can you tell I haven't had sex since you? Needy, needy...

Tell me if I'm offending you by talking like this. You told me you love sex, I am hoping maybe this way of talking is something you'd appreciate from me?? (I'm a man, don't ever know for sure how it is with a woman until she tells.)

Jen: Don't assume because you do not here from me that I have rejected you. It is not always that easy to be on the internet here. It kicks me off all the time.

M: Ok sweetie, I'll try to be more gentle with you. Today I'm ok with you being on singles sites and dating as much as you want, even having sex with another man (or woman) if that was your choice, I'd still welcome you back to my bed anytime you chose to come. I'd sure like it if you told me about it and how it was though, I want to live the fullness of your life experience with you, I hope you'll let me.

Chapter 28

Deanna: Hi! Michael, Your suggestion of Starbucks near where you live sounds good... probably won't have too much time after that as I have a dinner commitment back in Nanaimo later in the day. Just need the address & time you can make it. Looking forward to meeting you.

This just keeps getting better and better all the time. She's obviously not shy. But how long would it take to get her in bed first time she's at my place? Yeah, I like the thought of her. And her being in Nanaimo might be even better because when we meet for sex at that distance, we'll most likely make it a two or so night stand each time, I love cuddling all night, waking up with a pretty face next to mine. I like this, I'll try for a long hug when we get inside my place and see what sparks may fly... (Book Michael's back yeah!)

M: After coffee we can move your car to visitor parking at my location right across the street. I can meet you anytime on Sunday, just let me know. In fact if you're short of time on Sunday I'll most likely be home all day and night Friday and Saturday as well if you have any other suggestions. I'm not shy at all, I like the way this conversation is evolving, write as boldly as you want, I welcome your suggestions.

Jen: I am not doing any of those things except I have looked on the single sites. I sent a comment to the man telling him even though he gave me his phone number I would not be calling him. That ends it all. Nothing else. Your head takes you places I do not go.

M: My head takes me places *Mormons* don't go. Otherwise it's normal. That's why I suggest you go on Mormon singles sites and get off the one you're on, it would be much safer for you. The expectations of males on the Mormon sites would be quite similar to yours. Non-Mormon society is *very* different than it is with Mormons. I think you're way over your head on that site because you are naively expecting Mormon standards, it's just not so, you don't speak the language there. There should be plenty of Mormon males in southern California too who are on Mormon sites as well as in Utah. Just some suggestions, I really really care about you, I don't want you to get hurt.

Am I offending you by writing so boldly about sex? I will stop if it is so, but you need to tell me frankly, you haven't done that yet. All we have right now is *communication*. Please be fully open and honest with me so we can move closer to what you want in your life, I'm very flexible, I want you back.

It's possible that I could go the excommunication route and become Mormon again a year or so later. But I don't think I could ever go to the temple because there are so many of the beliefs that I now question. I know my kids (and you) would be happy if I came back even if I was inactive and now and then had a beer or a glass of wine. There are plenty of Mormons who do that. You know I'd be sexually faithful to you, always was, and our temple sealings would likely be restored so we could *both* have our hopes and dreams. Would that interest you sweetheart? If so, I could give you a letter to give to your bishop to get the ball rolling. It's not foolproof, I don't want to personally stand in front of 15 men again and bare my soul and personal history to them, it would have to be done in my absence. And they might want it done in Victoria where I do not want any contact with the Mormons at my home. The above idea came to me (now that there's renewed hope for us) as I walked the breakwater today. That was just before I saw a pod of four whales surface just a few yards away, then watched them swim away moving above and below the water. Boats were soon swarming all around them.

Talk to me candidly sweetheart, it would please me so much if you would do that, we need to try to get to know and trust each other again, the last couple of days took a heavy toll on that.

M: Once more I invite you to be completely candid with me, I feel that I may have offended you with my writing boldly about sexual things. I really haven't changed much inside, I don't write like to just anyone but I'm always writing stories with book character Michael in mind. Are you still wanting me to present as an LDS elder on the way to the temple would write to you? I can do it if you want, I still speak that language. Tell me please.

Linda: Next week? I should be finished that office move by then.

M: Let me know when and where you want to meet.

Linda: Will do.

Jen: What in the heck makes you think I am interested or doing those things. You know me better. What you have been doing is your choose not mine. Do you understand. Just because I am on a single site does not mean I am dating anyone.

That doesn't make any sense at all. If she's not interested, why does she spend all night every night lately on a singles site that she said twice she had shut down? I need to be very cautious with this woman, she is playing a dangerous game but I don't know yet if it's with me, with other men, with herself, or all three. I really should back right off sending emails to her except polite responses. If Deanna and I click, I need to keep it from Jen, it would do no good to tell her. Every time I have asked her if she wanted to know if I was sleeping with another woman or not, she hasn't responded. I think I have my answer for sure now, keep my stuff to myself even though not too long ago she asked me to tell her everything, that it excited her that I was with other women. (Yeah, several times she said that until I gave her a copy of my first eight books to read. I don't know if she ever did, most likely not more than a few of the sex scenes in the beginning. I told her all about Suzanne and DeLeon anyway, she wanted to know.)

I think she wants to be Mormon and wants also to be wild, but sees herself only as Mormon even as she spends hour after hour looking at photos of men, and most likely responding to their messages. What else could that ultimately lead to but sex with someone other than me? And she's offended if I suggest that she might do exactly that. I'm swayed much too easily by her, it's not the innocent kind of play we enjoyed in Victoria when she was full of life and fun and love for me, she has changed even though she denies it. I don't like that change, it demands much caution, I went way too far back to her today. Gotta be smarter and more disciplined around her. I truly might be much better off without her, it's just that it would be easy and comfortable to play house again. She indicates no interest in co-creating my dream with me, that *must* be my priority.

We're slip sliding away here, just a false start once more today when she convinced me that she still loves me and sees a future for us and I fell for it. I must turn it around so that *she's* chasing me, if that can ever be again. The only way I know that might help her move towards that is to stop sending detailed messages, only reply to hers. She knows there are hundreds of men available to her on singles sites, she's looking, maybe when she comes to her senses and realizes what she could actually have with and from me compared to going that route, she'll start moving back in my direction. Do I want that? I don't know, I thought I did earlier today but now I'm not so sure again. Go slow with her Michael, go real slow.

Yep, she's right back at it as I write this at 10:30 p.m. logged into singles. And she has changed her objective from wanting "friends" to wanting "a relationship". Right, not interested. Her only interest in me is most likely for backup. She's not going to share her life with me, has no intention of doing that, just sent that email today to tug me back, she knew it would work, I'll try to be cool, but not good at that. She'll most likely be logged in to singles the entire night. But she's not interested?? Who is she kidding? I guess she has no idea that I know when she's online. I've got to leave her to her own devices and see what she brings with her if she actually comes to visit me. For sure that would not happen if she had to pay for the flights herself. *Why am I doing this?*

Looking real good Deanna – and everybody else except Jen too. I may as well go to bed, busy day again today, too many contacts, I may have to get out of this and just meditate, finish editing the books, and BE immortal.

But you know, I told her today that it no longer mattered if she was on singles sites or dated other men. And surprisingly at that time it genuinely did not matter, why should it? I need to leave her be in peace, let her do what she wants to do and be ok with that, send those vibes if any. Who knows, maybe after that experience with other men she will come back much better for me. Just be happy about it and her Michael. *That's* the winning attitude…

I was up earlier today and noticed that Jen left the singles site about midnight. Maybe she's taking my advice about needing sleep, or just getting bored with what she was doing there? Anyway, it doesn't matter because as I arose from my bed a few minutes ago, awakened to another glorious day in lovely Victoria, some new thoughts flowed into awareness.

I'm not really like the person who penned those sex messages to Jen yesterday and she obviously did not appreciate them. (Or am I?) I think I may be doing my sabotage thing with her too, writing the words I know inside will drive her away from me because I know inside that she is not 'good' for me, meaning not necessary to fulfill my dream. I felt yesterday that she was drifting even further away after she read those messages, not wanting to be with a man such as I presented myself as being, yearning instead for the kind of man I once was, temple worthy Mormon high priest, bound to discipline and moral codes, valuing her as a business partner as much as wife because she's good at it and feels she is giving, doing her part, ok.

The thoughts that came into mind as I arose from my queen size bed this morning are that what has been driving me to get back with Jen is that I thought she would jump in and actively help me "co-create" my dream, and she'd be good at it, success would be guaranteed. She was already in that role when she visited last, but she removed that hat soon after she left, it didn't fit her well. I know now another mistake I have been dwelling on: I DON'T HAVE TO *DO* ANYTHING TO BECOME ADAM - I don't have to create or co-create or work at it at all to make it happen – I ALREADY *AM* ADAM! I don't need her to help me be that. *So why then do I need her?* I don't know! Loyalty maybe? Still in love maybe? Thinking of helping her have me again, the way it was but better maybe? I gave her up easily yesterday when I thought she didn't really want me, it was only when she came back with that single message about still loving me and looking for a future with me that I moved back alongside her.

I lingered in bed today because I was imagining myself immortal but still here on earth. Living in a beautiful home with all the trappings of wealth. Living with eleven beautiful women, the ones who will go with me to populate other planets. Not me and one and ten others as it would be in Jen's dream, it was not mine, but me and Eleven as ONE. *That's* my dream! And it's already created, I just need to relax and let it manifest, it's coming my way even this very moment, it IS my way. Did I write that clearly enough? In short, I don't need Jen to help me manifest my dream. So why, unless she chooses for herself to be one of the eleven equal wives in my immortal family should I be courting her with the expectation of living a normal life together again? That's not what I want, that's not what I am. I AM ADAM! *She remains my biggest temptation.*

So enough of courting Jen. She can visit, we can swap affection and sex as far as she will take it, but I will not make concrete plans for a future with her. She needs to know that so she can move on and find a man to her liking. She is gone unless she hungers for immortality and being among my Eleven as an equal. I can't move her towards that, I don't even want to right now. Let's see what happens when she comes if she does, I did a pretty good job of making myself disgusting to her Mormon way of thinking yesterday I think. So, get on with it Michael, enjoy life, enjoy Deanna if she comes and comes willing, she's a gift for the moment, and there are others appearing. My approach with Jen I think will be to tell her my dream as outlined above, and that my dream is where my mind will be centered from now on. She's welcome to visit and have sex if she wants, but I'm not about to share a roof with her for a long period of time *unless* she too dreams *my* dream and is content with it. Then we could live together, in that big house somewhere.

Just think of the influence those twelve powerful beings could have on this world's people. It would be a new paradigm, a planet of super beings. I need only to keep imagining myself in that big house with those eleven beautiful women. Not imagining actively as if to create, just content to be there with them. After all, *that's my dream.* For me at this point in my awareness my dream is big, from the point of view of me my real self and "Source Energy" there's nothing to it – it's done. *Just get on with being YOU Michael Adam...*

Sure, temptation's back. I go to the kitchen to get a mug of white tea and a small container of raspberry yogurt, come back and this just in:

Jen: I am traveling today and tomorrow. If I can email you I will. Love Jen

And I lose my tears and my heart again!!!!! She's SUZANNE all over again isn't she? Are all my potential wives like that, here to tempt and try, poke and prod and annoy until I become what they want me to be - until I become *Adam?*

M: Drive safe hon.

M: Are you going to Salt Lake City tomorrow then, or stopping along the way? Just wondering, you said traveling for two days on a trip that takes only five hours.

Deanna: Let's make it 1 pm Sun at the Starbucks for a 1st time "Meet & Greet"... See you soon.

M: I'll be there Deanna.

Deanna: Rec'd...thx for getting back, Michael.

Ok, makes her a better woman, not desperate, jumping in bed with me moments after we meet. If it's promising I can always go to her in Nanaimo early next week, sleep on her sofa if need be while we explore what there is to explore. Might be the best approach to a casual affair, I was too eager for her body and let her know, we haven't even met yet. Life's good, abundant with low hanging fruit ripe for the picking. Anticipation is fun while that big house is manifesting, I am becoming Adam.

Sarah: (pretty 63 year old on Abraham singles from Utah) Just read your profile, and liked everything you said. I just joined this site, and really don't know how to use it yet... Hope this message gets to you.

M: Well, this is most unusual, the first message I've received on this site since July, and huge bonus it's from a pretty lady. This site is almost dead, many of the members haven't logged in for years. The best alternative that I know of is Spiritual Singles.

Sarah: Oh, I had never heard of the other site... Can we email without going through this site? I find it a bit complicated - however, I am brand new at it - I'm sure it gets easier with practice.

M: Yes, I would like to swap messages with you. My email address is (insert)

Sarah: (by regular email) Hi... Yes, I think this will be much easier to chat this way! Can you tell me about yourself? I've never been to Victoria, but I've heard it's absolutely beautiful!

M: Victoria is a destination. I often see two or three cruise ships at a time docked just a ten minute walk from where I live. I lived in Utah before the divorce, ex still lives there but trying to sell the house. Been there?

Sarah: That's so funny! I just moved to Utah a couple of weeks ago after my divorce. I grew up in Salt Lake - moved to Las Vegas years ago - Never thought I'd come back to Utah, but here I am! Two of my sons and their families live here, so it's nice to be near them right now. What a "coincidence" huh?

M: I lived off and on in Utah for many years, love it there, even the heat in summer. My home was right up against a hill, so private we didn't even draw curtains at night. I loved the house, walked the hill almost daily for years. Ex and I drifted apart, we're still friends. She visited me a couple of weeks ago, needed a vacation she said. How long have you been an Abraham fan and what got you there?

Jen has not signed in to singles since last night so maybe it's not a going concern for her anymore, those all night sessions might have helped a lot with that. I should let it go of course but my heart flutters and eyes water with the very thought of her, there's deep emotion in me for that woman, I care so much. But now with that emotion on the surface I'm wondering why it would take her two days to complete what should be only a five hour drive. Is she stopping in Las Vegas along the way to meet someone, or just to have fun maybe? Overnighting with a female friend perhaps?

M: (to Jen) Journal September 4, 2014:

I need to be happy for her that she's got a life and is actively living it as a single, free to flirt and be sexy. She was like that when we met, yes, very much so, we had fun on the streets of Las Vegas, dancing and twirling, she innocent but alluring, a gorgeous sweetheart, drawing all eyes to her and then with envy to me. I tamed her too much being strict Mormon and all. I only wish she'd share her life with me, tell me about it as it moves along. I want to be there with her, intimately sharing each moment, but that's not going to be. She may tell me after the fact that she's been with other men, but I think it is only those few crumbs from her table that I will get to sustain me and keep me drawn out to her.

For months I have experienced surges of intense love, and sometimes a soft voice whispering *"I love you"*. I often pondered about that, who or what was I silently saying *"I love you"* to? Who was responding back? I concluded that such love was being directed to myself, more specifically to my higher self, the non-physical part of me, the part I once called "Heavenly Father" or "God'. It may be so, and it may be to more than one source that I am sending to and receiving love from. It may be that I've realized that I AM love and it's just an exchange of awareness with the universe. But today I'm wondering if that intense love that comes and goes involuntarily may be to and from my eleven Sister Wives as One? Knowing me, it makes sense to conclude that it is so…

Today, while I get my whole self where it needs to be to apply the full power of immortal bodies, as a general guideline what I want is an attractive willing woman to spend two nights a week with me or I with her. (Yes, Deanna might play that role perfectly, one week Victoria, she coming to me, the next week Nanaimo, I going to her.) Also, I'd like to have an ongoing open relationship with Jen. If she will allow us to have mutually satisfying sex even though she imposes some limits on what we can do, I want Jen and I to get together for two weeks every three months. And I want to keep generating stories for my books while not falsely leading sincere women along. (I'll be more careful from now on but will follow through with the women I am now in touch with.) I will of course pay great attention to Law of Attraction, making it up as I go along. Nothing is fixed, nothing should be, that's just the way life is, and it's wonderful, thank-you, thank-you, thank-you.

Jen didn't respond to my suggestion that I go the Mormon excommunication route, being baptized anew when that has taken its course. I thought that might please her. But she has become very much like Suzanne was, not responding to the content of my emails, just minimally staying in touch with a message of her own occasionally. Jen has her own agenda and that most likely includes finding a Mormon man to hopefully take her all the way to the Mormon dream that she continues to cherish. I'm ok with that, I wish her well. But I have once again placed a limited number on the women who will compose my immortal family – eleven, up from seven. So I'm no longer her backup, she would have to accept my dream while there's still a bedroom left in my house. Should I tell her that? Certainly not be email, but maybe when she visits, if she does. And maybe it would be wiser to not discuss my dream at all, keep our discussions down to earth and consensus reality, and enjoy each other's bodies.

Just thought of a way to get Jen out of mind: think of what she's doing the same way as I think about what my first ex is doing after twenty years apart – never give it a thought – don't care – her business totally – might work. Maybe keep saying to myself: *"I am free of Jen."* Shoulda done this pain thing a long time ago, why now? Maybe the very best thing would be if she wrote back and said she's not coming for that visit. That would give me some time to get over the emotion of her. After all she's the one who filed for divorce when I left to buy a motorhome and write books, my lifelong dream. When I did that she'd already been gone to visit family for two months and it looked like she'd be gone for months more to tend a newborn grandson. I seized the opportunity to pursue my dream.

Heather: Hi Michael: I wish I had known that you sent me two messages prior to our meeting on Tuesday. I would have acknowledged having received them and would have told you what a charming man you are for having sent them. I tend not to retrieve my messages or send messages when I'm in Victoria, preferring to use the telephone which, if I remember correctly, you prefer not to if you can help it. Anyway, it was a pleasure to have met you and I hope you do find your heart's desire. I'd hate to think that you would ever settle, Michael. Don't give up on love, no matter what. Cheers, Heather

M: Thank-you so much for those kind words Heather, so nice of you. I enjoyed our brief time together but as it often is when two hopeful singles meet for the first time, something undefined doesn't 'click' with one or both and they go their separate ways. That was my experience much as I think you are a great lady and a magnificent 'catch' for the right man. It is my hope that he's on the way to you soon...

Sarah: I was introduced to Abraham about 10 years ago... absolutely love their teachings! Wish I could get a little more consistent about staying in my vortex, but I keep doing my best... I've been to see Esther a couple of times - really enjoyed that! How about you? How did you learn about them? I found that my husband and I just wanted different things out of life... But we're still friends too.

M: Even when I was Mormon I was into metaphysical stuff so it wasn't surprising that when I discovered Rhonda Byrne and "The Secret" the teachings rang familiar. Then when I found that Rhonda's ideas came from her being on a cruise with Esther and Jerry Hicks, I checked out Abraham. I got a lot of their dvd's and books and realized somewhere along the way that it was most likely that my own non-physical entity was among the group called in our time "Abraham" - it was all too familiar to be otherwise. But I'm not a groupie, the only time I was in Esther's presence was at a seminar in San Antonio, then at her home with many others after for beer and barbie. What I like best about the teachings of Abraham is that it leaves you individual and free, not inside a box bound to somebody else's notion of reality. For me it's all-comprehensive because I find Abraham in myself. So what are the "different things" that you wanted and your husband didn't?

Sarah: Hi there... I could say "ditto" to so many of the things you just wrote. When I was a Mormon, I was always studying anything I could beyond that. I think the first book I read that spoke to me was Psycho Cybernetics, but I don't think I found it until I was about 17 or 18. Wayne Dyer's book, You'll Se It When You Believe It was another one of my early favorites. So happy to be on this side of all of that, but certain I still have a long way to go. A lot of good came from those years... "We can't get it wrong, and we'll never get it done," right? I would love to be able to say that I find Abraham within myself. I keep looking. I think Esther would say I'm trying too hard. I'm definitely not a groupie either, but I really enjoy hearing Abraham's words whenever I get the chance. Wow, you had a beer with Esther? How much fun!

So, in answer to your question, "What were the different things?"... there were many. He loves the nightlife of Las Vegas (which I loved too at first, but a little bit can go a long way) I love being with family and loved ones, having, meaningful conversations, and he loves being with people who were "famous in their own minds". And at the risk of sounding too conventional, I like being in a monogamous relationship, even if it's only for a time, and even though he said that was what he wanted, he really didn't. I'm not complaining at all... we had a really great time together for a lot of years! I loved it all, but I believe I've expanded beyond that now. Thank you for telling me about Spiritual Singles - I just joined, and it's so much fun to know that there are places where like-minded people can meet. I loved reading your profile. Thank you for sharing so much about yourself! Sarah

She sends me a canned message on Singles and I reply there, identifying myself.

M: I think you'll really enjoy Spiritual Singles. To me every contact I get there is as good as three or four on any other site. Of course you still have to cautious, but on that site I feel everyone's 'family', we all speak the same language so to speak. I just responded to your message there, not sure if you realized it was me, if not there goes Law of Attraction again it seems. But do put up your beautiful photo there too, you're a lovely lady. If your ex still lives in Utah and is still Mormon (mine is) and single, maybe we should get yours and mine together, do us all a favor.

But anyway Sarah although I enjoy our conversation and would like to continue if you do, feel free to send a good-bye if you want to, we live at a great distance so it's not likely that we will every meet. If you happen to get out this way though, let me know for sure, I'll show you around and if you're bold and by yourself you can stay at my place for a while. Take care dear one.

Sarah: (on Singles) Of course i want to keep talking through email! You're the only person I've chatted with on these sites. I sent you the hello just to let you know I saw your profile. I added a couple of photos, they just haven't been approved yet. Goodbye??? We just barely met! Are you kidding? Distance? It's all relative, right?

M: Virtual distance is relative, measured in microseconds through a series of servers I suppose. The world's virtually ours, time and space are conquered by technology, it's a great time to be alive and well on this beautiful planet.

Good choice Sarah, I'd like to continue this conversation as well. Just giving you an easy out because although airplanes still fly I'm not planning to leave Vancouver Island in the foreseeable future even if we arrive at a point where virtual's not enough. (We did meet on a *singles* site.) Speaking of which, on Vancouver Island there are nine women for every man. So it's a great place and time for single men, my inbox is virtually swamped with invitations. I'm getting to be a reasonably good conversationalist (never was before) from walk talks along the seaside, but am still looking for that elusive someone I want to suspend my singles profile for. Next scheduled meeting with someone new is still two days away, but hey, today hasn't happened yet. *Can you get here today?* Enjoy the day Sarah.

I've been successfully keeping Jen out of mind with the 'think how it is with first ex' technique mentioned above. But in the rare moments that I choose to indulge I crave Jen's presence and miss her like crazy. Hope her silence doesn't last too long, hope she comes to me soon. Where has she been for two days along the short way to Utah from the Los Angeles area? Maybe she'll send a quick note tonight, it's the second day of her trip to somewhere. Mustn't go there, hurts too much. But she *could* have had me, and chose not to do so. *Why* Jen? Why? *She's so SUZANNE!* Guess that explains it...

As I walk to and from the laundry room this morning I realize that I'm walking slowly, lingering in the hallway, hoping my next door neighbor appears, the attractive woman from Liverpool who I saw once in the elevator when my sister was with me. Next time I see her I may be bold enough to invite her to walk the breakwater with me if she's not wearing a ring. Yes, I crave the loving touch of a woman. I dream of my Eleven and how it will be, but I cannot seem to touch them, or feel their touch even though sometimes that happens in the night dreams. *Are we real?*

As I rewrite The Suzanne Chapters (which turned out to be my entire series of now unpublished books) the question passes through my mind about where Suzanne was for almost an hour after she arrived at the Las Vegas airport where she knew I was waiting to pick her up. You'd have to ask her yourself of course (she won't tell me I'm sure) but after observing how much alcohol she was consuming during our week together in Sin City, my best guess is that she was sitting at an airport bar preparing herself for our meeting, the first one since that night in Loa and her tromping away early the next morning. She had come I think to see if I loved her in the flesh after describing a much different woman in my books. Maybe she *needed* that drink if drink it was because yes, I was disappointed in her looks and I'm sure she knew it the quarter second after I turned and first set eyes on her in Las Vegas. Does that make sense to you? I'd still meet her again and spend a week or two of intimacy if she'd allow it. I may always be emotionally connected to the woman from Texas - WRETCHED SILENT SUZANNE!

As I take a break from rewriting my unpublished books and lie a few moments on my sofa, soft strains wafting from computer speakers, I feel again for who it is that I exchange those peak loves with. From my soul floats that love again this time accompanied with the image of billions of souls who come to earth with me to play out a grand production we created spiritually before we came. I love US, not just a mere soul group but EVERYONE. And I feel to record that love for you and acknowledge yours for me. Thank-you, thank-you, thank-you.

As I microwave a can of steak and potato soup for lunch I feel unbearable pangs of longing for Jen. I want her back and I want her back ALL THE WAY to me *right now*. Is she still connected from a distance? Does she feel my pain my yearning? Will she sway back to me her priority? This very moment *I'd marry her again!* Can a divorce decree be annulled?

And with that as usual comes another choice while I wait and wonder if Jen has urgently swayed back in my direction over the last two days of her silence. My guess is not, there's time left to explore the possibility of others. And if Jen writes soon to tell me she can't come for several weeks yet, then I have my answer. And anyway, come or not, I'm single, why should I not explore others concurrently 'just in case' as she now seems determined to do as well.

Sarah: Dear Michael, (Is that your real name, by the way?)... just wondering. Wow! You seem to be in a really great space and time, with the perfect circumstances for manifesting that "elusive someone you want to suspend your singles profiles for"... I truly wish you the best in that!... But, I'd love to have a chance to hold your hand too if I'm not too late! I think it would be fun for me to tell you a bit about my experience in this...

The other day when I messaged you from the old Abraham Singles site, yours was the first and only profile that caught my eye. (I had been tempted to join that site for a long, long time and suddenly, that was the day I was inspired to just do it.) Then when you mentioned the Spiritual Singles site, I went over and joined that one too. I was completely distracted though while I was filling out the profile and questionnaires because I was helping my little granddaughter with her homework at the same time. I need to go back and give it the time it deserves for it to be more accurate and heart-felt. I noticed you put quite a bit of thought and effort into completing yours. I loved everything about it!!! Esther always says, when you meet the right person, you'll just KNOW it, It will feel so right, and so completely natural and fun as you get to know each other. When I read the things you wrote, and the things you said in your profile, it feels so completely perfect in matching what I feel I've put into my Vortex! My friend and I both got goose bumps last night when we read through everything you had to say. I always thank my goose bumps for being a sign from the Universe that I'm in alignment with what they know is there for me.

So, when you meet this new lady in 2 days, it might be that perfect culmination of all things coming together for your good, and if that's the case, I do hope it's filled with wonderful synchronicity and alignment for you! If, however, you're left wondering at all about what it might be like for us to meet, I would absolutely love to come to Vancouver to see you! I can think of nothing more pleasant than walking with you wherever you want to take me. What a fun adventure! My schedule is quite open right now - I'm almost as free as a bird to go and do whatever happens to come my way. This is the first time in my life I've felt this way! What Synchronicity! In the mean time, I'm completely enjoying our on line conversations! You're a fascinating person! I'd love to know more about you, if I haven't said anything to scare you off yet. Never before have I had this sense of enthusiasm, eagerness, and friskiness about what may lie ahead. Did I say anything that made you wonder, or did I offend you in any way, that might have prompted the "Good Bye option" you posed? Hope not. Talk soon, I hope. Sarah

M: Sarah, I'm just a novice hobby writer finally addressing a lifelong yearning to author books. That yearning was quenched until a year ago by the harsh demands of consensus reality: raising kids, making a living etc. But the wow's on me Sarah! Although I have met several women on Vancouver Island and could meet a whole lot more (I'm real picky), somehow it always seemed that *she* would fly to me from a distance. (Yeah, really.) Now, that "she" could possibly be my ex who did fly to me recently and may want to return soon for a brief visit as the friends we are (maybe not, don't know yet.) I'm just being fair to you letting you know that she and I may or may not be done, though it's highly unlikely that we'd get together long term in the foreseeable future. Fair enough?

I moved to Victoria (not Vancouver) on July 1st this year after living in the USA for twenty years. Since that time I have been hoping to find an attractive (to me) compatible woman to explore Vancouver Island with me while the summer weather was still here. There were several potentials who came and went but it just never materialized. My thinking was to travel with my car for at least two weeks, maybe three and get to know the Island, staying in hotels and bed and breakfasts each night along the way. It might not take even two weeks to do that exploring, it's not such a huge island, but she and I could come back to Victoria for a few days in between ventures. Are you bold and adventurous enough to be that woman if our first few days walking and talking in beautiful Victoria work out well for both of us?

We'd need to do it very soon because winters in Canada are long and they arrive quickly once September has come. We could set a schedule that would work for both of us. I'd pick you up at the Victoria Airport and you could stay at a nearby hotel or at my one bedroom apartment if you're ok with that after we've held hands and talked a bit. It would be nice to be able to cuddle and talk into the nights after walking the seaside each day. We'd then decide on the road trips yes or no. If you kept your return date for the flight home open and can get away for an indefinite time, that arrangement should work for us. And of course you could go home the next day or whenever, your choice, I'd immediately get you back to the airport if that's what you wanted. (I think you're going to like me though, they all do.)

I'm very willing to explore these feelings and this opportunity that you are presenting us. I acknowledge the synchronicity involved but am experienced enough to know that Law of Attraction always offers a choice of several roads to travel down, none of them wrong. As I see the present situation, the *worst* thing that could happen for us is that our fun together turns out to be shorter than we had hoped. Thank-you so much for that wonderful invitation sweetie. *Wow, just wow* Sarah, I *must* meet you. Enjoy the day.

Sarah seems like the woman of my dreams right now. As you know from reading this journal, I've been trying to lure someone from a distance to come to me for quite some time. Regardless of the beautiful women in Victoria, *that* seemed right. This seems like a done deal, that's the enthusiasm and sense of urgency I had hoped Jen would have for me and didn't. Depending how she next writes, if Jen's only planning to stay a couple of days when she comes (tickets on me) I may ask her not to come, and invite Sarah to come next week instead. Sarah is familiar with and fond of Abraham, Jen's not. That should say a whole lot about compatibility where it really matters. Were those intense pangs for Jen that I experienced minutes before receiving Sarah's invitation to come to me *the pangs for a now lost love?* Could be, I'll go there...

Oresha: Hi Michael..... "Amongst Friends"... The "Man from Courtenay" turned out to be nothing more than "smoke and mirrors"... not at all the person he "portrayed" himself to be... perhaps even a sociopath.... at the least..... there's some personality disorder apparent.... Go Figure!... Well, it's back to square one for me I guess... lol I hope you're having a much better time of it than I am... Have a great weekend..... Ciao....

M: I'm sorry for that Oresha, he seemed like such a good match for you the way you and Kathy described him. Please don't think *all* writers are like that. On *my* front things are looking hugely promising. An attractive woman wrote to me yesterday from the almost dead Abraham Singles site that she joined yesterday and immediately found and liked my profile even though I live more than a thousand miles away. I noticed that she is living in the same Utah home town I love, where my ex still resides. I suggested she join Spiritual Singles, which she did. An hour or so ago I started feeling intense pangs for my ex. Almost immediately after I had those tamed I received a message from Sarah, the woman now on Spiritual Singles telling me about an amazing synchronicity that lead to her expressing eagerness to come to Victoria to meet me as early as this coming Monday. I thought about her familiarity with Abraham and her sense of urgency and eagerness for us to meet (she'd never experienced anything like that in her life) and I concluded that those pangs for my ex may have been *the pangs for a now lost love.* Wish us well Oresha.

Sarah: Michael, I can hardly believe this is all a potential right now! It's completely amazing to me! You wouldn't believe all the cooperative components that have come together in my life very recently that would give me the opportunity to do this with you - First time in my life when it would have worked out! I love it!!! What fun!

I've never had the opportunity to do something this adventurous in my life! Once, about 15 years ago, I had a good friend (platonic, although clearly he wanted more, but we were both fine with it) that invited me to come up to Denver to do some hiking and exploring with him. We stayed up late at nights, drank wine, ate good food, hugged, had great conversations, and there was no awkwardness at all. Nothing came of it... we were just too different in our wantings. He's now happily married to the woman of his dreams, but we still remain good friends.

In the case between you and I, it seems that could be the "worst case scenario"... But I would hope for much more of a connection, based on the little bit I know about you. You seem absolutely fascinating to me! If what you wrote in your profile represents you quite closely, I just can't wait to get to know you! I think it might be wise to share some of my most annoying personality quirks - I'm sure more will become evident, but if they're deal-breakers to you, it would be good to know up-front, don't you think? I have grown sons and their life-long complaint about me has been that I take too long to get ready in the mornings. Of course, being boys, they're in and out of the shower in 5 minutes and ready to go. I take at least an hour getting ready to go anywhere. I wash my hair every day, and start from scratch with my shower, hair and makeup. It doesn't bother me, but I know it can be annoying to some. I have friends and daughters-in-law who can keep up with the boys in getting ready. Not me. I also have to get my nails done at least twice a month, and that can be annoying. I think these things are pretty reasonable, but they may not be to some. I'll think of more, I'm sure, but if those aren't too big of an obstacle, maybe we could make a plan??? Talk soon... Have a great day! (I know you will.)

P.S. Fair enough! My ex is behaving in a similar way, it sounds like... Doesn't want us to be completely over, but I feel so right about it all that I see almost zero chance of ever going back to Las Vegas, and he sees zero chance of coming to Utah. We're just simply too different! Neither of us is right, and neither of us is wrong... it just is what it is. Two people who have experienced a lot of great times together, but can't figure out a way to be happy going forward. I'm so comfortable with knowing it's over, and looking to what lies ahead. I expect great things out of my life ahead!

M: If you are serious about coming here as early as next Monday, I am prepared to cancel my Sunday appointment with the woman I've never met, another one expected for next week with a woman in Victoria I've been swapping messages with for a lot of weeks, and to put off my ex if in fact she wants to visit soon. That's my commitment to you if that's what you are prepared to do. I think we should seize the day and explore the possibility of US that is now being presented, thank-you for that growing hope. Once we have met physically and spent a few days together we will each have a much better idea of whether or not this new finding is likely to lead to a long term relationship. It is my hope that it does, I'm well tired of the mating game. But if not, I think we'll have great fun together anyway.

Shall we leave the quirks and whatevers to discover in person as we go along? It would be more fun that way. However, I assure you that Victoria is a laid back tourist retirement place, I can't imagine us ever needing to rush anywhere in the a.m. and that hour you take making yourself look even more beautiful would speed by for me absorbed in my writing. If you stay any length of time I'll have to buy a sit down dresser with mirror for you, I hadn't thought of furnishing my bedroom for a lady when I bought my furniture, but there's room I think. That can easily be done but it would be best that you pick it out so expect to stand doing your makeup until we get that taken care of, might not take long.

Nails are fine but you'd be smart to tell me you're doing it for *me*, how could I ever complain about that? Just don't start eating crackers in bed my love, that might turn into a deal breaker when the crumbs work their way over to my side. And be aware that I was shorted on touch as an infant and need a whole lot of that. It's the touch of a loving woman that I have missed so much for so long. (With some good days in between of course.) Frequent hand holding, hugs and cuddles will keep this man happiest but he respects the need for individual time each day. When do you want to come Sarah?

Oresha: Good for YOU! I wish You the best... keep me posted.... Hugsssss...

M: (to Sarah) I'm off for my daily walk along the sea, back in about two hours. Should you write in the meantime, I'll respond when I get back as a priority. Book your flight one way or open end so we have flexibility? You have me so intrigued Sarah. Did I say excited? But you know, somehow it's as if we've already done this, you are familiar. Do you feel the same?

Oresha: P.S..... I didn't know there is an Abraham singles site! I'll go on there and spiritual singles.... also..there's another site..can't remember the exact name.. ttyl....

Sarah: When you say next Monday, do you mean the 8th? or the 15th? I think I might be able to do either one with just a little planning - How much fun!!! It sounds like you would have to change a lot of your plans, but is that ok with you? I love the whole idea of seizing the day! I love what you said about "Once we have met physically and spent a few days together we will each have a much better idea of whether or not this new finding is likely to lead to a long term relationship. It is my hope that it does, I'm well tired of the mating game. But if not, I think we'll have great fun together anyway." I completely agree! And it does feel like we've met before! I can't wait to see! And, by the way, the nails are definitely for you! I try my best to take good care of myself for the purpose of staying attractive to my man. I don't know how much you know about the female species (I'm sure you know a lot!) But so much of what we do is definitely with you in mind. And don't worry, I never eat crackers in bed! The crumbs are just annoying!

M: I'm thinking the 8th Sarah. Other than simply wanting to meet you asap we'll need a few days to explore Victoria, there's so much I want to show you. Then if we decide to do the Island we'd best get to that asap while the weather is still beautiful. Coming from summer in Utah you might enjoy the coolness, but for sure bring a sweater and jacket, evenings can get downright cold. Or if it's a matter of space and weight on the plane you could buy a jacket here of course.

Since I arrived two months ago it has only rained four or five times and then only a few minutes at a time. I think you are going to really love it here. As I did the ten minute walk to the sea this afternoon and first gazed upon it, snow-capped USA mountains across the strait, I was wishing you were here, it's a *perfect* afternoon, couldn't be better. Tide was in and the sea unusually smooth. I walked just a few yards from the Norwegian Jewel, a cruise ship docked near the breakwater, there's so much to enjoy.

You are making a huge commitment flying here Sarah so yes, I'll gladly change my plans so we can explore each other for as long as you can stay. You're doing everything I had hoped *"she"* would do, perfect marks, even about the notorious crackers in bed issue. And you know Abraham too, huge bonus, we speak the same language, can't wait to hold your hand and look into your eyes sweetie, wish it was today. Your man in Victoria

Sarah: I love that that you walk! I've never had very good luck in the past in finding someone who loves to walk, so I've walked a lot alone. It would be so much fun to have someone to share it with! I've already looked into flights - just tell me which day would be good for you - this Monday or next? Re the one way ticket - sounds good. I'm intrigued and excited too! Yes, I feel that we're familiar but this is more fun than ever! By the way, do you like wine?

M: This only gets better and better. Monday 8th go ahead and book, let me know what time you arrive. I enjoy wine, have some shiraz cooling, tell me what you want to arrive to. Do you like beer? We can explore those tastes too as we enjoy our nights together, there are two liquor stores less than a two minute walk from me.

Can this be real??? Who needs Jen and all her slip sliding away, me being her lowest priority. This woman is the total opposite – *and she knows Abraham!* Strange isn't it, that she comes from the same city I lived in and loved for many years, and where Jen lives to this day. Maybe we passed each other in the streets or stores, not knowing then that we'd be sweethearts and lovers.

Sarah: I love Shiraz and beer... And Cabernet and even Merlot. I'm so looking forward to this !!! I can't wait to see you! I've never done anything like this in my life before but it feels so good, inspired and aligned!

M: We'll walk across the street and get whatever you want when the shiraz is gone. Hope you pick a fast plane and find a tail wind. If your kids weren't visiting I'd say come tomorrow or Sunday, or tonight. I love your eagerness for adventure, you seem exactly who I've been waiting for. It's going to be so much fun with you, a dream come true, I just *know* it. Together we'll co-create whatever we mutually want - just *get* here sweetheart.

Sarah: I'm on my way!

She attaches maybe by mistake a link to her professional website. Bonus as far as I'm concerned.

M: That's impressive sweetie but am I going to get a bill? Should I still call you Sarah?

Sarah: Oops! I didn't mean to do that... I definitely would have told you but I'm such a novice at this I didn't want to use my first name until I knew you. I'm so sorry.

M: As far as I'm concerned it doesn't change a thing Sarah, I'm sure you would have told me as we got to know each other. I'm proud of your accomplishments, well done. I hope you will still come, I really want you to.

Sarah: I'm so sorry... I didn't mean for that to happen.. I'm such a novice at this I wasn't sure I should use my real name until I got to know someone.

M: I replied already but it may have been to a different email address. I don't mind at all honey, not at all. Do you mind if I continue to call you "Sarah" in emails? Tell me when to pick you up at the Victoria Airport.

It's 8 p.m. and Jen just signed onto singles, she's most likely home from who knows where. And as usual now I am not her priority, other men are, most likely because she has little emotional attachment for me anymore. She's just leading me along as backup or because she thinks I *need* her and she's being loyal. She goes to other men's messages first (not even Mormons so that gives the lie to that), mine are stale and waiting in her inbox. She knows that, she has made her choice.

I really hope it works out with Sarah, I must pull away from my ex, it's past time for that. As soon as Sarah confirms her flights I will cancel Deanna and pull back from everyone else. I'll wait to hear from Jen but will almost certainly ask her not to come if she still plans to. She has proven beyond all reasonable doubt that she is more interested in other men right now. I've been watching singles to see if she is duplicitous, going back to singles to write to other men before writing to me after a two day absence. She *is* duplicitous, that's a fact. I expect only a brief email from her and maybe not even until tomorrow. She'll feel she owes me a message and will have excuses, tired from her trip or whatever. I'd like to know where she was though.

I'm still not feeling close to Sarah even though I could quickly raise some tears for Jen. But that could change after Sarah and I spend some time together. It does seem strange though that such a highly educated woman as Sarah is could get such a crush on me so quickly as she says she has. How valid can that be? But flying to Victoria from Utah is certainly proof that she wants to be with me. Let's see what comes from this new development. *Could she be Kira?*

Sarah: I love the name Sarah. I was just trying to keep a small level of anonymity. I still really, really, really want to come and meet you! I'd love to be called Sarah in emails. I'm so looking forward to it! This has been an amazing couple of days for me! It feels like such a big turning point in my life that's been coming for a long, long time. Thank you for being a huge part of it!

M: Thank-you too Sarah. I too have outstanding things falling into place almost magically the last couple of days to make me completely open to you. We can discuss when we're together. Try to come early on Monday if you can, I can't wait to walk with you to the seaside in daylight for your first look at what I think is truly beautiful. Today would have been perfect. Maybe Monday will be too. Let me know when your flight is booked so I can make concrete plans and let people know, thanks.

This still seems like a dream, but I've felt it coming for at least a week now. I wrote in my journal a few days ago: *"Suddenly a moment later the sun has risen behind my curtains and I feel a great love coming into my life, I'd give all else away for her whoever she is... And I will, I will, she's coming!"*

My emotions aren't engaged (yet), it seems so familiar as if we'd already done that been there before. But maybe my emotions are simply locked away for a while to keep thoughts and feelings of Jen at bay? Life's so interesting, I'm sure it's unfolding according to plan... A little concern about Sarah is that she was opposed to her ex having polygamous desires. And I have those too! (Wonder how many Mormon men have those secret desires? They'd be excommunicated if they moved upon them in real life.) But if I need tell her my dream I can always say it's my "fantasy life" and separate from my real one, and that at present is true. Will I come to be so deeply emotionally involved with Sarah as I was/am with that wretch of a Jen who became Suzanne? Perhaps the deepest of emotions are feelings of *loss* rather than feelings of gain...

I'd like to be Sarah's exclusive and shut down my singles profiles if the physical test works well. Everything else seems to be in place, even just a four hour flight away, and for me it would be going 'home' to the city that I love. Suzanne when I took her there from Las Vegas commented on me not being available because I was still firmly attached to Utah (and my ex.)

Depending what Jen has to say in her now hours overdue message (that's hopefully coming) I think my best strategy would be to not respond to her for a day or two. Then eventually (because I don't want her phoning me out of sincere concern for my well being) I will send something like the following:

M: (to Jen not sent) A door closes another opens, everything is falling into place for me like magic and I am happy. We can continue to communicate but our personal paths are separate now, that was your choice. But I'd really like to receive updates on you and your family and be virtual friends, I'll always care about you. Tell me about your loves and prospects, I'll thrill for you, cheer you on, provide a sincere male point of view when asked. Take care Jen, I wish you the very best and much happiness, we had wonderful times together.

And Sarah is NOT on singles. That's a really good sign, she's not actively searching for another man like the others seemed to be even as they were investigating me. I'm hoping she's booking her flights and will get back to me, especially so I can let Deanna know not to come day after tomorrow. I think about one of the major points in Jen and I reconciling being that we wouldn't then have to sort through and become familiar with someone else's 'baggage'. But you know, after Sarah telling me about her family I WANT to meet her 'baggage'. I'm looking forward to it. Strange huh?

It's morning now and still nothing from Jen, third day. I know it has to be but I'm still astonished at how quickly and how irrevocably she dumped me, going from hot to cold in a day. As it was with Jackie, I think behind it, even though neither admitted it, must be another man she's interested in? Yeah, it hurts, but I'm not allowing myself to feel those feels anymore, not sure that's a good thing, just gotta get over her and let the feelings flow freely. I saw a vivid picture of Jen in my mind last night, thought she was thinking of me and got up to check for a message but no, false alarm, again. Is she waiting for me to message her again, thinking I'm still actively chasing her and that's a good thing? She already has unanswered messages from me in her inbox so I'm not about to do that. I'm hoping Sarah is solid, you'd think at the last minute like that she'd have rushed to book her flight. We'll see, still not feeling close to her, just words on the internet so far. Hopefully that will change on Monday. What a gal if it does, woman right after my own heart, could be a wild ride, hope so, hint of loving her now with those words written.

Ok, I'd been concerned that I had lost my inner guidance for a couple of days, concerned especially about the lack of emotion about

Sarah, everything seems perfect with her then why am I not loving her like I have so easily loved others? In the past that would mean that it's not going to happen, we may never even meet. But a few minutes ago still early a.m. as I write this, I felt again that sweet flow of internal revelation, the "still small voice" of God speaking to me. And with it came as often does, joyous feelings and understanding. I had fallen into wanting things to be a certain way rather than trusting that the very best would always come if I but stepped aside and let life flow. By wanting it to work out with Jen and to work out with Sarah concurrently I was creating resistance. Law of Attraction blindly serves us, supplying us what we desire, like the operating system of a computer, always there, always working according to strict laws, but unseen, forgotten to the most part. So those desires of mine to force life to manifest a certain way and none other were preventing the *fullness* of life as it could be from coming to me.

Think about it, have you not all your life had many intense desires for something to manifest exactly the way you wanted because you really wanted it to? And as time went on have not those intense desires faded away and gone time after time? Then why should today be any different? We are meant to just FLOW with the stream of life as it is brought to us effortlessly. It's the journey that is important, our task simply to *enjoy* it and be happy, always expecting more and better to come, as it will because *that* has become our prime desire. So I give up resisting, let life come, *bring it on*, I'll take it moment by moment, no longer try to shape it to please my ego and meager understanding; just accept and allow, knowing that it's going to be really really good that way.

Chapter 29

———⋄⊙⋄———

Sarah: Good Morning. This all seems so crazy! I'm absolutely loving it though! I have some work to do, but I can do it anywhere... do you mind if I bring my laptop and some work? It won't take up very much of our time. Do you have wireless internet? I'm having so much fun in the anticipation of this!

Gotta just *love* that woman! Could this finally be KIRA coming home? She even located in my home town, we might have 'accidentally' bumped into each other along the way and caused sparks to fly. She speaks Abraham, she speaks Mormon, she speaks ME! But I needed to leave Jen, and I needed to become a writer to record the deliciousness of our being together again. And so it was done, the stage is set, Michael and Kira arrive to an anxiously waiting breathless audience. We're *on* Kira...

M: Good morning darling. Crazy aren't we? But I too love careless abandon, life's so fun that way, stepping aside and letting it happen, knowing that the flow of unhindered *life* is always going to be really really good, bigger and better moment by delicious moment. That's what we'll have together you and I *because we're both insane and loving it.* Yes I have wireless, and yes I too spend much time on a laptop. We'll make sure we get to that every day, even as we travel we'll find places that have internet. We're a *fit* Sarah, I'm so happy, come soon...

M: (to Sarah) I love the name "Kira". Do you? May I call you Kira?
Sarah: I love that name!

From now on in these books instead of "Sarah" she will be "Kira". There, now that I haven't heard from Jen for several days I am beginning to transfer male energy to Sarah. I'm sure I'll fall in love with her easily, she fits all my hoped for criteria, even coming to me from a distance. I expect that we'll have the time of our lives whenever we are in each other's physical presence. She's shaping up to be my dream come true, the woman I will THROW myself into, maybe even Kira. Mmm - tall slim beautiful well-endowed blonde who speaks my language and takes care of her body for her man - *vivid, vivid.* Sure, I could marry this woman if all goes well during her visit and that's what she wants.

Kira: (formerly Sarah) Can you tell me what the cell phone system is like? Do I need to talk to my cell company to arrange for traveling abroad so that I can talk to my family?

M: USA cell companies charge roaming fees in Canada, quite steep. You can use my cell, I think I have a plan for USA, we'll take it with us when we travel. And there's always free internet video.

M: I shall call you Kira. (I tell her about my family.) Think you can handle all that 'baggage' if we get serious?

M: (to Kira) I looked over your photos on singles. Lovely grandchildren. And you Kira, *what a bod!* I'm going to have vivid dreams tonight for sure. You on the way yet?

Kira: As soon as I can! Thank you!

Kira: Your "baggage" sounds beautiful!!! I'm sure they bring you a lot of joy! I can't wait to introduce mine to you but I'm pretty tied up with what's going on this weekend...

Take note of that Michael, don't be concerned about silence this weekend, she's genuinely busy with her family.

Kira: I really love the name Kira! Where did it come from!

M: Since you know Abraham I dare tell you that story. We speak the same language you and I, I don't think it will mess with our hope for each other, I surely hope not.

Wow, feelings are really starting to flow for you right now, and it's not just that gorgeous bod either, though that's certainly a lovely part of it. (whew...) We'd darn well better overlook the age stuff and like each other when we meet, this could be real good. You've caught me at the perfect time to explore a possible long-term relationship if we're still talking a week after we meet, meeting physically is always a trying event. I've had two women tell me in the last two weeks not to "settle" but to wait for true love. One of them was a quality woman I'd just met who really liked me, but there was no felt connection for me. Right now I'm looking for that elusive true love to throw myself into. You seem perfect - and your own inner knowing knows that.

In 1984 I was living in the magical city of Victoria, British Columbia where I am now located. I was (temporarily it turned out) separated from my first wife who had told me she wanted a divorce. We were living in another province at the time. I knew I had to go to Victoria and I did. Victoria is my womb. Every time I stay in Victoria long enough I emerge a different and better man, like a caterpillar discovering wings. I was spiritually initiated there in Victoria in 1984. I don't know how long that took, I lost track of time as I was taught power, magic, the way things are as we walk within consensus reality completely unaware that in our ignorance and fear of the unknown we are being manipulated by others who know more. It was a great and terrible adventure. Sometimes I'd get so weak I couldn't stand, reach up for help and an unseen but felt hand would lift me to my feet.

It culminated in me sitting at the kitchen table in my rented apartment and writing an entire book in one sitting. There was more to come, even poetry, but eventually my fingers were too sore to hold a pencil anymore and I consciously quit. That book today is like a prophecy of my life in some ways. It's a seminal work, everything I think and write today is colored by that book. Over the last year I have come to realize that the book has a peculiar rhythm, the beat of a drum that I voluntarily march and wrote and write to, still do. That beat is drummed by Abraham. I have concluded that my non-physical entity is among the group called "Abraham". I am home in Abraham. I hope you understand and can accept this strangeness, I do actually function well in consensus reality too.

So why Kira? Here are quotes from the prologue to the 1984 book.

> "*Michael and Kira had been inseparable. Children of a god, in light bodies they had danced together among the stars for eons of time. The old gods had beamed with joy as this eternal dyad from the star system Kobol had flashed from planet to planet, ring to ring, system to system. Alive with light, joy, wonder, they had carried within them the rainbow spectrum and the heartsong that bid them and their festival of light welcome, and safe passage to anywhere in time.*
>
> *Yet even in those carefree innocent moments together, moments that on a planet like Earth would span millions of years in time, they had both known that one day they would need to create a space of their very own. Only then in the dominion of their own space and time could they*

consummate their love and create their own children, their own new dyads, from the endless sea of infinite elemental intelligence that they knew filled all space. This deep inner knowing, this knowledge that they would have to master gross matter in order to create their own worlds, is itself the restless foreboding that gradually weighed down the light bodies of Michael and Kira. It had forced them to become slow in their movements, clumsy in communication, and to descend into physical substance."

The book follows Michael and Kira as they "fall" from an innocent pre-existent state to meet on this planet as mortals, and go beyond. Michael and Kira's eternal love story makes for delightsome thought-provoking reading as plausible answers to the enduring questions: "Why am I here? Where did I come from? Where am I going?" are provided. The book puts the anticipated millennial changes in perspective. Only you, the individual reader will know for sure if this book is fiction or fact. Many "have eyes and see not" and "have ears and hear not". Yours may be suddenly opened and you may come to a startling new appreciation of who you really are...

I recommend this book to thinkers and serious seekers after truth, reality, and the meaning of existence. Others may simply enjoy the love story!"

Strange but I'm grounded, please come Kira. I'd like to say "I love you" but how could that possibly be? I've had more than one woman I was fond of go into silence and dump me after revealing such things as I just did to you. So I'm a bit on eggshells now, waiting for you to say you're still coming to explore us. Are you? Are you Kira?

Don't take me too seriously sweetie, as I compose messages I'm in character (like an actor) writing book manuscripts. You're going to like me when you come, I'm sure of that.

Kira: Beautiful, and yes, very different from anything ever written to me in this lifetime... I'm definitely coming! Nothing could keep me from it. I can't wait to see how this all unfolds. What did you mean about putting the age thing aside? We are a few years different in age, right?

M: Yes, the age difference should not be a problem for either of us, just the usual brown spots and stuff that happens as mortal bodies get more experienced. Twice recently I met with women whose photos on singles sites were at least twenty years old. I should have known from the stated age but when we met I had been (foolishly) picturing in my mind someone who looked much younger and was disappointed, not off to a good start. I don't think we are going to have that problem at all, some of the women I have met told me that I look younger than my photos. And I'm active, walking miles every day, you'll like me, and I'm sure I'll like you.

Kira: Everything you tell me gives me more hope for this new adventure working out just beautifully. You're absolutely intriguing!

M: Whew, survived that one. Should be fun...

M: Off for my walk, wish you were here, enjoy family.

Well, I think that's solid except I don't think she'll be here by Monday, maybe mid-week? So, here goes, cutting ties.

M: (to Deanna) I thought I should let you know that since I sent the last message I found out that a woman I've been communicating with for some time who lives at a distance will be flying to Victoria next week and may stay with me for a while. So I'm going to leave it up to you for us to meet briefly on Sunday, or wait until some later date when I am free and we can spend more time getting to know one another. Would it be smarter to just wait do you think?

Deanna: I think it would be smarter to wait until some later date but I so very much appreciate you being in touch, Michael. take good care.

M: You too, meeting's cancelled, maybe we can meet some other time.

M: (to Linda) I found out that company will be arriving from a distance next week and they may linger. So we're going to have to postpone our meeting, sorry about that. Take care.

Linda: No problem. Have an enjoyable visit - the weather should be beautiful.

Jen hasn't been on singles for 20 hours. But neither has she sent me a message. And you know what? It's just curiosity now that's driving my interest, wanting to know where she's been and what she's been up to rather than an emotional connection, her life is her own business. With Kira on the near horizon and my energies transferring to her, I think I've broken free of Jen. Celebrate with me? Cheers…

Kira and I are going to need some long talks but since she's opposed to polygamy, maybe I'll switch back to the safer Jen dream of one Eve but with sister wives part of our family. (I guess that part of my dream's not completely sorted out yet is it?) I can easily picture Kira and I among the Immortals walking this earth, doing marvelous works and wonders to help bring immortality to the willing ones of this planet. Maybe I don't need that big house, maybe our sister wives will join us later, maybe they'll be part of the same non-physical entities that Kira and I are sprung from? Maybe our sister wives will come when it's near time to go to another planet and begin our joyful mission of populating new worlds. And maybe there won't even be polygamy? *Strange huh what Kira coming can do to a man's dream?*

Maybe by straining for that dream I am creating resistance to the *fullness* of what could come, keeping it at bay when the Universe is ready already to make it happen? Relax and let go instead? But if Kira and I settle into times together and times not because our homes are at a distance, I might yet invite Jen to come on occasion, who knows how it will be - I once loved her, she once loved me. Maybe, just maybe until Jen marries again, Kira and I will have an agreement that would allow me to spend time with Jen and her to spend time with her ex? I'd be open to that. Maybe the best of two worlds for us? Dream along with me, but I love it when life *flows* - I think my darling Kira does too. Summer and winter home perhaps? Consider the possibilities… So with that melting of harshness felt for Jen and no deep emotional attachment left, I send the following.

M: (to Jen) Haven't heard from you for several days, are you doing ok?

Think I'll go walk again, physically restless, wondering where Jen fits into my life again. Maybe there'll be a message when I get back. She hasn't been on singles for almost 24 hours now. That's good I think, she's most likely home and busy, visiting her daughter etc. just not thinking of me. Or of course she could be with a man, not even home at all, logged into singles last night from there. Perhaps what was meant to be an overnight with him (or a female friend) turned into a several nighter and she's away for the weekend. I'm curious, we were close as few as ten days ago. Drat, I'm feeling for her again, I wanted those energies to be directed only to Kira.

It's now Sunday 4:30 a.m. not sleeping. I was just about to write that it is unconscionable for Jen to not have written to me by now so she must be somewhere where there is no internet. But no, she logged onto singles six hours ago. What's with that woman, how could she change so completely in just a few days, not even a friend anymore and no warning? I've got to get to the bottom of this.

M: (to Jen) You've made your point very clearly with your silence of many days that you don't even want to be friends anymore. I'll never understand how you could become such a different person in such a short time after all the history we have, but I'd at least appreciate a courtesy note saying that you are ok. I suppose my next step is to contact your daughter and find out if she knows where you are and if you are doing all right. Strange how it came to this, I'm not angry with you, what you do with your life is your business. I accept that we no longer have a romantic connection of any kind but can't we at least stay in touch now and then? Please assure me that you are safe and well wherever you are.

M: (to Jen's daughter) I'm getting concerned about your mom and wondering if she is ok. The last I heard was a quick note from her that she was leaving California to return home but that was quite a few days ago and I haven't heard from her since then. It's her business of course what she does but we were friends last time I heard so the unexpected silence is concerning, I hope she's ok. Please let me know if you're in touch and all is well, thanks.

Jen's Daughter: Michael, As you know my mother is quite the independent woman and answers her phone, texts, and emails if and when she pleases. She is fine... I have been in contact. At times, I have to hunt her down.

M: Yes she is independent and I'm happy for her, thrilled actually, she seems to be doing really well lately, glad she's all right. I just need to get used to the newness of her, I had been getting frequent messages so the sudden silence was of concern, especially when the last I heard was that she was traveling. I hope she and I (and you) can remain friends, we had a wonderful eighteen years together. Thanks, enjoy the day, hope you and your husband are well.

As I look back on my recent emails to Jen I can't blame her for being disgusted with what I wrote, all about sex and sharing the intimate details of her life, not willing to give her up. I'm thinking I may have been doing the usual sabotage thing to push her away because I was expecting a new love to come to me from afar. *And Kira has come!* Or at least says she's "on the way." What a miracle it is that is unfolding right now, life's so rich so good so abundant.

M: (to Jen) Ok, I now believe you to be safe and well Jen and I'm grateful. I understand too your backing away because as I look in my files I've been sending a lot of messages about sex and wanting to share the intimate details of your life, you must have found that disgusting. For all it's worth I apologize, it won't happen again. I was not yet ready to let you go. I really liked the woman who came to visit me in Victoria and was hoping she hadn't changed, but she did. I'm ready to let you go now, be at peace, I've tamed my emotional connection and now Law of Attraction can fill that gap and it will, as if by miracle. I hope the same for you. But I'd love to remain friends with you and pen pals if you will, we had wonderful years together. Life for us was real good, we did so much, I was happy.

The Holland America Amsterdam is docked near the breakwater as I write this, I think that's the one that carried us on that fabulous journey up and down the Amazon. There will always be reminders of good memories from the past, we shared so much, thank-you for that. Write when you will, tell only what you will, your messages will always be welcome. Enjoy the day.

Sarah: Good morning... Hmmm... Michael? Michael? I think I'll have to wait until I meet you to know which name seems to fit for me. I love the name Michael! I've never met anyone by the name of Michael... I just can't wait to meet you. I have so much I want to talk with you about! I love what you've shared with me so far! Yesterday was a day filled with lots of fun, mixed together with some emotion and craziness. All of my children were here for a sort of reunion. The kids swam all day, we barbecued and played together long into the night. Lots of friends stopped by... never a dull moment! It makes me feel hopeful when you tell me that you are a part of Abraham... I hope you can shed some of that wisdom and infinite intelligence upon me while I'm in your presence.

One more day of "fun" today then I can get on with packing for my trip to Victoria. I have to admit I'm a little nervous... I've never done anything even remotely similar to this in my life! I'll write again later today... I'd love to respond to some of your earlier messages. Big Hugs! "Kira"

M: Mmm, love those hugs Kira, want much more. Sure glad you are having fun with your family. Fittingly, that event too allows you time to yourself for a while now without feeling an *obligation* to be with them. (Though of course you'll always *want* to be.) It seems that the universe is conspiring to get the two of us together, I'm all for that. I want to hold you as we talk and renew auld acquaintance should past lives be really real. (If so we were close without doubt.)

One of my greatest joys in life is to stretch out on a sofa and watch my grown up kids interact with each other. Those are such choice moments, as if each child of yours was you - giving you extra eyes and ears and love to experience life with. Living at great distance for many years I haven't been as close to my kids as I'd like to be. Maybe that will change as my life partner when I find her and I focus on family and do those visits often while concurrently quietly co-creating and enjoying everything else we mutually want to manifest.

I'm curious about something and would like to get your opinion on it. It was disconcerting to me to discover several years after my first wife and I were divorced that I had already been talking for a minute or more with one of my kids I unexpectedly ran into and all along my ex had been standing right beside my daughter. She was invisible to me! I hadn't allowed her into awareness. We sure get emotionally connected to significant others over the years, the ties that bind I guess.

For many years my kids tried to keep me and their mother separate, but that was hard to do because we attend many of the same family events. It's awkward, but there is no potentially jealous other, ex never remarried. It was only last year at a week-long family reunion that ex and I actually sat down and shared a few minutes of (almost) normal conversation. I think some of the awkwardness has something to do with the fact that those delightful kids and grandkids share the same genes and exist only because *we* exist and mated as we did. That's undeniable, it's bigger than we are, and we know it. I cancelled all other commitments including that first meeting that was scheduled for today. And Jen (my most recent ex) has been completely silent for the last few days, most unusual.

I'm a writer of novels - in my books there are fresh Adam and Eves chosen from among the people in worlds like this one to populate new planets. It's kind of like the Mormon dream except that in this one, Adam and Eve (translated beings - immortals) are creating *physical* bodies, not the spirit ones the (rather vague) Mormon concept of "exaltation" seems to be about. But set that aside, just get that (nervous) gorgeous body here so we can get on with creating the comfyness of life together if that's how we choose it to be from now on. I'm almost certain that I'll like you just as you are: nails, dawdle and all. I'm ready for you, this is going to be good, don't you just *know* it? I'm here waiting for you, and hugs. Enjoy the day Kira.

If she asks if we should marry, I would say: "Let's give ourselves two years before we decide to formally marry or not. I've already had three wives, I no longer need the pride of ownership. And during those years should we want to spend time with our former spouse to work through desire and a better closure, then let's be content with each other doing just that, and fleeing swiftly back to the other each time it's done."

I don't wish to complicate matters at this time with too much sending of messages. (Been there, done that, didn't work out well, *or did it?*) The most important event is that Kira arrive and our hugs are satisfying, we see our soul in the other's eyes. So I won't put the following in an email just yet. I picture us at my apartment, me at my desk, she setup with her laptop on the kitchen table. She asks and I silently point to her laptop and move to my computer to send her a reply in writing, so you dear reader can share our lives with us. I have searched for Kira (I would write) for a long time, all my life maybe. A few times I thought I had found her. But it was always just my own long drawn out yearning, the other did not share my dream as I had dreamt it. So I began to think that "Kira" personified was just a lovely character in a book I once wrote. I began to think that Kira was just a concept, a concept that embodied *everything* I have always wanted. But *this* time, because of the way we come together, and the woman she seems to be: MAYBE SHE IS REAL!!

Kira just checked out my profile on singles, maybe to show another. Her mind is on me – unlike the Wretched One in the same city who seems to have forgotten that I exist. Or is it that the Wretched One is *orchestrating* this meeting of Michael and Kira, she the new Suzanne, the one who keeps the timing, the hidden director controlling the stage play? And that she knows my love for her, so she must step aside to let happen what now must, and thus she's silent? (I have a good imagination don't I?)

I think now as I am fresh from the shower that I want to be translated (made immortal) today so I can be there invisible the whole time Kira travels to me, she feeling my presence but not seeing. And then at the Victoria Airport as she comes through the doors she sees me standing there, completely confident, glorious, her Adam appears and he is magnificent. Her hand moves involuntarily to cover a quivering mouth, eyes watering as (unlike DeLeon and Suzanne) SHE COMES TO ME!! Will plays be produced to refresh that scene for all to see? (Yep, it's good.)

But maybe, the thought flows into mind, maybe it's that everything first needs to be acted out on the *physical* plane before it can be indelibly traced upon the soul. Maybe that's how we the ancient gods set it up in the beginning - if there ever was one - that souls, our creation through which we live and have our individual being, would be comprised only of an amalgam of *mortal* experiences. And if so, then Michael and Kira must make their coming together happen as it happens with mortals. Even though the seeds of immortality are already in their being, they must act *as if* they are mortal. And that's how it may be with the Immortals on this planet, if it's not too inconvenient, *they play mortal!*

Finally a message from Jen, days after I expected one. It's all business but that's the best way for it to be right now as I prepare for Kira to enter my life, maybe for a very long time. My energies transferred from Jen to Kira no problem, it's Kira I think about almost all the time. I will do my very best to make our story a success story, already I feel that she and I are one.

Jen: I am not trying to make any type of point other than I needed time to myself. Anyway you are the one that chooses to use only emails. I am home and I will give you an update on business.

Which she does, nothing else, not even a signature at the bottom. This lady is real ticked at me! I'm so curious as to where she was the last few days but I'll most likely never know – maybe she was home the whole time and I just imagined all the rest?

M: Thanks for this message, I just wanted to know that you were ok, the last message was that you were traveling, then nothing. That was highly unusual so I was concerned. Of course you need time to yourself and whatever you do is none of my business anymore. Sorry to bug you, I'll try not to do that again, I'm no longer emotionally connected. (I address the business issues.) Just in case you were still thinking of coming to Victoria, please don't, maybe sometime in the future we'll find that we have some time for us, it's certainly not that time now. Take care Jen, I'll always care about you, please stay in touch, I want us to be friends if you're ok with that.

Jen: I still love you but maybe we need a brake from thinking to much about getting together at this point. So I am friend. Our life had many wonderful moments.

Lovely, exactly what I needed right now, she closed a door I needed closed so Kira could step through another. And yet Jen opened a different door a crack. Who knows, if Kira's ok with it, Jen and I might spend some more days and nights together now and then. I'd like that, as long as it doesn't damage my prospects with Kira, Kira's my top priority, may always be from now on.

M: Friends it is, and yes we did, wonderful times indeed, I'll always cherish the memories. We'll just have to wait and see if there's any of our candle left to burn sometime in the future. Take care Jen, life's good.

M: If you have the divorce decree please send a copy of it to me along with the other stuff if you don't mind, thanks.

I saw four whales less than ten yards from the end of the breakwater a few days ago, and another seal eating an octopus. Two seals today as I was walking back. It's nice that you were here, you can relate to that. Enjoy the evening.

M: (to Kira) I wait with bated breath to hear of your imminent arrival, you thought it possible to be here tomorrow. I'm like you, I'd shoot for it, but have you booked your flights yet or will it be a day or two later before you can get here?

Should I be concerned yet? I know I must have faith and expect only the best, but I've been disappointed before and this has moved so fast that it is still just a dream that Kira could be here so soon. As I was conditioned to do by Suzanne, I'm on eggshells thinking that my last long message might have been so far out (Adam and Eve, though couched in a novel) that she is having second thoughts about this whole budding affair. Write soon my love, I must hear from you. She instantly responds to my bated breath message.

Kira: Oh my goodness... I was just writing to you! Here's what I had written so far... I'll send the rest in a minute or two.... Hi Michael... I'm going to use that name until we meet - it just feels right for now. I'm not looking forward to telling you this at all, but I think I'm going to have to wait until Tuesday to come. I'm so sorry - I really, really want to be there now! It's kind of a long story, but I've been waiting for the past 7 months to receive a document from my ex that needs to be signed and notarized, and he's telling me that he finally has it ready for me for tomorrow. Can I text you on your phone? Or would it be possible to talk???

M: Much as I want to be with you, why not take the pressure off and plan to arrive in Victoria on Wednesday? I'm fine with that, you might be more relaxed that way. Let me know.

M: I was hoping to hear your voice first time in person, but if it's important for you to call before then, here's my number.

Kira: No problem... I'll just keep writing to you. I wanted to share a bit more with you through email anyway. No, I really want to come Tuesday if that's still ok with you. Did you get my last email I sent right after this one?

M: Yes of course, please come Tuesday if you can do that, I'm so excited about seeing you.

Kira: That link you sent me from Phantom of the Opera was the most beautiful song I've ever heard!

M: It is a glorious song, served up perfectly couldn't be done any better. I'm not planning another round but if I was going to come back to his planet and had my choice, I'd want to come as a singer with the talent and opportunity of a Michael Ball or a Sarah Brightman. It would be so awesome to move an audience from tears to laughter and back to tears any given moment by the sound of one's voice. I'm not a singer but

I am a novice wordsmith. I think I'll soon have a glorious story to tell. It's the story of a perfect love, a perfect love gone right. Write that story with me?

Kira: You do write so beautifully! I would love to write that story with you! A perfect love gone right. Whew!!! What a night it's been! Everything that has to do with you has gone so absolutely perfectly up until now... I told my friend earlier that it seems too good to be true... However, I reminded her that I had given that story up a long time ago. Nothing is ever too good to be true - it's only meant to get better and better and better, right? That's my belief as I've come to know Abraham's teachings. Well, tonight I tried to book a flight, and as I was trying, the number of seats available were growing fewer and fewer and fewer... then I had to enter my passport number, and couldn't find my passport!!!

You know, I just moved here about 3 weeks ago, and tonight I couldn't find my most important file with all of my important papers in it (passport, licenses, etc...) I still have about 30 or 40 boxes in my garage that I haven't unpacked yet, and that was the only thing I could think of... that it was hiding inside one of those big brown boxes... I kept thinking of Esther/Abraham's words, "When you're feeling frustrated, fearful, worried, or anything else that's negative, you need to take the time to do something that will raise your vibration." So I just prayed... and prayed. And I found it! So, the end of the story is that I finally got it booked... (insert flight schedule) Does that work for you?

M: Let's write our story then, only *we* could get it right. *Anytime* is the right time for you to arrive. But are you aware that you have a four hour wait in Seattle? I saw some flights that were four hours total time from LAS to Victoria, forty minute wait in Seattle, but they may be booked. Glad you found your passport, nothing can keep us apart Kira except ourselves, and that's not going to happen. We'll have a night together before we get to walk to the seaside. Will we talk the night away do you think? Gosh I'm wanting to be with you. Only two more sleeps then... Good night sweetheart, I feel close to you, has it been a year already since we first met on the Abraham site? Your Michael

I awaken to this.

Kira: Hello again... This is my real email address... I created the singles one just for you since I was trying to be anonymous at first. I know I'll be in Seattle for a while, but the other flights didn't work. I'll have some time to get some work done while I'm waiting in the airport since I didn't get anything done this weekend. I'll see you Tuesday evening at 8:09. I'm looking forward to it so much!

M: Kira, You'll clear Canada Customs and Immigration in Victoria, it should be quite rapid. I'll be able to see the status of your flight from where I'll be waiting for you so don't fret if your flight is delayed or if Immigration takes a while, I'll wait for you. It's a very small airport, turn right as you come out of the final doors. I'll meet you close to there or failing that, at the nearby baggage carousel on the same level. We'll watch for each other, I'll most likely be wearing blue jeans (I dress very casual) and a long sleeve pullover, probably light blue or grey. Expect it to be quite chilly that time of night, you'll need a sweater or jacket, probably best to carry it on, you'll walk outside from the plane to the terminal, and again to my car. I'll try to remember to carry my cell phone but I never carry a cell so don't count on it, I may forget and leave it at home. I can't imagine it, I'm hugely excited about meeting you, but should we fail to connect (flat tire or whatever) wait an hour then take a cab for the twenty mile drive to my place. Buzz at the front entrance. Or if you prefer, check in to a hotel in the James Bay area of Victoria, the driver will give you the options, and we'll connect later that night or next day (call me.) Hopefully we won't need the redundancy. Here's my address. Enjoy the flight honey, just one more sleep and we're together. Should I use this email address now exclusively?

This too was waiting in my inbox this morning.

Kira: I can't wait to read all of your books! So many of the ideas are so familiar to me, and I can't wait to talk with you about how they were all created. I couldn't sleep last night for such a long time, so I read, and re-read your description of who you are in your profile on… It calmed my nervous worries and transformed them into hopeful anticipation. I've always had that since our first contact, but my old habits of doubt kept trying to nudge their way back into the mix. It was relatively easy to push those feelings aside while I had so much distraction with family over the weekend, but being here alone last night gave me a chance to really feel my feelings. It really helped to read what you had written. Then, the last thing before I closed my eyes and meditated myself to sleep, I listened again to the song from Phantom. The lyrics are so honest and beautiful! I truly hope, and fully expect that you are this person you present yourself to be. With hope and joyful expectation.

Kira: I forgot... With hope and joyful expectation, Your Kira

M: My Dearest Kira, I can feel your presence here beside me as I work my computer keyboard this early a.m. Tuesday September 8, 2014, the day before we meet for the first time in this present incarnation. It's a familiar presence, as if it has always been, that we'd never parted. Thank-you so much for coming to me, that was a component of my dream of Kira's coming, that she'd come home to me from a distance, you are playing your part perfectly, as always. In my 1984 book, Kira had gone on with the others to a planet among the Pleiades when earth as we knew it was destroyed. Michael had stayed behind to complete a task vital to the eventual return of humans to this planet. Who knows how it really was, or if it was, but my fantasy, my vivid writer's imagination, and Muse, wrote it up like this.

Michael was alone on Mu. He had chosen to remain behind to complete the record of his people, and to prepare a way for their return perhaps many thousands or millions of earth years later. He knew that his work, the dolphin project, must be completed to perfection. The aging process in Michael's physical body had been altered. As he moved his fingers through his long flowing golden hair, he remembered how exciting it had been when word had gone out from the temples that the secrets of perpetual youth had been restored to Lemuria. He remembered too the confusion the announcement had caused in the health professions and the economic sector. Somewhere, he thought, some hidden governing council must have labored hard to reach a decision to share temple secrets with the people.

Michael and Kira had been chosen among the first to be called to the temple. They hadn't really known why they had been chosen except that they had kept the laws of the land and given loving service to others. From the time of their first introduction, Michael and Kira each knew that they had known the other long before. They also shared a secret feeling that they would one day be called to a great work. As Michael waited for the dolphins to return, he admired again the perfect form of his naked hands and arms. He felt the throb of power that constantly pulsed through his muscles and sinews. His was a perfect body, a body like that of the gods. But Michael was lonely. He thought often of Kira who had left years before with the last remnants of their people for new homes among the seven stars. His mind scanned the centuries and retrieved the memory of how it had been when he and Kira had first entered the temple.

They were instructed to leave everything behind, to bring only the clothing they wore. It was a glorious morning, a magic morning from the very moment they left their home and saw the birds fly strangely, circling and calling softly above their heads. They walked hand in hand with peace in their hearts, and a strange composure settling upon their lips and countenance. Those who peeked out of their windows and saw them would say later that already Michael and Kira had been transformed. From the outside courtyard, the inner doors of the temple appeared to be as a polished sea of glass, spun perhaps from pure gold. They noted their reflection and saw that the sands of time had marked them in their mature years; matching wrinkle for wrinkle, contour for contour, form for form. They appeared to each other as identical twins; one male, one female.

Never before had Michael and Kira felt such a completeness of love for each other. The grip of their hands clasped tighter, forming a sphere, a perfect sphere. They passed through the inner doors of the temple. Some clocks would mark the time they remained inside as six hours, others as six days. Ancient legends would later speak of a temple and an entire city that had risen up to the heavens and disappeared completely from the face of the earth. But for Michael and Kira time had ceased to exist...

The clear crystal sound of the dolphins' light chatter brought Michael's reluctant thoughts back to the here and now of physical awareness. He knew the dolphins were returning through the underground streams to his retreat deep inside a mountain. They would be well fed from the teeming waters of the warm tropical seas that were slowly swallowing the landform of Lemuria; Mu as it had been affectionately called. For hundreds of years, the people of Mu had been forced to live in caves with narrow entrances to protect themselves from the giant beasts that had risen up upon the lands after the cataclysm on Atlantis. Atlantis was the other wing of the sacred eagle. The eagle, an ancient symbol of wisdom, was the shape of certain landforms known among the stars.

Lemuria was the continent that developed the intuitive spiritual parts of man. On Atlantis, souls incarnated to learn about technology, the forces of gross matter and physical manifestation. Atlantis was to ensnare, to weigh down. Lemuria existed to channel the higher desires, to lift up again. Between the two continents was a landform known as the center. For thousands of earth years, by consent of the rulers of both governing continents, the center was held in reverence and awe as a sacred land upon which only the gods and their apprentices, the initiates of the sacred brotherhoods and priesthoods, could dwell. For as long as the center was held sacred, the powers developing on the two continents remained in balance. Communication was maintained though special temples governed by the secret priesthood rings. The people were content for things to remain that way. Life was pleasant and good on Mu.

Only much later, just before the cataclysm, had the people any forewarning that something unusual had entered their world. They began to catch glimpses of strange lights in the sky; much higher up and faster moving than the common airships from Atlantis. They had become accustomed to the peculiar white-blue glow that surrounded the temples which only the priesthoods and their initiates could enter. But they began to hear rumors of people disappearing from their homes, never to be heard from again. There were strange stories of others who had been taken inside wondrous flying machines where they had been interviewed, probed, and examined by people who looked like gods. There were also the healers, the teachers, the masters of matter who came out from the temples. They seemed to defy all known physical laws. They spoke of a marvelous work and a wonder about to happen among the people.

Now, as Michael indulged his loneliness, he was aware that Kira, even though physically many light years away, was sharing these memories with him. Their training in the temple had brought them to an awareness that they had a special communication channel of their very own. This channel when they so desired could not be tapped by any other organized life form, except by a god of a higher order than they.

Michael felt close to Kira. Their minds melded often. But he wanted to be in her physical presence. He wanted to hold her tight in his arms; to press her body close to his yearning bosom; to gently stroke her soft golden hair, look into her eyes and say, "*I love you Kira!*" He wanted to comfort her now in their separation, and to assure her that again they would be together. In their loneliness for each other it seemed a very rough game this game the gods played to become themselves.

Together, Michael and Kira shared a magic language that formed the completeness of their eternal relationship. Nothing could approach the joy of watching Kira move. Every little motion of her body awakened waves of shared memories. Each tiny lift of an eyelash, each infinitesimal movement of her lips, each tiny quaver in her voice, brought back an ocean of associations, a sea of memories of endless other times in numberless other worlds when she had moved in exactly that same manner before; when she had spoken with precisely that one single haunting sound...

Moving effortlessly though the streams deep within the mountains, the dolphins homed in on Michael's thoughts. They flashed excited messages to each other, wondering what the young god would teach them today. The dolphins were pleased to be a vital part of Michael's project.

Slowly, inexorably, a deep rumble began within Michael's powerful chest. As the trembling rose it was shaped into a stream of sound that passed through his open lips; a sound that would have been heard from afar as the sound of the rushing of many waters; but there was no human left to hear... From Michael's Womb, Victoria, City of Victory, Earth Year 2014. Michael and Kira have returned.

M: (photos attached, two of me as boy, my siblings, cover of my series book 1.) I am that man Kira. You will find me ever so gentle, ever so caring and attentive, ever so loving. I have always been that way, only now the love is so much greater because I know that each time I look into your eyes I will see my own soul looking back at me, and it is beautiful. It's you I want, more than anything...

M: You will be in good hands Kira, I will guard and protect you as the greatest treasure I have, which you will be. Have no fear, you're going to like it here. And you are always free to return home to your family anytime you want to, there is my cell phone and internet video to keep in touch as often as you/they want. Otherwise, I will be pleased if you stay with me for as long as you want to, months even, *try for forever?*

My current plans are to stay on Vancouver Island, or maybe a trip or so to nearby Vancouver on the mainland until after Christmas. Then sometime in January I thought I'd go to Los Cabos for a few weeks to break up the wet winters common to Victoria. If we work out well and it fits into your plans perhaps you would join me in Las Vegas and we'd drive from there to your home for a few more of the winter weeks, or maybe combine that with Cabo or Hawaii perhaps?? Otherwise I have no plans for longer trips at present. On my bucket list is chasing down and attending every major musical production everywhere in the world where the presentation is in English. (Les Mis, Phantom, Mama Mia, etc.) Another alternative we can consider if you're into road trips is a motor home that I own, it is presently in a rental pool in Los Angeles. (Yes, there's a mortgage on it, but I'm on top of the payments.)

The above is just so you know my tentative thinking at the moment, and to calm those fears a bit dear one. We'll have lots of time to talk and plan a future for us should that become the mutual desire that I feel it will be. (We are quite capable of co-creating *whatever* we want: *"Yes, we can do that. Yes we can do that too."*) My thinking is that you will most likely want to travel back and forth to family and responsibilities in Utah before and after Christmas, and possibly to visit with your ex or another if there is as yet unfinished desire and closure needed there. (That's ok with me, I will always want you to be free, I just hope that you will always come back to me when that particular moment has run its course.)

Being of Abraham, I'm very flexible and quite unconventional, life is for fun. Whatever you do is (and always will be) completely up to you and will be acceptable to me. As we say of our children, I just want them/you to be happy and to be as fulfilled with life as they/you will allow. Just know Kira that my little apartment in Victoria is a home for you whenever and for however long you choose to be here - I'd be thrilled if it was often and for long periods of time, even permanent. So plan your trip accordingly. Eventually we might consider getting a better place in Victoria and have a summer and winter home in USA and Canada, or a single one in Bahamas or on a South Pacific island perhaps should we choose to do that. (I love the South Pacific - go native with me?) We deserve all the abundance that we will allow into our lives. I hope that helps.

Did I really write all that? I've never even met this woman before! But then, why should today be any different?

Kira: Is it true then that what I always tell my children - "nothing is ever too good to be true" is the absolute truth as long as we stay in alignment? I've always said that and wanted so much to fully believe it, but I never did completely... Until now.

M: It is true dear one, the universe is filled to overflowing with abundance - low hanging fruit ripe for the picking. Why settle on earth for pennies or even millions when we OWN planets? If any given mortal moment brings you disappointment, simply choose a new life in the next one. And in that next choose happiness. But the greatest love of all is that love which endures forever. You and I, we could find that love within each other. I want to *live* that story with you - the story of a perfect love gone right. Should Michael and Kira serve *that* one up well, it will be told to yearning ears forever by tellers on distant planets of how it was at the coming together again of Michael and Kira.

Come home Kira, a great love awaits you and me, even as I (always a visionary) foresaw and wrote in my journal a few days before you came to me eager and willing trembling on the Abraham site:

"That's how I see it in this moment of my longing. We'll see what comes through my doorway, it's open, wide wide open right now. My body is craving, my heart and brain are mush, my soul is yearning. Suddenly a moment later the sun has risen behind my curtains and I feel a great love coming into my life, I'd give all else away for her whoever she is. And I will, I will, she's coming!" Our song will be: *"That's all I ask of You"*. Our response to a difficult moment will always be: *"Love me, that's all I ask of you."* And thus we will always know peace between us, how could it be any other way? Your Michael

It could be that Jen simply wants to explore the world of singles and other men right now. But I think that with her continued silence she is internally aware of what is happening with me and Kira and that she needs to step aside right now. I've planted the seeds of freedom and an enduring but open relationship with Kira. So it's possible that Jen and I could still share the same bed on occasion for periods of time.

I'd like that, it arouses me to think of being solid with Kira and still able to share my body with Jen without sneaking or feeling guilty. (Kira having similar privileges.) I do think that Jen would welcome she and I occasionally sharing beds, at least until she commits to another man. Could Jen and Kira become friends? Or would such a thing not work for non-polygamous women who share the same man? Is my dream coming true, just not in the way I thought it would?

I'm freeing up drawers and closet space in preparation for the love of my life to arrive tomorrow night. I came across the dress I asked Jen to take out of my closet and she hid instead with a scribbled note: *"Can't help it I Love YOU!! babie..."* I won't throw anything away, there's no need for that, but I will tuck it away in an unused suitcase. I'll keep close too the twin hearts medal with chains she made for me. Perhaps the several chains are symbolic of a love that was stifling, the vitalness of freedom lacking. But yes, what you did and left behind in Victoria touches my heart my other love. This note is so you will know that should we never come together again or I never tell you, and you read this. On this day I still love you, but I'm no longer emotionally attached, we both needed that, thank-you for it, you were wiser than me to initiate it. I had to work through my jealousy and my fear of forever losing you should I let go too long, perhaps I already have.

I keep by habit checking singles and notice that Jen logs on and off. She's working it, trolling for other men as I trolled for other women. But today I am *thrilled* for her! I have cast off her chains even as she has unlatched mine, a grander life and love beckon now for both of us.

Jen: (she addresses some business and then writes) There is a big candle left burning for us in the future. I also cherish our time together. Love Jen

M: I look forward to lighting that candle again then. In the meantime each of us could become serious about someone else but I'll always try to make it so that whoever I'm with is ok with me spending a couple of weeks with you now and then, it would be such fun. I'd like to get together with you but I agree that now is not the time for that, perhaps sometime next year.

Have fun Jen, I'm hugely excited for you, even hope you *are* working singles sites now and meeting men, that's the way it should be. I was thinking that my initial suggestion that you go to a Mormon site might have been wrong. With non-Mormon men there's little chance that you would commit to a long-term relationship if you want to remain a faithful Mormon, perhaps that's what you are thinking. Enjoy the day.

Jen: I just came in from being outside. It is raining just right. Could not resist walking out into it to get that perfect rain and weather all over me. Hope it stays a nice slow rain. Love Jen

M: That kind of rain in the desert and the negative ions that come with it is as refreshing as those huge snowflakes that sometimes gently float down and melt on your nose in northern climes. It's nice to be talking normal with you again, thank-you for that.

Jen: These are the divorce papers. (attached)

M: Thanks for that. I'm surprised that we've been divorced for five months and didn't even know it, there's something broken in the system. But I'm glad of it because if we had known earlier we wouldn't have had those wonderful days together in Victoria. *Mmm, I want more of those!* Thank-you so much for coming and for being the beautiful woman you were when you were here, it was so encouraging, you'd already made huge changes. Wish I could see (and experience) you now.

Jen: I check the single site a bit but not doing anything. I am communicating with a man in St George but not sure if I even want to meet him. He looks like a good looking man but just don't feel like making the emotional commitment to meet someone. I did take dinner over to our neighbors yesterday and visited with his very nice wife. I can tell she is a capable and good woman. I could tell she wants to live and I think she will. Cooked a great roast yesterday and had my daughter and her husband over also. Think that's what I will have for dinner tonight. I got my airline credit card. I am suppose to have a free flight and one free companion ticket. Hope I do. Possibly we could go somewhere in February. Maybe your daughter could get you a week or two condo in Mexico.

M: It would be tons of fun to travel with you. My daughter already checked Cabo for me and it's compulsory all-inclusive, quite expensive. I can almost taste that roast, you're a really good cook, I had no idea how fortunate I was living with you. Maybe meeting the man in Utah would give you some experience that would help later with men you are more attracted to. You can always turn down follow ups and who knows maybe you'll want to spend some time with him anyway, that would be normal for singles, he's obviously very interested in you. I think you should let him spend some money on you, he'll enjoy that and it's always your own choice to get serious or not and to accept or turn down offers to take you out somewhere. (Or is it your fear that you might get serious? If so, can't help you with that one.)

Anyway just some thoughts sweetie, you are as free as I am to do whatever you want and to get involved with others as lightly or as heavily as you choose. We can't wait for each other to live our lives, I'm moving forward with mine. It has helped me a whole lot meeting several women since coming to Victoria, it might help you too to get out there and meet men?

M: Oresha, I think I've lost Kathy's email address so I'll direct this to you. I have company arriving tomorrow evening and they may stay awhile. I want to get "Somewhere in Time" back plus as many of the Abraham videos as you two can return, we'll most likely want to watch them. So please make an arrangement to drop them off tonight or tomorrow, thanks.

Oresha: How does tomorrow around 2:00 pm sound? Does that work for You? If not, please suggest a time in the afternoon..... I'll do an Abraham-marathon tonight and early tomorrow.. lol Your kindness in loaning the DVD's is greatly appreciated!.... I can bring back all the ones I have tomorrow... I'm trying to get a hold of Kathy to get them from her also... then perhaps, if you don't mind...once your "Guest" has departed... could I please borrow the one's that I haven't had the pleasure of watching...or watching again...lol ? The Somewhere in Time one will definitely get back to you tomorrow...Thank You. You must be getting excited about Sarah's arrival...

M: I'm waaay beyond mere "excited". Yes, let's make it 2 p.m. then, I'll watch for you in the parking lot, or buzz. Yes, of course you can borrow the dvd's again, it's just that I'm hoping she stays at least until Christmas. Turns out she was using her friend's name, her name is Kira.

Oresha: OK then.... I'll be there at 2:00.... got my fingers crossed for You and Kira!..

Kathy: Hi! Thank you so much I have watched all the DVD's and enjoyed each and every one of them! Have a wonderful sharing of time! Good luck... and know I am most grateful for the opportunity to view your DVD's...Cheers PS Oresha is picking up the last one and has all the others along with the movie... I tried to watch The Butler but it would not play on my computer...

M: Glad you enjoyed them Kathy, sorry the butler wouldn't play with you, it's hard to get good help nowadays. Take care.

It has been almost twelve hours since I last heard from Kira. But I don't see how the last message I sent would have driven her into silence and not coming, I thought it was exceptionally good. My guess is that she rushed off to Las Vegas for the night so she's closer to the airport. It's just that silence and I don't get along well post Suzanne.

M: Kira, I expect that you remain busy preparing for your trip to Victoria tomorrow. I just wanted to tell you that I've been thinking a lot of you today (as usual the last few days) and want to wish you a good sleep wherever you happen to find yourself this night. Take care, sweet dreams, we'll come together on the morrow. Let me know when you're at the airport in Las Vegas waiting for your flight to leave so I will know conclusively that this isn't just an exceptionally sweet dream that I've been enjoying. Good night Kira.

Have I done it yet again? There were others I once called "Kira" before I gave up the notion of her ever being personified and manifest. But this time there was so much more – SHE WAS COMING TO ME!!!!! I'm going to bed now not having heard from her for many hours. What could it be? No computer, no internet wherever she is for the night? Why won't she be considerate enough to write me? Doesn't she know I'll be fretting the day before she is supposed to come home to me and goes suddenly silent like all the others have done before, even my beloved Jen who left her skirt with me? But I must trust and hope that she is about the business of settling affairs to come to me for a long period of time. I will sleep if I can then get up in the night and see if she has written. Would that I was just making this up, that it was fiction. But it's too late now to choose not to be a writer, I'm too immersed, *why must I still feel the pain?*

Oh yes, the timing is perfect, this one is for real, SHE'S KIRA!!! I finished the last sentence and a message arrived that very moment, it always seems to be like that. I wonder who's *really* directing this play? Whoever they are they're really good at it!

Kira: This whole process has been so incredible! I can't wait to tell you all about it! What an amazing few days this has been! I've loved receiving all of your email messages - I think I'll be a little sad when they end because we'll actually be able to talk in person to one another. Do you think we can just plan on emailing each day? I'm staying in Las Vegas with a relative because of rain. They had to shut down I-15 - it was literally washed away in Moapa. I came through just before that happened. So many really interesting events. I'll leave here in the morning... will be there tomorrow evening. I can't wait to see you. Good night... I hope you sleep well!

M: I was just about to go to bed so tomorrow night would come faster, but I was concerned for you, not having heard for a while. I trusted though that you'd be about the business of preparing to come to me. Thank-you so much for writing, thank-you so much for being YOU. I'm glad you're in Las Vegas tonight so you don't need to do that drive tomorrow on top of everything else. I thought you would be, and what a blessing it seems that you were able to make it - *floods in the Mojave Desert!* The universe continues to conspire on our behalf. Maybe you'll get that tail wind tomorrow too.

You know I'm writing manuscripts for books as I go along each day so what I pictured was me at my desk and you setup with your laptop on the kitchen table. I foresaw us exchanging emails daily to add to the books we'll co-create, the story of our perfect love gone right. No, we won't stop writing sweetheart, we might even write a whole lot more, that's how I see it. *Gosh I'm wanting you...* Will we recognize each other?

$$Chapter\ 31$$

---◈◈---

I promised we'd get back to Michael and Jen before this book ended. When we left them Jen was visiting Michael in Victoria. They'd had one night that included a semblance of sex, Jen still being the Good Mormon Girl she wants to be.

Michael's greatest threat is an invisible man from the worlds of spirit who has a huge influence on Jen, or at least Michael thinks he does. "He" the only name Michael has for this newly revealed invisible entity recently demanded that Jen choose him or Michael to be her "Adam". If the choice was "he" Jen would have to take her life to be with him in the world of spirits. She tells Michael it wouldn't be suicide, she'd just die.

It seemed an urgent choice she'd have to make, that was just a few days ago. Even though Michael recently proposed marriage and Jen accepted, Michael's not sure as we rejoin them if Jen has firmly committed to him or is still wavering thinking instead of him that she might go with the man with no body or her new sexually aggressive friend Al. Or with another man, she has several waiting from dating site contacts, they call her occasionally. One of them, Henry, a man from California is thinking of becoming a Mormon. Jen felt real good when she talked to him on the phone about that. She felt that God had come to rescue her from Michael. They were at the time in the midst of a rather nasty exchange of emails brought on largely by Jen's fears that Michael will be sexually unfaithful to her or will want another woman. Jen told Michael that she has been lying to him and deceiving him and that it was "impossible" for them to ever live together for "many many" reasons that she never tells Michael about.

Yeah, I know too weird but this is a true story and they say truth is stranger than fiction. It is, I'm just telling it the way it really happened. How would you like to find out that the spouse you loved and thought you knew over the 18 years of your marriage had all along been secretly communicating with some invisible person who had it seemed by persuasion the power of life or death over her, and had secret sex with her in the night? Michael only recently found out about "he" who has apparently been in Jen's life a long time.

One morning she told Michael who was her husband at the time and had slept beside her that night that she had been made delicious love to when she was half asleep and it wasn't him who had done the deed. It seemed so real that she wanted to know if she needed to confess adultery to her Mormon bishop. Michael told her she hadn't been awake enough to take responsibility for giving permission to the entity to enter her vagina. So, pleasant as it was, she had in effect been raped while her husband slept unknowing beside her. Michael recently questioned the morals involved in that and Jen got in a fume, saying her angel was "good".

Michael knows that soon after Jen left from visiting him in Victoria she had a mysterious spiritual experience on the hill behind her home. That caused her to pack and rush off somewhere. She talks vaguely of being in the desert at night, the stars were bright. There's a time gap in Jen's life right there that has never been explained to Michael. He wonders if she has been sleeping with another man and hiding it from him (and maybe from herself?) but he doesn't know. He's determined to find out about that and the mysterious "he" before Jen goes home from her seven day visit as his fiancee.

As we return to Michael and Jen in Victoria, she's at the grocery store across the street shopping for a whole chicken to make soup for him. She wants to fatten him up, he needs it. Jen's (still) too fat, Michael's too skinny. Between the two of them can they, like Jack Spratt lick the platter clean? Let's peek in and see how it's going today, day three of Jen's seven day stay.

Presenting Michael and his ex Jen then.

Last night after the downtown movie I was lying naked on the sofa when Jen shut down her computer game and sat at my feet, angling her body as she asked me to massage her feet. Her robe fell open and I without thinking commented that she still had some weight to lose. That got her in a huff and she went to bed saying I am too skinny. I soon followed and found her dressed including her Mormon under garments. She knows I like to cuddle naked and won't remove her sacred clothing. Anyway in the ensuing brief chat she got up, said she didn't know where

587

to go, walked to the kitchen then came back saying she was flying home tomorrow (today as I write this.) I almost fell asleep then got up and stroked her hair as she played a mindless game, then took her face in both hands, kissed her, and said after looking deep into her eyes, *"You silly silly woman. You could have everything you want but you opt for a mess of pottage instead. Just stop fighting me, it's not a soft tender feminine thing to do, I'm looking for soft and tender."* (Or something like that.)

We went back to bed both naked this time and slept for seven hours, my longest sleep in a long time. We made love this morning but as usual not all the way, that would be against her Mormon beliefs, liberal as she is in interpreting how it should be done in the Mormon way of life. How strange and peculiar that life is, I never knew it until I stepped away from organized religion. There's so much good and loveliness among the people, yet so much fear-inducing compulsion to do it somebody else's way to reach the highest heaven.

She sleeps in as I write at 10 a.m. today, me naked as usual except a robe for warmth. Just before I got out of bed I told her of a new twist on my many year recurring dream of her walking away from me. Here's how it goes, she didn't comment.

M: (to Jen) In my dream this morning I lost sight of you and rushed into a series of twisting tunnels that eventually became a flight of stairs to climb. At the top there was a wall, a dead end, nobody was there. There was nowhere to go, nothing to do but turn around and go back to search again for you Jen. I'm looking for Eve and wondering if it's you. Is that what this past 14 months was all about? Me rushing across America madly searching for Eve when all along she was in the home I had abandoned, beautiful her in the back yard tending to the roses?

But back in the real world I'm engaged to this woman (Jen) who threatened only hours ago on the second day of her visit to walk away again, to fly home early like Kira did and maybe never again see or speak to me. Even the first day was marred with some contention. We are poles away from being deliriously in love eagerly waiting for our wedding day to arrive. Logic still compels, at our age we'd be in our 90's before we could accumulate as much marital experience with another as we could already begin with each other, for all that may be worth if anything real at all beyond the baggage.

And so if in the end she does smile happily as she said she would, her job helping me reach my destination finally done, and walks away with another Adam with a different dream, so what? At that point she will be gazing upon me Adam content in my Garden, with beautiful loving Eves who share and want my version of the dream. We're getting ready to populate our magnificent higher order planet with children made in our own image and likeness, as did Adam and Eve on this planet where I live and write these books. What would it matter in the end if Jen walks away to her own Adam and *his* dream? Perhaps Jen *is* the object of my quest, but like Kira she is Eve to another Adam, never having shared *my* dream for eternity. A bittersweet ending to my Becoming Adam books when I promised you a sweet one? Choose for yourself how to see it, as for me MY dream will have come true, I will have become Adam. Be happy for me?

It's just that every individual has the power to choose for themselves, and to dream their own dream. Like attracts like. Law of Attraction brings people close when they are dreaming a similar dream, or are walking a similar path. Along the way individuals (deliciously) make individual choices, flub lines, ad lib, and change their script so others must adapt. The end of any dream may come with different faces than the ones hoped for or started out with. But if the dream is big, the outcome expected, the end is sure. The dreamer *will* have his or her dream come true. What more could we ask for?

Before the drastic changes that Elaine suggested and I made, my books began with the following words:

> "It matters not where my consciousness centers in this life or the next, or what anyone teaches differently, or however I may be challenged and criticized by others who see it differently and want to sway me to their way of seeing it, or who say my dream is impossible. As my soul roams the universe it will always be with the utmost thought and fixed determination that I am becoming or that I AM Adam!
>
> Only in that manner can I create the reality I want for myself. Only with that strength can I attract the Woman

> *to me who is exactly as I am. It is WE who will populate*
> *newly created planets. That's what I want, that's what*
> *I am becoming regardless of any other soul who would*
> *tempt and beckon me into worlds of their own choosing. I*
> *am not theirs, they are not mine. The gods keep the timing,*
> *when the time is right for me, my well-beloved Eve will*
> *appear, and we will be ONE..."*

I ran the above by Jen and she likes it. It explains a whole lot in the beginning about what motivates Michael as he abandons home and wife and begins his quest to find Eve. So I put the above statement back into the introduction to my books. Even should this present mortal body of mine wear out and die, with my fixed determination to be Adam I will return for a fresh new body with my Eves trailing clouds of glory alongside, each of us becoming immortal together, then flying swiftly to our Sacred Mountain on another planet to plan and carry out our chosen version of eternity.

And what of Jen? Jen, like everyone has the power to choose. She *could* choose to be my Eve instead of that of another. She'd be different, she has a different version of my dream, but could fit in. I'll always leave a candle lit in my window so she can find me in the dark, a door open to step through into my waiting welcoming presence.

So, as Michael and Jen discuss his dream she comes to him today, looks up into his eyes and says, *"Can I tell you something about my spirit man?"* Of course I want to know and she says that he told her it was *her* choice, to accept me as her Adam, or to accept *him* as so. Jen tells me that her choice was me. And then, less than one minute later she completely contradicts herself (and admits it when I pin her down) and says that she and her other Adam will have spirit children and she'll happily send them to populate the physical bodies I and my wives create as we populate our planets. (We're moving right along here developing my *fantasy* dear reader. Hopefully you know me well enough by now to understand that when I'm speaking with Jen I easily leap from fantasy to real life and back again without a pause in the conversation.)

I tell Jen her fantasy about sending spirit children to me would never fit my dream, that the physical bodies I am responsible for in the same manner that Adam and Eve are responsible for mine will be populated by spirit bodies created by the Ones (God the Father and Mother) who created the spirit body that animates my own physical body. I tell her later after remembering something from my experience in Womb Victoria decades ago that maybe she and I will first create those spirit children, then *later*, physical bodies for them to inhabit when we do as we must do and cast them into time to learn how to become innocent again after passing through experience in worlds such as this one where contrast exists.

Poet William Blake's Songs of Innocence and Experience explain that concept well. This may be too strange for you but it's really not so far out, just ahead of its time as earth and its inhabitants move inexorably towards what some call "The Millennium" and others "The Golden Age". Read about quantum physics lately? E.g. *"What the Bleep do we Know?"*

This fantasy that I am outlining is an eclectic one that includes elements of Mormon belief. How could it not when I was Mormon forty years? Had I started this book with such esoteric stuff unless you were already steeped in metaphysics and spirituality or were acquainted with Esther Hicks and Abraham, you would not have bought my book. Dear Elaine pointed that flaw out to me so the book begins with real life conversation. You get bread and milk before meat and ale. We're dishing up prime rib and steak right now, your choice of beverage.

You see, in my dream of who I want to be as I become Adam, my objective is to create *physical* bodies for my children. In Jen's dream she and her Adam create *spirit* children, and have the option of also creating physical ones. (I suppose if one interprets the bible literally that would be similar to God the Father conceiving a child in the physical body of mortal Mary.)

My choice to create only *physical* bodies in my garden world was based on an experience I had during my retired unbusyness when I asked God to tell me how to survive eternity without being bored. (I didn't at the time believe in past lives, I do now.) A complicated scheme unfolded that taught me the secret to not being bored with life in the eternities was to have frequent out-of-this world SEX! I assumed that sexual pleasure was reserved for physicality, now I'm not so sure. Thus my desire to create *physical* bodies on into the eternities, the curse lifted in my worlds so Eve would bear and deliver children painlessly with fullness of joy. And she needn't bear many, I don't think Adam and Eve had many children of their own but their own soon multiplied exponentially.

That experience jolted me from my comfortable lifestyle and sent me on my quest for Eve perhaps in part because Jen and I at the time were not doing much for sex, and anyway I wanted to write a book and was searching for stories maybe as much as for Eve? The early Mormon dream that eternal families consist of one man and several wives crept in to my fantasy life and Eve became Eves. *Now that was really exciting!!* Especially in my unchecked imagination if I and my Eves were a family of equal spouses, all 'married' to each other, all loving each other, and my wives if they so chose were lesbian except for me their Adam. (I think it's a turn on for most men to see women making love with each other, it certainly is for me. And then to add *myself* into the equation, now *that's* the stuff of an eternity without boredom, a perfect dream!)

Ok, it's just a dream ladies, mere fantasy, *your* man has secret fantasies too, I just talk about mine. I DO live in the real world and when Jen and I are actually living together I will be sexually faithful to her because I know how important that is to her, as it most likely is to you as well. (Not everyone is like that. Suzanne would have shared me and we would have welcomed the other home when the fling was done, by then a different but desirable fruit tasted and filed in life's delightful experience. I loved her for that.)

There, you now know all there is to know about Michael Demers. Still love me? Did you ever? Hope so, you are important to me. I *am* Michael.

Yesterday was a day of peace in my apartment. So when I finished my washup last night and found Jen lying naked in bed with no covers on smelling like roses and dreamy eyed, I taught her some Tantra Sacred Sex as best I knew how. I began with sweet kisses and caresses to her head and face. Then with a hand on each side of her leg I lightly moved my hands and her energy from just above her knees, passing close to her vagina on each side but never touching. The energy was moved to her heart area over her breasts, touching nipples that instantly hardened, and above the breasts a bit. Then lifting my hands and moving them down to her knees to repeat. She exclaimed the whole time, she was feeling the energy movement and taking delight in it, the first time in her life she had experienced that.

I was never taught my cue but at some point I caressed her vaginal area and lightly massaged her clit. I asked her to tell me when she was nearing a clitoral climax and not to give in, we had not yet reached our destination, the valley of complete pleasure. All the while I was whispering to my lover that she was representing Divine Feminine, the sum total of all female energy, and as such was a Goddess. I repeated, *"Goddess gets what Goddess wants"*.

I was there I told her to serve and service her and was at her command. My penis was not mine to enter her, only if and when she asked for it. And then it was like a flashlight, lighting her up inside, penetrating even her heart. I represented and was Male Energy, the yang for her yin, daylight for her night. She entered my fantasy eagerly and soon her hips were moving up and down impossible to stop. She spoke some fantasy and when I moved two fingers inside and up to her G-spot and beckoned she was ready already, there with no need for a repeat back to clit and then inside again. She had already begun long rolling Tantra orgasms. I heard sounds I had never heard before. In them and in the wealth of pleasure on her face I was richly rewarded. She was my goddess last night, I served her well, she was a part of me. Only the eventual tiring of my fingers slowed it for her, she could have gone on and on and on. Perhaps at our age a vibrator would have helped keep her naked lying on her back legs open with careless abandon uncaring, fully immersed in the Valley of Pleasure.

Today it's noon and she's back at the grocery store, tonight is ballet, Nutcracker presented in Victoria by the Royal Winnipeg Ballet, my first ever ballet, and hers. As she was bathing I went back to bed naked then watched her dress, telling her that I could "take her" at that moment. She put on an exotic Roaring Twenties hat, came to me and as we touched we felt the connection I'd been expecting, a sweet spirit fell upon us and we knew in that falling that we could have a wondrous life together, it was up to us. The two essential ingredients were in place: being together physically, and not being contentious about anything. We talked about a future. I think it's going to happen.

And with that and Elaine's long absence, it was with complete sincerity that I spoke the words to Jen today, *"In the last 24 hours you have moved closer to me than you have in the last 18 months."*

We're going to be well together for a lifetime. And if in the end she walks away with another Adam, so what, it's her choice to do so, she has made it possible for me to BECOME ADAM.

This is book two of a series of four books. Read all four and follow the amazing saga of Michael, Suzanne, DeLeon, Carrie, and Jen. Truth is stranger than fiction, it's an incredible story. The ending is to die for!